KT-562-731

For James Hill, with all my heart

Contents

URSULA, UNDER

I Ursula

O N A CRYSTALLINE, perfectly blue morning in June, after a day of angry pewter skies and of sheeting, driving rain, we enter our story. Clouds pile themselves picturesquely, theatrically, like plump odalisques, against the blue, clear-edged and astonishing. The forest all around is a palette of greens. Wild chokecherry trees are in raucous bloom. It is as if this were the first morning of the world, perfect. Even the garter snakes slithering under roots, over rocks, over roots, through the grass seem a part of the day's jubilance. Dew on fat ferns catches the sunlight in bursts and disperses it, starlike.

We are just miles inland from the tip of the Keweenaw Peninsula of Michigan, which juts out into Lake Superior, the arrival point for the earliest hardy wide-eyed settlers arriving from the East on lake packet boats to stake claims and seek copper, well before the Civil War. Lifting off from a branch overhead, a red-winged blackbird calls out clearly something that sounds much like *kee'-we-naw,* the native word for "portage." Many things here that are not called Keweenaw are called its English equivalent, Portage, almost as if life were much like a brief transit across a wee stretch of land.

It is Monday, June 9, 2003. Our story itself began long before, if we believe that all back story is also story, that the underside of the iceberg explains what we see above: all those wind-sculpted shapes that, looking for all the world like praying hands, came to be called, by fanciful meteorologists, *nieves penitentes,* or penitents sculpted of snow. Still, a painful and highly unusual event happens this glorious morning, and it is through this tiny aperture that we enter our narrative.

We are at the moment seeing through the eyes of Ursula Wong, a child with dark Asian eyes, café-au-lait complexion, and a thick blond braid down her back that seems frankly too much hair for a two-and-a-half-year-old to have had time to grow. Ursula has had her second birthday on November 19. She is a child small in stature, five pounds nine ounces at birth and now just over twenty-seven pounds, as of her spring checkup. She wears denim bib overalls with a purple T-shirt beneath; in the cool of the morning she has insisted on putting on her purple hooded jacket for the weather. Snow mittens are clipped to the sleeve ends. Yes, they are purple too. It is perfect and cool in the sixties.

Her mother, Annie, says, "Honey, you don't need a coat. It's June." Her father, Justin, says to Annie, "She'll figure it out pretty quick. She'll take it off herself and think it was her own idea."

In a clearing a couple of hundred feet down an untraveled dirt track into the forest, a glade carpeted by short grass kept low by odd gravel-shot soil, Ursula is crouched on her haunches examining tiny white blooms on wild strawberry plants in the grass. Each tiny bloom is a star. Ursula is transfixed.

Ursula and her young parents have traveled almost five hours west and north from their home in Sault Sainte Marie, Michigan. They have spent the night at a Super 8 Motel in Houghton, a town that houses the state's mining college, now more diversified as mine after mine has shut down. The motel faces Portage Lake, and Justin, who is an installer of vinyl siding and gutters, has paid the five dollars extra for a room with a view of the lake and the opposite shore. They rarely leave home, and this overnight away is a treat.

Ursula has splashed in the pool and run around on the motel's wooden deck, puddled from the day's rain. She has giggled delightedly as with the heel of her hand she pounded buttons in the lobby vending machine to make foil packets of chocolate-chip cookies fall, *klunk,* to the bottom of the machine. Ursula has suggested in a business-like way that they might live here. Justin has reminded her that Grandma Mindy is back home, and her purple carpet in her bedroom and all her stuffed animals. "Oh," Ursula has said. "That's true." Sober as a church mouse, clear-spoken as a valedictorian.

The Wongs have come here because Annie, a librarian, has gotten a bee in her bonnet of late: she wants to know more about her great-grandfather's death in a 1926 mine collapse, and then more about his life. Seems dumb, she has said, to live so geographically close to it all and know nothing much about our roots.

So the previous fall they had gone to a commemoration of the disaster at the iron mine where her great-grandfather died, and now, several months later, in weather as lovely as Eden's, they have come to search out the site of the copper-mining camp where the family lived when her father's grandfather was a blond barefoot boy new to Michigan, new to America. Her father is foggy about family history, does not remember being told much; he is beer-sodden most of the time anyway.

Annie has spent the previous afternoon in the archives of the Finnish college across the lake, reading accounts of the 1926 tragedy an hour and a half south, in Rovaniemi, Michigan, while Justin and Ursula first nap and then dry-roast in the sauna until they glow. Ursula loves the sauna. She sits with a sober expression, for only a few minutes, nonetheless, and then says perkily, "I'm done," ready to move on to the next thing. She is after all two years old. "I'm not," says Justin lugubriously, peering out at her from under the wet towel draped over his head and then retreating back under. He takes sauna seriously.

So Ursula sits and waits, rolling her eyes in the way she has seen little Olivia do on old *Cosby Show* reruns, precocious, in charge but obedient. Ursula's swimsuit is purple, like her bedroom carpet and her coat and everything else in which she has a say, and she sits on the hot cedar bench on a small purple towel. She draws the line at the television dinosaur called Barney. "Get outta here," she says, when anyone mentions him, with an exaggerated wave of her tiny hands, dismissive, parodying someone else—maybe from Brooklyn—she's seen on TV.

Ursula's even having come to be—considering Annie's injuries (a fractured pelvis from a hit-and-run accident at age ten which also broke both her legs) and all the doctors' attendant warnings—is a miracle in everyone's eyes. It has occurred to Annie that the birth of any of us, our coming to birth at all, in light of all the hazards every ancestor faced, is pretty much a miracle too, and she has been chewing on this thought for several months.

While Justin and Annie are awed and protective toward Ursula, they also believe that she needs to learn to make choices from early on. So she gets to make choices. She is, as a result, a bright, perky child, astonishing everyone.

That evening, taking Ursula for a final packet of cookies, Justin hears the roar of the crowd on the lobby TV and plunks himself down between a tool salesmen from Ironwood and a grandfather from Escanaba who is en route to see his little granddaughter Ursula's age, in Bay Mills, and has stopped here to visit the shrine of a sainted priest-missionary for his wife, who has cancer. They are all watching the Stanley Cup playoffs. There is a television in the Wongs' room upstairs, of course, but the lure of the lobby and all of these hockey fans is irresistible to Justin. He drops into a chair and starts roaring with the rest of the men.

Out through the glass door of the lobby, in the twilight, the surface of the lake sparkles. Ursula stands waving her silver packet of cookies with a defeated look but also with flashes of a tiny anger. She makes an exasperated face at the desk attendant, as if to say, *Men.* The attendant laughs heartily. The New Jersey Devils are playing the Anaheim Ducks, and the Devils are on their way to shutting out the Ducks.

Justin does not know that two defensemen, one on each team, playing against each other, are actually related, at not so great a distance back in time, to his wife, Annie, who is here after all seeking out her ancestry, and neither he nor Annie will *ever* know it. On the Devils, Oleg Tverdovsky, from Donetsk, in Ukraine, is descended from an ancestor who migrated east; on the Ducks, Fredrik Olausson, of Dädesjö, Sweden, has hands shaped like those of Annie's great-grandfather dead in the mine, passed down from a shared great-grandfather of their own. The degrees of separation are considerable—the connections go back to the beginning of the nineteenth century—and no one is asking the question, anyway. Justin's high-school team in Sault Sainte Marie was called the Blue Devils, and he is rooting for the Devils.

The lady at the desk has a name tag that says EILEEN. She looks down at

Ursula standing rolling her eyes, waving her packet of Mrs. Fields cookies, waiting for Justin. "Who do you want to win, honey?" she asks.

"Well, who's playing?" says Ursula perkily, her eyebrows lifted.

The attendant is surprised at the response. What did she expect? "The Devils and the Ducks," says Eileen.

"I like ducks," says Ursula. "I hate devils. Devils are ba-a-ad."

The attendant laughs heartily. "They're not *real* devils," she says.

"I don't care," Ursula says. "I like ducks."

Justin and the tool salesman and the grandfather hear none of this. There is a great deal of roaring from the onscreen crowd as well. Pucks fly, ice shivers up in fine flurries, blood flows. All is adrenaline joy.

The attendant helps Ursula open the cookies and gets her some milk from the breakfast room, checking with Justin first in pantomime. Justin nods yes, but this is after all hockey he's watching: she might have asked him anything and he'd agree.

The Devils win, three-aught. Annie comes down in the elevator, using her cane, looking for them. She and Ursula and Eileen have a good laugh at the hockey fans. "She likes ducks," Eileen says to Annie, reporting the remark. "But she doesn't like devils." Eileen crouches to Ursula's eye height and high-fives her. "Gal after my own heart," she says, slapping palms.

They are driving today to the site of a settlement where Annie's great-grandfather had lived in his childhood, soon after he came over from Finland, the now overgrown location of an abandoned copper-mining community out toward the point.

On their way north from Houghton this morning they have stopped in Calumet to take a couple of pictures of Ursula sitting on the lap of the over-sized statue of Alexander Agassiz, Harvard naturalist, copper baron, and aristocrat, otherness incarnate and no friend to the hoi polloi. Still, his sculpted bronze robes are cool, and Ursula poses sitting on his knee as if he were a dear, loving uncle.

The plan is to have a picnic here—the glade looked inviting, and time is abundant—and to spend the rest of the day seeking out where the camp would have been. Camp Grit. *Its name must surely have been a joke,* Annie thinks—*or maybe not?* Nature has taken over again at the site of the camp,

perseverant, triumphing over all humans' intents. The land had been lev-
eled, entirely, but, the historian at the college has told Annie, the forest has
reasserted itself and is as thick as if it were first growth. The cabins will be
gone, even the traces of their foundations, he says, as well as all traces of the
two churches that came later on, whose bells were transported inland for
two other churches, both Lutheran, one Finnish, one Norwegian. Finns and
Norwegians did not worship together, even if both were Lutherans.

Perhaps, Annie thinks, all *traces of human habitation will be gone,* but still
she wants to see where her great-grandfather lived as a child. To set her feet
on the earth there and know it directly. Justin is less curious about his own
heritage.

Annie's father, Garrett Maki, spends most of his days and nights drunk
since her mother's death, eighteen years before, while Annie was in the hospital recovering from the crash that crippled her. Garrett is on disability now,
as a Vietnam veteran, but no one is certain just what his disability is. Annie
suspects—no, believes—that her father was responsible for her mother's
death: there had been a great deal of abuse, and Liz Maki died of a head injury the night of an outburst on Garrett's part. There were no witnesses, there
were no charges. Domestic violence was not a thing people were comfortable
talking about then. The eighties are as distant as the glaciers.

Annie walks with difficulty, always with that cane, and invariably wears
long skirts to cover her scars and her atrophied muscles. Justin is able-
bodied and hearty, half Chinese. He is known to local hockey fans as Wild
Man Wong. Annie and Justin are fiercely in love.

BECAUSE URSULA IS clamoring for lunch, they have pulled the
truck over onto a graveled apron of the road, then meandered through a
patch of woods, and are wandering peacefully in an odd clearing a short distance into the woods. They have no idea that this clearing once held the
boiler house of an old mine. The grass grows up through a layer of finest
ashy pea-gravel, a relic of the long-vanished brick structure. When the mine
was operating, the land was scalped clean: no trees anywhere. The forest is
thick again.

The fragrance of lilacs hovers in the air: there are wild lilac bushes to either side of the clearing. Lupines with their intense tiny indigo blooms poke up here and there. Clumps of wild lavender tuck themselves everywhere. Something else—a bush?—smells like licorice. Justin has set down the picnic basket in the grass. A tiny brown-speckled bird lands on its arched handle. Ursula chortles in delight and leaps to grab it.

"Nope," says Justin. "Birds are to fly." The bird, as if to demonstrate, lifts off. Ursula claps her hands in delight. Then she crouches again and tries to pick one of the tiny white blossoms. "Let it be," Annie says. "It will make a strawberry." Ursula rises to standing, her full height of two feet plus, plunks her fists onto her hips, elbows akimbo, and scowls in frustration: Here we are out in all this great sweet stuff and I can't do *anything*.

At the edge of the denser forest at the back of the clearing, there is a rustling sound. Papery, slight, but distinct in the silence. Ursula's head turns. A flash of white: a deer, venturing tentatively out of the forest, has spotted them, and turns tail to run. It is perhaps a dozen feet away. Ursula runs after it, squealing. The deer, of course, will not be caught, and there is nothing to say except "Let it go." Annie and Justin smile at each other, a moment too quick in its passing to run to the truck for the camera.

Ursula tiptoes dramatically, thinking perhaps of Olivia again—she watches those *Cosby Show* reruns, mesmerized, over and over night after night and can recite people's lines along with them. She cranes back over her shoulder at Justin and Annie to make sure they see her. They beam at her. She puts her finger to her lips: *Shhh*. Her back is to them. The blond braid down her back shines like silk floss in the sunlight, against the plum violet quilt of the coat. The deer is still in sight, a few feet into the leafy green shade of the forest. She is determined to catch it. The delight in her eyes is unmistakable.

She gives them a sign in mime: Watch me. Ursula's every gesture seems meant for the comedic stage. She is a natural. She tiptoes toward the tree line. The deer disappears deeper into the forest, as silent as breath. Ursula puts on a burst of speed, silent herself, looking back at Justin and Annie, steps into the trees, and disappears from sight. The only sound is an astonished tiny intake of breath from Ursula as she goes down, like a penny into the slot of a bank, disappeared, gone.

Annie looks terror at Justin, trips on the long skirt that covers her scars, lurches forward, and falls awkwardly onto her bare elbows. They sting and ooze blood. Justin is already at the spot where Ursula disappeared. "Oh, God, Annie," he says. His voice is barely audible.

Annie raises herself on her cane and stumbles toward him. They stand transfixed, staring down. The opening into which Ursula has fallen is amazingly small, and they can see nothing but darkness. They certainly cannot see Ursula herself.

Neither of them wants to call out to her, unconsciously afraid their voices will echo back at them from too deep an emptiness. Both of them think: *What is this? How deep?* and *Dear God, no.* Both of them think: *A mine shaft?* Neither says the word.

Annie had tried to imagine the shaft into which her grandfather descended one August day three-quarters of a century ago and from which he did not come out alive: fifteen hundred feet deep. No one could survive such a fall . . . but is this such a shaft? Annie is telling herself, no, it must be something else. Too small for a mine shaft, surely. Way too small. Then it must be a well. She heaves a half-sigh of imaginary relief. But what would a well be doing out here in the forest? The answer would be: The same thing as a mine shaft, serving a different landscape, a different time. And why in the name of anything would a well seem a relief? Her breath clutches up again.

Rough old timbers are laid across an opening in the ground six or seven or eight feet square. It is too early in the summer for much foliage to have sprung up yet, but each year it has grown up and died off, and grown up and died off, so the timbers remain exposed. One of those years, perhaps forty years ago when Justin and Annie's parents were in high school—and no one much has been here since, wandering into this forest which is after all nowhere—a tiny shoot grew up between the first and second timbers. As it grew, it pushed them apart, and it has become a tall solid tree, growing from inside the hole, through the timbers set into a collar to seal this shaft. As it happens, this is indeed a mine shaft, an air shaft, meant only for ventilation of the long since abandoned passages below.

Annie kneels painfully, all her weight on her cane, and calls into the darkness: *Ursula.* She can't tell anything about the depth of the hole. She calls again: *Ursula,* and then she sobs. She looks up at Justin. It has been a providence that Ursula was so close and they both had their eyes on her, or they might fall into blaming themselves or each other in their grief. Neither even considers that.

Justin's eyes dart wildly but his mind is clear. "How far would you say it was since we saw civilization?" he says. "Thirty miles?" He stops. "*Three* miles?" It could be either.

"The cell!" Annie says. "In the truck?"

Justin runs to the truck, his work boots seeming to shake the ground. The cell phone lies on the front seat, tiny and useless amid a scattering of animal crackers. In crisis the mind focuses on minutiae: he thinks, *Now is that cookie a rhinoceros or a hippopotamus?* He picks up the phone. No signal. *Of course, no signal: there are no towers out here in the wilderness.*

He tries to remember how many cars they saw on the road. All he can remember is the fat, furry rear end of a black bear cub shambling off into the trees near a river, and Annie trying to take a snapshot. He follows that rabbit trail into his mind and recalls the bright topaz eyes of what must have been a cougar just off the road as they drove up in the dark in the rain, the night before. But of course a car coming along the road now, Justin thinks, would be no help at all: none of *their* phones work either. A rusty dark red Subaru zooms by, heading north. The road is once again empty and silent, the sunlight bright and impassive.

Justin remembers a time as a teenager when his first car, a beater the color of pea soup, had stopped dead just west of Sault Sainte Marie at twilight. A passing car had offered to send help, then didn't. He recalls walking alongside the road in the dark, kicking stones, mumbling "goddamn fucker" again and again. Can't chance that kind of thing now. Trust no one. Justin has not trusted many folks in his life anyway. He carries a grudge about his father's having abandoned the family when he was three, not much older than Ursula is now.

Justin calculates the distance back to the last town they passed, Eagle River, and then estimates mileage forward to Eagle Harbor, next on the map. Forward seems best. He runs back to Annie.

She sits silent on the ground, her legs out painfully straight before her,

her eyes filled with tears. Justin's attention is drawn to the pattern of the fabric of her skirt: a pattern of tiny blueberries and green leaves. His mind is recording that to keep from attending to what has just happened. *Blueberries,* he thinks. *I never noticed that those were blueberries.*

The silence from the gap between the timbers is deafening, the darkness there impenetrable and magnetic as a black hole. They can see only a few inches into the opening: the leaf cover overhead is thick and the shade almost palpable. In the silence, the birds' twittering seems obscene, out of place.

Annie seems in a trance. She is not. This is just slow to register. Justin, however, is functioning in hockey mode: alert, aggressive, all nerve ends ready. "No phone," he says to Annie. "No towers." He sees the look of dismay in her eyes: lost, disbelieving. "I'm going to drive on to Eagle Harbor," he says. "I'll get help." He feels as if he will throw up his innards. "You can do this. Ursula will be okay." He sounds calmer than he feels. Annie just stares at him as if dumbfounded by his composure. "Look," he says, half-angrily. "Was she a miracle or *what?* So would God just let her *go* this way?" Annie can't believe he's talking this way. He can't stand for her to mention anything in the *vicinity* of God, shuts her down when she tries. All of a sudden he's preaching?

And of course Ursula is in no danger. Of course. This will all be explained in a moment. We're on an old *Candid Camera* show. No, *America's Funniest Home Videos,* that's it.

"Okay," Annie says, her voice belying her pounding heart. "Go then. I'll wait." She tries to think of something important to say about logistics, what he must not forget to do, but she can think of nothing at all. So she just repeats herself. "I'll wait." The tone is as if she were waiting her turn at the butcher's or the photo counter at Wal-Mart.

"Yeah, right," Justin says, his eyes wide with terror. He leans and kisses Annie on the top of her head. Her hair is warm. The pale skin of her part looks so vulnerable. He focuses on anything but that hole in the ground. "We'll get our miracle," he says.

"Hurry," she says, the audible quavering of her own voice this time scaring her. She squeezes his hand, and he's gone, the truck spraying up gravel.

IT WILL BE seven hours from now—Monday night—a news team on the TV will be helicoptered up from Marquette to broadcast nationally what is not this morning known to anyone else, what has not quite even registered in Annie's consciousness—before the remark is made. A woman her parents' age back in Sault Sainte Marie will be lounging alone in the newly remodeled high-ceilinged living room of the home she inherited from her parents, passed down from her grandfather the judge. Fried and sour after two gins, she will grumble at the TV screen, "Why are they wasting all that money and energy on a goddamn half-breed trailer-trash kid?"

Annie's mind is pulling up, as from a well, the tacit answer to that as yet unasked question. Annie cannot think of Ursula down that hole, so she thinks: *So many generations, back into history and then prehistory, all concentrated into this one little girl.*

This is the answer to the as yet unasked question, in backward format: this little girl carries with her the inheritance of generations uncounted, precious, induplicable. She is priceless, not only to Annie and Justin, but to the planet, the whole big fat blue-green ball hurtling through space.

As Annie's mind drops as far as it can conceive, down the dark hole of her own lack of knowledge about her own and Justin's families' past, an unfocused image of someone Chinese—male or female she cannot see, an older person, to judge from the posture and shuffling step; likely a male now, to judge from the shoulders and slight baldness, wearing a green gown—flits past her consciousness like a resurfacing memory of something she never knew to begin with.

She cannot flesh it out into focus so instead she begins trying to name the trees that surround her, to keep her mind off that hole and its darkness, and she cannot remember the names of the trees either. Her eyes fill with tears and, just for a brief second, overflow. The birdsong is deafening.

Justin heads north on the winding road, taking the curves too fast, hearing himself saying out loud to the empty cab, "Christ," again and again, and then "Crap," and then "Christ," and then silence.

2 The Alchemist's Last Concubine

OUT IN THE courtyard, a papery rustle of leaves from the little plum tree, then the near-imperceptible sound of what must be a thrown stone or a human step or the hoof of some animal on the paving bricks, then silence. Qin Lao, sitting alone in the near dark with a small oil lamp reading a manuscript, lifts himself, strong, a bit gingerly (for he is seventy-seven) on the arms of his chair, feeling with some pleasure how much strength he still has in his wiry limbs.

He balances, suspended for a split second on the chair arms, assuring himself with a sly smile in the flickering low light that his life force is full and intact. He feels with pleasure the play of the wiry muscles that rope the bones of his forearms, and he lets himself down, standing.

He walks in his soft shoes across the floor to the high window and climbs to a stool to peer out. He listens to the *schiff-schiff* of his leather slipper soles as he traverses the smooth stone floor. What would Zhou, his servant, be doing outdoors at this time of night? Zhou should have been asleep long ago, early riser that he is. Qin Lao steps up onto the stool and peers out the small opening.

Zhou is patient and useful, but this is not Zhou in the courtyard now: it is a deer, tall, full antlered, bending over the small bed of licorice weed that Qin Lao harvests to make elixir for Zhou's chronic excess of throat mucus. The deer is simply sniffing at the leaves, not eating. The servant Zhou is mute and has been ever since he appeared twenty years ago on Qin Lao's doorstep here, asking in signs whether he might be of use: at times it is only the clearing of his throat that tells Qin Lao where he is. The deer seems to sense that he is being watched, and he raises his head and looks around. No one? He does not look up high enough, to the small barred window up near the eaves. His nose dips back down to the fringe of the garden and nuzzles the leaves.

This is a deer of the species that, over two full millennia later, will be named Père David's deer, after a Catholic missionary from France, a man wearing a long dress much like the robe Qin Lao now wears. Qin Lao is thus not concerned that after thousands of years of this species of deer roaming Sichuan, some European will name the deer, claiming it for the West. Qin Lao knows nothing of politics and would not comprehend the search for power—imperial, muscular—that drives the soldiers and emperors of the world, before his own life and much later.

Qin Lao has a focus much more microscopic: as an alchemist trained in the disciplines and aspirations of third-century-B.C. Taoism, he seeks what he calls the elixir of immortality, but in a smaller, perhaps humbler way, hoping only to find the right recipe to extend his own life indefinitely and to pass that rare formula on. Qin Lao has often marveled in something like horror at his own intellectual pride, at the hubris of wanting his own life extended this way, of reaching out for immortality.

Not three kilometers farther up the winding road through the deep green trees into the mountains, the cinnabar mine is worked by slaves from the land to the northwest and by children, who fit in the small spaces in the mine's deepest parts and the high side crevices where no adult can climb. The slaves and the children quarry the reddish stone that will, once heated, surrender its mercury for the alchemical processes.

Qin Lao knows that several children have died this past year in the mine and been buried in the cemetery at the edge of the workers' compound. He has, not a month before, walked the road to the mine with Zhou, one cool morning. He has stood looking over the tiny graves, addressing the Great God in his heart: *Why these children, why death so young? Why am I—weak, foolish man, vain about my smooth skin and strong musculature seven decades and more into life, why am I given this chance to live on to so many times their years?* Still, he wants more. More life, more power-within.

Over the courtyard, the moon is high, just shy of full. Qin Lao looks up at the arc sliver of shadowy edge that hides from the light at the edge of the great circle. *So,* he thinks, *is the full truth: we are always near to its possession, yet never quite wholly arrived.* He does not like to look at the full moon when in all of its vibrancy it lights the sky: he thinks it bespeaks a false promise of full knowledge, full revelation.

The moonlight falls now like clear water over the courtyard and wall and the trees beyond, rinsing away the harsh glare of day, bathing the scene in a kind of pearlescent limpidity. The deer leans and sniffs, sniffs and moves. He looks up again: *Who is that watching me?* He paws at the stone border of the small garden and eats one small white flower, bright in the moon-light. Qin Lao, at his window perch, half coughs—the breeze is chill—and the deer once more looks over his shoulder. The moonlight on the back of the animal is a milky wash over the pewter gray hide, whose hairs stand out clearly in Qin Lao's acute vision.

Qin Lao half recalls a prophecy made by a soothsayer in this same village when he was very young, using the scapular bone of a deer. The bone had been drilled in a ceremonial pattern and then heated over a fire until the holes radiated cracks like the rays of the sun, which were then read as an or-acle. The exact words of the prophecy are something he has not thought of in years. He wonders now whether he can recall them. They said something about his old age. It was all an encoded prediction, in image and metaphor, but he could surely make sense of it if he could even recall it. He cannot. Here he is, in old age, and he cannot recall what was prophesied. Meng would remember, but Meng has been dead seventy years now, and the soothsayer, who would have been the age Qin Lao is today, has likely been dead just as long.

The deer's antlers are spiky and harsh in silhouette. Back of them, the soughing pines beyond the wall lay their branches against the sky like black paintbrushes, splayed by use. Qin Lao thinks: *The Great God is a wondrous calligrapher.* Then he prays: *Teach me to read these the lines of your poetry, o fair mysterious Tao. May I read the stark lines of pine branches, the paintings of moonlight, the characters flashed in the night by reflections of stars in the eyes of the deer as he looks up at me, never seeing me.* He steps down from his stool, being careful to hold up his gown. In the next room, Zhou sleeps on, under flat, weighty covers. In three hours the servant will be up drawing water.

Qin Lao does not know that in thirty-three years, out of the northwest quadrant of the Middle Kingdom, there will come a ruler who will unify all the states that now coexist, sometimes warring and sometimes in peace, and that that ruler will bear the same surname as his own, though he is no blood relative, not even in distant history's mists.

He does not know that that emperor will be revered and absorbed into legend, so that all his bloodthirsty purges will be set aside in the minds of both peasant and noble. People will with immense reverence speak of the great Yellow Emperor, Qin Shi Huang-ti, the Tiger of Qin, and believe that his tomb is at the deep center of a great mountain eternally guarded by robots with crossbows. They will believe that the emperor's coffin—cut of a single piece of perfect jade and incised with amazing designs—tiger, crocodile, tortoise, crane, marvelous fish with diaphanous wavering fins and tail—has been set afloat forever on a lake of mercury, silvery rich, in that great mountain's dark heart.

Should Qin Lao ever be told such things about the future, he would listen a moment and then think abstractedly, *Such things are possible.* He might try to recall whether he ever has actually seen a crocodile or whether the image is as vivid as that in his head only because he has once been told a tale of such beasts. Then he will return to his own work.

He does not know that the name China, which will resonate down the long halls of history, will come from this Qin surname, but via his non-cousin, now a young man with a long mustache several hundred miles away training wild horses and building a hunger for empire.

Qin Lao walks past the door through which Zhou lies curled, stokes the small stove with two more handfuls of wood, and goes to his own bed. When he sleeps—sleep is immediate—he dreams of a fish like the one on the emperor's jade coffin.

That next noon, not long after Qin Lao wakes, when Zhou has been down the mountain, in town, running the errands for hours—collecting the rents, buying several new vessels for sublimation, repairing the bright red left wheel on the cart—Qin Lao will suggest to Zhou that he take the cart six kilometers to the crook of the Huang He to the market to buy such a fish, fat and gold, to be cooked with red spice and ginger and thick purple onions cut fine, and deep greens. He knows Zhou likes to watch the great bamboo rafts that ride the mostly impassable river. He thinks of Zhou standing there staring mesmerized, as sunlight glints off the swift water's skin. He will tell Zhou that he will himself in the meantime do the requisite dealings with the cinnabar merchants, who like to cheat Zhou.

In the dream the fish waves its tail beautifully, as if it were one of the immortals who has transcended this life and become immaterial, one of the blessed *xian*. In the dream Qin Lao is very hungry, and his old mentor comes to him and says in that gravelly voice he had, "Empty your head, fill your belly." Qin Lao knows how to empty his head—he holds knowledge so loosely, like the reins of a nervy but wonderful horse. He knows, moreover, that to his teacher and to all alchemists the notion of a full belly means more, is a metaphor for a rich interior life.

When Qin Lao rises in very late morning, the house is in silence. Outside he hears fowl scratching in the dirt and a cart on the road very far away. He thanks the Tao for his hearing. He thinks of the black needles of the pines so distinct in the nearly full moon's light last night, laid against the gray-lavender sky, and he thanks the Tao for his still-vivid sight. He shakes off the crimpings of night in his bones and he stands. He puts on his slippers and goes to the door to the courtyard, unbolting it, throwing it open. No deer, of course. But he knows that he saw a deer. There is no entrance or exit to the courtyard: no deer could enter, as it is the center of the house. No deer once there could escape. The deer, nonetheless, is gone.

At the center of the courtyard at the heart of the house, in the cleared dirt space at the base of the small plum tree, he sees the evidence that, though the fish was a dream, the deer was not: a small pile of pelletlike deer scat. He laughs out loud.

He crosses the courtyard to the laboratory, smiling to himself and keeping his eye on the pellet pile as if it might take wing. He is thinking about the deer, transmuting, transmigrating, whatever it may have done. Surely it did not leap the wall around the house—it is over two meters tall.

Qin Lao lists off in his mind people he knows who would not believe him if he told them: they have the minds of merchants and artisans. *But,* he asks himself, responding to his own thought, if they have the minds of merchants, the arbiters of value, *why can they not see the value in moments of transcendence like these? Because one cannot put a price on it!* he answers himself. *Ah, that!*

He looks back at the deer droppings still beneath the tree, and he says out loud, "Priceless!"

He remembers what his teacher told him about merchant minds when he was a mere boy. There are those that are like a grub floating in a well or hung in a cobweb: the grub in its dry little casing is certain as it can be that the six extremities of the universe are bounded by its cocoon, and so too is the merchant. Any merchant. You need not bother yourself to attempt to communicate any least suggestion of the Tao to such a one, said his teacher, old Master Meng.

Qin Lao remembers the master's face lit by sunlight in the garden beside his house when Qin Lao was just a boy and was called Moon-Grabber, after his habit of reaching for the moon in the sky. He remembers the dark eyes of Master Meng. He recalls the exotic dark look of his cheeks, like tanned leather. Master Meng was of a different tribe, and from far away.

The teacher said to the boy: It is this "darkness" that is the gift of the Tao to me, leading men to deem me different and frightening, and so to send me off into the search for what is so much more interesting than the things of this world, beautiful as they may be.

Master Meng, three times that Qin Lao remembers, took the boy down to a stream, slower than the Huang He and much clearer, and placed a boat made of a nutshell, with a paper sail, on the water and sent it off downstream. The flash of the sun on the surface is beautiful, said Master Meng, and the movement of water, but under it all is the Tao, and he looked at the boy, and the boy understood.

Master Meng knew about the excrescences: those of rock, those of wood, those of herb, those of flesh and those that were called—for lack of a better name—"excrescences of the tiny."

"There are also jade-fat excrescences," said Master Meng. "They grow on jade-bearing mountains."

"I love jade," said the child.

"You love everything," said the master. He rolled his eyes. "We will mix this powder with the juice of cudweed gathered at the proper time of the moon, and this elixir, drunk with the proper prayers, will assist us to live to be a thousand."

"I cannot imagine," said the child, "living to twenty."

Master Meng said, "There are also excrescences from wood."

He took the child up a hill outside the city. He squatted on his haunches and plucked a truffle. "These, do you see, issue from evergreen sap that seeped into the soil a full thousand years ago, in the days when the diviners began to find dragon bones. Even before that. There are wood-resin mushrooms that shine in the night, luminescent as flames at the center of wax. There are peach-alum sorts that resemble a dragon."

The child said sadly, "I think that this business of dragons is meant to fool children. I think that this is only fairy tales."

"Truly," said Master Meng. "Truly, you sadden me, Moon-Grabber."

"You have taught me to speak my mind," the child said.

Master Meng sighed a great sigh. "There are herbs that work blessing and are said to have brought longevity, sometimes even immortality."

"Have you seen this?" said the child. "Have you known someone to mount to heaven without suffering decay?"

Master Meng did not answer the child. "There is an herb called the Buffalo Horn. It is over a meter in length. There is an herb called Five Virtues, which seems to resemble a towering hall. It holds nectar. I have seen one of these from several meters away, and it seemed to me there was a lavender vapor that rose like a smoke from its capital."

"And did you eat this thing?" said the child.

Again Master Meng quickly sidestepped the question. "My teacher sent a slave over the stream to procure the Five Virtues herb," the master said. "That slave's name was Withered Emblem. That slave fell into the stream and was washed out to sea."

The child began crying. "Why must we do this?" he said. "Why can we not just play hop-bones?"

"Perhaps you will be glad I have told you these things one day," said Master

Meng. "If you find a tiny excrescence—it may be shaped like a tiger or a fly-ing bird, it may be shaped like a lakeside pagoda—you must lift it swiftly from where it grows, with the edge of a bone knife, and the powder of this, once dried, will confer thousands of years upon you."

The child stared at him in silence.

"We may be out one day in the forest and I may be discoursing on these matters and you may look down and see a tiny man as tall as your foot is long, riding a palanquin hung with brocade or a horse with carved leather saddles," the master said. "If you reach down—as if he were some sort of doll—and lift him up, you will immediately become a genie."

"Will I be able to tell my good friends good-bye?" said the child.

"I do not know," said the master. "I have yet to see this thing happen. I only have faith that it can."

"I am hungry," the child said irritably.

"Then let us go in and eat soup," said the master. The soup the cook had made was aromatic and pale, with flecks of seaweedlike duck egg white floating in it in a way the boy always thought magical. There were small handfuls of pale green cabbage as well, and the boy loved to chase them. The cook ladled bowl after bowl for the pair.

Master Meng, later that evening, after the sun began setting, intent on finishing what he had started that day, told the child his own teacher had sworn by a formula he called the Tender. He promised that he would, the following week, show the child the actual ritual.

Qin Lao remembers himself at the age of nine years looking into the master's dark eyes and listening hard. He recalls watching as Master Meng mixed the formula: a paste or jam of cinnabar touched to the tongue and then swallowed. Master Meng had said, "If an adept will mix this paste with the juice of wild raspberries taken from below the tree line of the third mountain"—he pointed off to the west—"he can beget children at ninety."

Qin Lao had watched the master touch the thumb-sized dark hardwood spatula to his tongue, tip the paste onto it, breathe with his eyes closed for a specified number of breaths, and then swallow.

When this was done, Moon-Grabber asked, in his little-boy voice, "And why would a man want to beget a child at ninety?"

Meng had stared into the eyes of the child and said after a moment, "I am only forty-seven, child. How should I know?" He had called for the servant, who brought a plate of fruit. "Peaches, my boy. Eat. And raspberries too from the hill just behind us." As they ate, Meng had said, "Perhaps next summer I will take you to the Lake That Has Risen to Heaven and show you the mystery of Divine Cinnabar."

The child sat still, eating a crescent of peach, thinking of the moon as it looked when it was in this phase, sucking and listening. Master Meng would go on. One did not need to ask.

"We will prepare for that by eating the formula that is called the Divine Amulet, one hundred days. Then we will ride in a sedan car for three days, and when we arrive we will wash in the waterfall that comes down into the lake. I have seen a painting of this waterfall, but I am sure that the actual place is more beautiful. I will paint the paste of this cinnabar onto the soles of your feet and you will be able to walk on water."

The boy stared amazed. "Have you done this?"

"Oh, no," Master Meng said. "It is reserved for those who will become genies. You are of that race, and I am to pass this on to you."

"I am of this race, Master Meng?"

"Yes," said the teacher. "I believe that you are."

Moon-Grabber thought of the story he had been told about how Master Meng had found him on the terrace in a wicker basket, silent and wrapped in a blanket, and sucking on silk. Master Meng had said the infant looked up at him as if to say, "I am ready." The child was sure he had been left by a poor farmer who could not feed him, but Master Meng was just as sure that he had been left by fairies.

"Is the lake very deep?" said the child. He imagined his eyes were wide as the rim of the clay dish that held the fruit.

Master Meng had laughed uproariously.

Today, as he enters his laboratory, Qin Lao is remembering the morning so long afterward, that spring, when he found Master Meng dead in the garden on his knees, leaning over the herbs with a trowel, dead peacefully of what must have been a heart attack or an aneurysm. The child knelt and watched the corpse for a good two hours, waiting for it to wake, and when it did not, Moon-Grabber walked quietly into the village to ask someone to come and help him bury the body.

He did not question why Master Meng, who knew every formula for immortality, had died: he had died because he did not do something perfectly, as men most often do not do things perfectly. Master Meng said he knew no one who had attained immortality, but he had heard of five men who had done so, beyond the Huang He. He had said that the search still must go on and that the child would inherit his laboratory, to that very end.

The child had been sent, the week after Meng's burial, to apprentice to an alchemist named Hoptoad-Gold, in a great city three days' journey to the east, where there were no hills, where there were no evergreen forests, no deer. He had studied for over a decade there, in the pallor and traffic and commerce and dung of that city, until he was nearly grown, and then returned to the laboratory, which had been sitting gathering dust, undisturbed, as no one would dare tempt the fairies' wrath.

He knelt beside Master Meng's grave and he spoke the words into the soil, not knowing the ritual, trying to do what seemed right. He leaned over the packed earth and whispered into it, "I will do my best. I have learned many things in that city." That was all he could say. It seemed minimal. "There were no trees there," he added, as if Master Meng, down below the tamped soil, were casually listening. "Just dancing girls." He remembered their movements, like pine branches in the wind, and their songs, like the wind in the pine branches. He also remembered the lids of their eyes, deep and heavy above their dark eyes, and their soft hands, which waved and then beckoned and, as they passed by like the wind, softly touched his smooth young-man cheeks, stirring him.

"I go now to the work," he said to the master's grave and, pushing up on his strong young hands, walked to the laboratory and started dispersing the dust of a decade.

IN THE MIDDAY sun sixty-nine years later, Qin Lao decides that this afternoon should be devoted to walking and that he will walk to the cinnabar mine. He does not need cinnabar: his supplies are adequate for the vermilion pills he is decocting, half for himself, half for his friend Xu Xuli, the astronomer, who is eleven years older than Qin Lao and, Qin Lao believes, has been living on rice and dew for half that time. Xu Xuli often has drunk heavily when Qin Lao, an ascetic abstainer, visits; Qin Lao assumes that this is included under the heading of "rice," for indeed the wine is made of rice.

When Xu Xuli reaches the stage where he can exist on dew alone, Qin Lao knows he will be nearing the bridge to the land of the immortals. Qin Lao has never seen anyone do this successfully, but he believes that if anyone can do this thing it will be Xu Xuli.

At eighty-eight, Xu Xuli has outlived two wives, six concubines, and a pair of identical twin daughters who died at birth when he was eighty-two, his twelfth and thirteenth children. At present he has but three concubines, no wives. His eleven children have given him nearly a hundred grandchildren; those children have over three hundred descendants. Xuli has no need to worry, as some ancients do if they are without offspring.

Because Qin Lao keeps Xu supplied with the cinnabar pills, and because he is his dearest friend, Xu Xuli sees to it reciprocally that his descendants keep Qin Lao cared for. They bring him firewood and cinnabar, as well as bolts of silk cloth from his son the merchant in the south and jade and semi-precious jewels from his son in Ch'ang-an, which Qin Lao can trade for alchemical substances from the West. Qin Lao has rents for six houses as well, which provide him with income.

What Qin Lao does not have are offspring.

The year that Qin Lao had returned from his apprenticeship in the city of dust, a city that in Ursula's time would be called Chengdu, Xu Xuli was a thirty-one-year-old householder, a mathematician who studied the stars, with a young wife and a son, in whom he took delight. Xu Xuli had—to fulfill a vow his now deceased father had made, a decade before, to Master Meng—determined to find the young alchemist a suitable wife.

It was profoundly necessary to the energies of life—the *qi* force, the manifestation of the Tao—that the young man be provided with a mate, for the yin energies of the female were required to balance male yang. An alchemist must order all elements in his life in the proper proportions, and celibacy was intrinsically an imbalance: the male could not, deprived of sexual

intercourse, draw yin—as if he were the human equivalent of a tree orchid—out of thin air, after all! So Qin Lao would be found an appropriate
wife.

The wife had been found, in a village three days' journey to the northeast, the third daughter of a prosperous noble there. She brought a decent
dowry, and she was not unpleasant, though Qin Lao found his laboratory
more interesting. The woman's name translated as White Jade Blossom, and
she could dance beautifully and play three different instruments. She had a
natural scent that was pleasant—Qin Lao remarked, abstractedly, and—it
seemed to his new wife—perfunctorily, that indeed she smelled like a white
jade blossom.

"And what would that scent be?" said the young woman, wanting more
compliments. She hoped to hear that she aroused him as no woman ever
could and that her scent was the scent of the air that arose from the leaves
of the melon vines that climbed the trellis that shaded their eastern wall.

She waved her wide sleeves in the air, slightly, ever so slightly, to waft her
perfume to his nostrils. She wanted him to sniff it and to go on to say that,
furthermore, the magical red stone about her neck reminded him of the red
jewel on the forehead of the fabled Manchurian crane, symbol of true immortality, and that indeed she was his immortality.

She hoped that he would then reach over inside her gown, touch her first
at her navel, then travel the heel of his hand, the edge of his fifth finger,
whose nail was longer than the others, and smooth and round, down the
soft skin in the vast expanse between her navel and the place where the dark
downy moss started and then say that her small, almost childlike labia resembled cowrie shells, so smooth, so valuable, used for money since ancient
days.

His hand did not move to her robe but stayed poised in midair with a
brush he had inked, as he thought about something he seemed half unable
to capture.

The young alchemist was at that moment considering whether an herb
he had found up the mountain the previous afternoon was the cinnamon
onion for which he had been searching or only a near relation or counter-
feit. He was thinking about the instructions: that he would need to trek up

the mountain on a Six-Yin Day, with the Powers' Treasure Amulet attached by a thong to his waistband, that he would need to be leading a white dog on a leash and carrying a white chicken. He was wondering whether the chicken would have to be dead, and if not, how he could possibly carry it with any dignity.

White Jade Blossom was thinking about something else. She took the brush from his hand and put it back into the inkstand. She took his hand and moved it into the folds of her robe. Qin Lao, still abstracted, his eyes focused on a small black-and-white bird on the bare branch of a tree outside his open window, his thoughts on his work, was stunned to feel his fingers being led into the silky-wet flesh at the fork of her, astonishing him with its steamy and so alive heat.

He blinked. He was thinking about that chicken—would it need to be dead or alive?—and had not decided. He looked at the woman and remembered he needed yin, as a man who is not naturally thirsty is cautioned to get enough liquids. So he followed her into their chamber and did what he needed to do. It was all of a piece, this search for immortality.

In the third year of the marriage of White Jade Blossom to Qin Lao, Xu Xuli invited the young alchemist to his home. Qin Lao demurred, saying that he was decocting an herb potion that was a costly experiment. He had had to travel a full month to Mount Emei, southwest of Chengdu, to procure the plant in quantity and had had to hire three young peasant girls to pick the blossoms and dry them and press the leaves. He had then had to stay a full week after the harvest to wait for the plants to dry.

During that week he had climbed to the summit of Mount Emei, which was shrouded in fairy cloud 330 days a year. He had been told that if he should walk out on a certain path through the trees between three and four o'clock in the afternoon, when the sun was just there, peeping in through the branches at just such an angle, and the cloud was about, low to the ground—as it was almost every day—that he might be blessed with a halo of mist, the aureole of the Tao, a glow that would surround him and signify blessing.

On the third day of his stay at the mountain he climbed to the heights and walked out on the path in the afternoon when the sun was at the proper declination. He saw an elderly man robed in such a mist and a pair of little girls with a grandmother, all bathed in halo gold. The two little girls pointed at him and marveled out loud in their chirping small voices about his radiance, but he could not see it. He wished there were some way he could step outside of himself to see himself—in his mind, he was inventing photography—and lamented that there was not such a way. He doubted that aureoles signified anything and believed rather that this was some trick of the mist that was no respecter of persons.

That evening he descended the mountain. The following day he returned to his village with a servant and an entire cartful of herbs. Robbers never disturbed them with such loads. Robbers feared retribution from angry gods who would be—surely!—in league with the alchemist, and, moreover, robbers had no idea what to do with herbs in such quantity, even if they had great value. There was no black market in coltsfoot leaves.

Qin Lao had been keeping the fire alive for thirty days for this purpose, with three days to go. Sublimation was so time consuming, but it was a character builder as well: finding the herbs and the berries and leaves, and watching the fires, and procuring and melting the metals built patience. It was as if the refining process for the cinnabar had not its parallel but its precise human analog in the refining of character which was the fruit of this process.

Xu Xuli had said on the previous day that he would send a servant to watch the fire for a while so that the two men could meet and have a serious talk. Qin Lao said it was impossible, that he himself must watch. Xu Xuli waved a bamboo cane in the air and shouted so suddenly that his voice came out in squeaks. Qin Lao must come, and Xu Xuli would not take no for a response. His cane swished again. Qin Lao's eyebrows went up. He was not used to imperiousness in his usually mild-tempered friend.

The servant came and watched the fire, and Qin Lao rode in the lacquered sedan chair that Xu Xuli sent to his sprawling stone home with its screened-in verandas. Xu Xuli brought out a pottery jug of pale, strong rice wine and little cups. Qin Lao demurred: Surely Xu Xuli knew that an alchemist must not have strong drink any more than he might partake of animal flesh!

Xu Xuli shouted: Surely the essential nature of the Tao is not in rules but in knowing the essences of life and in setting priorities.

Qin Lao considered a moment. Such a statement did not seem shoutable, but in fact his friend had just bellowed at him. Qin Lao responded: Well, yes, that is true. The Tao does lie in setting priorities.

Xu Xuli said, "White Jade Blossom complains to my wife that you cannot be bothered with giving her children. My friend, is this so?"

Qin Lao sighed slightly and looked at the tiny rice-wine cups set next to each other on the low table. "Bothered?" he echoed.

"You have no son." Xu Xuli's tone was accusatory.

He poured rice wine into the cups. His tone changed. He leaned toward Qin Lao. He offered a cup of wine. "Here. Drink." He said it again. "You have no son, Qin Lao." His voice was softer, almost sad. "You cannot mean to neglect your wife?" He looked at Qin Lao's cup. "Drink," he ordered. "Clearly abstention from drink is not at this moment the Tao's true priority. Flexibility, friend, is the essence of the highest sort of man, is that not true? As the bamboo, though strong, must bend to keep its wholeness, so too must we."

Qin Lao tossed down the cup of wine. It burned his throat fiercely. He caught his breath, choked, breathed out gasping. He smelled the strong wine on his breath. Xu Xuli laughed. "Perhaps today you will not be Qin Lao, the timid young alchemist, but Long Wang, the Dragon King. Perhaps we will turn you into—"

Qin Lao held out his cup to his friend. "Pour then," he said. "Remember that I am the alchemist. I am the one who can change things to something else. You only watch the sky." Xu Xuli poured the wine.

Qin Lao thought about that word his friend had used, "timid," and felt something like anger. He drank down his second cup of rice wine quickly, in one swallow. "More," he said, extending his cup for refilling.

He thought about his own assertion, that he was the one who could change things to other things. He felt his mouth corners shaping an expression of rue. He had not intended that. It was the rice wine at work, undoing his normal restraints, his ability to hide behind the impassive and seamless-appearing mask he wore for others because Meng had trained him this way and Hoptoad-Gold had reinforced that.

"You are afraid of this thing," Xu Xuli said. "This fact. You are afraid of the fact that you are afraid." Xu Xuli leaned toward Qin Lao. He lowered his voice. He spoke comfortingly, reassuringly. "Other men have been impotent, friend. Surely you know the remedies, herbal and otherwise."

He got up and walked into the next room. Qin Lao stared after him, floating deep in his now somewhat sensitive skull on a sea of rice wine in a very small boat the size of a nutshell, a boat whose sail seemed to be taking him where it pleased despite his wishes. Xu Xuli returned with a silk purse the size of his palm. It was gray green with a geometric design woven into the fabric and with a red drawstring with tassels.

Xu pulled at the drawstring and tipped the purse into his own lap. In the taut skirt of his robe sat the envelope's contents: an ornate flat ivory ring, something over an inch and a half in diameter at its outer edges. The ring comprised two carved dragons whose tails locked at the bottom and whose tongues intertwined in a protruding spiral.

"With this," said Xu, "one can maintain vital strength in the member, and this"—he rubbed his forefinger over the nub of the spiral—"can afford much delight to the woman." He raised an eyebrow in what looked like slyness.

Qin Lao blinked. The drink had just hit bottom, in an explosion of warmth. He decided to take offense. It was a considered decision.

He rose slightly from his chair, then sat back down. He stared at the dragon ring in his friend's lap as if it would leap up at him. He stared in particular at the strange spiraling tongues and the hill of concentric small rings that they built. His censors down, he did not hide the look of horror this thing elicited. "Afraid, Xu Xuli? What are you saying?" Xu's remark had been made many minutes before, and Xu, as deep into the rice wine as Qin Lao, struggled backward to retrieve the reference. As the young alchemist challenged his friend—near pugnacious, and much unaccustomed for this man of such sanguine temperament—Qin Lao heard himself as if he were someone else, at a distance. He laughed aloud at that imagined far man's self-importance and silliness, then realized that that man was himself. He decided that he did not care.

Xu sighed. "White Jade Blossom has told Yao-niang—"

"That I, Qin Lao, am afraid?" roared Qin Lao.

In the concubine's quarters, at the far end of the house, there was a peal of laughter that sounded like silver beads rolling down slippery chutes. There were at least four women laughing. One laughed so hard she began choking. Xu Xuli frowned and ignored the noise.

"Not exactly," said Xu Xuli. "Not those words. Not the actual word 'afraid.' It is what I drew from my wife's telling of it," said Xu Xuli.

"Afraid?" Qin Lao's voice rose, not in denial, but in disbelief.

Xu Xuli frowned in astonishment. He was beginning to think that the truth, despite his first rash reading of Qin Lao's livid denial, might be more complex. "White Jade Blossom has told Yao-niang that you are very . . . timid . . . with her, and that this is why she has not conceived. She says there is no possibility—" said Xu Xuli.

"Oh, my wife is a terrible tale bearer, then," said Qin Lao.

"And is the tale true?"

"It is not." Qin Lao held out his empty rice-wine cup to his friend. "Oh, I do not believe my wife said this thing." He leaned forward into his own lap, moaning. "Is it possible that your wife has misperceived what White Jade Blossom intended?" Qin Lao looked forthrightly at his friend and hoped his head was as steady as he believed it to be.

Xu Xuli laughed and poured wine in both cups. "It is possible that my wife has misperceived"—his voice became louder and slower, deliberate, angry, delighted— "*every single thing anyone has ever said to her and that includes her lord husband.*" He drank down his wine. "It is possible that my wife wishes to stir up trouble—river-bottom silt—yes!—in this matter and cause the Huang He, as it were, to overflow once again, drowning whole cities, as it so often is wont to do. It is possible that my wife likes to make trouble. Yes, that is a possible thing!"

"Yao-niang?" said Qin Lao. "Your sweet Yao-niang?" He laughed heartily. Xu Xuli had complained more than once of his wife's slyness in matters where she had not gotten her way. "Is it possible that Yao-niang is envious of my wife's beauty and youth and would like to make trouble?"

Xu Xuli paused and thought about this. "Ah, my wife's beauty and youth! Those birds she has been watching fly, daily, daily, out each window she passes! Yes! Yao-niang is not pleased these days with what she sees in her mirror! Perhaps this is simply jealousy, malice, the entire cartload," said Xu Xuli. He recalled his wife, caught in an unwary moment when he had entered her quarters without announcing himself, pulling at the flesh under her eyes, making mouths at herself in the reflection in her washbasin. Her expression was one of dismay. Yao-niang, at thirty-five, was aging quickly, the quality of her skin altering from smooth to porous, the shapes of her skin about her eyes changing from taut to a soft relaxation, like wilted hibiscus petals.

"I believe," said Qin Lao, "that I am offended at your thinking I must be impotent, friend Xu Xuli. What foolishness!" His voice was mild, and slightly amused.

Xu Xuli stared at his friend, and his friend stared back. In Xu's look was incomprehension, shame at having been drawn into this, and a sense of how little he knew his own wife. In his friend's return stare there was a quality Xu Xuli had not seen in Qin Lao's quotidian moments unlit by rice wine: a fieriness, a sense that this unworldly alchemist might have his own very reasonable pride as well as his Taoist humility.

"Yao-niang has done her work then," said Xu Xuli. "She has set friend against friend, she has set you against your wife, and no doubt prior to all this, your wife against you."

"Yao-niang is a busy one," said Qin Lao. He could feel the rice wine in his sinuses, in his ears, beating against the backbones of his forehead like a liquid heart. He thought of Yao-niang's small dark eyes, and how he had suspected several times that there was something nefarious going on back of their darkness. He decided that perhaps he had not imagined her looking at his own smooth cheeks with a look that was not unlike lust.

Xu Xuli stopped, suddenly seeming sober. "Then why do you have no son?"

"It is not for lack of union," said Qin Lao. Qin Lao's eyes twinkled. "Perhaps you would like to observe this, if you do not trust your friend?"

"Observe?" said Xu Xuli. "*Observe?*"

"White Jade Blossom has no lack of passion," said Qin Lao. "Often, she runs just ahead of me, but I keep pace. My work is a weight on me, often: I feel as if I am carrying with me at all times, perhaps in the folds of my sleeves, all the cinnabar chunks I am heating to draw out the mercury. White Jade Blossom, by contrast, and unlike the servant girls, has nothing to do all day but to primp and play zither and sing silly women's songs. Thus she awaits me in our bedchamber with an alacrity that is, I believe, in large part simple anticipation of release from boredom. On the proper days after cessation of menstruation, we engage in the Nine Positions: the Turning Dragon, the Tiger's Tread, the Monkey's Attack, the Cleaving Cicada, the Mounting Turtle, the Fluttering Phoenix Bird—this is her favorite—"

"Indeed!" said Xu Xuli. "Did you say *observe?*" He was smiling broadly.

"The seventh position—the Rabbit Sucking Its Hair—this is the position we utilized yesterday afternoon. In the evening, the eighth, Overlapping Fish Scales. When I go home tonight, it will be the ninth, Cranes with Joined Necks." Qin Lao spoke these words with a soberness that might have seemed more appropriate in a lecture, perhaps on the applications of the western geometers such as Pythagoras to the astronomy Xu Xuli practiced and taught in his school.

He was not taking delight in the thought of his wife supine in their broad bed in the Fluttering Phoenix position or how that dragon ring might affect what he believed her already rather full delight. His eyes looked distant, as if he were back of his slight frown—begotten of rice wine now turning to an abstract nonsensory thumping—considering the diagram he had seen on one of Xu Xuli's scrolls, a leaning reed protruding from a pond's surface. As indeed he was. The accompanying text read: "In the center of a square pond whose side is ten *ch'ih* grows a reed whose top reaches one *ch'ih* above the water's skin. If one were to tug the reed toward the bank, its top would be even with the surface of the pond. What is the depth of the pond and the length of the reed?"

Xu Xuli stared at his friend, who was thinking hard about the geometric proof he had seen in Xu's own scroll. "What are you thinking, friend?"

"I am thinking, 'What is the depth of the pond and the length of the reed?'" said Qin Lao.

Xu Xuli, who had just picked up a cup of wine and sipped from it, choked with laughter, clear wine spraying in a fine mist from his nostrils. "The depth of the pond is irrelevant," said Xu Xuli. "And as for the length of the reed, I am certain you have in your scrolls the recipe for the enlargement of a lame male member by the application of stag-marrow salve—"

"I am not speaking in metaphors," Qin Lao said in consternation. "I was answering you directly. You asked what I thought, and I was thinking about the theorem you showed me, in your books."

"Oh," said Xu Xuli. "Then that is not the problem?"

Qin Lao shook his head soberly. He was not the least bit sober now. He was recalling another problem from Xu's books: "A tree of height twenty *ch'ih* has a circumference of three *ch'ih*. There is an arrowroot vine that winds seven times around the tree and reaches to the top. What is the length of the vine?"

The night before, this problem had come to mind when he had been engaged in the Hair-Sucking Rabbit with White Jade Blossom. It helped to conserve the sperm if he could concentrate his mind elsewhere. Then he controlled the situation: If he could distract himself with this geometry, he could prevent himself from losing semen at all. This way his yang would not be diminished and emissions could be kept for the times when White Jade Blossom would be liable to conceive. He had kept his eyes closed, and White Jade Blossom had no idea that he was doing square roots in his head.

He mumbled something to himself, not realizing that he had spoken aloud rather than simply thinking the words. It was of course the rice wine speaking.

"What?" asked Xu Xuli.

Qin Lao felt slightly foolish, but he answered. "I said that the length of the plant is twenty-nine *ch'ih*," said Qin Lao.

Xu Xuli guffawed. "Twenty-nine *ch'ih!* Your male member is twenty-nine *ch'ih!* Indeed, then, you must be the Dragon King."

Had Justin Wong, twenty-two hundred and several dozen years later, eighty-eight generations later, and directly descended from Qin Lao, heard Xu Xuli, he would have guffawed in turn, hearing the words in Chinese: Long Wang, meaning *dragon king*.

Xu Xuli, of course, would not have comprehended the pun. The English language would not come to be for long centuries yet.

"That is not what I said," Qin Lao said. He made a sound of disgust. "My friend, you are drunk."

Both men were speaking much more slowly now, as if, were they to rise, they might also walk much more carefully, holding their robes up about themselves and perhaps looking quite silly to all of the concubines, who were now—since they were certain the men were engrossed and unaware of their presence—listening through the wall.

Qin Lao shook his head no. "I cooperate," said Qin Lao. "Oh, indeed, I cooperate. And the reed, if you wish me to speak metaphorically, is quite happy to stand in the pond without drooping. Pointing straight up to your stars." He spoke more loudly than he knew. He stood and pointed his right index finger dramatically at the ceiling. Behind the wall there was a titter and then a guffaw.

Xu Xuli went to the doorway and bellowed at the women. "You go!" he said. "You *go!*" He was livid. He watched the eyes of the third concubine as she turned. This was a lively one. He caught himself. He yelled again and his voice cracked. "No more!" he said. He hoped that he sounded authoritative.

Qin Lao stopped and became even more serious than he had been previously. "Seeking earthly offspring and true immortality both demand that I give my full and intense attention to this matter. As a follower of the Tao, as a true alchemist, I can do nothing less."

"What, then?" said Xu Xuli. "What then is the problem?"

"Your wife is envious," said Qin Lao. "My wife—who is without guile—I believe—has no doubt told her all of this, down to and including the Hair-Sucking Rabbit, the Fish Scales, the Neck-Mated Cranes. Do you not then give her her due? Is this perhaps the source of her irritability?"

Xu Xuli roared with simultaneous rage and laughter. He slapped his thigh. He slapped himself in the forehead exasperatedly with the heel of his hand. "Yao-niang has done it again! Such consternation! The gods must be watching this show, thinking what fools these humans are!"

Qin Lao never mentioned this conversation to his wife. He did not believe that White Jade Blossom had pushed Yao-niang to this, and he did not wish to engage in discussion about it, fearing that perhaps he would then have to deal with a matter he had rather let pass unexamined.

Xu Xuli, by contrast, banished his wife—who had not been listening with the concubines to their conversation—to the concubines' quarters and did not see her for three full months. In the meantime, the fourth concubine took her regular place in her husband's bed.

On the appointed nights, Xu Xuli of course visited also with the first, second, and third concubines as custom specified. Yao-niang mewled like a cat but stayed out of his sight. The fourth concubine taunted Yao-niang with remarks about Xu Xuli's comments on the shape of her breasts, offering quotes and graphic descriptions. Yao-niang's nostrils flared with rage.

In the third month of Yao-niang's banishment, Xu Xuli's ministrations (on the schedule kept by his bookkeeper, along with the equally complex tax accounts) impregnated the third concubine with her first child. When Yao-niang was returned to the favor of her lord husband, she never again made such trouble. She seemed sobered. Even when, two months later, the pregnancy of the third concubine became an obvious matter, Yao-niang said nothing.

But for three more years White Jade Blossom, the wife of Qin Lao, did not conceive.

Xu Xuli at this point came to visit Qin Lao one spring evening. He said, "Soon you will no longer be young."

"I am twenty-six," said Qin Lao. He spoke the number as slowly as if he were squeezing a thick and resistant medicinal ointment out of a skin bag. He made an unripe-persimmon face. He seemed to be saying, Life is long. But then he recalled Master Meng's death at forty-seven, without an heir— unless he himself, the foundling in fringed blankets in the big wicker basket left on Meng's veranda, were considered the heir. But that was different.

For a moment Qin Lao looked off into the trees. He was thinking about where he might have come from: whether the farmer he still believed had left him on the porch for Meng to raise had ever seen him as he was growing, whether that farmer had watched him from a distance with pride, whether that farmer, who might be old now, or only the age of his master at death, was one of the men whom he saw in the town when he did weekly business.

Then he thought: *Perhaps I am totally wrong. Perhaps there was no farmer.*

Perhaps a young girl had relations with a wealthy, important man she knew would have her killed if she told her plight.

Perhaps, then, my father would have killed me inside my mother.

He imagined his poor mother slain by a blow from a brutal lord: a sweet young girl, no doubt, from whom he had inherited this slight crook in his right little finger. He mourned for her. He hated his horrible father, that violent noble. He frowned at the thought of his own never having come to see the light of day. He mourned his own death.

He stopped short in his thought. Then he thought, but did not speak, the words *Truly, I know nothing.*

"You are without an heir," said Xu Xuli, who had seven offspring by this time by his wives and eight more by his concubines. "You certainly know that." Xu Xuli waited until this seemed to have sunk in, like hard rain on packed earth that resists it. "I believe we can see," he said, clearing his throat, "that your wife is a useless one. That she cannot bear a child."

Qin Lao's eyebrows went up. His thin mustache drooped as he pursed his lips thoughtfully. "This is a matter about which I have begun thinking," he said.

"I have heard of a beautiful young woman over the mountain," said Xu Xuli. "First daughter of a landowner with a number of fine properties. The girl has very long hair." He indicated its length with a slice of his hand at the back of his own thigh, as if he were marking the base of his buttock.

Qin Lao's chin lifted in thought. He said nothing, but the slight flare of his nostrils suggested to Xu Xuli that he was resisting.

"Paugh!" said Xu. "It will increase your yin energy! It is the job of the alchemist to achieve unity in all the areas!" He tried to look as if he knew what he was talking about, though he wondered whether his words made any sense. He was after all an astronomer. He knew little besides mathematics and stars.

"Perhaps I would not have to neglect her, then, if this plan would increase my yin energy," said Qin Lao. He cocked his head slightly, considered this thing, and looked quizzical.

He turned away absentmindedly as if he were going back to his work, as if the matter had been settled, even though it was clear he was refusing to settle it.

"It is time to do something," said Xu Xuli.

"I have not thought long enough," said Qin Lao.

"Paugh! You could think forever, you . . . thinker!" shouted Xu Xuli.

"Perhaps it is not White Jade Blossom but Qin Lao who is at fault in this matter of the heir," said Qin Lao.

"What! The male!" expostulated his friend the astronomer.

"It is a possible thing," said Qin Lao.

He was thinking that perhaps he might have erred in dosing himself with alchemical elixirs, or in failing to dose himself. Perhaps, as an alternative explanation, he had siphoned too much yin from White Jade Blossom and diminished his male yang strength thereby. He considered that thought.

"Paugh!" said Xu Xuli. "We must find you a second wife!"

"Ah," said Qin Lao. "I am so busy already. White Jade Blossom would not be pleased if I neglected her."

"Then do not neglect her," said Xu Xuli firmly. "I will send a letter to the landowner tomorrow." He looked at Qin Lao as if to ask approval.

Qin Lao seemed neutral about the idea. He was imagining vividly: hair that reached all that way and what the girl might look like in his bedchamber, poised standing on the flat of the bed, like a child, her fair cheeks dimpled and her small hands in the air like two hummingbirds, bouncing slightly on the resilient moss mattress, arrayed only in her own hair, with the light on the sleek silky black, loosened from its pins, bouncing too. Still he appeared, to the gaze of astronomer Xu Xuli, almost indifferent.

Perhaps her teeth would protrude in a most ugly way. Perhaps she would have a harsh voice, or perhaps the abundance of hair would extend to the rest of her and she would be like the women a merchant had told him about, in the West, in the land that would later be called eastern Europe, who had hair on their arms and their legs, as if they were transmogrifying to bears. The traveling merchant had said, however, that these women had great strength in the act and that if he had been able to buy these women—they had not been for sale—he would have brought two or three of them home with the caravan.

"Shall I do this?" Xu Xuli prompted.

Qin Lao could not remember what Xu Xuli was referring to, what it was that he wanted or did not want to do. He was thinking about these bear-women the merchants had met in the very cold lands past the desert. He looked at him, puzzled.

"Shall I send for the girl?" Xu Xuli prompted.

Qin Lao remembered: this was not a bear-girl, but rather the one with the long black hair, bouncing on his mattress, candlelight gleaming off that silky black. "Do her teeth protrude greatly?" asked Qin Lao.

"Paugh!" said Xu Xuli. "If they do, just blow out the lamp! She will bring a grand dowry to you, my friend. She will give you an heir."

The young woman, whose name was Jo-lan, brought a grand dowry indeed. She did not have terrible teeth, though her face approached plainness which was not enlivened even when she wore cosmetics. Despite the fact that her hair was long, it was not shiny. Qin Lao was relieved that her demands on him were not extreme, and White Jade Blossom felt unthreatened. But no heir came from either wife.

In the twelfth year after Qin Lao had married White Jade Blossom, Xu Xuli decided that it was imperative that concubines be introduced. They were less complicated than wives, though they cost rather than bringing dowries. Still Xu resisted Qin Lao's suggestion that he himself might be at fault in the matter of this nonproduction of an heir.

Three concubines were bought. Qin Lao sighed and cooperated.

At this time, Qin Lao was making potions of "dragon bones," ground and mixed with herbs, as well as with cinnabar-mercury. Peasants found the bones buried in clayey earth pockets, not knowing that they were indeed fossils, bones of saber-toothed tigers and three-toed small horses.

They sold the bones cheaply, and Zhou ground them patiently.

One particular recipe for immortality which Qin Lao had found in Meng's pharmacopoeia called for the boiling of these dragon bones with certain powerful herbs, then grinding them into a fine powder which was packed into small bags sewn up from thin silk. The recipe called for the silk envelope of these ground dragon bones and herbs to be placed into the disemboweled and dried carcasses of dead Sichuan swallows. The swallow was then to be placed on the chest when one slept, and it was guaranteed that the morning would find the sleeper to have risen out of his body and become a genie. The swallow carcass was then to be burned. The recipe did not say that it might also be used to produce "immortality" in the form of a human heir, but Qin Lao thought that perhaps it was worth a try. So he had followed all of the steps and done this odious thing. He had even, because he slept on his side rather than on his back, bound the dead bird to his chest with broad ribbons.

The first concubine, who was to sleep with him that night, made furious noises about this, but he did his duty regardless—it was her fertile time— with the dead swallow strapped to his naked chest. In the morning he woke, and the swallow stank, and the first concubine had returned to her own bed in disgust. He assumed he had gotten something terribly wrong in the formula.

White Jade Blossom caught a spring cold, which worsened through summer. She took potions Qin Lao gave her, but she became pale and thin, her bones protruding as if they might cut her. Qin Lao could not have known that the cold was just secondary, and that White Jade Blossom had what would later be given a Western name, Hodgkin's disease, a cancer of the lymphatic system, which would not be treatable until about the time Justin Wong was born, twenty-two hundred and several dozen years later.

White Jade Blossom was buried wearing a gown far too big for her, tucked back behind her to cradle her closely. Qin Lao stood at the grave site and thought he would miss her.

Then he went back to his laboratory and worked on a potion involving the bones of a thousand-year-old variegated Power Tortoise. He immersed the whole animal—which Zhou had brought from a full day's journey upriver, in very cold weather—in sheep's blood, in a vat. It took a half-dozen sheep to provide enough blood. Because Qin Lao did not eat meat, he gave away all the bled sheep to the poor of the village.

Then he removed the shell, roasted it deep in a fire of mountain wood logs, and let it cool. He had Zhou grind the shell and then took a knifepoint's worth of the tortoiseshell powder three times a day until it all was consumed. Meng's recipe scroll said that at that point he would ascend into heaven. He did not. Again, he had done something wrong and must start over.

The second wife, Jo-lan, stayed healthy but did not conceive. The first concubine aged prematurely, her hair growing white and her menstrual periods ceasing. The second concubine died in a fall from a footbridge across a stream in flood, hitting her head on the rocks and drowning as she was swept away. Peasants recovered her body, and Qin Lao buried her in an appropriately less auspicious spot not far from White Jade Blossom's grave. The third concubine, like Jo-lan, wide of cheekbone like the dark people to the northwest, lived on uneventfully, learning to play the flute. She played songs that sometimes reminded Qin Lao of White Jade Blossom, in pale faded ways.

Qin Lao, now in his forties, still did not recall the prophecy by the old scapulomancer he had met with Master Meng: that he would have a child in his old age, a son, who would carry a sword.

If he had at this point in his life—he considered it to be old age—recalled this, he would have laughed. He lived on in peace with the plain Jo-lan, who had become dour with age and did not wish much contact at all and with his white-haired first concubine and his flute-playing third concubine. He did his duty, continuing to hope for a son.

Qin Lao, now fifty-seven, had managed his property and moneys well, with the assistance of Xu Xuli's bookkeeper. Possessed of more wealth than he knew what to do with at this point and still endowed with the mandate of Master Meng to keep seeking eternal life, he purchased from a rather peculiar peddler, who nonetheless seemed to believe what he was saying, a ginseng root that the merchant assured him was 297 years old.

The ginseng sat, brown and desiccated, in a box with carved floral designs on its lid and a cutout design that let the air flow into and out of the box. Qin Lao knew he had no way of knowing how old this root was or, in fact, given its advanced state of decrepitude, whether it were a ginseng root at all. It was said that after three centuries, the root changed into a man with white blood, which was the actual elixir of immortality. It was said that a single drop of this white blood would be sufficient to bring a dead man to life. In three years Qin Lao could test the theory. In the meantime, he worked in his laboratory.

It was at this time that the servant Zhou appeared. Qin Lao was grateful. He had not lost strength as such, but he had less inclination to physical labor and more of an urgent sense that he must work at his alchemical task.

The first concubine had become troublesome, as had the third. He essentially gave them to Zhou, who was certainly pleased. A mute servant had no reason to expect anything of the sort, no reason, actually, to expect any more than an occasional beggar-girl who had no other prospects and still would expect to be paid in food. Zhou knew other servants who had gotten into terrible trouble this way, stealing sheep to pay prostitutes, who gave them cankers for thanks. This saved Qin Lao from trouble, and Zhou worked all the harder, out of his own gratitude.

Qin Lao at this point had only Jo-lan to worry about. Jo-lan, when she spoke, had little to say except that she had wasted her life here with him and wished that she had never—twenty-five years before—left her father's home to come to this village that even the gods eschewed. Qin Lao asked if she would like to go there again. She seemed startled. Yes, she would. Would she like to go permanently? Her elation—the first he had seen in this whole quarter century—was extreme. Yes, she would love to go home to her father, who still was alive, and her mother as well. She would not have ever to come back here? No, she would not.

The following day Jo-lan told both the concubines that she was going away. They were overjoyed, because Jo-lan's depressive demeanor weighed on everyone within her sphere of broodiness. She instructed them to make a wonderful dinner for Qin Lao: a golden red fish she herself fetched from the river merchant's; crisp, soft, perfect vegetables; and a cool molded custard dressed with crystallized crescents of fruit she had bought at the market.

Qin Lao had no idea Jo-lan had such thoughts in her. He thanked her for the dinner. The concubines, watching from behind a curtain, remarked on the fact that she had seemed anonymous, somehow, all these years, but now seemed to be a real person in her joy at leaving.

That night Jo-lan entertained Qin Lao, who had not yet turned sixty years old, by demonstrating for him, and with him, the positions of Reeling Off Silk, Winding Dragon, the Kingfisher Union, the Pair of Mandarin Ducks, and the Bamboo near the Altar. Through all of this Qin Lao conserved his bodily fluids and did not ejaculate. He was, after all, a skilled Taoist lover—adept despite his taciturnity.

At the end, when he thought that he was near to calling a halt to the unsought festivity, Jo-lan executed the Wailing Monkey Embracing a Tree, and his seed left him despite all of his resolution, oozing like white lava.

Jo-lan, who was forty-two, asked whether he had now had enough. Yes, he replied. Good, she said. Now I will go to my father's. In the morning she left in a carriage. The dowry had long since gone into the alchemy. Jo-lan did not ask for it back.

Qin Lao, standing in the front door, waving, watched the carriage's rear wheels as she departed. He cupped his testicles in both hands and made an audible groan. From behind a painted screen inside the door, both the concubines laughed.

He went back to his laboratory and began work on a potion that involved the mingling of the dried and powdered remains of a ten-pound fungus that Zhou had procured—it was called the Express Token Mushroom— with the powder of a Flaming Brazier Mushroom.

The energy required in this one was great. He had consulted with Xu on the proper proportions, which seemed to be the secret key. Xu had thought that perhaps in the formulas Xu Xuli knew there was some elegant numeric relation—like that of the right-triangle theorem—that would mingle the powders perfectly. Once he had the proportions correctly divined, he would need to mix this with mercury in minuscule amounts, to form small pellets. He had not tried this particular method before.

He did not think of Jo-lan again until that night, when he lay down to sleep and his scrotum still ached terribly. He cupped his soft parts in his hands, pulled his legs up, and slept soundly, dreaming a dream that he would not remember, in which he crawled into a peach and became a preborn child again. Jo-lan had nothing to do with the dream, and he did not miss her.

Then he did not think of Jo-Lan again until the news of her death came, the following year. Her father's house had been broken into by robbers, and his treasure taken, and everyone in the house killed, for a total of seventeen people. Qin Lao could not imagine it. So much greed. So much death.

The third concubine became pregnant by Zhou. The child was a girl, who was sickly but had no deformities. The concubine did not recover from childbirth but declined and declined, an infection that would not be cured, the cause finally of her death.

Zhou sent the child to a woman in the village who had lost a six-month-old baby not three days before and so had milk in rich supply, and then he thought no more of it. A female child was not a blessing. A mute servant did not need offspring. The gods would approve his solution.

The first concubine disappeared not too long after this, for three days, and then as suddenly as she had left, returned. Zhou watched her and made signs to Qin Lao about this new strangeness that had come into her behavior.

Qin Lao had Zhou go into the village to find a young hunter who could trap an animal whose name he did not know, only knew as the "wind-born animal," the creature born of the wind. This animal would not die if put into a fire, could not be pierced with an ax blade, seemed somehow immortal. However, the animal would die at once—said the records of Master Meng—if reeds from the surface of a rock were stuffed up its nose.

The next step, Qin Lao told Zhou, was to remove the brain from the skull, mix it with crushed petals of chrysanthemum flowers, and take the powder obtained until it was all gone, one dose daily, as much as could be scooped onto the tip of a bone knife. This would cure such insanity as had come into the first concubine upon her return.

Zhou found a hunter who said he would go out immediately to look for this wind-born creature. Zhou was able to talk with his hands so expressively that even people who had never met him were able to understand. The hunter did not require a retainer, but Zhou gave him food for the journey: many bags of dried fruit and dried buffalo meat and several loaves of good bread. Zhou returned home from the town with chrysanthemums for Qin Lao to dry and to pulverize.

Zhou slept with the white-haired concubine and fed her pickles and soup every morning and evening. The fourth day after this she wandered away again. She was found in the heart of the village, hugging, so tightly it seemed she would break her, a three-year-old child she kept saying was her own.

Zhou took her home and gave her a sleeping powder Qin Lao had made. She slept through the next day. He brought her a red ribbon for her white hair, as if she were a small girl. She looked at him impassively, then laughed wildly, then went affectless once more. He slept in her bed again. There was no word from the hunter.

The fifth day, the concubine hanged herself from a tree two hundred meters behind the house but was not found—because of the thick foliage there—for two days more. Zhou buried her near concubines number two and number three, closest to White Jade Blossom's grave.

The following morning, before the sun had reached the tops of the bushes with cherry-hued flowers that lined the crest of the hill, Zhou and his master, Qin Lao, hired a carriage and had a man drive them—as if Zhou were a master as well—three days' journey, to the lake called Lake That Has Risen to Heaven, the lake where Meng had said so many years before that he would teach young Moon-Grabber to walk on the water.

And will you try this, the trick with the cinnabar paste? Zhou asked with his muscular, fluttering, heavy scarred hands, as they stood on the high ground and looked out over the blue water, mirroring sky.

I try many experiments, Zhou, said Qin Lao. Many fail. Failure in this experiment is too expensive. So, no, I think not.

He paused for a moment. If you would like to try this yourself, I have cinnabar paste in my bag, he said.

No, thank you, Zhou signed.

The two men stood silently, looking out over the mountain lake. Zhou's hands signaled: The water is beautiful.

Yes, said Qin Lao. Beautiful.

THE ALCHEMIST AND his servant lived together in the house with the courtyard for a dozen years and more. Peasants brought dragon bones. Others brought flowers to pulverize. Rents accumulated, taxes went out to collectors.

Qin Lao, in the forest to gather a fungus that Master Meng's records said was to be powdered and mixed with juice of the cowherd's berry, encountered a fox. The fox slithered, frosty and fiery hued, around the side of an ancient tree, then stopped and stared at the alchemist. Qin Lao stared back. He had lived seventy-five years and had never seen a fox, up close. But then why would he have?

Qin Lao had heard a story told by an old blind woman about a fox. The old woman, who had great-grandchildren running about her as she told the story, lived in a village where Qin Lao had gone to collect a root needed for a salve he was making.

The old woman was sitting at a roadside near a shrine to a fox-god. Qin Lao had seen many of these but had not thought about them, because his mind was usually occupied with whatever ingredient he needed for his work at that particular moment.

The old blind grandmother said that when she was a young girl in a village far northeast of here, a young woman had been buried. Two years later, she had said, a mysterious fox had appeared in the village, acting as if somehow it had been domesticated. It hung about people when they were talking together, as if it were someone's red-furred, white-tip-tailed lap dog. It heard everything about this girl's death, from relatives and friends who had been talking out in the village square. Then the fox disappeared.

Three days later the girl who had died came back. She spoke reasonably. She said, no, she had not died, she simply had gone to visit cousins at Six-Pine Lake, past the trail to Two-Pine Mountain. The girl's hair was in the same pair of tight coiled braids as it had been when they saw her last, dead.

Everyone stared at her and no one could talk, the old woman said. Everyone questioned his or her senses. Everyone knew they had seen the girl dead: very pale, very dead. Yet she looked just the same as she had looked before she had fallen ill. This girl's name was Lady Jasmine Yi. She had a space between her front teeth that was quite distinctive and, oddly enough, men thought beautiful.

After a short space of time, the great-grandmother had said, two men became enamored of her and began to compete for her favors. No one knew where the girl lived now, for her parents had moved away to the city. But each afternoon, the girl came back to the village square where the men played their games. Ultimately the two suitors went out of the city arguing which would have this girl, this Jasmine Yi. Neither returned. Both were found dead, of knife wounds, in each other's arms, under the tree where the girl had been buried. A fox hung about as the bodies were carried away.

The old blind woman shooed her grandchildren away from the road as she talked. "This girl was not a girl but a fox," said the grandmother. "She lay with both of these men and bewitched them. She caused them to die." She shouted at her grandchildren, who had wandered away. She could feel their absence acutely.

As if Qin Lao were a child who could not understand, she spelled it out for him. "This girl was really a fox who had wiggled its way deep into the grave and then slipped into the body of Jasmine Yi. When the fox had performed its nefarious deed, it returned the girl's body to its coffin and once again became a fox."

Qin Lao thought about the old grandmother's tale. He had once before heard tales like this, several tales about foxes who actually were succubi, she-demons who came to men and had sex with them then took their souls. He had not heard any particulars before this story. The way that the old woman told the tale—her hands moving animatedly in the air, her blind eyes closed but her eyebrows mobile about them—made him believe that this could very well be a true story. One never knew.

THE VERY AFTERNOON after Qin Lao, at seventy-seven, living alone with old Zhou all these years, sees the deer droppings in the courtyard, and laughs—*Priceless!*—Zhou returns from the market late, empty-handed.

He signs: They had no fish.

Qin Lao, usually detached from earthly matters to the degree that Zhou has often to bring him his food and remind him to eat, frowns irascibly. He feels astonishment at himself. "No fish!" he says to Zhou. "No fish! I have never heard anything so absurd."

Zhou signs: No one has caught a fish in three days. The merchants say it is an omen. His eyebrows leap about as he signs. He makes guttural noises.

Qin Lao sighs. Zhou has brought nothing but noodles and a bottle of glue and some pieces of leather to repair an apparatus in the laboratory. "Then we shall have noodles for dinner," he says, and Zhou cooks them.

The following day Zhou is about to return to town to try again—Qin Lao seems oddly determined to have this fish—when there is a rap at the door. He answers it. It is a girl, perhaps fifteen years old. She is wearing a dark cape and carrying a heavy satchel. She seems to have come from some distance. She seems very weary. Qin Lao's is the farthest house out from the village, and it is the first house she has come to.

"I need work," she says. "Do you have work?"

Zhou frowns. Probably there is work, but he does not want a woman around. It has been fine without them. They are so much trouble. He shakes his head no and is shutting the door when Qin Lao walks in, startling him.

"I heard the girl's question," says Qin Lao. "Did you tell the girl there was no work?"

Zhou nods yes.

"Well, then, open the door again," Qin Lao says. "We have many garments that need mending. You are slowing down, and we can use someone young and strong. Furthermore, perhaps she can cook better than you, or cajole a fish out of the merchants when you cannot." Qin Lao has never spoken curtly to Zhou. Zhou is astonished. He stands aside.

Qin Lao takes his place in the doorway. "And where have you come from?" he says to the girl.

The girl gestures away behind her, up the road. As she raises her arm, the cape looks like a wing. She says simply, "That way." Her eyes look very tired.

"Very far?" says Qin Lao.

"Many days," she says.

"And so are you very hungry?" Qin Lao asks.

"I am," she says.

"Well, you can come in then," Qin Lao says. "Zhou will give you some bread and some fruit and when you have eaten and rested you may go into the village and barter to get us a good fish for dinner. My servant cannot seem to do this."

Zhou makes a hurt face. His master has never spoken this way to him or about him. Zhou signs, in the shadows, You are like a woman approaching her menses. He knows that Qin Lao will not see him.

The girl does, however, and he thinks he sees a smile flit across her lips as if she has understood, though of course she cannot, for this particularly subtle piece of sign language is one only Qin Lao and Zhou know.

The girl stays in the concubines' quarters, which Qin Lao asks Zhou to sweep while she is bartering for a fish down in the village. As Zhou sweeps he makes sounds in his throat which Qin Lao knows are grumbling.

Qin Lao says, "You are envious."

Zhou signs back, You are senile.

Qin Lao laughs. "Sweep, Zhou."

The girl gets a fish with no trouble. The quarters are swept and she is installed. She assists Zhou with the marketing. Yes, he is envious, that is abundantly plain, but the girl is quite useful at mending and cooking.

She has been three weeks in the house. It is late one evening and Zhou is asleep. Qin Lao is lonely. He goes to her quarters and asks through the door whether she can play instruments, as he would like to hear music.

"Only the flute," she says. "But I have no flute. I sold it two days' journey up the road to pay for lodging."

Qin Lao asks, "May I come in?"

She stands back to let him pass. He goes directly to the shelf where, for all these years, the flute of the second concubine has sat, wrapped in its cloths, and takes it down. The girl's eyes widen in delight.

"Will you play for me?" Qin Lao asks. "The song of the Heavenly Carp?" He hums the tune.

"Ah," the girl says, "that song. In my village we call that song 'Rain and Mist.'" She looks somewhat abashed.

Qin Lao startles slightly. "Rain and Mist" are emblems for sexual intercourse. Since ancient days, it has been believed that thunderstorms are the offspring of the mating of the sky god—who is male—with the earth goddess. Thus rain, clouds, and mist are all erotic rather than meteorological in connotation. He is astonished to hear the girl speak this way.

"I am sorry," she says. "*You* sang the song."

"In this village, that song is called 'Heavenly Carp,'" says Qin Lao. "Surely it would be proper for you to play a song called 'Heavenly Carp.'"

"Surely that would be proper," the girl says. "But it is cold here. May I sit by the stove? In these quarters one must stay beneath covers after the sun goes down."

"Let us go to the stove, then," says Qin Lao.

The girl plays the song, and though Qin Lao has asked her to play "Heavenly

Carp" all he can think about while she plays is rain and mist. He feels something rise in him that has been long dormant.

It is well known that men at the age of sixty are to cease intercourse, but men of seventy require the female energy to keep warm and maintain balance. Qin Lao has not had a woman for twenty years.

The girl finishes playing and looks at her master sitting quietly in his chair. He looks back at her. "Rain and mist," he says musingly.

She giggles. "You said to play 'Heavenly Carp,' master, and I played 'Heavenly Carp.'"

Qin Lao rises. He walks across the few feet of space between them. He drops a small brush, with which he has been idly playing, next to her foot. She reaches to pick it up. "No, no," he objects. He leans, himself, to pick it up. As he starts to pick it up, he brushes the hem of her dress on the way down.

"Oh," she says involuntarily.

"I am sorry," he says.

"This is fine," she says.

His hand picks up the brush and as he stands up touches the side of her foot. "I am sorry," he says.

"This is perfectly fine," she says. "But I am a virgin."

He leans to help her to standing. "This is exceptionally fine," he says. "So too am I."

And they laugh, and he takes her to his bed, where it is much warmer for both of them. She demonstrates no positions. She lies very still as he straddles her. He feels his elderly bones as dry, brittle twigs in his flesh.

"I am very old," he says.

She takes him in her small hands and she warms him, as if he were a stick to build a fire. She is so adept that he wonders about her assertion that she is a virgin. But indeed she is, and she shouts when he penetrates her, and the morning shows blood on the covers.

Zhou is furious. Qin Lao asks whether he would have preferred to be the recipient of these attentions. Zhou makes motions that are not polite.

There is no way, of course, Qin Lao can know why all these years he has not been blessed with a child. A modern fertility-clinic lab technician could do the tests: it is indeed, as Qin Lao had thought, his own "fault." He has had an enzyme problem that has prevented his sperm from penetrating the membrane around the egg of every woman—all five previous wives and concubines—with whom he has mated. There is nothing in alchemists' lore that addresses this, even obliquely, misguidedly or accidentally.

Once, however, one night when the moon is nearly full, not quite full, at the stage Qin Lao loves because it retains mystery, nine months after the girl's arrival, these enzymes do their job. No lab technician, even today, could say why. Perhaps it is miracle, perhaps only fluke.

Qin Lao, when he hears of the girl's pregnancy, finds his eyes filling up with tears. He cannot believe what he hears, and he cannot believe he is crying.

He cannot know that this child will be a boy and will grow to be a soldier in Qin Shi Huang-ti's army, that a terra-cotta statue of this soldier will be buried in the tomb in Qin Shi Huang-ti's imperial capital Ch'ang-an—later Xi'an—that the features on the terra-cotta statue will be uncannily like his own as a young man.

He cannot know that the tomb builders—though not his son, who will bear a sword for Yellow Emperor and who will father more sons and who will die in old age in the capital, prosperous—will be shut into the tomb at the last, that their cries of terror, their wild beatings on the door, will be ignored by those who are heaping earth over the door.

He cannot know that in the late twentieth century, after excavators unearth this tomb and men stand in wonder staring at this vast clay army, a young girl coming through the exhibit that this tomb becomes, after paying her fee, will point out to her mother the crooked and most lifelike little finger of this soldier, so like Qin Lao's own. Justin Wong's little finger on his right hand will bear the same slight crook.

The mother will say distractedly, "Yes, dear," and, having no idea that the terra-cotta statue is a remarkable likeness of the sole son and heir of Qin Lao, alchemist, and having no sense of the mystery of it all that would allow her to marvel, even if she did know, will instruct the child to tie her shoelace—she points to the lace sternly—so that she does not trip and tumble into the subterranean channels of the exhibit.

When the young woman who has come caped to Qin Lao's door with her satchel gives birth to the child, near Qin Lao's seventy-ninth birthday, the child is indeed a boy, and fat and rosy. His hair, the moment the birth blood is washed from it, stands up, a soft, full brush, as if he is astonished. The girl lies exhausted but smiles and takes the boy to her breast. The child smacks and nuzzles but does not quite suck.

The midwife says, "There is too much blood." The midwife administers the proper drugs, but the girl just keeps bleeding.

The girl lies smiling, the tiny moon-faced boy wrapped close to her.

"Does it hurt?" the old man says.

"Oh, no," says the girl. "It is peaceful to bleed to death."

"Please," Qin Lao says. "Do not bleed to death." He pleads with her.

She makes a weak smile. "I do not believe that I am in control of this matter," she says.

"Please," Qin Lao says again. He seems to be addressing the Tao, all the stars of Xu Xuli, the universe canopy, life itself.

The girl continues to bleed until all of her blood is spilled, into the sheets that have been brought to sop it up, and then she lies still.

Qin Lao is crying. This girl—she has never told him her name and so he has called her simply Sparrow—is the only one that he has ever loved. And he is crying.

The midwife takes the child from the arms of the dead girl and hands it to Qin Lao. She covers the dead girl's face.

Qin Lao raises the boy, with Zhou's help, and does not die until he is grown and gone off to the army.

IN THE VILLAGE a story springs up that the girl had been Zhou's daughter by the concubine, who had been given away. The story holds that the child's mother had left the village when the baby was very young and that this girl was on her way back to her village of origin. There is no reason—except a desire for some orderly explanation—to think this true.

Another story holds that the girl's name had actually been Tian Hu, Heavenly Fox, and that she had been magical, not human.

But that of course is mere foolishness.

3   Justin

DRIVING NORTH, JUSTIN is thinking of . . . nothing. His eyesight seems almost irrelevant, as nothing he sees seems to reach his brain. His sense of smell, however, is overwhelming him, pushing him to the brink of tears. The smell of animal crackers and an open package of baby wipes fill the truck cab. There is the scent of some potent South Sea island flower in the tanning oil Ursula got into this morning, opening the top silently back in her seat and rubbing it on her tiny cheeks: they only knew when they smelled it. Annie had laughed and taken it away. In the rug behind him there is a smell of pickle juice from a jar Ursula had inadvertently dumped over last night as they drove. He heads like a train through a tunnel north toward Eagle Harbor, where there surely will be someone with a phone.

He imagines Ursula in a *Star Trek*–style teleporter. He doesn't realize where that thought even came from, but on the truck radio, a Scottish accent in a reporter—rather less intelligible than the TV Scotty's watered-down version—has tripped him back into his teens when *Star Trek* occupied real estate in his mind. *Beam her up, Scotty. Beam Ursula up*. He realizes this must look like praying.

He says it again, but out loud this time: "Beam her up, *anyone*." He clears his throat and roars "God" in a tone that fills the truck's cab. He yells, "If you're God, if you're there, show me." Then, for good measure, he yells, "FUCK!" He figures if God is there in the way his mother believes—and sometimes Annie does too—he can give Justin slack. There seems nothing else he can say. Thus "fuck!" becomes a prayer, like incense rising. Irrele-vantly he thinks of Byzantine monks, and onionlike Russian turrets, Rasputin, the Bolshevik uprising, anything but Ursula down that hole.

Beam her up. He remembers the kid who was his lab partner in high-school biology, the Trekkie, pale guy with dreadlocks, and always Hawaiian shirts, even in the dead of winter. Kid goes on about how they could do that, the teleporter number. He's saying to some girl across the aisle who asks, "No, no, it's not like the vacuum tube at the bank drive-through, not hardly. Dude, it's about entanglement. That's, like, photons of light but they've got related properties even when they're far apart. You do something to *one* of them and the *other* one changes."

Justin is staring at him over the fetal pig split down the middle and pinned to the dissecting tray. The smell of the formaldehyde, so much stronger than when they did the frog, is enough to make him retch. The dreadlocked Trekkie, by contrast, is grooving on it, as if it were, say, a roast chicken. "Oh, man, yum," he says. Justin is mesmerized by the intensity of the way he just keeps on talking, juggernaut talk. "You do something to one photon, like instantaneously the other one is going to change too." Justin clicks in deeper then. This is kind of interesting. Dreadlocks starts droning on about technicalities, and Justin zones out, bombing back in when he hears the guy say, "Yeah, Einstein said something about it." Justin perks up. Einstein and the teleporter? The guy says, "He called it something like 'spooky action at a distance'" Peculiar laughter from someone.

The girl who had asked says, "So when are they going to be able to do this? Like soon?" Justin's lab partner says, laughing, "Not before the week-end." Much laughter, and the teacher at the other side of the lab shooshing everyone. Justin remembers the hula girls on the Trekkie's shirt, almost as if they were come alive, dancing, the swooshy straw sound of their skirts. He recalls Kenny Marineau lifting the lungs of his pig as instructed to look at the heart and, clumsy as usual, slicing right through, so the heart comes free. He holds the tiny thing, the size of a nut, in the palm of his hand. "Oops," says Marineau, and guffaws. Beautiful, amazing, and Marineau making the usual idiot faces.

Justin cannot help thinking of Ursula's heart: *Let it still be beating,* "Let *her have grown wings, and be hanging in air like a dragonfly* . . . He hears his own pulse in his ears, *kachunk, kachunk.*

Justin does not look at the digital clock on the dashboard, its numbers changing constantly, moving forward through history while Ursula is down that hole, no ticking sounds, just silent unstoppable movement through history, one second at a time, those squared-off digital numbers in glowing green the color of leaves with the sun flashing through.

On the roadside, a deer newly dead, its head flung aside like an ingénue posing, the white of its throat stark and beautiful. Justin does not see it, nor has he seen the one he passed a mile ago. He does not realize that the angle of the neck was what summoned the image of that fetal pig. He does not see the squirrel splatted out flat on the center line of the road. He does not see the tree canopy or the blue sky.

IN THIS MEMORY that flashes by, with Justin's attending almost not at all, outside the window the snow is falling silently: thirteen inches of it so far this week, four and a half of them just that day, Thursday. It is January of 1995. The cushion of it muffles every sound. Cold northern sunlight spills through the windows onto the blue-gray painted wood floors, the color of navy destroyers. The windows are iced, in scoop patterns that cup the pane bottoms. The glass itself is old enough that looking through it is like peering through ice that has just formed up, overnight, in late fall, at the edge of the pond. The sunlight spills onto the narrow beds' coverlets in their separate rooms. Green needles up high catch the snow and release it in sparkling, bright showers. The silence is tender and impenetrable, soft-pedaling the songs of a few little nondescript birds in the birches nearest the little house.

As she takes in the half-sound of the birds' twittering and only partly articulates the thought, Mindy Ji Wong calls from the kitchen to her son Justin, in his room, "Jus, what does it mean to 'soft-pedal'?"

Justin Wong, twenty-two, long-haired, and very *American* Chinese American, wears headphones and sits cross-legged, in socks with matching holes on the balls of both feet, on the destroyer blue floor of his room. He has just settled in to listen to the *Eagles: Their Greatest Hits* and is banging his head to the tempo of "Take It Easy." His hair is soft black Chinese, and he wears it tied back as ancestors in China might have worn theirs, but his ponytail is a musician American's. His hair moves to the beat. He is mouthing the words. Mindy Ji Wong has heard it a million times. She knows what he's mouthing, even though she can't hear the CD. "Aw, Ma, cripesake, you know what it means. Jeez. You'd think you just got off the boat." He yells because he hasn't taken off the headphones. He keeps rocking and mouthing the lyrics.

Mindy Ji Wong is making a gingery rust-colored dough for the cookies that Justin likes best. Her wooden spoon is held up in the air as if, from Justin's vantage point, she's a medieval seige catapult ready to fling the dough at him—he makes moves to cover his head and yells "Incoming!"—but, no, she's just talking. "No, I mean literally, honey. Like, in a piano. What's the 'pedal' connected to and how does it make anything go soft?"

He takes off the headphones and presses Stop on the little pewter-colored CD player perched on his abdomen. He sighs and looks up at his mother in mock exasperation. "Okay," he says, "so you have these strings and these hammers." He is drawing the guts of the piano in the air in front of him. "So the hammers like vary the quality of the sound, see? And there's two or three strings for each note, depending."

"Depending on what?"

"Let me finish, Ma. When you use the 'soft' pedal what it does is it kind of shifts the hammers so they strike one less string." He flips a little latch or switch on his CD player and retreats back into listening mode.

"What determines whether there's two or three strings for a note?" she persists.

Justin turns off the Discman and feigns tearing his hair. "*God,* Ma." He hears himself, and he knows she will say he's blaspheming, so he decides to retrench on that. He smiles dopily. "God determines it, Ma." In the kitchen her Bible is open beside the bowl, pages spread wide to the beginning of the Gospel of John. Justin tells her she can't think about anything else but God.

The next time he says that she will doubtless say, "I can think about pedals and strings. I can think about birds in the birch tree. I can keep the proportions of ginger to cinnamon straight and triple the molasses while I'm doing that. While I'm reading the Gospel of John. I can think about more than one thing at a time. Unlike some of us. Unlike disadvantaged biracial youth from broken homes, with one-track minds."

"Fine," she says to him now. "Guess you don't *want* cookie dough. Probably shouldn't eat it, really. Raw eggs cause salmonella anyway."

He gets up laughing and wrestles the spoon away from her in the kitchen doorway, barking video-ninja yowls. He scrapes batter from the spoon with his straight white teeth. He makes animal moans of delight. He is a full foot taller than his mother. Mindy Ji Wong is two inches short of five feet. The height is a gift from the American father he cannot remember. He goes to the pottery bowl that sits on the counter in icy white sunlight and scrapes more dough from its sides. He walks off with a fist-sized chunk of it balanced on the spoon. "Just a nip," he says. "Just a tad."

"Fine," she says. "*Get* salmonella. Turn into a salmon and swim cross-country all the way out to Vancouver. Say hi to your uncle Wong Xin Li at the China Doll drive-through for me. Eat some memorial Puget Sound crab-meat *jiao-zi* dumplings—with Auntie Liu's special secret Hebei Herb vinegar soy sauce—for me, when you get there." Mindy Ji Wong goes back to stirring the thick heavy dough, with a new spoon.

Justin settles back down, clamps on his headphones and starts swaying in time to a song. Mindy Ji Wong looks over at her son and smiles. She knows he is listening to "Peaceful Easy Feeling." She knows the rhythm.

There is something about the way his lips curl that recalls his father, whom she hasn't thought about in, oh, weeks. Well, maybe days. She looks at the cut of his shoulders, and that is his father's too, sturdy and broad. Mindy Ji Wong smiles, trying to picture him in coolie pajamas in a gold mine in California or in the brocades of an ancient Chinese emperor. It's a silly picture. Justin Wong would look like an American with a Chinese face. Except of course for the lips, which are the lips of his father. The last contact Mindy Ji Wong had with Justin's father—and it was only a one-way contact—was hearing him when he played his harmonica on *A Prairie Home Companion* years before, in 1985.

IT HAD BEEN in wintertime, like this, and Justin had been asleep in his bed. She had climbed up on the roof—the reception was bad—to listen to his part of the program. She had listened to Garrison Keillor's monologue back in the kitchen, with all of the bad reception crackling, filling in the gaps with her imagination. It was a story about someone's aunt Mildred in Alaska.

Justin had woken up when the front door slammed and had followed her out. He startled her. There she was, up on the housetop in her flannel slippers, crouching Asian style in the snow on the roof. He was twelve.

Back of her there was a sky clear and black as Mindy Ji's hair: millions of stars, more of them visible to the naked eye than ten-year-old Justin had ever seen. His ma, crouching down in the snow, her long flannel nightgown beneath her robe trailing in the roof snow; his ma, squinting off into space as if scouting for Rudolph.

"Are you out of your mind?" he had yelled up to her. "What the hell are you doing?" He had always liked to think that he was the adult.

"I'm listening to this blues harmonica player on *A Prairie Home Companion*," she said. "Nothing unusual."

Justin stood transfixed. He was in boxer shorts and a tattered Wolverines T-shirt. "You don't mean—" He stopped.

"Yes. Your father," she said.

The following week he had opened the drawer in the dresser where Joe "Rapdander" Cimmer had left his harmonicas when he moved on, when Justin was two, one Friday morning in 1975. Justin had been playing with pots and Tupperware, thwack-bang, and looked up at his daddy's back, the worn boots, the jeans, the green-plaid flannel shirt. Joe had headed south to a Friday night gig at a dive outside Grayling and never come back.

Mindy Ji had been puzzled, but then life had never been highly explicable. Joe had not given a sign of unhappiness, not half a sign. Mindy had been working then where she was still working now, at a greasy spoon downtown, near Soo Locks, cooking and waiting tables.

She said nothing to anyone about Joe's disappearance, not even to the baby-sitter. Joe was gone for months before she mentioned his leaving.

One of her regular breakfast customers had asked about him. "No, I haven't seen Joe in a while," she said. That was all. A smile, neither rueful nor wistful. She was at the Superior Market, the only place to get fresh meat to order.

"Goddamn," the butcher said amiably. "Taking this inscrutable Oriental gig just a bit far, are you not?" The butcher had a way of talking like that. He had gone off to college and come back that way. He had always watched Mindy Ji with an interested eye.

"Could you get me a pound and a half of that veal, ground real fine?" Mindy said, ignoring him. "Wrap it and I'll come back for it when I clock out."

"Want to go to a movie, then, if your man's left you?" the butcher said.

He was at least ten years younger than Mindy Ji.

"I don't believe," said Mindy Ji. "Thank you." And that had been how it had gone for ten years. No dates. No thoughts of dates, just a daily waiting. Not the butcher. Not the baker, not the candlestick anything.

Mindy Ji Wong clocked in, clocked out, heard Joe Rapdander Cimmer on the radio, thought about how mysterious life was and how very lovely the eyes of her little boy were.

JOE'S HARMONICAS LAY in a nest of white handkerchiefs, each individual instrument wrapped in two layers of finely crosshatched white linen. There was to the ten-year-old something incredibly sacred about this. He leaned into the nest with his nose as if he hoped he could perhaps smell there the scent of his father and know why he'd left. He smelled nothing of his father, only something like spicy leaves.

"That's called sachet," said his mother, watching him. "I put it there."

He looked up at her with a second unformed question. She shrugged pretty visibly. She couldn't answer it.

One day when he was fifteen he took out the harmonicas and began fooling around. Mindy Ji Wong didn't know he was doing this until he was two months into messing around with the instruments and she walked in on him one day. He was playing something of Eric Clapton's. She cleared her throat behind him. She skipped the preliminaries, as if she had been expecting this all these years. Genes.

"Joe knew him," she said. "He played with him. You have probably heard him, on one of those albums."

"Whaaat?" said Justin Wong. "Dad? Eric Clapton?"

"You got it," said Mindy Ji Wong. "When his child fell out of that window and died, I believe your father was with him then. That's what I was told, anyway."

Justin made an agonized groan, as if he had just been forcibly linked at this tender age to all the pain of the world. He thought that thought: *I have just been tied in to all kinds of stuff I didn't even know was mine, and . . . God!*

Mindy Ji Wong looked at him and said, "Maybe you *have*."

It seemed perfectly easy and right, but it took several minutes after she left the room for Justin to wonder what had made her say that. He hadn't said anything.

When he was seventeen he had gotten his very first gig. He graduated from high school and went to work installing drains and downspouts and awnings and sometimes aluminum siding. He played in a club out near the reservation called Boo 2 Soo, and in two years he had become a local legend on a small scale. He did not have a gig moniker yet, like Rapdander. That would come if it came, as would fame, which was not the point anyway.

Now, ON THIS day of the snow weighing down the tree needles in glorious sunlight and cookie dough ready to go in the oven, Mindy Ji Wong calls in to her son, "When that's done, can you bring my books back to the library?"

Five miles into town is the library. It is five minutes from closing time, the warnings have been sent out over the loudspeaker system, and all of the patrons have been flushed out from between stacks. Back of the circulation desk is a blond girl, her complexion like raw skimmed milk, her eyes pale lake blue back of her rimless librarian glasses.

Justin is checking out, with a stack of hardbound Agatha Christies piled on his hands, all the ones Mindy Ji asked for plus one more he thinks she hasn't read. He has a book for himself about jazz funerals in New Orleans, and another one that is a book of full-color photography of computer-generated fractal images.

Justin is deep down inside himself, thinking about the gig coming up next week, at a little theater in Ironwood, thinking that he's got to call the promoter. There are three things that he has to ask him, and they are . . . he tries to dredge them up.

"So you're into Hercule Poirot?" says the librarian.

Justin is thinking of the ticket booth at the little theater. It's something about tickets he's got to remember. Right? Tickets?

"Hmm," he answers without having heard her.

"Which ones have you read?" the librarian says. "Have you read *By the Pricking of My Thumbs*?"

"Errgmm," says Justin. She's not quite breaking through the fog yet. He has heard the word "thumbs" and is trying to put that together with Ironwood.

Silence. She's waiting for him to come out of the cave.

"Uhhh," he says, looking out the library's glass doors at the quick-darkening evening, then looking down at his stack of books, "these are for my mother. She mainlines the stuff."

The sky outside is inky dark, and the streetlight illuminates a pocket of it right in front of the door: in that pocket, tiny white snowflakes fall thick and fast.

Justin is thinking that there's an odd cast of color to the sky tonight, as if the blue black were semitransparent and back of that was a red-brown color. He starts writing a song in his head, minor-sounding, plaintive. It seems at this point to be called "Prune Juice Sky."

"So," says the librarian, and the word is weighted, *down, down, down,* like a stone going into the lake. "So. Are you into mysteries?"

Justin lets go of the song, files it away for another time. He is checking his watch and thinking about whether he has enough for a six-pack of Red Dog at the Sav-U. "Am I into mysteries?" he says. He's surprised he remembers the words. He repeats it as if he were being held hostage at gunpoint and had to respond to get out of here. He shakes his head like a dog coming in from the snow. "I am not into mysteries," he says. His voice is uninflected. He is looking off at a tapestry of the Upper Peninsula of Michigan, done by some ladies' club, Rotary auxiliary, whatever, back of the checkout desk. He is looking hard at the ornate knot of gold thread they have used to indicate his town, Sault Sainte Marie.

"Two kinds of people in the world, ma'am." He says it in a voice that sounds suspiciously like a Joe Friday imitation, but is only half meant to be.

He is looking down at the toes of his leather boots, thinking he mighta-oughta get them recapped. "Two kinds," he repeats. "There are people who like mysteries and then there are people who think life itself is a mystery. Me, I don't like mysteries."

He is thinking of the big bad bass Hohner he has seen that afternoon in Nick and Nebo's pawnshop window and whether after this gig he will have enough for it. Needs some polish, but that silvered side will gleam under the lights, that mother-of-pearl will pearlesce.

"Your mom's into fractals?" the voice says, through these layers of space.

"That would be yours truly," he says. Why is she talking so much? He looks behind him, to be able to say, everybody else is waiting, but they're not. He is the only one in line.

"Jazz funerals, then," she says.

"Mine also," he says. He is thinking about whether it will snow Friday and so whether they will have to ask the guy with the four-wheel to drive.

She surrenders and hands him his books. He has not looked at her once.

"Due three weeks from today," she says. She seems to sigh.

Justin looks up at her then, at the sigh. Her eyes are just so pale. Finn, no doubt. The whole Upper Peninsula is overrun with them. *Why's she sigh-ing—asthmatic?* He makes a polite but perfunctory smile, picks up the stack of library books, and heads out to the Sav-U. His leather jacket flaps open slightly and Annie's eyes slide to the T-shirt: a motto on a ribbon flying in a breeze reads SEAMLESS AS A DREAM.

She swirls on her stool and stares at the wall behind her for a minute. She is thinking about whether in fact a dream is seamless. She considers dreams she has had and whether the collage effect is without seams or whether it is like a patchwork. She lets the question go. She thinks of the slight whiff of clean young-man hair that wafted over her as she was checking out Justin Wong's books.

Annie picks up a worn leather-handled cane and moves gingerly to the door of the office. She leans on the doorjamb. "He came in again," she says to her friend, a dark-haired young woman with a name tag that says TASHA. "At least *part of him* came in. Total space case, I guess."

"Men," Tasha says. "Comes with the gender."

"He did not even look at me," she says, "until the very last second. And then he didn't see me."

"Annie," says her friend, "give him time. It took Gilbert sixteen months to notice I lived next door, no matter how many times the post office mixed up our mail."

"He's gorgeous," Annie says. "And even if he's a space case, he feels brilliant to me, sounds that way. Jazz funerals. Fractals."

"He plays out at Boo 2 Soo," says her friend. "Fridays and Saturdays, nine to one."

"Whaaat?"

"Harmonica, girl. Saw him there last week," says Tasha, pulling up overdues on her computer screen. "Gilbert and I went out there with this guy from his store, and I heard him play. Good stuff."

"You rat," says Annie Maki. Her voice is a soft, smiley voice, a voice that seems to have a dimple. "You didn't tell me."

"Just did," comes the answer. "First chance I had, girl."

Annie flushes with delight. She picks up her cane and stands without its help. She brandishes it at her friend like a sword, like a musketeer. Her skirt is floor length and covers her fragile legs, rendered half useless ten years before, the same year Justin stood watching Mindy Ji crouched on the roof to hear Rapdander play on *A Prairie Home Companion*. She herself cannot crouch or kneel or walk unassisted anymore. She swims twice a week for her muscles. She always wears long skirts, usually pale colors, like her hair, like her eyes. The skirts are most often in small floral patterns.

"Furthermore, his blood type is A positive," she says.

"How in the world would you know that?" Annie says, blushing with something like anger and embarrassment.

"Reference librarians know everything," Tasha says. "And for whatever they don't know, they know the sources. I just asked my bud at the blood bank if they'd gotten any Chinese blood lately, and if so what kind. I did see his bumper sticker. I read everything."

"Subtle," says Annie.

"My specialty." Tasha shrugs. "It's the company I keep."

"*Rain Man*," says Annie. This is their joke: that like Dustin Hoffman as an autistic savant in *Rain Man*, Tasha remembers the oddest facts.

"Some days are slow." Tasha shrugs.

Annie goes to the front door of the library to lock up and pull the shades. The snow is still making itself picturesque, as if Sault Sainte Marie were enclosed in a paperweight. Annie locks the deadbolt and reaches up to pull down the shade. Outside the library, a truck is parked, shiny metallic blue green, the color of water at night in a swimming pool in Hollywood, California, where Annie Maki has of course never been.

The truck is striking in its shiny cleanness: the snow has been steady this past week, and more is expected, so nobody's washing their cars. But Justin Wong has taken the company truck to the car wash en route to the library. The side door of the truck says: SOO GUTTER, SEAMLESS GUTTERS AND MORE. Beneath that there is that same ribboning motto: SEAMLESS AS A DREAM.

Justin Wong has walked down the block to mail something, and now he steps back into view. He climbs into the truck. Starts the engine. Pulls away. On his rear bumper it says: GIVE BLOOD. PLAY HOCKEY.

Annie Maki sighs when she sees this. Something in her like a final tumbler in a tiny lock makes a click that's nearly audible. The librarian is in love.

IN THE TRUCK heading north to Eagle Harbor, Justin's mind is still hovering in midair, something like praying to James Doohan—the actor who played Scotty—on the starship *Enterprise*. He prays, *Beam her up*. He has traveled 2.2 miles along the asphalt in the time it took for us to look at the memory that zoomed past him at an oblique angle, on no road, heading for . . . us.

Justin reaches Eagle Harbor, passing a few houses on the way, recalling instances when he has wasted time trying to find someone home when no one was home, and he heads for the harbor, which must be the center of town. He pulls his truck off the road. He steps out into the breeze whipping off the lake and breathes in, deep, intentional. *What next*, he thinks. *Who now*. He turns and runs to the nearest house, a little white box with a glassed-in porch and a look of desperation. He is thinking as he runs that he could have stopped at *any* house if this is what he was going to do anyway.

An elderly woman in pink sweatpants and sweatshirt is watching the television, Court TV. People are yelling at each other about the sale of a motorboat, and who owned what part and why. The woman is thinking she had better talk with her kids about selling the house to the real estate developer who keeps pestering her, also that she cannot trust her son Chet, so maybe she'll ask his wife, who has more sense. Justin has to ring the bell three times before she hears him.

When she comes to the door he can barely speak. I need to call 911, he says, before he realizes or plans what he's going to say. Then he realizes that's right. 911. He says, Do you have long distance? He will need to call his mother too. She will want to be here. No, the woman does not. I could give you some money for a long-distance call, he says, before it registers that she has said she does not have long distance. He dials 911. He starts to give the information. He tells the operator to hold on and runs out to his truck.

The woman stands staring after him, with the front door and the aluminum storm door hanging open. She has not heard all he's saying and doesn't quite understand. Justin is checking the mileage, which he has jotted down to give rescuers coordinates. He comes thundering in again and then suddenly slows down as if something had calmed him. He has no idea why: perhaps an intuitive sense that he will burn out and collapse if he doesn't manage this better. He does a quick subtraction. Yeah, south down 26, he says. I'll park the truck on the road when I get back there. Silver '99 Dodge Ram with a quad cab. Sign on the door, SOO GUTTER.

ON THE TELEVISION a fat man wearing what looks like a bowling shirt with a tie is ranting about something. Justin wants to put his hand through the TV screen and yank the guy out by his throat: *My daughter is down a hole, fuck your motorboat, goddamn your beer belly, goddamn fuck that dumb-ass bowling shirt,* he is yelling inside his skull, dropping himself—as if down another hole—to the level of Court TV.

"Just hang up the phone, sonny," says a voice. It's the lady who owns the house. She can see he is frozen in non-thought. Justin is standing with the receiver in his hand.

He looks hard at it. *How did* that *get there*, he thinks.

"Give it to me," she says. She has not heard everything he has said, but enough. She replaces it in its cradle. "I can call my pastor," she says. "And my son Layton. He's strong. My other son, Chet, he's no help in a crisis. *Zero* help." She shakes her head in dismay.

"No, thank you," says Justin. "I just need to get back." Then he remembers he hasn't told them to call Mindy Ji. He picks up the phone and dials once more, gives them her phone numbers—home, work—and hopes the lines are clear. He takes off like a shot, out the door. He has not said thank you, but surely she knows.

By the time Justin rounds the bend southward and loses sight of the harbor in his rearview, the woman is back watching Court TV: There is a dispute about who owns the outboard motor and a red-enameled box of fishing lures. A blond heavyset female judge looks bemused and contemptuous. This stuff on the TV might as well be a dogfight, a cockfight, a cricket fight in Qin Lao's village.

4 The Caravan-Master's Lieutenant

T HE SWOOP ARC of the flight of the hawk barreling inland off the waters of Lake Köyliö in the south of Finland is invisible in the air. Nonetheless in the mind it is silver and scimitar shaped. The hawk scuds down toward a clearing in the birches along the shore. The surface of Lake Köyliö in the morning light looks nearly identical to the waters of Portage Lake, outside the Super 8 Motel in Houghton, Michigan, with the hills rising beyond it, the morning of Ursula's accident, almost thirteen centuries later.

Two thousand miles east of Lake Köyliö, in terrain the maps of the day call the Untrustworthy Mountains, on the ancient Silk Road, a nameless brigand on horseback—swarthy, short-tempered, idly biting his grease-blackened fingernails—lurks edgily behind a rock cliff. His horse whinnies and paws at the hard ground. A caravan carrying pepper and spices, bolts of silk, and packets of jewels and carved jade and ivory westward from Ch'ang-an, the Xi'an of today, lumbers toward him. That caravan is tiny in the distance, over several rises and falls of the land, but he calculates that it will reach him about sundown, which will be perfect. The thrill that the brigand feels is the shape of that hawk's flight so far to the west.

The young woman watching the hawk hurl itself toward her knows nothing of Turkish brigands except by hearsay, though she knows of the Silk Road. She is thinking simply: *How beautifully that hawk flies.*

She stands in the door of the sauna her father, a cloth merchant, has built for the family's use and, simply out of noblesse oblige, for the use of

certain neighbors and servants. It is springtime—late April—and she is rejoicing in the sunlight after so much long darkness. She is taking delight in
having survived a hard winter, when 20 of the village's 150 have died. Three
hunters have been lost to wolves—the winter was cruel, and the wolves who
would usually stay far from humans have been far more hungry—and fear-
less—than in another year. Several children have died of winter illnesses. A
young man bled to death when, chopping wood, his ax slipped and slammed
into his right leg; the young woman watching the hawk had used her best
knowledge as an herbalist but the ax severed an artery and, in the torrent
of blood, there was really no use or hope. The annual quota of elderly
women and men have died, several in sleep, three in falls. One woman not
yet quite old enough to die naturally of old age has been taken by paroxysms
rumored to have been sent by the curse of a witch. Most painfully, the
young woman's best friend, Piia, a married woman her own age, has died in
childbirth, of a weak heart. The child within her died in the dark, struggling
toward the light, and then suddenly—nothing. The cemetery up the hill
from the village has grown. There has been a great deal of stone gathering
to cover all the graves.

The young woman who stands in the door of the sauna hut transfixed by
the hawk's flight is Kyllikki, daughter of Rauno. She occupies a peculiar
niche, one of privileged marginalization, in this village. A fever at the age of
five left her deaf, so greatly diminishing her ability to speak that it finally left
her. She is unmarried because she refuses to marry; her father, three times
a widower, does not object. She makes herself sufficiently valuable in her father's home that there is no need to insist.

It is not that no man would want to marry a deaf-and-dumb woman:
among the men there is a loud joke that that is the ideal. She knows this; she
picks up the innuendos, which often take the form of blatant physical com-
edy. She goes every other day to a grove in the forest where there is an ancestor shrine to petition and placate. *Please, do not let my father die. Please,
may things stay as they are.*

Kyllikki wishes, as she watches the hawk riding its downdraft of cool air,
that she could have its freedom. Being excused from the duty to marry is not
enough: she wishes to be excused from the law of gravity, the law of mor-

tality, the law of logical limits. Her isolation in this silence has made her a kind of pagan monastic. Christian missionaries with their hard teachings and territorial agendas have not yet penetrated this far north, and will not for a couple of centuries. The brutality of nature nonetheless occasions in some Finns a numinous awe akin to that of the monks and nuns in their damp cloisters near the Mediterranean Sea.

In Kyllikki, daughter of Rauno, there is a natural asceticism whose aspect would appear wholly in place if she should be transported on that hawk's back to the south, say to Italy, and dressed by lay sisters as a novice in robe, coif, wimple, and veil, with a rosary hanging from her cincture, and an olive-wood cross. None of this, of course, is known to her.

She is not consciously thinking of music either: deaf since the age of five—fifteen years now, twelve since the death of her mother in childbirth —though in the profound silence of her skull, as in an underground cave, she remembers the sound of the strings of the kantele. Bach's first suite for cello will not be written for another millennium, yet she seems deep in her inner spaces to know the tune: the cello playing an undulating riverscape, a forest of wandering squirrel trails, a path through a wildflower meadow, a deep, dark, fern dell. She hears this melody in deep interior ears, hundreds of miles away from where Bach will write the music.

Kyllikki shivers from a chill blast of wind off the lake. The hawk boomerangs now, up and away. Her cheeks are flushed from the heat off the sauna stones. The warm bread aroma of beer poured out onto those stones—a luxury that would scandalize if anyone knew, but she can neither hear nor speak, after all, and so feels some redress this way—fills her nostrils, making her stomach growl hungrily. She smells the world keenly, a partial compensation for the excision of sound.

She crosses the hard, upsloping ground between the hut and the stream. There is still ice clinging to the stones of the stream's shore in late morning. She slips out of her heavy wrapper, splashes in the stream for a matter of seconds, and climbs out making sounds of cold shock in her throat that she can feel but not hear. At the place where she bathes is a tree in the lowest branch of which is the skull of an enormous bear that has been there since her childhood. It is said to be the guardian spirit of this stream. She stands in a slight moment of suspended thought as she stares at the bear's skull, dried and discolored green gray, holding the ashes of small sacrificial offerings of herbs. She slips into her wrapper and crosses the ground to her father's house.

Kyllikki goes about her chores listening to something inside her that is a very close semblance of Yo-Yo Ma's rendition of Bach's first cello suite. As she does midday milking she hums, unaware, and then feels her skull vibrating with the unaccustomed music. A young servant girl in the barn is startled by the odd unearthly sound, and she runs out the door into the sunlight in fear, before she realizes it was just her young deaf mistress, singing, without any words.

THE BRIGAND BEHIND the cliff in the Untrustworthy Mountains will have swooped down on the caravan by evening, killing two camel drivers and taking their soft leather bags of gold coins. Not so many coins— their goods have not yet gotten to market—but a robber does what a robber must do, he thinks. All in a day's work. As he rides away he rips his teeth with great relish into a peppered cold leg of roast lamb stolen from one of the dead drivers. More satisfying in the short term than coins and well seasoned.

KYLLIKKI SITS AT her loom in the afternoon with the shutters of the room thrown open, weaving a wool stole of precisely the color of blue she has wanted all winter. Her father has gotten the dyes from the East. Her eyes will look so very blue when she wears this that men making jokes about deaf girls will stop in their tracks and stand silent, confounded.

As she weaves she is thinking of the last Bear Feast before the illness that took her hearing—pneumococcal meningitis, which the people called only "the fever," mysterious as any other ill. She remembers only the fever itself, a red glow inside her head, pulsing, a furnace, her stepmother and sister and two servants hovering over her as she walked the edge of death's cliff and stood there with her breath held, and then came the silence. The Bear Feast had been one of the favorite times that intrigued her as a child, perhaps *because* women were kept away, and of course children as well.

She had crept into the clearing that time—she was barely five years old—when she saw the flames rising and filling the night. How could she not go, even if she had been told she would anger the gods and the spirits?

She hid behind a great stone in the forest, watching her uncle Sulo, who had killed the bear, taking the part of the bear in the dance and the spectacle, full of drink and some herbal drug potion, his eyes glassy and rolling. The heavy, blood-smelling pelt was thrown over him, covering his head, only his unshod feet showing. From under the pelt, Sulo's roars sounded variously sublime and unearthly, or comic, or simply bored and tired, as if he resented this. At one point he vomited on the ground, loudly. She had no idea whether that was part of the dance or an accident. Then he went on with the dance. She had asked her aunt the reason for all this. "Stop asking," the woman had said. "It is men's business." Later on, even without the power of speech, the child still probed and aggravated, with her eyes.

Her older brother's friend Seppo had said the Bear Feast was the most important ritual of all, the one celebrating creation, the one that brought power. If we do not keep up this ritual, he said, we surely will die: no animals will fill the forests, the spirits will desert us. The bear, he said, dropped to the earth from the sky, slipped from the slick fur of the shoulders of the Great Bear in the stars, and the bear is our brother now.

So we kill our brother? asked Kyllikki, puzzled. And eat him?

"Stop asking," her brother said.

The bear was our brother, superior to us. We were not to ask what that meant. We could not pronounce the bear's name: it was sacred. We could not say *karhu*. We had to speak sidewise, in euphemisms, out of reverence. We could call the bear Otso, the "apple of the forest." "Apple?" said little Kyllikki, before her accident, when she was first learning to speak. "Apple?" We could flatter the bear, calling him mighty master, Suuriherra. We could hide our fear and call him Mesikämmen, lazy one with honey on his paws. We could call him our cousin, Tatinipoika, the son of our aunt. But we could not say *karhu*. "I don't understand," said the little girl. "Explain."

Some said that the child had been punished not too long after this night by the spirits for too many questions, that the ancestors had rendered her mute for her impudence and curiosity.

In the clearing as she watched from the shadows the men danced, became sweaty, shed their clothes, and wearing nothing but paint, began performing lewd motions on themselves and one another whose point eluded her. Then she realized: One of the men was portraying a bride, a woman, and another man played the part of the bear. They were coupling. This was to ensure success in the hunt and to please the bear's spirit, the dead bear, the brother-bear. The secret ritual performed in the dark six weeks after a person died, to separate him from the living and bond him to the dead, was called a "wedding" as well. Everything in their rituals was a wedding of one sort or other.

She put her head in her apron in disgust and perplexity; she rocked and keened in her throat, and finally, after she had listened to all the growling and chanting enough that it wearied her, she crept away none the wiser and lay on her back in her bed considering whether she wanted to become one of them—an adult—or whether she might just stay a child. Adults surely seemed to hold desperately to illogical ideas and to be truly incurious. She decided she might just not grow up.

FIFTEEN YEARS LATER, the girl who resolved she would not grow up *has* grown up. At her loom she muses, feeling the thwack-clack of the shuttles in the bones of her arms. She wonders what life might have been like if that fever had not taken her hearing, if she had been married off. She decides that is a fruitless inquiry.

A servant who comes through the room, bringing a heavy white cheese in its skin, cradled like a baby, watches the deaf mistress weaving in silence as she passes through and thinks: *Thank you, my ancestors, that you have given me intelligence, not like the mistress, so wealthy, yet so much like an animal or a statue, insensate.*

Kyllikki's eyes meet the servant's, reading the error and arrogance of her thought clearly. She thinks: *But I have my own kind of freedom.* That flashes in her eyes. Then she looks away.

At the far end of the village, her house backing up the woods, lives the only other woman of marrying age who is not married. This is Vappu-Loviisa, whose name is lovely, connoting springtime and blossom. Loviisa is our own "Louisa," a name not much heard in our day but a lovely name nonetheless. This woman is not herself lovely. She has a reputation as a dabbler in black arts and is said to be able to seduce men with her spells.

Seduce men? Kyllikki thinks. *She must have to render them insane first.* The woman is a tower of suet and charcoal grease, and her hair is a matted mass, white as snow despite all her filth. Kyllikki has heard—or *understood,* since she cannot hear—that Vappu-Loviisa was responsible for the death of the tanner's wife's baby. It was said that the tanner had come to the hut of the witch seeking a charm against an enemy and that the witch had given it gladly. Then, because the economy of the witch is that way, no prices posted, Vappu-Loviisa had demanded that the tanner mount her like an animal, right there. The tanner had told the tale and enlivened it with vivid descriptions of the witch's enormous pale breasts like the jellyfish at the shore, but with nipples as black as the lips of a dog. He warmed to his tale and described nether lips spread like the doors of a cellar, as she stood there, inviting him. "Flapping," he said, "like the sails of a ship from Jerusalem!"

The men laughed uproariously, and they told their wives. He had rejected her, of course, the tanner said. He laughed in contempt. He had paid her in game for the charm—several hares and a half-dozen fowl. He would use the charm when the time came, he said. The enemy was in a village a day's journey inland. The charm would play a prank, no more. The enemy had tricked the tanner out of some hides, and the charm would just pay him back. The story spread quickly.

In the alternative version, it was said that the tanner had been revolted, then petrified, at first, but finally, after a draft of some sweet hot drink that the witch gave him, decided there was no help for it. It was said that he had in fact mounted the witch, had spent several hours at Vappu-Loviisa's. She had after all given him the charm.

Then he returned the following month, and again the witch demanded that he lie with her. He forgot what he came for, lay with her, and left. There was no moon, and a light, early-spring snow had been falling.

When the tanner staggered home, his wife was asleep and knew nothing of his absence. In the morning, their child lay dead in its basket. The charm had not even been used. The tanner walked about in confusion, bewitched; his wife keened, rocked, tore her hair. Vappu-Loviisa went about her business, her wild white hair seeming to glow in defiance. It was said that that was the start of the parade of men coming to her hut in the darkness.

Kyllikki is beside and beyond herself trying to fathom this. The woman stinks. Of course, most of the men stink as well, though the stench that they carry is of sweat, and work. Vappu-Loviisa carries the smell of vinegar and bile and something resembling decomposing bodies nearby, just out of sight. She uses no one's sauna. The purification of that ritual is utterly foreign to her.

Kyllikki goes to her grove and burns herbs to the ancestors asking protection from this woman. The glances she throws Kyllikki's way are venomous. Kyllikki feels like a fish in the mouth of a fox or a bear, struggling feebly, when the witch looks at her this way. She has worked out a system of signs within her household, and the elder of the cooks, Ruusu, can communicate with her quite well, by hand signals.

Kyllikki leans down and touches the woman's face, finger to cheekbone, as the cook shells beans, to beg her attention. She says to Ruusu in sign language: I feel frightened. Her sign for this is a cowering rabbit, her two fingers up at the side of her head, as rabbit ears. She pantomimes huge, nasty hair and her eyes roll.

"Oh," says Ruusu. "The evil one!" She laughs easily, as if to discount her evil and call her simply unpleasant. She has a name-calling sign for the woman: *luukynsi*, or bone claw. "You are frightened of *her*?"

Kyllikki makes the sign for *question*. Then she says: *Eyes. Hurt. Me.*

Ruusu keeps shelling her beans. She says, simply shaking her head no: No, you do not need to be frightened of her.

Kyllikki again makes the sign for *question*. *Question. Kyllikki. Do.* So what then do I do?

Ruusu says nothing at all for a moment. Snap, snap, go the beans.

Kyllikki says it again: *Question. Kyllikki. Do.*

The cook wipes her forehead and sits up straight. I will send your brother to tell her, says Ruusu. *Ruusu. Send. Brother.*

Can it be that simple? thinks Kyllikki.

Ruusu sends Kyllikki's older brother, Topi, who is tall and fair-haired and respected by everyone in the village for his bravery and handsomeness. He has a prominent brow seeming to bespeak intelligence, and flattened cheekbones that give his face a look of imperturbability, a lake on a windless day. Topi nonetheless returns disoriented, his eyes agog, his brows high up under his hair in frank consternation, swearing loudly that Vappu-Loviisa stepped out of her hut, lifted her skirt to her knees, and pissed a reeking yellow cataract violently on the ground before him, in a standing position. Like a man, he says, shaking his head as he tells the tale. Ruusu tells Kyllikki's father. She says it seems to her that the piss must have splashed on the brother and cursed him, because he is as confused as the tanner had been.

The story passes around the village and is magnified in the telling. When it gets to the house of the blacksmith, Vappu-Loviisa has grown taller than Topi, and the stream of witch piss has increased to flood proportions, with a sound as of an avalanche.

By the next house, there are boulders rolling on the waves of the flood.

By the time the story reaches the cheese maker's cottage, the mention of the witch's having pissed like a man does another leap: Vappu-Loviisa has in the story grown a penis the size of a bull's, which she flings about like a club or an octopus.

It is all about terror, and the power of story, and Vappu-Loviisa may or may not hear the specifics but she knows she has cowed Topi. That is all that matters.

Kyllikki's father, Rauno, goes to the witch's hut, and a lovely young woman wiping her hands on her apron comes to the door, a woman the father has never seen. Her eyes are dark, and her skin pale as milk. Rauno asks uncertainly for Vappu-Loviisa. Suddenly, though he has lived in this village for his whole life, he feels as if he is a foreigner. He is disoriented.

Oh, she is over the mountains, says the young woman.

Over the mountains? says Rauno.

Buying amber, the young woman says, for her charms. She smiles sweetly.

As Rauno turns to leave, he notes something odd about her hand as she smooths her hair: she seems to have an extra finger. Kyllikki's father comes home puzzled. Within the hour, others report seeing Vappu-Loviisa variously behind her hut at the village's edge, at the stream, and coming out of a cave half a mile from the village. No one ever again sees the young woman that Kyllikki's father had seen, so no one can verify that extra finger.

A story starts up that Vappu-Loviisa is a shape shifter. That the young woman was actually Vappu-Loviisa herself. No, no, says a neighbor, I believe she has a cousin from the other side of the lake who must have visited. Surely if she is a human being, she must have kin. And she has lived here for years, has she not?

No one can quite remember when she came. It was a few years ago, yes, perhaps. Someone lived in that house before she did . . . We cannot remember. But where did she come from? The woman seems to make minds go foggy. Certainly it is plausible that she could have had a cousin come on a visit. Still, nothing can be proven. Small as the village is, still the witch's power grows in the minds of the villagers as the story expands.

At the moment all this—witch piss, consternation—is going on in the little village on Lake Köyliö, which has no name except perhaps "the village of the sled dogs," other matters are transpiring even farther east on the Silk Road than the small matter of the brigand and the quick double murder of the camel drivers. The dogs in question in Kyllikki's village are dozens in number, Finnish arctic sled dogs with the coloring of foxes and the strength of Samoyeds. No other village nearby has so many.

A caravan that has gone out two years before from the area around Savonlinna, in the southeast of Finland, has made its way to China, to Ch'ang-an, to trade furs for Eastern goods, and is wending its way back west toward Europe now.

On its journey out, having traced first the route that not long after came to be called the Ox Road of Häme, then headed south through Europe on the route that Christian pilgrims took to the shrine of Saint James—Santiago de Compostela—in Spain, the caravan has turned southeast, to Constantinople, further southeast through Anatolia to Aleppo, to Baghdad, thence eastward in a ragged dog-leg line to Hamadān, Ravy, Nishapur, Bukhara, Samarkand.

At Samarkand they have turned eastward to the teeming Chinese capital, Ch'ang-an, with its population in the eighth century of two million, the site of the city which is in our own time called Xi'an.

The men, the carts, the camels—bought en route and soon to be sold back—have done their business in the imperial capital and headed west. They are back again in Samarkand. The city has been conquered by the legions of Alexander the Great, a millennium earlier, in their sweep across the continent.

It is not yet the Samarkand of today, of brilliant blue-tiled domes and blue-enameled facades, dazzling the eye of the traveler and making the city seem to bleed itself ethereally upward into the sky, as if it were becoming transparent. All this blueness will not come until Tamerlane makes it his Mongol capital, centuries later. But the skies above Samarkand are as blue as the skies above Finland, an astonishment. Indigo, rich, the color of kings and of emperors. The city thinks itself the equivalent of Rome or Babylon, and its decadence rivals theirs.

Six roads converge inward, asterisk-like, from the city walls to the heart of Samarkand. There, in a hexagonal plaza of pale packed dirt, a throng of artisans and merchants hawk their wares. The caravan master clearly is fascinated by—and drawn to—this metropolis, which is called by many the "city of famous shadows." It is in one of those shadows—a narrow street, a barely flickering torch—that the master has been knifed. On the journey out, he has said to Olavi, his young lieutenant, that somehow he felt that his life would end here. But of course he is still quite alive.

Only a few years before this, the emperor of China laid heavy restrictions on trade, making it an offense to export yak tails, pearls, iron, or gold. This does not mean the trade stops. The traffic continues, but more carefully. Silks are restricted now too. The traffic in brocades and damasks is secretive, and the value of the goods fluctuates as the danger lessens or intensifies. Chinese officials are careful to collect extravagant duties, yet merchants from the West still make dazzling profits. The caravan skirts the southern perimeter of the Gobi desert and then traces the arc of the northern boundary of the Taklimakan desert.

At the far west of China, the caravan takes on a great deal of apple green jade from the nearby mountains, most of it cut into smaller pieces by artisans, though they have managed two camels worth of the larger chunks. These will fetch amazing prices in the West. Already in Ch'ang-an they have traded their precious furs for a great deal of milk white jade carved into thumb rings and earrings and bracelets and hairpins. At first the master has thought this not worth the time, given that these objects have no function that is familiar in the West.

Olavi, like Kyllikki, can communicate only in signs. He has been deaf from birth. Olavi argues, in support of this trade in jade: *Exotic. Sells. Itself.* The master looks at him curiously. He signs back: *Not. Object. As-object.* Having navigated those rapids of semantic difficulty, the master is amazed at the enhanced depth and subtlety of their ability to communicate.

Olavi signs: *Object. Tells. Story.* He holds up to the master, in the glare and spice smells and hubbub and dung of the outdoor bazaar in Ch'ang-an, a pen holder carved of jade. *This. Of-writer.* Ah, agrees the master, nodding. *Writer. Connected-to. Pen-holder.* The master nods even more soberly. *You. Tell. Wonderful. Story.* The master's nod is almost imperceptible, very much comprehending.

"Ah," he says, forgetting for the moment that Olavi is deaf, "you're suggesting that what will fetch enormous prices for these—and fetch those prices honestly—is in essence to soak them in stories first, marinate them like meat, tell our own true and gutsy stories from the trip, and the stories of Chinese gods and heroes that we have heard en route."

Olavi, who of course knows none of the words and cannot read his lips, nods vigorously and slaps the hand of his leader hard in joyous agreement. Clearly the master has understood. Olavi signs: *You. Remember. Stories.* His boss laughs.

He signs in response: *I. Have. Poor. Memory. . . . Memory. Your. Job.*

Olavi laughs then and signs back animatedly: *Therefore. You. Must. Tell. Olavi. Many. Stories. Before. You. Forget. Many. Stories.*

And so evenings are taken up with the leader's telling Olavi every story—every anecdote, every fable of gods or heroes—he has heard in Ch'ang-an, translated to him at the first level of sea change by the one member of the caravan who can speak Chinese, a driver, stories told by priests and pharmacists and old women in the bazaar stirring steaming pots of noodles and broth. As quickly as he tells the stories to Olavi, he forgets them. But Olavi remembers in vivid detail.

They are now mere miles from the burial places of both the splendiferous emperor Qin Shi Huang-ti and the short, quirky, unknown failed alchemist Qin Lao, ancestor of little Ursula Wong on her father's Chinese side, as Olavi will be ancestor to Ursula on her mother's side.

No one—neither the ancestor on her father's side nor the ancestor on her mother's side—is thinking of Ursula Wong or asking whether she will—as Jinx Muehlenberg in her cups demands drunkenly of the air, as she watches the rescue attempt on television—be worth all of the money and time that will be lavished upon the attempt to pull her safely out of the mine shaft. News of the accident has passed from the 911 dispatcher now to the mine rescue team head. Word spreads out quickly all over, weblike, to the team members, but no one yet knows how deep Ursula has fallen or whether she is alive: if alive, whether she is injured, and if so, how badly.

THE MASTER AND Olavi barter in the market for pendants and brooches as well as for a large quantity of the exotic jade discs, perforated at the center, which the Chinese believe carry solar effulgence and grant the one holding them great peace and power. As curiosities they have bartered for jade incense burners and sacrificial vases to be used on the altars of ancestors, as well as for sacred peaches and pomegranates carved of white-and-red jade.

Olavi signs to the caravan master, grinning: *Your. Job. Find. Peach. Story.* That is to say: If you want someone to buy these, you'll have to enhance them with stories. The master frowns. This is difficult.

Olavi signs: *Story. You. Find. Sell. Peach.* Storytelling will be the key to profit: the buyer will buy *ambience* rather than *object*. He makes the sign for where this will happen: *Way-back-home.*

So the master works with his translator-servant (whom he pays with extra rations of wine) to seek out particular stories. He signs them to Olavi nightly, and Olavi commits them quickly to memory.

They have bought ivory combs whose backs are carved with exotic Chinese blossoms and whose intricate bas-relief panels are stained a deep red hue. They have bought ivory fans. They have bought enormous amounts of fine fabric, in bolts, some of it legal, some of it illegal and thus well hidden. They must protect the fabric well from rain and sunlight too. Even the caravan master, with his scruples and sense of integrity, sees the momentary whim of an emperor to whom he does not bow as being something to which he is not held accountable.

They have bought spices, which bring many, many times their weight in gold. Dozens of large bags of spices, which parceled out become thousands of small bags of spices, take not a quarter of the carrying capacity of a single camel, a "ship of the desert."

They have bought pepper and pepper and more pepper, which fetches great sums at home, and they have bought spices whose names they do not know, which the traders carrying them north from the warmer lands call "star spice" and "new moon taste" and "the tongue-jewel of the rajahs." Olavi signs to the caravan master excitedly, concerning the last: *See! Story! Sell!* Do you see what I mean then? The story embedded in the object brings the object alive and will fetch a fine price for us?

But there is more to be traded: at the far west of China, the caravan heads north to trade for horses, the so-called heavenly horses of Ferghana. There is no need to scout up stories to enhance the horses' value: everyone knows that these horses originally were water born, in a mythical pool into which a tall waterfall fell, making music. The horses are dun colored, some of them bearing two or three tigerlike stripes on their backs, and beautifully muscled. It is said that the horses were originally dragons, not the fearsome beasts of medieval Western epic but rather the spirits of power and change. It is said they can render themselves visible or invisible at will. They reveal themselves in storm clouds and lightning, and Chinese children frightened and delighted at watching a rainstorm are told that the momentary gleam seen on the leaves and trunks of trees after rain are the scales of dragons.

Not all of the men are needed to bring back the horses, but the master adjudges that on balance, it is imperative that they stay together, not separate. He cannot manage half the company and give the other half to Olavi: they must work together. These animals, carefully bred for almost a thousand years and unique in all the world, are beautiful and swift and incredibly expensive. The master says they will perhaps be able to afford a half dozen, but that if they can bring them safely back home they will fetch astronomical prices.

The dull-eyed drivers and laborers—men who need supervision, have no families, are not householders—prefer to be told what to do, have no stake in this, as they will not partake in the profits. They care little about how long this takes, or what treasures they carry, as long as they survive the trip and are paid their scant wages.

In Samarkand the caravan master has been knifed outside a smoky tavern with loud music, which Olavi cannot hear, by a red-haired Western courtesan employed to attract the merchant trade, and the caravan has been delayed for months. Two of the men disappear in the interim and take mistresses. In China, it is the law that such men must stay and that the women may not leave; here in Samarkand, by contrast, no one knows what the law is. The men are quite gone, unfindable, regardless.

The caravan master is slow to heal, the vanished courtesan will not be held liable for the act, and matters seem at this point to be disintegrating. The caravan master summons Olavi. It is the younger man's first journey, but he is quick and well organized. The master signs to Olavi that he must make arrangements to leave as soon as possible. He signs: *We. Must. Leave.* His hands seem to be a flock of wild geese heading west as he signs *leave*.

He makes the sign for *winter* and extends his hands helplessly palms up as if to say, We will be at its mercy if we do not hurry. Olavi nods agreement and sets about making lists and plans. He can work well with numbers even if he can neither hear nor speak. He is highly capable.

Within days all is in readiness. A Chinese herbalist has made a fatty yellow paste they can carry with them to keep the caravan master's wound dressed. They stock a great quantity of it for the journey. The master is indispensable. It is decided that he will travel in a lacquered palanquin until he heals. The palanquin is inset with a design made from bits of nacreous shell that has come inland from the sea several hundred miles with traders.

The master makes a great joke of this and then signs to his assistant that his embarrassment at being an invalid will be more than offset by the money he will get for the palanquin when the caravan reaches Constantinople. His young assistant laughs at this. It is a joke between them that the master loves money indeed. No opportunity for honest profit passes him by, but he will have nothing to do with dishonesty. This is why Olavi is his lieutenant: the young man has a reputation of integrity to match his quickness.

After many days back on the hard, dry white sun-baked earthen road, they endure a full day of the most persistent mirages they have yet seen, shimmering out ahead of them—pavilions and temples and even entire walled cities that waver in the heat and then dissolve into pools of pink reflectivity in the sand when the caravan reaches the crest of the rise.

There are auditory hallucinations of bustling town noises, crowds, music for dancing girls, bells tinkling, horses whinnying and neighing: everyone but Olavi can hear these. He can discern from the spooked, vigilant stillness in the countenances of his trail mates—their eyebrows looking as if they will jump off their foreheads and run away—that they are hearing things.

The camel driver nearest him, whom they had picked up in Turkey on the journey out, a man with a stained, puckered face and a left ear whose tip has been lost to a sword, describes the sounds with hand signals and charades. The drivers are accustomed to communicating routinely in signs, as they pass quickly from one area's language to another, and their makeshift sign language serves equally well—or badly—everywhere.

The driver makes signs to say *I*. Then *Hear*. Finally, *Huge-flock-of-twittering-birds*. Olavi has no notion what huge-flock-of-twittering birds might sound like. He imagines vibrations that he has felt in tiny bells, and he paints in his head the colors of sunset or just before dawn. He adds in the taste of a tart fruit he tasted in Xi'an, at the far end of the road where they turned around, and the taste of a brown-red spice that they sampled there also, rubbed into pork flesh and crackling from fire. *This,* Olavi imagines, would be the sound of a *huge-flock-of-twittering-birds.*

The caravan comes suddenly to an oasis fenced around by sand-binder trees and irrigated by a sophisticated system of underground tunnels. Pears grow here, pears said in an ancient story to have been watered by the blood of a maiden protecting them. The story attributes the pears' succulence and rich taste to the sacrifice of her blood. Olavi tries not to think of the story later when he eats the pears.

There grow here also heavy bunches of fat grapes in arbors. Olavi has never had such fruit, and delighting in the smooth damp jade texture of them on his tongue, he eats too many and is within the hour overcome by diarrhea. The camel drivers slap their sinewy thighs, lean as dogs', and they laugh uproariously. Olavi's face is so pale it is green now.

The master laughs too, to such an extent that the wound in his side breaks open again and starts oozing. He moans and holds on to his bandaged ribs, tears of hilarity and pain mixed together. Olavi signs to them all that they are fools, a slap of the heel of his hand to his chin, his fingers dancing off into the air in dismissal, a movement that would be recognized in any language. They take grapes with them when they leave and will need to eat them before they go overripe, but Olavi remembers the wrench in the gut and the sweat on the brow, not a good sweat like the sweat of hard work, and he partakes in moderation.

Huge stupid bullies with swords serve as guards to the caravan. They have lost no one to bandits, and they will not. They make it through the Tian Shan Mountains without losing a single animal or driver.

THAT WINTER, THE caravan has reached Constantinople, having sold off the camels at Aleppo to a foul-tempered Trebizonder for more than the master—who is by this point sulking that he is not yet well enough to ride a horse and thus still is in the silly palanquin—expected. Olavi has paid off the drivers, and the much reduced party has crossed into Europe.

An early ice storm stops them and their wagons at the Vistula, in what will come to be Poland, in a town whose name in their Slavic dialect means "delay," and no one can tell them why. After the ice storm comes a heavy rain, which freezes, and before that can melt, comes the snow. It is useless to try to go on. The town has two inns, either of them willing to put up the party all winter, so seeing no alternative, they choose the one whose innkeeper's daughter is less pockmarked and hirsute.

The winter is a hard one. Fights break out among the men. The master is tired of their company, tired of their boorishness. The horses of heaven seem puzzled at what they are doing in such a reduced state, in the barn of a Vistula innkeeper, with a half-dozen cows and six times that many cats, half yellow striped, half gray. The daughter of the village blacksmith, a quarter mile away, will be in the Polish lineage of Joe Cimmer, father to Justin Wong. Olavi and one of the men tend the animals and they have all the cream, eggs, and cheese they can eat in return. The master insists that the men who do not work must pay, and much grumbling ensues: We did not bargain to be here. We are not farmhands. The master gives one a cold stare then and says, "Oh? What *are* you, then?" The man does not answer but looks away.

IT IS MARCH now and as the master and Olavi are warming their too-long-idle hands at the inn's fire, the master says it is time. Finally. The master has healed, in this enforced rest, and is irritable wanting to move on. When the snow melts and the puddles evaporate, the grass sends up blindingly green shoots, the mud hardens into solid ground, and they are off. One of the drivers—it is impossible to know which, as several of them seem to have had a roll with her—has gotten the innkeeper's daughter pregnant. As the men ride off in their wagons—a half dozen of them are riding the horses of heaven, far less fine dray horses pulling the wagons—the innkeeper's daughter, her eyes red and watery, stands in the door of the inn wringing her apron, pursing her chapped pale lips, and scowling at no one in particular. Her stomach is already big and round. The master rolls his eyes at Olavi as if to say, Louts, brutes, asses, but really what he is saying is that he is anxious for home.

And suddenly it is June, they are on the Häme Ox Road again, and they can almost *smell* home. The master asks Olavi to deliver the ordered goods to the towns just west of Turku before he takes off for his own home in Savonlinna. Olavi next then must sell off the goods they have purchased in the Orient on speculation. He signs to the master: *Question. Olavi. Do. How.*

The master remembers all the evenings on the trail, his telling and Olavi's remembering stories, to use in that process. He signs back with a grin: *This. Plan. Not. My. Plan.* He pokes his tongue into his cheek and looks away. He points to a trio of hawks gliding silently overhead, swooping in and out of one another's path, weaving a fabric of sky, warp and weft, and he winks. He means, It's your problem now, I know you can do it. And by the way, how do you like those hawks?

So this is how Olavi comes to the village of the sled dogs, in an ox wagon packed with dyes, silks, jades, spices, ivory carvings, and all manner of stories.

KYLLIKKI SITS CURLED into herself on a huge smooth rock set into the earth at the lake's edge, shawl-wrapped against the evening chill. Not three yards away, tied to the shore, is a fishing boat the curve of whose waxy wood keel she is admiring. The late sunlight hits it and turns it, and everything around it the color of wild roses or spilled wine. The edge of the water, where it is shallow, is clear, and Kyllikki watches small fish darting about there, and a quick, slender water snake, and small clouds of bugs hovering.

The quiet of being away from the village with all of its hubbub—the animals quacking or mooing or bleating or neighing or throwing their heads around ringing the bells on their collars, the voices of small children shrieking in glee or in protest—is wasted on her, of course. She has silence constantly. But there is a visual silence about sitting down here by the water that pleases her.

She can see the far shore of the lake rising rocky from the water's edge. She can see the lake bottom as it tilts away from her, down, down, to darkness. Near the shore where the water is mostly clear, the round pebbles at the bottom appear green as jade to the eye above.

Kyllikki remembers a dream, suddenly: the way the stones draw her eyes downward dredges the dream from her night memory. Just before waking this morning the dream came. She turned under the heavy bedcovers in her cupboard bed and in the flash of light that entered her head as she rotated she saw the brief vision, a still image. She has had these vivid dreams ever since childhood, ever since the illness.

It is her impression that the village shaman, Perttu, at the east of the village, on the edge of the forest, is not a true shaman who has visions and dreams that see into more earthbound realities but is rather a blustering charlatan. He cultivates fear as his best weapon. He can neither trap nor hunt well, and he knows no trade. But he blusters as if he were born to it, and she sees through him. She says nothing: she only stands and watches him as he passes, and he throws her evil glances, feeling seen through.

Ruusu has chided Kyllikki repeatedly: He has *power,* don't tempt him. And Kyllikki has made a small child's sour face, puckery: No, I am not afraid, he is a fool. Ruusu makes signs in the air with her hands in the direction of the shaman's departing back, signs meant to ward off his evil eye. Kyllikki flicks all her fingers in dismissal: *Poof! Nothing! Insect-cloud!* That is her view of the shaman.

The dream this morning was typical—images whose import she cannot sort out, though their aura is strong and mysterious. In the dream she sat beside a pond, which must surely be this lake—there is no other lake nearby, and no pond whose water is this pewter color. There are many marsh ponds —from which later Finland will take its name, the land of fens—but they are green, every shade of green. So the water in the dream is surely Lake Köyliö. It is clear as brownish Baltic amber.

In the dream as Kyllikki peers into the depths of the lake, she spies near shore a small, dark-furred animal, a beaver perhaps, though it seems somewhat large for a beaver. Suddenly in the dream she has stepped into the water, and the weight of the creature is heavy and frightening against her leg. She steps back out, and the animal does not so much step out *with* her as simply materialize beside her, huge and dark. It is a bear, and the flesh of its dark flanks sways like terrible leaden curtains on its bones, menacing. The creature in her dream is on all fours but its back is the height of her shoulder, a gigantic bear indeed.

The dreaming Kyllikki this morning struggled awake making formless sounds in her throat, but she could not break the surface. The dreamer asleep watches the bear shamble up the shore, feels the earth shudder, trembles herself. The bear turns to look at her, with a look in its dark eyes that is almost human, and then enters a house at the top of the hill as if it were the owner. Kyllikki in her dream knows that the bear is not dangerous— powerful, yes, heavy with power, but not dangerous. Still she is terrified. And then she wakens, her heart pounding rapidly. She is sweating with the anxiety of the dream and the heaviness of the coverlets.

She rises with sweat on her brow and goes outdoors in her wool wrapper, wearing woolen stockings under her nightgown, and wooden clogs. The sky is not yet turning purple with dawn. It is still violently, peacefully, perfectly black.

She looks for the bear, the stars that shape the great bear against the bowl of the heavens. She cannot find it. She goes indoors again and lies down but cannot sleep, just lies there till first the waxy smell and then the flickering of Ruusu's candle in the kitchen promise some company, and the day begins.

IN LATE MORNING NOW, the soft leather bottoms of her sandals allow her to feel the earth through them. She moves her feet around in the short grass and feels small stones, and a dried blossom that crushes beneath her sole, and then something beetle-sized and hard. She reaches to pick it up. It is a fisherman's sinker, a weight for a net. She picks it up, brushes off the mud. She walks down the water's edge and lays it on the seat in the boat.

This boat belongs to Akseli, the owner, who sells fish to many of the villagers, including her father's household. Akseli's wife has a harelip, and Akseli has twice in a moment of daring (daring himself, daring her to report) stepped close to her when no one was looking and placed a calloused fish-smelling fingertip lightly on Kyllikki's upper lip, saying the word *raunis*. Beautiful.

She has simply stepped away, pulling her brows together in a contained fury he can read as clearly as she read his own meaning. Akseli's wife is her friend and a kind person. She has lost both of her children in the last three years, a boy of three to drowning, a girl at birth, born blue and not breathing, and she has a taut look about her, as if one more loss will make her rise like a bird and disappear. She has signed to Akseli: *No. Your. Wife. Beautiful.*

The surface of the lake, pewter hued in daylight, is the color of wine now. A silver fish leaps up and falls back. The ripples spread in a split second across an acre's worth of lake. The sun is about to dip back of the trees.

Kyllikki is not seeing in front of her—cannot imagine—a very quick happening three centuries in the future, when this village will have become a town. This will happen in midwinter, when the lake is covered by ice a foot thick and only those willing to chop through it and sit with their lines, teeth chattering, have any fish to eat. A British missionary-priest, Henry, will be martyred by means of an ax thrown by a drunken peasant, right here on the ice of Lake Köyliö, and become in the process the patron saint of Finland, Saint Heikki, with many stories forming up to dignify the confused political realities as well as the low-life shape taken by the martyring.

Kyllikki feels someone behind her and startles. It is a strange young man, one she has never seen, leading his sparrow-colored horse—one she has similarly never seen—by its bridle. The young man is dressed in peculiar garb, a Parthian tunic and leggings he has adopted on the journey, for comfort. He says nothing, just approaches and stands silent. Perhaps he expects her to say something? She says nothing. The air seems to crackle. Finally, she signs to him simply, touching her mouth, shaking her head no; then touching her ears, shaking her head no. I can neither hear nor speak.

The young man smiles broadly. He clearly understands. He signs—and she understands—*Take. Me. To.* He is thinking: *Take me to whom?* He signs: *The-one-who-sells-goods.* Merchant.

Kyllikki signs in reply. *Yes. My. Father.*

As they walk together up the slope from the water's edge, she keeps her eyes on him the entire time, as if he will vaporize, as if he were a product of her own mind. A fever-dream. She is wondering where he has come from, so foreign, why his eyes are so dark, whether his people are Lapp, to guess from the odd boxy shape of his head.

It is an afternoon that changes everything, as brief unexpected intrusions of the unforeseen often do in the lives of us all. Kyllikki's father is clearly astonished, as is Ruusu, the only mother figure in Kyllikki's life now.

Kyllikki's father, the merchant, communicates easily with the young man and is eager to buy from him. Bolts of well-wrapped fabrics—silks and exotic brocades—are pulled out of Olavi's horse cart. Dozens of tiny jade and ivory statuettes of Chinese goddesses and gods are laid out along Rauno's huge table. Bags and bags of spices from the wagon change hands. Yes, Rauno can sell these. Rauno roars in delight, not at the profits, but simply because this is such a surprise, on this routine afternoon in the village of the foxlike sled dogs.

Ruusu makes sounds of amazed awe deep in her throat. She throws Kyllikki glances that Kyllikki cannot interpret, except to know that they are asking her questions she is not prepared to answer. Thus Kyllikki looks away when Ruusu's eyes ask: Is this young man not handsome, Kyllikki? Is it not amazing that he too can neither hear nor speak?

Kyllikki's eyes are fixed glazedly on the tiles surrounding the hearth, counting something inside her head to distract herself.

Ruusu's glance says: Kyllikki, here is a husband for you!

Kyllikki looks out the window, having seen the glance despite herself. The shutters are open and the day is brilliant blue. A bird swoops on a tiny current of air, like an acrobat from the Chinese court on a silken rope, down from a century-old evergreen tree at the edge of the forest, beyond the near houses. Kyllikki occupies herself wondering what that tree will be used for when it is cut down, wondering what that bird's name is. It seems to have a glint of oily dark blue in its feathers, but it is not a crow. She wonders if it has a song, and then she remembers when she could *hear* song. Tears leap to her eyes. She scowls and blinks back the tears.

She looks up at Ruusu, who is grinning knowingly at her. *No, Ruusu,* thinks Kyllikki, *you have no idea what I am thinking. I am thinking about a day when I was a little girl and could hear everything you can hear now. It was dark outdoors, and candles flickered indoors. A woman sang to me. Perhaps it was you, perhaps not. The song was beautiful, and it involved a bird that carried messages from the sky to the earth. But stop looking at me! The young merchant has nothing to do with me.* Kyllikki flashes an angry look at the cook. *Leave me alone.* She wipes at her eyes with a sleeve.

Her father pulls his attention away from the merchant's goods and tugs at her shawl to attract her attention. *Question. Kyllikki. Ill.* Kyllikki: What is the matter? Are you ill?

On the sill of the window, the blue-glinting blackbird is preening its feathers. Kyllikki scowls at the bird, as if this were its fault. She thinks: *What is the matter with me?*

She signs in response to Rauno's question: Yes, I am ill. I must leave.

Ruusu follows her out of the room, grabs her head roughly, turns her face to Ruusu's own, and signs to her: *Illness. Never. Heal.*

Kyllikki's eyes challenge her: What in the *WORLD* are you talking about?

Ruusu signs it differently. *Love. Same-as. Illness.*

Kyllikki grabs Ruusu's bony wrist: *Stop. Talking.* She taps the back of the old woman's hand as if to chide her. *Stop. Foolishness.*

Ruusu signs it again: *Love. Same-as. Illness.*

Kyllikki makes a groan that is audible. She tries never to do this. It feels so out of control. The smallness of her world demands that she control it all. She signs: *Crazy. Old. Woman.*

Ruusu signs it again: *You-be. Not. Afraid.*

Kyllikki throws her shawl more tightly about her, though the day is not cold. It is a gesture of defiance. Ruusu is smiling delightedly, and Kyllikki cannot for the life of her think why.

Ruusu grabs the girl's face again, roughly, to force her to look the old woman directly in the eye. In huge gestures, she signs: *Finally! Finally! Husband-of-Kyllikki!*

Kyllikki stands solidly, with a look as of iron or stone to her jaw, and signs to the cook: *Kyllikki. Never. Marry.*

IF KYLLIKKI WERE in the China that Olavi has just left, almost three years before, she might be a part of the Golden Orchid Society, girls sworn never to marry, each for her own reason, but wrapping her determination in legitimacy with the mark of the Golden Orchid. Some of these women in China are courtesans; some, virtual nuns. Kyllikki falls into the latter group. In the village of the sled dogs there is no such club.

Kyllikki adds then, pointing back into the room where her father and Olavi are still inspecting the merchandise, somewhat less forcefully: *That-boy. Perhaps. Has. Wife.* The look in her eyes is of vulnerability.

Ruusu laughs uproariously and in the next room Rauno scowls and calls out to her, "Ruusu! We cannot hear ourselves talk!"—which of course makes no sense, as he and the boy are communicating through gestures.

Ruusu says mockingly, "Indeed, Rauno? You cannot hear your own silence?"

Olavi is meanwhile watching the father's eyes to gauge what he values most among these items and yet in which he will try to seem uninterested. It is the way of the eternal merchant. Rauno is in return watching the boy's eyes to see how well he understands Rauno's motives. It is an obvious dance, they both know it, but neither man smiles in acknowledgment.

Through the doorway, Rauno can see Ruusu holding his daughter's shoulders and chiding her. Kyllikki shakes free and runs outdoors. Ruusu laughs aloud, not meanly, but with delight. Still, her delight takes no heed of Kyllikki's discomfiture. When Rauno calls out to Ruusu, Olavi can see from the fire in Rauno's eyes and the way that he rolls them in frustration or pique that he is being twitted by the cook in response.

Olavi tells yet another story in signs, as he has earlier counseled the caravan master to do, to enhance the value of each artifact. Lifting an ivory carving carefully from its supple leather wrap, he lays it in Rauno's broad hand. It is the diameter of a small apple, and its carved bas-relief depicts a pair of mandarin ducks, facing each other. Olavi decribes with his hands the function of this item in Chinese dress: it is a girdle brooch.

Then he signs, *In-this-place* . . . here, in the village of the sled dogs . . . this man's girdle brooch in China becomes . . . *Woman's. Shoulder. Brooch*. He indicates the tips of each shoulder, where women in eighth-century Finland place the two brooches, often chained together in front, holding the drapes of their garments firm. Thus what is a man's girdle brooch in China transmutes to a woman's shoulder brooch here.

Rauno cocks his head trying to imagine how people in China must dress. He cannot. Olavi sketches for him, and Rauno ahhs appreciatively.

But Rauno has an objection. He signs: *Far-far-far. Excess*. He signs: *Not-useful. Here*.

Olavi argues. *These-mandarin-ducks. Equal. Marriage*.

Rauno waits.

Olavi signs: *Bride. Wears*. He pauses. *Therefore. Cost. Reasonable*.

Rauno is listening to scuffling in the next room. It is Ruusu trying to force Kyllikki to sit down and pay attention to her, physically holding her, and Kyllikki protesting. As Kyllikki pulls away from Ruusu, her sleeve knocks a clay vessel from the table, and it crashes to the floor.

Rauno shouts to Ruusu, "Quiet in there!"

Ruusu shouts back, "Mind your *own* business, master!" She is not accustomed to taking his scolding without retort, and given that she is also his unacknowledged bedmate, Rauno has less leverage than he often imagines.

Olavi stands before him in the profound silence of the mute, looking deeply into his eyes. He cannot see what Rauno is thinking, but it seems it must be deep. As he stands holding the girdle brooch with its carved mandarin ducks, this piece that might have been worn by a nobleman in Peking and has instead crossed the earth, Rauno's gaze has wandered off out the window and is lost in the middle distance.

He is thinking of the most recent pair of ducks that he has seen, at the reedy edge of a nearby lake. He is remembering the gleam of the late sunlight on their backs, a rich topaz gleam in the oily brown feathers that seemed to speak to his heart about the swift passage of time and the approach of death. He remembers his own father's death. Everyone has said to him that he looks exactly as his father had in his earlier years. So next he sees his own death, and Kyllikki's need for a protector.

Olavi does not see this or think this, but suddenly he too is thinking of ducks in a marsh, in a fen near his home many miles north of here, as if the thought had migrated sidewise.

Rauno does not see this thought of Olavi's, but he in turn sees in his mind's eye the fen nearby, inland from the lake, not far from the bog where the ritual sacrifices have been performed, not as regularly as in some other places, but whenever it seemed the spirits needed some appeasing.

In that bog by the time of this spring afternoon are fully five dozen sacrificial bodies, mostly young men and women in their prime, but also children and the elderly, as each shaman in turn has decreed, citing the will of the spirits. A number of times the alleged will of the spirits has fallen upon a person, young or old, who crossed the shaman's will or glance with a look or an act of defiance or fearlessness.

Rauno remembers the confusion in his own mind, the pain and the joy, when Kyllikki was such a little thing and was almost taken by the fever, and then when she woke deaf and went dumb, and it became a blessing to him. The shaman had decreed the year before that she would, when she came of age, be sacrificed in the fen, to the gods, because she was such a beautiful, perfect child. Surely her glance in the shaman's direction had been just as piercing then as it is now. Rauno had grieved at that announcement and gone into the forest and groaned and then finally screamed his grief, so that the birds lifted off their branches in a cloud of wing beating. One did not challenge the shaman's choice. One was to be grateful.

But Rauno did not want his daughter to die that way, and he was dubious that any of the other sacrifices—the ritual last meal of grains and fruit, the ritual rope about the neck, the drop into the swamp, and the rest of the family gone home to grieve, hoping the sacrifice had been as necessary as it was said to be—had any efficacy, in any event.

After Kyllikki's hearing and then her voice left her, by the next year it was clear that she could not any longer be set aside, sanctified, as a sacrificial victim. In her place a girl of her own age had been chosen, a girl with no apparent flaws like Kyllikki's, and that girl's body lay in the fen now, with all the others.

Rauno went into the forest again and made a sacrifice of grain to the gods or spirits who had protected his daughter from death by rendering her deaf and mute. A fox who came out of its hole nearby cocked its head at the man's odd keening song of gratitude, and Rauno went home to his daughter who would never hear him again.

Now, fifteen years later, with Kyllikki unmarried and this amazing young deaf-mute merchant standing before him, Rauno begins to think of a possible plan for his daughter's provision. He is imagining a grandson with the square, boxy head and small dark Lappish eyes of this Olavi.

He reenters the dialogue. *In-this-place,* he signs. *No. Wedding.* His eyes search the young man's eyes. *No. Need. This-ornament.*

Olavi is several steps ahead of the older man. He dances around the trap—which is to his perception not in fact a trap at all but a diversion from the mercantile transaction—in order to tell his story of mandarin ducks, to engage Rauno's imagination.

Olavi's fingers fly in the air, describing a moment: a fowler in a Chinese marsh stalks his prey. He covers his head with a pierced gourd, which to the ducks lighting on the surface of the water will appear to be simply an empty calabash floating out from the shore. Rauno understands and is transfixed by the image. The fowler grabs the swimming duck by its webbed foot and drags it under, breaking the neck with a quick squeeze of a strong fist, and bagging the fat bird. This bird is clearly not a mandarin duck.

Rauno is astonished. Before he can react, Olavi tells another story, the sort with as little plot as the story he has just told: that in Chinese imagery, the mandarin duck—so called because it is the noblest or highest of the duck family, as Mandarins are the noblest or highest of the Chinese people—is often pictured with the lotus. Olavi unrolls a bolt of heavy jade green silk into which is woven a pattern of lotuses and lily pads. The sunlight from the window dances across the ripples of its smooth surface. A dragonfly in a pale bronze hue flits through the scene.

Suddenly Rauno thinks again of the bog where Kyllikki would have been lying dead now, beneath the surface, with all of the men, women, and children sacrificed to the gods the shaman seeks to placate—in the process consolidating his own shamanic authority—had she not been felled by that providential fever.

Olavi is talking with his hands about a dragonfly that he saw over the Imperial Canal in Ch'ang-an and another that he saw in Samarkand. His eyes are animated. A story need not have a plot at all if it has image and animation.

Rauno stops him short with a heavy hand on his arm in midair. *No. No. No-need.*

Olavi can see the pique of fascination in Rauno's eyes, and he puts up a finger to tell the man to wait. He goes out to his cart, slamming the door with the heedless force of a man who cannot hear the slam. He returns with another bolt of brocade whose repeating pattern is of peach trees in blossom. He says this is also called the Fairy Fruit and that while it is claimed by the Persians, the Chinese say it actually originated in China.

Olavi has a map he folds out for Rauno's inspection to show him both places. He looks to Rauno for the same excitement he feels. Some of it is there. Rauno knows of Persia too, as well as India.

Rauno has, however, never seen or tasted a peach. Olavi tries to describe with his hands the taste and texture of a peach. It is a futile effort, with the little he has at hand for comparison. If only there were an infant in the room, and he could pinch its little cheeks between his fingers! If it were summer and the wild strawberries were out he could use their taste for a comparison.

In the next room, a clatter. Ruusu has dropped a stack of wooden bowls. She calls in to Rauno teasingly, "I hope I am not destroying your peace!" She laughs. Then she drops them again. "And now. Was that worse?" Rauno chides her but there is a smile on his lips. She calls in, "Kyllikki has run off in a lather. I believe you need to make a proposition to this young man, that he take her on as a wife. Unless he already has one!" Ruusu's laugh is energetic and loud, as if anticipating a good outcome.

Olavi unpacks a package of small, carved boxes. These are carved of the wood of the peach tree, he says. In the palace gardens of Xi Wang-mu, the Queen Mother of the West, he explains—mouthing the name for Rauno—there are said to be trees on which grow fairy peaches that ripen only once in three thousand years. Once eaten, they confer immortality upon those who eat them.

Immortality! says Rauno, miming the pains of old age. He is only fifty-two.

"Ask him!" prods Ruusu.

Olavi lays out a line of nested boxes. He displays three necklaces made of the seed of the peach. All comprise intricately carved beads strung on knotted silk. These are often used as wedding gifts, he says, because the peach is the fruit of immortality.

Rauno signals for Olavi's attention, clears his throat. *No. Weddings. In-this-place,* he says. But then he ticks off on his fingers the number of young women who are of marriageable age. Four. He does not include Kyllikki in his count. Two of these young women may be married off within the year, he considers. Their fathers may wish to buy wedding goods.

Olavi sees he is changing his mind and signs *Not-true.* He grins. *Question,* he signs, in large gestures, as if shouting.

Well, actually, Rauno signs, I was not thinking of those two young women. Yes, I suppose I might want to buy some of your silk, and perhaps other things. The silk will make coverlets.

Olavi says: *Question. Daughter*. He tries to think of the word and fails. He uses the word he uses when he is trading. *For-sale*. In the moment, the mute young man is without words.

Rauno makes an offended grimace. It is entirely theater. He is delighted.

Olavi remembers the look of the sunlight coming in through Kyllikki's hair, as she had stood by the window. His hands shout: *I. Marry. Her.*

Rauno tries to continue his grimace and instead he breaks into a great broad grin and embraces the young trader. In the next room Ruusu whoops and runs in and hugs both the young trader and her master.

Kyllikki, meanwhile, unaware that the deal has been sealed, is running pell-mell in the other direction, off into the forest. She might as well be blind, besides being mute and without hearing, for all that she sees. She runs like a madwoman. The floor of the forest is damp and spongy under her feet. Squirrels scatter as she runs, spilling nuts; a tiny green snake slithers out of her way a split-second before her right foot lands where he had been.

A spotted deer at a distance, bending to eat flowers from a bush, startles as the earth shakes beneath her, perks up her ears, sniffing on the slight breeze the aura of a human: the milklike scent of the perspiration in between Kyllikki's breasts, the flowerlike scent of her hair, the lanolin scent of emollient, gotten from her father's sheep, that she uses to smooth the dry skin of her hands, red from laundry, and tame her wild pale hair that strays stubbornly, night and day, from its bands and its ribbons.

Kyllikki flies by; a pair of mourning doves coo in astonishment on their branch; a cloud of swifts rises from the higher branches of the same tree, into wide sky and out over the beach. Kyllikki collapses at the edge of a brook too wide to leap and too deep to wade across. Breathless, she throws herself on the ground weeping, and not in grief.

THE WEDDING WILL be at the Midsummer Feast, in the village of the sled dogs, and in the meanwhile Olavi will finish his route, many miles north to his people near what is today Vaasa.

The fathers of the three other marriageable girls are consulted, and Olavi sells a good deal of the silk he has brought as well as a number of ornaments and boxes made of semiprecious stone. Rauno weighs out a random assortment of coins—some Arabian, some from what is today Germany, some from as far as Persia—on his little mercantile scale. The coins have the value of the metals' weight; their face value means nothing in this foreign land.

Olavi's purse is filling fast, and he is becoming aware that he may be in danger of robbers again. He makes arrangements for Rauno to serve as his banker in his absence, and the deal is sealed.

Rauno, astonished to realize that he has just engaged his daughter to this young man, and in so doing turned upside down every absence of hope that he had for her, as well as every determination she had for herself, walks to the forest's edge and calls for her: "Kyllikki!" No response. He calls louder. His voice carries and echoes. Then he hauls himself up short. Kyllikki cannot hear anything: what is he doing! He has not called her this way since she was five years old. It is as if she has come alive again.

He plunges into the forest to find her, bellowing despite his remembering that she is deaf: "Kyllikki, Kyllikki." When, following the same path she followed, he finds her beside the stream, fallen asleep, he sits down beside her and waits until she wakes, so that he can tell her the news of her impending marriage.

She sits up shaking her hand, which has gone to sleep where it was folded beneath her, and she is astonished to see Rauno. *Father*, she signs. *Question. You-here.*

Rauno signs: *Kyllikki. Marry. Merchant.*

The look of dismay or delight or both that flits across her countenance takes Rauno aback momentarily: Have I done the wrong thing? Kyllikki cannot think of a response. She composes her features as if herding geese or sheep: eyes, stay closed; brow, stay smooth; lips, betray no emotion.

Rauno signs: *Question. Kyllikki. Happy.* Kyllikki looks off into the deepening shadows of the tree line across the brook. The deer she had startled has hovered there since she crumpled, standing watch. Rauno sees her meeting the deer's gaze, steady and animal-like, and turns his head quickly.

The deer startles and flees. Kyllikki signs only one word—her hands speak loudly now—in response to her father: *Surprise.*

Rauno and his daughter walk home in the twilight. When they arrive at the house, Rauno asks again: *Question. Kyllikki. Angry.*

Kyllikki says again, her fingers flying: *Surprise.*

She turns to go to the kitchen to help Ruusu make supper, then turns back to face Rauno. She signs to him: *Father. This-thing. From-the-gods.*

THAT EVENING OLAVI will come to visit, and in front of the fire he will make a betrothal gift to Kyllikki, a pair of ivory girdle brooches gotten in Ch'ang-an, which will become shoulder brooches for a merchant's daughter in the south of Finland. They are the circumference of the top of a pop can in Michigan over a millennium later, that Annie Wong set in the cup holder in Justin's truck as they drove out from Houghton, and they are carved of finest ivory. In bas-relief on one is the symmetrical inward-facing pair of mandarin ducks Olavi had shown to Rauno. On the other is an asymmetrical composition, also carved shallowly in ivory: the blossom-twined trunk of a pine tree, curved like a crescent moon, and in the scoop of the tree, a pair of cranes, one with its head up as if listening to the sky, the other with its head down, seeming humble or puzzled or pensive.

Olavi signs to Rauno: *Cranes. Mate. For-life.*

That evening Olavi sleeps beside Kyllikki in the cupboard bed where Kyllikki has slept for years. They both lie restless. They have not yet gotten to know each other enough to do anything but breathe in unison and lie listening to each other's breath. Olavi turns on his side, smoothes Kyllikki's hair, with his right hand, again and again, as if she were a fine horse or dog. He can smell the wax of the newly quenched candle on the shelf inside the bed doors; he can smell the natural flowery scent of her hair. Kyllikki is amazed at the feel of his bristly cheek against her skin when she lays her hand there, to trace the line of his jaw. She holds his jawbone tenderly, this boy her own age whom she met only today. How can things happen this suddenly after so very long? She sniffs like an animal into the curve of his clavicle. He rouses slightly and she smells the male sweat of him. She frightens herself and pulls back, clearing her throat. In the next room, Ruusu is listening, her ear cupped to the heavy wood door. Kyllikki, knowing Ruusu's inquisitiveness and her habits, imagines the older woman there and sighs.

She kneels up, vigilant. She can hear nothing, but she can sense presence. Kyllikki leans over and put her finger over Olavi's lips in the dark, the mute silencing the mute. All she means is: First, I must get up. She opens the doors to the bed carefully and pads barefoot across the floor. She stands silent until she sees Ruusu's shadow move in the light of the candle, and she pounces like a cat.

Ruusu shrieks in astonishment. The light of the candle is enough that Ruusu can read Kyllikki's signs: *Ruusu. Go. Away.* The shooing of her hand seems to say: very far away. Ruusu pouts. Kyllikki signs: *Ruusu. Go-to. Rauno.* Ruusu sulks.

Kyllikki wishes she knew a sign for reciprocity, the Golden Rule she has never heard spoken except sidewise in partial Finnish proverbs as her father has translated them for her, in signs. She wants to say, Do unto others as you would have them do to you, but the concept is abstract. She cannot think what her options are. The candlelight flickers about them, making their shadows dance. So, to simplify, Kyllikki signs loudly to Ruusu. *Kyllikki. Tell. Rauno.*

The older woman's eyes widen, and she scurries away. Rauno would banish her to the barn for this. She signs back to Kyllikki: *Yes. Yes.* She rolls her eyes exasperatedly. *The girl has no sense of fun,* she thinks. She sneezes into her sleeve, and she goes on up to Rauno's bed, where he snores like a walrus.

Kyllikki stops at the hearth, lights a new candle, and takes it back back to the closet bed. She closes the door, and sits smiling at Olavi, her shawl wrapped about her. Olavi looks at this girl to whom he has just betrothed himself. She signs to him: *Tell. Kyllikki. Story.* She smiles and he watches the candlelight dance on her cheeks. She specifies: *Desert. Story.*

She waits, and Olavi begins signing, there in the candlelit closet bed. The story involves an encounter his caravan had with a party of Chinese traders, "mute barter," as they call it, in which each party leaves their goods laid out in a line, then withdraws. No language is shared, and so Olavi—mute as he is—is at no disadvantage. The opposing team brings out the goods they

propose to swap for these. Goods are added and subtracted until a satisfac-
tory bargain is struck.

Olavi describes the morning of the transaction in question: hazy, misty,
breaking out into brilliant blue by the time the trade has been effected. He
describes the look on the face of the toothless Mongol trader in the Untrustworthy Mountains when he offers a box cut of jade set with tourma-
line and a single small moonlike pearl in exchange for the two brooches that
have become his betrothal gift to Kyllikki, daughter of Rauno.

The Mongol trader's expression is a look first of disdain, then of interest,
then of assurance that he has the better of the deal . . . and the deal is made.
Olavi has told him a story about the box. The story involves a heavenly creature, a *xian,* the milk of whose white mare produced first the moon, then
the stars, then the very pearl that adorns this tiny box. The Mongol trader
is transfixed by the story, of course. Kyllikki is equally transfixed by the telling.
The candle keeps flickering.

Kyllikki signs: *Question. Story. True.*

Olavi signs: *Question. Which. Story.* Obviously he has embedded several.

There is the story of the Mongol trade mission, the explanation of the
Silk Road custom of mute barter, the myth of the origin of the celestial
lights, and the story of the mythic origin of the pearl.

Kyllikki signs: *Question. Every. Story.*

Olavi laughs. The Mongol trader and his absent teeth are real, mute
barter on the Silk Road is real, but the heavenly mare and the moon and the
stars and the pearl were inventions of the moment. Kyllikki laughs delightedly.

Olavi signs: *Story. Bought. Brooches. For-Kyllikki.* He is so pleased with
himself.

Kyllikki smiles in amazement that she is here, in this bed, this candle
flickering, this man telling her stories. She imagines him to have a near-
bottomless store of them, and she is of course right. Just this one trip to
China across the Silk Road has supplied him with stories to last his whole
life, but he will keep accruing more, his life long, every day.

Olavi leans forward to where Kyllikki sits hunched over in her gown and
shawl. Like a drunken man he leans forward, his head heavy against her col-

larbone. He sniffs the milky smell between her breasts. He nuzzles into her shawl. She taps him atop his head. Look at me, her eyes say. He sits back. He looks directly into her eyes. She throws off the shawl. His breath is even, and hers synchronizes with his. She unties the lace at the neck of her gown and lets it fall away. Her breasts are fuller than he has expected and more lustrous in this low light than he might have thought mere human skin could be. His mind begins writing a story about a heavenly creature, a *xian,* whose skin is pearl.

He sinks forward onto her, and there is no more sound except their breathing, until after an hour of this turning and sighing, and rubbing and kissing and rubbing some more as if they would polish each other to a high luster, Kyllikki's voice, so strange, so seldom heard, erupts in a cry like a strange bird's. Upstairs, Ruusu is asleep, and in the tree branches outside the window of their room, a mourning dove wonders what bird that might be.

OLAVI'S JOURNEY NORTH is swift, only three months, and the wedding happens soon on the heels of his return. Rauno has hoped, of course, that there would be a child right away, because that is the custom: to prove fertility is the first duty, before the marriage itself. But there is no pregnancy. Ah well, this union clearly is fated to be, regardless, and so it will be done.

Olavi's profits from the trip are enough to build a house for the couple and so that too is done. For three years there is no child, and Rauno takes ill. It is cancer, before cancer has a name: prostate cancer, which grows and eats his bones, and he lies dying miserably for two years while Kyllikki nurses him and Olavi takes short trips into Russia and Germany.

Vappu-Loviisa continues to cast evil-eye looks at Kyllikki, sidewise, when she passes her, and to snort and spit and growl indecipherable curses and charms in Kyllikki's direction. She lays a dead rat at Olavi and Kyllikki's door, with a charm around its neck. She daubs the corners of their house, in early morning, before she thinks anyone is awake, with bear grease and her own urine mixed with herbs, muttering curses the whole while.

Kyllikki is astonished when she almost walks into her as she is going out to milk the cow. The witch is fatter and uglier than ever, and there is a rumor that she has killed another infant, perhaps her own, though no one can imagine that she can still breed. She has told some other woman, who passes the rumor along, that she has put a spell on Kyllikki, that she hates the young woman more than she has hated anyone, ever.

Kyllikki is somewhat unnerved by the thought, but she stands her ground when she sees the witch. Kyllikki in her devotion to her father's illness garners a sense that life is a good deal shorter and more precious than she had known —she is only twenty-two now, and she feels as if she has lived lifetimes.

KYLLIKKI STEPS OUT onto the packed dirt in front of their cabin one morning and Vappu-Loviisa steps out of her own cabin, quite a distance away, though it seems far too close. No one else is out. It is a strange moment. Vappu-Loviisa is wearing only a shift: her pale fat legs seem to glow sickly; her horny feet seem not quite human. Her hair is a nightmare.

She stands glowering at Kyllikki and muttering a curse. She leans and picks up something from behind her on the ground—Kyllikki can see that it is a tiny skull—and she holds it out before her, chanting words Kyllikki cannot hear but whose import is clearly malevolent.

Suddenly Kyllikki realizes what the witch is doing and has already done: she is cursing her, perhaps cursing her childless, perhaps cursing any progeny she may have. The skull is an infant's.

Kyllikki feels herself seeming to grow. She sets her feet apart. Vappu-Loviisa steps forward, still muttering her curse, the tiny skull held out in front as a talisman of the worst evil she can conjure. Kyllikki takes one step forward. She focuses hard on the witch's hair, which has always made her feel bilious. Vappu-Loviisa keeps muttering, cursing.

And suddenly, as Kyllikki stares so intently, the witch's hair bursts into flame. Vappu-Loviisa screams and throws herself onto the ground writhing. Kyllikki stands transfixed and terrified. It is as if her glance has effected this strange, terrible thing. She does not know what to do: she cannot imagine getting near the witch.

She runs to her father's house to ask Ruusu, who is hard asleep in her own corner of the kitchen, but Ruusu cannot be woken. Kyllikki runs upstairs to her father. He wakes and hobbles down the stairs, leaning on

Kyllikki. He is intent as the head of the household on handling the matter, despite his illness. By the time they are out of the house it is clearly too late: Vappu-Loviisa has run back into her own house, and the entire structure is on fire, from the bottom tier of logs to the roof of thick thatch. No other dwelling is near enough to catch fire, but the house is close enough to the forest to be a danger to the whole settlement. Kyllikki and Rauno can do nothing but stand watching in a kind of wonder, and perhaps relief.

THE HOUSE BURNS quickly to the ground. The ashes smolder all day and all night. Acrid smoke, peculiar smells—flesh, potions, who knows what. The following day someone poking through the remains says that there is no skeleton there of a woman, only of a pig . . . and nearby several tiny skulls. Ruusu is interpreting for Kyllikki. Kyllikki's eyes widen in horror, and she runs away to the line of poplars at the edge of the forest and vomits until she can vomit no more. Rauno dies while Olavi is on another trading journey, to what today is Estonia, and on his return Kyllikki is gaunt and grieving.

OVER TWELVE HUNDRED years later, in a day when missiles controlled from a distance are capable of traveling across the world to destroy perceived enemies, no one is thinking about a repulsive woman with fleas in the village of the sled dogs. If however one were to question whether Vappu-Loviisa's formless curse, meant perhaps to visit sterility on Kyllikki, perhaps to visit tragedy on her offspring, could circle the earth that long, suspended in air, hurtling toward Michigan, one might well ask.

In any case, Ursula Wong in the newness of the twenty-first century is the only child of Annie Maki, who is the dozens of generations along offspring of Kyllikki and Olavi, and Ursula Wong has just slipped down that mine shaft.

IT IS NOT LONG after this that Olavi and Kyllikki trade Rauno's house, now that he is gone, to the wealthiest man in the village, the fur trader. They give their own small house to Ruusu, and they take everything and move north to the land outside Vaasa, where Olavi's people are from.

For a millennium, for forty-eight generations, the area is home to the people who will eventually be ancestors to Marjatta Haapalehto, Ursula Wong's great-great-grandmother, who will marry the schoolmaster Emil Palomaki, and beget Jaako and the others, then immigrate to America, and Jaako will become Jake Maki who will die in the collapse of the Meridel-Pflaum mine outside of Rovaniemi, Michigan.

For a thousand years, peacefully, outside of Vaasa, these people live— well, not totally peacefully. An old woman will die falling off a cliff in the twelfth century, not long after the missionaries have come to convert the Finns to Christian thinking; a five-year-old child will die of being beaten by his uncle in the sixteenth century; a mother of three pregnant with some-one else's child will be killed by her paramour, but not until she has taken her place in the line of succession by way of her second son, who will be Marjatta's ancestor, who will be a duke, of all the silly things to be, and then die in a battle over nothing for a king he does not wish to serve.

The tiny skulls in Vappu-Loviisa's charred ruins indeed were of infants; we cannot speak of the pig's skeleton. Whether it is the witch's curse, who can say, but Kyllikki and Olavi go childless for three decades, and suddenly, after her menses have ceased and Olavi's hair is white as winter, Kyllikki finds herself pregnant, as if in a fairy tale.

In Italy, decades before, the caravan has stopped at a monastery and Olavi has learned there some stories from the Bible. The story of which he is thinking is one that parallels their story, at least in part. An old man named Abraham and an old woman named Sarah have a child at even more ad-vanced ages. They name the child Isaac. Kyllikki cannot hear the name in her mind's ear when Olavi shapes the word with his lips as a suggestion. No—she shakes her head—that will not be the child's name.

Olavi thinks of another story he heard, from the Bible, in that same place. A story a bit more off the beaten path, the monk said. A prophet, a dresser of sycamore vines, who went about telling people to live their lives simply. Olavi likes the tale, in the way that he likes stories that have little plot but a great deal of substance.

We will call the boy Aamos, he says, this boy who is born when his mother is well over fifty, and his father is white-haired and walks with a cane, and they do.

5   Annie

I N THE SHIFTING leaf shadows of the forest north of Eagle River and south of Eagle Harbor, Annie sits vigil, refusing to let her mind go down the hole just a few feet away from her. There is not a sound but the birds and the breeze. She remembers the piece about her great-grandfather's death in the mine shaft: fifteen hundred feet down. *No one could survive a fall like that,* a voice in her head argues. Annie slams a vault door on that. We have no idea how deep that hole is. *It could be something other than a mine shaft,* she thinks. *But what?*

She imagines the Tenniel line drawings for *Alice's Adventures in Wonderland:* Alice drifting, pendulum, pendulum drift, her skirt ballooning out, a lovely parachute. Yes, that would be nice: Ursula drifting, drifting like that and landing on a pile of quilts at the bottom, with bunnies from Beatrix Potter. She starts humming the tune Ursula's music box plays, "It's a Small World." *Let the world be a lot smaller, and the hole not so deep or dark,* she prays. *Let the miracle happen, whatever the miracle is.*

SHE REMEMBERS A simpler time, before her own accident, which could have easily been the end for her. "The essay contest is not mandatory for everyone . . . but," says Sister Brendan Louise (standing before the class in her old-style habit, her square hands with their childlike spatulate thumbnails stuck into the pleats of her heavy black bodice), *"it will certainly be mandatory for Annie Maki."*

The saggy flesh around Sister Brendan Louise's pursed mouth wobbles righteously. She pulls out a man-sized white linen handkerchief and reams both her nostrils with relish. The class, mostly eleven years old, loves it.

"Get the good Sister a spoon! For her boogers!" says Skip Halvorson, in a stage whisper, in Father Mick's Irish accent. Much laughter from all around him.

"Hah!" says Kristi Olkkonen, Annie's best friend, leaning across the aisle while the laughter subsides. "Lucky you."

"Complain to Father Mick," says Skip, making a megaphone of his test paper. Skip rarely talks to girls, so there is something of radical daring in this. "Mickey'll get you out of it. Unconstitutional, that's what it is." The sixth grade has been studying the Constitution, and this sounds newborn fresh and sophisticated to Skip. "It's against the thing about life, liberty, and the pursuit of happiness, eh," he stage-whispers.

Annie smiles nicely at Skip. "That's the Declaration of Independence," she says. "It's okay, though. I'll do it."

"Man, am I glad I'm not smart!" says Skip. "They always make *you* do the extra stuff, Annie. I'd sue 'em."

"It's all right," Annie says again. And she thinks: *I can do this with the tip of my little finger, and there's that prize dangling out there.* Some patriotic organization is sponsoring this essay contest. It's for the whole state, and there is a first prize statewide for the best essay by a boy and another first prize for the best essay by a girl. Each first prize is a bicycle.

"All of you take out your penmanship notebooks," says Sister Brendan Louise. She seems not to have noticed that for thirty years no other teacher in spitting distance—or perhaps the whole country!—has been doing this. Penmanship notebooks indeed! But Sister Brendan's students learn an elegant hand, strokes that are bird-wing smooth, and Annie's handwriting when she is grown will bear Sister Brendan's mark.

"My goodness, you write like a girl from the nineteenth century!" a teacher in high school will remark.

"Sister Bully," Skip Halvorson mouths sidewise, leaning across the aisle and repeating with delight, for the thousandth time, the name he has concocted out of Brendan Louise.

Three days after the assignment is given, Annie has settled on her topic.

The subject for boys is "A Michigan Hero for Our Times" and for the girls "A Michigan Heroine for Our Times." There is not yet much concern in the schools about either sexism or drugs, so the word *heroine* evokes no smart-alecky wisecracks from anyone.

Annie knows nothing about her own ancestry, or she might have written her essay about Marjatta Haapalehto, her great-great-grandmother from Finland, whose hair shone so like her own. Annie would have liked her.

Instead, she reads a couple of articles about a woman name Julia Kate Peterson Clapper, who took over the Graveyard Point Lighthouse on Lake Superior after her husband, the lighthouse keeper, died young of a stroke. Julia Clapper then tended the light for thirty-six years, raising and schooling her children on the rocky point of land, alone.

Annie knows that her great-grandfather died in the Meridel-Pflaum mine accident, but she knows it only vaguely, in a way that does not probe at the truth—as a tongue might probe at a bad dental cavity—any further. The idea of a mine frightens her: she feels no connection to mining, cannot imagine anyone going down into a mine, every day, descending into the dark.

She seeks the light. She wants to go not down, but up. That's the pull, the attraction, the beauty of this lighthouse business. It's light, and it's up, and Julia Kate is a woman that Annie at ten can visualize and appreciate.

As Annie's mother, Elizabeth DeBruin Maki, has done, Julia Kate had lived her life without much help from her husband—though Liz's husband, Garrett, is slouching as usual on the couch in the living room, wearing an old army fatigue shirt—his name is right there on the tape—just Maki—and drinking vodka from a Welch's grape-jam glass with Fred Flintstone driving his stone-wheeled car around and around it.

Annie can understand Julia Clapper by way of knowing and admiring her mother. Annie has a fierce little set to her chin when she thinks about this. She will *not,* she vows, unlike her mother, find a man like her father, and sometimes she wishes he'd simply die—of something or other—and leave Liz and Annie alone in the world.

Liz is a nurse at the hospital, working the night shift more often than not. Annie loves to help her iron her uniforms, permanent press but still wrinkle prone: the smell of the sizing, the smell of the iron heat are lovely. Soon the fashion will change, and no nurse will wear white, but Liz is at the end of the tradition. Liz tells Annie one day that the ironing is a way she has of holding up her head just a bit, knowing she's starting the day freshly ironed. Annie is not sure what she means by that, though she has the sense that her mother has put up with more than she knows.

Annie writes her essay about Julia Kate. Julia Kate making her way out to the end of the wooden pier to light the beacon there, with high, danger-ous, cold blue-green waves washing over her, drenching her, Julia Kate hold-ing on coolly and confidently to the rail as if all Lake Superior concentrated into one wave could not dislodge her. Julia Kate teaching her four children, all daughters, penmanship (she thinks of Sister Brendan Louise here): curls on the capital Ns and Ms, noodlelike loops in the os, loping, smooth curves melding letter to letter. Julia Kate lonely and sturdy and bright and au-tonomous. Shipwrecks are averted and passengers from unaverted ship-wrecks are dragged out of the sea by this short, feisty woman in her bright red rowboat.

ANNIE REMEMBERS MOMENTS with her own mother, dancing in the kitchen to "My Sharona," a song her mother always loved. Goofy moves, rocking and twisting and both of them throwing their hair around—un-dersea creatures, anemones, hydras—gyrating, giggling, then Garrett com-ing in boozy, growling in disgust, "Jesus Christ, are you out of your fucking minds? Women!"

She remembers even earlier times, marching around the kitchen with Liz, banging pot lids and playing kazoos and singing along with Bob Dylan to "Rainy Day Women #12 & 35," whose lyrics suggest that everyone ought to be smoking dope, though in the memory Liz seems to be crying a little bit, and Garrett meanwhile is sitting there dozy and watching their loopy parade. Annie did not realize until years later that Garrett had gotten a couple of habits in Nam and that one of them was marijuana. She tries to imagine Julia Kate cutting loose this way, in order to write a scene in her head with Julia Kate with her children, and cannot, so she leaves out the idea altogether.

In the state capital at Lansing, the committee has no difficulty naming

Annie's essay the first-prize winner in the state. It has life, says one. Originality, says another. Look at this little girl's handwriting, says an older woman. She writes like my mother, Palmer *R*s and all.

The winner in the boys' division—half a head shorter than Annie, and a bad speller—writes an essay about a University of Michigan football player, Harlan Huckleby. The judges sigh. The only other essay they even halfway consider has taken Henry Ford as its subject and said nothing new, Model T, American ingenuity, blah blah blah. The wooden perfection of the prose makes the judges think that perhaps he has lifted segments of this direct from an encyclopedia, and though they do not check—it is not the least bit interesting to them—they are right.

The six-hour car trip downstate, across the Mackinac Bridge and its sweep of blue water against the springtime blue sky, is a delight to Annie. Her mother takes off work and drives her, and they stay overnight in the Red Roof Inn on I-696. On the way, they sing silly songs in the car.

Photographers take pictures that will appear in the newspaper in Sault Sainte Marie. Annie and the boy winner, along with two of the judges and the governor himself, are in the picture.

The bike is a bright fuchsia pink, with white streaks and flashes and with turquoise fringe streamers flying from each handlebar grip. Annie has had a bike before, but not such a lovely one.

IT IS THE SECOND of June, summer everywhere else but still spring in the Upper Peninsula. It is a Saturday morning, and Annie is meeting her mother at church to help out with the Blessed Virgin's altar. Liz is an old-fashioned Catholic, the youngest woman in an altar society dominated by elderly women: her life blooms novenas to Our Lady of Lourdes, to Saint Dymphna, the patroness of nervous breakdowns, and to Saint Jude, patron of impossible causes.

Liz prays nightly, when she goes to bed, when she's working days, with a sky blue crystal rosary she has had since she was seven. Often she falls asleep praying, when Garrett is out or already asleep, and the rosary skitters its way out of her fingers when she turns in her sleep and slides across the bed. Several times Garrett, climbing into the bed shaky with drink, has lain down on it, cursed and flung it across the room, slamming it against the wall. Three or four of those times the chain has broken.

Liz has brought it to the jewelers, Sclafani's, to be fixed. The jeweler, a son of the Sclafanis, with a terrible name—John Bosco Sclafani, named after Blessed John Bosco, the boy saint—had had a crush on her in high school, all four years. He has lost a good deal of his hair now and has never married. He asks, in a flat voice, with an eyebrow raised, "What, is Garrett rampaging again?"

Liz lets her eyes drop to the glass display case. In a very small voice, she says, "Please."

The man behind the counter says, "Lizzie, if you ever get tired of that, let me know. I'm still waiting."

Liz looks up at him, pleading. "Bosco," she says. "Don't."

"He hits you," the jeweler says, daring her. His jaw is set. She looks down at his hands. They are clean, his nails neatly trimmed. He wears no jewelry besides his watch, nearly thin as a coin. He takes a small white envelope with the rosary in it from a tray in a drawer.

"No," she says, looking into his eyes. "He doesn't, Bosco. Garrett isn't, well, Francis of Assisi"—here she breaks into a brittle half-laugh, hardly recognizing the sound of her own voice— "but no, he doesn't hit me." She is lying. She doesn't like lying, but she doesn't see an alternative today. She has to defend Garrett to Bosco; she has to defend herself against the truth.

"You let me know anytime, Lizzie," the jeweler says. He puts his hands flat on the glass of the display case. He slides the rosary in its white envelope across the glass of the counter to Liz. "No charge," he says.

On the rosary's silver-filigree crucifix, as Annie dangles it out in front of her, almost the size of a library card, hangs a small silver Jesus, his head rolled to the side, his shins looking skinny and vulnerable. When Annie herself was seven, she had hung the rosary around her neck and preened before the big oval mirror of her mother's dresser. Liz laughed. "Not around your neck, sweetie," she said. "It's not a necklace."

The concept of the rosary is foreign to Annie, a centuries-old piece of Catholic practice that has not passed down into her generation. Annie lifted the crucifix from her chest and held it at arm's length to inspect it. "I don't get it," she said. "Why they killed him. He never did anything bad, right? So why would they kill him?"

"Out of envy," said Liz. She admired the light reflecting off her daughter's hair and did not realize why she said what she said next. "They just couldn't stand all that light in him." Little Annie, her blond braids looking for all the world like her great-great-grandmother Marjatta's at the same age, took the rosary to the window and held it up in sunlight. The prisms dispersed the light into wild rainbows against the far wall.

Liz spiraled down into her own silent prayer where she stood, recalling scripture passages from the Good Friday. *They have pierced my hands and feet: they have numbered all my bones. People with easy lives, she thinks: They don't understand this at all. They just stand outside suffering as if it were a museum diorama of, say, early Lake Superior Indian life*—she is thinking of one she has seen—*an anachronism, a curiosity*. Her spirit recites inside her, *Not one of his bones shall be broken.*

She remembers Father Mick's gory didactic sermon: that a death by crucifixion was a death by asphyxiation. That if the crucified did not die quickly enough the Roman soldiers would break their leg bones so they could not support themselves, and their lungs would collapse.

Liz felt sometimes as if her own lungs would collapse, in this life with Garrett and the anger he brought home from the war. She kept praying for Garrett, who seemed somehow to be lost down a well. She visualized her prayers as the bucket, and daily she cranked the thing toward the surface.

ON THE SECOND of June 1985, not much after 9 A.M., while Garrett is still knocked out on the prickly green living-room sofa where he has fallen asleep the night before, Annie climbs on her bike with its flying turquoise plastic fringe of handlebar streamers. Those streamers always remind her of football cheerleaders' pom-poms. On the way to her goal of being a movie star like Mia Farrow, she wants more than anything else to be a pom-pom girl for Soo High School in three or four years. Her hair and the turquoise streamers flying out behind, Annie heads up the street to the church.

The wind on her neck feels so good. It presses the nylon fabric of her girls' size 12 parka against her still perfectly flat little chest. The sunlight seems part of this breeze somehow. Annie thinks of the generic grace before meals that begins "Thank you for the world so sweet," and she says it inside herself, a stand-alone zoom-up prayer.

She dislikes the rot-smell of the flowers when she cleans the vases and the feel of the slime that they leave behind, but she does like the feeling of getting it all done and putting the new week's flowers, the regular florist's delivery, into the vases. The Blessed Virgin's eyes are downcast, looking straight at Annie's work. Today Annie will stand flame-colored swords of gladiolus in the big cut-glass vase with the ferns, and the Mother of God will approve.

There is a four-way stop at Greve Street and Easterday Avenue. Annie stops at the sign, dismounts halfway, looks down the street, and gets up and takes off again. She is halfway across the intersection when a flash of light at the corner of her eye astounds her, and then she is hit, full force, from the right side, the impact throwing her up and out of the street onto the grass and against a tree. She sees nothing of who or what hit her, not even a suggestion of color: she experiences only a flash of terror and light, and then the unearthly soar through the air and the landing, so hard she is sure she is dead, although she is still conscious.

In the driver's seat of the bronze-colored Cadillac that speeds away, fifteen miles over the speed limit, Jinx Muehlenberg, thirty-five years old, divorced now six years and here for the reading of her uncle's will the day before, leans into the steering wheel muttering, "Jesus, shit, Jesus, oh, fuck, goddamn kid, Jesus, shit."

JINX HAS SPENT the night in the king-sized marital bed of an insurance man named Philip Carbo. When Jinx knew him in high school, he was "Crusher" Carbo, first-string quarterback for the Soo Blue Devils, and as far as the high school girls could see, the hottest thing going.

Philip Carbo now has his own insurance business on Portage Avenue, with two agents and two secretaries he calls "my girls." Carbo is married to a nurse at the hospital, who often works the same shift as Liz Maki but this week is out of town for her own uncle's funeral in Grayling.

"Hey, yeah," Carbo says on the phone at his office when Jinx calls the day before, "funny you should show up. The ball and chain is out of town for her *own* dead uncle." The way he says "ball and chain" tells her he loves his wife, even if he talks this way.

"Symmetry!" Jinx says, and she laughs a discordant laugh. Her second husband had turned to her, the day he left, and called her laugh Fingernails on the Blackboard.

"Beauty!" says Phil. "Get your buns over here, then." He pauses for a second, as if to consider whether to go further. The pause is almost infinitesimal. "Park your car in the church lot, eh? We'll have some fun." Jinx remembers aborting his baby in high school. He never knew.

The morning after, with the heavy silk drapes shut tight, she is walking naked around his bedroom, rubbing the fabric of his wife's dresses between her fingers, squirting his wife's perfume into the air and sniffing it.

"Hmmph," she says. "So you never had kids." There is a question implicit in this.

The man is lying back on his pillows rubbing his stomach, beefier and hairier than she remembers. "Yeah," he says. He sounds sad. "We went to the clinic. They said first that it was her, and then they decided that it was me." He seems suddenly defeated, saying it.

Jinx turns around and sees the expression. She cannot think why, except that it will give her a feeling of power, abstract and raw—she can almost see blood, a red veil coming over her eyes, the iron-rich smell of it, as a tiger dreams gazelle haunches, steak—but she says, "Hey, that's funny." She picks up a negligee of his wife's from the half-open top drawer of the dresser and puts it on.

"Funny. Why funny?" he says. He is still lying back on his pillows, moving his hand slowly in meditative circles in the springy hair that surrounds his navel. The seaweed and old-fruit smell of cooling rank sex hovers like a thick cloud in the air of the bedroom, just over his head.

"Because you got me pregnant in high school. I never did tell you." She lifts her chin to the side and looks at him curiously out of the corners of her eyes: How is this striking him? And isn't this just the most perfect moment to tell him?

His face has gone slack. His unshaven morning look strikes her as heavy and uncouth. She feels her mouth corners curling up into a smirk.

He sits up straight. His face is drained, ghostly and fat-looking to her, behind the morning beard.

"Don't worry," she says. "I got rid of it."

He starts—unbelievably—crying.

"Oh, shut the fuck," she says. "I took care of it, don't worry. It's not like there's a little Crusher Junior out there somewhere and I'm here to hold you up for support. Jesus. My father paid for it."

She tosses his wife's negligee across his hairy, salty nakedness and laughs at him as she leans into her little flame-colored lace bra. For a split-second she thinks: *That was thirteen years ago.* She refuses to admit the next thought: *I could have a kid almost a teenager.*

She picks up her matching panties from the floor. She looks over at Phil, whose big hands are spread wide over his whole morning-shadowed face. He is doing something funny with his shoulders: they're shaking. *Good Christ,* she thinks. *What an ass.* She opens the top drawer of the dresser. It is his wife's lingerie drawer: silky white and pale beige and pink panties and bras, neatly folded, fill the drawer. She drops her flame-colored bikini panties into the drawer carelessly and closes it. She puts on her slacks without underwear. "Hey, guy, I'm outta here," she says easily.

She shuts the door behind her. She thinks she hears him on the other side of the door, moaning. She is only half aware of the smile that spreads across her face as she walks to her car, two blocks away. She does not realize that she is gunning her motor loudly or that she almost hits a fat brindled cat scurrying out of her way as she pulls out. She does not see the stop sign she barrels through.

When she arrives at her parents', she unreels the garden hose and sprays the bumper, hard. A ragged piece of Annie's pink sweatpants fabric is hooked onto the bumper, and there is blood on the chrome and the fabric. Jinx is disconnected from all this: That was just a bad dream. Good. The grille is dented. Not much else. She surveys the near-imperceptible damage with a relief and delight. The shred of Annie's sweatpants washes away, in the runoff, into her mother's ripple-edged bed of petunias.

Not once does she think again of the little blond girl—yes, she saw her, at the very last minute, and the white gold of the blond hair was striking—lying back there in the grass. No one has seen the accident. Annie is stunned beyond calling out. It is only a half hour later, when a delivery truck comes by and sees the bike lying partway into the street, that anyone calls for an ambulance. Thus Annie is still lying at that horrible angle against that tree, stunned, while Jinx Muehlenberg is hosing off her Cadillac's bumper and grille.

At the church, Liz is saying to one of the older ladies, "I wonder what's happened to Annie. She's always so punctual, ever since she was tiny." She is worrying that it has something to do with Garrett, his perhaps refusing to let her come.

"Don't fret," says the older woman. "She'll show up any second now." It is over an hour before Annie is in the ER and able to give the attending physician her phone number. The nurse calls the number; nobody answers. Garrett is still asleep on the sofa and the phone rings while he sleeps.

It is a half hour more before Liz, in a panic, calls the hospital from the phone in the church sacristy. "Yep," says the intern, "we do have your little girl here. We'll need you to come down." Liz, in her fright and concern, still has energy to be offended at the chiding tone of that last comment: As if! My Annie! My treasure! She does not let on to the intern that his tone incenses her: what would be the point?

Jinx sidles into the kitchen of her parents' house. "Gotta get the nose back to the grindstone," she says casually. It is a joke wasted on her mother, but there is no grindstone. Jinx serves as a volunteer two afternoons a week at the art museum in Grosse Pointe, just to feel as if she is working. She lives very well on a small percentage of the income from her investments. Her broker is good.

"But, Jinx, darling, we were going to go shopping this afternoon! You said you weren't going to leave till tomorrow," her mother protests. Her mother's eyebrows are raised in distress. Jinx notes with a bit of a shudder the drawn-on look of them, their too-red look, their crookedness.

"Things change," says Jinx. "That's real life." She shrugs an easy shrug. Everything in her is tight as a drum, always. She has a look that is slightly arch, above the easy shrug. This is Jinx: toxic-waste theater, masquerading as casualness. Her ex-husband had said it, just after he filed for divorce, and she had laughed loudly. At that moment she had resolved to take him for everything he had, and she had done it. It seemed only reasonable.

The police report says simply that Annie did not see the car. There is really no evidence to go on. No one saw the accident but Jinx and a big muscular yellow Lab owned by a family in the middle of the block, a pale big-eyed dog standing and staring, then walking away to his freshly heaped-up blue plastic dog bowl of Gravy Train.

Jinx puts the whole matter out of her mind, clamping down the lid like a steel trapdoor. She leaves town, and she does not come back for another three years. When she does return, she avoids that intersection, though not consciously. When she returns, Annie is in high school, but not on the football field as a pom-pom girl. She walks with a walker now and can't even navigate the bleachers for football games, so she gets to sit right down in front.

This time, when Jinx returns, she calls Phil Carbo again. "So what's up, Crusher?" she says, lightly. "Want to get together?" There is a heavy silence on the other end of the line. "Hey, did we lose our connection?" says Jinx. Her tone is brittle. "Is the phone company falling down on the job?"

"Phone company's fine," Phil says. "Yeah, we sure as hell lost our connection, you goddamn bitch." He puts down the phone carefully so as not to break the receiver.

He does not tell Jinx that his wife left when she found the flame-colored panties and that he has spent the last three years celibate, penitent, trying to woo back his wife.

His wife does not share private business at work, but Liz Maki knows she has moved out of the house she had shared with Phil Carbo and that she seems even after all this time drained of her blood, pale, and wounded. The name of the woman with the panties has never been mentioned, and Phil Carbo's wife herself does not want to know.

Annie is in the hospital for months after the accident. There are cuts and abrasions, of course. Her shoulder is broken in the fall, there are serious subdural hematomas where her head hit the tree, with attendant headaches and blurred vision, but the legs are the real problem, both of them fractured in multiple places.

There will need to be surgeries, say the doctors, and the surgeries come, over a period of years. The long bones grow differently from others, say the doctors, nodding mysteriously, and this kind of surgery is complex. There has been a ring fracture of the pelvis. The surgeries will need to be done downstate, at the University of Michigan.

Annie will have to be driven there a number of times, by a nun from the grade school, who does this because no one else can. In the hospital, Annie will be alone. She will do a great deal of reading, and she will come to hate hospital smells with a passion.

Liz Maki remembers the doctor saying the words, and the words drifting away, through the closed window. "She likely won't be able to have children," the doctor says, dispassionately. "She's lucky to be alive." Liz Maki cannot register all of it, and within the week Liz herself will be dead.

ANNIE, DESPITE ALL the cautions, goes on to have Ursula, and she sits now at the mouth of the shaft down which Ursula has fallen, refusing to consider the possibility that Ursula is already dead. In her mind an image of a sparrow flits through, and she knows it is Bede's sparrow, Bede the so-called Venerable, the monk who wrote an early history of England.

Bede had written at one point that the brevity of life is like the passage of a sparrow through the uppermost point of a church, flying in out of the dark through one tiny window and out through the opposite window. Her mind refuses to go there: it shuts down when the terror that rises every few seconds in her transforms that sparrow to Ursula herself, a flying child, her blond braid trailing behind in the wind. No, Ursula has not gone out again into the darkness. Annie refuses even to think that.

Yet her mind, which of course is less under her control at this point in her life than it seems it has ever been, stumbles as in a dark forest, tripping on roots, remembering that doctor's words—that she will never have children—and wondering whether this is punishment for her defying that. *No,* she tells herself immediately. *This is not punishment . . . This is . . .* but she has no alternate explanation.

Suddenly, across the screen of her mind's eye is stretched a scene that sends her spirit into an agony: the memory of people jumping from the top of the World Trade Center not two years before, and the fade-out, and all of the aftermath. A voice inside says: *And you might as well hope Ursula is okay as you could have hoped one of those people would bounce and fly.*

Under her breath Annie responds to that voice, with only the trees and the wild creatures listening—within earshot that would be several rabbits, a number of birds, a few snakes, several butterflies hovering, and a cloud of pesky blackflies. She whispers something she never says, having been brought up by Liz to believe it a horrible thing to say. She says, "Shut up."

The silence in the forest resumes, and out on the road a motorcycle speeds by, its rider thinking of nothing but the pizza he will have when he gets to his girlfriend's house, a few miles ahead: double cheese with sausage.

6　The Minister of Maps

W AN LI, THAT irascible emperor nobody ever saw—he was given to mystery—born eighteen hundred years after Qin Shi Huang-ti, had given Wong Shao-Long the title of minister of maps. It was the first year of the seventeenth century C.E., the same year that, in England, William Shakespeare threw in his lot with six other men and bought the Globe Theatre. China, of course, knew nothing of England, of Shakespeare.

Of all China, only the emperor, Wong Shao-Long, and a few navigators and makers of maps knew that the world was enormous and that it was round, a globe after which one might name a theater thousands of miles away.

Shao-Long's new position had not existed until the Italian Jesuit priest, Matteo Ricci, had come into favor with the emperor twenty years before. Ricci had pleased the emperor by guessing correctly what might intrigue him in the way of gifts. After years of groping his way toward Peking, Ricci had wanted more than anything else the emperor's favor, which would give him respectability and would by extension ratify the intellectual worthiness of his doctrines. It was a step toward bringing the gospel to China.

And what did please the emperor, when it came down to it? The first offering of gifts Ricci sent up to the emperor, through the offices of the shrill, alternately domineering and obsequious palace eunuchs, included religious artifacts about which the emperor, it was hoped, might become curious. The bright representational painting style of the day that pleased Europeans often frightened the Chinese, who were used to sketchily brushed subtlety and muted hues—as if the subjects of the pictures would come alive and step out of their frames! In this bright Western style there were a little contemporary painting of Jesus and a newly done picture of Christ with his mother and his cousin John the Baptist as well as a more pastel, less perspective-bound, less lifelike antique oil painting of the Mother of God, in a silver frame.

The sedan-load of gifts borne by native manservants included further devotional items similarly intended to pique the curiosity of Wan Li about Christianity: a crucifix encrusted with varicolored precious stones as well as with relics of canonized saints—a lock of hair, a finger bone—encased in nuggets of bright stained glass; an ornate copy of the four gospels; and a gold-thread-bound breviary filled with the prayers that the priests, in their priestly ritual, were instructed to recite every three hours, day and night.

Not knowing what else might intrigue the emperor, about whom so little was known and about whom no gossip seemed able to circulate, Ricci included a unicorn's horn (taken, oddly enough, a decade before, from a rhinoceros on the African continent, and relayed through Portuguese traders in Macao). Such a unicorn's horn was said to be flawless protection against all disease for the emperor. Surely this would be welcome.

As European visitors to North America would do—the English would plant their little huts in the soil of Jamestown, in Virginia, in just seven years—Ricci offered the natives (in this case, the native emperor) trinkets as well: a variety of brightly colored European belts, a number of mirrors, a variety of glass bottles. He sent two lustrous prisms whose stark geometric shapes, hung in the sun, made rainbows that danced in the air, across the intricately carved wall panels, on the ceilings, across the faces of the courtiers who dangled them before the emperor, back of his screen.

Further, in the hope that the emperor might be drawn to the idea that association with the Jesuit foreigner would open doors to worlds unknown, Ricci sent a copy of the best atlas available to him, Ortelius' *Theatrum orbis terrarum*. Knowing that the Chinese considered themselves the only civilized nation on earth and believed there were no lands worth investigating outside of their borders, Ricci took the great risk that the emperor might be offended by this, fly into an imperial rage, and have the middle-aged Jesuit beheaded. While it was the dream of converting the Chinese to Christianity that energized him, if in the course of this he should be put to death, Ricci was ready. Martyrdom did not terrify him, but instead rose to his nostrils with a sweet oriental scent, as of the incense at High Mass.

He sent a clavichord no one in the emperor's court could conceivably play. He sent two different sand clocks. He sent a tall, imposing clock in a fine carved wooden cabinet, with weights and a pendulum. He sent a small delicate gold-plated clock the height of a vase for spring flowers, a clock no taller than the upraised ears of a palace-garden rabbit, a clock that could stand easily on a table, which struck the hours and worked by means of tiny spidery springs.

It was these last two gifts, carried ceremonially in the rosy gold light of dawn into the Forbidden City, past the five elephants that guarded the South Gate of the palace, which proved to be the bait that caught the emperor, like a fat palace goldfish, its diaphanous fins waving languidly, on Ricci's hook.

Ricci, back at his apartments that dawn, closed his breviary after the recitation of the Divine Hours, knowing that his gifts were in transport. He sighed. He imagined the elephants: he had seen them before, many times. They were washed and oiled and perfumed daily, but still they were redolent with giant-mammal musk. In his mind's overeager eye, he could just see the sedan with its bearers passing the huge beasts and entering the gate. He sighed again as he imagined them inside the walls.

Thanks be to the God who made heaven and earth, he prayed. Praise to the God who made men who made atlases, prisms, and clocks, with which he had baited the hook with which he would catch Wan Li, who fancied himself the Son of Heaven, and teach him about the true Son of God.

From that time on, the emperor needed the Jesuit. Because he could not pronounce the "r" sound, he transformed "Ricci" to "Li." Matteo was easier: it became "Ma-tou."

Can you come teach my foolish and stupid and clumsy servants to regulate these miraculous clocks, Li Ma-tou? Will you demonstrate this clavichord for my courtiers, so that they can in turn demonstrate it for me? Will you teach them to play it? Li Ma-tou, do you have more detailed maps of this world you say encircles the borders of my Kingdom at the Center of the Earth?

And so, as Li Ma-tou in response to the emperor's entreaties produced more maps, there grew the need for a Ministry of Maps, to administer the collection and decipherment of the documents, and to protect them from those who might use them to undermine the emperor.

In Europe there had been little information about this vast land of China and much speculation. It was said that China was filled with pygmies and one-eyed men, fabulous fighting storks and jewel-guarding gryphons; it was said that there were men in China who lived nourished only by the scent of the fragrant spices for which China was so renowned and for which Europe salivated; it was said that in China was to be found the tomb of Adam himself, on an island in a lake of tears wept by the first couple after their dreadful fall.

Mandeville had written two centuries earlier that beyond the mountains of India, it was said that diamonds grew like "hazel-nuts, and they are all square and pointed of their own kind, and they grow both together, male and female, and are nourished with the dew of heaven, and then engender commonly and bring forth small children that multiply and grow all the year."

On European maps, past the boundaries of the known territories, cartographers penned on the waves of the sea, "Here be dragons." China was not on their maps, but if it had been, mapmakers would have alleged that here be one-eyed men, here be men who comb silk out of trees, here be some men who live without heads but have eyes on their abdomens and others whose feet are so large they can lie on their backs on hot afternoons and shade themselves with their feet as umbrellas.

Those maps would not have been able to indicate, as was the truth, that here be broad boulevards, printing presses, paper money, coal for heating: the mundane truths of daily life in the imperial kingdom. But the knowledge of these amenities would have presented a philosophical difficulty: How could the Chinese have these things if they were indeed savages? And if they were not Christians, how could they be other than savages?

For their part, the Chinese called all Westerners "barbarians": their language sounded to the Chinese like a garble—*bar bar bar*—and clearly they believed Westerners had not advanced as the Chinese had, a belief that was in many respects true.

Wong Shao-Long was summoned, by a letter from the minister of the Office for Transmitting Memoranda, from his estate near the clear green-blue Lake of the Fragrant Pomegranate, to the palace. The estate had been given to him as part of his benefice when he was named third vice-deputy of the Ministry for Ministries, fifteen years before. He was a geographer by training, and in all this time his training—gotten on maps of a tightly constricted world beyond whose borders lay nothing at all—had lain useless.

Wong Shao-Long's heart beat in pitty-pat tremulous anticipation. His life had not gone well. Perhaps now. His first son had died at birth, and the geomancers said this was a sacrifice to the Immortals, on a much smaller scale, of course, but similar to the equinoctial border sacrifice required of the emperor to maintain the fertility of the kingdom. The geomancers asserted that this sacrifice would redound to Wong Shao-Long's eventual glory.

His second son had died before his first birthday. Shamans were consulted, and Buddhist bonzes, and no one had an answer. In the silence that followed the burial of the small boy, who had just learned to walk, and who was named Luminous Small Dragon (his father's name meant Exquisite Small Dragon), a daughter was born and died, and a second daughter lived only six days.

For five years Wong Shao-Long serves, childless and in personal shame but refusing to banish or replace his wife, as the minister of maps. In the reception room of his grand home is a clock much like the one that the Jesuit had given the emperor years before. There are not more than a dozen of these in all China. Shao-Long loves to hear the clock strike—it is so exotic, so very Western!—but each dying vibration reminds Shao-Long that life is short, that each hour passed is one more hour lost from his life. He is a minister, yes, but he has no heir.

And then, in the year that is labeled in the Western calendar 1638, over two dozen years after the death of the venerable Father Ricci, when no one is watching for this—because his wife, Crane, is by now well over thirty years old, with raven's-feet at her eye corners and silver threads invading the deep thick black gloss of her hair—his wife is once more with child.

A third daughter, born far too early and small, does not breathe right away and is left for dead, the placenta thrown over her face by the two midwives to smother evil spirits which might escape and fill the room. The midwives are busy tending to Wong Shao-Long's wife—his only wife, whom he has refused to replace or supplement despite her failures—and do not see the baby's hand—protruding only slightly from the pile of livery tissue—twitch, and then its tiny foot; nor do they then see the bloody placenta slip smoothly off the child, who struggles out from beneath its red burden.

Because they are soothing, and crooning over, the now enervated Crane, who is anguishedly bemoaning her failure yet once again to provide her husband with a son or even a living child, and wailing that surely her lord husband will not be merciful yet this one more time, the midwives do not hear the girl child's first small intake of breath, then its throaty miniature coo, then its first tiny cough. Until the amazing small child opens her mouth wide and sings out, "Yaaa-aiii!" in a tone far more like that of a cello than might be expected of a new infant, no one knows she is alive.

"Oh! Oh! Oh!" say Crane and the first midwife, in concert. The second midwife, who has been laboring too long over the mother without heeding her own nature's call, loses control of her bladder at the shock and stands bewildered in a puddle of her own urine.

"The child is haunted! Evil spirits have taken over the corpse!" says the first midwife, in a voice shrill with terror. "Smother her!"

"On the contrary, give the child to me!" orders Crane. She no longer sounds weak.

The second midwife stands paralyzed in her lake of urine, which is now spreading wider upon the tile floor. The first midwife yells, "Evil spirits, oh honorable mistress!"

"Evil spirits, indeed! Evil spirits do not give an infant breath! Give me the girl!" Crane instructs.

The first midwife lifts the bloody child and holds it out gingerly before her at arm's length, muttering a spell.

"Oh, oh, oh, my beautiful little one!" Crane sings. "See all her wonder-ful hair! Like thick feathers plastered down on a new chicken! See her bright eyes!" She nuzzles the baby's skin, which smells like egg and like blood and like flowers. She nuzzles the baby's damp hair, which begins to dry and to stand up like spikes, like soft porcupine quills, like milkweed.

The first midwife, standing at a distance, notes the limp, useless look of the infant's legs and turns away, frowning to herself in perturbation. She will not tell the mother, not now. Crane will not want to hear such ominous tidings. The father will surely choose to expose the girl to the elements and let her die, once he knows. It will not be the first midwife's responsibility, then. She looks over at her assistant midwife standing there in the fear-induced puddle and starts to laugh broadly, hysterically, great gasps of laughter. She grabs a quilt for the mother to wrap up the spiky-haired baby, who is sucking on Crane's index finger with great noisy eagerness.

The child is named Ming Tao, brilliant peach, the luminous fruit of im-mortality.

THE DAUGHTER IS fifteen now, and past the age where she would have been married off. Indeed, her legs are useless, as the first midwife had intuited to be the case. But the first midwife's contingent prediction has not come true: Wong Shao-Long, rather than ordering the child's destruction, dotes on her.

It is clear she will never walk, and so he has had carpenters construct a little cart for her, in which she may get about in the women's quarters. The characters for *luck* and *happiness* and *immortality* are painted on the three sides of the cart, and a pull handle attached to the front. The maids take her wherever she wishes to go, within the narrow confines of the women's wing.

Crane has died three years into the child's life, of a hidden heart ailment that is not known to the doctors in the way that doctors today think they know what has caused a death. Crane dies, in the minds of all those around her, of Death. Wong Shao-Long, despite the horrified responses of his fel-low ministers, lavishes all his attention and pride on the child. He takes two new wives and a half-dozen concubines, but they do not satisfy him.

Because Wong Shao-Long has risen in dignity and power over the years, he has been able to expand his estate. His fields are extensive, and from the hill on which his estate is so beautifully situated, his daughter, Ming Tao, lifted by an attendant, can see for miles. Her name means "brilliant or luminous peach," and her father adjudges that it was well-chosen.

Because she is a cripple, she will bring no bride price at all. She pushes this aside. She has her father's devotion. She talks with him morning and night about geography, about government intrigues, about agriculture and horticulture, about religion and music and nature. She needs no husband. The curse of her useless legs has given her a freedom she knows she would have no other way. She will never have to fear the wrath and the whim of a husband, as other girls she has known have had to do, growing from playful youth into a dreadful subserviency.

A friend two years her elder has hanged herself with a silk rope from the crenellated wall of her new husband's estate, having sent Ming Tao a letter the day before: *Your little cart's blessing is true. By contrast, I will die of this misery, marriage to this man.* The friend had been married for only four months.

WONG SHAO-LONG, who had been friends with Father Ricci, has continued his relationship with the Jesuits who follow him. They talk about maps: Father Ricci had put out three editions of a progressively more detailed map of the world, and Shao-Long had talked with him as he worked on the details of this, in the light from the best window, in midday until the light lessened, at four o'clock.

Shao-Long especially wants to know more about all of these new lands he has never seen before. The Americas are like a withered vegetable vine, off there to the west. China is right in the center. Ricci does not want to alienate his hosts, after all: their favor will pave the way for the gospel.

Wong Shao-Long and the Jesuits talk about history. The Portuguese Jesuit who follows Father Ricci asks Shao-Long about stories he has heard, that Christian missionaries have been here, a thousand years before, and that there are pockets of Christian believers all over China. Shao-Long shrugs and says he does not know. He has never heard anything of this. The Portuguese Jesuit says that he understands there are also Chinese in the direction of Turkestan who retain only vestiges of Christian practice—the

Adorers of the Cross, they are called—and would the minister of maps know anything of these people? No, Shao-Long says, he would not.

The Portuguese Jesuit says that he understands that there are also Jews, somewhere in China. Would this be true?

Shao-Long says, "It is a pity, indeed, that a stupid man like myself should be the minister of maps for the entire Middle Kingdom, but that is the case. I know nothing of any of these peoples. Can you forgive me?"

After the Portuguese Jesuit, who is in his thirties, departs for Macao, leaving a Portuguese colleague twenty or thirty years older behind in Peking, a French Jesuit replaces him, a young man reputed to be an intellectual prodigy. The Jesuit mission goes on, despite the inaccessibility of the emperor.

The following year, when Ming Tao is sixteen years old, Shao-Long asks for baptism for himself and his whole household. The Jesuits are overjoyed. The household numbers seventy-three: Shao-Long and Ming Tao, then the cooks, gardeners, builders, bearers, physician, tutors, soothsayers, weavers, basket makers, seamstresses, grooms, coopers, chandlers, and so on. Wong Shao-Long has decided that all will be Christians. This will add to the tally of the saved, and the Jesuits will write back to Rome about their new success.

On the late-summer evening Shao-Long determines that he will offer this entire house for baptism, he tells his daughter about it, in a great flush of joy. "It has taken me many years to make this decision," he says. He beams at her.

She scowls back. Her black hair lies pressed to her forehead, damp with perspiration. "You have taught me to think for myself," she says.

"Yes, and of course you are pleased," says Shao-Long.

"Of course?" Ming Tao scoffs. "Indeed not!"

Shao-Long is astounded. He has had many heated discussions with this girl. She has not been raised like a woman, though she has had none of the mobility of even a normal woman. Yet she is this independent!

"My daughter!" Shao-Long chides.

"You will not tell me, Father, that I am to be pleased," Ming Tao says.

She sounds like a dowager empress! Shao-Long at this moment questions his whole way of rearing this girl. But only for a second.

"I will decide this matter for myself," Ming Tao says.

Outside there is a rumble of low summer thunder, the promise of evening relief after the long bright day's heat.

Shao-Long says weakly, "But I have already told the priests from the West and they have written to Rome. Do you want them to find that they have lied?"

"Indeed not. That would be extreme dishonor." She does not say everything that she is thinking, namely, that the word "lie" is not the word he is seeking. "Simply replace me in their tally with someone else," she says. "Find someone from your friend the minister of foreign cargoes' estate to fill my place, until I should decide what I will do. Their pope will not care—or even know!—whether one of the seventy-three is from the neighboring estate. Furthermore, I have not said I will *not* agree to be baptized. But I will indeed *decide for myself,* Father."

A whistling sigh of resignation escapes the minister of maps. "As you wish," he says. He mops his forehead in the late-summer heat. He pauses and looks out the open doorway of the room into the courtyard. "And how will you make this decision?" he says.

"As we have long had our talks, Father, and I have learned from questioning you, I can question the priests also," Ming Tao says. "Then I can see whether they have any truth I should wish to embrace."

Shao-Long laughs as if his daughter has lost her mind. "You have never spoken to any man but your father," he says. "This is not possible." He frowns, because she is smiling broadly as he says this.

"I have spoken to your concubines' sons," Ming Tao says.

"Ahhhh, they are simply boys," Shao-Long counters.

"I have spoken to the vegetable gardener and to the keeper of the fish-pond," Ming Tao said, challenging.

"Indeed, my daughter, you have *not!*" he expostulates.

"Heaven and earth did not collide when I did this," Ming Tao says. "I was simply able to find out from the vegetable gardener that, yes, we were having squash blossoms for dinner, the first time, and the second time that he had a peculiar look on his face because he was considering whether to stake the peas high or low, and the third time . . . well, he told me a number of interesting stories about his own daughter, who is blind."

"Indeed, my daughter, you did *not!*" Shao-Long moans.

"It was you, my father, who taught me to be interested in everything. It was you, my father, who taught me to ask questions. You, Wong Shao-Long, taught me that my world is far wider than the distance my little cart can take me."

"Oh, daughter, the Immortals punish me for my indulging you!"

"From the keeper of the fishpond I learned how fish are bred and, as well, how humans may be conceived," Ming Tao says. Her eyes sparkle naughtily.

Her father looks apoplectic.

"Of course, I knew this information already," Ming Tao says. "From your second concubine, as well as from my friend Mountain Song, as well as from my auntie, your very fat sister—"

"Ming Tao!" says her father, and then he bursts into laughter. He laughs till he cannot laugh anymore, wiping the tears from his eyes. He is thinking of what a sweet little girl his older sister had been when they played together fifty years before and how bloated, like a dead animal floating downriver, she has become today. "But I must admit, even though I am her devoted brother, indeed, she is fat!"

Ming Tao laughs with him. The girl has a slight dimple when her face is animated. It is a pity, he thinks, that she is lame.

"My sister is as fat as a water buffalo!" says Shao-Long. He looks around him as if to assure himself that there are no gods in the room to dispense retribution.

"If she jumped into the fishpond, the fish would be thrown out, as far as the estate of the minister of foreign cargoes!" says Ming Tao, and they both laugh. "And the keeper of the fishpond would not be pleased. No, he would not."

"My daughter," Shao-Long says soberly, recomposing himself, "you know very well you should not have talked to these men."

"No stars fell." Ming Tao shakes her head haughtily. "No windstorms arose. I do not believe I have displeased the gods," Ming Tao says.

Shao-Long groans. Outside a long low growl of thunder threatens rain. Still no rain comes.

"I will talk to the priest," says Ming Tao. She makes that dimple again, though her will is like iron.

Shao-Long rises to leave the room. He smooths the skirt of his robe. He smooths the hairs that escape from near the end of his queue, which extends down his back to his waist. He wipes his perspiring brow.

Ming Tao addresses his back. "You want your whole household to be baptized, Father, am I correct? Therefore, as I said, I will talk to the priest."

Shao-Long repeats after his daughter, compliantly, defeated, willing to compromise, "Yes, you will talk to the priest. Through the grate, daughter. Not face to face."

"But, father!" she protests.

"Were I the minister of foreign cargoes—," Shao-Long begins.

"Yes, yes, I know," Ming Tao says, joking fiercely, straight-facedly. "You would have had me whipped with leather cords like a slave, and exposed on a mountainside," she says. "You would have had me sold to an African trader. You would have had me pickled and sliced and put into one large barrel and sold to the Tartars for a very small sum, to be eaten in Tartar meals out on the steppe. But you are not the minister of foreign cargoes, and moreover, he is a benevolent man himself, as you well know. You are my father, the minister of maps, and I am the daughter of whom you are proud, despite my withered limbs."

Shao-Long leaves the room, shaking his head. *What have I done?* he thinks impotently yet delightedly, as he has thought so many times before. I have raised more than a son. The Tartars themselves might go pale at this girl.

As he pads down the hall in his soft slippers to his own quarters, he giggles under his breath to himself. Behind his back, a servant girl makes a hand sign to another. The master has lost his mind, finally, she seems to indicate. This is a gesture that she has made many times before, but really she does not mean it. It is a sign of affection.

The servants seem to identify with the strong-willed Ming Tao, who has managed so many times to extract from her father rich or plenteous rations for the servants or special concessions: if a girl who is crippled can have this much power, the servant logic goes, then perhaps there is hope for us as well.

. . .

OUTSIDE, THE RAIN comes down, in thick silver sheets. Clouds of steam and splashes of rain bounce from the long-heated stones of the courtyard. Shao-Long, reaching his chamber, sits in an enormous dark chair with carved arms too high for him, the minister of maps looking somewhat like a child, staring out into the rainy night.

The elderly Portuguese Jesuit, Joao Maria Fereira, is summoned to persuade Ming Tao. The baptisms will be the following week. There is much rush and bustle to ready the ceremony, which will involve also a high mass.

"Well, then," says Fereira through the dark wooden screen, perforated with tiny quatrefoil holes, to Ming Tao. "What is it that you desire now to know?"

He cannot see her face, only hear her voice. Through the screen he smells a fragrance like peaches. His Chinese is decent, though his pronunciation is wooden, his buzzing Portuguese sibilants everywhere, his vowel tones so bent that Ming Tao must listen closely, sifting with her ears, to make sure which tone—hence which word—he intends.

"I have spoken at some length with my father about the ideas you teach," says Ming Tao. "Many of them are congruent with Chinese natural philosophy. Many of them, on the other hand, clash violently with the Chinese conception of man's nature. Yet more of these notions are simply outside of the natural and require some explanation." She pauses. "I would like to know about the doctrine of the incarnation," says Ming Tao. "I should like to know about original sin, and why it is called *felix culpa,* the 'happy fault.'" I have innumerable questions about transubstantiation, and purgatory, and the papacy. In any order you wish.

"I want to know about the stigmata of Francis of Assisi and the death, on an island just off our coast, of Francis Xavier the Jesuit. I understand he lay longing toward China and died of his longing. Perhaps you can explain to me why he was not allowed to have the fulfillment of his prayer, to come into China. Your god teaches—my father says this—'Ask, and you shall receive; seek, and you shall find; knock, and it shall be opened unto you.' If this is so, why then was Xavier's prayer not answered by your god? Surely it would have been to his glory?

"I want to know about Jews and why Christians hate them, if Jesus, your god, was a Jew. I want to understand where heaven is, and whether the Chinese Immortals are there along with your saints. I wish to understand the virgin birth." She stops her long rush and sits silent.

Fereira crosses himself and prays for the help of God. "It is, of course, not necessary that you understand all these matters before your baptism," he says. "It is necessary only that you give assent to surrender your spirit to grace, and later understanding will come. Many faith doctrines are mysteries."

Ming Tao has grasped, from the very first words of Fereira, that he is no match for her mind. "Do *you*, then, understand transubstantiation?" she challenges him.

"It is not ours to understand. It is ours only to give assent," says Fereira.

"Ah," says Ming Tao. "So you did not mean it when you said understanding would come once I gave assent."

Fereira sighs. He thinks of the young French Jesuit, René Josserand, pacing down in the courtyard, waiting for him, and wishes that he might be already outdoors and leaving with Josserand, walking together, nodding their heads about this young woman, heading toward the caravansary where their horses are tethered.

Or, then again, he thinks, as an alternative, Josserand might venture indoors, having perhaps picked up his distress tingling and crackling on the clear plasma of air floating out to the courtyard. Josserand could come to his aid. The young man's mind is quicker. He is full of fire. He would not react so lugubriously, so defeatedly.

"The baptism is in six days," says Fereira. "It would be far better to submit first and then to ask your questions."

"Or, perhaps," says Ming Tao, "to submit first and then to forget about asking my questions. Am I correct?"

On the other side of the screen, Fereira sits silent, his breath leaking out of him. Does the conversion of this household rest in the hands of this prickly young lady? Will her father postpone the baptism until she consents?

Fereira cannot see Ming Tao's quick dark eyes, the buffed-smooth almond-shaped fingernails of her hands, the intricate latticed ice blue and fern green of her silk brocade robe, and neither can he see her withered feet, bound in black cloth and hidden beneath the intentionally overly long hem of her garment. He has been told by her father that she is lame, and that is all.

Ming Tao will not ease his discomfort. Both sit in silence, a silence that is more painful to the priest than to the girl. On Ming Tao's side of the screen, a servant girl scuttles by. Ming Tao signals her something silly with her hands. The servant girl giggles. Fereira squirms, hearing this, feeling that someone is laughing at him, and his power is nil.

Then he says sullenly, "You are not seeking baptism."

"I am seeking answers," Ming Tao says.

Fereira says, "Perhaps I am not the one who ought to catechize you."

"Why is that?" asks Ming Tao.

"Dear young lady, I am slow," says the Jesuit. "I was fifth in my class, but I cannot keep up with you. Perhaps it is simply my age. I am sixty-six now."

"And will be sixty-seven," says Ming Tao, suppressing laughter.

"Yes," says Fereira, exhaling.

"Chinese revere great age," Ming Tao says.

Fereira cannot tell whether she is mocking him or attempting to be genuinely respectful. The effort of speaking to this girl is light years beyond him. "Great age cannot keep up with great youth," says Fereira. "I do not wish to delay the baptism through my ineptitude. Perhaps I should send a substitute who could respond to your questions with more energy."

"A substitute?" asks Ming Tao. Fereira can hear her perking up.

"I have an associate, a young priest from France, newly arrived, who has come with me. He is out in the courtyard. Perhaps he and I together could be of more use than this old man, alone."

"I do not believe that my father would sanction this," says Ming Tao.

Fereira has not thought of the obvious sexual danger the girl's father might perceive in the young man. After all, she is lame, and invisible as well as unreachable, back of her screen. Furthermore, Jesuit celibates, cerebral, militantly disciplined, and possessed of pride in their identity, are *genuinely* celibate, unlike unintelligent, dissolute orders of which Fereira has heard secondhand. There is no danger on this front at all.

"Nonetheless, I shall ask him," says Fereira. "I will go now, to arrange for your father's permission. Tomorrow I shall return."

"Good," says Ming Tao. She will wait for the sunset and watch the phoenixes of the clouds illuminated in shimmering pink light, and then perhaps she will believe in Resurrection, an idea of the Christians' that the Chinese tales of the phoenix make somehow seem credible.

THE FOLLOWING DAY Father Fereira comes again, with young Father Josserand. Behind her screen, Ming Tao cannot see either of them. But she has arranged to be brought to a window as the two priests approach, by a servant girl whose silence she has bought with a length of fine, thin brown-and-gold geometric-print fabric and a length of yellow to serve as trim. The girl is devoted enough that the fabric would not have been necessary, but Ming Tao loves to give these things and the girl loves to serve.

From the window, Ming Tao watches the arrival of the two priests, who habitually wear the garb of Chinese scholars as Father Ricci did. Fereira is thin and slightly bent. As he takes off the black veil he has worn riding across Peking on his horse—this protects him not only from dust but from having to stop and greet everyone that he meets—Ming Tao notes that Fereira's hook-nosed face is livelier than his voice. His curly gray eyebrows are continually raised as if in astonishment or as if awaiting attack.

Father Josserand is taller than Fereira and more solidly built. While all Westerners' faces are strange—such big bulbous eyes! such protuberant noses!—Josserand's face, when he removes his dark veil, seems in some way to please Ming Tao. He appears intelligent, kind. His shoulders look as if he could slip his hands under his big horse's belly and carry the animal across the courtyard, with no help.

His voice, when it says a simple hello through the quatrefoil perforations of Ming Tao's protective screen lined with white silk—so that none of her can be seen at all—is a pleasant voice. Ming Tao tells him this. Fereira looks over at Josserand, who does not know how to respond. Women do not speak this way. On the other hand, he has never spoken to a Chinese woman, except to a servant. Fereira shrugs. Josserand indicates in signs that Fereira is to speak for him now. "Father Josserand sings," says Fereira. "He was a boy soprano in the cathedral choir in Lisbon."

"Oh my," says Ming Tao. "He is a eunuch then? Eunuchs have a great deal of power here."

Josserand's voice, deeper than before, as if to be certain he proves his assertion, comes through the screen. "No," he says. Then he says it again, a few notes lower. "No, I sing tenor, and, no, I am not a castrato."

"Excellent," says Ming Tao. But the tone of her voice is so neutral and noncommittal that neither priest knows what to say. "Shall we then discuss the stigmata?" And so they do, for over an hour, ranging from the issue of hysterical manifestations to the question of the expiatory power of blood.

Father Josserand, who has studied the Old Testament with the scholars in Paris, says through the screen, "When Adam and Eve first knew themselves naked—first experienced shame—and the Lord God made garments for them, he made those garments of animal skins. Which of course would mean that he first killed these animals.

"Imagine these animal skins! Ripped from the dead bodies of—what, bears? some sort of larger fur-bearing creature to be found in Eden, and peaceful creatures, as even wolves and foxes and lions and bears then were, undeserving of death themselves? Imagine animal skins covered with blood on the inside, and the Lord God smearing blood over the naked and shamed bodies of our first parents!

"This would have been the first instance of death in the Bible, the deaths of these animals to cover Adam and Eve's disobedience. In a real way, then, as well as a symbolic or spiritual one, sin brought death to the world. But the blood of that death covered the shame of our first parents."

On the opposite side of the screen from Ming Tao, who has listened to this tale in silence, Father Fereira's mouth gapes open. "I have never heard that, René," he says, as if Ming Tao could not hear him.

"In Paris, I studied with Protestant scholars, Joao," says Josserand. "They do an earthier species of exegesis."

Father Fereira wants to ask how Josserand came to study with Protestants—heretics—and whether therefore anything they might teach could have credibility. Whether on this basis the pope might even revoke René's ordination, if he knew. But the story René has told seems rather beautiful in its own grisly way and even, deep down, true.

SINCE THE CONCEIVABLE revocation of René's ordination is clearly not possible or even useful—in fact, there is far more work now than the few fathers here can do—Fereira does not even ask.

"Well, then, shall we move on to the subject of sacraments?" says Ming Tao. "I should like to begin with baptism." She hears Fereira clearing his throat hopefully on the other side of the screen. "Father Fereira," she prompts him, "I did not say I should like to begin by *being baptized*. I should like to begin to *learn about baptism*."

Father Josserand leaps in front of the throat clearing of the elder priest. "This is appropriate," he says to Fereira, answering an objection he knows that the priest will make. "This is highly appropriate."

Fereira grumbles. "You do it, then René."

"Baptism," the younger priest begins, "is a drowning, a death, a surrendering, a going under, as well as a washing, a cleansing, a sign of renewal. When the catechumen is immersed in the baptismal flood, as the earth was immersed in the flood in the day of our ancestor, Noah, the sins of one's earlier life are eradicated."

"But I have been told that in baptism there is no real 'going under,' only a sprinkling," says Ming Tao.

Fereira clears his throat again. Ming Tao is beginning to develop a lexicon of throat clearings. As Father Fereira's previous throat clearing signified his hope that Ming Tao's mention of baptism was actually prelude to her asking for baptism, this next throat clearing is a signal to the younger priest that perhaps this is dangerous territory. Populated by Protestants.

Ming Tao can hear that. She goes on. "Young priest," she begins, "I understand you have not been here long enough to see our annual dragon-boat festival, with the grandeur of its dragon-boat races."

Fereira clears his throat again. This time it means: Do not allow her to divert you. Then Ming Tao hears a thud, of flesh-cushioned bone hitting flesh-cushioned bone. Clearly it is the heel of the younger father's hand, coming down hard on a knee. Is it his own knee, in exasperation, or the knee of the older priest, in rage? This she cannot tell.

René says, "No, I have indeed been in South China for three full years already, and I have seen these races. There, since I arrived from France, I have been studying Mandarin with a tutor, so that I could come to the capital."

"Excellent," says Ming Tao. "Then you understand the import of these rituals?"

"Yes," says René. "I am told that the dragon, in China, is believed to exercise control over rainfall from the heavens, and to have a particular affinity with rivers. Lakes. Streams."

Ming Tao can hear the older priest, two feet away on the other side of the screen, struggling in his throat as if he were in the grip of a stroke or a heart attack. Then she hears him whispering in French, which she does not understand, a stage whisper louder than his normal voice, "René, this is pagan *merde*. The girl is trying to drag you into the sewer."

René Josserand laughs a big laugh. He responds, in Chinese, without attempting to mute his voice, "Joao, no girl—and no dragon—can drag me down from the cross of Christ. This is mere metaphor. Symbolism. The girl does not believe that there is an actual dragon upstairs, with a bucket."

He turns in his chair and his voice comes direct at Ming Tao through the white silk cloth back of the intricate-perforated lacquered screen. "Dear lady, you do not literally mean you believe in a dragon in the sky. Do you?"

Ming Tao, on the other side of the screen, laughs. "If, as my father has instructed me, you literally believe in a three-personed god in heaven, and if you believe that the two persons besides the Father are animals—the Lamb of God and a spirit who appears as a white dove coming out of the clouds—why then can there not be a dragon as well?"

René Josserand slaps his knee in great jollity. "Indeed! A veritable barnyard in the sky! A divine zoo for the delectation of the angels!"

Ming Tao laughs. "Perhaps you can teach me about the Gray Goose of God, and the Octopus of God, and the Salamander of God, and so on."

Josserand roars in hilarity.

Fereira reaches desperately, fumblingly into his bag and pulls out a small, glass-stoppered bottle of blessed holy water. He sprinkles it out with a flick of his fingers, at himself, at Josserand, at Ming Tao—which is to say, at the screen. Ming Tao sees the white silk darken with the water and is slightly mystified. "This is sacrilege," hisses Fereira at René. "This is abominable filthy talk!"

"We are all being baptized," René says to Ming Tao. He laughs loudly again. A manservant leans in through the door behind the two priests, wondering.

Ming Tao says, "Last year at the dragon-boat races in June, my father tells me that one of the rowers fell overboard and drowned. This was considered a good omen, because a sacrifice to the dragon-god is held to be promise of rain and prosperity for the year. This, indeed, proved to be the case." Ming Tao twists a handkerchief in her hand as she speaks—it is a gesture not so much of anxiety as of excess energy—and then stuffs it up against her mouth so that she will not laugh out loud. Her maidservant, a square, muscular woman who is moving silently about the room behind her, dusting the furniture, looks curiously over at Ming Tao and smiles. She misses the intent of the wit, but she can tell that her mistress is twitting the priests. "Would you say that the sacrifice of the rower is not unlike the sacrifice of Jesus Christ so that the earth can be saved?" Ming Tao asks. Again, she presses the handkerchief to her mouth to suppress a giggle.

"The death of the rower is an accident! An act of stupidity! Clumsiness! Falling over the prow of the boat because he did not know how to handle his oar and then being eaten by river rats and devilfish!" says Father Fereira. "The death of Jesus Christ was an intentional act, indeed the most intentional act of all history."

Josserand leans over to the older priest and whispers in such a tone that Ming Tao can hardly hear him, "Joao, few Chinese can swim. Surely in your missionary training—surely in your experience—you were taught, you discovered, that it is not politic to insult those you wish to proselytize. The Franciscans may do that, but surely not the Jesuits!"

Ming Tao goes on, imperturbable. "Would you say that the sacrifice of the rower was a sort of baptism, that immersion in the waters of the river, a death, a surrendering, a going under, as well as a drowning, so that even though he was doubtless an infidel like myself, he might have indeed gone to heaven?" she says.

René Josserand is amazed at the way the girl is able to repeat, verbatim, his earlier characterization of baptism. "Only God Himself knows," says René.

"Old priest," says Ming Tao, addressing Fereira. "I find the young priest's way of answering my prickly question to be very inspiring. Very humble. Is this your answer too?"

Fereira, ready to leap in to correct Josserand, to insist that, no, there is no comparison with baptism, and that the Great God of Heaven certainly—and with a slavering gusto—condemns to the bright flames of sulfurous fire all those who will not accept His baptism, is silenced. His breath escapes him, a slow leaking admission of defeat. "Yes," says Fereira, "this also is my answer."

"Well, then," Ming Tao says. "That is excellent." The tone of her voice says clearly that the tables have been turned, that the older teacher has, fully against his will, become the taught. "We are finished for today."

Fereira says, "But . . . but . . . but . . . the baptismal ceremony is next week!"

There is no response from Ming Tao. Behind the screen, they hear a scraping—this is the maidservant lifting her mistress from her chaise, the chair's legs scraping against the tile floor—and then the feet of the maidservant shuffling away heavily, as she carries her young mistress, draped across her strong arms, useless legs with their useless huge unbound feet in their black wrappings, off to another chamber.

Fereira and Josserand rise to go. Fereira shakes his head, mumbling.

Josserand helps him out of the room. "This is an . . . unusual situation," he says. "Catechizing a woman . . . who is . . . so sequestered."

"The sequestration is not what is unusual," says Fereira. "In normal circumstances, we would not be allowed—or required!—to speak with the woman at all. Normally, the head of the household would instruct the women of the household, and offer them all for baptism. We the clergy would see them only at the baptism, and thereafter they would hold prayer services of their own in the women's quarters."

"Without the Eucharist!" Josserand says.

"Indeed," says Fereira.

"This is scandalous!" Josserand says. "To draw them to the faith and to refuse them nourishment! How can we do this!"

Fereira is rather dumbstruck. "Ehh, errh," he says.

"And you would have the father of the family, the head of the household, who has only just begun to learn these truths himself, teach the rest of the household? Why, I cannot begin to imagine what perversions of doctrine must then ensue!" Josserand says.

They are into the front hall now, and the servants are shuffling about them, gathering their cloaks and hats and pressing on them packets of sweetmeats that Wong Shao-Long has had made up, tied in elegant bundles and stacked in heavy silk bags.

"You have never seen this young woman?" says Josserand.

Fereira startles slightly at the tone of this question. It is inappropriate. What could it matter? And why does the upstart young priest even ask? "Of course I have not seen her," says Fereira. He bristles.

"*C'est dommage*," says Father Josserand. "If one were to judge from her voice, she must be quite beautiful."

The following day, as the two priests are returning, Fereira turns to Josserand as they ride through the crowded streets. He shouts something at the younger man over the noise of the hooves and the carts and the vendors. Josserand indicates by signs that he cannot hear at all. Fereira shouts again, and again Josserand makes hand motions with his right hand, handling his horse's reins with his left, to say, I cannot hear you. A third time Fereira tries, and suddenly, as he is halfway through what he wishes to say, all the noise in the street seems to stop simultaneously, and he is shouting into the silence, ". . . our *last chance!*"

Josserand laughs at the volume and urgency of his voice in the quiet. Laughter is not the response that Fereira wants. He scowls, but of course Josserand cannot see his expression, through the thick veil. "We will do what we can," Josserand says. "The conversion of souls is the work of the Lord, and He calls whom He calls. I recall that our Lord said to His dear apostles, 'You have not chosen me, but I have chosen you.' Therefore we must relax."

"*Relax!*" shouts Fereira across the distance between them. "The ceremony is set! It is five days away!"

"Should the Lord not decide to choose Ming Tao today, then indeed we must bend to his will. I will, in that event, choose a suitable person from the neighboring estate, as Ming Tao herself most sensibly suggested to her father, to make up the tally." Josserand looks straight ahead, but beneath his veil he is laughing at what he terms Fereira's exteriority: a concern with numbers, with appearances, matters René often finds laughable.

As things happen, Ming Tao wants to know why the Lord God, knowing Adam and Eve would sin, made them anyway.

"Free will is the glory of God's creation," says Father Fereira.

"And yet you do not wish me to exercise *my* free will," she says.

Father Fereira grits his teeth and is glad that this is the last time he will have to do this. He recalls René's reminder: the work of conversion is God's own, and he ought not to feel a failure.

"Do you genuinely believe that, Fathers? Both of you? That free will is the glory of God's creation?" Ming Tao says through the screen. Father Josserand is thinking that he smells a scent like the heart of a peach, a rich oil or essence pressed from the peach nut, wafting through the screen. Father Fereira smells nothing.

"Yes, I do believe that," says Josserand. "And it is, as you rightly point out, a terrifying doctrine."

Father Fereira clears his throat. Ming Tao can hear that this particular clearing of the throat means I do not care to answer that question, young lady, and moreover I find you quite irritating.

"Do you know the tale of Nu Gua?" asks Ming Tao. "It is one of the Chinese tales of the creation."

"Tell us," prompts Father Josserand, coaxing.

Ming Tao hears the frustrated whispering chiding of Father Fereira: "Do not waste our time listening to pagan palaver!"

Then she hears the response of the younger priest: "Is it not clear to you yet that the girl does not wish to be baptized? Continuing to harass the young lady is in fact a waste of time. 'Unless the Lord build the house, the laborers labor in vain.'"

"What silly saying do you quote me this time?" snaps Fereira.

"Yet another silly saying from the Bible," Josserand answers mildly.

"Accch, Protestants," says Fereira. "They ruined you, René." He is apparently forgetting about free will. Then he remembers. "And you let them." It is at the moment in the conversation at which René quotes Psalm 127—"unless the Lord build the house"—that Fereira determines that he will write home to Rome, he will see to it that Josserand is recalled. *We cannot have Catholic priests quoting the Bible the way this young upstart does,* he thinks. *As if that were the basis of what we're about.*

Ming Tao continues as if she has not heard all the whispering. "Nu Gua was a goddess who was half human and half something else. Some say snake. Some say dragon. At any rate, she did not have legs."

"Ahh," says Josserand, audibly.

"She was alone, in the newly created world, and she was lonely. She wanted company," says Ming Tao. "She wandered about creation in a limited way, hampered by her lack of legs, enjoying the beauty of this world but feeling the loneliness. She sat down by a river and scooped up some sand and clay from the riverbed. She sculpted the clay into a little figure much like herself, except that she gave it legs so it could move about easily."

"Ahh," says Josserand again, but unintentionally.

The older priest opens his mouth to speak, and Josserand can see without doubt what he is about to say: "In Christianity we do not believe in goddesses. There is one God, and He made all things." So Josserand puts his finger up to his lips to silence the older priest. Fereira starts to say something anyway. Josserand picks up Fereira's walking stick and knocks him on the knee, pretending that this is an accident. "Aieee!" howls Fereira.

"Nu Gua came to understand that, in the cycle of life, she would need to provide these creatures with a means of perpetuating themselves. And so she made them male and female," Ming Tao says.

"Just as the Lord God did," says Fereira.

"Ah, Father," says Josserand, with his tongue poking into his cheek. "Is that in the Catholic Bible or the Protestant Bible?"

Fereira scowls in rage at the younger priest. Ming Tao can feel the look through the screen, as well as the younger priest's delight.

Ming Tao goes on. "There is another tale about Nu Gua. It is said that there were only two people on earth, Nu Gua and her brother Fu Xi. They wanted to marry, but they did not feel that incest would be proper."

"Indeed!" says Fereira. He leans over to Josserand. "Do we need to hear any more of this?" he asks. "This is vile to be forced to listen to."

Josserand dismisses his objection. He speaks to Ming Tao rather than to Fereira. "In some sense, yes, I suppose that if the first two people on earth came forth from the same father, then, yes, we might term them brother and sister. Thus Adam and Eve, in the Christian creation story, might also be termed brother and sister."

"Father Josserand!" Fereira fumes and hisses, unable to contain himself.

Josserand wipes from his own forehead and cheeks the spewn spittle of Father Fereira. Unseen by Ming Tao, he bows to the older priest rather comically, graciously, in his seat as if to say, Thank you for the shower.

Ming Tao says, "But these two wanted to produce children and they could think of no other way. So they went to the very heights of Mount Kunlun, in the west of the Middle Kingdom. In the cool air of the heights there they each built a fire out of logs and brush, and they watched the fires burn." She pauses, imagining those fires burning.

On the other side of the screen, Josserand too imagines the scene. Fereira is cradling his head in his hands, nodding twitchily.

"It came to pass then," Ming Tao says, "that the smoke from the two fires began to join together, twining like a braid. It was from this that Nu Gua and Fu Xi came to understand that the gods blessed their plan to populate the earth this way, a way that someone else might have called incest."

Father Fereira says, "The human heart is desperately wicked."

Josserand twits him. "That is from the *Bible*, Joao. Jeremiah the prophet."

"Hold your mocking tongue, René," says Fereira, under his breath. "The human heart in its unredeemed state justifies anything that it decides to do." He makes a sound of disgust.

He speaks with the air of an outsider, as if he himself did not have a human heart, thinks René.

Ming Tao says, "But is Father Josserand not correct in saying that Adam and Eve were as much brother and sister as Nu Gua and Fu Xi? Were not Adam and Eve then incestuous also?"

Father Fereira leans forward into his lap and makes a sound in his throat that Josserand cannot decipher. It is not, in any case, a positive sound. He sounds to Josserand like a cat coughing a hair ball.

Josserand tries not to laugh. He says to Ming Tao, "You are blessed with a first-rate intelligence. I will not ask you yet again whether you would like to be baptized with your father's household, as I can see that you would not. I do trust that the Lord, if he wants this for you, will so move you. As for myself, I will provide the substitute. Tomorrow I will ride to the estate of the minister of foreign cargoes and choose that substitute, someone to replace you in the tally."

The following day Josserand goes alone to the neighboring estate of the minister of foreign cargoes. Fereira stays behind at the Jesuits' residence with the shades drawn, drinking tiny Chinese cup after tiny Chinese cup of a hot herbal potion the priests' old cook recommends for intractable aches of the head and the neck.

At the residence of Liu Wei Hua, minister of foreign cargoes, René Josserand rests, waiting, in an ornate and comfortable armchair. He gazes out over the lily-thick pond, where dragonflies buzz and frogs burp, through the dark lacquered lattice. His eyes follow the shapes of the latticework, up, over, down, over, till he is dozy. When Liu comes in, he is startled slightly at the sound of Liu's footsteps. He struggles out of his somnolence, trying to ground himself. *Ah, yes. I remember now where I am, and why I am here.*

Liu listens to Josserand's plea—may I have just one person? please? for the baptism?—but does not answer. He sits in silence for a moment, gazing out at the dragonflies' filmy cloud of fat gnats hovering over the pond lilies. Then he turns to Josserand.

"We do not have enough commerce with France," Liu says.

Josserand, surprised, waits to hear more. Prior to Ricci's time here, the Chinese have not wanted much contact, much less extensive commerce, with Europe's barbarians.

"This is your birthplace—France—is it not?" says Liu.

"It is," says Josserand.

"How long has it been since you have been in your own land?" Liu asks.

"Seven years," Josserand says. "Three years in Macao before I came to Peking, three years in Ceylon, one year on the ocean in transit."

"How long will it be until you return?" Liu asks.

"Oh, I have committed my life to stay here," says Josserand. "The emperor, as you know, does not take kindly to persons who are merely visitors. We must promise to spend our entire lives in China or we may not enter at all. I will die here," he says earnestly.

Liu looks peacefully out through the lattice. A dragonfly swoops, and another behind him, in green opalescent stitches through the air. Josserand watches the same dragonfly.

He does not know that the older priest has sent word home to Rome that Josserand will be returning on the next carrack. *Entirely too independent of mind,* Fereira has written. *A dangerous young man.*

But he has a heart for China! A heart for the Church! says the Italian priest at the Peking mission. A heart for the Gospels!

Joao Fereira has ignored the Italian. He cannot forget the young priest asking what Ming Tao looks like. He cannot forget the young priest saying "Adam and Eve" and "incest" in the very same sentence. And he will not forgive what he believes, in his selective memory, to be wholly Josserand's fault, for his having given up so easily: that Ming Tao will not be a part of this baptismal ceremony. Josserand will be sent back to Rome, and that is that. A ship will be leaving within the month, and Josserand will be told—not face to face, but in a formal letter, in Latin on parchment, delivered from Fereira's room to Josserand's by a manservant—next week, after the baptism, that he will be on that ship.

"Is France very beautiful?" asks Liu. "I have heard from a previous priest that this is the case."

"Yes, very beautiful," says Josserand. It is a subject to which he warms to with ease. He paints word pictures of the French sun filtering through the leaves of vineyards in the south, of the same sun filtering in through the tall windows of the donjons of châteaux, of the light of dawn washing down into narrow Parisian streets.

"You must long for your home," says Liu. "You must miss very much all this beauty."

Josserand is surprised. He has genuinely forsaken his earthly ties, a forsaking that his priestly training had urged on him gradually, prying his soul's fingers off his possessions, his self-will, his prospects of progeny. "Indeed, no," says Josserand. "Heaven is my home. I do long for heaven. France, I can carry about in my memory: all of these pictures I shared with you."

The two sit staring out at the lilies and dragonflies.

"Will you tell me about the great temples of France?" says Liu. "From the previous priest I heard stories that there are mysterious windows of glass in these temples, as high as the heavens themselves, windows of many colors that tell ancient stories. Have you seen this story-glass also?"

"Ah, the cathedrals!" says Josserand, lapsing unconsciously into French. He knows no equivalent word in Chinese. Liu attempts the word and cannot handle it. Both men laugh. "Indeed. Sainte-Chapelle, in Paris, is one of my favorite places to pray, of anywhere I have been. This is three or four hundred years old—"

"Very new!" interrupts Liu.

Josserand pauses. "An interesting viewpoint," he says, "that three or four centuries is a brief period. I suppose this is the Chinese perception, and it is instructive." He pauses again. "Perhaps the Chinese are closer to God than we rough Europeans. I think that would be God's perspective as well."

"God's perspective!" Liu echoes, in wonder. "How can you know what your god thinks, indeed?"

"The psalmist says, 'For a thousand years in your sight are as a day that has just passed, or like a watch in the night. You sweep men away in the sleep of death; they are like the new grass of the morning: though in the morning it springs up fresh, by evening its is dry and withered.' This is in the Bible, our holy book, which speaks the thoughts of God," says Josserand.

"Indeed, this is very Chinese," says Liu. "And this book must indeed be a wise book, for surely these must be the thoughts of God."

Josserand's heart beats a tiny bit faster. He loves these moments of bridging the cultural chasm. He cannot understand Fereira's fears of the Bible: indeed, daily, at all the liturgical hours, the Jesuits themselves are required to recite it! And yet Fereira—and most of the others—fear venturing out into what they seem to see as its wilds, without the rod and the staff of the Vatican at their necks, curbing them like stinky wandering sheep. Liu sees the beauty and truth of it so clearly, so easily. *Praise God!* thinks Josserand.

"Tell me about those great windows," says Liu.

"Oh, at Sainte-Chapelle it is not the pictures themselves but the great sweep of the glass and the play of the light through the variegated expanse of it that lifts the heart," Josserand says. "This was a royal chapel, for Louis IX. There are processions of bishops—"

"In your tradition, do men become hardened and stupid when they rise to power, as happens so often in China?" asks Liu. His candidness is refreshing to Josserand.

"Precisely," says Josserand. "All the bishops in this glass procession have the same arrogant gaze, the same wretched nose. One assumes that a single man was the model for them all and that that man must have been the presiding bishop, immortalized as all the bishops. I have tried not to look at those windows. They are not conducive to prayer."

Liu shakes his head in agreement. "Always in life one must ignore some things in order to focus on what is more worthy. And is there another window that is more worthy than this window of many identical bishops at Sainte-Chapelle?"

"There is a beautiful window called the Apocalypse window," says Josserand. "In this window, Christ appears with a two-edged sword—which stands for the Word of God—between his teeth."

"Ahhh," says Liu, visualizing this picture.

"There are many symbols worked into the window as well, from the Book of the Apocalypse. Seven of this and seven of that. Seven-branched candlesticks."

"Numbers are very Chinese as well," says Liu, obliquely, and Josserand nods in agreement. Indeed, how could he not agree? he thinks.

"At the cathedral at Chartres, which is much grander, indeed—my weak words cannot describe the scale of this cathedral!—there is one window that I love very much. It is called the Jesse window." Josserand's hands describe the shape of the great church and Liu's eyes follow. "Jesse was the ancestor of Jesus, who is the Son of God."

"Ancestors are very important in China," says Liu. "We would understand this Jesse window. Tell me about these ancestors."

And so Josserand does, for over an hour. Liu wants to hear all known details of the lives of the forebears of Christ, and Josserand obliges. The sun starts to sink, and Josserand says, "But I neglect the one reason I came here." He explains that his superiors would like one more person to take part in the baptism the following week. He shrugs, in some embarrassment. He says, "The daughter of the minister of maps does not wish to participate—now—and I think that is reasonable. But Father Fereira insists that we must provide the full complement, baptize the exact number of souls he has sent in his report to Rome. I wonder whether there is anyone in your household who might wish to substitute for the daughter of the minister of maps."

"This is a difficult matter," says Liu. He twists his forehead into a knot. "Is it necessary that this person should understand these matters? How could one come to understand these matters so very quickly?"

"I agree," says Josserand. "Father Fereira, however, believes that the numbers take precedence, and I am in obedience to him."

Liu laughs. "Perhaps I have an answer that will suit us all," he says. "I have a servant who is rather . . . silly. His mind is not everything that it should be. Still, he does his work. He will be glad to submit to your ceremony, I am sure. He agrees to anything I ask him. Will this do? If so, in exchange for this favor I do for you, will you come here and teach me more about all of these ancestors in your sacred book? I should like to hear fuller stories, for instance, of the shepherd boy who became a king."

"David," prompts Josserand.

"And of the prostitute who harbored spies," says Liu.

"Rahab," says Josserand. "Perhaps she was only an innkeeper."

"And the others. I do not remember them all. You went quickly," says Liu.

"I did," Josserand agrees.

Josserand sits dumbfounded. Can it be this easy? "Let me understand you clearly. If you do me the favor of providing a servant to submit to baptism, you will then—in exchange!—do me the further favor of allowing me to teach you about our Lord?" He sits with his head cocked, his thoroughly pleased smile screwed slightly, as if he had eaten a sour fruit, his hazel eyes looking intently into the near-black eyes of Liu.

Liu nods soberly. "Is this acceptable?"

"This is most acceptable," says Josserand.

"The servant of whom I speak has a nickname. The others all call him simply Bald Silly, and he does not take offense. He is an assistant collector of night soil from all the latrines on my rather extensive estate." Liu sweeps his hand slowly through the air, indicating the majestic sweep of the property. "This little man delivers the waste to the gardeners, who in turn produce squashes and lettuces, peas and melons, for our table. He is most imperturbable. I have, making my monthly rounds of the estate in my sedan chair, seen him standing staring at the sky, at a bird flying over or something else, leaning on his shovel, with flies on his hands and his lips and his eyelashes. He does not flinch; nor does he seem even to blink."

"After baptism, he will be expected to come to Mass," Josserand says. "Will he do this?"

"This can be arranged easily," says Liu. He contemplates for a moment. "Actually, I should simply make arrangements to give the man to my neighbor, the minister of maps, so that he will be part of that household. He has no family here. Surely the minister of maps can use another night-soil collector."

Josserand is at this moment seeing Liu as the key to more souls, visualizing Liu leading his entire household up a gentle incline of clouds toward the rich gleaming wood-and-bronze gates of heaven (which in his mind's image he unconsciously models on an amalgam of the gates of the Forbidden City and the doors of Chartres Cathedral). "God bless you, indeed, oh Minister of Foreign Cargoes," says Josserand.

THE FOLLOWING MORNING, Bald Silly is summoned before the minister of foreign cargoes. He is a rather brown-skinned man, short and wiry. He has been scrubbed clean by another servant. He is not wholly bald: wisps of colorless hair, leached by premature old age, scraggle from his scalp here and there. He smiles, he scrapes, he bows. He agrees with anything and everything he is told. He bows again.

He is amazed when the minister of foreign cargoes offers him a plate of melon. He gobbles the melon and puts the plate into the waistband of his pants, where he secures it as best he can and then stands very still so as not to lose it down a pant leg.

"Do you understand?" asks the minister of foreign cargoes. Then he checks himself. "Of course you do not! But then, it is not necessary. This afternoon you will go, in a cart, to the estate of the minister of maps."

"In a cart?" says Bald Silly, amazed.

"I am having a number of items delivered to the minister of maps. You will be included in the load," says the minister of foreign cargoes.

"In a cart!" repeats the man, as if he were, in a silver flash, being translated to the moon in the wheelbarrow he uses to move human feces.

THE LETTER THAT Father Fereira has sent to his superiors in Rome, informing them that Father Josserand will be arriving as well, is en route back to Europe. The letter will take a circuitous route, and it will not beat René Josserand back to Rome.

Josserand is detained with a fever on the island of Hainan when his ship is blown off course. He is precariously ill for months, and when he recovers it is the wrong time to sail, because it is now the monsoon season. In his isolation Josserand has time to consider his dire situation. He has moments when he thinks he may find a way—how? how?—to reenter Peking, to persuade Fereira, and then moments when he thinks that his life is over, that being sent home is so shaming that he would prefer to have died with his fever.

Yet he does not die. The following season, he is able to take passage on a ship, thinner, paler, and with just a bit less hair. When he arrives in Rome, he is ready for whatever chastisement is waiting, hoping simply to be sent right out again, to be useful in the missions, anywhere, wherever God should decide. He knows that there is little likelihood of this.

But on his arrival, matters are muddled: it seems that Fereira has died in the interim, his death the result of an aneurysm, though because it is the seventeenth century, just like everyone else, he dies of Death.

If Josserand but knew: Fereira in his dying moments has tried to blame the mortal bursting of a blood vessel in his brain on the younger priest, but when he has pulled at the sleeve of a fellow Jesuit, attending him on his deathbed, to tell him, "This is Josserand's doing," his voice has failed him, coming out as a thin, useless squawk.

As Fereira dies, a look more of frustration than anything else comes into his eyes, and the attending priest, a Castilian friend of René Josserand's, looks up at the agonized figure of Christ on the crucifix twisting his head to the skies as if to say, *Eloi, eloi, lama sabachthani?*

The Castilian is thinking of all of the stories of wondrous deathbed utterances of canonized saints and remembering that the last thing he heard Fereira say, several hours before, after a dinner of duck wrapped in soft pastry, was, "I have such damnable gas. I will need to move my bowels tomorrow. I haven't since Thursday."

When asked whether Fereira had said something at the last that should be written down for the order, in case there should later be a move to canonize the Portuguese priest, the Castilian suppresses a smile and says, "Nothing. Blessed silence."

He will confess this peccadillo at his weekly confession on Saturday. Best not to make a fuss, really. Look at what kicking against the goads brought dear René.

Even the Castilian, René's closest friend in Peking, is not aware of the last events of René's tenure here. No one is aware, except for Ming Tao and Bald Silly. At the high mass for the baptism, René has assisted. This will be the only time that the women of the household will see a priest in person, at the baptism. Ming Tao has attended the mass out of sheer curiosity. She plans to ask thousands of questions of the two priests the next time they meet.

She brings a secretary to the mass, and the secretary sits beside her, making quick notes when Ming Tao leans over to prompt her concerning matters about which she wants to remember to ask. In what sense is the Eucharist Jesus' body and blood? Is this not, then, cannibalism? Does the participation of three priests in this ceremony, when only one is required, make the magic more powerful? Where does the incense come from, and is this sort of thing not derived from ancient pagan Chinese rites, and is that not a scandal to Father Fereira?

Father Josserand cannot help but see her, though he is not introduced. Her face is clear and her eyes very quick: he notes this. From a distance he cannot see much else, except that she is bound into a specially made chair that will be carried out by two attendants. Once he thinks he catches her eye and that she seems to be signaling something to him. But he cannot be sure.

After the baptism, Fereira, having caught in the corner of his eye Ming Tao's attempt to communicate something—hello?—to the young priest, decides that he must put a stop to this. While Ming Tao wishes to continue her sessions of instruction, Fereira refuses to let Josserand participate in those sessions. But Fereira has forgotten that he himself cannot answer Ming Tao's questions. So there can be no more sessions at all.

There are several days of silence.

Ming Tao hears, through the servants, that Josserand is going home, back to France, in some sort of disgrace. The following morning, after she has slept, she takes up her brush and writes a note herself—her secretary does not need to be involved in this. She then has the note carried by Bald Silly to the Jesuits' residence.

"This is from my father to the French priest," she says. "Give this money in the pouch to the servant you deal with, and say he is not to involve old Fereira." She gives an additional sum to Bald Silly, who will use it to buy a small idol, though he is a Christian now, by fiat of the minister of maps. Do I wait for an answer? asks Bald Silly. She indicates no, that the job is then complete.

There is another full week of silence, and then Bald Silly is summoned back to the Jesuits' residence. He returns with a packet for Ming Tao, sent by Father Josserand. The gatekeeper shrugs and lets the small, silly man in. He wonders why such an idiot is sent on errands that must be important.

FATHER JOSSERAND NEVER comes back to the estate of the minister of maps. He is in the greatest pain and conflict of his life to date: to this point he has been a success, his parents' pride, a lion of learning at the seminary. What right has that ignorant tyrant Fereira to send him home? The thought of the windows of Chartres Cathedral, that he will see again—in a year, he thinks—is no consolation at all. He has just settled in.

And so, in a gesture of hope and defiance, he responds to the peculiar request of Ming Tao. He considers this strange petition from several angles. He walks as he thinks, striding muscularly up and down in the Jesuits' cobblestone courtyard. Then he thinks as he rides, in the countryside, his heavy cape flapping like sails in the wind. He rides without a mask and unconcerned for bandits. Then he thinks while he sleeps, through thick heavy white dreams like clouds in fine paintings of South China landscapes, through dreams flimsy as wings of dragonflies over the pond of the minister of foreign cargoes: dreams of fish swimming up river rapids, of fish throwing themselves into the nets of fishermen, of talking fish promising strange rich perverse destinies whose morality—despite all his training in logic and epistemology, moral philosophy, and exegesis—he has no way of genuinely comprehending.

He considers Ming Tao's argument that this request of hers is no stranger or more dissolute—*in fact a good deal less so!* she writes—than Adam and Eve and their incest. They had no other way, did they? She argues that she has no other way, either, and that he will be gone to the other side of the world. She says: No one will ever know.

René Josserand can hear petty, sophistic legalistic arguments in his head, arguments not worthy of his intelligence. *If you cannot decipher the morality of this act, you can at least confess it later and be forgiven.* This is an argument that will not play for him.

If he cannot be comfortable that his gift to Ming Tao is a selfless gift, he will not comply with her request. There is certainly no self-indulgence involved, he thinks—though the likes of Fereira would see the whole matter as only self-indulgence. There will certainly be no contact that will sully his Jesuit virginity. So he resolves to comply.

He sends Bald Silly with his well-wrapped package to Ming Tao. "Hurry!" he says. "Do not stop on the way for a game of bones! I want to see you here again within the hour." He points to the twelve on the standing clock. "Do you understand? When the hand points here?"

When the servant returns, slightly early, out of breath, perspiring mightily, he says, Did you stop for a game? No? Good! Did you give money to the servant who answered the door, and insist upon secrecy? Very good! Here, take this rosary for yourself as a reward. Good man! Good man! Now forget this.

"Forget what?" says Bald Silly, and at this moment Josserand sees a flicker in the servant's eyes that makes him wonder whether the old man has been acting the idiot role all his life. Then the flicker is gone and the idiot smile is back. Bald Silly hangs the rosary around his neck and departs, with a quick little step that looks like a dance. Josserand shakes his head in amusement.

UNTIL RENÉ JOSSERAND leaves China, he never sees Ming Tao again, never sees her at all after the single time at the baptismal mass. It is while he is recovering on Hainan, thin, pale, and wondering whether his life will henceforward serve any purpose at all, that Ming Tao gives birth to the child, a son. At this point he has truly put the matter out of his mind. After all, what are the chances that such a fool gesture would come to fruition, indeed?

Fereira is dead, even the Castilian Jesuit friend of René Josserand has no idea of what has transpired, and Ming Tao's father—new Christian that he is, who cannot decipher how literally to take these doctrines—surrenders to her argument, that this is indeed a virgin birth. It would have to be. Wong Shao-Long knows—can conceive!—no other explanation.

A stoppered jar of vital fluid, carried between estates by a fuzz-pated dancing, babbling idiot? Absurd! A kitchen tool for basting fowl, employed by a virginal girl, all alone, to inseminate herself upon her wide bed? Even more absurd! Conception upon the first contact, as happens so often, unwilled, in the normal course of human relations? Well, then.

Josserand's vineyard-swarthy French complexion might as well be Chinese, and his Western features do not overcome the strength of Ming Tao's. The birth is easy and normal—it is only the mother's legs that are useless—and the child's appearance is wholly Chinese.

For the child's birth, his grandfather, Wong Shao-Long, sets off a display of fireworks over the Lake of Three Dragons, which connects to the Lake of the Fragrant Pomegranate. The lake's islands each look from a distance like the back of a dragon—in Chinese, *long*—writhing up out of the water.

The fireworks display that welcomes the first full moon of the New Year is the only one that is larger than the one set off by Wong Shao-Long to celebrate the fact that, finally, after so many years—he is fifty-six!—he has an heir. If one were to calculate the amount of saltpeter that goes into this display of the joy and gratitude of the minister of maps, the sum would approach three or four battles' worth of gunpowder in the wars then being fought among the nations of Europe.

Wong Shao-Long does not wish to make more of a public point of his daughter's child's "virgin birth" than happens naturally—he does not wish to be called to explain, even in conversation, what he himself does not understand—and so the display of fireworks goes up unannounced, everyone for miles wondering what the occasion could be.

The colors and shapes of the fireworks are nothing short of amazing. The Chinese are masters of this art, from earliest times. Green sparks grow up, up, up, like the reeds of the lake and then from them shoots forth a silvery dragon, whose red tongue darts out and then back, and then all the display—green leaves, dragon, fire tongue—vanishes in midair over the lake.

Ming Tao watches from her bedroom window, wrapped in quilts against the cool evening. The sky is incredibly black, as if the Immortals have sucked out all color and light for this one night, to make an entirely perfect backdrop for the celebration of the birth of her son, who is at her breast, under the coverlet, making small smacking sounds, testing the skin of the nipple with his tiny tongue.

Ming Tao thinks a tiny oblique thought: *And no man has ever seen these my breasts, or touched them!* Because she is so essentially virginal, it has never occurred to her that a grown man might do precisely what this tiny man under the covers is doing now, kissing, exploring.

Innumerable tiny golden fish dart through the black of the night, back and forth, back and forth, and then out of the hand of the earthbound master of the pyrotechnic display raises a giant blue fish made of light, who devours all the little fish.

A silver display forms a circle high against the black sky that those who are watching can tell is meant to be the moon; then, within it, the ears of a blue rabbit spring up, then the whole rabbit. It is the hare in the moon! There, beside him, a cassia tree sprouts! Oh, there, he pounds out with his pestle the elixir of immortality! And, as suddenly as it has appeared, it all dissolves into a trickling shower of silver.

The beauty of the display augurs well for the life of the newborn. The child grows in age and grace quietly, sheltered on the estate of the minister of maps, loved by his mother and all of the servants, especially Bald Silly.

THE JESUIT SUPERIOR at Rome, having had no special affection for Fereira, does not much credit the dead priest's indictment of Josserand.

Josserand's credentials prior to this have been unimpugned. "But then, well, then, what shall we do with you, now that you are home?" the superior says, bluff, a little too loud, ushering Josserand into the parlor three days after his arrival. He is slapping René on his back. René, unaccustomed to this, not expecting it, feels frankly faint with relief.

"Oh, we must use you wisely now. Come! You must be so fatigued! Here! Have a seat! Have a glass of wine! Take a cushion! The good sisters at—what is that convent down the alley?—well, they have embroidered these. The gold thread—is it not beautiful? Prop yourself! Here! Take a footstool. Tell me, tell me about all that has happened."

René, as may be imagined, does not tell him all that has happened, but he does have a number of marvelous tales, and he does have a way with the telling of them. The evening passes in a garnet haze of Jesuit burgundy from the estate of the family of the novice master.

René rises within the order to a position of some importance. He loves to call himself, jokingly, the minister of maps, because there actually is a good deal of work he must do with cartography, as he handles logistics of the worldwide mission activities of the Jesuits. He reads about Paraguay and dreams of going there.

THEN IT IS recorded that in 1658, at the age of thirty-eight, René Josserand lands on North American soil. His diary pages—incomplete due to an overturned canoe, a house fire, and the expungement by an envious superior of certain passages whose prose could be called nothing less than radiant—tell of his arrival at Montreal, his paddling off in a canoe with a fellow Jesuit named Martin Quenard Le Boite into the country of the Onondagas.

We follow him across what later becomes New York State. Here, on a minor feast day of the Blessed Mother especially dear to Le Boite, a day whose sky is a more opaque gray than René has seen since a day in monsoon season off India, his diary records that the two priests build a chapel outdoors in a clearing next to the water. The "chapel" is a framework of knotty twigs covered with native blossoms and leaves. The floor of the forest is covered with dried leaves, all color drained out of them.

The two priests embellish the framework of twigs and vines with five pieces of red yarn that have unraveled from Le Boite's scarf, tied into tidy small bows, at the corners of the lean-to and at the front center. The bows are meant to emblematize the five wounds of Christ.

IN JOSSERAND'S JOURNAL we read this passage:

I watched as my brother priest Quenard tied each bow tenderly, veritably like a woman. The little strings whipped in the chill wind. Against the flat pewter gray of the sky, just the hue of a bowl I recall at my aunt's as a child, their red color summoned in me feelings of marvel. I recalled the blood of Christ, shed for my many iniquities. My comrade's hands in the cold seemed so white and so small. The shape of the shelter recalled to me a crèche, a simple Nativity scene with fewer than a dozen statues, in the parish church of my youth. I was moved to tears.

I stepped forward to Quenard, took both his hands in mine as if simultaneously to bless him and to stop him, and, as the tears fell on the sere brown leaves, recited out loud in Latin there in the chill forest the Confiteor, for all the sins of my life that brought my Lord to the Cross. Quenard, who is a more silent sort, frowned at first and then, when I reached the phrase that calls all of the angels and saints to behold my confession, joined in. One felt those angels and saints indeed, hovering over the dried leafless branches, like the "great cloud of witnesses" written about in the Epistle to the Hebrews.

A later twentieth-century historian has suggested that this entry gives rich reason to think that buggery was going on and goes back to find support—a flash of color here and there, like a red scrap of unraveled yarn in the naked trees of René's life—in his earlier journals. René Josserand, hearing this, would laugh hugely. The two friends say mass for each other. On a rise in the distance, they see Mohawk Indians watching them but have no contact with them.

Many Jesuits have, by this time, died at the hands of various Indian tribes. While among the Jesuits it is believed that there is no greater or more glorious destiny than to be martyred, and many do seek out that martyrdom, both Le Boite and Josserand prefer to stay on earth as long as they can, to go as far as they can into this new and fascinating continent.

René Josserand, whose own hands are so fine, the hands of a French gentleman (though Quenard makes no mention of this in his journals, Quenard being far more the mathematician than the poet), thinks often of the mutilated hands of their predecessor, Isaac Jogues, whose fingers were said to have been chewed off by Indians to whom he was trying to bring the gospel. He reconfirms with God in his prayer, contrary to the seeking-of-martyrdom spirit of the age, *Well, Father in heaven, thy will be done, indeed, on earth as it is in heaven, but my own personal preference would be a quiet death in my bed at a very advanced age, and only then heaven, thank you.*

Jogues has visited in 1641 the spot where twenty-seven years later fellow Jesuits would found the mission of Sault Sainte Marie. There, brought by word of mouth flowing like rushing river water, two thousand Chippewas gathered to meet the priest and his partner Raymbault. Jogues addressed them in their own language, then went on with his journey. He was not able to return, his own martyrdom intervening.

When Jogues had entered the seminary, his novice master, Louis Lalemant, asked him, formulaically, what he was seeking in joining the Society of Jesus. Jogues had responded laconically, "Ethiopia and martyrdom." Lalemant—who had two brothers, Charles and Jerome, in Canada, and whose own nephew, Gabriel, later died at the stake at the hands of his own would-be converts—had replied, "Not so, my child. You will die in Canada."

In 1668 other Jesuits return to the *sault*—not an actual waterfall as the old French word implies but the rapids of the Saint Marys River where it exits Lake Superior heading south through Munuscong Lake, swooping west and then southeast again through Potagannissing Bay, thence into Lake Huron.

Three hundred years later, at a tricentennial celebration of the founding of Sault Sainte Marie, for which the city has a commemorative medallion struck, Justin Wong's mother, Mindy Ji, meets his father, Joe Cimmer.

The following year Mindy Ji and Joe will attend Woodstock together. A renowned news photographer will take a snapshot of Mindy Ji dancing there, covered head to toe in mud, wearing a halter made of a bandanna, her hands in the air, the shapes of her breasts against the the sunset sky defined in a way that might stop a sculptor's heart, their nipples erect and seeming to be pointing somewhere.

Mindy Ji's facial features cannot be seen—they are behind her raised left elbow. The photograph appears in a number of full-color newsmagazines, including most prominently *Life*. Mindy Ji never sees it. It is at Woodstock that Joe Cimmer will meet two of the musicians with whom he hooks up for a number of years, launching his career in earnest.

At the tricentenary celebration both Mindy Ji and Joe are long-haired and fresh-faced and tie-dyed, and their look is brand new to the world, non-derivative. Joe is playing a Dylan riff on a street corner on his harmonica, and Mindy stops to listen. She drops a shiny silver half-dollar into the violin case—*violin case?*—he has laid out beside him in the grass at the edge of the sidewalk. His eyes are closed and he is cooking.

When Joe finishes his song, he opens his eyes and reconnects with the world. Mindy still stands contemplating him. "What?" he demands, hearing his roughness, but thinking his tone is no ruder than this girl's stare.

"Two things," Mindy says. "One, that was nice. Two, your violin case is far out." She walks away.

He looks down at her half-dollar dazzling in the sun on the red velvet, then he looks up again at her, walking away. Her blunt-cut black hair is so thick. It pools at her shoulders, then plunges again till it reaches her waist. The skin of her legs, brown and smooth beneath her cut-off shorts, seems to take in the sun and convert it to some kind of lotion-of-pearl.

Joe Cimmer runs after her, grabbing up his violin case with its rattling seventeen dollars' worth of change—most of it from the night before, laid out to attract more—and calls out, "Hey, Injun Princess!"

THREE YEARS AFTER the founding of Sault Sainte Marie, in 1671, René Josserand arrives, having traveled overland and by canoe from Montreal through what would become New York State and the territory between. He has read the writing of an earlier Jesuit, speaking of this territory.

Josserand dips his oar into the water and then draws it up out again, and a flash of half-memory flits past his mind's eye: Ming Tao asking wryly, through the white silk of the carved, lacquered screen, whether the drowning of the dragon-boat oarsman might be considered a sacrifice to the dragon-god who brings the rain. He dips the oar into the water again, almost angrily, because at this moment the Christian idea of martyrdom seems no less silly than the death of Ming Tao's story's drowned dragon-boat oarsman. He does not wish to entertain this thought.

He recalls the words of that earlier French Jesuit whose journals he has perused, whose descriptions lit passions in him that he knew were in large measure human adrenaline and daring; nonetheless, the Holy Spirit still hovered there, as a later Jesuit, Gerard Manley Hopkins, wrote, "with warm breast and, ah, bright wings."

> We have long known that we have the North Sea behind us, its shores occupied by hosts of Savages entirely unacquainted with Europeans; that this sea is contiguous to that of China, to which it only remains to find an entrance; and that in those regions lies that famous bay, 70 leagues wide by 260 long, which was first discovered by Husson, who gave it his name but won no glory from it other than that of having first opened a way which ends in unknown Empires.

There is little about the day to day of this journey that smacks of glamour. There are wretched rapids to the rivers that overturn the boats dozens of times, causing a frightening concussion to Josserand with an aftermath of recurring headaches, and a ripped thigh muscle and broken elbow to Le Boite. There are raggedy shorelines to the lakes that, because of the danger of the beautiful but treacherous open water, necessitate closely hugging the ins and outs of the wild coast and thus doubling the distance.

There are rumors—transmitted through Indian guides—that an epidemic has overtaken the tribes native to the lands they are passing through, an illness marked by ravening hypochondria and an insatiable cannibalistic taste for human flesh.

There are swarms of fat bloodsucking insects and leeches and snakes whose benignity or danger is uncertain. Le Boite is allergic to the sting of one of the breeds of insect that attacks them and is deathly ill from it, but allergy as a concept has not yet been invented. He soldiers on, and the priests move out of the insect's territory into a new insect's. His skin becomes leathery thick from his scratching.

The corn the priests carry for nourishment is far too heavy for the canoes when afloat, and it rots or is stolen by bears when cached for a day or two's explorations inland under trees on the shoreline. What few dried berries hang on the bushes, left over from summer, appear to be succulent, elysian, to the famished pair. One of the varieties of berries—tested the day before with a minuscule sampling—makes Josserand fall onto his face and vomit copiously, blue-red berry vomit, into the cushion of leaves until he prays for death, which will not come.

All in all, the task is insane and impossible.

Josserand focuses, in the clouds of the meat-eating gnats and the growl-ings of his own diarrheic intestines, in the midst of impassable rapids, bear-rifled provisions and oaken oars shattered on river rock, on greater things: the salvation of souls and the finding of the Northwest Passage.

He is divided in his mind as to which is nearer to come in time, and though he knows that his own particular task is the former, he would not mind being in on the latter. To think of it! A passage to China! Such a dis-covery would wrap his earthly life, like a little red string neatly tied, with the symmetry of a white package. This symmetry is, he meditates, a gift given to few, while the lives of most men (it does not occur to him to think of the lives of women) fritter and ravel and dissipate into the ether like the dew of a summer morning.

Having arrived on the second of May 1671, Josserand is involved in the preparations for a great public council to which all the tribes have been invited.

The tribes are not told that the purpose of this ceremony is to take pos-session of all these lands for the great king of France, who is at this moment beginning construction on his rococo château at Versailles. He is not think-ing of this ragged country or these ragged priests any more than he is think-ing of colonizing Uranus.

A spot on high ground has been selected for the ceremony, by a Chip-pewa medicine man and a fur trader jointly, which overlooks the village of the Chippewas and the Saint Marys River. A great wooden cross is constructed and planted. It catches the sun off the water at dawn in a way that gives Josserand an unbearable pressure—the kind that precipitates prayer—behind his breastbone. Natives from several tribes, even as far as three hundred miles away, come, by land or canoe, to the spot.

The superior of the mission, Father Claude Dablon, raises the flag of the king of France, Louis XIV, and looks out across the wide blue river that, like a mirror, reflects the blue sky. A dense flock of small, flittering dark-winged birds crosses his vision and is mirrored back from the skin of the river. He thanks God for creation.

He thinks, a bit uncomfortably, how delighted, in his detached mercenary way, the king will be at all the resources here, when they are all revealed. France has iron, as does this area of New France, but it has no copper like the copper that Dablon has seen the natives extracting from the rich copper mines on the Keweenaw out to the west of here. Why, he has seen a huge boulder—six or seven hundred livres!—that he deems to be almost pure copper. He has seen deposits as well at Thunder Island, Isle Royale, and Chagaouamigon Point. Surely there must be rich stores untold yet undiscovered.

As his gaze sweeps out over the natives, he thinks of their copper almost with nostalgia, as if it now belonged to the fat king far across the sea, who cannot count his wealth. There is something that makes Dablon's soul writhe at this: he is a pure heart like Josserand, and he is entwined in— indeed, risking his life for—this enterprise, which for the king is at base about empire and resources. His own superiors soberly assure him that martyrdom here will mean heaven.

He blesses the great crucifix on the hill. He looks down at the natives who gather at the base of the rise. He recalls times he has been moved to laughter by their well-meant ceremonial gesture of tossing fragrant brown snuff, reverently, at the smaller, ornate golden crucifix that he uses when he says mass. Here, on this beautiful morning, no one tosses snuff at the cross: it is far too high and the breeze off the water too strong.

The missionaries sing the "Vexilla," and all the scruffy French trappers who have come from miles around for the ceremony—some of whom are even clean-shaven for the occasion!—sing along, most of them mangling the words. The priests have handwritten several copies of the lyrics, but few trappers can read. The Frenchmen's voices can hardly be heard: the wind catches their voices and swallows them, but down below the tribes watch them opening and closing their mouths like baby birds waiting for worms.

Muskets are aimed high into the blue morning air and discharged noisily. The tribes below shout in delight. They have never seen or heard anything like this. They will soon want to trade furs and fish and anything else for the magical muskets these white men have. Such lovely noise, such sweet smoke!

DURING THE CEREMONY René Josserand, now forty-three years old, has a brief moment of wondering where this will all lead, a sense that some kink in the movement of history is happening, that in a decade or three, surely in a century, no man present will recognize the land on which they stand.

Distracted as he is—in the way we all are at moments of great ceremony, a kind of blood overload too rich for the everyday mind—he remembers irrelevantly, out of nowhere, a young woman on his family's estate in France—a serving maid of his mother's—who had had a child out of wedlock—a scandal!—and that he heard she said to her friends: But I was with him only *once!* How can this be? The shred of thought produces in him a small agony, and he finds his mind slipping greasily backward to the question that he has allowed to rise only a few times in these intervening years: could there have been a child? Once more the muskets discharge. A bird falls from the sky. A bearded trapper laughs as if this is delightful, hilarious.

IN CHINA, THE son of Ming Tao and René Josserand is now sixteen years old. He will inherit Wong Shao-Long's estate, as René would have inherited his own father's property had he not entered the Jesuits. The boy's name is Yi Peng. He is handsome and strongly built. He will be a scholar of languages who will rise high in the government, and he will be an ancestor of Justin Wong as well as of another ice hockey defense player, Gong

Ming—a woman!—who plays in the Winter Olympics in Nagano in 1998, five years before Ursula's fall into the earth.

René Josserand, the unknown father of Yi Peng, will be, through all the hundreds of generations of Justin's ancestry, the only Caucasian in all of his lineage before Joe Cimmer and no one—not even Yi Peng himself—will ever know.

On the spot where the ceremony is held, declaring the land Louis XIV's, spruce and pine and deciduous other trees are planted by the priests, and a forest grows up in a very few years. Quickly the location of the precise historic spot becomes first confused, then forgotten.

The place where Dablon has planted the large outdoor cross lies within the mobile home park where Justin and Annie and Ursula live: Narita Pete's twelve-by-sixty-foot mobile home covers the spot.

For over two hundred years, the land has lain untouched. Then after World War II, a returning veteran, a Chippewa who has lost an eye on D day—not two hundred yards down the blood-sloshed sand from the lifeless body of the French grandson of Annie's great-great-grandmother Marjatta, the son of her lost daughter, Susu—buys the land and clears it for a trailer park.

After the war, people in Sault Sainte Marie wonder where all the prosperity is, all the good money that they are assured is the fruit of war, because here, there are so many soldiers who come home shell-shocked and unable to settle back down in their families. Little tin trailers—temporary!—are parked on the spot, but some of these veterans live in their little tin trailers until they die, not sure what happened to the lives they had planned.

The precise location of the first timbered mission structure, down on flatter ground nearer the river, is now obscured, covered by a brand-new upscale convenience store where Justin likes to go, on the occasional Saturday night when he does not have a gig, to pick up a six-pack of Mexican beer and a shrink-wrapped chunk of pale Danish Havarti cheese with dill that Annie likes. There is something just a little goofy, incongruous, about the luxury of this place: all kinds of wine, European-named mineral waters, on Sundays a stack of the *New York Times*! No one at all, not the historians, certainly not the owner of the convenience store, a high-school classmate of Mindy Ji Wong, knows the mission was here.

A half mile away, on the spot where the tall tree that made the huge cross was cut down, there is a fudge shop frequented in summer by all the tourists who flock there to visit the Soo Locks, the "fudgies" about whom the locals make jokes but on whose trade they are so dependent. In the fudge shop the tourists buy T-shirts with pictures of huge freighters out on blue water or passing through the locks, with colorful maps of the Upper Peninsula, or small cedar souvenir boxes with faux-velvet lining, or trivets embellished with pictures of deer grazing forestland. Outside the fudge shop a neon-hued windsock flaps and puffs in the breeze.

THREE CENTURIES EARLIER, René Josserand baptizes as many dying Indians as he can reach. Even against the will—or despite the lack of understanding—of the recipient, baptism of the dying can be valid, a quick way to heaven, is the theology. Several times, he does this surreptitiously. Once, a mother brings him a dying child. He asks to baptize the tiny girl. The mother says no, she just wants him to make her child well. Does he not have some medicine? Josserand, despite the scruples at forcible baptism that are beginning to nag at him, dips his finger into his canteen and says *Ego te baptizo* over the child as she lies weak and barely breathing in her mother's arms. When the mother is wiping her eyes—there is a great deal of spicy fat-smelling smoke in the lodge—Josserand makes the sign of the cross on the child's forehead with the water from his canteen. *In nomine Patris, et Filii, et Spiritus Sancti.* He names the child for Saint Anne, the mother of the Blessed Virgin Mary. That evening, the child dies.

He tells the mother that he is sorry he had no medicine. He wants to tell her that he has sent the tiny girl's soul to heaven and will meet her there when he himself arrives, and would the mother not want to meet her there too? But he does not. It is too dangerous.

He baptizes an entire village of natives the following year, at the request of their chief. At the ceremony, looking into the eyes of a young native girl he is baptizing, he recalls the brief glimpse he had had of Ming Tao at the baptismal mass eighteen years before, and how clear her pale skin was, how bright her eyes.

Then he remembers Bald Silly and the foolish, intent, wondrous look on his face as he went on his errand, back to the estate of the minister of maps with his tightly wrapped parcel. That look, even in memory, still makes him laugh, so again he laughs.

The sunset out over the lake—flashy red, brilliant gold—is astonishing that night. The birds sing more beautifully than he has ever heard. Perhaps, he thinks, his senses are coming alive, in this hard wretched life.

He thinks about the question that an old unchurched trapper asked him the previous week, begging his pardon for the profanity, but Father, what in the name of the holy balls of Jesus is your damned priestly celibacy meant to do?

He said to the man, thoughtfully: to consecrate me, to concentrate me.

The trapper had laughed at him, right out loud, then grabbed his own leather-breeched crotch, front and back, comically, mockingly. Holy piss, he shouted, my own holy shit!

That night, as René Josserand sleeps, a medicine man, who has just been told after the fact by someone else the significance of the ritual in which he has participated that afternoon, puts a tomahawk deep into the skull of René Josserand, aged forty-four.

His body is thrown by three newly baptized boys, instructed thus by the witch doctor, into a nearby river. It floats downstream for several miles, then snags on a tree trunk stripped clean by a windstorm. Crows peck out his eyes like fruit, and larger scavengers take out his heart and entrails.

His body slips softly back into the water. His skull, with its enormous fissure, washes up on the bank of a river near what is today a small town called Paradise, near Tahquamenon Falls. Mud covers it immediately, and then weather and time claim it equally.

It is still there today, undiscovered, four and a half feet into the rich earth, beneath leaves, grass, and clay, never touched by a gravedigger's hand, the rest of his bones scattered over an area of twenty miles. There are local postcards, but none of them says, "Paradise, Michigan, home of the tomahawked skull of René Josserand," because no one knows.

French Jesuit records call René Josef Augustin Josserand a North American martyr. In the parish church near his family's estate in France there is a window, commissioned by René Josserand, on his return from China and before his departure for North America. It bears at the foot of its walnut frame a now darkened donor plate engraved with his name and the year. It is roughly modeled on the Jesse window of Chartres, showing forth in pictures in stained glass the ancestry of Christ. Tourists often remark on the beauty of that window's Rahab, whose brow is broad, clear, and pale and whose dark eyes sparkle like Ming Tao's.

7   Justin and Annie

AT THE ISLAND—she likes to say the word, magical, "island," because it sounds to her as if Atlantis had risen again—Annie sits on a high stool slicing scallions for what she calls her Flying Finn chicken-cheese-and-cumin enchiladas. In a blue wedding-gift pottery bowl, neat as if she were on some haute cooking show, Annie has piled the ripped chicken, capping it with plastic wrap, which clings to the bowl's sides and gleams in the island light.

On the handled boom box on the island is piano music. The last tune was indigo hued, batik-ish, melancholy, as if Debussy had written it on a trip to India, but it was somebody else's; the tune playing now sounds triumphal, as though some rotund latter Napoleon were marching into town, hand stuffed into his vest, his thoughts behind his shiny forehead on his next conquest.

"Do you *like* that stuff?" Justin says, walking in, polishing a harmonica. He is screwing up his face, as if to say, *Eeyurk*.

"The one before, yes. This one? No."

"Good," he says. "I was hoping that I wouldn't have to return you to your father, for reasons of very bad taste." He kisses her on the back of her head, sniffing her freshly shampooed hair. "*Ay, caramba*," he says, deadpan. "You *mucho piaoliang*, missy."

"That means pretty, right?" she says. She tosses her almost dry hair in the warmth of the room, and the smell of hyacinth wafts from her. Through the window, bright late afternoon sunshine falls across the wooden cutting-board island top.

"Yep," says Justin. "Means how its sounds. *Hen piaoliang.*"

"You know, though," she says, "I distinctly remember you saying right there at the altar, 'For better or for worse; for richer, for poorer.' I don't think exception was made for bad taste." She waggles an eyebrow at him as she slices a fragrant thin green shoot of onion, slice slice. The longitudinal fibers protest slightly as they give way.

"Not even if you started liking Barry Manilow?"

"Not even," says Annie.

"Well, good, then," says Justin. "Just testing."

"Not even if you stopped wearing deodorant altogether, husband, and smelled like that roadkill skunk we passed last month," says Annie.

"*Me* no hit skunk," Justin says. "*Me* fine driver."

"Nonetheless, you've forgotten deodorant many a day," Annie says.

"Keeps my boys at a distance," says Justin, in a silly deep voice, working his armpits like a bellows. "Don't like to be working too close."

"I still love you," says Annie. "Even when you reek."

Justin picks up a green onion and chews on it. "As well to be hung for a sheep as a lamb," he says. He makes a proprietary grin. There is a dimple much like his ancestor Ming Tao's that lurks in his left cheek: this sardonic look draws it out, and instead of looking wry he looks childlike. He breathes out fiercely. "Dragon reek," he says.

"Yiii," says Annie. "We've still got the garlic to do too. Oh, goody."

He stops and looks at her in wonder, as if he has never seen her before. "Damnedest thing, Annie. I don't *get* it, but I believe you *do* love me. Even when I reek."

"And you love me. Say it."

Justin clutches at his throat and makes gagging sounds. "Llllghhh. I llll-ghhh. Luh-luh-luh . . ."

"Asshole," she says lightly, tossing her head at him. He blinks at the sun glinting off the pale yellow of her hair. It is a hue seldom seen except in small children.

"It's the white guy in me," Justin says.

"Dude," says Annie. "You're the scion of ages and ages of deep, rich lacquer-red Chinese blood. Zillions of ancestors. Only your father is white."

"In my throat," Justin says, mocking gagging sounds. "Hanging there on my tonsil. Little white guy. Can't you hear him? Glllgg. Glllgg." He pretends to choke slightly. "I think he has a hard hat on. Sticks in my craw, eh."

"He's like, what? The size of a raw oyster?" Annie grins. She's still cutting scallions, slice slice, scraping them with the heel of her hand into a small green-white mountain. "Does he look like your father?" Annie says.

"Maybe." There is an odd lift of the eyebrow and odd intonation in the word. They have rarely mentioned the man whose harmonicas sit in the drawer.

"Your father's not here," Annie says. There is a dark, Byzantine sadness to her tone.

"As in, Our Father, who art in nowhere-we-know?" Justin says. "As in hollowly echoing be thy name?" His jaw is clenched, his dark eyes narrowed.

Annie is picturing some mythic whale's belly-sized cavern into which Joe "Rapdander" Cimmer disappeared, over twenty years before. She can hear the walls of the whale's belly echoing: *Justin o Justin o Justin*. But Justin has always been right here, so Joe can't be looking for him. She redubs the scene: *Daddy o Daddy o Daddy*. It was Joe Cimmer who walked away.

The voice is Justin's, but as a preschooler. Annie is furious. Give blood: play hockey. She doesn't know whether she wants to shoot Rapdander Cimmer for what he has done or to hold out her arms and beg him to come home to his child, now grown to a man, so all this can heal.

"Acting like some kind of jerk won't make that all better." Annie looks up at Justin with a combination of sweetness and pleading.

"You want me to say something sensitive. Right?" He is serious. He is not mocking.

She nods as she slices, calmly. The sunshine has moved slightly, its angle sharper now, its hue slightly hellish. *This time of the afternoon,* she thinks, *reminds us each day that we're mortal: it says, the end's coming, repent, repent.* She marvels at how the sun keeps up its rounds and remembers a number of reasons she keeps on believing in God. She ponders the differences between white and green onions, in chemical terms. Why she cries when she slices the white ones and seems quite fine now.

"You want me to say that I glllhhh . . ."

"Aw, Jus, you've said it so many times . . . I was just wanting to hear it now . . ."

"Okay. Me try," Justin says. "Shall I compare thee to a summer's day? Thou art more lovely and more temperate. Rough winds do shake the darling buds of May . . ."

"Oh, Justin," Annie says. She feels a warmth in her collarbone, a heat, as if marrow were melting and rising in her, as if she were a fever thermometer. The marrow liquefies, thins to salt water and tries to spill from her eyes. She refuses to let it. She blinks. "Oh, shit," she says.

"Great response," Justin says. He intones as if it were a news headline, "Ice hockey goalie learns Sonnet 18 to seduce Finn chick; Finn chick responds with 'Oh, shit.'"

"Run that back past me again?" says Annie. "You learned that for me?"

"Like who else would I have learned it for but a librarian?" Justin says. "That Koko-Doko gal with the close-set eyes out at the Dairy Dreem? That waitress at Boo 2 Soo, with the collagen lips and the boob implants?" He stares at her stunnedness. He smiles quietly, pleased at his little surprise. He recites the entire sonnet for her, quietly.

The sunlight seems stage-managed: it has softened, accentuating the broad smooth shape of Justin's brow, which Annie thinks is likely Joe's, as it is not Mindy Ji's. There are no pictures of Joe around, or none that she's ever seen.

She is so taken by Justin's recitation that she cannot meet his eyes. She looks anywhere else: at his brow, at the harmonica in its white handkerchief nest in his hands, and then up at the little opal-glass bird with clear cut-crystal wings—one more wedding gift—that hangs in the kitchen window above the sink. Light rays splinter into flame-colored and blue violet darts, shoot off, and then diffuse into the shadowy interior. A draft of air jiggles the bird dangling on its few inches of fishing line. Then Justin finishes. They sit in silence a moment.

"I learned it two and a half years ago, Annie. Before I knew your name. I just never did have a chance to use it on you."

"I was just too easy, right? Too available?" Annie says. She remembers all the times at the library, Justin moving through with the armfuls of mysteries for Mindy Ji and seeming unable to notice her.

"No, I was too—eee, er, um—shy," Justin says. He makes funny eyes that mean: I saw you, Annie, every damn time, and I couldn't believe you were looking at *me.*

"Jeez," Annie says. "You? Shy?"

"This shyness stuff is site specific," he says. "You need help with these onions here, lady?"

She passes him instead a block of cheese. Its holes are exquisitely tiny. "Lorraine Swiss," says Annie. "Lorraine is a region in northwestern France. Mostly Catholic. Four million inhabitants. Wheat, barley, oats, wine, and iron ore."

Justin stares at the tiny perfect airholes in wonderment, holding the lacy cheese up to the light. He is thinking about lots of Catholic churches with banks of candles flickering and melting down in their shadows. He is thinking about fields of barley, and what they would look like, and where did he hear that line anyway: among the fields of barley?

"I don't know how they do it, make the holes, but if you'd like to know I can find out," Annie says. "Maybe some kind of belching process, the opposite of kneading dough or carbonating pop."

"This is precisely why I married you, Anne Marie Maki Wong," Justin says. "I needed a reference librarian around to tell me how they get the holes into Swiss cheese, and what might be the relationship of those holes to iron mining and the papacy."

"Not really Swiss," Annie says. "Alsace borders on Switzerland. Lorraine is in France."

"Thank you," says Justin, with great *courtoisie,* bowing low, the silver harmonica in his hand slicing an arc through the sunshine. "You are more than I could have dreamed, Annie."

"Oh, hush," Annie says, laughing. "Give blood, play hockey. Did your mother read all those mysteries you checked out, anyway? What was it, three a day for a couple of months?"

"Every one," Justin says, sober as that. He makes a scout's honor sign with the fingers of his right hand, emphatic in the air. Then he winks. "Every goddamn one."

"So you know how to do garlic?" says Annie. "Remove the neat little casing—use the knife partly, and partly your thumbnail—then stack up the fat little cloves, and then slice them small."

"I can do this thing," Justin says. "Ow!" he yells, smacking himself in the forehead, slapstick.

"Don't give blood *now*," Annie says. "Wait till you play hockey. Did you know a girl in high school named Heidi Kolmar? Behind you, ahead of me."

"Nope," Justin says. "I only had eyes for you."

"You didn't know me in high school," says Annie.

"So then I was totally blind," Justin says.

"Heidi Kolmar went to Smith College," Annie says.

"Big whoop," says Justin. "I went to Soo High School."

"She got Julia Child's old room in the dorm," Annie says.

"Big whoop," says Justin. "I inherited Julia Child's hockey goalie gear."

"I mean, we are doing this Julia Child thing here, aren't we?" Annie says, as if to ground them in some kind of logic, as if she were the official librarian and Justin the court fool, announcing this to bleachers full of seraphic spectators. "That was what made me think of it. This lovely kitchen you've made me. The sunlight. The neat little bowls of stuff. This is such pleasure." She looks about her as if heaven will be anticlimax.

"Big whoop," says Justin. "Big whoop that Tidy Heidi has Julia Child's dorm room. Me, I've got Julia Child's shin pads. Her jockstrap. Her little embroidered Smith College puck cover that matches the toaster cover. These items rule."

On the radio is a song that sounds Gaelic now. They sit and slice scallions and garlic and listen. The sun recedes back of a huge spruce that shades the window, between their lot and the next one, the trailer that must be the oldest in the park, flat blue painted and looking as if paint is all that's holding it together. Someone in that trailer turns on a light in the living-room window. From where they sit, the light turns the desolate little tin box to a cozy den, something out of a children's book, a place where furry brown rabbits live, reading and murmuring and making tea.

Justin finishes and pushes his bowl toward Annie. "Good enough?"

"Perfect," she says.

He pulls out a length of clear plastic wrap and rips it off. He caps the bowl.

"Perfect," she says again. He goes to the sink and he washes his hands. "Use the lemon juice," she says. "It gets out the garlic smell."

"I knew that," he says, indicating that of course he didn't. "I don't wear Julia Child's crotch guard for nothing, you know. I'm no fool."

He uses the lemon juice, rubbing it in, feeling it burn in the tiny cuts he brings home every day from his work. Then he washes again. He dries his hands on his T-shirt. He reaches for Annie's hand cream that stands next to the sink. He rubs it into his hands.

Annie is thinking about the idea of rabbits living next door and admiring the look of the light in the blue trailer's window. She is thinking that she is so grateful for all of this. She is thinking that fine Eastern colleges, faux Cotswolds cottages costing a mint, and vacations to all kinds of wonderful places are nothing compared to what she has: garlic cut perfectly, Justin, that light in the window next door and the dark spruce tree silhouette overhead, a chance to know anything she wants to know—barley in Alsace-Lorraine—at her job, and get paid for it. She is thinking she loves her new life. She is thinking about her old life, and Garrett's drunken rages. She cuts that off.

Suddenly she startles. "Yiii!" she shrieks. "Whoa! What are you doing?!"

Justin is under the island, sitting on the floor, pulling her sandals off, then her thick heavy ribbed socks.

"Hey, hey! That tickles!"

He is creaming her feet with the cocoa-butter hand lotion.

"Ooh! Justin!" she says, settling into a sigh as the tickling gives way to a feeling of simple rare pleasure. "Oh," she says, quiet. "Mmm," she says. "How am I supposed to cut these onions?" she says.

"You're not," he says. He keeps massaging, spreading the fragrant cream over the top of her foot, under the soft, bridgelike arch beneath. He slips his fingers into the spaces between her toes, all at once, *sloopsh,* then individually, slip slip slip slip. She feels the cream turning to skin, or her skin to cream. He wipes off the excess onto his T-shirt.

"Really, Justin," she says. She's not really protesting. She's quiet.

He is rubbing his right thumb across and around each toenail in turn, in descending order, and his left the same, in a symmetry she can feel though not see. "This little piggie went to Mackinac Island," he chants. "This little piggie stayed home. This little piggie had garlic enchiladas. This little piggie had none." He grabs hold of the little toes, yanking them softly in unison. "And *these* little suckers cried, 'Wee wee wee want to be Julia Child, all the way home!'"

He climbs out from under the island and stands. He takes the knife from her hand—she is sitting there holding it useless in midair anyway, lulled and semistunned by the foot massage, held captive by cocoa butter—and he puts it down on the cutting board. He lifts her from her high, tall-backed stool and carries her to the sink.

Her long skirt trails down as she lies across his arms. Her feet look so white, exposed, as if they've never been used at all, like Justin's ancestor Ming Tao's. Her toenails are smooth and square, broad as a child's, white as anything, as wide as they are long. He holds her in the crook of one arm and turns on the water at the sink with his free hand.

"Wash hands now," he says, in a comic robot voice. "Official instructions from Julia Child."

She washes. It takes a long time. She is soaping and soaping her hands, first the froth, then the cream, then the long, steaming-water rinse. Justin is holding her cradled across his strong workman's forearms as if she weighed nothing at all.

"We go living room now," he says. "Next step in recipe."

Annie leans her head on his shoulder. "You got this from Julia Child?" she says.

"So far," he says. "The next page was torn out of the book. From here on in, I improvise."

He lays her down on the rug, in a nest of floor pillows. He kisses her stomach up under her long loose shirt. He marvels at her skin, how soft it is, even in darkness how white. He chews on her white cotton bra and then works it off, down around her waist. She is making soft sounds in the twilight. He is humming something to her.

Annie says. "Mmm. That's nice." The music on the radio, a sound behind his humming, enters her lulled state. "Mmm," she says. "Sounds like topaz. Topaz light." It is piano, a Liszt or a Chopin.

"Today," she says, semidreamily, semisensible, "there were a whole rowdy bunch of kids, say eleven or twelve years old . . ."

Justin unhooks the hooks on her soft little bra and throws it across the room. It *thucks* quietly against a calendar from a Chinese restaurant—a picture of a tile-roofed pagoda on an autumn hillside—and falls, draping itself over a lampshade. In the dusk, one ray of light strikes the red leaves of a tree beside the pagoda. The tree's leaves match the tile roof.

One afternoon not too long before, Annie has stopped in amazement to look at the picture: free calendars with one picture to cover the whole year tend to go invisible after a while. It occurs to her that what astounds her is those red leaves: the coming of autumn is proof that in China time actually passes too. In her mind China is one vast tableau and removed from time.

But she is not looking up at this now. Her eyes are closed. She is making small, unintentional, catlike sounds, stopped in her story about the library by Justin's breath tickling her bare midriff skin in the dusk. She sighs and starts again.

"There were all of these kids in today," she says. She feels the tip of his tongue in her navel.

"You just keep talking, library lady," he says, lifting his head, grinning a quizzical face right into hers. "What's the deal?"

"I just want it to go on and on," she says. "I'm a speed bump in your road to whatever. I'm slowing you down." She wraps her arms around his head and pulls him to her. "Oh, Justin," she sighs. His dark hair is so soft in her hands. She works her fingers in circles behind his ears. Perfect delicate bones that hear music. His hair so like something else: what, mimosa?

"I'll 'speed-bump' you, girl," he says.

She laughs. "Not just yet, please?" she says, ruffling the fringe underneath his hair, the vulnerable top of his neck. "Anyway. All of these kids. They were doing a project together, and loud, and they wore me out. When they left, I thought I'd make a phone call I needed to make, to a publisher. In Vermont. One of these small presses, pure and surrounded by woods and fields and so on. Toll-free. I love to make toll-free calls."

"You know what I love?" Justin says. He is making the quirky smile, dimpled and wry. "I love knowing that, no matter what I do, I cannot distract you from all this blather about rowdy kids and your toll-free calls. That I cannot drive you totally wild."

"Oh, trust me," she says. "You are doing this thing. Oh. Yes. Anyway."

She tries to start again. She stops and catches her breath deeply, suddenly. "Oh," she says.

The room is quiet for a moment except for the Liszt, over past the small mountain of fragrant green onions. The shadows overtake the whole living room. The only light on is the one in the kitchen, above the small island. From her vantage point on the floor, Annie can see the bare lightbulb from beneath, so she scoots aside, letting a plant on the room divider block the glare.

The cloud of red leaves on the hillside calendar tree winks out as the light through the blinds slides away. The tones of the piano are delicate. In a far room in Annie's mind, a couple long dead dances in that sweet topaz light. The woman is wearing a taffeta gown, the color of toffee. Her partner is bowing. The shadows are maybe a half hour earlier than this, as if dream trailed reality timewise.

"Oh, Justin," says Annie. "Slow." It is a request. Soft. Her breath merges with the Liszt, which becomes transparent, jewelly brown light, the color of the fields of barley in the song Justin tried to remember. The song is Sting's. There. That's it. Neither of them is remembering Sting.

Justin is up under Annie's long, baggy shirt now, his whole head, softly licking her nipples.

"I was just going to say," Annie says. She cannot remember what she was going to say. "Oh," she says instead.

She is quiet for a minute. The partners in her half-dream are walking each other through some eighteenth-century dance. In their room, the ceiling is concave, ornate, stark white, but it is two hundred years ago and it is getting on into sunset, so the light is oblique and resinous. Is this a mazurka? A waltz? Annie makes a librarianly resolution to look this up later. She feels Justin's tongue trail left to right across her breastbone and circle the sugary skin of the other breast's soft nipple. Oh.

She starts again. "They put me on hold. For a minute, two minutes. The Muzak was beautiful, though, something like this Liszt—whatever—so I just held on and held on. Maybe ten minutes. Just sat there with the phone to my ear, zoned, looking out the side window, just holding on."

"Are you holding on now?" Justin says. His voice is a whisper.

"Oh," she says, involuntarily. "Yes. Oh, yes. Yes, Justin. Oh oh." Her hands lie limp for the moment beside her head, and she is breathing a soft even rhythm. Her pale yellow hair seems to have its own light in the dusk, spread out over the rug. Annie scoots herself backward and grabs the legs of the magazine table beside the couch. She holds on.

She feels her skirt slipping away, as if caught in a quick high wind or a midocean maelstrom. She feels her heart slipping away, like a cooked onion layering out of itself, whoops, and where is it going?

Justin tries to remember what life was like before Annie and cannot. Her hands come up around his head and then he is down, down, a dark cavern, sweet. He cannot remember the route back to the surface of earth, and he does not care.

WHEN THEY WAKE, it is wholly night, perfectly quiet. On the island, beneath the one lightbulb, the bowls and the onions and garlic sit waiting.

Annie's bra hangs from the lampshade, a silly, limp testimony. Her long, batik-cotton skirt drapes the TV. Justin's boots are flung halfway across the floor of the kitchen, and one of his socks. They are wearing their shirts. Only shirts.

"What was that you were saying?" says Annie.

"That oh-oh-oh business?" says Justin. "Or the, like, oof-oof-oof stuff."

"Yeah, that," Annie says.

He climbs over her, making a childish, devilish grin. "Are you saying you want more?" he says. His tone is mock shock.

"Mo-o-o-re?" Annie echoes. Her tone is the tone of an orphan in *Oliver*.

"Okay," Justin says. "I'm easy."

It is 1 A.M. by the time Justin lifts Annie into the shower and they stand, holding on to each other for what seems dear life, beneath the hot water. It pours on them, torrents.

"Tomorrow, what say I cook those enchiladas?" says Annie. She can still smell garlic on Justin's hands as they brush away her long, wet hair from her eyes. Annie remembers the song called "Tomorrow" from the musical. Justin insists the musical is named after his wife.

A wide-eyed orphan, an evil red-haired woman, a good ending nonetheless.

ANNIE IS GLAD they are under the shower. It masks her tears. She is thinking of something she saw in a book that came through the late check-in last week, a collection of Wallace Stevens's poems. The day was slow. Nothing was doing. Tasha was running an errand. So Annie sat several minutes just flipping through Wallace Stevens.

"Death is the mother of beauty," the line went. She thought about that: *If we didn't have death, we could not half appreciate what we have now, its mortality, ephemerality, vaporousness.* She does not say any of that now.

"Oh, I do love you, Justin" is all she says.

Justin thinks something he cannot explain, as if he were picking up Mars on his fillings. "Death is the mother of beauty," he thinks, or he hears. He half imagines his own death: it would have to be past the half-century mark. It would have to be way the hell past that.

Or maybe his truck will turn over, and land in the river, upside down, and he will in panic not remember how to roll windows down and escape, and so will drown terrified in a very small space, or maybe he will become weirdly ill with some sort of thing no one yet has identified and die young, next year.

Perhaps, on the other hand, despite all the doctors' best guesses and cautions, Annie will conceive, and there will be a whole line of children come issuing forth, like sweet cooked onions, like Russian dolls inside of Russian dolls, how many years? Is the end of the world anywhere near?

Because her head is burrowed into Justin's clavicle, sharp little brownish bone under the honey skin, she does not know there are tears on his cheeks as well. Justin holds her close, standing there under the shower, and feels the bones of her spine, her fine vertebrae. He fingers them as if she were a flute. They are out in some southwestern desert, his mind says, and here comes the wind blowing through. It is hot, as if from a blast furnace. It dries them. It sings desert songs.

Annie leans against his hard flat stomach, her weak legs braced by his stronger ones. She is thinking about her scars, down there, the scars from the accident, scars from the surgeries, her pale legs' bowing where, after the surgeries, the outer bone grew faster, more eagerly, than the inner.

She is recalling her father sitting at the enamel-topped table in their little kitchen, one afternoon when she was in high school, drinking and brooding and sucking his cheeks in and staring at her as she propped herself against the sink's edge and wrestled a jar lid and tried not to look as if this were a difficult task, much less as if she were trying hard to keep her balance.

"Going to need to get college, girl," he had said, as if she had not already led her class all three years and applied for six scholarships. "No man in his right mind is going to marry a cripple." He said it so lightly, as if he were not trying to drive a stake through her living heart. "Going to need to support yourself, girlie." Annie looked at the stuff in his glass. It was clear, though she knew it was not water. She wrestled the jar lid free without his help, out of fury and goodness, smiling peacefully.

She is recalling Justin's lips kissing those scars, the first time, in the front seat of his truck, running his lips up and down the scars, trailing them as if he were playing harmonica, as they sat by the river at night, a full moon. She is recalling the way, afterward, by the river two years ago, he brought out the harmonica he always carried, the small one, and played Clapton's "Wonderful Tonight" for her, and the way that she told him the stars were applauding. She is recalling the way Justin kissed those scars again tonight.

She leans back against the molded-plastic shower enclosure and looks into Justin's eyes. She parts his lips comically, as if she were a horse vet inspecting his gums. "Is that damned little white guy still in there?" she asks.

So he says the words that she has wanted to hear. He tells her he loves her. The little white guy on his tonsils is gone. Then he tells her how long this will go on, this thing that he has not been able to say: till the greenhouse effect does this thing and that thing, till their great-great-grandchildren are coming to see them in the old folks' home and they've got liver spots on the backs of their hands, and loose neck flesh and earlobes that dangle like turkey wattles and they're older than Sarah and Abraham, till some cheesehead goalie from Saskatoon, Saskatchewan, retires.

He holds her close.

There is only one towel, a huge one, pale yellow. They step out, and Justin wraps them up together.

"One Sino-Finn enchilada," says Justin, "coming up."

"No more coming up," Annie pleads, leaning against him, laughing and laughing, and he unwraps her—after all, they have been pretty much dried by the desert wind—and takes her into the bed, where they sleep soundly.

TIGER LILIES ARE everywhere on the walls, trumpeting orange. Tasha's living room in this old gray-shingled house set smack up against the sidewalk, amid piles of hardened grayed snow, is in stark contrast to the exterior. The doorbell rings, and it is the last guest, Narita Pete, whom Tasha does not know. Narita's life with Annie as a neighbor at the trailer park does not intersect with Tasha's life with Annie at the library.

This is a baby shower for Annie, it is mid-October 2000, and an early, sloppy snow from the last half hour lies on the ground. Narita remarks on the fire in the fireplace: Ooh, what a nice one. On the mantel above are knicknacks she likes too. The fire makes crackling sounds, the hickory logs' fragrance fills the room. Yum, says Narita.

Starting to snow yet? asks Tasha. A little, a dusting. Narita settles into a corner of the sofa and observes the crowd, which is not really a crowd: a couple of women from the library, Justin's mom, Tasha's neighbor who had nothing else to do.

Tasha's husband, Gilbert, shuffles through making self-conscious faces. "This better not be contagious," says Gilbert, and everyone laughs stupidly. Gilbert does not want a child until they have a better house, until he has been promoted to district manager, until Tasha has gotten her master's in library science. Tasha shrugs. You know, maybe we'll never get there, she says. Maybe I'll kick his ass out too. Everyone laughs. *Candy* ass, she says, winking.

Tasha passes cut-glass cups of punch the color of the tiger lilies. Where's Annie? says someone. Is her mother coming? God, no, comes the answer; her mother's been dead since she was ten. Lord, says the woman, I knew that. I'm so stupid.

Tasha says, "She asked Justin to take her out to the cemetery this afternoon because she said she wanted to talk to Liz. She says she doesn't want her to feel left out of the pregnancy, so she goes out there and talks to her, sort of, in her head I guess. Giving her updates: ultrasounds and whatever. Telling Liz she wishes she could be in on the real thing."

Creepy, says someone.

THE LATE LIGHT is starting to fade, and the snow falls steadily in the dusk in the light from the streetlamps. Suddenly Annie and Justin arrive, Annie's cane clumping up the stairs. Shhhh, everyone. Bing bong, bong bing, sound the Westminster chimes bought from the hardware store when they remodeled. Huge sound, enormous dignity, weird, disproportionate.

This is a surprise: Annie really does not expect anyone else to be here but Tasha and Gilbert. She thinks she and Justin are coming to dinner. The cars have been hidden. Surprise! comes the shout, and Annie gasps in genuine shock. Light snow covers her hair. She is wearing a gigantic sweater of Justin's, tweedy and rough—because nothing much fits, these days—over a long skirt. Tears rise to her eyes. "You *guys!*" she says. "You sneaks!"

Justin sees Gilbert back in the kitchen and tears a beeline through the hubbub of the shower. Justin has for Gilbert the kind of patronizing tolerance that real musicians have for dabblers: Gilbert was a drummer in high school and played with two local bands, Neon Fly and the Dachau Lampshades. Neither went anywhere, but Gilbert still thinks of himself as a possible star, somewhere down the road. Justin has tempered his contempt for Gilbert, to please Annie, until they have become something like friends.

A log crackles and falls heavily in the fireplace, and people startle. "Nice trip to the cemetery?" says Tasha wryly. She thinks the dead need to stay out of sight, out of mind.

Annie wrinkles her forehead: regret, dismay. "It's beautiful out there," she says. "No snow left on the headstones from last week. The crocuses I planted last month at the border of her plot were there, though, under it all. In the spring they'll be poking their heads up. Bright purple. Like little tropical birds."

The headstone is rosy-hued marble, polished. Annie picked it out, when she was in high school, after Garrett had left the grave without a headstone for five years. Annie paid for it with baby-sitting money, and the monument guy, knowing the circumstances, had given it to her for half price, without telling her that he was doing it. It says simply, ELIZABETH DEBRUIN MAKI, 1949–1985.

It is a single plot. Garrett will not be buried there, he says: he will be cremated, and have his ashes thrown into the middle of Lake Superior, "from the deck of a goddamn taconite freighter," he says. He seems to think this is a gesture of independence, but in his isolation, he would seem to have no one even to scatter his ashes for him.

A border of morning glories, a vine, is sandblasted into the pink marble. Free, said the monument guy, wishing that he could give the girl more: what would he give her—fireworks like the displays Ming Tao so loved four centuries earlier, fountaining up pyrotechnically out of Liz Maki's headstone to promise Annie in some kind of skywriting that life goes on?

Annie thinks, standing there at the foot of the grave, and there are no other words for it: *Come back, Mom, I need you here.* She tries to remember Liz's face and can conjure up only the secondhand images, the photos she sifts through, again and again, in the boxes: scores of pictures, but all still and static.

In the truck, the same dun silver color as the dismal day, Justin rolls down the front window and yells to her, "Hey, Annie. Come on. This just makes you sad. Jesus. Get back in." The people at the shower are waiting, but Justin can't say that. He is not good at this kind of thing, keeping girly secrets, game playing. Hockey, okay; baby showers, forget it.

She motions him to patience and stands a while longer, gazing at the headstone, the tree nearest, with its leaves all gone, at a black bird hovering—a crow? The kind that eats roadkill? She scrapes that thought quickly aside, and she reminds herself that surely her mother deep in the earth is all bone now. But then she remembers the pictures she has seen of saints incorruptible, cased in glass, Saint Theresa, the Little Flower, whom her mother so venerated: in her glass case in France, looking as if she is sleeping and no more than that.

Justin in the truck is not thinking about his ancient ancestor Qin Lao. The fact that Qin Lao's grave had been excavated by a team of Swedish archaeologists in the 1920s, who published their findings in Swedish, in a Swedish journal that even Annie has never heard of, is of course unknown to him too. That team of archaeologists included a distant great-uncle of Annie's once removed, whose father had been on the team of the Norwegian scientist Kristian Birkeland, who at the turn of the twentieth century uncovered the secret of the aurora borealis. There is a picture from 1902 posed in Arkhangelsk, Russia, of Birkeland, looking dapper and fey, "with three assistants and a Samoyed guide," the caption notes. The last is in fact no Samoyed guide at all but a dark-eyed half-Lappish first cousin of Marjatta Haapalehto lost to the family history. Justin further does not know about Qin Lao's son who is memorialized in the terra-cotta army of Qin Shi Huang-ti at Xi'an, the clay soldier with the infinitesimal crook of the little finger that he has passed down to Justin Wong. Justin is not thinking about his ancestor Wong Lin at the grave in California, sitting and missing his own wife, Daisy, and—right there at the graveside—finally breathing out and then not breathing in. Justin knows nothing about him, and his picture in Mindy Ji's box of old family photographs is not annotated.

Annie has finished her visit at Liz's gravesite now and has made her little ritual walk, slow and in today's snow rather sloppy, around the plot to the graves that surround her mother's—"Just saying hi to the neighbors!" she says to Justin. There are several very old graves in the vicinity and Annie likes each time she visits to stop and nod to them as if she had known them. One she especially likes is the double plot of John and Comfort Stowe, a stark stone carved with the likeness of a dour angel above their names, dead within two years of each other in the 1880s. Comfort, she thinks, what a name, what a good thing to be. Lucky John.

ANNIE AND JUSTIN are at the shower now. Murmurs, the passing of punch, tiger lily hued, and lemon bars. Remarks about Annie's girth. Logs readjusting their positions in the fire like someone who has been sitting too long, twigs snapping. Out in the kitchen, men roaring in laughter.

Something heavy dropped, and a scramble. Tasha calls in, "No hockey in the house." It's not funny, but the women laugh in the way that at showers people laugh at nothing, to cover the genuine terror of whatever is about to transpire, in this case, a birth, to a young woman who had been advised not to get pregnant at all.

What are you going to name her? asks a librarian. Her? says someone else. Does this mean you had an ultrasound? Yeah, they're routine now. We're thinking, says Annie. She catches Mindy Ji's eye. Obviously she has discussed this with Justin's mother.

"I had a dream last night," Annie says. "I had been looking at a book of paintings at work, by a fifteenth-century artist named Memling. Checking it in and I just got distracted. The Last Judgment, a lot of that kind of medieval thing, but there was one in particular that caught my eye. Saint Ursula, a medieval kind of legendary, wafty, not very historical kind of saint. A picture of a woman with—"

Mindy Ji takes a quick astonished breath and closes her eyes in the way she is wont to, when this kind of thing comes on her. "Annie!" she says. "A woman with a veil and a cloak, right?"

"Right," Annie says.

"Lots of *little* women under her cloak."

"Right," says Annie. "The supposedly eleven thousand virgins, which I'll bet were eleven at most and three decimal places got added somehow." She says to Mindy Ji, puzzled, "You know that painting? I never saw it before."

"No, I don't," says Mindy Ji. "That's just in my head. I dreamed it last night. In the dream, there was that woman, with all the little women under her cape, and *you* came in, and you were *her* mother." Mindy Ji stops and frowns. She says, "They were on a ship, right?" Annie says yes. "Now *that* is weird. What does *that* mean?"

No one knows what to say. Narita clears her throat uncomfortably. Everyone sips punch. Mindy Ji tends to stop conversations this way sometimes.

Out in the kitchen, Justin stomps his feet as if in the stands at a hockey game. Some great joke. Maybe just news about somebody Justin and Gilbert knew from high school.

Annie sits thinking about the painting, which is somewhere in Europe, in a shrine, among multiple paintings of these little virgins embarking and disembarking from ships on a mythic voyage they are supposed to have taken from somewhere to somewhere. Sails puffing out, much traffic on the docks, someone being efficiently martyred, by means of a sword, on board ship in the middle of all the humdrum loading and unloading.

Annie sets down her punch cup. "The baby's name," she announces— not having to consult Justin, who has said that he will make the decisions about which third world countries to invade or not, thank you, but that the naming of babies is totally Annie's department—"is Ursula Elizabeth De-Bruin Maki Wong." She is surprised at hearing herself poke the Maki name awkwardly in there, despite Garrett's brutality, despite his ignoring her all these years, despite her terror of him still.

THE C-SECTION the following month, the nineteenth of November, is difficult, and the baby is smaller than the doctor had thought she would be, a little over six pounds. Big enough, nonetheless.

Justin makes it through the wait in the pacing-and-prowling area—a C-section of this sort does not allow fathers or anyone else in. Still, once the baby is born, he finds himself frightened to death at the thought of it all, after the fact, and the second he sees the baby, he faints, something he has never done in his life. The starch goes out of his legs, and his head goes woozy and then black.

So there is Annie, still in Recovery, knocked out, due to the complications of the pelvic ring fracture from the accident and the uncertainty of how this will go, and suddenly now here is Justin, crumpled in a heap on the floor next to the empty bed in Annie's room, the nurses scurrying like rubber-soled ants to fetch orderlies, the amazing new baby all rose violet, snug in its pilly white blanket in the arms of the nurse.

Ursula's hair at this point is jet black: it will not turn blond until she is three months old, bit by bit, until one morning she will look like a little tow-headed Finn, but with Mindy Ji's eyes and that gorgeous bronze skin.

She is wiped clean of waxy birth residue and blood, blinking up at the overhead lights in amazement. She resembles nothing so much as an exotic fruit, discovered on a distant vacation, but with a human face not unlike Justin's.

Mindy Ji in her paper hospital gown and paper mask, the only available family member, cradles the infant. A pudgy orderly, grunting with the effort, helps Justin up. A nurse swipes smelling salts under his nostrils. Ursula's little face is purple as a pansy, and Mindy Ji is thinking: (1) my beautiful grandchild, sweet baby, you look like a little bear, all that wild black hair, that face like a fist; (2) poor Liz in your grave, that I never knew, I wish you peace and I promise I'll take up the slack for you; (3) and, by the way—a message from one chamber of Mindy Ji's four-chambered heart to another—where are you, Joe Cimmer, grandpa to this little wondrous thing who—oh, Joe, I know it—would just pop your heart?

THE NOTIFICATION HAS come in the mail: Narita Pete has won the ten-thousand-dollar second prize in the Hefty bag sweepstakes she entered six months ago, and Narita heads out her door yelling, ululating like a fool. Annie hears the whooping outside. Narita runs headlong, barefoot, across the patch of dry dirt with its patches of straggly grass, between the Petes' old gray trailer and Justin and Annie's. She waves the letter above her head. "Ten! Thousand! Dollars!" she shouts. Her voice breaks in a squeal. "Ten! Thousand!"

Annie opens the door, thin metal, light on its hinges, and wobbly, and seeming ready to break off right there in her hand. She stands staring.

"Dollars." Narita says, flat, stopping, blinking. She feels a little silly and waves the paper limply. "Do you believe it?" she says, in almost a whisper. "It's real."

"Let me see," Annie says. "Come on in." Indeed it is real. Narita sits down at the kitchen island, plunks her elbows on the counter, and puts her head in her hands, just disbelief. "Oh, wow!" Annie says.

"You know what I'm going to do, honey? I'm heading across town to the dealer's this afternoon and figure out what we need in a new house. Start putting together an order. Yes ma'am! Is Little One sleeping? You gotta come with me. You're the one with the taste, girl. This here is a down payment on a new mobile home, with maybe some furniture. Whoa, honey."

"They make you pay taxes on it," Annie says. "Don't forget that." She is smiling at Narita's clear delight. Her husband, Henry, drank them into debt for years, but he's been dry and nearly sane now for a couple of years, since sometime during Annie's pregnancy with Ursula. He works regularly, and they can qualify, but they have no down payment piled up.

In Ursula's bedroom there is a scuffling sound: Ursula pulling something down from the dresser, maybe the stuffed polar bear, and the thump of something harder, maybe the canister of wet wipes. Then her little music box starts up, a blue bird with a pouty-mouthed beak that reminds Annie of no one so much as Shirley Temple. When Ursula pulls its string, the blue-bird box plays "It's a Small World" again and again and again.

Narita stops a minute and consults some list in her head. "I wonder how many entries I sent," she muses. Narita has one cupboard in her kitchen set aside for this. She has taped a fancy little Magic Markered sign on its door: KONTEST KUBBARD. Her letters are wizened and crooked, like someone's polio-withered leg. Annie's not sure whether she means to be cute or just can't spell *cupboard*. She keeps contest newsletters and coupons and stamps on the shelf there, and index cards, paper, and scissors. Annie has sat with her several times while she has written out entries: her name and address and so on, sometimes a phrase in big, fat, markered block letters, like DR. SCHOLL'S FOOT POWDER or GO FOR THE GOLD or SPA-BY-THE-SEA/BATH CRYSTALS SOOTHE ME.

Narita says, "I think maybe I only sent five to this one. I think I only had a half-dozen stamps that day, so I sent five to this contest and one to a contest with a Jeep Cherokee as first prize." Narita's car now is a huge seventies-green gas hog that Justin calls Wei Long, Noble Dragon.

One afternoon in Narita's kitchen Annie has watched her letter those Spa-by-the-Sea sheets of paper until the letters swim in front of the eyes of both of them. "Yiii," says Narita. "It makes you either love whatever the stuff is or hate it. You get hypnotized." She pauses for a second. "I think I hate these. I've never bought any, but I think I hate them."

"They smell pretty good, actually," Annie says. "Sort of like melon."

"Maybe someday," Narita says. "Maybe if I win I'll buy me some." The prize in this contest is a trip to a spa by the sea, somewhere on the west coast of Mexico. She imagines Henry on that trip, his careful, recovering-alcoholic walk in his little high-heeled cowboy boots, his spindly legs and his barely restrained little potbelly. She sees him with his dark serious Chippewa face with its sunglasses, sitting stiff and unrelaxed at a beach table with a white canvas umbrella. He looks as if he feels out of place.

"So," says Narita now. "Hey, I hear Little One in there, shaking the crib like a gorilla babe. Whoa, honey, she is one beautiful child. You are so blessed. I'll go bring the car around. I got to call Henry at work and tell him I'll pick him up, and call my sister in Colorado and tell her, but I won't stay on the phone, I promise. I'll probably have to leave a message on her stupid machine and listen to that whole schmoozy song about angels she's got on there, but it'll be quick. Oh, and Cherine." She rolls her eyes. Narita's grown daughter, Cherine, has not been pleasant with her lately, and Narita cannot imagine what she will say when she tells her she's won ten thousand dollars. That her Escort just died again and is in the shop, her boyfriend has vanished the week the rent is due, she's about to run out of cigarettes and she needs money? "Well," Narita says, "maybe I'll tell her a bit down the road." She grins in childish delight. "You can hardly hide a brand-new double-wide, eh."

"I didn't say I was going with you to the dealer's," Annie teases.

"But you are," says Narita. She winks. "I'll be back in a jiff."

At the dealer's Narita aims her car straight for the space beside the double-wide whose vinyl siding is baby blue, the same color as Annie and Justin's trailer. "Some fancy-ass parks, they won't let you have blue," she says. "Only earth tones. My sister out in Littleton, that's the way her park is. Not even white allowed. Too glarish, or something, she said. Earth tones." She shakes her head: what is the world coming to? "You can see the mountains from her park," she says. "Real hard. Gray. Plain old rock."

"Fancy-ass parks, I know nothing about," Annie says, deadpan.

The sales agent is there the second they are inside the door. He sticks out his hand. "Royce Biever," he says. Annie tries to think what he means, as if this were an alien greeting. "That's my name," he says.

"Mrs. Pete's the shopper here," she says. She balances Ursula, nine months old, on her hip, and she uses her cane.

"Yeah," Narita says expansively. "I like this one." She tries to contain herself.

"The Monaco," Royce says. "You've got all the upgrades on this one— your master bath with the Jacuzzi, your oak-veneer cabinets with your frosted-glass inserts, your sculptural carpets." The carpets seem carved and are twenty years out of date. Annie imagines Cheerios burrowing underfoot into the sculpture. She knows Henry would have no opinion on the subject of carpet style. She visualizes his taciturn, impassive face. She makes a sidewise swipe of her eyes in Narita's direction. "I'd pass on the sculptural carpets," she whispers.

"Yeah, the minute you say it I know it," says Narita. "This is what I needed you for, sweetie." She is running her palms deliciously across the kitchen countertops, the color of spinach soufflé and resembling genuine stone. "This is pretty, huh?"

Annie nods yes. "They might have some simpler cabinets, cheaper," she says. She looks at the price list. "If it were me, I'd put that six hundred dollars into, oh, a real fireplace instead of that creepy little electric deal."

"Really?" Narita says.

"Kind of weird you can have a real fireplace in one of these. I would *love* that, myself," Annie says. She has no memory in her cells of her ancestor Violeta as a child at the court of Gustavus Adolphus, squeezing around behind the servants' backs as they sit huddled at a huge fireplace. Or maybe she does, when she longs for a fireplace.

"For the difference I can get a *fireplace?*" Narita says. "Six hundred dollars?"

Royce is standing back listening. "Just feel free to go on, miss," he says. "You're doing my work for me." He grins in a way that is a combination of appreciation and smarminess. His teeth are uneven, and he has a serious underbite. "You want to see the bedrooms? Your master in this one's got your walk-in closet and your cathedral ceiling."

They follow him down the hall. Ursula, looking as serious as Newton atop his tower proving out gravity, leans and drops a fat crumb-dusted raisin from the depths of her jacket pocket into the carpet's deep serpentine curves. The raisin disappears. The bedroom is huge. Narita moans with pleasure. "Oh, jeez, Annie, look at it." Annie does. Narita peers into the master bath. "Oh, honey, check this out!" she squeals to Annie. "Gold faucets! A whirlpool! That neat little window!" Royce is lingering behind in the bedroom, just listening around the doorframe.

Annie whispers, "Lose the gold faucets, and really, I don't like that window, myself, but if you do . . ."

"You think?" says Narita.

"It's awkward and weird-looking," says Annie, "trying somehow to look elegant. Cheesy."

"Cheesy, yeah," whispers Royce under his breath in the next room, agreeing. He smiles to himself. This sale will be a breeze.

"Okay," says Narita. "I trust your taste. Henry says whatever I want is fine with him. What about the skylight?" Narita says.

"Skylights are good," Annie says, decisively. She sighs. "Hey, I think I'm going to have to sit down. This baby is getting pretty heavy right now." Ursula is clapping her hands and throwing her weight around. Eighteen pounds is not all that much but Annie can't carry her long.

Annie heads out to the living room and settles into the not particularly comfy sofa with Ursula, who is getting restless and wants to crawl, while Royce and Narita finish up their tour. Annie pulls her keys out of her purse to amuse Ursula. There is a tiny flashlight on the key chain. She shows Ursula how to turn it on and off.

After a couple dozen ons and offs, the flashlight stops working. Annie picks up a newsmagazine from an end table. On the front cover there is the tear-streaked face of a distraught mother. A few hours south in Michigan, a six-year-old has shot and killed another six-year-old. Ursula wants to see the picture.

"No, honey." The baby grabs at the magazine and crumples the cover in her fist. Annie leans over and picks up another one. It's about hunting. She passes the gun ads and finds a nice picture of deer in the forest, standing staring straight at the photographer. She thinks: *Next minute he was probably dead.* Ursula leans into the magazine, presses her lips to the full-color photograph and gives the deer a big sloppy kiss. Then she tries to snatch away the first magazine.

"Cry!" she says, getting a look at the picture of the bereaved mother on the cover. "Mommy cry!" Annie is still astonished when Ursula talks. This is new, and earlier than Annie expected.

Annie hands Ursula off to Narita while she navigates the stairs, and they cross the parking lot to the office, an even more palatial model called the Medici. Royce mentions this as they are settling down to the table to talk terms. He says, "Me-DEE-see." He says, "When the product literature came in I thought, what? Funny names." He shrugs.

They do the numbers. Yes, with a down payment of the after-tax portion of her prize—which she'll get by the end of the month—Narita and Joe can afford this, based on Joe's job at the plant and Narita's at Taco Bell. Yes,

Royce should be able to get it built and shipped in by the end of next month. They make them custom, he says. Individual.

Narita is deciding: Should she order the model with closer-together studs for strength? (Annie nods yes.) Should she get the glass door in the kitchen even if they can't build a deck right now? (Annie nods yes; Justin will be glad to help Henry do that next summer.) Annie makes her way to the front bay window of the Medici, looking out onto the parking lot.

She blurs her eyes and sees instead in her mind's eye the shore of Lake Superior, some distance out of town, a parcel of land that she has picked out in her imagination, and her own dream house: huge, smooth, honey-colored logs, a second-story porch looking out over blue water, a fireplace with water-washed stones. Already the fire is roaring. There's bread in the oven, some fragrant kind, shot through with small chewy seeds. In the living room there is a dog, golden colored, lying asleep on a big rag rug. She can hear Justin's truck in the driveway. It's sunset.

"Okay, then," says Royce behind her to Narita. "I'll hold on to this order form while I check out those questions you had, like whether those King Louie mirrors will fit in this model . . ."

Narita looks over at Annie, and Annie nods silently and lets her lids drop, no. "Forget the King Louie," Narita says.

Royce is scribbling on his pad. "Oh!" he says. "Did you want built-in shelves in the pantry? That's extra."

"As opposed to what?" says Narita.

"No shelves," Royce says, looking blank.

"If there's no shelves, I don't see how you can call it a pantry," Narita says. "Otherwise it's just a closet, eh."

"You have a point there," Royce says. "But I don't make the rules." He makes a crooked-toothed smile.

"You can give her the shelves, Royce," says Annie. "Come on."

Royce says, "Pardon?"

"Throw in the shelves, guy," says Annie. She says it with motherly authority.

Royce sucks on the end of his pen. He clears his throat in a way that suggests it's his brain that he's clearing. He says, "Well, okay."

"And a living-room set," Annie laughs, feeling her oats. "In blue. Like this one here, but in blue."

"I can't do that," says Royce.

Annie turns to Narita. She smiles nicely. "You know, there's another dealer out the highway where we didn't look yet—Wilderness Homes." There is a new park adjoining the sales lot. Annie tries not to laugh at the name. All the models sit on an asphalt lot, and the new park is sterile, over-civilized. Annie loves their trees, even loves the muddy road that winds up the hill to the park, would not move to a concrete-paved park for the world. "I went to grade school with the son of the owners. His name is Keith. He had a crush on me when I was twelve, even though I was in the hospital most of that year. He'll get us a deal."

"Okay," Royce says, sighing. "The shelves in the pantry. The living-room set. You probably mean with the end tables too, right?"

"Yep. And the coffee table," says Annie.

"You want to order the front and back stair sets?" he asks. "Those are extra."

"Oh," Annie says. She thinks a minute. "What's the alternative to stairs?" The doors are waist height off the ground. "You have to have stairs, right?"

"I guess," says Royce Biever. He sounds slightly sheepish.

"Wilderness Homes says their stairs are free," Annie says, adjusting Ursula on her hip. "I saw it in their ad."

"Take the stairs!" Royce says, in a tone of voice that shows he's just passed his limit.

"Put all that in writing," says Annie. "When Mrs. Pete comes back I'll come too, Royce. I'll bring you a present, for being such a peach of a guy."

Royce perks up. He stands watching the women as they leave.

Over Annie's shoulder, Ursula smiles and waves at the salesman as if he had treated her to ice cream and told her wonderful stories and thrown her up into the air and caught her. Royce Biever blinks in amazement. His girl-friend has been nagging him to get married and have a couple of kids. He resists mightily. So now here is this little girl with the beautiful dark eyes— what is it that's so exotic about those eyes?—and that stunning white hair, like a dandelion puff all around her head, and this little girl loves him!

In the car, when they are out of sight of the salesman, Narita breaks into a roaring guffaw, leaning over the steering wheel. She laughs all the way to the next intersection. Ursula is staring at her, perplexed. When she finishes and wipes her eyes, she says to Annie, "You were great. But what present? What was that all about?"

"Mindy Ji ordered this thing from the Fingerhut catalog," Annie says. She likes to listen to these Christian radio programs in the bathtub, you know? So she ordered this gizmo, a toilet-paper holder with a clock-radio built in, not to mention an emergency siren. She ordered one, and *two* came, so she gave me one. I didn't know what to do with it. So it's a thank-you for Royce Biever, see?"

"An emergency siren?" Narita says, incredulous. "A siren? For what?"

"I don't know," Annie says. "I suppose if you have, like a really big turd you weren't expecting and you need the emergency services people out. Or something." She tries to keep a straight face. Then she bursts out laughing.

"You're lying, girl," Narita says.

"No," Annie says. "There's a siren. About the turd, I just made that up."

"Turd! Turd!" Ursula chants, clapping happily.

That night, Justin and Annie are eating their dinner at the high table, and Ursula is in her high chair throwing nuggets of King Vitaman. Finally she has to be taken down from her chair. The sun has just sunk behind the trees, and the room is swallowed in shadow. Annie lights a couple of candles on the table. Ursula is crawling around the room, pulling a lost toy from under the sofa, crumpling a newspaper, snuffling into the soft belly of a stuffed dog she finds wedged on the shelf with the encyclopedias. She crawls under the table.

"Ursula, under," Annie intones, in a voice that says she is reciting this.

"Utha, unna," says Ursula, looking up at her parents from under the table, and claps her hands in delight.

Annie makes a roller-coaster motion with her hand, for Ursula. "Zoe, zooming," she says, and Ursula parrots it. "Zoe, zoomee. Zoe, zoomee."

"Gitche Gumee," says Justin. He shifts. "So what's this I hear about a sweepstakes, and a new double-wide for Narita and Henry?"

The drone of their talk lulls Ursula, who flops her head onto her arm and falls asleep on the rug. Their talk zigzags into their own dream—a log home out on the shore—then goes on, a version of Royce's walk-through. They decide on a dove gray Jacuzzi with handholds that Annie can manage and slate in the foyer and rocks from the lake for the chimney surround. Justin is talking about his friend who knows a mason outside Marquette who has done lots of these and works out of love, for barter.

"What could we barter?" says Annie. They're stumped. "Hockey lessons?" says Justin. A kid from Marquette would have been born in skates: silly. "Your cardamom bread?" he says. "There is an idea. *I'd* drive 150 miles—" the distance to Marquette—"for your cardamom bread."

They move on to the imaginary master bedroom, and they give it a high ceiling and a clerestory window. They've done this a dozen times, each time slightly different. The time before, Annie had installed in the same place an old glass panel with stylized Art Deco roses she'd seen in a house in a magazine. They cannot conceive of having the money it would take to build a house. Still, they keep planning it, so they'll be ready.

THE SKY ABOVE the trailer court is leached white by the cold. It is 2002, and the rains of October have taken down much of the overhead foliage already, though the scattered pin oaks hold tenaciously to their small leaves, so metal-like, looking as if a sculptor has cut them out with a blowtorch and carefully left them to rust, until spring, when the tree will drop them.

The wind howls through the trees as if through a copse of reed whistles. The Petes' garbage can, an old galvanized one, tips over onto its side and rolls clattering into the rutted drive, its lid careening off into the bushes beyond. A red plastic fire engine belonging to the grandchild of someone across the road wafts featherlight through the yards, unstoppable.

Ursula runs about the living room clapping her hands in terrified glee. "Pook!" she shouts, "Pook!"

"No," Annie says reassuringly, in the tones of a mother who doesn't talk babytalk, who talks to her child as if she were as bright as herself. "It's not spooks, it's just the wind, it's just a *sound* like a whistle, that's all." Annie makes a whistle and a silly face.

"Pook 'issle!" Ursula exults. Annie smiles, imagining what goes on in her head. Ursula runs into Justin and Annie's room and comes back with a large pearlized bass harmonica. She blows into it, slobber spraying everywhere. The sound is great, a low-pitched whine, a whale's fart, a dog's gut rumble.

"Oh, riiight!" agrees Annie, laughing "That *is* what it sounds like."

She leans to take the harmonica from Ursula. "This is Daddy's, okay? You have a whistle in your toy box."

"Har-moni-caaaaa!" shouts Ursula. Her longest and most complex word. "We'll get the whistle now for you," says Annie. "This one is not a toy." Ursula throws herself on the rug and pounds with her fists. "Har-moni-caaaa!" she insists. She caterwauls.

Annie nods her head stoically, quietly, no: you will *not* scream me down. Annie hears a thud and looks out the window. An ornamental shutter. painted bright red again and again, too bright for the dun day, has blown off the oldest trailer within eyeshot and slammed into the trailer next door to it, the one that belongs to the elderly lady who goes every night in a taxi to that bar down on Ashmun. Every time Annie sees her leaving, she watches the bony discomfiture of her walk, which seems to bear its own death wish within it; then when she sees her come home again, unsteady with liquor, she thinks, *Oh, God, let me live that long, but dear Lord, let Justin too. Give us grandchildren, and peace.* Annie's crippling and Liz Maki's premature death made her very old, very young. Overnight.

"You want to read a book?" Annie asks. Ursula stops crying instantly. "You see?" Annie says, no nonsense and grinning, speaking to Ursula as if she were a decade older. "I *thought* that was fake."

Ursula wipes her eyes with her fists. "Somebody's tired," says Annie. Ursula runs to her bookcase, losing a huge blue bunny slipper on the way, and rummages. The books are wedged in together, too many of them for the space.

Ursula pulls on the spine of one and a dozen slender picture books tumble out. "Oof!" she says, falling backward, books everywhere. Atop the shelf, a doll falls over, and the lamp wobbles then settles. Ursula puts her feet— one slippered, one not—straight up into the air, and wiggles her toes.

"Very pink," Annie comments. "And smelling like string cheese, ooo-eee." This is very funny to Ursula. Much giggling.

"You want Winnie?" says Annie, holding up *Winnie-the-Pooh*. No Winnie, yells Ursula. She holds up another book. "You want Clifford?" An enormous red dog fills the front cover. No Kwiffer, Ursula shouts. "You want Little Bear, my little bear?" says Annie. No Weedo Bear, says Ursula. "Okay, says Annie, "*You* tell me what you want."

Ursula looks sober. "Annie, Annie, all about," she intones, as if it were in Latin and she were the pope. A smile of delight breaks over her face. She feels she has done some transgressive grown-up thing, speaking her mother's first name that way.

The book is an oversized alphabet book, well worn, a page per letter. The illustrations, by an artist whose work Annie knows, are light, agile line drawings with watercolor, perhaps tuned more to the eye of an adult. Annie snuggles into the sofa and Ursula climbs up onto her lap, careful of the places that hurt. As always, when Ursula crawls into Annie's lap, she leans to kiss her mother's legs through the skirt, carefully on the bone shield of the knee, a ritual. "Get beddo Mommy wegs," says Ursula.

On the first page, as Annie runs her finger across to show Ursula, are only those four words: *Annie, Annie, all about*. The Annie of the book looks much like Annie Wong—long blond hair, good cheekbones, glasses down low on her nose when she reads—except that of course the book Annie is mobile. She is everywhere. The Annie of the *A* page is a librarian too. In the picture, the old-fashioned library shelves stretch to the very high ceiling. There is an Art Nouveau chandelier. The artist has clearly had fun. Annie is climbing up the rolling ladder to pluck a book from a high shelf. But she is everywhere else as well: at the checkout desk, stamping a little boy's book. Mysteriously perched on the ledge of a high window, releasing into the bright day a bird that has flown in by error and become flustered. Sitting on the front steps of the library, next to the stone lion, basking in the lovely warm sun. There is a wash of gold over the whole picture: the oak of the shelves gleams golden brown, motes of dust dance visibly in the gold shaft of light that streams through the high window. The translucent glass of the chandelier is a pale white gold.

This book is very special to Annie: Justin had given it to her early on when they had begun hanging out—never did "date," she thinks, just take a ride and talk, go for a beer and talk. The gift of the book had moved Annie deeply. A child's alphabet book, from this hockey-playing blues musician in the old pool-colored Soo Gutter pickup? There must (she had thought) be a great deal more than she had guessed inside of him. Mystery.

Ursula yells, "Now *Betsy!*" and Annie reads, "Betsy . . . beneath the bridge." Ursula runs her small index finger over everything on the page, cataloging and naming. Stones. Water. Shadow. Meadow. In the same order each time that they read the book, as a child needs. Betsy wears a green checkered dress and has auburn curls that dance about her shoulder blades. Betsy is not everywhere, all about, like Annie. She is only beneath the bridge, poking a stick in the stream. Through the arch under the bridge we see a meadow where dragonflies hover. The whole scene is green tinted.

"What do you think she is doing?" says Annie, an old routine. "Tuttles!" says Ursula. "Turtles?" says Annie. "I thought you said last time she was finding her bracelet." "I *fib!*" exults Ursula, in rascally glee. She chortles.

"Now Camiwwa!" says Ursula. "Camilla, collecting," says Annie. Camilla is dark-haired, and she wears a blue shift to her knees. She meanders along the seashore, picking up seashells and washed-smooth stones. At the moment she has just found a round pebble of blue glass and is holding it up to the light. Her wicker basket is blue. Her hair ribbon, brilliant indigo, whips in the breeze. The sky is a wash of gradations of blue, flecked with feathery clouds.

"Dana Dana Dana!" chants Ursula, maximum volume. "What is the *matter* with you, crazy person?" Annie laughs. "Dana, dilly-dallying," reads Annie. Dana, in a white nightgown, is heading up the stairs, her candle in its dark candlestick white, the walls all around her white, the toy rabbit she carries white too. She does not want to go to bed, and we can see it in her expression, resistant but awfully sleepy.

THE TRAILER DOOR flies open, and it is Justin. "Daddy Daddy Daddy!" shouts Ursula, rushing him. Annie winces as Ursula jumps from her lap.

"What are *you* doing home?" says Annie.

"Just a drive-by eating," says Justin. "Gotta go back. Wanted to grab a couple of kisses from my woe-men." Ursula smacks loudly, plasters his face with kisses. Justin grabs several slices of bread and smacks them onto the counter. Ursula grabs at his pant legs. "How do you like this wind?" he says to Annie. Weather is one of his favorite subjects. He works in it, as Annie does not.

"Who has seen the wind?" Annie recites from Christina Rossetti, a poem that Ursula knows from another big picture book. "Neither you nor I: / But when the trees bow down their heads, / The wind is passing by." Ursula runs to the window seeming to think that perhaps *this* time she will see the wind.

"Jeez," Justin says. "Ask a simple question, get a librarian answer." He slaps an entire package of lunch meat on three sandwiches and squirts mustard loudly from a plastic bottle.

"Fart!" shouts Ursula in toddler delight at the blurbling sound of the mustard squirt bottle.

"You married the librarian," Annie says. "Nobody made you." Big grin.

"Aye," says Justin, in a *Braveheart* brogue. "Aye, lassie, that I did, and the luckier I." He swoops Ursula up in one hand and twirls her around. He drops her back on the sofa, kisses Annie on the cheekbone, touches Ursula on the tip of her nose, and heads out into the wind with his pile of sandwiches flapping. The door won't close, with the wind, and he pokes his head back inside. "By the way, short person," he says to Ursula, "*you* are the fart, not me." He pulls the door shut behind him.

Ursula giggles. "Daddy talk silly," she says solemnly, analytically, to Annie.

"He does," says Annie, agreeing soberly. "Do you want to finish the book?" Ursula flips through the pages. No, she does not want to see Emma entertaining, serving tea to stuffed animals propped at a table, with tiny teapot and cups to match. No, she does not want to see Fiona, ferrying her dog in a rowboat across a stream. Nor does she want to see Gillian growing, marking her height on a chart on a vertical ruler on wallpaper that shows umbrellas and ribbons and bouquets in lavender, seeming to fall from the sky. She does not want to see Hedy hemming, Iris imagining, Johanna juggling. She flips wildly, all the way to the back of the book. Annie thinks it's a wonder the book hasn't torn to shreds by now.

"Ussuwa!" she exults. "Ussuwa, unda!"

"Ursula, under," Annie reads. The Ursula in the book is blond too, with big brown eyes like Ursula's own. Annie imagines when she looks at the page that the picture child has an Asian cast to her features, but she argues back: *That's only my imagination.* Ursula on the page is under a kitchen table, with sheets and blankets draped all around. A sense of safety and bowerlike enclosure pervade the scene.

She lays the book aside and hugs the little girl close. *Amazing,* she thinks. She had never imagined, with her body so badly broken, that she could have a child, nor that a guy with as much life in him as Justin would have been interested in a "cripple," as she calls herself in her head. It is her father's voice that speaks the word.

THE DARK TWO-LANE ribbon of state road swerves into the forest and narrows. The trees press closer to the asphalt, like gawkers. Ursula smashes her nose to the window in her little seat behind Justin, breathes out a fog on the glass, squeals and claps her hands in delight. The canopy of spindly bare branches overhead, meeting above the road, makes a cozy tunnel, and even though the leaves have all shriveled and dried and dropped off, the lattice of branches shadows the road and shuts out most of the sun.

"Oooh!" says Ursula. "Like my house!" she shouts. Well, yes, the feel of the forest is like the woods around the Wongs' trailer back home, three hours' drive east, if this is what she means, Justin thinks. "Castle!"

"Castle?" says Justin. No buildings are anywhere near.

"She means," Annie explains, "this looks like a picture in that huge book. You know, where the forest grows up around Sleeping Beauty's castle. All you can see in the picture is trees, with a little glint of color off in the distance, deep in the forest. That's the castle." It never ceases to amaze him, the way Annie can read her mind.

"Gotcha," says Justin. The entire bookcase in Ursula's room is filled with picture books, many of them from the library sale, others presents from Mindy Ji or Tasha. Then there's the bookcase in the hall and the one in the bathroom, for crying out loud. Not to mention the piles on the sofa and next to her bed. "Unh-*hunh. That* picture."

They have driven here this morning, the week before Ursula's second birthday, for the ceremony at the dedication of the new monument at the site of the Meridel-Pflaum disaster. Jake Maki's name is there on the bronze plaque, along with all the others who died in the mine collapse, though his body and the six others who were pulled out of the lowest drift are not entombed along with the rest, in the now capped and fenced shaft just a few hundred feet into the woods.

JAKE MAKI, SUPERINTENDENT, it says at the top, in letters carved into the bronze. It seems somehow to Annie as if this makes him responsible, as if he had had or should have had some superior powers, the power to stop the cave-in, surely the power to save all those lives that were lost. Annie gets angry as she realizes she's thinking this. *He was only twenty-nine!* she protests, deep inside herself, as if someone were blaming her great-grandfather for the collapse of the mine. No one is, of course. Twenty-nine: Justin's age. A very young man.

The little girl who held her mother's blue crystal rosary up to the light and watched the prisms' rainbows dance does not pray, grown up now, the same way her mother did. Times when her mother would have retired to the chapel grotto of her heart, where little stubs of white beeswax candles flickered, Annie climbs up on her soapbox inside—her spirit does not need a walker—and yells at God instead.

It is this outrage in her that calls out to the bluesy free-floating rage that Justin carries around with him: each of them shelters the other, holds the other, rocks, croons, comforts. A therapist would tell them, solemnly, as if it explained away anything, that Justin finds in Annie his own version of Mindy Ji, her spunk, her cookie dough; that Annie recognizes in Justin the anger of Garrett and wants to heal it, despite the fact that her mother could not with all her buckets of prayer haul Garrett up out of his darkness.

Justin could live with this, though he has no use for what he calls psychobabble. He senses clearly the solidity at Annie's center, as at Mindy Ji's. He would say, Okay. So fucking what?

Annie would resist mightily. Justin is nothing like my father, she'd say. She would start to say more, but it all would devolve to a condemnation of her father for the waste of her mother's life . . . She cannot go there, for it takes her into the dark, to the unanswered question of Liz's death once again.

And so she would clamp her lips shut, and lean over and hold tight to Justin's forearm as if to reassure him—of what, she doesn't know. In the process of squeezing Justin's arm, wordless, feeling the clench of her heart, Annie would remember her mother repeating, *But Annie, before he went off to the war, he was not this way. He was a gentle spirit.* And that would just make it all worse.

AT THE MERIDEL-PFLAUM monument, a granite obelisk at the edge of a parking lot set into the forest, Ursula fidgets. Meridel-Pflaum no longer operates their three mines in the county: over the decades one after another has shut down. At their peak they had provided a quarter of the country's iron ore, says the speaker. Ursula wriggles down from Justin's arms and tries to waddle away. He scoops her back up. A representative of the company is talking at great length about progress in mine safety, quoting statistics.

Annie wishes he'd have pulled in some human stories. But then, she thinks, what would he say? Here are the names of some miners today who have *not* been lost? Only loss makes a story. Things going well makes no story at all. Then the Meridel-Pflaum guy says all of the mines are shut down. "Now *that* is safety," Justin stage-whispers, leaning over to Annie.

A woman whose great-grandfather is entombed in the mine speaks, with tears in her eyes. She tells a story of him as a teenager, singing at a church service, and she tells it as if she had been there, though he died two decades before she was born. She holds up his picture, an enormous enlargement. In the picture he is bright-eyed and yet somehow sad in anticipation, as if he had recently been told his life would not go on much longer. She makes the audience want to exhume him, resuscitate him, have him sing "Amazing Grace," right there on the spot. The man, a Cornishman, is in the woman's eyes a hero, as if he had given his life that she might live. *That's better,* thinks Annie. *A story, at least.*

A state legislator launches into a speech about legal initiatives he is cosponsoring, to allocate funds to find and cap old disused mine shafts that dot the area, both here and out in the Keweenaw, in the copper country where Jake Maki lived as a child. Annie tries to imagine that terrain, where she has never been. She listens a while and then tunes out. She is tired of standing and makes her way back to where she had seen Justin and Ursula. They are nowhere in sight.

She finds a bench and wraps herself tighter in the shawl she has thrown over her coat. Justin has probably taken Ursula to get something to eat. Little Debbies, Ursula loves to shout. Brownies or oatmeal pies, something she can sink her teeth into. Not chips or candy. It will be fine: Justin will sniff them out.

Annie snuffles her hot moist breath into the fringe of her shawl, to warm herself. Someone else might get up and stomp around to keep warm, but she cannot. Tears rise to her eyes but she is not sure whether they are from the wind or the rage and self-pity she tries to tamp down, again and again. People who don't know her up close think her a gentle spirit, submissive. Only Ursula comforts her in that respect, that rage and that self-pity, though Justin can hold her and make her feel loved. It is as if the little girl is the healed version of Annie. All of her hope for redemption and healing is balled up there.

Annie peers around searching for Justin and Ursula but cannot find them. She twists and dips her head till she sees Ursula's red snowsuit, Mindy Ji's gift the previous Christmas, the color of Qin Lao's cinnabar, a flash in the gray day, which she wears despite the fact that there is no snow yet, and Justin in his tan Carhartt jacket carrying her on his shoulders.

All this blather about sacrifice reminds Annie of World War II speeches, overwrought with myths of heroism. In Annie's eyes all of that business— as well as her father's time in Vietnam—was a pathetic bloodletting, no more. Garrett had brought home a Purple Heart from Vietnam: he had happened to be hit by a stray piece of shrapnel from a detonated mine. His best friend in his unit was point man on that patrol, Liz had said. He died. Blown to pieces. I don't think your father ever got over that.

The young man who had died had been third in his high-school class, from somewhere out west—Utah? Colorado?—and he and Garrett had met in AIT—advanced infantry training. The guy had been planning on going to dental school on his return. Liz tells this to Annie when she is nine. Annie remembers her mom's face when she says that Garrett was different before Vietnam. She has never known what to do with that information, so she shuts that vault again. Slam. Maybe later.

A band from a nearby community college strikes up a song, off-key and unrecognizable. Annie watches the face of the tuba player, a thin, young man whose cheeks bulge like a frog's, rhythmically, with each note. His hat tips precariously forward as he plays, and he is struggling to read his music without losing it. She imagines him in a Budweiser commercial, on a lily pad. She surveys the backs of the crowd, because from her bench she can no longer see the speaker's platform, though she can hear the speaker's voice when the wind is blowing the right way.

In the back row of spectators she counts three Detroit Pistons starter jackets and two coats she knows came from Wal-Mart, because she has seen them hanging on racks at the Wal-Mart at home. One has fake fur at its neck, and Annie thinks, *It's from a fake fox,* and almost laughs.

Justin is limping slightly from an accident the week before: a scaffolding slipped and dropped him three feet, spraining his left ankle and doing—the doctor who's checked him says—potential nerve damage, not terrible, only slight. His loping walk is only slightly altered, but each time Annie sees him wince when he puts his foot down wrong, she feels mortal and misses Justin as badly as if he had died in the fall, even though he is there in full view.

Even from this distance Annie can see the gleam of Justin's broad forehead. He hates to wear hats, so the most recent stocking cap Mindy Ji has knitted him is stuffed into his pocket. A loose lock of black hair is sweat-pasted to Justin's skin. He's talking nonstop to Ursula. From the lilt and bob of his head, it would seem he is telling her some silly story. He is beaming with pride, as if he were parading this beautiful little girl for everyone. *See our miracle?*

She feels herself anticipating a time fifty years in the future, their old age, and Justin dying before her. *Men do that,* she thinks. It makes her just furious. She imagines Ursula grown, a grandmother herself. She visits his grave with Ursula, her hair now white and tied back in a knot, but in the imagining she does not include her walker. It's not conscious, but just as in her mind she leaps on her soapbox and yells at God, in her vision that takes her to the middle of the century, she see herself without her walker, whole.

Annie navigates to the side of the gathering where she can see to the front. Someone places a wreath on the monument. The flowers are garish and bright, unnatural colors in the November day. The ribbon is plastic and terrible. Annie thinks: *Why are we here? Why did I insist we come?* Yet it is, after all, *her* grandfather who died here, not Justin's, who died of old age before Justin was born. She thinks: *Neither of us knew our grandfathers, both of us had fathers who were not really there.*

The ceremony seems interminable. She checks her watch. It has been twenty minutes so far. Next up is a young English professor from a nearby university. The introducer says he has degrees from Johns Hopkins and Syracuse and has published an essay recently in the university's literary magazine, about searching through slag from the mine, and finding garnets: a metaphoric meditation on the meaning of that. Annie hears herself sniff. But that's nothing new. Everyone knows that. There have always been garnets in slag. He has also published two books of poems with a press in Nebraska whose name no one but Annie has ever heard.

Annie dislikes the man immediately. As he meanders into his talk, he seems to weave in and out of an accent whose genuineness she doubts deeply: what, pseudo-Welsh? She has an impulse to pull herself up onto the platform and order him down. There is just something obnoxious about the toss of his forelock and the fact that on this cold day he has ostentatiously taken off his coat to speak, displaying the beautiful hand-knitted sweater beneath.

Annie is guessing its price as she watches him unfold the manuscript of his speech, as slowly as if he were eighty. She is sure that, unlike Justin's stocking cap, it has not been knitted by anyone who loves him, but by desperate widows somewhere in the Hebrides in their dark cottages, trying to keep their fires going.

A silk paisley scarf in rich russets and browns wraps lightly, tenuously around his neck, and threatens to blow away in the wind. Annie wills that to happen: *Blow away, please blow away.* She inspects her own anger: This young man has done nothing but appear callow, for less than a minute. Why is she so angry? She looks around again for Justin and Annie. She wonders whether her anger will turn her into a witch in her old age. Then she thinks: *Old age? What makes me so sure I will live to be old? My grandfather died at twenty-nine, the same age Justin is now.*

She leans on her walker and cocks her head, watching the poet-professor read, somewhat calmed. She chides herself. He turns his head just slightly and she realizes what her rage is about. His face is a good deal like the face of her grandfather, in a picture on a poster her father had, in a black plastic frame, facedown in the desk drawer.

JAKE MAKI FOR COUNTY MINING SUPERVISOR, the poster announced. Its date was two months before the collapse of the mine. Jake Maki, the little boy his mother Marjatta had hoped would become a teacher, something respectable and on the earth's surface, winds up instead down in the mine, and the mine falls in on him. Annie feels tears in her eyes and does not even blink them away. The wind is harsh. *No one cares. Why is* anyone *here anyway?* Annie swipes at her eyes with her shawl.

The young poet is quoting from John F. Kennedy's *Profiles in Courage.* Annie finds this odd for a poet. Perhaps somebody has told him this is not an audience to whom to quote Rilke. That he ought, in his pseudo-Welsh way, to ring this particular grating chord. He is saying: These men buried deep in the earth beneath the feet of all those present—these men are all heroes. The crowd applauds.

The young poet reads from Kennedy's *Profiles in Courage:* "For without belittling the courage with which men have died, we should not forget those acts of courage with which men have lived. . . . A man does what he must— in spite of personal consequences, in spite of obstacles and dangers and pressures—and that is the basis of all human morality."

Annie is not sure he believes himself. This poet looks as if morality is not his usual terrain, as if he would have preferred to talk on the subject of paisleys, or terza rima, or the dumbing down of American college students at the beginning of the twenty-first century. Or then there was that silly riff on those garnets in slag, but he's been asked to do this, and he will, damn it.

He says, simply, These men went to work. They supported their families, as men did then.

Annie hears this as an oblique and effete attempt to be somehow femi-
nist, to acknowledge that women work now. *Okay, poet. Women worked then,
too. They just didn't get paychecks.*

The poet goes on, on the subject of heroism as demonstrated in the life
and words of John F. Kennedy. Annie wonders how long this silly man
thought about this—five minutes?—and whether there wasn't someone
else whose words he could be citing. An iron-mining poet, perhaps? Is there
such a person? When Kennedy was a young naval officer, he had his boat
sunk out from under him and survived, says the poet who looks like Jake
Maki. He turns his head again, that way, to knock his forelock out of his
eyes, and Annie confirms the resemblance, uncanny.

As a librarian, Annie is aware that this generation of schoolkids does not
know that fact about Kennedy. As they do not know many facts at all: *Ex-
cuse me, miss, is the Civil War the same thing as the Battle of Gettysburg? Pardon me, did Eli Whitney invent something, or what? No, just tell me, okay? I
don't have time to go find the encyclopedias.*

She approves despite herself of the way this poet presents it, straightfor-
wardly, without condescension, but she feels angry again at all this dumbing down. She does not know that Marjatta would have been even angrier
at the way matters have gone, given all her hopes for this new land.

The poet says: "When JFK was asked how he became a hero, he replied,
'It was involuntary. They sank my boat.'" He pauses, expecting some sort of
response. The audience is waiting for him to explain. He clears his throat.
He brushes away his forelock with the back of his hand.

Annie can stand no more. Clearly the poet has nowhere to go with this.
Kennedy's humor does a terrible dance, out of context, a dance of the bones.
What will he say, that these men entombed in the mine were not voluntary
heroes? Will he make a joke, as JFK had? But it was his own life, and he lived,
even if to be cut down at Dallas, by whomever, why ever. And what will the
audience, many of them the descendants of these men whose names are
there on the bronze plaque, do then—mob him?

Just then she sees Justin coming toward her and simultaneously she hears
Ursula calling, "Mommy, Mommy." She is still up on Justin's shoulders. Annie turns and mouths it to Justin: *Get me out of here.*

Justin frowns. *Why?*

Annie says it out loud. "Let's just go."

Justin places his right hand on her back as they walk, balancing Ursula with his left. When they get away from the crowd, he says, "What's the deal? Overload?"

She looks at him and starts to cry. "Maybe. Displacement. That damned poet looked like my great-grandfather who never got to see his kids grow up."

"We couldn't find Little Debbies," says Justin. "No vending machines anywhere."

"Yeah, well. That too," Annie says, laughing through her crying, as if the seventy-five years' past disaster and the absence of oatmeal-pie vending machines were of equal weight.

"No Debbies!" says Ursula. "Let's find a store."

"Chill," says Justin. "Grandma Mindy made cookies. They're in the car. Chill."

"I want De-e-e-ebbies," Ursula intones, and Justin groans.

"There are no stores," Annie says. "You know you love Grandma Mindy's."

Ursula starts up a moan. Justin can't stand it when she moans. He wants to pull Little Debbies down from the trees for her.

"She'll be fine," Annie says. To Ursula, she says, "We've got egg salad, honey, in the truck, and juice boxes, and Fruit Roll-Ups, and Grandma Mindy's cookies, with raisins—"

Ursula says, "I saw a store! I saw a store!"

"Fifty miles back," says Annie to Justin. "She means that convenience store near Seney, with the antlers on the wall."

"Debbies!" shouts Ursula. "Debbies!"

"Grandma Mindy's feelings will be hurt if you'd rather have Debbies than her raisin cookies," Justin jokes. "She'll be ticked."

"Tick!" shouts Ursula. "Tick-tock! Tick-tock!"

Justin takes his hand from Annie's back and sways Ursula side to side, pendulum-like, a bedtime game.

"Tick-tock!" she shouts, distracted. "Tick-tock. The mouse run down!"

8   A Foundling at the Court

D ARKNESS ENVELOPS STOCKHOLM almost round the clock at
this time of the year. As the year rolls downhill into the drear
purgatory of the winter solstice, three hours of weak light
in midday are the sole evidence that life even half-intends to go on. It is in
midafternoon of the winter solstice that the strange event happens, in the
gray-gold ombre period, not quite full dark, perhaps three o'clock.

A silhouette of indeterminate gender, dressed in a raggedy wool cape almost to the ground, appears in one of the castle's minor courtyards, climbing down from a tradesman's carriage. The figure is off-loading crates,
setting them near the door leading into a basement hall, doing this in perfect silence.

The figure stands, considering, then climbs up into the carriage again
and pulls out from under a blanket a high-handled raffia basket. The bulk
of the basket is awkward, though it does not seem heavy. The shadowy figure holds the basket away from its body and walks with some difficulty. The
rounded paving stones are icy. The fountain at the center of the courtyard
flows in summer with clear water and the wiggly diaphanous swimmings of
golden fish. Now it is still and dark, though it is not frozen over because a
spring empties into it from underground. The figure walks to the rim of the
fountain, runs a hand as if in a final check over the pitch-besmeared bottom
of the basket, sets it in the water, then stands back and muses as the thing
floats. So strange, in the half-light: the black water reflects the sole lantern
in the scene, hanging from a stone wall near the tradesmen's door.

The figure tugs hard at the bellpull. The white-capped head of a kitchen maid appears in a window just above.

"Yes?" she calls down.

"Cheeses from Holland!" announces the figure. "Brown rind and red rind. All excellent."

"What did you say? Did you say cheeses?" the maid calls.

The caped figure seems to reconsider. Perhaps some other item will seem more urgent.

"Flowers from the . . . ambassador," says the caped person, a revised attempt. "For My Lady Queen, in celebration of her giving birth to an heir."

"Hardly!" the maid shouts down. "The child was a girl, and it's said it was born with three teats and fur all over its body and a caul over that. Hardly a matter to celebrate!"

"They have come from the far Azores," says the figure, a clearly feigned harshness. "If you do not hurry your insolent buttocks down here they will wilt, or freeze, and we will have yet one more international incident on our hands. Hurry!" The figure climbs into the carriage, puts a whip to the horse's flank, and rides clattering over the cobblestones into the night.

The maid closes the shutters and turns to consider. *My insolent buttocks,* she thinks, for she has indeed heard the second series of remarks, as the wind shifted. She laughs, imagining her buttocks talking back to this man, if indeed—as the timbre of the voice seemed to suggest—it was a man. Then she thinks: *Flowers?* If somehow indeed there are flowers down there at the door they will freeze in a moment, and I will be flogged.

So she takes up a lantern and hastens down the narrow, curving stairs, catching her breath in astonishment as a rat slips from a crevice and darts across her path. She unbolts the door and stares puzzled at the stack of crates. Flowers? In crates? She tries to lift the top one. Indeed, it is empty. And so is the second one in the stack. She is puzzled. A piece of paper flies loose from the second crate's side, where it had been loosely fastened.

"Look in the fountain," it says. She feels a smile unfolding itself in her face. What is this game? She is one of only a few servants here who can read: she deals with the tradespeople's bills, and so she must both read and calculate. The crates sit helter-skelter now, all three light and empty and scattered. The paper is in her hand. She goes to the fountain.

On the skin of the water, which reflects back her candle now as well as the wall-hanging lantern, there is a dark basket, finely and tightly woven, like a little boat, floating. She cannot reach it from where she is. Are the flowers in here? She circles to the far side of the fountain. A sound, like a cat, a slight mewling, from under the blanket inside this basket.

She leans out over the water, holding her shawl close, trying not to lose her balance, and grabs for the handle. That mewling again! No one here needs a basket of cats. She remembers the rat on the stairs and rethinks that. She wonders how deep the fountain is, whether it extends into the earth like the shaft of a well. She stretches herself out over the dark water, the fringe of her shawl just dipping into the water, and with two fingers hooks the handle and pulls it to her. One more mewl. She hauls the basket out of the water.

She sets it, dripping, on the smooth stones of the courtyard, and unfolds the blanket. *My God, a child!* Not many days old, wild dark hair, tiny black eyes hardly open, fat red cheeks, fists unclenching and clenching again and then opening once more! She throws the blanket back across the child, covering it entirely, and scurries up the stairs, wailing with strange consternation. She does not even realize the wail is coming from her. The baby wails with her, muffled and scuffling under the shawl.

In the servants' quarters there is much hubbub now. Two days before, a maid has given birth to a child who died without drawing breath. No one has known what to do: the birth was a surprise, and the mother lies bleeding weakly in her bed, and the maids flutter and whisper, terrified. Of what, they are not really certain.

The dead child is laid on a shelf in the basement, coins on its eyes, not an arm's length from the palace stash of lingonberry preserves for the breakfast bread of Gustavus Adolphus and his little-loved, whiny queen, Maria Eleonora. No one but the palace maids knows that the child is there.

The second day, a middle-aged pastry cook, taking matters into her own hands, has a tinker cart the body to the church, where he leaves it on the step, bound up in a blanket and laid in a basket not unlike the one in the fountain. The old sexton, folding the blanket aside, mutters, from Jeremiah, as if soliloquizing before an audience of none but the stars, "The heart of man is desperately wicked: who can know it?" He arranges for the child to be buried in the paupers' section of the churchyard.

The very afternoon the tiny dark-eyed child is arriving at the palace, announced as a cheese or as flowers, the dead child of the maid is laid in the earth, the gravediggers arguing whether the hole is deep enough, whether the earth is too hard to keep trying. One of the gravediggers is very drunk, the other too tired either to argue or to dig. He leans instead on his shovel handle and cradles his head.

The maid who has scurried up the dark, winding stairs with the live child is making noises no one can decipher, as she sets the basket down on the kitchen floor. "In the fountain!" she says. "Eeyow! Woo! He was yelling. Oh, aaargh. About cheeses from Holland! My, eeee! About flowers from the Azores! And then . . . there's this *baby!*" She sets down her lantern and stands, fists on her hips. The blanket flaps around, seemingly of its own accord, and the baby yowls, startling the kitchen maids.

A matter-of-fact woman, several times a grandmother, picks up the basket and heads for the bed where the mother of the dead baby lies in her postpartum moaning. The wooden heels of her shoes knock loudly against the stone floor. The heel noise resounds in the passageways and echoes off the walls.

"Here! Sit up!" she orders. "None of that!" she chides. "Nurse this child."

The girl rolls over, groggy, and half sits up. She blinks for a moment in silence. "What did you say?"

"I said sit up." She pulls the girl to a sitting position. She unlaces her bodice. Her fine full white breasts pop out, pink-brown nipples erect. The grandmother-maid leans over and hefts the girl's full bosoms as if they were melons at market. "Ooh, good ones!" she says.

Something in her remembers suddenly when her own breasts, now shrunken dugs, were this lovely. She will tell her husband about the moment, the memory, that evening, and he will say, smiling, "Yes, and I remember too," and place his hands on her, and say then, "Come here, old woman."

"Your hands are cold," says the girl to the woman now.

"This is not your own child," says the woman, to make sure the girl is not disoriented. "You know that."

"I know that," the girl says, devoid of emotion. "My child died."

"Nobody knows where this child came from," says the woman. "Just feed it. For now. Keep it quiet, and keep your nice titties from going to fever."

The child belongs to a Forest Finn girl, gotten off a rye farmer from deep inland who had already had a wife. The rye farmer owned the girl, in some kind of arrangement the girl had not understood, but only recently had he explained to her that his rights extended to her bed as well. She was the only girl on the farm—there were three male farmhands—and she could not ask the mistress, of course—what would she say: Oh, mistress, the husband says . . . ? Oh, mistress, the husband wants . . . ? No, this is an unworkable proposition: if she desires to eat and sleep, she must comply, and in silence. The rye farmer has a fat white hairy belly and tits like a woman's. His teeth are bad. His breath stinks.

The rye farmer's father had emigrated to Sweden a quarter century before, crossing the Gulf of Bothnia with most of his village to start a new life in the forests of the interior there. Still, they were Finns, remained Finns: they lived among Finns, they spoke Finnish, they grew rye like Finns, and like Finns they burn-beat the forests.

This burn-beating—*huuhta,* in Finnish—is a technology ages old, used all over the world by tribal and nomadic peoples, to compensate for bad growing weather: forestland is burned, carefully, skillfully, and rye seed sown in the ashes for a phenomenal return.

The Swedes, blessed by better weather and unaccustomed to this way of farming, for some years manage to ignore the Finns: they are out of sight, out of mind. In the past few years, however, available land has begun shrinking as the population expands. There is pressure to get rid of these crazy Finns who will go burning the forests down—no one knows why, they just know as God's truth that all Finns practice witchcraft and moreover get ninefold and twelvefold returns on their rye seed. Thus, counting in the fact of the practice of *huuhta* itself, Finns are thrice suspect.

The Forest Finn girl has, when her belly begins to show, run away to the capital, thinking that when the time comes to deliver she will think what to do. But then she comes suddenly to delivery, and as the woman in whose barn the girl has taken shelter cradles the child in the crook of her arm, admiring the sweet roundness of her head so soon after birth, the Forest Finn girl suddenly dies: closes her eyes, fades quietly, instantly. As she breathes out, she thinks, as if agreeing to her own departure, of the rye farmer's hairy white belly and dark, sour breath that smells like nothing so much as it does like a horse's fart, and she gives a small laugh, then expires.

The midwife's husband, who delivers goods for a cheesemaker, agrees to take the child somewhere. Somewhere safe, says the midwife. It must be safe. "Perhaps the palace?" her husband proposes, in a tone that seems half joke, half not. He laughs heartily. "I hear the new daughter there is a bit of a monster. Perhaps they'll exchange her for this one, and this one will be the queen, and no one but ourselves will have an inkling."

They laugh, and it is too absurd, but he does it. The midwife's husband has a reputation as one who will never pass up a dare or a practical joke. What in life, the midwife and her husband ask each other, is not absurd? They fold aside the blanket that covers the child as she sleeps. "Like a little bear cub," says the midwife. "Pikku Pentu," says one of the Finnish maids, peering over her shoulder. "A little bear cub."

And so the child of the toothless rye farmer comes to the palace of Gustavus Adolphus and his German queen, Maria Eleonora. She is a peculiar "twin" to the newborn Christina, the heir to the throne: the two have been born on the very same day, the eighth of December, 1626. The third child, the tiny corpse interred in the paupers' quadrant of a Lutheran parish church on a small island in the Stockholm archipelago, is also a girl. The third child, never named, will never be mentioned to either the first or the second.

The girl-child of the toothless rye farmer and the dead slave girl becomes the delight of the housemaids, who raise her in common, in their own quarters, though Jasmin, the wet-nurse, spends more time with the baby than the others. As the first months of her life pass, the infant's hair and eyes change color: her dark hair progressively vanishes and is replaced first by a naked head and then by white tufty chick fur; her eyes lighten until they are an extremely pale blue.

No one knows who her mother and father were, but a note in the basket that floated the baby in the fountain had said, as if in the baby's voice, *I am a Finn.* "Nonetheless, very likely very fine folk, to look at the little one," says one of the housemaids. The child has the looks, in her facial bones, that its wretched father had had as an infant, the birdwing shape of the bones above the eyes that in the father came to seem a wretched and permanent scowl; the tip-tilted nose that in the child is pert and delicate was in the father discolored by drink, its nostrils distended in a sneer of unearned pride. How easily do we fall from our first beauty!

"Perhaps the mother was a witch," says another servant. "Any Finn can curdle milk or give you smallpox just by thinking about it."

"I know it," an old woman concurs, her eyebrows lifting in terror and assurance. "They know spells. They can fly. They can change themselves into birds or reindeer and spy on us." She shakes her head earnestly.

"Not true," says someone else. "I lived with a Finn milkmaid once. She was just like us." No one seems to be listening to her.

"Perhaps the child was gotten rid of because the father was afraid of being transformed to a reindeer," ventures a maid.

"Men!" expostulates another. "Always afraid!"

The wet-nurse, Jasmin, has a great deal of milk indeed, and as she nurses the child, it grows chubby and round. One afternoon, nursing the baby while she is wrapped in a purple blanket, her face peering out of the middle of it as out of the petals of a pansy, the wet-nurse names the child Violeta, in her own mind, and it does not occur to anyone to ask about a name until months have passed. "Violeta," says Jasmin. "Violeta Solveig."

"But Solveig is a Norwegian name!" protests the laundress who has inquired.

"Is that not the same as Finn?" Jasmin asks. She is suckling the child at the moment.

"Not at all," says the laundress.

"Oh," says Jasmin flatly. "That is strange." So, odd as it may be, the child's name is Violeta Solveig. While Swedes and Norwegians down the centuries will each make jokes about the other, no one outside of Swedes and Norwegians will ever understand the hilarity—or aversion—such a name might evoke in a Swede.

As for the distinction between Swedes and Finns, that will remain a shape-shifting dance until 1917, at which time Finland is no longer Sweden's and no longer Russia's. But then in the Second World War, all the games start up once again. In the Sweden of Gustavus Adolphus, no one knows how many times borders and flags will shift, nor does anyone care.

IN ANOTHER PART of the palace, the infant Christina is being raised, the child who will, as her subjects assert, "by the grace of God"— rather, of course, than by accident of birth—become Queen of the Swedes, Goths, and Vandals, Great Princess of Finland, Duchess of Estonia and Karelia and Lady of Ingria.

It is a miserable infancy. The hair that has covered her body falls out, and she looks far more like a human being. Yet she is a homely child.

In later years, troubled by a curvature of the spine, Christina will believe that she has been repeatedly dropped on the floor by her mother, who she is sure hates her, as well as by servants at her mother's behest. When she poses for paintings, the portraitists invariably choose one of two options: to pose Christina at an angle or simply to falsify.

Maria Eleonora, frail and isolated, has created her own society within the circle of her ladies-in-waiting, brought from Berlin. She dotes on her handsome and well-loved husband, the king, who, in the manner of nobility of the time—as of any time—has had his rascally affairs of the heart and the loins before he has been matched up with her just-right blend of frivolous prettiness and dynastic suitability. Ten years before Christina's birth, he has sired a son, Gustav Gustavsson, off a girl in Vasaborg, but the son is ignored as a possible heir.

Gustavus Adolphus shares Maria Eleonora's dilettante quirk for architecture. Together over glasses of dark red wine brought from the Mediterranean, they play at night with maps of the kingdom and more detailed maps of the numerous small islands that dot the Stockholm archipelago, the king discoursing for the queen's delectation about how he will transform this wretched collection of single-storied turf-roofed houses that surround the turreted castle into a city of beauty. But of course this is more about power, his own, than about architecture. The king has played the lute for years, as easily as if he were a swarthy papist Italian, and now he begins to import for his queen fine court musicians.

The queen had lost a pregnancy a year after their marriage, and then a daughter, who lived only a few months. She whined and wished for Berlin and then whined some more. Two years before the birth of Christina who would be queen, Maria Eleonora had, in advanced pregnancy, gone with her husband, the king, to review the fleet. The warships were moored within view of the palace, just across the water off the island of Skeppsholmen. It was a lovely cool day in the calm of autumn. The queen boarded the royal yacht. Suddenly a great wind arose. The yacht tipped violently, scooped water, threw itself back, nearly upright. The king, alarmed for the queen's safety, instructed his pilot to head back to shore, immediately. The queen debarked, white-faced from the terror of the capsizing and awkward with the bulk of the child. She climbed into a carriage and came to the castle over roads rutted by autumn rains then hardened to nastiness by the cold.

Not long after she arrived at the palace she exclaimed, "Jesus, I cannot feel my child!" The legitimate son that Gustavus Adolphus has longed for was born dead. Maria Eleonora sank into despondency. The king had to go abroad once more; the queen was hysterical with grief. There was now only one surviving male heir in the Vasa line. The king's brother had died three years before in battle, leaving as the only Vasa qualified to fill the Swedish throne one Władysław IV Sigismund of Poland.

Władysław IV Sigismund of Poland, oddly enough (or reasonably enough or absurdly enough) will, by way of a youthful dalliance unknown to historians, become the Polish-American runaway harmonica player Joe "Rapdander" Cimmer's—Tsimmer's—ancestor, a baker's dozen generations removed from Joe:

1. Władysław Sigismund's bastard son grows up in his mother's ancestral village to be a shoemaker.
2. The shoemaker's daughter, to her family's shame, marries a gypsy and gives birth at the age of seventeen, in midsummer 1702, in a bright green gypsy cart, in what is today Romania, to
3. a daughter who marries a house carpenter and at the age of forty, her hair fast graying, gives birth to

4. her eleventh child, a much-cosseted musical prodigy who after his mother's death when he is in his teens, oh, sigh, becomes an itinerant musician. In the course of his foolish and mostly misspent life, he nonetheless travels as a pilgrim to the Holy Land: there, as he trudges up Mount Horeb for the view, he decides to convert to Judaism. Upon his return to Eastern Europe, fulfilling a vow to his dying mother, he weds a homely but buxom cousin, with whom he produces in 1776, as across the Atlantic a number of colonists are signing the Declaration of Independence

5. a deaf daughter with beautiful hazel eyes and chestnut hair that falls in ringlets, who cannot hear her father's music—which handicap he in his fatalistic and guilt-ridden way ascribes to the sins of his youth—who marries a quiet man who does not mind that she cannot hear him, as he does not talk much anyway, and she is a delight to his eyes. This chestnut-haired daughter of the Holy Land pilgrim gives birth to

6. a tall, strapping son with extremely acute hearing and a head for business, who becomes a prominent tradesman in Kraków, a purveyor of goods to the Jewish quarter of the city.

7. Of his seven children—not seven *sons*, which occurrence would have been seen as the ultimate biblical blessing, but seven daughters, who make him blissfully happy nonetheless with their devotion— the third daughter produces

8. a nearsighted son who becomes mayor of a prosperous and well-kept town on the Vistula whose name means "delay," a town that had been the wretched village where Olavi's caravan spent the entire winter so many centuries earlier.

9. The son of the bespectacled mayor, lamed by an epidemic but blessed by his father's prosperity, spends a good part of his childhood playing in the organ loft of the small local Catholic church and becomes—though he still is a Jew—a renowned liturgical organist as well as the composer of several masses, including a requiem now well-known but ascribed to someone else.

10. The second child of the Jewish composer of masses is Joe Cimmer's

great-grandmother Iva Tsimmer, who emigrates to America in 1902 and gives birth in Brooklyn, New York, to

11. Joe's grandfather Josef, after whom Joe is named, who does not wish to be either a Jew or a Pole, Americanizes his name to Cimmer and, in a spirit of adventure as well as to evade a murderous creditor, moves west to Detroit and produces

12. Joe's own father, Lukas, who upon his graduation from high school — an accomplishment that amazes his father, who has called him a "useless lout" ever since he could walk — heads north from Detroit. He aims for a town with what he considers a lovely name, Mount Pleasant; finding it flat as a griddle, he keeps heading north and settles in Big Bay, to work at a sawmill for Henry Ford. Lukas is, of course, the paternal great-grandfather whom Ursula Wong, dropped precipitously on June 9, 2003, down a hole in the forest between Eagle River and Eagle Harbor, Michigan, has never known.

13. The long-vanished Joe Cimmer, thirteenth-generation descendant of Władysław IV Sigismund Vasa of Poland, does not know this either. His father, Lukas, has vanished when he was a toddler, and with him all history. Only a fragment of his own family story had come down even as close as his grandfather, a vague tale about an unspecified ancestor having been a Jewish organist in a Catholic church in Poland. Even this memory had been lost when Josef Cimmer, tone-deaf and immune to both music and story, moved westward and started all over, as if it were the first day of the world.

Of course the long-vanished Joe Cimmer does not know this either. Does Joe Cimmer matter, for he is so very long gone? Are not all the rest of these people gone, behind the veil of time? Are they not, nonetheless, all in Ursula's blood? But of course this places Sigismund of Poland — among all these others — in the lineage of Ursula Wong. But then who except a half-dozen historians, mumbling in their beards and stroking their leather elbow patches, has today ever heard of Sigismund of Poland?

· · ·

IT IS URGENT, in January of 1626, that Gustavus Adolphus produce a male heir, and it is in response to this urgency rather than to the whinings of Maria Eleonora that the king agrees to have her join him in at Reval in the gray depths of winter, when travel is wretched and the king himself opines to his attendants that the gloom of winter is minimal compared with the gloom that comes over him when he looks down the hall of the second half of his life and considers that Maria Eleonora, now seeming to loosen her grip on reality, will be there the whole way to his grave. But he must have an heir.

By April, when the royal couple returns to Åbo, which will become the Turku of today, the queen is once again pregnant. There will be no mistakes this time. The queen is coddled and confined. The astrologers and the herb women and leeches work overtime to ensure the fruition of this tooth-grittingly intentional pregnancy.

The powerful cries of the infant heard outside the door of the queen's room seconds after delivery set up an immediate belief: a son has been born! The astrologers have predicted a male heir, and of course they are right!

But then it turns out they are not. The king's sister, Catherine, lifts the infant from the arms of the midwives, whose eyes are averted in fear that they will be blamed for this terrible happening. Catherine carries the hairy, red, penis-free child quite naked on her outstretched arms to the king. No words need to be said.

The king, however, is pleased, in his staunch oblique Vasa way. He proposes to Catherine, "Sister, let us instead of bemoaning this birth as a tragedy, thank God instead. I hope that this girl will be the equivalent of— nay, the same as!—a son to me. I pray that he will preserve her! She should prove to be clever, since even this young she has deceived us all!"

Ah, but the king is more often than not off to battle. His default enthusiasm for turning this girl-child into a king is not shared by his neurasthenic and self-absorbed queen, who frames the identity of her daughter as one more confirmation of her inadequacy, one more siphoning-off of the attentions of her dashing husband the king.

The king, seeing Maria Eleonora's dramatic deterioration in starkly framed spurts as he does, coming back from his battlefield sallies, begins to fret seriously about the state of Maria Eleonora's mind. It is becoming more and more apparent that she is not merely neurotic, eccentric, unpleasantly quirky: it is clear that the queen has gone over the falls in a fragile bark, left the river of sanity, and gone adrift in the open sea.

In consultation with his advisers, Gustavus Adolphus frames a document assuring that, should he meet his end earlier than he might hope—a not unlikely prospect, given his near-constant presence on one battlefield or another—a guardian should be appointed for the queen herself, to keep her in check, and others to help raise his daughter, who must be more than a queen, who must be king.

ALMOST FOUR CENTURIES later, in Sault Sainte Marie, Michigan, Annie and Justin have made Ursula's nursery—a ten-by-ten-foot room in the mobile home—their idea of everything beautiful for a little girl, as if she were the only child ever, unique, a snowflake of a star blinking once in the vastness of space. On Ursula's doorknob hangs a tiny pillow with pink-and-purple faux needlepoint letters on burlap: THE PRINCESS SLEEPS HERE. On the thin walls—they buckle when leaned on—hang pictures of angels and Disney characters. On the dresser, a music box with plaster doves in a water globe that plays "Love Makes the World Go 'Round." Over Ursula's bed, a mobile that sways in the heater vent, quilted hearts and bears. Tiny white Christmas lights drape her curtain rods, looping in scallops for Ursula to watch in the dark until she drowses off to sleep. On the shelves, a collection of stuffed toys: several Dalmatians, a giraffe with a neck that looks broken, a number of cats and kittens, a sober-faced elephant, cartoon lion Simba and his mother, Sohrabi, fresh from the African veldt.

While the rest of the trailer is carpeted in gray, Ursula's room's carpet is a bright purple, her own choice. At the carpet store she has padded right to the huge upright remnant, standing next to a bright green, Sequoia-thick Astro-Turf roll, and patted it confidently with the flat of her tiny white starfish hand. At home that morning, while Ursula was eating her oatmeal—slapping the quick-cooling surface with the back of her spoon, making splashes that landed in her hair and three feet away on the wall—Annie had said, "What color rug do you want on your floor, honey?"

This is the kind of conversation Annie's friends find peculiar: they cannot conceive of consulting a child. Ursula puzzles a minute over the question, her spoon in midair. "What color do you like the best, Ursula? Daddy will take us to pick out a rug today. Carpet. What color do you want for the floor of your room?"

Ursula giggles the yodeling, half-insane-sounding laugh of the normal two-year-old and yells, "Poopoo!"

Justin walks in pulling on a sweatshirt on over his old holey T-shirt. "Why is this short person yelling about bowel movements at the table?" he asks, drily. To Ursula he says, "Hey, that sign on your door says Princess," he says. "Princesses don't yell about poo-poo. Feces. Excrement."

Ursula giggles louder and tips over her oatmeal bowl. "Poopoo!" she says again. "Poopoo!"

Annie says, "Translation problem." She is wiping the oatmeal with her right hand as she leans on her crutch with her left. "The young lady is answering her mother's question. Her favorite color. It's purple." Again Ursula yells it. She claps her hands. More oatmeal spatters.

"Banzai!" says Justin. "We head to Karpet Kastle for nice poopoo carpet."

THE NURSERY WHERE the real princess, Christina Alexandra of Sweden, is being raised has none of the conveniences of Ursula's trailer-park nursery. The sole window is too high to see out of. The walls are stone, cold and dark, icing up in winter from moisture and breath and the dampness that leaks through the cracks of the shutters; in warm weather sweating cool dampness that draws little Christina to stand with her cheeks pressed against their dark roughness. There are no pictures or mobiles or twinkling lights.

In winter the floor is like ice, so fur rugs—none of them purple—are laid across it, two deep, and Christina is allowed to crawl and roll about on them. The toys that Gustavus Adolphus has brought her from all of his travels are either too beautiful to play with or too plain to interest her. The nursemaids find this baby heir to the crown strange: she has an oddly adult face, not chubby and pleasant, unevocative of joy in those around her.

Christina depresses the staff, who are wholly unable to amuse her. The queen, Maria Eleonora, has of late taken to her bed more often than not, and the king is away at war, consolidating the kingdom. His visits home are so filled with statecraft and the quelling of palace intrigues that he is hard-pressed to find time to spend with his baby daughter. Her mother babbles on vacantly, giving orders that are immediately superseded by palace staff. The infant is lonely and bored.

Thus it comes to the nursery attendants that they ought to bring the princess a companion, essentially a live toy. The baby girls are not yet a year old when the plan is implemented. The little Finn foundling with the partly Norwegian name has been cosseted by her surrogate mothers, who love to dress her in lavender and violet remnants of fabric—rich brocades and moirés like the princess's own. These they cadge from the palace seam-stresses.

Violeta is all things the princess is not: round-faced, jolly, sparkly-eyed, happy. She has no parents, and yet she is happy and well loved. The maids clear their plan, through a lady-in-waiting who has access to channels of power, with Axel Oxenstierna, the king's right-hand man, whose intelligent guidance will carry Christina well into adulthood. The child is a foundling, yes, they say, but has been raised in the palace since birth.

Oxenstierna scowls slightly. "How can she have been raised in the palace without any one of us knowing?" he asks. The three nursemaids shrug their shoulders. Each looks to the other foolishly, brows raised, seeking answers. "Disorder?" asks Oxenstierna. "Do we live in such disorder here?"

The nursemaids misunderstand. They do not know the word and have not caught his meaning. They seize on his hypothesis. "Oh, yes," they agree smiling in unison. "Yes, Lord Chancellor, that is correct, indeed we do." The speaker beams as if exhilarated at her revelation.

Oxenstierna laughs. He has not gotten to be the king's trusted right-hand man by being dense or a fool. This is wonderful, he decides: the princess will be amused, and all this whining—on top of Maria Eleonora's—will be at an end. *We will celebrate this,* he thinks, *that we live in disorder: that in the palace itself there are foundlings who grow up in dark corners, to serve the kingdom in such odd ways, when they become needed.*

Violeta and Christina, born on the selfsame day, spend their childhood together, several hours a day. They take naps in beds that are side by side, at times in the same bed. The nursemaids throw a single coverlet across them on the rugs when they play themselves to sleep in the afternoons. The fairer child amuses the princess.

WHEN THE KING comes home from his wars he is as little as possible with the queen, who spends hours dressing her hair, powdering and repowdering her face until she resembles a ghoul. The king comes to the nursery and plays with the two girls. He enjoys the little Finn's sprightliness: it is a counterbalance to his daughter's lugubrious temperament.

There is a moment now and again when Christina notes this, in the way that bright children are preternaturally aware of what is going on under the surface with adults, and lowers her head and scowls for a second in envy. As the two little girls grow and walk and then run, they move from the dark, shuttered palace out into the fresh air, as boys might. Christina is a willful child, who wants to swim naked on the beaches of Stockholm, wants to run and ride ponies and, when she is old enough, horses. She wants to learn archery and to hunt rabbits and deer. The king approves all of this and says that in a couple of years she will be able to ride with the hunters. After all, she will be king.

In the meantime, the little girls ride their ponies, all year, even in winter, in snow, and sing and shout as they ride—Violeta teaches the princess wild Finnish songs that she has learned from the maids—and they fall off their mounts and sprain their arms and scrape their foreheads, and are perfectly happy. The maids in the palace are astounded: these little girls off in the care of the ruffian grooms! The other girls who come to the nursery quarters—cousins and the children of nobles—stick to more delicate, ladylike pursuits. Christina is glad to have Violeta along, wild as she herself is. Oxenstierna, informed of it all, nods gruffly, approving, and so does the king, from a distance, for he is off now at the wars for months that stretch into a year and then two.

When the girls are six all of this changes. The king dies in battle, the much loved and somehow seemingly invulnerable king, and there is a hole in the world, a dark, sucking vacuum. The girls discuss this as they traipse through the forest with bow and arrows, hunting rabbits with Christina's entourage trailing by only a couple of dozen feet.

"I know that he is dead," says Christina, "but he has always been gone so much that it feels no different now. It seems still as if he might come riding up." She is shuffling through the dry grass, kicking stones with her fine leather boots with their silver clasps. She is only six, but she speaks with the assurance of a child well past twelve.

Violeta has grown apace, the two of them studying languages and history with Oxenstierna, precocious and eager and apt, and learning to operate as if they were not girls, but young men, asking philosophical questions and daring the unknown.

"I wonder who my father is," says Violeta. Christina stops in the path and looks at her in astonishment. A brown rabbit with a startlingly white breast hops across the path, and the princess does not even see it. "I have never known," says Violeta.

"God's blood!" says the princess, who loves to swear like a soldier and is not corrected for it by the maids and the grooms, though Oxenstierna will not tolerate it at all. "I had never thought about that! You have no father!" She pauses. "Your mother is one of the maids then," the princess says. She rides the declaration slightly uphill, as if it were half question. It has never occurred to Christina to question this. She finds her own mother dispensable, superfluous; it has never occurred to her that anyone should need a mother. Violeta seems, in some half-conscious realm of her mind, to exist only to amuse *her*. Why then should she, of all people, ever have needed a mother?

"No, not one of the maids," says Violeta. "They care for me. Only that. I was left as a foundling. Here at the palace."

"God's wounds!" says the princess.

"I was floated in a basket in the fountain in the tradesman's courtyard," says Violeta.

"Like Moses," says the princess.

"I had not thought of that," says Violeta. "How peculiar! How wonderful!"

"Oh, look!" shouts the princess. Another brown rabbit, white-breasted and fleet, leaps across the path. The entourage, hanging back at the discreet distance the princess insists on, moves scuffling forward along the path, single file, as the girls take off into the woods, through the brambles. The princess's arrow strikes home and the rabbit falls dead, dark blood drooling around the place where the shaft has pierced the white breast fur. The princess crows in triumph.

THE QUEEN IS returning from Germany now with Gustavus Adolphus's body, and Violeta will go with the party to meet the ship that brings the fragile queen and the embalmed body of the king, in his heavy and horrible casket, home. Violeta is useful and can entertain the young princess en route in the carriage—play games, do sums, recite French verbs competitively as both girls so love to do.

It is summer, and the king is seven months dead. Gustavus Adolphus had become separated from his men in the early-morning mists of battle, then shot in the back and dragged along by his horse, trapped ignominiously by his spurs in his stirrup. He was felled by one more shot as he lay thus trapped, dangling from his mount, bleeding profusely, onto and into the bleak, dry, November-hard ground.

The girls are taken to the shore, the ship docks, and the queen disembarks with the casket. Christina is hugged mercilessly by her mother, crushed into the folds of her dress as if Maria Eleonora would break her like pastry. Violeta stands to the side, glad of her orphanhood, grateful that this silly hook-nosed, powder-faced woman is not her mother. She stares hard at the casket as if waiting for the king—whom she has always liked greatly—to rise up in his hearty way and say that this is all a joke. She pities homely Christina, soon to be queen of the realm.

Now Maria Eleonora is entirely devoid of moorings. The girls are kept at the castle at Nyköping for a full year; the king's embalmed body is kept in its casket in state in the Great Hall the while. Christina must sleep with her mother in a grand bed over which is hung, in a jeweled box fashioned of filigreed gold, the king's heart, which the queen has insisted be scooped out and saved for her personal treasuring. The queen cries day and night.

In the mourning-draped rooms of the palace the girls must be quiet and still, and they hate it.

Christina says, "This is my mother, the queen." She plunks down an ornate wooden doll dressed in finery in front of her friend Violeta. She makes a small reedy voice: this is Maria Eleonora's. "I am so miserable," intones the doll. "Oh, my husband is dead and my life is worth nothing." Christina says, "This is my father the king, risen up from his casket." She makes a deep voice, much like her father's. Violeta marvels at her gift for mimicry. "My queen, your life was always worth nothing. I placed myself in the path of that musket ball to get away from you."

Violeta says, "Do not be cruel, Christina."

Christina looks at her pale little blond friend with fiery outrage, then stops. She says, almost submissively, in a voice that is hardly her own, "Well, then."

Violeta says, "I miss your father too, Christina." And then both girls cry. The nursemaids, standing outside the door, peer in, perturbed and astounded.

Christina turns to them and glares. She picks up the father doll and says, in her father's voice, "Go away, silly women." The maids fall back like waves on the shore and vanish. Both girls guffaw in delight at this seemingly magical power: Violeta, of course, has no such power at all.

Christina wipes her eyes on the sleeve of her gown. She is not used to crying. She gets onto her knees and walks the mother doll across the room. "Walk, walk, walk," she says, with each step. "Walk walk walk walk."

She is near the high window. She holds the doll with one hand and pulls up a chair with the other. She climbs on the chair. She holds the doll in her left hand and braces herself against the wall with her right. The shutters are open against her mother's orders—strict mourning is to be observed—but when Maria Eleonora is in another part of the palace Christina insists to the nursemaids that they let the air in, and they will disobey her mother more easily than they will come against this willful child.

The doll wears a choker of tiny real pearls and a collar of hand-tatted lace, tiny shoes made of deer hide. Its blue eyes are genuine jewels, semi-precious stones. Christina makes her mother's small, reedy voice. "I cannot go on living," she mocks. The girl holds the mother doll high and she speaks in her own voice. "The decision is yours, Mother," she says, and she aims the doll carefully for the aperture in the stone wall, then lets fly. The doll soars through the opening, without hitting the curb or the lintel, and out into nowhere. Three stories below, it will crash to the courtyard stones.

"Christina!" chides Violeta. She can feel her own face pale with chagrin at her friend's cold, unchildlike rage.

"I know," says Christina, with an icy calm. "And yet."

DOWN THE HALL they can hear the noise of the dwarves, their throaty voices singing one of the queen's favorite songs. This will mean that the queen is there, visiting them: they will sing for her, perform their acrobatic feats, leaping and rolling and then piling themselves into pyramids, telling dense, foolish dwarf jokes till the queen's desire for all this is sated.

"Those horrible, horrible people," Christina says. "No. They had no choice in their state, but my mother does. She is the monster, to take such delight in monstrosity."

It is usual for royalty of the time to keep hunchbacks and midgets and freaks about for entertainment, and Maria Eleonora enjoys them enormously. Among them is a man who was born without legs but can do such amazing things: the queen loves to see him scoot across the floor like a little frog—she calls him Froggy—and swears he plays the lute almost as well as her dead husband, who was a master of the instrument and knew all of the newest Italian songs. There is gossip that he sleeps in the bed of Maria Eleonora, but no one can say this is true.

IN THE WINTERTIME, heavily salted meat and fish constitute much of everyone's diet, the royals as well as the peasants. Beer and wine are the usual drinks for all, even for children; oddly, milk is an unusual drink for Swedes until years later. Water is thought unsanitary, and with very good reasons. Christina eats heartily but cannot stomach either beer or wine, while Violeta, like most children, drinks weak beer several times a day.

One morning when Maria Eleonora is out of her quarters Christina sneaks into her mother's boudoir and discovers a stash of rose water the queen mother uses to wash her face. "Look at this!" says Christina to Violeta. She pours some of it into the washbowl, scoops it up with a dipper, and drinks it. "Oh, oh, oh!" she groans gloriously. "This is wonderful!"

"You had better not," says Violeta.

"Do you think it is *poison?*" Christina asks. "Set by my mother to trap me and kill me?" She laughs contemptuously.

"It is only that she will . . . be angry . . ." Violeta stammers.

"Indeed!" says Christina. "But I have had so much salt cod I am dying of thirst, and I will have some rose water!" She pours more into the bowl, dips it up with the dipper, and drinks. In the large cut-glass reservoir rose petals float and flutter as she sets the decanter down.

"I would not like to see you beaten," says Violeta.

"Beaten!" Christina exclaims. "I am queen!"

IT IS WEEKS BEFORE Christina's daily thefts come to be noticed, and when the levels of the rose water are discovered to be low, with no explanation, Maria Eleonora berates the maids, who protest their utter innocence. They have no idea Christina is up to this mischief. When one of them is stationed behind a curtain to watch—as if this rose water were liquid jewels—she is put in an awkward position. She must tattle on the little queen. She quakes in fear but tells the truth.

In consequence, Christina is beaten, slapped about the head and face by the queen herself, her skin broken by the large stones on the queen mother's rings. When she falls trying to run away, she is beaten on her back and shoulders with the queen's shoe, her hair pulled to make her stand up, her dress ripped. She sits astonished, holding her hands latticed over her face for protection as her mother rails at her. Finally Maria Eleonora desists and departs.

Violeta has been in the adjoining room, hiding in an alcove, covering her ears against her friend's cries. When she sees Maria Eleonora leave, nursing her own hand where she has injured it in flailing at Christina, she runs to Christina's aid.

"Oh, Christina, Christina!" Violeta cries. "Let me help you." She runs to Christina's side.

Christina pushes her away. "Don't touch me, Finn pig!" she screams.

WHEN THE GIRLS are eight, it is decided that there must be a royal portrait of the little queen, so a painter is commissioned. The sittings seem endless, even though the artist needs Christina in person only for the smallest portion of the painting.

While Christina resembles her father far more than her mother—and this has been a source of repeated irritation to Maria Eleonora, sending her careening off into fits of mourning, which reek of a fury that Christina lives and is queen while her husband is dead and she herself relegated to the margins of palace life—in the painting as it develops Christina's face is far more her mother's.

Violeta attends all the sittings. She works at her needlework—even at the age of eight she is accomplished at intricate, tiny embroideries—and looks up at Christina and makes silly faces to amuse her. The artist slaps himself on the head in frustration again and again when Christina moves.

"My neck grows stiff," Christina says. "If you should like to paint me in my coffin—my mother might like that so much better, with her passion for tiny caskets and all things morbid—perhaps I could be more cooperative."

The artist has heard of the little queen's barbed precocity but still is astonished to hear this.

"No, Your Highness," the artist says. "I can accommodate." He punches himself in the chest like a papist making a quick mea culpa.

"Excellent," says Christina. "Then you will not mind if my sweet sister, Moses, and I chat while I pose."

"No, Your Highness," the artist says. "Go right ahead, indeed."

Christina and Violeta chat on, about all sorts of things they have learned from their new tutor, Johannes Matthiae, and other assertions—absurd ad hoc lies presented as facts—that Christina throws in, to confuse and astound the humorless eavesdropping painter.

As the painting proceeds, Christina's soulful, doelike, but even at this young age shrewd eyes are modified to resemble more the delicacy of her mother's, and her chin as well. Maria Eleonora natters about, insisting to the artist again and again that he refine her daughter's features.

Finally the painter goes to a portrait of the Queen Mother and begins to mold himself consciously to the task of replicating that portrait. The more he does this, without foregrounding what he is so intentionally doing, the more the Queen Mother approves.

In the portrait, Christina stands in front of a window—realistically copied from the actual window behind her—which frames an entirely concocted scene that never was there: ships, a river that curves away into the distance, a range of ethereal mountains.

Christina's hair is enormous and pale beneath her small filigree crown, and her pearl-and-jewel-bedecked green-and-gold brocade dress looks as if it weighs a ton, as indeed it does. The artist has actually painted the garment hung on a wood mannequin while Christina and Violeta are out hunting deer with the groomsmen. The gold-fringed gloves and the ropes of pearls and emerald barrettes that appear in the portrait have all been added by the artist, who paints from the actual objects, but hung on a peg, not on the young queen, who despises such ornament.

"You look far more like a miniature of your mother here than like yourself," says Violeta, when the painting is finished.

"Indisputably true," says Christina, "yet Oxenstierna has taught me that as queen I must choose my battles. This is not a battle in which I choose to engage. On the one hand, I would prefer to resemble myself. On the other hand, what does it matter? When I am older I shall have my portrait made as I should like it to be. And perhaps by the grace of God my dear mother will die and be out of the way sooner rather than later." The child who speaks this way is eight years old.

THAT EVENING IN the maids' quarters there is good-natured bantering among the women, the Swedes and the Finns among them throwing barbs back and forth at each other. The day's work being done—a rare thing, for is work ever done?—they settle on stools and piles of rugs around the fireplace and begin telling tales as they mend capes and stockings for winter, which is coming on fast.

The fireplace is cavernous and the stock of logs piled there burning bright two feet deep. The flames crackle and pop and cast lickety-split dancing shadows across the faces of the servants gathered around.

Two fat cats prowl through the gathering, nudging past feet, slipping under skirts, being sheltered or shooed. One woman sneezes and knocks a big yellow cat aside with her knuckles. The cat yowls. The woman keeps sneezing and cannot stop. Two more servant women join the gathering, wandering in with big bowls of the Finnish *keitto,* milk and potatoes and fish boiled together, which has been the servants' dinner. No one points out that there really is little distinction between the Finns and the Swedes, among the serving women. They all eat the *keitto.* The two women's eyes scour the room in the flickering darkness for stools on which to sit. They have been tending to visiting nobles' needs during the supper hour and missed their own meal.

Violeta wanders like one of the cats, snuggling up first against Jasmin, who for three years had been her wet-nurse and who now saves her tidbits of pastry from the royal kitchen, French pastry with lemon and apricot fillings, and tiny meat pies—venison, pork (which Christina herself will not eat), and lamb. At eight Violeta is wise about the eyes, if one were to look closely—how could she be otherwise, exposed as she is to a full day of all of the lessons the little queen herself must learn, in order to govern the kingdom like a man: Latin, philosophy, French, mathematics, rhetoric. She is small-boned, with the gaze of a tiny adult but the rosy fair cheeks of a pale-skinned Finn child.

Jasmin, exhausted from the day's work, is falling asleep as she sits, and Violeta extricates herself from her nest at the woman's side, so that she will not be trapped by the woman's bulk—for she has grown hefty—as she begins to fall deeper into sleep. She scans the room for someone else to sit with. "Come here," says a voice from the shadows, and Violeta obeys. It is another of her foster mothers, the woman who has taught her braiding and tatting.

Now one of the Swedish maids tells the old favorite story of the bear: how it envied the fox its bright red coat and thought it must have one just the same. "So the bear asks the fox," says the woman, "'Where did you get that? For I must have one every bit like it.' The fox tells the bear," she says, "that he has just climbed up onto a hayrack and set it on fire, and the color of the fire made his fur the same. So the bear does this too. Stupid bear! And of course all that happens is that his fur catches on fire, and to this day the bear's fur is black from being burned, and singed on the ends to boot."

Everyone knows the story but loves hearing it again. "Aye, envy is such a terrible thing," says another maid. "But do you know, our own little bear, Pikku Pentu here, does not live up to her name."

"How is that?" says Violeta, to whom the old woman is referring.

"I see you in company with the queen daily," the old woman says. "And I see that, unlike the bear who envies the fox's coat, you do not long after her riches or royalty but simply stay in your own skin contented."

"And why should I long for her wretched life?" says Violeta. "My mothers love me." A murmur of approval goes up from the circle of women.

As adolescence approaches, Christina begins to be interested in the boys in a bold new way, though Violeta stands back from this flirting. Christina does not quite yet understand the implications of her status as queen, that any pairing will be decided by counselors, not by her heart or anyone else's. She rails on to Violeta about the rudeness of the palace boys.

"Perhaps," Violeta says, "it is your overeagerness which puts them off." Her voice is even and soft, but it cannot soften what she is saying. Christina is furious.

"Overeagerness!" Christina bellows. "Indeed!"

When Christina is in this mood there is no dialogue to be had. Violeta changes the subject. "We should go and have our costumes for the ballet's finale fitted. The seamstress was wanting to finish the ruching," she says.

The boys are all in a room overlooking the water, doing pliés with the newly imported French dance master, Antoine de Beaulieu, practicing for the middle scenes of the ballet in which all of the palace children are involved. The boys are the huntsmen. Three small-boned girls play the deer. A trio of violinists repeat and repeat a two-minute-long melody. Beaulieu, shouting commands in French over the music and waving his hands, runs the boys through the dance of the deer until everyone is ready to scream with frustration at his perfectionism.

Christina's cousin Karl Gustav breaks rank and runs over to them. Beaulieu shrieks curses. Christina snaps her fingers imperiously at the

ballet master. "Relax, monsieur! It is time for a respite!" There is such authority in her voice that it never fails to astonish newcomers to court.

It is Karl Gustav with whom the queen will fall deeply, passionately, in
love. Christina imperiously orders the ballet master, "Go have yourself a
glass of wine, monsieur! Have an orange! Indeed, have two, and for the
blood of Jesus' sake take your time!"

Ultimately it will become clear to everyone that attempts to marry
Christina off to anyone at all are doomed. This doom proceeds not only
from her personality and her unwillingness to conform herself to ideas of
"femininity": it proceeds as well from her father's early determination that
she be raised with the canny, suspicious instincts of a king.

But Christina does not yet see herself as others see her, and she imagines
herself quite as lovely as Violeta. In her lavender dress with its deep purple
bows, Violeta might well be taken for royalty. In her constant awareness that
she is in this company solely at Christina's whim, she holds back and is ever
retiring and reticent.

The boys begin to pay attention to Violeta, and there are moments when
Violeta sees flashes of jealousy in Christina's glance. Violeta is politic about
this: she teaches Christina how to unfurl her fan with more delicacy, how to
dance with more lightness in her step. She braids Christina's hair in intricate shapes which bring great raves from the other girls and from a couple
of the boys as well.

But Christina is far too impatient to sit for hours for the mere sake of girl
vanity and begins wearing her hair rebelliously loose and unkempt, winding up looking more like a rollicking cavalier than like the gossamer nature
sprite she fancies she resembles.

WHEN THE GIRLS are twelve there is an outbreak of chicken pox
among the palace children, and both Christina and Violeta are stricken.
They are kept in separate sickbeds, Violeta in the servants' quarters, in the
dank normal dark of that place, and Christina in her own bedroom, hung
with heavy darkening drapes. Somehow, to the medicine of the time, light
seems an enemy.

When they recover, Christina's face is heavily pockmarked, while Violeta has scars only on her back and the tips of her shoulders and those scars do not show when she is dressed, not even when she wears formal dresses with low-scooped necklines. Christina's scars are on full display.

One beautiful morning the following spring, the palace children are assembled for a lesson in geometry. It is early May and unseasonably warm. The girls ostentatiously wave feather fans to move the air. Johannes Matthiae draws a large isosceles triangle on a large slate. His voice drones on, monotone, as the children's eyes wander out the window. A bird alights and everyone's eyes are on it, willing it to fly into the room and disrupt the lesson.

The tutor drones: Euclid blah blah equal angles blah blah then by contrast blah blah (he says, drawing a new figure) unequal angles and so blah blah then . . . If in Greek *iso* means "equal," is this (second figure) then an isosceles triangle?

The bird has lifted off the windowsill and flown away. A number of the children are watching it. Others nod in the warm morning. Violeta has heard the tutor but does not wish to volunteer first. This is so simple, but everyone else seems to be dreaming clouds and birds.

The boys who are discussing Christina's pockmarks are still whispering. One of them points out in a stage whisper that on her lower left cheek, still rosy raw, is an isosceles triangle made of the scars of the pustules. On a puff of sudden quiet in the room, the words travel to Christina's ears. Her face reddens.

Violeta leans over to her and whispers, "Pay them no attention, Christina."

Christina answers the tutor, as if none of this were going on. "No, of course, that is *not* an isosceles triangle," she says.

"Correct, indeed, Your Majesty," says the tutor.

Christina looks at Violeta's smooth cheeks as the little Finn leans near to reassure her. Christina is offended by that perfection. Something in her rises up to blame Violeta, as she had also blamed Violeta for her mother's beating because Violeta had warned her. At that moment she sets her heart like flint.

THE FOLLOWING DAY Violeta is told that her presence at tutoring will not be needed. The day after that she is told she will be going on a journey, and the third day her bags are packed and she is set in a carriage. Her old wet-nurse cries and the other serving women are distressed. No one knows where she is going, but it is whispered about that clearly this is Christina's doing, that she has been envious of Violeta her whole life, and how could we ever have expected anything else?

Violeta is sent to be a serving maid, or perhaps a tutor, to the family of the commandant at Elfsborg, an island in the harbor off Göteborg. The cross-country journey will be beautiful, and the family is said to be kind, but Violeta's heart is wrenched. Christina has been her friend, closer than a sister, but, indeed, as the maids all had said, how could Violeta in common sense have expected anything different?

She tells herself she has been blessed to have all of this time at the palace—*Twelve years! An education! Mathematics, ballet, geography!*—and that simply having been spared being drowned at birth like a rat is more than she might have expected from life.

In the interior of the carriage, alone, she lets herself cry, just a little, and sings a little Finnish song that says, in essence, "Life is as hard as the icy rock under the turf, and we slip on it sometimes, and then we get up to find life is as hard as the icy rock under the turf, and we slip on it sometimes, and then we get up . . . ," and she sings it until she is laughing right through her tears.

The carriage jolts along the rutted roads and Violeta holds tightly to the door handle. She is musing on providence: whether there is such a thing as God's will for her life or whether this is all happenstance. She and Christina have had discussions with Oxenstierna on this subject, and it has always been clear that Christina is in a far better position than Violeta to choose to believe that God plans her life for her. The divine right of kings, when it is on one's own side, tends to lead one to side naturally with divinity.

And yet, Violeta thinks, *that in itself is a danger.* Christina is rough and irreverent on the subject of God and indeed—as Violeta has once or twice pointed out to her—has set up her own will as a god. Christina has laughed at this, as if to say, And what is wrong with that? When Violeta answers, "Thou shalt not have strange gods before me, not even thine own girlish will," Christina laughs again, harshly, and changes the subject.

Violeta, holding hard to the door of the carriage as it hurtles through the ruts, decides to come down on the side of an intricate providence, telling herself despite all that this will be an adventure. At just this instant a wheel rattles loose and flies off. The driver reins in the horses so hard that Violeta is thrown from her seat, sustaining a knot on her forehead which turns blue and gives her a headache that will not subside for weeks. I wonder, she thinks, half-laughing to herself, what God had in mind there, since I have decided this all has some meaning.

In her lap, along with her sewing pouch, a packet of hard rye biscuits, and a wax-wrapped ball of cheese, is her diary, a small book bound in brown leather. Christina has always kept a diary—it is one of her duties as queen to record her activities for posterity—and the previous year in a moment of tenderness or ownership she has given Violeta a journal for her own use.

At the time, the girls had been doing needlework with the ladies-in-waiting. Sunlight streamed in, unfurling in ribbons through the high narrow window. One of the palace cats meandered among the women. Violeta thanked Christina profusely for the book. "But what shall I write?" Violeta said.

"All that you do each day," Christina said.

"But for whom to read or for what purpose?" Violeta asked.

"For your descendants," Christina said.

"My descendants?" said Violeta. It had never occurred to her that she might have descendants. Her parentage was a blur, her future even more so. "Descendants." She spoke the word oddly, as if she had chomped down on a pebble in a mouthful of porridge. "But what shall I write? My days are as uneventful as that cat's. What should a cat write? 'In the morning, I drank a saucer of milk and slept in the sunlight. I picked up a ball of yarn as I walked among the women, and carried it off to my corner. I napped. In the afternoon, I drank milk, I napped.' And so on. My own diary could not be much different. All I could write would be that I attended Christina, returned to the servants' quarters, then the next day I attended Christina and returned to the servants' quarters," Violeta says.

"Oh," said Christina. Her own diary had not reached the stage where she

reflected on anything at all, so she could not proffer the idea that the mea-
gerest life should offer much meat for deep introspection.

THE FORT AT ELFSBORG is a surreal affair, a fastness of inward-
leaning trapezoidal stone walls set into a compact flat rocky island, midbay.
The peak of a tower that flies the blue-and-yellow flag of the Three Crowns
and the roofs of several varied smaller buildings rise above the walls.

As the tiny boat in which Violeta is being conveyed approaches the rocky
shore, the small well-defined gray-green waves seem to grow wilder, making the landing difficult. Violeta, huddled against the cold spray in the stern
of the craft, is not certain she wants to land at all. Her disorientation is pervasive. She has never lived anywhere but the palace.

She certainly does not remember the shed in the rye field where she was
conceived, or the basket in which she floated on the skin of the water of the
fountain. The feeling of coming to this place is as the feeling of one who has
drifted in a dream, rudderless, and wound up nowhere at all. The shore
seems infinitely distant. The sandy flat ground inside the fort walls supports
no vegetation, is more like that of the Middle East—starkness and sand—
the lands that her ancestor, Olavi the merchant, has traversed on the Silk
Road—than that of the rest of Sweden. Nine centuries' worth of merchants
and fishermen, weavers and herbalists, carpenters, singers of tribal songs,
cart builders, stonemasons, one paralytic, one mayor, one rye farmer, come
between.

Violeta climbs out of the rowboat onto the Elfsborg beach, her knees
buckle under her, pitching her to the damp sand. She is overcome, suddenly,
by the movement of the waves and the rebelliousness of the cheese, bread,
pears, and beer she has had for her lunch, and she vomits copiously.

Standing before her is the commandant, a tall muscular man with small
Swedish eyes and a round head of thinning straw-colored hair, in his full
dress uniform. "Welcome," he says, bowing from the waist with great ceremony, "to your new home." Violeta thinks: *Well, then, I will spend my life
here, as a teacher, but this will be fine too.*

. . .

THE DOG SLED belongs to the leprosarium of Saints Lazarus and Magdalen on the island of Glöskar, the island of lagoons, behind Violeta across a good mile of thick, solid, unyielding sea ice, and so, technically, it is criminal theft for her to take it and its two dogs. Glöskar is only one of the thousands of islands in the Åland archipelago, set into the Baltic Sea smack at the crossroads of trade between Sweden and Finland.

The leper colony's silly name comes, as come so many names, from compounded mistakes. Someone remembers that there was a leper named Lazarus in the Bible, and then someone remembers that Lazarus who was raised from the dead had two sisters, Mary and Martha. The two entirely separate Lazaruses become conflated; Mary Magdalene seems to someone to be a combination of both of them, though of course that is a different character too. Mistake piles on mistake, and thus goes the world.

Violeta is heading out west toward Föglö on the pearly white ice, in the beautiful morning. She is thirty-eight years old now and has been captive in the leprosarium since her son Carl-Marcus's fourth birthday.

She has not wound up spending her life on Elfsborg as she had assumed when she landed there: she had married the tutor of the commandant's son and emigrated to New Sweden, the land that is today New Jersey, Delaware, and Pennsylvania. This abortive emigration will never be known to the family history. There had been a terrible voyage, on which her new husband, Per Marcus, was thrown overboard by one of the convicts sent to populate the new colony—a convict who was in fact one of the dwarves so beloved by the queen, who in his turn mysteriously vanished over the side of the vessel.

A tall and well-muscled Ethiop slave of some erudition, Oscar Lucassen —he had been freed by his Danish master for his excellent services—who was also a passenger on the voyage, had been given the task of serving as Violeta's protector. Oscar Lucassen spoke Portuguese and Dutch as well as Swedish, Danish, and a northern Abyssinian dialect; he was glad to recite the Twenty-third Psalm in the African dialect for anyone who asked, dropping to a dramatic basso profundo when he spoke of the valley of the shadow of death, but then reassuring his listeners quickly, with a brilliant smile, that he was an unregenerate pagan who simply appreciated excellent poetry.

Two weeks further along on the voyage, Oscar Lucassen took Violeta aside and told her in confidence just how her husband's murderer had died. The wife of the Lutheran pastor on board, he said, had suggested that since he was no Christian, he might consider whether there was something he could do to protect others from the wretched dwarf. Oscar Lucassen had told the story to Violeta with great dry humor. "Perhaps it was something I ate," he said, rolling his eyes. "When I eat shellfish, I experience spasms in my bowels." He made a face of comedic pain.

"The night of the dwarf's untimely end—it was after our dinner hour, though we had had only biscuits and cabbage soup—I had a terrible spasm in my *hand*. Highly unusual. I had picked up that little man by his throat ruffles and held him out over the side of the ship, to, oh, *frighten* him into what your pastor's wife might call 'the fear of God,' when all of a sudden—"

Violeta clapped her hands over her face and guffawed in disbelief. "A spasm in your hand!" she said.

"Indeed," said Oscar Lucassen. Your pastor's wife suggests that as I am not a Christian, I cannot be held to Christian rules. In fact, she avers, an inversion may be at work: she says that this accident—this fortuitously timed cramping of my hand—may well buy me entrance to your Christian paradise."

Violeta sat stunned but a fine smile spread over her face. "Sir," she said, "I can do no less than tender you all of my gratitude and to hope that I may repay you somehow, someday."

Violeta served briefly as tutor to the girls in the house of the governor of the new colony, Governor Ridder, upon her arrival. The child conceived on the ocean voyage grew inside her unmentioned as she went about her duties, beneath voluminous gathers of high-waisted skirt, until two months before its due date, when she revealed the pregnancy to Oscar Lucassen, who went to tell the news to the governor on her behalf.

"This is not a good situation," warned Oscar Lucassen. He did not refer to the pregnancy but looked around himself rather ambiguously, out the windows, over the river. "I believe you should return to Sweden. Per Marcus's lands seem very fine." He had read the deeds and documents. He was not a fearful person at all, and Violeta could not for the life of her see what he was referring to as the "situation."

Violeta said, "Per Marcus wanted to make a success of this venture. I will see it through as he would have done."

The child was born and named Carl-Marcus. A new governess came for the Ridder household. Violeta insisted on buying—for very little money— a small plot of land and a cabin from a couple who had moved north to the settlement which would later become New Amsterdam and then New York. That couple purchased a piece of land a good distance out into the wilderness, not far from the plot on which was later built the brownstone little Ursula Wong would applaud nightly at the opening of her beloved *Cosby Show* reruns. Ursula would say, "That's where Olivia lives!" Annie would say, "It's a story, honey," and—their ritual—Ursula would reply, "Good stories are *real*, Mommy!"

The cabin was the sort of assemblage of logs and mortar chinking which originated with Forest Finns in Sweden and which, in the new land, became the standard dwelling, the frontier log cabin which few Americans would ever know to associate with its Finnish origin. It had a steep roof with a carved ornament at the peak, a fireplace of huge stones from the river's edge, a dirt floor, a single room with a sleeping loft.

It was the only house that was for sale, and it was cheap, but it was the ornament at the peak that so connected with Violeta's heart, assuring her this was to be *her* house. The piece of wood, cut out in a wondrous design and painted iron-oxide red like so many houses in Sweden and Finland, was clearly someone's way of bringing the civilization of Europe to this wild land.

Violeta thought: I will live here as a widow, and I will bring Per Marcus's dreams to fulfillment in his name in the New World.

Oscar Lucassen continued to live with the Ridders and to teach the boys there. The pastor tried to convince the man to convert to Christianity. Oscar Lucassen asked the pastor to leave him alone in his heathenness. The pastor persisted.

Oscar reiterated without elaboration, "This is not a good situation." Still she could not see what he was objecting to. Violeta charged off the truculence to his constitution, which she deemed exotically pessimistic.

She made friends with many of the Indians, who were in general very compatible with the Finns making their homes at the forest's edge: the

Finns and the Indians had the same sense of being part of nature rather than its master, a wildness which scared the more civilized Swedes. At this stage in their history, Swedes, like their peculiar abdicated queen, longed to be French more than anything: decadence, ah, give them decadence.

Violeta was visiting, in the depths of a bleak November, the fort at Tinicum—named from the Indians's *tennakong* and later to be called New Goteborg—to trade with a fur trader there for some skins for the winter to come. Oscar Lucassen had brought Violeta to Fort Tinicum in a horse carriage.

A lantern was knocked over while Violeta was in the fort's yard, and the fire flared up quickly, licking at the fort's timber walls, roaring toward the sky, rolling black clouds of belching smoke. She wrapped the baby tightly in its blanket against her shoulder and ran, but the gates of the fort were locked tight. She realized she was trapped.

She recalled fainting at Per Marcus's death and was conscious that if she were to faint now, her child would die with her in the fire. She fought her wooziness. From out of nowhere, it seemed, she was grabbed around the waist, and as if by miracle, the gate flew open, jimmied by a muscular push of what seemed superhuman strength. It was Oscar Lucassen.

He carried both her and the child away from the river, to a point as far from the fire as they could stand and still see it. They stood watching in silence until the fort was gone.

"May I offer an observation?" said Oscar Lucassen.

"May I guess at its nature?" asked Violeta, seated against a tree with Oscar Lucassen's greatcoat over her head like a lean-to, and Carl-Marcus burrowed to sleep in her shawl. She paused. "Might your observation be something to the effect that this is not a good situation?"

"Indeed," said Oscar Lucassen. "Perhaps we should return to Per Marcus's lands."

And so they did return, the three of them, with Oscar serving as Violeta and the boy Carl-Marcus's executor and protector.

VIOLETA TRAVELED TO the nearest town in the settlement, Wicacoa, today's Philadelphia, to embark for Sweden. The ship meandered downstream, past Fort Christina, and for only one second Violeta connected the name to her childhood twin: Fort Christina became today's Wilmington, Delaware. Violeta and Carl-Marcus returned from New Sweden to the estate outside Uppsala, where the ancestral home sat intact, its furniture shrouded in spooky cloths bathed in the dust of several years. Oscar Lucassen came along in tow as protector and tutor-to-be for the child.

The family home was intact, its furniture covered with spooky cloths bathed in the dust of several years. The fields were still being cultivated by tenant farmers. The road was in good repair. The house had a single chandelier much like the ones in the church in Uppsala, but smaller.

In that grand house on the hill, with its French decor—pastel trompe-l'oeil murals and fine crystal chandeliers—and its stables with fine horses and its three-score gray sheep munching grass, Violeta had stood looking out of the front windows of the house, thinking of the Ninety-first Psalm—"Angels bear me up, lest I dash my foot on a stone—" which Oscar Lucassen could also declaim with great drama. Then she had said to herself aloud, "So then I shall live my life *here,* and it will be just fine."

BUT THAT DID not happen either, just as it had not happened the first few times that Violeta had made such predictions. When Carl-Marcus reached the age of four, Violeta had found herself leprous. The disease had incubated since her early childhood in the palace's servant quarters, picked up from a serving maid now dead and lying in a churchyard outside Uppsala, her bones in the earth crusted and deformed from the disease. Violeta was diagnosed in short order and sent to the leprosarium, to live out her life.

At the leprosarium, she had not said even once, not even in her deepest recesses in moments of darkest despair, "Then I shall die *here,* and it will be fine." There was no resignation despite circumstance: Violeta continued to hope against hope.

THIS MORNING, AS Violeta heads away from Saints Lazarus and Magdalen, across the ice, her state of mind is far from clear. She is thinking of the wretched leper who only yesterday exposed himself to her and pushed her to the ground in the snow. She is thinking of her son, Carl-Marcus, and of his legal guardian and surrogate father now, Oscar Lucassen. Confusedly, she means to escape from the leper colony on Glöskar and finally come home to stay, at the family estate. This of course cannot happen.

It is 1664, and she is thirty-eight years old. It is only four years until Jesuit missioners will plant their cross at Sault Saint Marie, Michigan, far across the world. Among those priests, of course, is René Josserand, ancestor to Justin Wong, who will become husband to Annie Maki, descendant of our Violeta, now wrestling the reins of the dog sled on the Baltic ice.

The sky is a fierce, defiant blue, cloudless. The horizon seems to recede infinitely. Föglö is only a memory from the last time she has come near there, in a fishing boat called the *Saint Peter*. "The stupidest of the apostles!" the man tilling the rudder has said. "The one who could never get anything right!" The man tilling the rudder, of course, is a leper too. Lepers are as various as anyone else: it is a disease that knows no social class, and no one knows a thing about it at this stage in history.

Violeta is not thinking about the problem of possible criminal charges for stealing the sled. Glöskar has no sheriff, and no one is following her. Were she to think about it, she would giggle: indeed, where would they put her? No jail would have her. Her face has the appearance, a horrified observer has once said, of rotten cork; her hands are crippled and the finger bones inside melted away to the look of candle drips, useless.

She wears heavy mitts in the extreme cold. Her feet in felt boots have not yet begun to go gangrenous, but she has observed with alarm the progression of these changes in others and has been thinking since the summer that this would come to her soon.

Under the gray cloak, its moth holes carefully darned, and the unwieldy sealskins that shield her from the cold, she wears the russet robes of the leprosarium of Saints Lazarus and Magdalen.

Out in front of the sled, the pair of dogs, Princeps and Ullo, bark spiritedly in counterpoint into the overbright day; their breath curls upward in white puffs and dissipates. Princeps's gray ruff around his white neck fur and his bright blue eyes make him a handsome animal; he is chesty and brainless but fast. Ullo is dull brown, leaner, even faster. The two are poorly matched: they strive against each other in harness. Violeta holds on to the reins with difficulty and a great deal of pain.

LEPROSY HAS INCREASED in Sweden and Finland so greatly these past years that whole colonies have formed up, at the command of King Karl Gustav. Prior to this, lepers simply were asked to stay clear of the healthy folk—or at least those without the disease. They carried small brass bells or carved wooden clappers, and bowls for alms. But with the rise in the number of cases, the king has established a hospital—in a manner of speaking—on Glöskar and had the king's wardens round up every leper in the islands as well as on either shore, Finland's or Sweden's.

Glum are the boatloads that pull into Glöskar: purulent, nodular, misshapen, sans toes or noses, looking despairingly down the short slope of a life spent with wretched, decomposing strangers whose only connection is that they are rotting together. Churches are commanded to send moneys and supplies to the nearest leprosaria. Some do. Many do not.

Nobles, and the king himself, occasionally make donations of lumber or money with the notation that this is being given "for the good of their souls," as if the action were placing a star on their heavenly charts, as if Luther had never determined that God did not operate that way, as if the Reformation had not happened.

Violeta's eyes are—this is part of the illness—devoid of their old keenness; still, she can still see the far shore, where no lepers may go, and yet where she is heading. Her features have disappeared behind the lumps and dunes of coarse flesh that disfigure her face, once so lovely.

Christina might find this some satisfaction, Violeta has thought more than once, if she were to see her now. Christina has spent the time in between becoming the political creature her father hoped to see in a son, a hardened and petulant woman not unlike the mother she so despised. She has converted to Catholicism—*what?*—and traveled south to Rome. Her life has been harsh and loveless, and yet a Spanish diplomat has called her "the biggest harlot in the world."

While Violeta has not kept a diary as Christina counseled her, not since her first one was swept overboard on the voyage to New Sweden, Christina has indeed recorded her every thought. She writes of her conception of herself as a "superman," the likes of whom the earth has rarely seen. She copies a maxim on the relationship of royals to their spiritual directors into her diary, tears it out, and rewrites it, as if she cannot bear to let it go:

Confessors of princes are like men engaged in taming tigers and lions:
they can induce the beasts to perform hundreds of movements and thou-
sands of actions, so that on seeing them one might believe they were com-
pletely tamed; but when the confessor least expects it, he is knocked over
by one blow of the animal's paw, which shows that such beasts can never
be completely tamed.

She blots the ink on the second version, sighs satisfaction, and pictures
herself as a lion in an equatorial jungle with palm trees and bright sun. She
sighs again. There is one swift second in this period when she remembers
Violeta, and she thinks of her not judgmentally but simply distantly, as a
small violet in a pot upon a windowsill, on the same day she has described
herself as both lion and superman.

Christina falls in love, passionately and uselessly, with a cardinal of the
church, Decio Azzolino, who has a reputation for dalliances with stage ac-
tresses. At the very second Violeta is struggling on the ice with Princeps and
Ullo's reins, Christina is sauntering with Azzolino through an orangerie, an
opulent glass-enclosed greenhouse filled with orange and lemon trees and
other delicate plants, as well as decadent *putti* and nymphs cast in copper
and turning a wonderful green.

As our Violeta drops the left rein onto the ice and Princeps leaps onto
Ullo's neck, Christina is leaning her ungainly head backward beside a wilt-
ing palm tree in the orangerie in Rome—looking less graceful than painful—to form up a witty retort to the cardinal on the subject of Portuguese
portraiture. Christina laughs with what she assumes to be charm, and the
cardinal looks over her shoulder at a sad tropical bird flitting miserably
about up near the frosted panes of the greenhouse roof, bonking its tiny
skull again and again on the panes.

VIOLETA'S HEAD IS fogged with the wretched anxiety of the last days:
voices clamor and pound in her brain. The voice of the warden of Lazarus-
Magdalen, Lars Nikolas Lefthoven, harangues the group at assembly: *You*
worthless, perverse spawn of Satan! You rotting sons of basilisks! You purulent
useless whores. Violeta remembers the abuse verbatim, as well as her own in-

ner replies as she sits there determinedly knitting despite her hands' pain: *And why are we useless whores, warden? Because we will not lie beneath you?*

There is the imagined voice of the king, in the letter read to them: "It is the good pleasure of the Crown to insist that the parishes of Saltvik, Vårdö, and Finström return immediately to the payment of fitting allotments toward the support of the lepers of Glöskar." The voice of the new king, Karl Gustav, Christina's cousin and their childhood playmate, in Violeta's head, is not much changed from the schoolroom. The edict is impotent, as there are no sheriffs to enforce it. Lefthoven is without power himself, and lepers have no way of insisting on anything.

There are the voices of various lepers. The voice of the man with the terrible uneven loping gait—seeming to insist, by his attempt at speed, that he is not crippled, when indeed it is excruciating even to watch him—whines that Violeta has taken his bowl, again and again. The man's mind is gone, his rant incoherent. The voice of the woman who has slept next to Violeta in the women's hut rasps in her head: *Give me that, give me this, give me the other thing.* Usually it is a blanket she demands, or a bandage, or sometimes Violeta's bread.

There is the voice of the man who, the day before, pinned Violeta against the shed wall and then knocked her onto the hard ground and insisted on having his way with her: his voice in her mind is groaning, and there is even a stench to it. Though she escaped, leaving the man standing trouserless out in the snow, that moment determined her to take off in the dog sled, this very day.

Then there are the voices of Oscar Lucassen and her son, Carl-Marcus, whom she has not seen since he was five, since the leprosy showed itself and she was forced here. Oscar's consistent deep rich basso is unforgettable. Carl-Marcus's voice is as it was in early childhood, piping, calling out to her as he comes running up the path from the pond to the house, on the land that her husband, Per Marcus, had left to her. He holds out before him in offering a small sweaty handful of clover flowers and wild violets. The large sleek black retriever, Herr Svartz, who is his constant companion, runs at his heels, his pink tongue wagging. "Mor, Mor!" he is calling: mother, mother, in Swedish. "See what I found for you!"

Violeta is suddenly overcome by great hot tears. Carl-Marcus has gone to the university to study by this time, she knows this from letters. He will be a scholar like his father. His voice in adolescence deepened to bass, though not to the great depths of Oscar's. She has not heard that voice. She wants to see him, right now.

His image rises before her eyes, much like his father in musculature and strawberry blond hair, his hair having however the wild wiry texture of her own. His eyes are the very image of hers; never having known Per Marcus's parents, much less her own, she has no idea that Carl-Marcus is his paternal grandfather's double, in almost all respects. She cannot know that his handsome aquiline nose is his grandfather's: when she last saw him it was only a button. She wants to tell Carl-Marcus he has made everything in her life worthwhile. Just one more time she would like to see him, just one more. *Please, God, once more.* She wants to thank Oscar Lucassen.

Princeps and Ullo suddenly break apart with a huge burst of vitality, having gnawed through their harness and tugged it apart into ribbon shreds. They rip one rein out of her hands and leap dancerlike into the air, as if gravity has been rescinded. They bark wildly and take off running in the direction of Föglö, on the horizon. Violeta, aching in her missing of Carl-Marcus, is too overwhelmed by her feelings to let the extremity of her plight penetrate. Oh, the silly dogs, she thinks. They will come back.

To fend off her fear, she begins to hum, in the full beautiful voice that has continued to astound the other lepers and the warden, proceeding as it does from this little woman whose bodily frame is decaying around her. The dogs grow smaller and smaller as they head toward Föglö. Their yipping is carried back to her on the wind, happy and free. The fragment of rein in her hands hangs limp and useless.

The tune she is humming comes up from some deep place in her. She follows its curves, trying to remember in what hymnal she learned this song. She cannot remember, but she continues to hum, as if despite the ice that surrounds her, she is a spring, and the music is issuing from a crevice deep in the earth.

Her voice follows the leaps of the dogs in their joy, and though she cannot know it the melody she sings is identical to the motif in the final movement of Beethoven's Sixth Symphony, the "Pastorale," which will not be written for almost two centuries. When Beethoven conceives it, he will think that this expresses in song the fresh, calm time after a thunderstorm in spring.

Violeta, under her sealskin and rug in the dogless sled, the reins ripped to tatters and lying beside her on the frozen sea, nonetheless hums the same tune: the dogs' escape has indeed ended her storm, her struggle to hold on, and a kind of peace washes over her. She is so tired from the sleeplessness of the last week, and the wrestling with the decision to run away and the counterpoint fear of not running, that she sighs and thinks vaguely: *A nap would be excellent.*

She wiggles under the robes to generate warmth in her body. The face of Christina at age seven, when the girls are out together, chasing birds in the spring in the palace courtyard, giggling wildly, rises before her mind's eye. In the distance the dogs are just specks on the ice.

An image of Oscar Lucassen pops up as if this were a puppet show: Oscar is bending to talk to Carl-Marcus; Carl-Marcus is four, his eyes wide with wonder as Oscar Lucassen describes his birthplace in Africa in great detail. Her mind's eye remembers the wonderful smell of him, like good clay. In the daydream Carl-Marcus and Oscar are outdoors on the family land, where Oscar now lives alone as conservator, where Carl-Marcus comes home on school holidays. In three years he will bring back a bride, the daughter of a professor at Uppsala, who resembles his mother in her youth, and in four years there will be a daughter . . . whose cheekbones will pass down the ages to Anne Marie Maki Wong, and then to Ursula.

An image of a seven-branched candlestick—she cannot think where she saw this—arises in Violeta's mind. Seven flames flicker wildly on seven pale thick tallow candles, as if in a high wind. Faces she cannot discern seem to peer out from the flames, as from curtains. Violeta fights a powerful need to sleep. In the distance the dogs have disappeared.

Violeta closes her eyes and sees Carl-Marcus nestled against her breast two hours after his birth, when huge dark Oscar Lucassen arrived to see him for the first time. Oscar Lucassen is glowing with pride and joy, as if the child were his own, and indeed he will treat the boy as if he were.

As it happens, the feisty dogs are captured the following day—by means of a length discarded pork intestine—by a butcher in Föglö, who cannot imagine where they came from. As it happens as well, the third day it snows, and the snow covers the body of Violeta and the sled, until from a distance the whole seems to be a small, somehow unnatural hill.

The dogs in their squabbling have taken the sled quite a distance off its trajectory. Since only a very occasional skater or sled ever passes between Föglö and Glöskar—there is little traffic with the lepers, in winter's depths none at all—and the sled has gone far off course, before the spring thaw melts the ice underneath the sled runners, no one ever sees the small unnatural hill that is Violeta the leper, dead of the cold. When the ice melts she sinks quickly, silently, with her conveyance, into the Baltic, to become meat for submarine scavengers as had her husband, Per Marcus, out in the Atlantic, as well as the wretched dwarf his murderer.

In June of that year, folk all around are preparing for the Midsummer Feast, born in pagan antiquity. All night there are bonfires in the cool air, and dancing and often debauchery, to which dour pastors most often turn a blind eye, sighing. On godforsaken Glöskar, three of the least-ill lepers hang a *Midsommarstong*—a Midsummer cross—with looping chains of flowers. Indoors by candlelight, the warden of Lazarus-Magdalen writes up his annual report. No one in Stockholm, to which his report will be carried by boat, and then by horse post, will read it anyway. As he tries to recall the name of that eaten-away little woman who disappeared, stealing the sled and the dogs in the bargain, to report that, if he should, he cannot. Still, in his mind, oddly, there hovers a scent of wild violets.

9 Jinx

JOE CIMMER IS up in the cab of his truck, in the driver's seat, surveying the lot of the Z-Bay truck stop in Sheilah Falls, Montana, as if he were in a Tarantino flick and the action were coming up any time now. Joe has been gone from his family now for too many years. On the road, time does not pass the same. The lights are hellish and dazzling, casino-like.

The cigarette smell of the previous driver assigned to the truck hasn't faded, though Joe's had the truck for eleven months. The blue-gray upholstery is marinated in smoke. It riles Joe. He's in recovery from that particular vice and steeped in self-righteousness. How anybody could have lived like that is totally beyond him. It's two years he's been a nonsmoker.

The lot's a dark carnival tonight, backlit by the purple-and-emerald-green sign of the Z-Bay convenience store. Even the diesel pumps look kind of extraterrestrial. Diesel-odor thick air. Human-stockyard piss smell rising off the asphalt. Wretched hot night, no breeze for relief.

The hookers are crawling, as usual, but it looks as if what they want tonight isn't so much the buck as simply cool, wet air-conditioning. Joe is observing a transaction not fifty feet away: the woman is long-limbed and verging on stringy, a carny look. Her bright red dyed hair is ratted up with clawlike clip combs through which the light from the purple-and-green sign comes shining, eerie. She looks as if she has gotten here hand over hand on a vine hung with flat fifths of whiskey. She reminds him of someone, he can't think who.

He's betting himself that poor sucker in the Peterbilt is going to let her into his cab. He can see from here, she's got those flashy acrylic nails, talon-like, painted unnatural colors, jukebox hues. Joe can't see that she's got lit-tle crappy flamingos there too, and paid extra for them, but she does. She's tapping her nails rhythmically, *dada-rttt, dada-rttt,* on the passenger win-dow the guy has rolled halfway down to talk to her. Joe wants to climb back into his sleeping compartment, crank down the AC, eat a fried pie. Drink that quart of milk he bought a few minutes ago in the Z-Bay Quik-Stop, be-fore it goes lukewarm.

The gal with the jukebox nails keeps hanging on to the guy's running board. She's wearing these white vinyl boots that come up to here, and this chick's shorts are short. Joe wants the transaction over. It always makes him feel better to see someone else fall into what he won't, ever again. Makes him feel like a conquering hero, when the guy takes her in. *Win-win,* he thinks. The guy gets what he wants, and Joe—the invisible watcher who wants to feel he's on moral high ground—does too.

But the girl gives up finally. She lets go and swings down to the asphalt. She turns and gives the guy's tires a kick with a toe of the white vinyl boot, which glows weirdly in the lot light. She wipes sweat from her forehead with a hanky she pulls from a shorts pocket, then she moseys along to the next truck in line.

Joe loses interest and climbs back into his sleeping compartment. He set-tles down with a *USA Today* he picked up in a booth at a McDonald's not far from Missoula. There is a ketchup blot on the front page of the *Money* sec-tion. He feels like an astronaut circling the earth, high up, higher even than when he is in the driver's seat. He is not in this world that he reads about.

The paper has news of another suicide bombing in Israel, a sidewalk café, a terrorist group taking credit for it; an Israeli bulldozer is trying to ram, to crush, the house of a Palestinian family, and a couple of old ladies are stand-ing in front of the dozer refusing to move while a few little kids gawk. There is another famine in Africa, kids looking dry-skinned pale for Africans, hollow-eyed, balloon-bellied. Prince William poses—photogenic, narcis-sistic, preening—with a new girlfriend or fan. Joe can't be bothered. The girl's eyes are pale and sad, like a Weimaraner dog's, and her lipstick looks like something out of the sixties, pink white.

Joe wonders what it would be like to come home at night, to pick up the morning's *USA Today*—no strangers' condiments spotting it—and sit down on the sofa like what he calls a "normal stiff." To come home to a wife who cooks dinner and then maybe watch an hour of TV. Dull TV. Perfect, a perfect life.

He remembers Mindy Ji's cooking: the dish she called Chinese sauer-braten; her "Chinese" corned beef and cabbage with butter and salt drool-ing off; her "Chinese" custard pie with the surface that cracked like the cracks on the tortoiseshell oracle bones she had shown him in books; her "Sichuan" coleslaw, for godsake—she'd tell him that, laughing, pushing the glass bowl at him across the old wooden table: just plain, pale coleslaw with little soft flecks of pimiento.

Joe has driven past their old place in Sault Saint Marie on three different occasions since he left, tentative passes, not having half an idea what he'd do if he saw either of them—first three years and then eight years after he left, on visits back to the area. Then again last year, he had routes that took him nearby, the most recent time delivering Polaris snowmobiles to dealers' showrooms.

Again he'd seen neither hide nor hair of her. But why would she still be there? The first two times he'd looked in the phone book. No Mindy. He wondered if she'd just picked up and left or married some guy who came into the restaurant. No, she was just unlisted: too many breather calls, but Joe had no way to know that. The last time he passed through he hadn't even looked in the directory: if he had he'd have seen a new listing: Wong, Justin, and Anne Marie.

HE HAD STOPPED trying to visualize Justin grown: in his mind Justin was still almost three years old, standing solid as a little tank by the fence. He was waving, his hand sloshing back and forth like a little wind-shield wiper, his bowl-cut shock of black hair blowing up like silk fringe in the wind. Joe had tried to explain to himself why he'd left, years ago, and had never come up with an answer. Fear, sure, but of what? He could not have told anyone.

But nobody asked. He had gone on the road with a different band, then switched again, always thinking that in a month or so he'd pick up the phone and give Mindy a call. He'd be sheepish. He couldn't explain to her either. He remembered trying to tie knots years ago when he was a Boy Scout, and doing fine with that, but when it came time to untie them, he was at a loss. He had really made a knotty mess this time. It seemed unundoable.

His own father, Lukas, had left his mother when he was three. He felt as if he were on cosmic autopilot, repeating a riff till the world's end. By the time he got out to the West Coast two years later, procrastinating month after month, spinning out good intentions, Justin would have been in kindergarten, and Mindy would surely be married to somebody else. She'd have filed for divorce and it would have been posted in the paper or whatever they do. No response, so they'd have given it to her. Made sense, made damn good sense. Smart woman, that's what she'd have done.

So he stopped thinking he'd call. Better, probably. Better for her.

Maybe somebody who could give her what he couldn't: good money, a new house. The house would have a brick front, oh, hell, maybe be all brick. A long driveway, three-car garage. Somebody who could raise his boy the way he would never be able to: maybe to be a doctor, a lawyer. He tried to picture Justin now and could not: it was always the three-year-old face on the now grown-up body, Joe's height but without the paunch. Gorgeous kid. He had seen Keanu Reeves in a movie when he was younger and thought: *Will he look like that?* That had become an advantage today, the half-breed part. Affirmative action now. Hey, who could figure the world today, what would come next?

Joe tried to imagine Mindy Ji transformed from the hippie girl she had been into a cool subdivision mom—sleek little haircut, that shiny black hair razored saucily, expensive clothes bought from a New England catalog—driving a compact car. Or maybe an SUV. It would be silver. A golden retriever with all kinds of energy bounding out of the backseat, Justin chasing him. Justin was fifteen at this point, when Joe was concocting alternative lives for them, but there in the film in his mind was Justin's three-year-old face again.

Joe was angry at the usurper, this guy who had stolen his Mindy. Wait!

If she'd remarried, maybe there were more kids, and Justin was a big brother. He was imagining twins, a couple of little girls who looked like Mindy but paler because the usurper was white. Some fat white jerk. *Like me*, he thought, pressing his palm to the fifteen pounds of belly he'd put on recently, after the ten he'd put on a few years before. He was imagining Mindy Ji pregnant with twins, several years before. They'd be in grade school now. He was furious.

AT THIS POINT (Justin fifteen, the interloper and the little twin Mindy Ji clones nonexistent) Joe was still playing in L.A. but ready to give up the life and go over the road. It had taken a dozen years to dull the edge of the faculty in him that gave rise to his music, but yep, he was now to that point. He took a class at a truck-driving school—he would be reimbursed for the tuition the minute he finished and hired on the spot. There, he had done it. A whole new nonlife and the death of hope. Excellent.

So Joe is back in his bunk now, with all the lot lizards prowling the Z-Bay asphalt. He pulls out his wallet from the back pocket of his jeans. Cloudy plastic sleeves sheathe two snapshots of Mindy Ji and two of Justin. There had been a fifth picture, of all three together, but years ago Joe had put it away somewhere for safekeeping—and also because it just made him hurt to see it. He pulls the back-to-back pictures of Mindy Ji out of their sleeve.

There's the one he took of her on a great fall day, what year? Sometime during the Vietnam War, under the trees out in back of the house. The leaves swirled around their feet, yellow and brown, dry and shiffling: he recalled standing ankle-deep in leaves to take the picture. Mindy Ji was clowning on a stump, with a round terra-cotta pot balanced atop her head, and wearing a silly face. Her orange blouse made her look part of the autumn landscape. Her shoes used to look weirdly unfashionable to Joe when he'd look at the picture, but now the clunky seventies style had come back. The other picture is a photo-booth snapshot, caught at an odd moment, with a look that is Mindy Ji's quizzical, out-of-this-world face. Joe puts them back into their sleeve.

The smaller picture of Justin is from the hospital, a strangely faded newborn portrait. His face is dark red against the pale crib sheet and squashed, like an old apple gone soft; his eyes are slits, and his balled-up fists like a tiny boxer's are caught in midair. In the second picture, a snapshot of Justin on his second birthday, he is sitting on the wood floor, shoes and socks off, little brown toes splayed as if to let the breeze blow between them. He is holding one of Joe's harmonicas, and the look on his face is one of wonder. Joe slips these pictures back into their sleeves too.

There is a rap at his cab window up front. He raises an eyebrow and ignores it. *USA Today* is going on about baby-boomer teen-consumer profiles relative to Gen X teen-consumer profiles. The gist is that there is more money around and more stuff. News, right? The rap comes again, and he hears a voice. "Joey!" It's coarse, it's cajoling. It's loud. He can hear it through the rolled-up window.

He frowns. Who the hell? Nobody calls him Joey. Nobody. Nobody here even knows him. What the hell! He crumples the paper and slams it against the bed. He pokes his head out. It's the redheaded hooker.

"Get lost," he says flatly. Then he rolls down the window a couple of inches. "And where the hell do you get off calling me Joey?"

"That's my old boyfriend's name!" she says, sprightly, as if that means something. "And your name is right there on your, um, truck thing." She pronounces it: "Joseph Kimmer."

He doesn't correct her. This is not a conversation he wants to go any further.

"So why don't you let me in, honey?" she says.

"No, thanks," Joe says. "I gave at the office."

"Gave what?" she says. She laughs a half-cackle of a laugh. Something about the laugh is familiar.

"I've got work to do," Joe says. "You too. Move along." He winks genially, but his patience is short. "Check out that razzle-dazzle rig over there. The black with the flames painted on. Now *there* is a guy who is looking for action, I'll bet you."

"Not you, Joey? You're cute." She smiles, and the fallen-in quality of her cheeks shows. Joe figures her for thirty-three but she's looking like forty-five right there around the eyes.

"Not me," Joe says. "But I wish you the best. You and all of the other ladies. Tell 'em what I said, that I gave at the office, okay? That they don't have to bother knocking."

She harrumphs. "I got nothing to do with them, Joey," she says, dismissive. "You got to be lonely tonight," she suggests again, her voice lilting up on the question. Then she shrugs, gives up, and swings down from her perch, heading toward the flame-detailed black rig Joe had pointed out.

As she walks away Joe sees the flashing lights of the diesel island peeking through her high, teased hair. Dispassionately he watches the odd, high-school-athlete way she swings her hips. Volleyball player, he'd bet. She turns sideways and waves back at him. Joe thinks, Goddamn. Jinx Muehlenberg—that's who she looks like. That bitch.

BOLTS OF FABRIC—a half dozen of them—stack high on a table across the room from her, next to one of the floor-to-ceiling windows with their dozens and dozens of mid-nineteenth-century panes. Light from the tall window falls on the fabric stack. Jinx Muehlenberg is drinking gin right now, in a fat rocks glass from Caesars Palace, where her parents went for years on their vacations.

She is not watching the play of the light on the fabric or thinking about the fact that the sunlight this afternoon is the same sunlight that has fallen on Michigan since it belonged to the Chippewas, and even before that, since it belonged to the mammoths and saber-toothed tigers that lived at the edge of the receding glacier. Same sunlight, huh? she would say if this were pointed out to her, and look at the speaker as if he were cuckoo.

The bolts of fabric are a deep forest green lit with small flicks of flame red and yellow. Their paisley pattern—based on a shrimp-shaped blossom known only in India, and named after mills in the city of Paisley, in Scotland—means nothing particular to her, does not ignite joy or passion in her. The bolts in the upstairs bedroom, similarly, piled on the heavy dark dresser that had been her grandmother's, mean nothing to her in themselves. They are green on a white linenlike ground—"celadon green," the designer had called it. Jinx had replied "whatever" with such a flatted affect that the younger woman, whose name was Laurel or Lauren or one of those poured-in-a-perfect-mold sorts of names, stared back oddly. The design repeats and repeats: a classic flowering Tree of Life pattern rooted in a rocky mound.

Rich as both patterns are, still to Virginia Jean—"Jinx"—Muehlenberg they are just random emblems of control and autonomy. That is to say, her own. Marking her territory. She's redoing the house—this house that she has always hated, this millstone around the neck, this thing that ties her to roots—to make it fully hers, to claim it, since she has no goddamn choice.

Her father's will specifies that the house cannot be sold for fifteen years, and other significant moneys are contingent on Jinx's abiding by that clause. Her father had been such a hard one. She feels his hand reaching up out of the grave and pulling at the pants leg of her purple-pink nylon warmup suit as if this were a zombie flick. He couldn't be content just to die. But then, she thinks, laughing to herself, *He taught me everything I know.* How she chose the fabrics: Well, here were some colors that seemed not to bother her too much. They disappeared when she was looking at them. She said that to the designer. The designer gave her that look again.

"That's a sign of taste," said the girl, who could not be more than twenty-six. She was working hard at working with Jinx.

"Taste, schmaste," said Jinx. She was not uncomfortable realizing that this was her father's voice rising up in her. He had said that very thing twice or three times. There is no one in this town—this *damned* town, she calls it, invariably—whom she intends to have over. But now that her parents have died and left everything to her, the properties here and downstate, the trusts, all three businesses, she will make the house hers.

Her plan, now in progress for several weeks, is to expunge all the "family stuff." She will get rid of the dour sepia portraits of ancestor judges and family groups posed out in front of the mansard-roofed house when it was still raw and new, every group with at least one face blurred by impatient wiggling while the photographer made the exposure. She will have someone haul off the tall dark-cabineted hall clock with Westminster chimes that reminded her of childhood nights when she could not sleep and heard the tolling at each quarter hour. She will unload the goddamned many-ton cast-iron daybed upstairs for whose retention the Lori or Lauren girl keeps softly arguing.

"Can't you see it with, oh, one of those antique toile de Nantes coverlets, brownish rose, don't you remember, in the Jouet catalog? Oh, it would be beautiful, Ms. Muehlenberg! The bed in a smooth cream enamel . . ." she rattles on happily, in her imaginings—mornings awakening in slanting pink sunlight, that kind of thing.

Jinx cuts her off short. "Would you just . . . would you can it about toiles de Nantes? Could I not one more time hear that toile de Nantes crap?"

The decorator bites her ripe little cocoa pink lower lip but will bring it up later, for sure. She is a feisty girl, for all her delicacy. No one will ever use the room anyway, she will argue—this is most likely true—and it is easier to redo the room than to move out the monstrous curlicued iron thing she deems so exquisite. The daybed, she argues, will be out of sight, out of mind. "Decision making by gravity," she tosses off, in a bit of fatalist logic, which is not her own but which she thinks—correctly—will make sense to this prickly client. "Think of how much you would have to pay local help to get the thing out of here." The designer has heard Jinx use this very phrase contemptuously—"local help"—as if everyone here grunted rather than speaking and had close-set eyes, signifying that cousins had mated again and again in the family tree.

This is the piece of the Lori girl's logic that finally will do the trick, this appeal to contempt for the locals. Next will go the forties and fifties and six-ties stuff her mother and father held dear, in what she calls their "hideous fat-ass nouveau-riche taste." There are several huge reproductions of hunt-ing scenes and mythic white fat, marbled goddesses, with huge gnarled off-green trees making massive and velvety shadows. In the paintings there are black-and-white spotted dogs everywhere and hunting horns propped about. A horse or two flares its nostrils and shows its eye whites in shadows thrown by the tree branches. The originals of the paintings must have come from some small country in Europe. The frames are baroque, gilded wood.

There are several smaller clocks around the house that had been her mother's. The woman loved clocks. A cuckoo clock from the Black Forest when they were there not too long after the war, before Jinx was born. The year, maybe, the first child had died in infancy, hit by a delivery truck in the driveway, the son she would replace. The trip to make them forget that. Jinx brings to her mind's eye the snapshot of her parents, Marva and George, posed on that trip in front of the gate of a German death camp, with odd looks on their faces—pride? puzzlement? In her mind her father wears lederhosen, but that is only her imagination. There is a porcelain clock with a small china figurine of a girl, blond and braided, swinging a pendulum, *swing* swing, *swing* swing. A framed picture of her mother as a girl in Wisconsin, with red braids and pink plastic frames to her glasses. A perpetual clock in a glass dome. A plaque that her father had been given by the Elks Club, with three different years engraved on it, for something or other. All this has to go.

Jinx needs no clocks at all in the house: somehow, time grieves and angers her, in its feeling quite beyond her control. Her digital Seiko is fine, thanks. It can wake her up, even those mornings when the night before she has drunk too much, its small beep almost a bird's heartbeat, yet just enough.

ON THE EARLY evening of the day Ursula falls down the hole—Justin has reached Eagle Harbor and the rescue team has been alerted, and quickly the TV news teams and the press are converging—Jinx is slid down into the heavily embossed salmon-and-gold brocade cushions of the sofa her mother had bought the year she was a junior in high school, in '66. The loll she affects is a stiff loll, her repose slightly starched. She is trying to balance herself and not slip from the sofa. Her slipper bottoms are slick: she has just noticed this as she has tried to push up and sit straight, and they've slipped on the plush of the carpet. *Got no traction,* she thinks. She says the word aloud, "traction," just to hear the sound of it. "Traction."

She is three-quarters drunk. She holds up her rocks glass in front of the TV and swishes the single ice cube—a little chill, but no serious dilution—and the olive around. *Olive?* she thinks. *Who put an* olive *in there?* Through the glass and the distortions of cut glass and cube of ice she looks at the bright colors of the TV screen as if they were a kaleidoscope.

"No, I am thoroughly inebriated," she argues, with no one.

On the TV screen the emergency management team swarms. A young woman who has been flown in from somewhere civilized—where, Detroit? Chicago? Minneapolis?—is giving an update. "Brandi Chandler-Greene here," she is saying, "bringing you updated coverage . . ."

Jinx quickly squashes a soft rubber nub on the palm-shaped remote control in her hand and wipes out the sound. Jinx grew up with no one but Finns and Germans and the descendants of French trappers and then the local Chippewas. She hates what she calls "black folks" with a passion more expectable in an Alabama sheriff from her parents' day.

"I don't *think* so," she says in the direction of the screen, far too loud. "Oh no no, my honey brown honey, I really don't think so." She takes a big swig of her gin, as if it were water. "No, not *Brandi Chandler-Greene*, sweetie. Come on. What's it really? Taneesha Laqueesha Green?"

She scoots her bottom back slightly onto the sofa cushions. Her nylon warmup suit, which she routinely wears around the house after her shower, has no more traction than her slipper bottoms. The towel around her hair starts slipping free, and several hunks of wet hair freshly rinsed in Deep Auburn escape. She fishes the fat pimiento-stuffed olive out of its floaty place deep in her gin—"Who cares who put it there?" she says out loud— and sinks her teeth into the flesh of it. She sucks out the pimiento like a human Hoover—she says that word aloud also, "Hoover," to the empty room —and sinks into a shallowly buried recent memory, interred alive.

SHE IS REMEMBERING a twilight evening the previous week. Out front was a pickup truck parked near the steps, from some workman or other. She had just come down, after taking her shower. Dusk had overtaken the house while she was upstairs. She had fallen asleep for a while, just before that. No light was on downstairs. The shadows were deep.

On the porch, she sensed movement. She stood back in shadow to see who this was. A young man, propping a ladder, just briefly, to retrieve a tool or some such, from the edge of the porch roof. She watched as he climbed. Tight young butt. Nice strong legs in those jeans, thigh muscles outlined as he moved, through the worn denim. Lots of dark hair, tied back at the nape of his neck in that ponytailed sixties way that had come back.

Chippewa, maybe? She sniffed, flaring her nostrils. She had known Chippewa boys in grade school and called them all Cochise. Something in her liked the rich way that they smelled when they sweated in gym, and another thing in her fought that down as if she were wrestling an alligator. In her freshman year of high school there were nothing but dumb Finns and Chippewas, besides herself. *Aryan*, she liked to call herself, joking or not. She complained to her father, who at the end of the term sent her downstate to a boarding school run by an order of Polish nuns.

The beds in the dormitory were like short gravel driveways, the food something out of a dour Victorian novel she'd never read and did not ever want to. She was forced to wear uniforms, green-and-brown plaid. Each day she got demerits for breaking the uniform code: she wore knee socks, a neck scarf, costume jewelry (dangling mesh earrings, a charm bracelet), purple eye shadow, which her best friend at the time said made her—with her auburn hair—look like a whore. She did these things one at a time or together.

Her father gave money to build a school chapel. The bright geometric stained-glass windows on either side of the small altar said, in brass tags at their bottoms, on the left, GIFT OF GEORGE MUEHLENBERG, and on the right, GIFT OF MRS. MARVA JEAN FEDERER MUEHLENBERG.

The nuns kept Jinx on. In the summers she got sent to camp in Wisconsin.

The uniform business was more than a game: it was an obsession. The prefect of discipline, a Prussian general of a sexless nun, rode her little cart in the school hall giving out chits for detentions, Penance Hall. Jinx called her mother long distance and stormed and whined, and her mother sent her brand-new twenty-dollar bills and called her Honey and asked if she'd like a new angora sweater or something, and said maybe she could catch a twin-engine down to Detroit in a couple of weekends and they could go shopping, and wouldn't that be a fun time? And how was Sister Ann Stanislaus? Was she well?

Jinx watched the young workman. Since her second divorce, she had disconnected herself from anything that resembled hope, as previously she had unhooked herself first from any semblance of faith (that at the convent school), then from love (in her first marriage, to the fat broker who had looked, up front, like a reasonable, grown-up deal).

She remembered the boys in high school, the backs of station wagons, the one in particular where she had cut herself rolling over onto the harp that was that boy's sister's. The transport of the harp was the reason the family had bought the big car at all. She remembered that boy sucking her blood as her hand ran red, and the way she could feel her own lip curl back as she watched him, disconnected, sucking and licking her wrist like a dog, like a vampire. She recalled looking down at her own body, naked except for her shoes and socks, and smelling all of the mess they had made, and laughing hysterically. She did not remember where they had been parked, whether there were trees around, or that there had been a star shower that night that could be seen far and wide. She had not known about the star shower until afterward, and would not have taken the trouble to watch for it if she had known.

She remembered the abortion that following spring, just two weeks before Formal, and the look on the face of the doctor, who did this on the side, on the q.t., but everyone seemed to know anyway. The look on his face, she thought, would have seemed right in place in the picture at the death camp, standing smiling next to the tall crematorium chimney.

The smile on his face was a rictus. "And, according to this chart, this is your third?" he had said. "I suggest more care, young lady."

Jinx remembered her quick response, not out loud, but inside: *Fuck you.*

She remembered her next response, which seemed to give her more control. "You've been paid," she said. "Can the advice."

She still now this evening over thirty years later, watching this young workman on the porch—despite the absence of faith, hope, or love—could feel something like lust. She was feeling something resembling that now.

But this was not her usual sort of thing. "Usual" might mean striking up a conversation about the shitty service in first class with a man in an airport VIP lounge or in a hotel bar. The light could be right or wrong, atmospheric or fluorescent: it did not matter. The man could be porky or wizened, all wiry gray or looking as if he were auditioning for a role as a stand-in for Robert Redford fifteen years ago.

None of that mattered. She was just hungry: aesthetics, irrelevant. If she were hungry she'd tear into any gristly roast, any cheap loaf of white bread:

it did not matter. The gin she was drinking would probably rot her gut, but it was bought at a very good price by the case, wholesale, and it did the job.

But at this moment the impulse wakened in her by this young workman proceeded from some other place. This was not indiscriminate ravening. The chill twilight behind the boy was rich as a rainbow, shot with purple and red and a streak of remaining bright sky so white it looked silver. It framed the young man in a startling, beautiful way she did not want to ac-knowledge. In profile she saw that his nose and cheekbones seemed un-Indian. She watched as he wiped his brow with his forearm, a flannel sleeve over his T-shirt.

She was wearing the warmup suit she wore around the house, standing in shadow against the wall, back of a lamp table. Her eyes traced the shapes of the young man's biceps in his rolled T-shirt sleeves. The belt loops of his jeans stood out in high relief as she stared, and his shirt stuck to his body with workman's sweat. She could see the muscles of his left side rippling under the T-shirt as he reached for the overhead gutter, working loose a piece of metal or branch that protruded. She could almost see dark hair un-der his arm.

She unzipped the front of the warmup jacket. In the half dark, the sound of the usually silent plastic zipper seemed incredibly loud. She stepped out of the running pants. She had never had to fight her weight like her cousins and took pride in her tight small hips, though she did nothing to keep them that way. For a moment, she stood in shadow, without the pants, jacket half off, and then slipped her hand inside the jacket and fondled her left breast, rolling the nipple between thumb and forefinger.

The boy seemed to be ready to descend to the porch now. He shifted his weight on the ladder's top rung. She leaned forward and tugged at the lamp cord. The light came on. He was a pretty boy. Ah, no, not Chippewa. Maybe Chinese. He did not see her there yet, a dozen feet into the interior of the house.

She moved her fingers around her own nipple like turning the tiny knob on her car radio. Right station, yes, this was right, a station she had never picked up before, but interesting. How long had it been since she'd had any-one? Long calendar pages, all of their squares empty, empty. Who cared if it had been six minutes or sixty years, really? She hated time and she detested the god who invented it. That god smelled like the false teeth of Polish nuns. That god rode a cart in the hall like the prefect of discipline handing out Penance Hall summonses.

She smelled her body in salty heat. She knew that the light from the lamp lay across her white flesh just as she had intended, perfectly oblique. She passed her left hand, somehow with a flourish, like a stage magician's, across the bright bush of her pubic hair and slipped her thumb into it, backward, nudging her nail against soft flesh and hungry nerve. "Ah," she said, involuntarily, and heard herself say it. She shifted the heel of her hand slightly. She made another small sound of something like simple surprise.

"Okay," she whispered. "China Boy. Look here, China Boy." She moved slightly in the light, but only slightly. On the porch, the workman stopped, sensing movement, and squinted, not sure what had changed since he climbed up the ladder. Was it the light? The living-room curtain liners were closed, but they were that sort of nylon the sixties liked, almost completely transparent. He could see a woman's shape, standing back near the wall. What was she doing?

She pretended not to see him. She let the jacket fall back from her breasts, which were full and pale pink, their nipples erect and side lit. She closed her eyes. She had seen that the China boy had seen her now. *Good,* she thought. *Excellent.*

She isn't. Is she? the boy thought. He stood, a fistful of branches pulled free from the gutter in one hand, transfixed, disbelieving.

Goddamn, she thought, peering out of the slits of the corners of her eyes, *I'll bet he's fine-looking up close.* The twilight was closing in, back of him, quickly now, all that aurora effect being swallowed by night. *Not much more than a teenager,* she thought. *Just enough.*

She slipped off the jacket entirely and was all white skin passing through the light for a split second. She picked up the towel she had used for her hair. She wrapped herself in it, casually, as if she did not see him there stunned at this spectacle. She did not look at him. She walked slowly diagonally across the room, first into and then out of the light, into the deep shadow of the front hall.

She heard a sound on the porch, then a light, agile thud on the packed dirt in front of the porch. He had leaped down. Of course. He was wearing those workman's boots. Sure. He could do that. Was he chickenshit? Was that the thing? She went to the door. The lock stuck. She swore under her breath.

The lock came undone. "Okay, China Boy," she said. "Time for some Chinese take-out. Fortune cookie say . . ."

She stepped, in her towel, into the doorway, and looked to the left. He was gone. The silver truck, almost invisible in the shadows now, started up.

"Fuck," she said. "Almost." She turned and went inside and slipped on her pants, then her jacket. She thought of the look of his well-muscled back as he climbed the short ladder.

Now, a week and more later, she lounges diagonal in her gin, staring at the faux gems on the toes of her soft leather slippers, the kind she had always mocked when her mother had worn them. She would not wear her mother's, though they were the same size. But now that her mother was gone, she could wear them herself without seeming compromised. She had bought new ones just like the ones that her mother had worn.

"Shit," she says aloud, to no one. "I paid for them, didn't I?"

Brandi Chandler-Greene talks intensely into her mike, gesturing in the direction of some movement in the near background. She has expressive eyebrows, and her makeup is flawless.

Behind her, the camera and rescue crews move about. Jinx Muehlenberg sees a blond girl in a long skirt leaning on a young man with a dark ponytail. She makes no connection to that stuff last week.

"All of that goddamn money and energy," she says, under her breath. "Wasted." She takes a drink. She feels her brow tight, slightly awry. "Wasted. On that goddamn half-breed trailer-trash kid."

AT THE MINE shaft north of Eagle River, it is late afternoon before anyone else has arrived. Justin and Annie spend three hours breathing as shallowly as they can breathe, holding each other, trying not to look at the clock in the truck too often. Justin yells "God" every once in a while, a roar. They try to drink tea from a thermos. It tastes like piss. They sit staring at each other. Life has been leached of itself. The shadows move, and they breathe, and the birds call out. "*That* is a red-winged blackbird," Justin says. He can say nothing else. "We've just got to trust that they'll get here," says Annie. So they choose to wait, since they cannot do anything else.

The dispatcher at 911 has said to Justin there's *one* rule he must follow when he gets back.

"What's that?" Justin says.

"Do not do *anything* near that hole, guy," she says. She wants to call him "hon" or "sweetie." His voice is a lot like her son's. She wants to hug him through the phone. "First rule of rescue," she says, "is not to create any more victims."

"*What?*" Justin says, as if she's speaking in proto-Vulcan.

"I said *do not go near that hole,*" says the dispatcher. "Understand?"

Justin is just realizing she's right, that that will indeed be his first impulse when he returns: he can already feel it arising. He'll say, "Goddamn it, I'm not going to wait for those fuckers," and think he can do anything he needs to. After all, this is his child. He does not respond to the dispatcher.

The dispatcher says, "*Justin.*" It's like a slap to wake him. She says, "I'm a mom, Justin. I know what you'll want to do. You'll think you can do it yourself. *You don't know what is down there.*"

Justin says, "*Ursula* is down there. My little girl."

The dispatcher says, "Justin, if you so much as touch one of those logs laid across the hole, you could dislodge something that will send your little girl to her death." She is thinking of mine shafts she's heard of in the area, incredibly deep. Journey to the center of the earth. "If it's not a mine shaft it could be a well. Either way there is going to be water down there. The mines fill up when the pumps stop working." She is talking before she considers too carefully. Maybe she shouldn't be saying this, but she thinks: *If he goes back there and tries to get her out, I'd die of guilt if something worse happens.*

Justin says, "Oh, *crap.*" It is a moan.

"I know," she says. "You feel helpless. But you don't want to make it worse."

"How could it be *worse?*" he says.

"Your wife could wind up a widow, even if they save your daughter."

"Crap," Justin says again.

"Promise me you will not touch anything. Not a log."

"Check," Justin says reluctantly.

"And you'll stay away from the edge of the hole. Stay back maybe six feet. You don't want to unsettle any loose earth, okay?"

"Check," Justin says. "*Oh, crap.*"

So ANNIE AND Justin sit almost motionless in the grass, waiting. At one point, Justin suddenly imagines Ursula crawling up through those logs as if this all were a joke, *surprise!* He cannot stand it. So he goes to the truck and he gets his harmonica. He will distract Annie. He will play every song he knows or doesn't know.

He begins with her favorite, the theme song from a French movie he's watched with her at least three times, thinking maybe he'll give her the video for Christmas if there's a way to get hold of it. The movie is called *Manon of the Spring,* and there's a harmonica solo in it, Verdi's "La Forza del Destino," plaintive, enormously sad, but still mysteriously hopeful. Tears well up in her eyes but do not spill.

"Do you want me to stop?" Justin asks, thinking he's done the wrong thing.

"No," she says. "Don't stop. Don't ever stop. Just keep playing until she is back on the earth again."

The sun sinks lower. First to arrive, almost at the same moment, are the interviewer and camera man from the ABC affiliate in Marquette, who have helicoptered into Eagle River, and a geologist from Houghton whose neighbor, a state trooper, had phoned, off the record, and said, Maybe you'll want to get up there.

The rest of the news team is setting up some miles south, in Eagle River, at a campground that has been designated "command center" for what is now termed "the incident." It is the closest available building for coordinating the media without getting in the way. Thus Justin and Annie have seen no one yet, and it feels as if nothing at all has been done. They can scarcely breathe. Other news teams are en route, varying distances away. A God's-eye view would see them converging, but God is not the one who is antsy for reassurance.

Gunnar "Swede" Maguire is a retired geologist who has mapped all the abandoned mine shafts found to date, for the state DNR. He has a habit of cocking his head to listen, hard; he wears a canvas slouch hat that he doffs in a courtly, somehow touching way when he speaks. A heavy forelock of stark white hair falls across his forehead as he speaks, and he tosses it back. He speaks with animation. His wife tells him he might as well be French, the way he talks with his hands. He has driven his rusty Jeep up here from Houghton the second he got word, with his wife running behind him insisting he take his big thermos with coffee, and several white-bread cheese sandwiches, and a baggie of dried apples from their tree. He pulls into the clearing, parks, and leaps out, running toward Justin and Annie.

"Oh, Jesus," Swede Maguire says to Justin, the minute he is introduced. He sounds as if it's taken his last breath to say this. He claps his big arm around the younger man's shoulder, shaking his head in grief and concern. He has been talking out loud to himself in the Jeep on the drive up. Remorse, self-beration, arguing back at himself, putting himself in the place of these young parents. Swede's kids are grown and have kids of their own. This little girl down the hole is the age of his granddaughter Caitlin. "Oh, Jesus, oh, Jesus," he says again.

Justin is standing beside his truck now; Annie is lying across the front seat, amazingly, blessedly—Justin thinks—half asleep. Justin cannot imagine how she can sleep unless her head has just shut down on her. He wishes his own would shut down on him.

"I've had nightmares about something like this happening," Swede Maguire says. "Every once in a while, even though we did everything we could to be thorough. I thought: Got to be one or two more shafts out there that we missed, eh. Or maybe a hundred. You can't be everywhere at the same time. We were here, this very location, but by my records it was August when we came, and the grass would have covered the site, I mean totally. Probably flowers too, shit. To put the frosting on the cake, in a manner of speaking. It would've looked like the rest of the ground, solid." He talks like a man skiing moguls, forcefully, zigzagging, unstoppable till at the end he brakes in a dry spray of verbal snow.

The team from Marquette pulls in not two minutes behind him.

Brandi Chandler-Greene and her cameraman run at Swede like linebackers, wanting immediate footage. Maguire's eyes focus on the reporter's dangling bronze-colored earrings. He thinks: *Gorgeous woman, but they should have sent someone else. Or*—laughing to himself—*no one at all, so they could actually* do *this thing, whether it is a rescue or an exhumation.*

Brandi Chandler-Greene, up in his face now, is on a roll: Is this a mine shaft? What is it? Tell us how this shaft got missed, if it *is* a mine shaft, and if it's not a mine shaft, what it *is*. Tell us who, and what, and why, exactly and right now. Tell us who you are, anyway. Tell us tell us tell us *everything*.

"Look," says Maguire, moderating his exasperation. "You people have got to realize up front that we don't know everything. Cannot be everywhere. Life is still just damn dangerous, even if we're not on the top of the World Trade Center with lunatics crashing in setting the world on fire." He looks at the man with the minicam.

"Who are you?" says Brandi Chandler-Greene, while her cameraman shoots. She sounds almost like a child, but she's just new at this.

"Turn that thing off, would you. Goddamn it. Have some respect." He hears his mind—the mind that sent up the term *exhumation*—emending that to "respect for the dead," but he refuses to think that.

Brandi Chandler-Greene turns, in a regal gesture, Cleopatra-like, to her cameraman. She says—in a tone that implies she is doing this of her own free will, suggests that the initiative is *hers*—"Okay, turn it off."

Swede Maguire says, "And keep it off." Both of them nod like children, in agreement. "And erase whatever you took just now." The cameraman looks to the reporter, and she says, yes, delete it. He gives his credentials. He says, "I am not here officially, in any way. I just live close by, that's all." He pauses. "And because I live close by, I do happen to be the guy who did the maps of all the abandoned mine shafts for the state, when that came up as an issue." He pauses again. "Do you know there are tens of thousands, literally tens of thousands, of abandoned mine shafts all across the country?" Clearly she doesn't. *Pretty much nobody does,* he thinks.

In his Jeep he's got binders and folders and maps of the area, but already he thinks he knows what this shaft will turn out to be: part of a system already well known, extensive, pre–Civil War, just a shaft they missed. Swede feels the earth underneath him in a different way from all these lay folks who think it's solid: in his mind's eye, which is reality, it's honeycombed, literally "under-mined," with tunnels and shafts, miles and miles of them in each system. He figures that this one must be Sac-Trevelyan. He'll check the charts later to see if he can connect this location to a particular drift or leg of it.

Brandi Chandler-Greene's mind is racing hither and yon. She is thinking: *How can we tie this to the World Trade Center?*

Swede Maguire sees her thought, at an angle, almost as if her head were transparent. He feels as irritable as a man flayed, his skin scraped away. He tries not to turn it all on her, so he makes an observation indicting the whole world instead.

He says, "I swear, people have turned into vultures today. On the one hand, they think they're immortal. On the other hand, they want to know someone else *isn't,* that somebody's been sacrificed to the maw of the gods of death, so *they* are safe now. No different from South Sea Islanders and their volcanoes."

Brandi Chandler-Greene is thinking, *He's a slippery one. Complicated.* But then she thinks: *Well, thank God he didn't call* me *a vulture.* Except of course that he did.

Maguire says, "Look, if you want to talk off the record before all the equipment gets here, and we agree ahead of time about what you will say on camera, and what I will say in reply, I'll play your media game. Otherwise, no go, lady."

The reporter looks at him and thinks: *He's our expert here. We have to play this as it lays, by his rules, if we want footage to sandwich in. This is going to be a long night.* Capitulating, she says, in a tone of more solidity, "Okay. So tell me what you know." She dismisses the cameraman, who seems relieved and goes to get trail mix and juice from his backpack. After that, a cigarette.

Swede walks the reporter away from Justin's truck. "We've got maps," he says. "I did the maps myself. But this territory is wild, and I do not doubt that down the road—I mean in the future, not literally *'down the road'*—he says this when he sees Brandi Chandler-Greene's wondering look, out toward the road—"we'll find more shafts. Do I blame myself? What do you want me to say? That I do? Mapping every abandoned mine site in the Keweenaw was a fool's errand, and I was the fool who knew more than any other fool, is all. We did everything we could, and still I expected, deep in me, that something could have slipped by us."

"And how would that have happened, that something could 'slip by'?" she asks. Her tone is accusatory, has a little Möbius twist to it. She wants him for an ally; still, she's already putting in the stiletto.

"Look, lady," says Swede Maguire. "This country started to be mined by the whites way before the Civil War." He stops and thinks, *Oh, hell, so I have to be careful about racist language here? I cannot be right.* "Not a whole lot of regulation of *anything* then. Those folks were coming out here from the East with dollar signs in their eyeballs, and they dug where they wanted, and they walked away when they failed or the mine played out. The records are spotty to nonexistent. It was a miracle we could do even what little we did."

The look in the reporter's eyes is one of surprise. A cloud of tiny blackflies converges about her hair and she bats at them. They dissipate.

"I see you're getting a clue," Maguire says, salty. In his mind's eye he imagines a boat tying up at the tip of the Keweenaw, at Copper Harbor, a man whose face he cannot see, staking a claim with the land office on the island offshore—after all, there were no roads inland then—and setting off into the trees with a half-dozen men and mules and tools and maybe a woman or two. Swede Maguire's wife, Delayne, is his mainstay. He imagines a wife like Delayne, and a man with more balls than he believes he himself has. He cannot imagine the gumption it must have taken to come here in the earliest years of settlement.

Brandi Chandler-Greene considers Maguire's face as the afternoon angle of sun sharpens his features. He has had his sixtieth birthday the week before, with his four children and seven grandchildren at the house for the cake and balloons, two of them under a year old, three younger than Caitlin. For his fiftieth, they had had black balloons that said OVER THE HILL, so they didn't do that this time. Maybe way too much closer to true, he'd said.

Brandi Chandler-Greene is twenty-five and has grown up the daughter of a first-generation communications executive in Atlanta. This country is alien to her—she feels a slight resentment that she could not start out in a more congenial climate, but her old-fashioned father has wanted her to get some soul, some experience, which is hard to come by now—and this man she must interview might as well be from the next galaxy. But he interests her.

She took very little history in college, and remembers less. Her wanting to work in the industry—maybe stage, maybe screen, maybe TV—started when she played Sacagawea in a sixth-grade play for a parents' assembly. She loved the fake buckskin dress and the way its fringe dangled, and she got a kick out of carrying her papoose on her back. It was as unreal as a fairy tale.

"Say some guy from the East comes out here across the lakes and stakes his claim," Swede Maguire continues. "There's maybe not a record of that— things got lost. Say a land agent dies of a fever and some of his stuff goes missing. Rowboats sink. Fires eat buildings. As far as record keeping's concerned, those first miners might as well have been the Indians who were here mining the copper six thousand years ago. Did you know they did that, a huge amount of mining?"

He can see from her look of astonishment that she does not. "Yep," he says.

Brandi Chandler-Greene feels she has walked into an avalanche. To Swede Maguire she says, "Indians?"

"Yep," he says. "A mysterious, vanished race. Working this area from 6000 B.C. to maybe the time of King David of Israel, 1000 B.C. They left no records: no dwellings, no cave drawings, nothing but lots of pits for storing copper and the copper itself—*Lake Superior copper*"—he says this proudly, proprietarily—"in native cultures of Indians all the way down to South America. An intensive mining enterprise. Must have taken literally *thousands* of miners, and artifacts in every Indian culture along a zigzag north-south line almost to the straits of Magellan."

Brandi Chandler-Greene is a bright woman, but she is overwhelmed by all this. She tries to remember the location of the straits of Magellan. They sound vaguely like veins that wind out of someone's kidneys, to points unknown. She doesn't know what to say next to Swede, whom she has underestimated, so she says, "Wow."

SWEDE SAYS, "GEOLOGICAL history's long. Humans appear for a split second, dig a hole, and go away. The trees grow back, and a whole lot more vegetation. Mystery reasserts itself. Yeah, I think that this hole is a mine shaft, if that's question number one."

Brandi Chandler-Greene writes down *mine shaft yes*, the number *six thousand*, and those three words—*mystery reasserts itself*—thinking somehow she will use this. She will ask Swede to do this whole riff once again, for the camera, and he will comply.

AT THE NEWSPAPER south of here in Calumet, a thirty-three-year-old employee named Chad Karvonen—whose great-grandfather died in a copper mine accident with an ore cart run amok, though that fact has never impressed itself on his consciousness as noteworthy—has, two hours earlier, sent out a dispatch over the wire service.

The message is simple: a little girl is down an apparent abandoned mine and emergency services are being sent to the scene. Chad Karvonen's great-grandfather had played tag daily in summer in the trees with little Jake Maki, when he lived as a child at Camp Grit with his mother, Marjatta, and stepfather, Isak: again, no one remembers this.

"HOLD UP, HOLD UP, hold up," chants Toby Root, the guy down at the camp in Eagle River who has been designated interim incident commander in all this bureaucracy, at least till the rescue team from Traverse City gets here. Toby's ancestors came to the copper country right about the same time that Annie's did, but they never crossed paths, and Toby Root, never having had curiosity about his ancestors, has no idea they were Finnish. The name was changed from Ruutila to make them Americans, and they wanted to forget about the Old Country.

There is a sense at the camp as well as at the glade north of Eagle River where Annie and Justin and Swede, and now the news team, are gathered, of everyone's holding their breath and of nothing getting done, though behind the scenes a million things are happening.

The folks at 911 have been told that in this situation they'll need to call Copperland Search and Rescue. They do that, and a man at Copperland tells them, Well, this is beyond their scope, really, their scope is dealing with rock climbers. "High-angle rescue," he says. "Besides," he adds, "we don't have many of them anymore, that's not as big as it was a few years ago when all those bonehead college kids were climbing like spiders all over the cliffs and getting themselves stranded."

Toby Root thinks of the title of a movie he saw come on TV, but turned off a half hour in: *Where Angels Fear to Tread. That's what those kids would do,* he thinks. *Go where even angels wouldn't go after them to save their lives.* Toby Root laughs at himself. And these kids do this rock climbing all for the hell of it.

"I want all of you people to get back to the road," he says "This is a matter of the little girl's safety. You get near the hole, you're like a herd of buffalo overhead, you can dislodge earth and timbers and kill the kid." He thinks, *If she's not dead already, a pile of bloody mush, which is more likely.*

Toby Root remembers the only mine accident he's heard about any time recently, a flood in the Quecreek mine in Pennsylvania the year before: nine guys trapped underground, no fricking way they would get them out though in the end they did, and Toby Root's head had felt as if it would burst with disbelief at the news. He remembers trying to put himself in the place of the families up there in whatever that building was, waiting for news, but he couldn't do it. Failure of imagination. He has gotten the multigas meter dropped into the shaft as far as it will go, but it stops at about twenty feet, as if it has hit bottom. At that point, the reading is fine. How deep is the shaft? No one knows.

Toby Root has a minicam with an attached light dropped on a cable to the place where the gas meter stops. All he can see is that the shaft takes a dog leg downward, off into more darkness, diagonal maybe at thirty degrees, the angle at which the ore slopes off toward Lake Superior, down under the lake bed.

The dispatcher at 911 feels as if her throat will close up. "Call the state agency in Lansing," says Copperland. "It seems roundabout but it's the way it's done. Gotta follow procedures." There is a tone of detachment to his voice that the dispatcher does not like. Rescue personnel are supposed, like doctors, to be detached to some degree, but there is a tone of selfish relief in the voice of the Copperland guy that says, "Better you than me." The little girl down the hole somehow does not exist.

The dispatcher, a mother with three teenaged kids and one more in grade school, feels a kind of compassion the Copperland guy does not. Still, she wants, less like a mother than like a barroom brawler, to put her fist through the phone and open her fingers and grab him by the throat. She's feeling what Justin is feeling.

Instead she says good-bye, nicely. When she hangs up the phone, she lets out a yell, there in the office, alone, an interminable-seeming high-pitched groan, till that breath is gone. She composes herself and goes to the next phone number, the urban search-and-rescue group.

She is sent from one phone number to the next until she reaches a civil engineer in Jackson, Michigan, far to the south, the contact person for the team who says, okay, he'll take over now.

She says, "Meaning you'll do *what?*" He says he will go down the phone tree, call the guys in Lansing and Detroit and Pontiac, who will then call the search-and-rescue squad nearest the site of Ursula's fall, which is in Traverse City, six hours south of Eagle River in the Lower Peninsula. "Traverse City!" she says. "Traverse City!"

The engineer echoes her, "Yes, Traverse City." He is calm.

The dispatcher mom can hear the shrill desperation in her own voice when she says, "You know what? I grew up in Muskegon in a big family. When I was a kid if we'd act up my mom would say, 'Do you want me to send the bunch of you to *Traverse City?*'" She doesn't *care* how she sounds.

The engineer downstate in his car on I-94 has no idea what she is talking about.

The dispatcher says, "That's where the state mental hospital was. The loony bin." She catches her breath. "Do you understand there is a tiny little girl down a mine shaft while you people sit there like chimpanzees eating bananas in your *phone tree?*"

The engineer says, "Ma'am, you've got to calm down. Be part of the solution, not part of the problem." The dispatcher is sure now, she wants to throttle him. He says, "First rule of rescue is not to create any more victims by doing this in a disorderly manner. We don't trade a life for a life."

"You know what?" the dispatcher says. "I think I'm talking to a recording, that's what. I'll just try to get hold of a real human being." She is holding the phone away from her, looking at it as if a mongoose and a cobra were about to explode out of the mouthpiece. Then she realizes that he has just said to her what she had already said to Justin. She is almost gagging.

"It's out of your hands now, ma'am," says the engineer. "We'll handle it." Then he thinks again. "No, there's something that you can do. Call the Red Cross. The rescue crew will need food. Search out whichever contractor in that area does road repair for the state department of highways, and get him to truck the lighting equipment up there. That will be a *big* help." He pauses a second. "And ma'am," he says, "trust us, would you?"

The dispatcher's emotional circuits have blown by this point. She can say nothing. The engineer says, "Hello? Ma'am, are you there?"

She says quietly, "I'm here." Somehow the fact that he obviously realizes the complexity and has a plan calms her. To this point she has felt as if she might have reached a phone booth on a highway and is talking to a random passerby wearing a tutu and a propeller beanie.

"Okay," he says. "Get the Red Cross there, and the lighting equipment." He adds, "Oh, and some Porta Potties."

The dispatcher is suddenly confident this will be done right. The mention of Porta Potties does it. Click. Having four children has taught her that anyone who understands this part of life is grounded in reality.

"I can do that," the dispatcher says.

"Great," says the engineer, who is turning his car into an Arby's drive-through. "And you'll trust us?" Out his driver's side window a scratchy voice at a nearly inaudible level is saying, in the tones of a cartoon mouse, "May I take your order?"

"Right," says the dispatcher to the engineer. She'll trust them. She doesn't know whether she will, but she really has no choice. She'll call the Red Cross now, and then the guys with the lights. Then she'll figure out who might have Porta Potties.

Toby Root is bustling around, not officious but clearly in charge anyway. Still, he can hardly wait till things get going and someone relieves him. This is a wretched, trapped-in-amber feeling.

. . .

MINDY JI HAS borrowed a car from her boss at the restaurant and taken off even though it's the lunch rush and there is nobody else to cook. Go on, go on, said her boss, who is almost family after all these years. Jesus, that sweet little grandbaby, he had said, hugging Mindy Ji and giving her the car keys. Let us know when you know anything.

Mindy Ji drives like a bat out of hell the whole way across the UP, not watching the speed limits, yet nobody stops her until she is coming around the bend onto the crescent sweep of road that skirts the gorgeous broad bay at Baraga. A state trooper pulls her over, and Mindy Ji, in a lather, explains. He quickly decides to give her an escort the rest of the way.

Forty-five minutes after the crew from Marquette arrives, Mindy Ji pulls in. The local sheriff has arrived, with a young, wide-eyed deputy. The sheriff has brought his RV, a rickety old thing he uses for hunting and fishing. The inside of the RV smells like old fish and beer. There are cardboard signs around making stupid jokes about rifles and boats and trout. The RV was handy, is all. No one knows what to do.

Justin and Annie are collapsed into themselves in the living room of the sheriff's RV, in camp chairs, and are breathing as shallowly as they can, as if conserving the oxygen in the universe for Ursula.

"You can't trade a life for a life," Toby Root says, with an air of having said it in training a hundred, a thousand times. "We have got to ensure the safety of the rescue crew. We have got to have everything we need before we go down there." Annie and Justin both look as if their heads will explode. It is the third time within the hour that they have heard this. They try not to look at each other.

Toby Root is at the site now and has just taped a flow chart to the dry-erase board propped against the wall. Apparently rescues are as formulaic as everything else in the world has become: Annie muses stunned and open-mouthed on that diagram: what the duties of the safety officer might be, and why he is higher than the operations chief, and what hazard control could mean. She wants to grow wings, and dive down that hole, and swoop back up with her baby. For an instant she pretends that this is indeed why life deprived her of her legs, so that for one brief moment it could give her wings in exchange. Life itself is a vast field of hazard this evening.

Poking out from beneath the slick white board, on which are scrawled a few illegible notes from the chief to himself, and some phone numbers, are several boxes of crackers of various kinds: white cheese, yellow cheese, bacon, rye. "Help yourselves," he says, when he sees them looking strangely at the boxes, as if they were corpses protruding from beneath a bed.

Annie cannot imagine eating. Justin scowls out the window, wordless and stiff. "Suit yourselves," he says, trying to be both pleasant and *real*. He is thinking of his children at home, all three in high school: *My God, what would I have done?* "This could be a long night," he says. That remark is repeated again and again.

MINDY JI IS OUT in the clearing now, being interviewed by someone from CNN who has just arrived by private plane with an entourage. He is a pale man with square glasses and a comb-over who came in with his antennae up in a way that made her angry.

She has told CNN that Annie and Justin will not be talking to anyone, period, so what does he want to know? They're not on camera yet. She pulls out a picture of Ursula outside Narita Pete's trailer, the old one. This is Ursula, yes. Last fall.

Why does Annie use a cane? She was hit by what we assume was a drunk driver, says Mindy Ji, when she was ten.

How are the parents taking this? Mindy Ji has an impulse to say something sharp. Instead she says, "'The Lord is near to the broken-hearted.' Psalm 34:18." She smiles oddly—this is a canny move to fend off future prying— and darts a look quickly at the man's eyes, which seem to roll backward threatening to show their whites. She knows it was just the right thing to say and tries not to show what she knows. She is reminding herself of a saying of Jesus', not so widely known: "Be wise as serpents and innocent as doves." Mindy Ji has to work at that, the "wise-as-serpents" part.

She pulls out a snapshot of Ursula that she just had printed at Wal-Mart the day before, Ursula with her hair loose, pale as flax, eyes onyx dark, standing on a chair in Mindy Ji's kitchen, holding up for the camera a spoon blobbed with cookie dough. Mindy Ji counts the chocolate chips in the dough in the picture, the same move that Justin's mind keeps making, distraction.

The pain is too great, so the mind takes a shoot-the-chute into inanity. The camera guy from CNN focuses on Ursula with her spoon and her cookie dough.

IN THE SHERIFF's RV, Annie's eyes are glazed over: on the television, a commentator is analyzing Gwyneth Paltrow's penchant for picking bad-boy types who look as if they have beriberi and comparing how many days' growth of beard each is sporting. The pictures are laid end to end, a half dozen of these young men. Annie sighs. Justin has said at the first that Annie resembles her. This always gets under Annie's skin, she can't say why. Gwyneth Paltrow talks, but Annie has no idea what she's saying.

She presses the remote. An infomercial for acne cream with graphic shots of acne blemishes, looking like the geology of a pink moon. She changes the channel. A zipping, zooming NASCAR race, crowds in a frenzy, oh, yes, just what we need.

She stands with difficulty and tries to navigate around the furniture in these close quarters. She's looking for Mindy Ji. She wants an update. She thinks she may die on the spot. She tries not think of Ursula twisted, still, no longer breathing, in darkness, so she thinks of Gwyneth Paltrow's perfect legs, perfect hair, days and nights filled with money and fame and scruffy wrong choices in unshaven men, her whole life underfurnished and sad.

Justin has migrated outdoors and is sitting under a tree playing his harmonica quietly to himself. It is the same song he had played for her earlier, before all the hubbub arrived with the news crews, "La Forza del Destino," the Verdi.

His eyes are closed and he is picturing a scene from the movie. The little blond shepherdess with the porcelain skin who reminds him of Annie so much—her hair, her soulful delicacy—leaps like a mountain goat from crag to crag, in the film clip in his mind's eye.

But Annie cannot even walk without her cane: the thought stops him in midmelody—as if Annie's accident had just happened all over again, on top of Ursula's—and he opens his eyes. There is Annie before him, and her cane, and her now very sad eyes. He clamps his lips together, closes his eyes, and keeps playing for her. There is nothing else he can do. Maybe this will keep Ursula breathing, a kind of magic, a charm.

Annie is thanking her stars for Justin. She has no idea that Jinx—a person utterly foreign to her—had been so struck by the look of Justin the week before or that she had so incredibly done what she did. Justin had set it aside as a dissociated moment of which he could make no sense at all and asked his boss without explaining whether he could be put on a different job. *Sure, Justin, no problem.* Annie has no idea that Jinx Muehlenberg, eighteen years earlier, in June of 1985, maimed her.

SOMEONE WHO CALLS himself the temporary hazard control supervisor has arrived. This is Bobby Vachon, who has driven up from Republic Mine, Michigan. Even though, in addition to Toby Root, someone from the local fire department has dropped a gas meter on a rope down the hole and found the air safe, he does it again. The state team does not leave this stuff to volunteers. He strides into the RV announcing himself loudly. Justin and Annie are on the sheriff's nasty little sofa.

Justin stands up, furious. He wants to deck him. He counts to ten under his breath and Mindy Ji says, "Justin, he's just doing his job."

Justin says, "Or not." Bobby Vachon says the readings checked out, that the air is fine, no toxic gases.

"They already did that," Justin barks.

"It could change," says Bobby Vachon. "We've got to keep monitoring it."

"At this rate," says Justin to Bobby Vachon, "you might not have her up by her birthday." Justin is without realizing it imagining her alive, simply sitting at the bottom of the mine shaft on the bathroom stool she uses to brush her teeth, making a great deal of blessed toothpaste-slobber mess. Maybe she is sitting with her legs crossed, tapping her foot, with a little pursed mouth like Olivia on *The Cosby Show.*

"Her birthday?" says Bobby Vachon. "When's her birthday?"

"November," grumps Justin, acerbic, flat.

"He's just worried," says Mindy Ji, reassuringly. She half tackles Justin, as tiny as she is, throwing her weight against him and toppling him onto the sofa next to Annie. "Sit down and try trusting the man," she says. She is looking him smack in the eyes, and she's smiling. "Try trusting God."

"I think I'll trust Scotty," says Justin, with a gray look on his face that Annie has never seen. Not despair, not hope either.

Annie starts crying, the first time she's cried through all this. She can't stop.

10   A Wastrel Killed by a Snail

THE TIDE IS still out. Along the beach that trails from the tip of Point Olvidos, the strewings of amber and greenish and black seaweed form themselves into patterns. Chen Bing is walking barefoot in the wet sand, savoring the feel of the waves lapping up, lapping up, under the soles of his feet and then sluicing out again. His dark pants are rolled to his knees. His jacket—much too large, in order to accommodate extra clothes in winter—hangs almost that low. His wool watch cap is pulled over his ears, because it is moving on toward evening and a chill is coming on. He sniffs, because he has the remnants of a cold, and in sniffing he smells the strong salt and seaweed smell.

It is 1851, and he has come to the Monterey Bay area of California from the south of China, two years before, in the first wave of those wild for gold. He has not yet been able to get to the gold fields, but he says to himself: *I will get there, I truly will get there.*

He has passed the Carvalho Creek outlet into the bay and headed away from the village. He aims back inland now, having come around the point. The rise of the short cliffs is on his right. The crevices in the rock that harbor the abalone are half a mile ahead. The huge snails in their striped crenellated shells are a delicacy much prized in the restaurants north of here, in San Francisco. Their meat is served in the form of steak, with a saffron rice dish alongside, and slices of orange.

He is remarking to himself upon his thoughts and emotions, attempting without much success to describe them: this is the eternal habit of feckless men in distress, talking to themselves in slow deliberate fashion about what they are doing, so that they will not go crazy.

I am collecting abalone.

The sand is so fine.

What is that feeling? It is a deep sucking *feeling.* He says this each time a wave pulls back and flings itself into the ocean. *I know what I'm doing. I know what I'm going to do.* He truly does not.

Chen Bing is reading the patterns of flung seaweed as if they were characters, rich Chinese ideograms from the early Han dynasty, readable by the grandchildren of Qin Lao in the days when they were first codified. Some of them—lazy and strung out—resemble *xing shu,* the lovely italic script used by calligraphers; others, more formal and clearer, resemble *kai shu,* the regular, more easily readable script. He is reading the patterns because his mind is dense with fear and confusion, and he wants direction. He is, however, *not* thinking how crazy this is: to be reading the seaweed for omens, for portents, for simple directions.

Chen Bing, thirty-two years old, only two years in California, carries a pail for collecting the succulent mollusks. He is distracted, and he is walking slowly. The pail bangs against the small knob of bone at the outside of his knee. He smells the salt of the water and his own sweat. He sighs. *It will all be clear soon,* he thinks. He turns to look out at the water. The sun is lowering quickly. Its rose-colored light spreads across the bay's surface so beautifully. He might be the first person on earth, he is so alone here.

He reaches into his pants, whips out his sad mollusk of a limp penis, and pisses into the bay. Once more, he sighs. It is this mollusk that has gotten him into the trouble he is now in. It is this mollusk that got him into the trouble before, that caused him to flee from Huizhou. He has an impulse to rip it off and fling it into the sea. He recalls tales of court eunuchs in ancient days, guarding the concubines, and wishes that he had been castrated as a child. *No, I do not wish that terrible thing,* he says to himself. *I will solve this. In the future, yes, I will do better.*

He thinks of men he has until today scorned: the poor Chinese who have coped less well than he has with the dislocation of this new life, the men who go crazy. He will not go crazy.

He thinks of the silly man they call Dim Sum, though that is not his name: Dim Sum shuffles ceaselessly about Point Olvidos and the Bishop's Way settlement talking singsong to himself in Chinese, begging noodles and nights' sleep in toolsheds.

I'm talking to myself, he says to himself, in English. *No, you're not,* he answers himself. Then, in a third voice, he curses loudly at both of the voices, in Chinese.

He remembers the three local Chinese who have hanged themselves this past year, none older than forty. Ung Wah, who had worked a small plot and sold vegetables, very successfully, and then sent back to China for two of his brothers, had suddenly come unhinged one day and hanged himself from the tree that shaded his pole beans. It was said by one of the brothers that he had received mail from China the previous week but had not disclosed the contents of the letter. The brother said he had seemed "fragile as paper" since then, but no one could recall a single utterance or gesture that would give a clue as to his suicide.

Joseph Bow Quong, the odd young man who had been converted to Catholicism by the friars, and thus gained his name for the saint who was the mission's patron, had worked furiously for the squid dryers, every day, many hours. He seemed almost to be pushed by demons, unable to rest, but he pleased his Chinese employer in the extreme. Joseph Bow Quong had walked out to the point on a Saturday afternoon, stood watching the water—Chen Bing wondered if he had pissed into the bay—then gone back to his rooming house and hanged himself from the kitchen light fixture while everyone slept.

Moon Yick had saved up enough money in Santa Cruz, serving as purveyor of festival and funereal goods to the Chinese community, to bring a young woman from Jiangmen to California to be his wife. The young woman, who was very beautiful (Moon Yick had received a small portrait of her a year before from the professional go-between) had been raped on the ship, in mid-Pacific, by the first mate and most of the crew, until she was unconscious, then thrown overboard.

Moon Yick had sighed and told his friend Louie Ah Bo, prosaically, with resignation, that he simply would have to start over. Louie Ah Bo, much relieved at his friend's resolve, told others at the Six Companies meeting that evening at the Powder Mill that Moon Yick would be fine. Moon Yick in the meanwhile climbed on a chair in the storeroom, threw a heavy rope with a noose at its end over a rafter and then kicked it out from beneath himself. The following morning Louie Ah Bo had found him.

CHEN BING REMEMBERS these men and he thinks: *I will live. I am not Ung Wah, not Joseph Bow Quong, not Moon Yick. I am Chen Bing and I will live.* He looks up as a gull passes overhead, loosing its bowels so close in front of him that a white-green splat falls on the knuckles of his right hand as it swings out before him. He curses all birds.

Over there on the sand out in front of him, flung up with the last tide on the sand, a character drawn in seaweed that means "expensive," "valuable." It is also the character for the cowrie shell. Chen Bing thinks of that sweet, shell-shaped place in the fork of the body of a woman. *I will not think that,* he tells himself. *That is hardly the proper thought now.* He realizes he is standing there with his organ in his hand, the entire ocean gawking. He curses aloud and replaces himself in his pants.

There, to his left, newly thrown up by the waves, is the character for the verb "struggle," "wrestle." Hah! It has the appearance of two parties with their fists up. He thinks this might well be his signature: *Chen Bing, man who wrestles himself.*

At the Santa Cruz Congregational Mission for Celestials he has heard a sermon preached about Jacob's wrestling with the angel of the Lord. It had been a hot day, and he had found himself dozing, but the story aroused his interest. The Franciscan mission had an ever-burning light next to the altar, like that at the Chinese temple. The padres' chapel thus seemed, strangely enough, more familiar to the Chinese, with their twin beeswax smells and twin flickering-flame ambiences, than this straitlaced bright-daylight mission.

On the other hand, Reverend Arledge is very strong on teaching ethics, which reminds the Chinese of the Confucian base of their culture, and strong on encouraging assimilation to dominant culture, which the Chinese want dearly. They want to become Americans, while the good padres want them to become saints, citizens of the Catholic heaven, disdaining this world. Thus, far more of the Chinese come here, to the Congregational mission.

Furthermore, the padres do not preach, do not tell stories of prophets with fire from heaven, and huge whales who swallow men who try to run away, and wicked queens who fall from windows and break open like melons on the stones of the courtyard. The padres just murmur and finger their beads.

Chen Bing knows that the biblical Jacob struggled with the problem of women: he can understand this from his own life. This is human, even if Jacob is not a Chinese, a "Celestial." Jacob had an innate tendency to deceive: this too Chen Bing can understand from his own forays out of the clearings of truth, into underbrush, into deep woods. Jacob slept with his head on a rock: he can understand this. Chen Bing might as well sleep with his head on a rock, for all the actual sleep he can manage, these days. Jacob found himself wrestling all night with the angel. Had Chen Bing not seen the ideograph for "struggle," for "wrestle," back there? He turned to look. The beach seemed miles long.

The pastor, Reverend Henry Hiltz Arledge, had opined in his sermon — hands waving, the spread of wide gestures like grand broad wings — that this was no regular angel, no garden-variety cherub or seraph, but the Angel of the Lord, which is to say (here he nearly whispered, catching — in a weird, upside-down sort of way in the hot still air of the church — the attention of all of the congregants who were still awake), *the Most High Himself.*

The tone in which the Reverend Arledge made this pronouncement set Chen Bing's teeth on edge. He had always known about ghosts and immortals. He knew there were such things. He had never come in touch with such things, but he knew others had. Here, on the world's other edge, a pale pastor talking about the same thing! These angels must pass over national boundaries easily.

Jacob, despite all his failings, had been renamed Israel and then had become the father of a very great nation. Chen Bing understood this. *A confused and dispersed nation, as well as a great nation,* he thought. A nation preoccupied, if Chen Bing were judging aright from the things he had heard in the Reverend Arledge's sermons, with ritual cleansings and animal sacrifice, sacrifice not unlike the ancient Chinese border sacrifice ritual, except that these Hebrews in Reverend Arledge's stories were obsessed with tassels and unleavened bread and a bush that burned. Chen Bing had not put these disparate emblems together yet in any way that made sense.

Before him, across his path, written in seaweed: "prisoner." The ideograph shows a person—a simple forked creature—enclosed by a box. The seaweed enclosure drapes perfectly, hemming in the small forked seaweed man. *Yes, I am a prisoner,* Chen Bing thinks. *I have imprisoned myself.*

He turns and keeps heading toward the rocky cove where he has made his best finds. Today is a holiday. No one is out collecting. He will be able to gather everything he sees, without interference. *You are greedy,* he tells himself. *No, you are practical,* he argues back.

In front of him, across the dark sand, lies the character for "household," "family," drawn in seaweed: it is a picture of a door, the door of a household. One cannot have a family in this circumstance, and yet what can one do? He thinks of the young laundress, Lily Sing, back at the mission, expecting his child. She has a harelip which is badly sewn. He wonders whether the child will bear the mark also. He imagines the look on the rubicund face of the Reverend Arledge when he has to tell him about this, the widening of the pale eyes, the mouth clenching about its teeth. What then? He cannot imagine.

Back home in Xin Ning, where he had had status in the community, where he had owned a store and a two-story home with a stable (though he had won them gambling), he had done the same thing and then procured an abortion for the girl. The girl had died of the infection, and he had had to flee for his life from her relatives. *Will you never learn?* said the voice, then. *Will you still not learn?* says the same voice now.

The cove with the rocky nooks where abalone attach by their muscular suckers and hold on tight is just ahead. The light is diminishing quickly. The shadows will fill the cove and he will not be able to see. He hurries. He carries his pry bar in his right hand, his bucket in his left. The water is cold around his ankles now. He half sneezes. The shadows rise quickly.

. . .

THE FOLLOWING AFTERNOON they will find his body, the dark
jacket slipped up around his head so that he appears to have been decapi-
tated, the loose drawstring pants washed away in the tide so that his tight
brown buttocks flash the sky. There is no dignity in this, but then dignity
has not been the leitmotif of his life.

Reaching out with his pry bar to lift a foot-long abalone from its rocky
perch, he loses his footing and drops the bar. It vanishes instantly out of
sight into the rising dark water. Extended out over the rock promontory to
pull at the creature with his bare right hand, so as not to waste this trip, this
afternoon, this abalone, he becomes trapped. The creature has clamped
down, hard, on his hand. He cannot pull free. He tugs and the muscle clamps
tighter. He screams. His scream sounds like a woman's. He is ashamed, then
decides that in this circumstance his tone of voice is a matter of little import. There is no one to hear him. It is a holiday.

He decides, finally, that he will wait, that his patience is long. His self-will
has seen him through so much. He will wait out the creature. His hand
smarts terribly, the wrist clamped and bloody, the fingers inside the shell
paralyzed with the chill under the water. He waits.

He is praying to Jacob's angel at the wrestling rock, to Confucius, to a virgin with stars and roses in her serape who has appeared to a mestizo shepherd somewhere south of here. None of them seem to hear him.

He remembers the statue of the Blessed Virgin, pale-skinned, with a
crown of stars, at the Franciscan mission, which had banks of candles and
lace altar cloths seeming somehow Chinese, so unlike the Congregational
mission. Chen Bing prays in his desperation to this Blessed Virgin, though
he does not know what to call her. *Star Lady,* he says. *If you make this snail
let me go, I will give half of my money that is in my box to your mission.* He
waits, as if for response from the sky or from the stubborn snail. The sky
does not speak; the snail does not free him.

If you make this snail let me go, he says, *I will be a gentleman to Lily Sing.
I will do the right thing.* He sighs, even thinking that. That will be difficult.
Doing the right thing, in Chen Bing's experience, was seldom enjoyable.
The abalone does not respond. Chen Bing wonders whether the Star Lady
is in any way moved by threats, but he cannot decide how to threaten her,

and he does not think in his situation that he ought to take frivolous chances. Things *could* get worse, though he cannot think how.

Back at the mission, Lily Sing lays her hand on her belly—the reverend and the schoolmistress have not noticed yet that she has rounded up—and thinks of Chen Bing, but with a slight irritation. She hopes the child will not be a boy and have his devious and irresponsible manner. She has no notion that foolish Chen Bing is here in the cove, trapped by a mere foot-long snail with a muscle as tenacious as his own stupid resistance. A snail, indeed, with the tide rising.

The Reverend Arledge, who has no idea of Chen Bing's plight either, recalls him, randomly and evanescently, at this moment, at his devotions, wondering what it will take to save the soul of such a hardhead. The reverend thinks: *He seems impervious, so taken with every story he hears from the Bible, remarking soberly to everyone on Samson's stupidity, David's stupidity, Adam's stupidity, but somehow unable to make application of it to his life.*

Clamped down on by the valve of the murderous dumb abalone, Chen Bing distracts himself remembering stories he has heard at the mission. He is trusting that something he does not know about biology will be his salvation, that when the water rises and the abalone is beneath the surface, it will let go of his hand in order to drink. Or some such. Whatever an abalone must do. He knows no more about the abalone than he knows about the Star Lady. So he thinks about stories meanwhile.

He recalls the character back there in the sand: "prisoner." It does not even occur to him to think that he is the prisoner of the abalone. He is sure that this is temporary. He thinks of quicksand pits he has heard of where one can drown if one dares to struggle. He tells himself to relax. He thinks of the straw children's toy, the monkey trap, in which the only way to free one's fingers, again, is to cease struggle. He has now ceased to struggle.

He chides himself for his words about prison. These are not the right words. These are words that will defeat him. He must say positive words. *I will find the way out,* he thinks. No, he decides he will go beyond that. *As Israel fathered the twelve tribes, so too, from Chen Bing shall come a great nation.* He snickers at himself.

The tide rises. He snuffles and bargains and begs of the Christian god and the Italian Saint Anthony whose statue graces the Franciscan mission with all of the pretty bells, as well as the Celestial Immortals. *O, hear my plea.*

As the fast-rising tide comes wicking quickly up his pant legs, he remembers the tile-roofed house in Huizhou where he had met that limping girl. He remembers the room where they had sat drinking tea, he remembers her very small hands cupped around the teacup as she sat, he recalls the bamboo-shaded pagoda where they had met secretly, evenings.

As the rising salt water soaks his shirt, he prays to any ancestor who might be listening—this would include Qin Lao, this would include anyone at all—to kill the snail, so that it might release his hand. Yes, that would do the trick.

He remembers the girl's body, pale in death, how her eyes seemed so sunken and her cheekbones dissolved away, how her breasts caved in, their nipples dark, raisinlike, shriveled. He had marveled the first moment he saw her in death that wherever she would go now, it was likely her limp would not matter. He had always felt her superior. Now he was not certain. Would she be able to fly? Would she become a demon and seek revenge on him? Had she placed this snail on this rock and enticed him here? One could not know at this moment.

As the water reaches his armpits, he remembers the smell in the hold of the ship, all the money he had to pay those Spaniards for that rank, dreadful passage. He remembers the dead man beside him one morning when he woke, whose bowels had released in the night, and the money he took from that dead man's cloth wallet. *The dead,* he had told himself, *do not need money.*

He remembers his own little strongbox at home and how when Lily Sing had asked him to take her into Monterey to get some salve for the sore that had ulcerated on her back, he had said he could not help her out but that it was not anything to be concerned about, that indeed these things healed themselves. He remembers why he crossed the ocean: to find the "gold mountain" about which everyone in Toi Shan and Xin Ning and the rest of Guangdong had heard in such profuse and extravagant detail, to dig the gold here and become a rich man.

In the strongbox he has enough money to get to the gold fields and more. When the water is at his chin, he begins panicking. He reaches under the shell with his left hand to try, by main force, to pry all of it free. He imagines the snail smirking, deep in its shell, in its triumph. He thinks of a character he has not seen in the stragglings of bulbous seaweed: the ideograph for *shan,* mountain. He loses consciousness. The tide swallows him. He does not have to struggle with the anguish of the drowning as he dies. Death comes, so simply.

His body floats in the tide, anchored by the hand clamped in the shell, like a pennant of fleshy seaweed. When the tide recedes, the abalone releases its prisoner for its own abalone reasons, and his body is left flat on the dark wet shore sand. He is found at half-past low tide. The seaweed that drapes him—if anyone were thinking in these terms, but of course they are not—is the ideograph *suddenly.* It comprises an image for rain and beneath it, a single bird. In the minds of the makers of language, rain comes on a dusty plain, *suddenly.* A flock of birds flap their wings, and the flock rises as one.

SUDDENLY, LILY SING is alone with this child inside her. Suddenly, his father back in Huizhou has no son, even though he has disowned him years before and thinks of him no more than once a week, and usually with gratitude that he has grown and gone. Suddenly, it is the future.

IN THE FASHION of Americans, Lily Sing names her child after its father. She has taken the news of his death in stride, indeed with a kind of relief that she will not have to deal with this man anymore. In fact, she has laughed in her small narrow bed at night, giggling quietly into a shawl, at the thought of his bare buttocks facing the sky in death, his hand still caught in the shell of the stubborn abalone. She has laughed until she cries, and at that moment she feels the first stirrings to life of the child within her and stops in astonishment.

The child is a girl, with great black puffs of hair and with fingers that curl and uncurl slowly, like flowers opening. The day after the birth Lily Sing and the schoolmistress sit huddled together watching the child asleep on her back in the dresser drawer. They are using the drawer as a cradle until the one being donated from someone's attic arrives. Together the women decide that the child must be named Daisy Chen.

"You are far better off without Chen Bing," the schoolmistress says.

"I know this," Lily Sing says. She nods her head in deference, though the schoolmistress treats her as if they were peers.

"You can stay here as long as you like," says the Reverend Arledge.

"You are kind," Lily Sing says. She curtsies to him, as is her habit.

The child is the joy of the mission. In ceremonial photographs from this time, taken inside the mission in front of a painted photographer's backdrop which looks like a stiff, heavy curtain, the Reverend Arledge is white-bearded and stern, though a hint of a smile plays about his lips. These pictures are highly unusual for the day, but the photographer is a young man who is very determined to see the possibilities of this new form of art.

One of these pictures has surfaced in Mindy Ji Wong's box of photos, its paper stiff, breakable, brownish. There is no caption or inscription. Neither Mindy Ji nor her mother or father could say who these people are, but the picture has been in the family for years.

The schoolmistress, whose name is Jenny O'Deal and who later will marry the Reverend Arledge, a good twenty-five years her senior, is pale and wears tight-waisted dark skirts with white blouses pinned at the neck with a scrimshaw brooch. In the pictures it cannot be seen that the lacy-edged brooch reads, etched into the whale-tooth ivory in intricate letters, the motto ALL FOR JESUS.

There are usually twelve adults in every picture: one might guess that the reverend, who is composing the groups for the pictures, thinks about twelve tribes a lot, twelve apostles, 144,000 redeemed. Lily Sing is invariably one of the twelve. Others include an assistant schoolmistress and several Chinese who live near the mission.

In all of the pictures, Daisy Chen is standing in front of the group, from the time she can toddle. In one of the pictures, she is a small blur, like a comet, actually toddling through the extended length of the exposure required by cameras of the day. At times Daisy Chen wears Chinese garb, pajama suits appliquéd with small elegant finishings, shapes that resemble the mission's porch gingerbread. Other times, she wears American dresses bought by Miss Jenny O'Deal, with white stockings and hair bows.

. . .

WHEN DAISY TURNS five, Miss Jenny O'Deal, who has the previous year become Mrs. Reverend Arledge, gives birth to a son, who becomes the new joy of the mission. Lily and Daisy leave not too long after this, as it is time.

A Chinese landholder, Tim Tandem Ho, has come to the mission and asked to see Lily, the day of the birth of the Arledge's baby son, William. Tim Tandem Ho had gotten his name from a stunt on a bicycle some years before, when as a new immigrant, he juggled and did tricks, also playing harmonica on the dirt streets and collecting coins in his hat. Lily, summoned from the kitchen where she is starching and ironing the front parlor's curtains, scrutinizes Tim Ho with a look somewhere between puzzlement and a sense of a miracle rounding the bend in the road. She can almost hear this miracle's hoofbeats.

Tim Tandem Ho introduces himself. He is a mustard farmer from the Pajaro Valley, not far to the east, and he says is very prosperous. Lily does not need to be told this: she can see his stiff, new dark gray suit and his shiny, new oxblood-leather boots with their ornate peacock designs on the sides. Tim Ho holds a perfectly white western hat on his hands.

She says, in the straightforward way that she has, "You are *prosperous,* yes. But are you *comfortable?* I mean, in that suit?" Her speech is nasal and somewhat impeded by the harelip, which is poorly sewn.

"I am not," says Tim Ho, much relieved to discern so quickly the freshness he has been informed is characteristic of this laundress. "I prefer to wear working clothes. For today, this seemed better."

"And what is special about today?" Lily Sing asks. Tim Ho is listening to the nasality of her speech, and he finds himself oddly charmed by the way her voice spirals up through what must be strangely shaped passages created by her slight defect.

"I have come into town to make a young lady a marriage proposal," Tim Tandem Ho says.

Lily Sing wipes her hands on her apron. The starch leaves a bluish white residue. "You are wanting the Reverend, then," Lily Sing says. "You are wanting to make some arrangements, I assume."

"No," says Tim Tandem Ho. "This would be to place cart before horse."

"I am sorry?" says Lily Sing. She finds his speech charming but incomprehensible. Reverend Arledge is rather more sober, and none of the Chinese who come to the mission are witty.

"I will need first to ask the young lady," he says.

Lily Sing is not sure what he wants her to say. He is standing quite still, and he seems hardly to be breathing. He is holding his hat on his hands. She is wondering—looking at his eyes, which are twinkling—whether there is a giant white chicken beneath the hat, ready to come flapping out at her. She does not actually yet know he can do magic tricks, but several layers beneath her skin, yes, she knows this, and this is why she thinks of the chicken.

She says, "Is this a Chinese girl?" She cannot imagine Tim Ho courting an American, but she knows no other Chinese girls here.

"Yes," says Tim Ho. Then he is silent.

"Does she work for Americans?" Lily Sing says.

There is a thud and a clack at the window. It is the bird who has been trying all afternoon to get in. Sunlight falls through green leaves, new as it was outside the windows of Qin Lao's house in Sichuan, fresh as it was outside Rauno the merchant's house, in the village of the sled dogs: the very same sunlight. The reverend has said that morning, in a rare joke, that the bird is a seeker of truth; Lily Sing has replied, in her muted adenoidal tones, which are also somewhat wry and cynical, that the bird is simply stupid.

"Yes, she works for Americans," Tim Ho says, astonishing Lily Sing, who is distracted by the bird. "She is a laundress."

Lily Sing's heart leaps up. *There is another Chinese girl here, and a laundress! Oh, to have a friend!* Lily Sing makes a small laughing sound, joy. "Do you have a picture of this girl?" she says.

"Yes, I have such a picture," says Tim Ho. He reaches into his pocket. He pulls out a photograph. It is one of the twice-a-year group photographs of the crew at the mission. Little Daisy Chen stands in the front, looking straight at the camera with a half-scowling, half-dozy look.

Lily remembers the day of the picture. Daisy had not had a nap, and this was the photographer's fourth attempt to capture them all still at once. Lily looks into Tim Ho's face. She herself is in the front row, between Lam How and Jim Koo Yi. There are no other Chinese girls besides herself in the picture.

At this moment Lily Sing feels as if she had swallowed a large, heavy thing, an American silver dollar perhaps, and it had lodged back of her breastbone. She feels her heart thumping against the broad coin.

"I have come to propose to the girl in this picture," he says. "But as I do not know her well, and as I am not an educated man, I do not have proper or flowery words. I am only a grower of mustard, though I do grow a *great deal* of mustard." He pauses. "I have a large house with a pillared porch. This is very unusual for a Chinese."

"Yes, this is unusual," says Lily Sing. She waits to hear what more he has to say. She is watching his face, which is smooth and broad at the cheekbones, with contrasting dark, wild eyebrows.

"My house has carpets from Belgium." He says this word as if it were "bedjum." "It has a piano, though I cannot play it. I understand that this girl does play piano."

Lily Sing keeps looking straight at him. She is trying to discern whether he is about to dissolve, like a statue carved of sugar outdoors at a fair, with rain threatening to fall. She nods neither yes nor no. She clears her throat slightly.

"I have purchased a large library of sheet music," he says. "Three books of hymns. Also European composers. Also popular songs. The fireplace in the parlor of my house is surrounded by Dutch tiles," says Tim Tandem Ho. "The pictures on the tiles are very pretty, all blue and white, like Chinese pottery. My stable has six horses."

The bird peck-pecks at the window. A full-body thud and a fall to the ground. A regrouping, then an assault on the glass, beak first.

Lily Sing keeps on staring straight into Tim Tandem Ho's face, almost as if she wishes she could unnerve him and send him running, like Jonah, to some other errand. She wonders whether a large scriptural fish would then cough him up on the back steps of the mission and she would still have to deal with this matter.

"The Reverend Arledge suggested this course of action to me when I came to him to ask whether he knew a suitable wife. The girl would have to move to the Pajaro Valley. As you know, there are few Chinese women in this part of the world. I require a wife." He shrugs, speaking matter-of-factly.

Then he stands still as a mannequin, with his white hat held out on his hands.

Lily Sing stands dumbfounded. Tim Tandem Ho has a smooth boyish face, unlined but not with the smoothness of idiocy. His tight pigtail, the queue that is typical of Chinese males in America until the Chinese revolution in 1911, hangs down the back of his suit jacket to his waist. He is certainly clear-spoken and skilled in English. She cannot tell his age.

Daisy comes running into the room, her own long, slim black braid — which matches Tim Tandem Ho's queue — flying. She is chanting a song about bees. She stops short, as if she has run into something, when she sees the face on Tim Ho and the face on her mother. Both seem *caught,* or if Daisy Chen had known the image to which to attach what she sees, they might seem to be spinning in one place, like a pair of gyroscopes, silently whirring.

Daisy Chen, a child with a serious manner and an early determination in her own mind that something is wrong with the world, stands still and says nothing. She has not inherited Lily Sing's harelip: her tiny mouth is like a primrose. Time and time again in Daisy's infancy, Lily Sing has taken that small, sweet pout between her fingers and blessed it. For a full minute, all three stand still and say nothing. Underneath it all, there seems to be a whirring, which is clearly distinct from the hum of the insects outdoors.

Then Lily Sing turns to her daughter. "Daisy, this is your father," she says. "Your new father. The good one. The one you prayed for in your night prayers, last summer."

Tim Tandem Ho turns to the child. He bows. "Would you like to wear my hat, Daisy?" he says. He holds the hat toward her. She does not respond.

Daisy scowls at her mother. "How does *he* know my name?" she says, as if feeling invaded. "Did you tell *him?*" The pronouns are intended to make the point that he is clearly an outsider.

"Would you like to know my horses' names?" says Tim Tandem Ho. He does not wait for her to answer. "Their names are Wing, Yellow Emperor, Mustard, Diablo, John Quincy Adams — we call him Quincy — and, the prettiest of all, Lady Snow. Your mother will like Lady Snow."

Daisy looks to her mother for clarification.

"They all are too big for you, Daisy," says Tim Tandem Ho. "We will find you a pony."

"A pony?" asks Daisy. Her eyes are alight. "A pony?"

"Unless you would prefer to ride on a pig. In the Pajaro Valley, people can do as they like. We could provide a pig," Tim Tandem Ho offers, his eyes twinkling. "Very pink, with a side saddle."

"No, thank you," Daisy says, very proper. "I think I will just have the pony." The tone is as if someone has passed a tray of tarts at a reception and she has opted for gooseberry. Something as small as that.

LOCAL LEGEND HAS it that the mustard Tim Tandem Ho grows so well on his farm had been brought to the area by Franciscan friars, many years before, that sandaled brown-robed contemplatives had scattered seeds alongside the roads so that the missions along the coast would be linked by this path of gold: riotous gold mustard blossoms along both sides of the road in springtime.

It has not yet become what it will become later, a primary crop in the area, but Tim Ho has the golden touch with this crop, which others still seem to think nothing but a wild nuisance. At harvest time the tall plants wave in the breeze like gold froth on Pacific waves, wafting their yellow fragrance downwind. The evening sun strikes the gold with a special immediacy and glints off at such an angle that Daisy Chen thinks of Chinese fairy tales about the Eight Immortals. The plants are nearly a dozen feet tall, a veritable forest of gold. Daisy Chen loves to run into this forest and play hide-and-seek with the children of the farmworkers.

WHILE IT IS THROUGH Daisy Chen's descent from Qin Lao, the alchemist, that we trace Justin's, then Ursula's lineage, it is a fact that Tim Tandem Ho's can be traced back to Qin Lao as well, hand over hand following the thread through a different winding passage of the genetic labyrinth.

Four generations forward from Qin Lao, the old alchemist who had thought he would never have offspring—dead many years by that time, after his only son came in his very old age—that son has had five children, who have produced among them thirty-one grandchildren, who then have produced one hundred four great-grandchildren.

Daisy Chen is descended from the youngest daughter of Qin Lao's grandson who bore the nickname Gold Bug, because of his early interest in metallurgic alchemy; Gold Bug had died young, leaving nonetheless three offspring. That youngest daughter had been called Gold Butterfly.

Tim Tandem Ho is descended from that same Gold Bug's *oldest* son, the first brother of Gold Butterfly, who became a scholar. This older brother was a man with an abstract habit of mind who grew crabby and fat in his old age but who as a young man had been quite as cheerful as Tim Tandem Ho. That scholar had been called Shining Carp.

Neither Lily Sing nor Tim Ho, of course, knows these things. As they stand, on the day of their first meeting, in the kitchen of the Congregational Mission for Celestials, memorizing each other's face, with the silly bird throwing itself at the window—*thuck, thuck*—neither is speculating about these unknown degrees of relatedness—which have, across two thousand years, become nearly uncountable.

Daisy Chen, by the age of six, has let a cuticle of fear and caution grow all the way around her heart. So, despite the fact that her new father calls her his Pajarita Amarilla, his little gold bird, she holds herself aloof. He buys her the promised pony, which she names Jacob, because she likes all of the stories about Jacob that she has heard at the mission. She stays aloof as she rides Jacob, as if she were in some way paying Tim Tandem Ho back—a surrogate punishment—for what Chen Bing had done to her mother. But no part of her realizes that she is angry at Chen Bing. Not at all.

A traveling photographer takes a portrait of Daisy seated on Jacob, wearing a white fringed vest and elaborate buckskin boots. Daisy scowls into the camera as she had done when she was two, back at the mission. One of these pictures is in Mindy Ji Wong's box, and on the back of the brittle old paper in Lily Sing's spidery hand is written *Daisy Chen Ho*. Daisy does not use the name Ho for herself until she is seventeen.

Lily Sing has not told Daisy Chen the full story, only that Chen Bing had left her alone in her plight. Daisy Chen does not have in her mind the image of Chen Bing, butt-naked to the inlet sky, clamped at the wrist by the fierce abalone. She does not know he died before she was born. She does not know that, only moments before he died, he was recalling the same stories that are her favorites now.

She imagines him a prosperous man living somewhere south of here. She sees herself as his beloved child to whom he will be coming home when whatever is holding him loosens its grip. Daisy Chen, over her early years, has developed in her mind a story in which Lily Sing's harelip and frankness are what drove her father away. Had it not been, she thinks, for Lily Sing's stitched lip and wry manner, she would have had a good father, not this silly Tim Tandem Ho, with his mustard fields waving, with his constant attempts to amuse her and make her smile, playing his silly harmonica, doing tricks on his bicycle. She does not really understand—because she is so thoroughly the center of her own universe—that Tim Ho would cut out his own heart with a spoon to have this child love him. Eleven years Daisy Chen lives on the mustard farm of Tim Ho, holding her heart back. She is tutored at home. She learns to play the parlor piano quite well and especially loves the sonatas of Schubert.

Though the first seven years of the marriage are barren, ultimately Lily Sing gives birth to three more children. Daisy resents them all. Lily turns herself inside out, as does Tim Ho, trying to make her firstborn smile. Her identical twin brothers, Harry and Harvey, seem to Daisy to attract a disproportionate amount of attention, and the youngest, Jenny, named after Reverend Arledge's wife, is the prettiest, easiest-smiling child ever to have been born for miles around, in the memory of anyone living.

In the summer of 1867, when across the continent the War between the States is over but there has been very little recovery, a friend of Tim Tandem Ho's dies. He was a merchant with stores in San Sabas and San Felipe, both patronized by the Chinese as well as many Americans and Spaniards. The family must travel to town for the funeral.

Daisy Chen, sixteen and haughty, rebels. She does not wish to go with the family. She stands with her feet apart and tells Tim Tandem Ho for the thousandth time that he is not her father and cannot tell her what to do. Lily Sing slaps her face and says she is a terrible little witch, and then grabs her daughter to her and hugs her in grief, crooning. Daisy Chen is amazed at the strength of this feeling. She never has understood love. She does not know its name when she feels it so pervasive in her mother's crushing hold. She stands back in silence and stares at her mother.

"You are correct, Mother," she says. The reversal is swift and astonishing. "I will pack Jenny's clothes. I will say no more about this. I have been in the grip of demons. Please forgive me." They go in the buggy to town, and Daisy is placid and helpful. She braids her three-year-old sister's hair. She packs apples and pickles and boiled eggs and bread in a large willow basket with a handle like a swan's neck.

Tim Ho's friend, the deceased, made a good deal of money from his store, in which his younger brother is partner. One of his best-selling goods is opium. Its sticky, dark mass is kept in brass boxes and smoked with friends in the makeshift room at the corner of the store, curtained off with heavy floral-embroidered satin, while in the rest of the single-floor establishment, mothers and children shop for domestic necessities. The smoke lifts in thin puffs and then tendrils out the small high window to the alley.

The store also sells, for medicinal purposes, sea horses, horned toads, and a number of the same herbs Qin Lao had spent intent, puzzled afternoons hunting and gathering and processing, thinking, *Will this one work? Why?*

The store sells ornate carved boxes and functional tin and brass boxes, for foodstuffs and opium. The store sells embroidered-cloth Chinese shoes, dried squid and sea cucumber, skin creams and wound salves in small, round red and black and gold tins covered with very small Chinese characters. The store sells Chinese ink and the brushes required for it. It sells paper and incense and fans for the afternoon heat.

Because of the prosperity of the deceased, his funeral is large. An outdoor altar has been built to hold the ceremonial herb-laden fragrant roast pig. Framing the pig is a dazzling blue sky, and the wind is a light one, a pleasant one. Daisy leans over most uncharacteristically to Tim Ho and whispers in his ear, "Perhaps that is the pig I said I would not ride when you married my mother. I must apologize to him as well." Tim Tandem Ho looks at the girl in amazement.

The funeral procession takes the longest possible route through the little town of San Felipe. Tim Ho rides his friend the opium dealer's favorite horse in the procession. The horse has a long pale mane that is braided with silver and red ribbons, and a complex matching ribbon braid trails down and around its tail. Tim Ho looks at the finery and hopes the horse has no need in midparade to stop and do its duty: the apparatus would seem to impede such attempts.

The firecrackers are shot off again and again at the head of the procession and by mourners lining the roadside. The air fills with the gunpowder smell, which overpowers the fragrance of roast pig and then lets it rise again. The fireworks are intended to frighten away evil spirits, who take advantage of this brief time between death and burial to attempt to steal away the soul of the newly deceased.

To further protect the corpse, to distract predatory devils, a man has been employed by the merchant's survivors to toss scraps of red tissue paper into the air and in the dirt of the street along the route of the funeral procession. This is silly Dim Sum, who will be paid in rice wine. The demons, it is said, must leap through the pinholes punched in the center of the scraps and in so doing will be kept off the deceased. This has gone on for centuries, and no one can say it does not work.

Lily Sing, emboldened by Daisy's unaccustomed gestures in apologizing to her and in suggesting to Tim that she should perhaps apologize to the roast pig, decides that this may be the moment to tell Daisy the truth. As the procession passes in front of them, banners high, horses shying at the firecrackers, Lily leans over to Daisy and says, "Daisy, death is a terrible thing sometimes."

Daisy looks at her mother as if to say, Sometimes?

"There are times when it is more a blessing," says Lily.

"To whom?" Daisy asks.

"To the dying sometimes. To the survivors sometimes." Lily is not looking at her daughter as she speaks. She is watching a man in a dragon costume dip and sway in the funeral parade. The gunpowder smell is thick.

"This merchant?" Daisy says. "Is this the person you're talking about?"

Daisy is wearing American clothing: the white batiste blouse, the long dark skirt. She has not worn Chinese clothing since she left the mission and came to live at the farm of Tim Ho. Her accent is wholly American. East of the Mississippi River, the country is recovering from the Civil War; west of the river, huge crews of Chinese and Irish and other minority groups are pushing the railroad, from both coasts, toward Utah, where they will meet in two years, joining the coasts, this amazing feat. Daisy is part of this new America. When she says "Is this the person you're talking about?" she sounds very distanced from the Chinese culture, from the merchant, from her mother and Tim; in the shapes of her speech she sounds not Chinese at all.

"No, not this merchant," says Lily Sing. "It is your father about whom I speak."

Daisy pauses. "Tim?"

Lily smiles. "I am glad you said that," she said. "You never have said that before. But, no, not Tim. Your father."

"Chen Bing?"

"Yes. Chen Bing. I have the idea you have an illusion about him. A story that you have made up."

Daisy stares at her mother. It is not a glowering stare, but it is harsh in its visible fear at what Lily might say.

"Chen Bing died, Daisy, long ago. *That* is the way that he left us," Lily said. "He told me that morning that he was coming that evening to bring me good news, and I waited and waited but he did not come. I was not surprised. He did not often keep promises. The next day he was found by men who were gathering abalone. He was drowned, facedown in the sand, his hand caught in the shell of an abalone. His pants had washed away." Lily thinks: *I did not need to tell that last part.*

"Do you mean this was good that he died?" Daisy says.

"Let us rather say Tim Ho has been quite a blessing to you," Lily says. "You have had a life in the country. Piano lessons. A pony. The twins. Jenny."

At this moment, after braiding Jenny's hair in the morning, Daisy can think of the younger siblings as a blessing; the day before, she would not have been able to. Daisy is looking into her mother's eyes as if she has not seen her before. The parade goes on, noisy and dusty and endless, in front of them. Someone is waving a noisemaker with long tassels, and the tassels slap Daisy across her eyes. She blinks.

"We had a good life at the mission. We have had a good life with Mr. Ho," Lily says. She has always called her husband Mr. Ho. Even in the dark of their bedroom, she has addressed him this way. It is somehow more an endearment than a formality.

Daisy nods in agreement. The moment is like the still, stunning moment when a wild horse is suddenly tamed. A banner passes before them in the parade. It is an ancient Chinese blessing, and it contains the character for "suddenly."

Two years later, Daisy Chen Ho marries a young supervisor on the Southern Pacific Railroad, a young man named Wong Lin who had worked on the crew that completed the last leg of the transcontinental railroad that same year, 1869. In celebratory photographs taken of that crew, Wong Lin is a muscular young man with a broad white grin: from the look on his face, one would think he had done it all himself, there is that much glowing pride.

One of these photographs, in reproduction, lies in Mindy Ji's picture box. Names of all the Chinese laborers are listed on the back in Chinese. Wong Lin is just one of them. His name is not isolated or highlighted. His face is in the picture, his name is in the list, but to Mindy Ji, who does not read Chinese, Wong Lin, Mindy's great-great-grandfather, is just one of the crowd there. She has never heard his name.

That sense of ownership in Wong Lin's broad grin is what has brought him to this supervisory position, a most unaccustomed position for a Chinese. The workers respect him. He has broad hands and a keen sense of organization. He knows how to divvy up work and to delegate. He can motivate others. He tells jokes no one has ever heard. At times he reminds Daisy of Tim Tandem Ho.

There is no picture of Wong Lin and Daisy Chen at their wedding. It is an American wedding, and Daisy Chen, who has always been an American, wears an American dress, aqua blue moiré, with extravagant leg-of-mutton sleeves. The Reverend Arledge performs the ceremony at the mission. The Arledges' younger son, Etheridge, serves as a ring bearer. There are no other attendants. As her husband pronounces the pair wed, Mrs. Jenny Arledge, in the second row of chairs, realizes that Daisy will be leaving them, a fact whose full impact has not yet hit her. She begins to cry very loudly, to sob, and then to try fruitlessly to mute herself.

The bride and groom, standing rod straight in their wedding finery at the front of the church with their backs to the congregation, turn and look at Jenny. Daisy's hair is done up in such ornate fashion that she moves her head stiffly as she turns to look. Ivory pins with silver tips protrude slightly from the dark piled mass of her hair. These are the same pins Jenny wore at her own wedding to Reverend Arledge.

Jenny sobs until she chokes. Then she starts laughing, and everyone in the church laughs, and the whole ceremony is disrupted, with the bride and groom laughing until they have tears in their eyes, because life is just so absurd, so absurd, going on this way and going on, everyone being born, marrying, going away, dying, coming back home in the looks in the eyes of their children, passing it down, not remembering, doing it all again.

FOR THEIR HONEYMOON Wong Lin and Daisy travel to San Francisco and register in a hotel with a lobby that is shadowy at every hour of the day. In the morning the shadows are misty and pink, in the afternoon blue green because of the drapes drawn against the harsh sun setting over the ocean. The lobby has tall, fountaining palms in pots that bear Greek bas-reliefs. It has tight, uncomfortable sofas and hard wooden benches like pews.

Their bridal suite has lamps that shed delicate magical gaslight about, on the floor and the drapes and the wallpaper and the tall, nearly black wood of the bedstead. Into the bedstead are carved grapes and ribbons and something else no guest has ever been able to make out.

As Wong Lin in his nightshirt blows out the candle beside their bed, Daisy Chen, turned toward her side of the bed, hears herself sigh. Is this sound resignation? Fear? Hope? Longing?

Wong Lin says in the dark, "Mrs. Wong?" There is no answer. He says it again. "Mrs. Wong?" Again no answer. He can hear her breath in the dark, steady, slow. She must be sleeping! He has no idea whether this is his new wife's habit, falling asleep as if dropped from a cliff—how could he know! —but he lies on his back beside her in an odd consternation.

Daisy Chen, her long black hair let loose, falling down the back of her white cotton nightgown to her waist, lies very still. She listens to Wong Lin sighing and clearing his throat and making sounds of bewilderment—*ohhh, ehhh*—as if he had been asked to lift something unliftable, overwhelmed by the very prospect. She hears him settle down to a soft sighing, as of resignation, yet not quite. She lets herself drift into half-slumber.

She feels his hand on her back, stroking her hair. His hand seems to span her entire back. "Mrs. Daisy Wong," he says. "This is your husband." He speaks as if from a very great distance, as if, in fact, he were speaking to her on a telephone which will not be patented for another seven years. He runs his right hand down her hair again, three times, four, five. As his hand passes over her shoulder blades he marvels at their fineness.

Daisy is beginning to have a half-dream. It involves waves coming in on a shoreline, white foam, sunlight making small stars on the water. It overlaps with a memory of the carriage ride here, with a memory of her first pony, with an ephemeral memory of the dream father she had constructed out of her wishful imaginings. *He* would have stroked her hair this way. He *would* have. She sighs.

Wong Lin's hand insinuates itself inside the dark, heavy curtain of his wife's hair at her waist and he rests his hand there, very patiently, carefully. Daisy blinks in astonishment in the dark. His touch is peaceful and firm, but it is not a touch she has ever known, not a friend's, not a father's. She works very hard at controlling her breathing, and yet she gasps slightly. She wonders if Wong Lin has caught that.

She thinks: *I suppose through the ages that brides have all had to go through this moment.* She feels the moment to be a dark tunnel, not long, with escape into some vista beyond the rock mountain a prospect not far ahead. It does not occur to her that this would not shock or terrify every woman. After several moments, he moves his hand to her right hip bone and rests it there. *She is like a bird,* he thinks. *Bird bones.* He realizes this thought had been born in the moment he touched her thin shoulder blades, wing bones. For a moment he thinks she might fly away.

He says, "Daisy Chen, turn to me."

Obedient, fearful, she does. In the moonlight that comes through the window he can see her face in amazing detail. He traces the thin crescent of her right eyebrow with his index finger. He sings a child's song to her softly, in Cantonese. It involves a magical clock and a waterfall. It sings about time passing swiftly and water that runs over rocks and drops down, down, down to a blue pool. The refrain is repetitive: *down, down, down,* with an up-lilt to the words.

He does not know that the beautiful shape of the bones of Daisy's brow has been inherited from a great-grandmother on Lily Chen's side, a wealthy woman in Chengdu renowned for her beauty and cruelty, who—if she had still been alive when Lily Chen's mother gave birth to her with that cruel harelip—would have instructed the midwife to hold the child struggling head down in the nearest stream, until the struggling should cease and the infant go limp in death. Girls were no blessing, this was an old truth, but a child with a defect was cursed by the Immortals, and a girl-child with a harelip would rarely be allowed to live. Lily Chen would have died, and Daisy Chen would not have ever been born.

Wong Lin remarks to himself on the stark beauty of that brow. He does not know that the shape of her nostrils is much like the nostrils of Chen Bing's own mother, a dignified woman who wrung her hands, mourning her son's wretched unfilial roistering and, from the age of fifteen, whoring.

"Daisy Chen," says Wong Lin. He moves his hand down the front of her nightdress, six inches, twelve inches. His hand stays still on the flat of her abdomen. She is holding her breath. Something in her says again: this touch is not a father's. She has been told what to expect. She braces herself for it.

Wong Lin sees her clenching her teeth, and he says softly again, "Daisy Chen." Her childhood name, as he says it in this oblique moonlight, is a blend of reassurance, promise, and a chiding for her fear. He cannot see Daisy Chen's hands: they are bunching the handkerchief-soft white top sheet beneath her chin in a terrified pucker. In the moonlight the sheet seems to glow.

Daisy is thinking, in a kind of terror, *My father would not have done this to me.* But, as the children attending the nearest Catholic mission school learn, and as Ursula Wong's mother, Annie—who attends Catholic school more than a full century later in Sault Sainte Marie—will learn, it is said that as God knows everything, that includes what has been, what is now, and what will be, as well as what would have happened *if.*

What would have happened *if* Chen Bing had lived is that he *would* have, one day when Daisy was four years and two months old, moved his hand down her body precisely the way that her husband is doing now, and down, and down, then continued this without the knowledge of Lily Chen for a half-dozen years until Daisy—who would still have possessed, in her genes, the fragility and need for protection that showed themselves first in her childhood defensiveness and now in her wedding-night fear—would have run from her father one hot summer day in fear, in inability to withstand this even one more day, right there in the village, into the path of a horse run away with his buggy, and died at the age of ten, stopping the lineage of Ursula Wong—who would of course never have come to be—then and there.

"Daisy Chen," Wong Lin says for the third time, "I want you to know that life is long. I am patient." His broad hand still rests on the flat of her abdomen at her waist, and though this pains him, he actually means this.

Daisy bursts into tears. "Oh, my husband," she says. "Thank you, thank you. Someday very soon I will be strong." She burrows her head into the curve of his collarbone. He sighs, and she sighs. They sleep.

The second day of their honeymoon, in a restaurant a half mile away, they have dinner on pearllike white dishes. They order abalone and saffron rice. Wong Lin makes his broad grin. "You might order a cordial," he says. "This can also give strength." Again, that broad grin. "Would you like a cordial, my wife?"

She nods yes and drinks the strange, heady cherry brown stuff like a medicine. Her eyebrows rise, and she coughs. She clears her throat. "Oh, my," she says. "Perhaps this is more strength than I know how to use."

Indeed, it is. The marriage of Daisy Chen and Wong Lin is not consummated for several months. Wong Lin travels for the railroad and so is out of town half the time. He has hoped that these absences will indeed make the heart grow, if not fonder, then more supple, more ready. He decides finally to go to the reverend, who goes to his wife, who goes to Lily Sing.

The two women take Daisy for a walk on the dusty road that leads out from the town's edge one evening two days before Wong Lin is due to come home from a trip for the railroad. They walk in their high-buttoned shoes through a thigh-high field of wild white snapdragons. Each of them bends to pick a blossom now and then. Daisy listens more than she talks. She squeezes one white blossom near the end of a stalk between her right thumb and forefinger over and over again, without recognizing the tic as a way to distance all of this painful business. No one thinks to question how or why a whole field of snapdragons, every one perfectly white, has come to be there, growing wild as Tim Tandem Ho's mustard once grew.

The following weekend, the deed is done, the marriage consummated, with the shedding of much earnest sweat on Wong Lin's part, and a modicum of blood and tears on Daisy's part. By the end of a year, the matter is lost in forgetfulness, as if the painful time had never happened.

In 1871 Wong Ah Lee, Daisy and Wong Lin's only child, is born. He has his mother's facility for adaptation—hard won, that facility—which might be seen as the gift of forgiveness. He has his father's drive. He has the intelligence of them both. He sprouts his first two teeth early, at five months, and walks alone at seven months. The Arledges treat him as if he were their grandchild as well as Tim Ho and Lily's.

The child is well loved, and the proverb that says "A child who is well loved has many names" bears itself out in the life of little Wong Ah Lee. Reverend Arledge tends to call him "Abraham," saying soberly that the American translation of "Ah Lee" is "Abraham Lincoln," whose picture hangs in the two classrooms of the mission school. This is another rare joke on the part of the Reverend Arledge. He says, further, that Ah Lee has the set-jaw determination as well as the sense of humor of the sainted liberator. Wong Lin, though only in his head, calls him "Al," thinking this will in some oblique way make him more American in a climate that is becoming less and less friendly to Chinese.

IN A PHOTOGRAPH in Mindy Ji Wong's wooden box, there is a picture of Daisy and Wong Lin and little Ah Lee taken when the child is three years old. On its reverse, there is only the notation *1874, Ah Lee. Intelligent.*

Mindy Ji Wong has not in all the years she has owned this photograph known that this child grew up to be her great-grandfather.

Whenever she has looked through the pictures, the thought has struck her: *That child looks mischievous.* Also: *That child looks something like Justin at three.* She has mentioned this, once, to Joe Cimmer, years ago, before he left. He has said in reply, in his laid-back, ironic way, "*All* Chinese look alike, babe." Then he has kissed her.

THE WINTER THAT Ah Lee is seven years old, there is a terrible accident at the Sanborn Tunnel where Wong Lin has been working as a supervisor. Two Chinese crews are tunneling toward each other through the mountain. The coal gas trapped in the mountain is being burned off, as it routinely must be. But something goes wrong. Oil spills and catches fire, sending a wall of flame through the tunnel. The tunnel itself functions like a huge cannon, and the explosion sends railroad cars outside the tunnel flying. Amazingly enough, no one is killed by the explosion itself, or by the flying cars, but five Chinese die of their burns.

Wong Lin, who is on the other side of the mountain at the time, is himself unharmed, but he is furious at the carelessness that he feels has caused this explosion. He makes a great deal of noise about safety precautions. The Caucasian bosses will not listen.

Nine months later, in late autumn, a crew of twenty-three—twenty-one of them Chinese—are working, twenty-seven hundred feet into the mountain. At this time, Wong Lin is on business in Santa Cruz, having been given more duties and a slightly more dignified title, though no raise in pay.

A pocket of gas, undetected, is ignited by a small dynamite charge. An enormous roar wakens the Chinese workers camped outside, who rush into the tunnel to save their fellows. When they are fifteen hundred feet into the mountain, another explosion rocks the mountain. Twenty-four Chinese are killed instantly; the remaining seventeen are burned so badly that no one who ever sees any of those who survive—and ten do—can forget the Sanborn Tunnel Terror. The odor of roasted flesh is talked about there for years.

Reverend Arledge says it is God's grace that Wong Lin has not been at the tunnel. Wong Lin says, "Is it God's grace that my friends *were?*" Reverend Arledge says nothing. Wong Lin asks again. "Is it God's judgment on them, then?" he says.

Reverend Arledge sighs and says he does not understand God's ways sometimes. He sighs, and then he edits that. "At least a third of the time," he says, to put a number to it, and he purses his lips in perplexity.

AT FIFTEEN, AH LEE begins working with Wong Lin on the railroad, assuming that he will in time move into his father's job. When he is sixteen, Daisy contracts an infection that leaves her bedridden: he stays home to nurse her. When he is seventeen, Daisy dies and is buried beside Tim Tandem Ho and Lily in the small family plot inside a wrought-iron fence underneath a tall willow tree, on the farm, which is now being worked by Daisy's twin brothers.

When Ah Lee is eighteen, Wong Lin suggests that it is time for him to "see the world," that is, the world of the railroad. He gives his son a railroad pass and several months to travel the country to scout whether there is perhaps somewhere else that they might resettle. Wong Lin has decided that, yes, he can leave Daisy's bones here: what he cannot abide is *being near them.* Several evenings a week when his father is home, Ah Lee finds him out brooding beside the iron fence and sometimes talking out loud to Daisy. Yes, Wong Lin can leave if Ah Lee finds a place for them.

So the son sets out, by rail, as a scout. Wong Lin, depleted by Daisy's death and the mysterious death by lynching of a Chinese friend, is working as a supervisor for a small private railroad in the Pajaro Valley. Ah Lee writes home once a week, and his letters pile up, a travelogue. Wong Lin's hopes rise as Ah Lee moves east: perhaps there is new life to be had somewhere else. He visits Daisy's grave frequently.

Ah Lee writes home that he has arrived in Michigan, a small town near Detroit, and that he thinks perhaps here is a place they might settle.

Father,
    I calculate that Detroit is a place where you might start a business with your savings. I believe that as your physical strength will surely

*lessen in years to come, you may wish to consider such a course of action.
As yet I do not have a clear idea what sort of business might be appropriate, but I am consulting with others on your behalf. I am certain, of
course, that you do not wish to enter into the sorts of work to which Chinese have become habituated over these forty years since our people have
come to these shores.*

Had Wong Lin received this letter, he might have waved it in the air,
laughing, and remarked upon the polysyllabic diction, "Ah! My son, the
professor!" with some pride. Since Ah Lee's early childhood, his precocity
has been his father's delight.

Wong Lin, however, does not receive Ah Lee's letter.

The day before Ah Lee's letter arrives in California, Wong Lin is visiting
Daisy's grave at twilight, and talking to her in the lavender light. "Mrs. Wong,"
he says, "this is your husband, come to visit you in the evening." Then he sits
quietly for a while. Without thinking about it, he finds himself singing his
wife's favorite song, an old South China song taught to her by Lily Sing.
Years before, he has heard Lily singing this, in her snuffling way, as if cotton
were stopping her singing, one evening on the porch, facing the sunset. He
looks up at the big house's porch and remembers that. It is a song about a
wife left behind in South China and waiting for her husband to come to take
her back to America.

> Flowers again shall be my headdress,
> Flowers indeed. My dear husband will soon return
> From the Gold Mountain, from the Coast
> of the Gold Mountain, to bring me to that place.
>
> Ten years I have waited for him.
> I have spun at my wheel, I have sung songs.
> The water is wide.
> Oh, my husband is coming!

As Wong Lin sings, tears rise to his eyes. He remembers Daisy in her
white cotton nightgown, with that soft white sheet bunched beneath her

chin in fear, in the honeymoon suite of the grand hotel. Tears course in rivulets down his cheeks. Wong Lin is just fifty-two, not an old man, but he feels ancient. He hopes that his son will write soon. The previous week's letter has been waylaid by a postal mishap, and he misses his son.

Before he can rise to go home, Wong Lin clutches his side, suddenly, and sits back down on the outdoor bench next to the grave plot. He makes not a sound. The last sensation he experiences is the overwhelming fragrance of the lilac bush six feet away, which is in full bloom.

He is found later that evening by Daisy's brother Harvey, who knows where to look for his brother-in-law. Many evenings Wong Lin has fallen asleep here, sitting up on his little bench, in the peaceful twilight near his wife. Twice he has taken a cold from it. Tonight, despite the identical look of him when Harvey comes smiling to shake him awake, Wong Lin is dead, his heart stopped like a clock as he breathes in the scent of the lilac.

AH LEE'S LETTER is a day away, heading west. The previous letter will not arrive at the Wong homestead for weeks, having been diverted to some dusty post office where no one is paying attention. As for mail heading east, it is several weeks more before Ah Lee receives news of Wong Lin's death.

Ah Lee, who has picked up the much-traveled letter at the local post office, sits down with the letter from his uncle Harvey, and he is hard-pressed to think at all. He walks along the Huron River at a curve of the stream where gray-green willow branches hang over the grayer green river and he watches the sun glint from its lightly roiling surface. He still is unable to think.

So after he walks, he sleeps, in his rooming house, a dark green three-storied affair owned by a Mrs. Dahl, the widow of a moderately successful Norwegian immigrant storekeeper.

Ah Lee has seen, the first week of that month, the two lines of eroding painted letters memorializing Mrs. Dahl's husband, two decades old, on the windowless, brick side wall of a dry goods store downtown, as he walks up Ann Street toward Main: FRIEDRICH DAHL, PURVEYOR OF SUPERIER QUALITY WARES.

He smiles at the misspelling. He then, in a mind cartoon he hangs above his own head like a small cloud as he walks, mentally sketches himself smiling at the misspelling. He does have this habit of mind, of distancing himself from immediate experience in the way of the intellectual. He jokingly captions his mental cartoon self-portrait: *China Boy Smirks Superierly.*

Ah Lee is a spelling snob. He laughs out loud at his own silly snobbery, as he walks. A young couple walking toward him pull closer to each other in slight alarm. He imagines they think him eccentric or worse. He makes a faux deranged smile at them and tells them brightly, in Cantonese, that it is simply that his father has died and he is beside himself with grief. He senses that there are tears lurking just millimeters inside the curve of his eyelids. Consequently, he works hard at not blinking. The effect this produces is a terrifying stare. The young woman puts the back of her hand up to her face to shield herself from this inexplicable display of emotion.

As Ah Lee continues on up the hill, he says aloud: *Are we not somewhere near Lake Superior here? Should people in this town not know the spelling?*

AT NIGHT, HE twists in his sheets in his narrow bed, which being next to the window is at night too cold and in the morning far too filled with hot sunlight to luxuriate in late sleeping, despite the absence in his life at this moment of pressing appointments that would force early rising. His dreams are not memorable, but he wakes with a sense that he has dreamed of mustard in bloom and of a starker western sky, suffused with reflected light off the Pacific. He cannot remember those California dreams, but they ache with loss.

He eats Mrs. Dahl's gravied meat, thick roast cooked so long it falls off the bone, and her noodle-and-white-cheese pudding, as thick and unyielding as a mattress. He listens to the slow, perhaps melancholy, perhaps only peaceful, liquid melody of an old popular song. He recognizes that song, floating on the breeze from the next house. The wife in that house plays at this time each evening, unfailingly, and her playing is graceful. The song is called "To a Wild Rose."

It makes him feel that he must know at this moment how his father felt when he was young and fell in love with his mother. This business of romance is a matter that has not occurred to him more than once or twice, the thought that he might wish to take a wife sometime. He sees many years of education and preparation ahead of him before his adult life begins, and he focuses like a mule, blindered.

A fair-haired young man across the table from Ah Lee watches Ah Lee's distracted pause, his listening, his musing, with some interest. The thought occurs to him: *Do Orientals have feelings the same as ours, or are they different?* The young man is from a farm in deepest Ohio, on his way to Detroit to seek his fortune as a salesman of farm implements, and he has never met anyone Asian. His assumption—based on the one previous occasion when the thought has occurred to him—is that the feelings of Asians—or Eskimos or Africans or Bushmen—are alien, unique.

Ah Lee walks after dinner, alone, and he stops at a tavern. The bartender peruses him as if he were an artifact walking and talking. The man, whose thick, dark handlebar mustache is waxed, has never met anyone Chinese. Ah Lee watches the ends of the bartender's mustache waggle as he makes mouths of perusal and consternation, staring point-blank into Ah Lee's face over the varnished bar top. Ah Lee, standing with his shiny-shoed foot on the brass rail, stares back at first and then grins. The bartender is taken aback. "I am an American," Ah Lee says. The bartender blinks in surprise. "I have an American haircut. I do not chew American tobacco, but if I did I would expectorate my American mastications into your American cuspidors."

"Hey, boy," the bartender says. He is not sure about those words.

I piss like an American, Ah Lee thinks, but does not say. *All Americans piss precisely like Chinese.* "I am hardly a boy," says Ah Lee, with no inflection at all, and certainly no inflection the bartender can take as offense. He has heard others call black men "boy" in precisely the challenging tone the bartender has used. "I am of an age to drink your whiskey and am sufficiently solvent to pay for it," says Ah Lee. "With requisite courtesy to leave you a fine tip, as well."

He leaves four coins as a tip on the bar for his double whiskey and goes to a glass-varnished dark corner table. He feels the bartender's astounded, perplexed eyes on his back as he walks away. He broods and drinks. He notes the other patrons, watching him out of the corners of their eyes—*A Chinee! In a suit coat, and drinking whiskey!*—and then he goes back to the rooming house.

He hears grumbling and laughing through the walls of his room that night, young men his own age and older men his father's age, and he feels disconnected from all of it. They are all in transition from something to something else; he himself is just stuck, like an insect in amber.

For three days Ah Lee is unable to make a plan. Then, the third day, late in the evening, his mind seems to rise from the dead. A young man comes to the rooming house at dinner talking about his life at a state university only a few miles away, two towns to the west. He is entering his third year at the university and he seems an exotic to Ah Lee: he is not only a reader but a practical man, intent upon the study of metals technology as well as conversant with all sorts of literature by writers Ah Lee has only heard of, never read.

Ah Lee feels the first whiff of evening breeze sniff at his neck. Mrs. Dahl's summer kitchen is attached directly to the house, and in consequence the point of a summer kitchen—to keep the heat out of the living area—seems to have been lost in the process. All the heat of her afternoon's cooking gathers and hovers and settles and will not leave. The air is steamy and heavy and thick. Dinnertime is invariably an exercise in endurance for Ah Lee, who does not love heat. As he eats this evening, perspiration drools down the hairs at his neck into his collar. He makes a resolution to get a haircut tomorrow.

He has had a momentary impulse one afternoon to tell Mrs. Dahl jokingly that Chinese cooking is much quicker and would not turn her house into a steam bath this way, but he senses that her small blue Norwegian eyes, set in those powdery pale puffy cheeks, would startle at the remark like a window shade slapping open, her pupils contracting, unable to discern whether he is serious, and if so, what he actually means.

He has overheard her telling her daughter one day that this young man, this Chinee who looks like a gentleman, really is not like the rest of his kind. In her eyes and the eyes of most people she knows, Chinese are crazy and uncomprehending as well as inscrutable.

"He speaks English like an American," Mrs. Dahl tells a neighbor in praise of her new California-born boarder. Her own English is heavily accented, the torque of the fjords on her vowels, her consonants bent as well.

If Ah Lee were to suggest to Mrs. Dahl even jokingly that she learn to cook like a Chinese woman, in order to keep the house cooler, all her solid approval of him would melt instantly. If he were to respond to her comment—put forth in his absence—and say that indeed he *is* an American, as he has told the bartender, she would be nonplussed in the extreme, despite her assertion that he is not like his own people.

THE NEW YOUNG man at the table, an engineer-to-be whose name is Albrecht Hagedorn, shovels stringy green beans in white gravy into his mouth as he talks about Greek plays and mathematical perplexes, talks about pretty young ladies in white blouses and dark skirts, talks about green hills and views of the raw new town set in the low, rolling hills that the river has formed in its years of meandering through the countryside.

He goes on all the way through dessert—a three-berry cobbler dribbled with thick cream—about a huge new gymnasium that has expensive equipment imported from Europe. He says its landscaping makes it look like a sort of temple, and then adds, "Perhaps it is." He swallows a large lump of piecrust, washes it down with a big gulp of water from his sweating glass, and then he talks some more.

Ah Lee feels the breeze on his neck again and thinks he can adjust to the difference in the sunlight and the weather here. He resolves: *I will stop having those California mustard-field dreams. I will look to the future.* He listens to Albrecht with the sense that this monologue is meant specifically for him. Now he can pursue education: Wong Lin's savings—not huge, but enough—will be coming to him. He knows he himself is not meant for business, but for learning.

He thinks that perhaps he will read the plays of Aeschylus—about whom his table mate Albrecht has been going on—and (he thinks now in the mode that has always thrilled his dead father, always so proud that the son of a railroad man should have the heart of a scholar, from infancy) perhaps he will even read them in the Greek. He resolves further not to become a soft, flaccid man in all his studies: he will lift weights at the wondrous gymnasium. He imagines himself with firm, hilly biceps. He smiles.

Already, while the last slices of cobbler are being cut and passed and spooned into boarders' mouths, he is making a daily schedule in his head, for the next few years. He is feeling the sweat that continues to roll down his neck, from his hair to his collar, and onto his smooth hairless shoulders beneath the starched white cotton of his shirt.

In the morning, at breakfast, Mrs. Dahl keeps talking, as she pours his tea and serves him his oatmeal. She is going on about peonies, how her white peonies are in bloom, that they are Chinese flowers, that he ought to take a stroll in the garden late in the day when it is cool. She chatters. "And when their petals are gone," she says, buttering her homemade bread for him alone, as no one else has come to breakfast that day, "there will be a brief time, perhaps two weeks, and then my tiger lilies will bloom. Do you like tiger lilies?"

"My grandmother was from South China," Ah Lee says. "Her American name was Lily." Mrs. Dahl slathers his bread with peach jam from the blue-and-white pottery jar on the table. He does not say, *My father has very recently died, and I do not know what to do or to say,* but his sadness pervades his remark about Lily, as if his grief really were for her. As perhaps, in part, it is.

Ah Lee, absorbed with thoughts of the autumn to come, of burying himself in books and of lifting weights, pays little mind to the tenor of Mrs. Dahl's attentions: she waits on him as if he were a young prince, or perhaps as if she were in love with him, though this is clearly not possible, since he is twenty and she is at least fifty-five, her woolly hair steel gray and pushing at the confines of its snood.

She butters his bread as if he were the emperor of the Middle Kingdom. She is unaware that she is doing this, and she could not stop herself even if she understood. Outside the window of the dining room, knotty bright red roses climb a white trellis. They enter her consciousness halfway as she is pouring cream onto his oatmeal and somehow become a part of her delight in the moment. She *cannot,* of course, be in love with Ah Lee, in any real-world sense. He is Chinese, and she is a mercantile Norwegian immigrant widow, old enough, conceivably, to be his grandmother, if she had hurried. It is Ah Lee's smooth face and courtly manner of doing each thing he does that touch his landlady.

Gertrud Dahl, a dozen years past menopause and on the far shore of a wide moat between herself and Ah Lee, will not make it into the family tree of Ursula Wong, but perhaps she hovers there today anyway, like a firefly, loving Mindy Ji's great-grandfather in this partial, adoring, uncategorizable way, during these very few weeks this hot summer, before Ah Lee is quite a man.

THAT FALL HE enrolls at Ann Arbor, known by this point as the finest academic institution west of the Alleghenies. The university is sixty-plus years old. The lawns of the academic buildings are unmowed: their grass, bright green in some places and parched in others from all of the summer's heat, waves like the mustard fields of Tim Tandem Ho.

Inside stately classical buildings, the clicking of Ah Lee's heels on the marble floors sends up echoes that fill the grand lobbies and staircases all the way up to their high ornate ceilings. Ah Lee inhales the damp granite smells and he loves them. He haunts the library; he sniffs the itchy redolence of old-book dust in ecstasy. Ah Lee has been transported to the eighth heaven.

In Ann Arbor, Ah Lee moves into a boardinghouse for male students recommended by Albrecht, the third-year student from Mrs. Dahl's. The two become fast friends. Ah Lee's new friends insist that he must have an American name, and they extract his new name from his initials, A. L. He is Al now, as is Albrecht, and the two are "the Als," or "the Twins." Everyone seems to think this hilarious, though neither Ah Lee nor Albrecht does. The bonding is mutually beneficial: Ah Lee misses his father as a friend, and Albrecht has always wished for a younger brother. Something in each of them transcends the racism of the society that is the matrix for this friendship. They are always startled when they find themselves stared at.

In Albrecht's final year, Ah Lee's second, Albrecht insists on taking Ah Lee home with him at Christmas. As they head north and west, the terrain changes: first flatter, then hillier than it was in the southeastern corner of

Michigan. The trees thicken, and the daytime shadows in the stark cold sunlight grow longer and broodier. Evergreens start to outnumber deciduous
trees; as they head north, the trees' leaves become thicker and the forests
greener. Ah Lee has never seen anything like this. The snow changes from
graying melted and refrozen patches here and there to a deep, sparkling
blanket of perfect white. They change from a train to a buggy, and the fragrance of the pine needles rides the cold breeze to their nostrils. Despite the
wool scarves wrapping the bottom halves of their faces, they can still smell
the pine, and to Ah Lee the scent is amazing.

Two villages away from Albrecht's family's farm, when the roads are
no longer passable to wheeled vehicles, they transfer themselves and their
Gladstone bags and their paper-and-string-wrapped parcels to a huge dark
well-worn sleigh piled with blankets and heavy, fringed shawls. It is evening
when they arrive at the switching point, and Ah Lee feels momentarily irritable: *Will we never get there? Should I have stayed in Ann Arbor and studied my Hebrew the whole Christmas holiday? Is this day forty-eight hours
long?*—and, as all human beings are wont to think when we are most tired
and cranky, *What is the meaning of life?*

He settles himself in beneath a pile of pale knitted shawls and a plaid
blanket the colors of both the twilight sky and the pine-needle canopy. The
horses finish dropping their steaming apples into the snow. The driver snaps
the reins and they move out. Ah Lee's heart is moved in an odd new way.
The lavender sky turns to purple, and stars come out. Back of those pin-
pricks of perfect white light, the sky goes blue black. Ah Lee stares at the sky,
grateful, transfixed.

Next to him, under his blankets' weight, Albrecht is collapsed, asleep, before the sleigh is fully in motion. *How can he sleep?* Ah Lee thinks. *This is as
amazing as the first evening of creation.* But Albrecht has seen it before, has
grown up with it. Ah Lee imagines his friend as a child in all this beauty, taking it all now for granted. He wonders whether Albrecht, viewing Grandpa
Tim Tandem Ho's waving acres of mustard fields, would have felt the same
awe. He thinks not. He mutters into the blankets a phrase he recalls from his
mother's nightly Bible readings, "The earth is the Lord's, and the fullness
thereof."

When Ah Lee first came to the university, he had had a deep sense that he was finally "home," the place his mind had always been seeking. Now, heading north, there is a different sense, that of reorienting to a new geographic "home," perhaps the sense of rightness an explorer feels, finding a new place that is nothing like the place he came from but that feels so right.

Later that night, the two young men lie on their backs on the matching hard-mattressed twin beds in Albrecht's old room. Too much of Mrs. Hagedorn's coffee, and neither can sleep. Ah Lee tries to explain this deep sense of his to Albrecht and cannot. Albrecht, less verbal, less concerned with these matters—articulation, distinction—shrugs and says simply, "It's home," as if the fact that it is *his* home is quite enough to explain the leaping of his friend Ah Lee's heart.

In the morning Ah Lee wakens early, when he hears stirring down below: the hard shutting of an exterior door, the stomping of boots to kick off snow from the first morning trip to the barn, the clanking of the big coffee measuring spoon against the enamel coffeepot. He lies still on his back. He knows no one here except Albrecht. He looks over at Albrecht, asleep like a statue. He knows his friend will sleep for hours. He is home, and he is constitutionally a late riser: sleep is his natural element.

Ah Lee walks in his socks across the cold bare floor to the window. The sun is starting to rise, out across the smooth rise of the pasture, the sky paling to pink from the lavender it had been when they climbed into the sleigh—as if these two pieces of sky were the bookends of the night and he had been summoned from sleep to observe this fine symmetry.

He breaks the thin layer of ice on the water in the porcelain washbasin sitting on the dresser and splashes his face with it, splashes his hair with it, combs his hair down plaster flat to his scalp. He can by dint of long practice part his hair mirrorless in the dark and does so.

He cups his hand against his mouth to smell his morning breath, makes a small sound of disgust, rinses his mouth with the washbasin water and swallows the residue. He takes out a tiny bottle of wintergreen-scented stuff and tips it onto his tongue. He dresses and cleans his nails with a small implement from his watch pocket. He tiptoes out of the bedroom and downstairs, his nose leading him like a dance partner in the path of the aroma of coffee.

In the kitchen, Albrecht's mother and father and sister, Charlotte, are seated in silence, their matching coffee cups and saucers—a pattern bought from a catalog, dark red line drawings of a Southern plantation home, pillars and moss and hoop-skirted ladies—set before them. Ah Lee makes a great deal of noise entering the room: the door sticks and he trips on the sill; then, in catching himself from his almost-fall, he knocks a small statuette of a shepherdess onto the floor. It does not break. Ah Lee does not know what to say. He picks up the shepherdess and replaces her on the corner of the sideboard. *An odd spot to be, in the first place,* he thinks.

Mrs. Hagedorn looks up taciturnly, or as if she were nearly deaf. "Oh," she says. "Good morning." Then she looks back down at her coffee cup. She gestures wordlessly to the coffeepot, dark blue and starred like last night's splendid sky. She points to an identical dark-red-and-white cup and saucer already set in one of the empty places. He pours, he sits. The chair makes an inordinate amount of noise, scraping the brittle linoleum. The Hagedorns sip their coffee in silence.

Ah Lee sees clearly that this is the family's habit, and yet his tongue runs unwilled out ahead of him. He begins discoursing on coffee and its Ethiopian origins. "Ethiopian shepherds discovered the wonderful properties of this bean when they saw that their flocks stayed awake all night after they had nibbled the beans from the bushes," he says brightly.

Mr. Hagedorn makes a small growl in his throat. He is clearly not a morning person. "And did you also nibble the beans from the bushes?" he says dourly.

Ah Lee clears his throat in chagrin and drinks his coffee silently. Even his slight slurps seem rude intrusions into the Germanic silence of the Hagedorn ritual. Charlotte Hagedorn, almost three years younger than Albrecht and a pretty ash blond girl whose features are her stern mother's, but softened, winks at him across the light of the oil lantern. She flares her nostrils in a way that makes him laugh. He spews coffee through his nostrils, and Charlotte giggles, not a whit of contrition in her. They sit drinking coffee in silence until the sun is fully up. Albrecht, upstairs, snores on.

As Mr. Hagedorn is gathering his shopping list for the feed store and Mrs. Hagedorn is clearing the table, when Ah Lee has left the room and is perusing the spines of the books on the parlor mantel, Mr. Hagedorn says, "Goodness gracious, that Chinee talks up a storm." Mrs. Hagedorn nods agreement.

THAT EVENING WHILE Albrecht is working on his stamp collection, Charlotte Hagedorn takes Ah Lee into the hayloft. Her parents have gone to the church in the village. Charlotte says she would like to show him a bird's nest and perhaps he can name it for her, with his vast knowledge of so many subjects. While he is standing atop a small pile of hay bales to see the nest, high on a rafter, Charlotte down below, standing in shallow straw, slips out of her dress and stands in the lamplight in her eyelet camisole and ribboned pantaloons. As he turns to ask her whether she has ever seen this bird, he blinks in astonishment. She does not give him time to assimilate any of this.

"Come on down," she says. "I can show you another nest then." He leaps lightly from the bale. She steps out of her pantaloons. The blond brown hair at her crotch looks gold, fiery, in the lantern light. Her bare skin is so very white. Her navel, he thinks, is so small and so flat it is like a skin buttonhole stitched into her by some marvelous seamstress.

Ah Lee, subverbalizing to regain his sense of control in the moment, in his vast astonishment, thinks, *Would it not be more usual to remove the upper, um, garment first?* He is at a loss to name that garment. He cannot take his eyes from that bush of gold. In his union suit under his trousers he is hard as iron. "Miss Hagedorn!" is all he can think to say.

"Oh, I think you might call me by my given name," she says. Her own eyes are fixed on the front of his trousers. "I see you appreciate this?" There is an audible twinkle in her words.

"Appreciate?" Ah Lee says. He can feel that his eyes are wide. He can see where her own eyes are focused.

She unhooks a thousand or so tiny hooks at the front of her camisole. "One intuits that you are a virgin," says Charlotte. "Indeed, I am too."

"I was raised by a mother who was born in a Congregationalist mission," Ah Lee says.

"And I am a baptized and versed-in-the-whole-catechism, confirmed

German Catholic," Charlotte says. "Most of the time. But I understand that Martin Luther—responsible for the development of all the Protestant faiths —had philosophical problems with celibacy himself." She sighs. "It is *so* isolated here. And God is *so* forgiving."

She drops her camisole lightly and soundlessly into the straw. Her small, round breasts are pink in the lantern light, their nipples so pale he cannot judge the place where they delineate themselves from the milky pale skin around. Her nipples stand upright, and the rest of her skin turns to gooseflesh in the chill. "Why don't you take off your clothes, then, and make me warm?" she says.

"You are a *virgin?*" says Ah Lee. "This bold?"

"Perhaps it does not require practice," she says. "Only the sheer isolation of this barn, on this farm, in this deep heart of Michigan, and those deep black Chinese eyes stumbling into my kitchen at breakfast."

"Indeed," says Ah Lee. He tries to think of an argument, mind over body. "Your brother will surely come out looking for us." He thinks further, ever the proper grammarian: *My* eyes *did not stumble. Eyes do not stumble.* He despises his own pedantry.

"Albrecht has some new stamps for his collection that came in the last post from New York," she says. "He *loves* stamps."

And indeed he does. Charlotte and Ah Lee have each other, creatively, this way and that, several times before Albrecht thinks to inquire absently of himself—and without follow-through—where they might be, this long. At this moment they lie in the hay, Charlotte's flat pale abdomen glazed with white drool, dried and sugary, Ah Lee astonished and smitten.

"And *still,*" she says, smiling, "I am a virgin." He has not penetrated her, because she has led him elsewhere and elsewise. She has, however, shown him how to please her, three times to his once, and indeed he has done so. "And so too are you."

"Do I take it that you mean you have done *this* before? You seemed to suggest that you were *innocent.*" Ah Lee does not know whether to be delighted or affronted.

"Oh, no!" she says. "I mean, yes. Indeed, I have never done any of this."

It is clear, unambiguously, that she means it. Her smile is broad, wholesome, open. "But it really is *very nice,* isn't it?"

"Very nice," Ah Lee agrees. He blinks in amazement at her.

She sits up and looks at him lying back in the straw, naked and sweating, and then she kneels up and looks at him some more. She smiles at his limp penis, lying across his leg. "Silly thing," she says, and touches it lightly with her index finger. It springs to life. "Oh," she says." Then let us try *this.*" She takes him into her mouth and he grows beyond her capacity to contain him. She chokes slightly and pulls back. "Your skin is so soft," she says. "And so . . . *interesting.*"

He lies back and lets her do anything she wants. He thinks he may die of this, perfectly happy. He wonders about Martin Luther, whose story he does not know but will look up in the library on his return. At breakfast the two will not meet each other's glance for fear of someone else detecting the changed state of matters between them.

The following evenings, Ah Lee sits up in the parlor with all of the Hagedorns while Mrs. Hagedorn reads to them—Longfellow, long passages from the Book of Job. Charlotte plays the piano, Albrecht pores over his stamps at a side table, Mr. Hagedorn snores in his chair. Neither Mr. nor Mrs. Hagedorn seems to notice a thing. Albrecht has shown no suspicion, not even mild questioning in regard to their relationship, which seems publicly quite polite, distant, appropriate.

The third night of the visit, Charlotte takes Ah Lee into her own bed deep in the night, and this time, they do the whole deed. Charlotte bleeds like the proverbial stuck pig.

"Oh, my," is all Ah Lee can say, swiping at the blood all over his own loins and stomach.

"I do all the laundry," she says, matter-of-factly. "There is nothing to worry about."

But indeed, on Valentine's Day Charlotte sends Ah Lee a card with pale pink ribbon threaded through eyelet lace, saying, on a small piece of onion-skin paper, separate from the card, that there is something they both must consider; that perhaps, recalling their holiday visit, he will know what she means; and that perhaps he can find occasion to come to the Hagedorn homestead on some pretext, rather soon, or that she will find some pretext to come south. She says, "I do not know whether to fear or rejoice, but I find myself doing both at the same time."

The card is of a heavy paper, six inches by four, with edges cut in semicircular scallops. In pastel colors it pictures a small boy and girl with a wagon, and a floppy-eared dog the color of Charlotte's strawberry blond hair. Charlotte signs the card, *Your friend, Charlotte Hagedorn.* Her handwriting is perfect, the serifs on her capitals seeming somehow like the lacy tips of the wings of black-and-gold butterflies Ah Lee remembered from Tim Ho's fields in bloom.

He holds the card to his ear, strangely, half aware that he is doing this peculiar thing, but he still cannot hear the tone of her words. Is she terrified? Is he misinterpreting the situation? Is she talking about something other than what he is thinking? What *else* could she possibly mean? He ponders and pauses and then he thinks: *Was this a trap? Was Charlotte in all of her seeming innocence looking for a way off the farm?* His bowels clench.

Ah Lee writes back to Charlotte, asking to meet her in Grand Rapids at a church conference in the last week of March. There is a speaker there who has been a missionary to China, and Ah Lee has already made plans to go hear the man. The idea of an American's going to China to save heathen souls—for this is the way the enterprise is framed up, with the word *heathen* used in the announcement Ah Lee reads in the newspaper—intrigues Ah Lee. He is quite disconnected from this: he thinks of himself as wholly American. The "heathen" are entirely *other*.

Charlotte writes him that she will come, that his plan seems good. In her reply Ah Lee does not sense anything to reinforce his fear that this had been a plan on her part. He decides that indeed, if she should be with child, he will marry her, whether her father is pleased with the idea or not. He is certain that this is the best course of action.

There will be no trouble about money: he has his father's inheritance, and though he had hoped to go on in his education, he can instead start a business as he and his father had originally planned. He is thinking about this in some detail. He is thinking a stationer's, perhaps. His academic inclinations might be, at a second remove, somewhat satisfied in that line of work. Or perhaps a bookstore, near the university. Yes, that would be better!

He takes walks in the winter night visualizing where he might put up a building for this purpose. He imagines the town spreading out quickly, and so he does his scouting on the frozen-mud outskirts, on wagon-rutted streets, which he senses will soon be the heart of the city. He passes an Italian grocer's establishment and looks up at its sign, newly repainted—the store is now seven years old: It reads EST. 1882. The letters and numbers are gilded bright.

He passes by in the daytime again and admires them. He visualizes his own name in similar letters above a storefront: BOOKS AND STATIONERY, A. L. WONG, PROP. He tries on the prospect of that. He muses that life does not always conform itself to our first choices, a business he already knew, of course. In this circumstance, feeling himself locked into a life wending a different route through the world (*to the grave*, he thinks, gloomy and silly), he feels further pricked, as if by a sharp needle probing a deep splinter. He laughs out loud. No! This is no time to be mourning. He is to be a paterfamilias now!

The third week of March, Charlotte Hagedorn, 153 miles to the northwest, goes out at night skating on a pond near the farm. She is wanting the moonlight, needing the time to think. She says nothing to her mother, who would not approve of her daughter's being out after dark by herself, anywhere at all.

She places her hand on her belly as she rises from the fallen log where she has sat to lace on her skates. Her belly has started to feel almost imperceptibly rounder, tighter, down low. It is not an unpleasant sensation. She makes her way to the edge of the pond and pushes off.

She is humming a hymn in her head, something she has heard at the German Catholic church. She is thinking about the Virgin Mary, how she must have felt when the fleshly reality of being stuck with this pregnancy and no husband in sight began dawning on her. *Of course*, Charlotte thinks, *Mary of Galilee, unlike me, was not playing the minx in the hayloft.* But then she thinks of Ah Lee's smooth cheeks, dark eyes, and square hands. She mouths "angel" aloud in the dark. She watches her breath shape a question mark in the dark air.

Distracted, she skates onto an area of thin ice, and the ice gives way. There is no one to hear her cries, as there had been no one to hear Chen Bing's cries almost half a century before. Charlotte is astonished by the blackness of the water. Her mind is alert. She thinks: *This is a strange thing to happen. I have never known anyone to fall through ice.* She certainly does not think: *I am about to die.*

She sinks first and then rises up underneath the ice. She feels her long skirt and her three flannel petticoats becoming heavier, heavier—how can this be? Surely they have taken in *instantly* all the water they can absorb. The heaviness is bred of the fight of her muscles against the dawning consciousness of her plight, and the absolute, terrible weight of her skates, which seem suddenly to be made of lead. The ice that she has fallen through is so thin: barely past sherbet consistency. Yet she has in her struggling moved away from the warmer-water pocket produced by the swift current of a stream entering the little lake, and she is back now under a more solid sheet of ice. Charlotte, fighting the heaviness of her skirts and skates, thinks: *Surely the ice will give way from below? After all, it gave way from above!* She knocks at the ice from below, with what almost seems a politeness. *Hello? World, ahem, let me back in? Please. Oh, my, I am eighteen years old and there is a very small child underneath my heart.* She is not sure the universe hears her.

She stops thinking and tugs at her skate laces desperately, fruitlessly. She is swallowing water. She tries to unhook her petticoats, hoping somehow that her skate laces will come unraveled by virtue of her thrashing. Her hands are frozen and useless. She tries now to push at the ice with the top of her head. It seems solid as rock. She can get no force into her pushing. She seems to be turning to stone. She opens her mouth to cry out, as if from some crevice in the mud of the shoreline a battalion of rescuers—what, Charlotte, beavers in their hibernation?—surely must materialize. And so Charlotte Hagedorn drowns, in far more agony of spirit than Chen Bing, unconscious, had had to know. She pushes blindly upward at the ice, only three feet away from the airhole, until all goes black.

At Charlotte Hagedorn's funeral, Ah Lee is stoic with grief. To his friend Albrecht and his family, the young man's absence of emotional display makes sense: in their perception, Charlotte had been nothing to this slightly exotic young man but the briefly met sister of his best friend.

Thus his grief is interpreted as politeness, just as Charlotte's pounding desperation beneath the ice showed itself to the eyes of the stars overhead as nothing at all, simply stillness.

IN 1973, IN a ragged half-moment that is the opposite number of the half-moment of the death of Charlotte Hagedorn—it is an unusually hot summer afternoon, bright and merciless, an afternoon for which Charlotte Hagedorn's farmer father would have given sober German thanks, at the dinner table—Mindy Ji, seven months pregnant with Justin, is sitting on the steps of the old, gutted church where she and Joe Cimmer have been living for over a year, fanning herself with a cardboard fan. She is going through a box of what she calls "stuff" that she has taken out of the attic of her father's house after her mother's death. Pictures, letters.

She comes across the Valentine card Charlotte Hagedorn sent to her great-grandfather. She looks at the signature: *Your friend.* She has no idea who Charlotte Hagedorn could be. The onionskin paper with the note telling Ah Lee, sidewise, of her pregnancy, is not there. Mindy Ji flips it aside and goes on to the rest of the items in the box, oblivious. Justin has wedged himself up full length, underneath the right side of her rib cage, and she sighs, like a building creaking and settling.

ON THE MORNING of Ah Lee's graduation the following year—the weather is sweltering and Ah Lee perspires and grumbles in his heavy dark baccalaureate robes—Wong Ah Lee meets, in the alphabetical lineup to receive diplomas, the young man whose last name is Wollaston. He is a hearty, bluff fellow who seems to love everything, even the heat.

"Ah, perspiration!" he effuses. "Blessed sweat! The gift of a provident creator to keep us cool!" He wipes at his broad, smooth high forehead with a large handkerchief. His hairline is already, at twenty-one years of age, visibly receding. This simple physical fact—the expanse of the brow—seems to endow him with a look of wisdom. He shakes Ah Lee's hand with an athletic heartiness and a firm grip that make Ah Lee look down at his fingers when

Wollaston lets go, to make sure they are all still there. *One two three four five.* Yes, they are, though the knuckles are aching and smarting.

"Call me Wolly," the young man says, with the fervor of a salesman. He smiles broadly and turns away, toward the front of the line.

Ah Lee lifts his chin in the slight breeze that rises momentarily. He ponders that business: "gift of a provident creator." Odd thing to say in this context.

Wolly wheels around suddenly. "Say!" he says. "I know you!" Ah Lee blinks in surprise.

"You were in the astronomy survey, three years ago. That class of Professor Hall's. I was, er, a bit lacking in my trigonometry background, if you will recall?" He laughs at himself. "You helped me. I could hardly forget your face. Not many Orientals in these parts!" Wolly laughs in a fashion that spells itself in the air, audibly: "Ha ha."

Ah Lee remembers now. Wolly has grown several inches since then, and put on a good deal of bulk.

After the young men have passed across the stage to receive their diplomas, Wolly asks what Ah Lee will do now. Ah Lee shrugs. He hopes the shrug does not look sheepish, but it is the truth. He has been paralyzed in his decision making.

"Come, come, come!" exhorts Wollaston. "Bright as you are!" He shakes his head in disbelief. "Why, you knew those logarithms like—" He snaps his fingers. Even the snap of his fingers is larger than life.

They are standing at a long table where sad- and excluded-looking uniformed employees of the great university are ladling punch from an enormous bowl into handled glass cups. Wollaston stares into Ah Lee's face, seeming to see the perturbation there. "Now, now, now!" he says. His habit is to say three times what someone else would say and let go. "We can't have that!"

Ah Lee says, "But that is the truth."

"Where is your family?" Wolly says, suddenly changing tack. "Introduce me to them. I will tell them how you saved my neck in Astronomy 1. Why, my boy, what you taught me set me on a course of studies I would never have thought of pursuing. I took Astronomy 6 this last term with old Asaph

Hall, and made a solid B, which my father, the reverend, will tell you is nothing short of a miracle. So. Where is your family?"

"Dead," says Ah Lee, without inflection. "My mother died of an infection she contracted when I was fifteen. She lasted two more years. My father died of grief the summer before I matriculated. I have twin uncles and one aunt, and they write me a joint letter each month, like clockwork. But I cannot introduce you to them. They are not here."

"Then . . ." says Wolly. "You have no family here to celebrate with you?"

"None," Ah Lee says. He tries not to sound defeated. He tries equally hard not to sound calloused or isolationist. Then suddenly he thinks of Charlotte Hagedorn and the smell of the hay in the barn that first night, and tears rise in his eyes.

Had Charlotte Hagedorn lived, he would have (this is what God knows, God who knows what *would have been* as well as *what was* and *what will be*) opened the bookshop he once had imagined, in the first block of West Liberty Street, where the land dipped to the railroad tracks, in the very spot where today there is a rare book dealer, Charlotte would have given birth to twin girls, and the couple would have had to deal with a great deal of prejudice at their odd union.

Ah Lee thinks if Charlotte Hagedorn had lived, he would have had a family of his own to be here . . . but then he stops himself. Had Charlotte Hagedorn lived, he would not have been here at all. The tears well and flow, one drop from the right eye, a meandering trickle from the left. He is utterly ashamed of himself.

Wolly Wollaston, bluff, gruff, and hearty, and thinking that Ah Lee is mourning his parents, says, "Well, well, well. Come meet *my* family then, my good man."

Wolly Wollaston, as it turns out, has been hired as a junior lecturer on astronomy for the Chautauqua circuit. He will travel with a troupe of lecturers and entertainers all summer, throughout the Midwest. A population hungry for culture will welcome them. Wolly will deliver one lecture, "If the Three Wise Men Were Here Today," to mixed crowds of farmers and laborers and schoolteachers and merchants who flock to the big brown tents. He will deliver this lecture again and again, twice a day, for a total of seventy-five lectures this coming summer. And then, in the fall, with the substantial money that he has earned, he will board a ship for Europe, to study astronomy with a renowned German professor whose work he has read and admired.

"The crowds love it," Wolly says. "I talk about the Star of Bethlehem and various astronomical hypotheses to explain the phenomenon scientifically, and then at the end I roll into a flabbering spiel on the idea that the more we find out about science—biology, geology, astronomy—the more we see God in all things."

"A . . . *flabbering spiel?*" Ah Lee echoes. They both break up in laughter. "Do you mean this all seriously?"

"Oh, indeed," says Wolly. "The Chautauquas, you know, were started by the Baptists to integrate culture and faith. They are today becoming broader and more . . . entertaining, at times. I see my role as education of the masses. Culture is for all, not for"—he makes a grand sweep of the hand indicating the green lawns of the university and its tall cool marble buildings—"the *privileged,* among whom I include ourselves, of course."

"There are those who would disagree with you," says Ah Lee. "On that business. The William Jennings Bryans of the world are outnumbered, I fear, by the modernists and evolutionists."

"In my talk, actually," Wolly says, "I contend that it is not only possible but mandatory that a man of faith be a modernist. While I don't address the topic of evolution per se, I do contend that our ideas ought to—*have to*—evolve as our knowledge accretes." He sets his chin at an angle and looks hard at Ah Lee, as if trying to discern just where Ah Lee himself stands.

It is that single word, "accretes," which galvanizes Ah Lee's dawning sense that there is something here for *him.* He remembers Wollaston as the foolish freshman he had been, thin of vocabulary, spindly weak at trig, and he is amazed at the fruits of education in this young man, his peer. He can see them so clearly. "Accretes," indeed. Wollaston would not have had the metaphoric-conceptual framework for that thought three years before.

A light blinks on at the back of his skull. Perhaps, he thinks, as he wipes a pink drip of pallid and sugary punch from his chin, there is something that he himself can do in the context of this fascinating Chautauqua phenomenon, to which he has paid no attention before today. Perhaps there is a job for him.

Ah Lee indeed finds a job here, a career. He is offered a contract by the same Chautauqua which employs Wolly Wollaston, that very summer. As chance or providence would have it, a Chinese professor of history in his fifties employed on the circuit for many years has died of injuries sustained in a trolley accident during the winter. This professor has been delivering two talks in alternation, "Marco Polo as a Johnny-Come-Lately," and "The Chinese Ideograph." Each has drawn many listeners, though the former draws more. The latter, an explication of the pictorial nature of written Chinese, demonstrates the evolution of the Chinese character from extremely early times up to the present.

"Ah, there it is again," says Wolly. "Evolution."

"In the general sense of the word," says Ah Lee.

"As opposed to . . . ?" says Wolly.

"As opposed to the capital *E* Evolution in which man moves up from the primeval slime to grow legs and then hair and such, and earns diplomas," says Ah Lee.

"You do not believe Darwin's theory then?" Wolly asks.

"I believe," says Ah Lee, "that my ancestors who lived before the earliest emperors were as subtle and bright—and also as confused and confounded by life—as we are, you and I." He of course knows nothing about Qin Lao. Could not. But he has hit the nail right on the head. Direct hit. "Beyond that I cannot go, and my small human brain is so limited that I feel I must choose my battles."

"Indeed," says Wollaston, cocking his head to consider the implications of this. He hears here a humility he seldom has heard in a scholar, and he does consider Ah Lee a true scholar.

"Some matters on earth are a mystery," Ah Lee says. "I do not feel the need to dispel *all* the mystery." He might have added that indeed he does feel a need to go as far as he can go in the discovery of the truth, whether that be 3 percent or 97 percent, but he stops there, as if at the Holy of Holies, at the impenetrable curtain around the mystery.

The director of the Chautauqua, whom Ah Lee meets in Detroit, is far more a businessman than a scholar, more a marketer than a thinker. When Ah Lee proposes that he change the content of the dead professor's lectures, as they feel uncongenial to him, the director says, "Uncongenial?" and looks at Ah Lee in perplexity.

"They don't feel as if they are my own," Ah Lee says. "For indeed they are not."

"Oh. Well, *change* them then," says the director flatly, his hands raised to the ceiling. "Just keep them Chinese. Anything Chinese. Yeah, that's good. Do what you want. Just Chinese. Chinese *stuff.* Folks out there love that. Exotic." He goes on with what he was doing, paperwork, adding short columns of figures.

Ah Lee walks away bemused. His smile grows broader as he walks. By the end of his three-mile walk through the heart of the city, he knows. He will give two lectures, one on the Forbidden City in Old Peking, this one with lantern slides.

The second lecture will be on the Chinese written character, but with an emphasis on a theory he is developing: the idea that the Book of Genesis was known to the ancient Chinese, that their border sacrifice rituals were in fact related to their knowledge of the story of Adam and Eve, and that the Chinese written characters themselves demonstrate this knowledge.

When Ah Lee reports these to the director, the man says, "Good. Good." He waves him away absentmindedly, then calls him back to see a proof copy of a poster announcing his lectures. The poster calls him Professor A. L. Wong. The director calls him "Al."

"No," says Ah Lee, "not Al. That lacks dignity."

The director ignores him. Then later, alone, in a moment of loony lucidity, recalling Ah Lee's protest, he alters the poster to read "Professor Alabaster Wong."

Ah Lee is appalled, nearly apoplectic when he finds out. "That is not my name!" he shouts. But the posters are out, and plastered on every post in the first town.

"Alabaster," the director says, rolling the word on his tongue like paté. "That has dignity."

"Do you know what it *means?*" says Ah Lee. He has an image of himself shaped in stone, in the Greek fashion, ludicrous, wearing a toga for dignity—as the statue of Alexander Agassiz, on whose lap Ursula has her snapshot taken so many years later, wears judicial-appearing robes. It is so silly. "Do you know *Alabaster* is not even a name?"

The director laughs. "Well. It is now."

In the three weeks before the Chautauquas heat up and roll out, Ah Lee constructs and polishes his lectures. He listens to Wolly Wollaston (who is now billed as Professor Rogers Burbage Wollaston, his full name) declaiming his own speeches. Ah Lee models the oratorical style of his gregarious friend.

Ah Lee has taken Professor Trueblood's classes in elocution and oratory because they are recommended, never thinking in his wildest dreams that he will ever be asked to speak in public, much less be offered the opportunity to make a career of this. He has laughed at his own pedantry; now he is being asked to capitalize on it! It is a strange world.

IT IS NOT until 1915, during the war, that Professor Alabaster Wong begins to formulate his wondrous, outrageous idea. He has never wanted another woman after Charlotte. It is not that he lacks the usual hungers: it is simply that some guilt in him weighs him down and makes him sure he would be, well, a weight, well . . . (he laughs as he thinks it!) an *albatross!* to any woman, bring her to her doom as he brought Charlotte to hers. *Alabaster the Albatross!* he thinks. But here is his idea: he wants a child anyway.

He places an advertisement in the newspaper in Detroit, seeking a young Chinese woman who would like to marry a professor and return to China. He receives seven replies. He travels to Detroit and meets five of the women. The other two have sent photographs.

One of the women he meets has something about her movements that reminds Ah Lee of Charlotte Hagedorn. Over tea in a tearoom in Detroit, near the river, Ah Lee asks her her feelings about having children. The young woman says politely, oh, of course, that this would be understood.

Ah Lee asks how strong is her desire to return to her homeland. Here she waxes poetic: she lauds the vegetation of South China, she recalls her best friend there fifteen years ago as a child, she recalls a dragon-boat festival, which seems to have been the highlight of her life. She bursts into tears at this last, and she begins going on in Chinese about the terrible isolation that she feels in America.

"Then I will be direct with you," says Ah Lee. "I have a great deal of money. I have made this on the Chautauqua circuit." He might as well be speaking a foreign tongue. The young woman waggles her shoulders as if to say, Okay, well, what?

Ah Lee continues. "I am afraid my advertisement was not as direct as it might have been, but then, given the constraints of etiquette, perhaps it *was* as direct as possible." He sighs. He folds his hands in his lap. He refolds the napkin before him on the table. He looks around at the other patrons in the restaurant. He lowers his voice. "I am *not* looking for a wife. I am looking rather for a woman to give me a child, a woman who will then go back to China to stay. There will be no further connection."

The girl's head is lowered. She peers up at him quizzically through plucked-thin dark brows. She would have been willing to marry this man, just to get back to China, but now he is telling her he will send her back *without* expecting her life to be spent with him in exchange for the journey? All he wants is a child? She sits silent, uncertain that she is hearing him rightly.

"There is of course significant cost to you. At least one full year of your life, perhaps longer. I am not certain how long a child takes the breast."

"And then I may go home to South China?" she says.

He nods yes.

"Well, oh, certainly, yes. Oh, my, yes, do you wish me to sign papers?"

"Papers?" says Ah Lee. He has not thought of this aspect of things yet. But he has a friend who is an attorney. Yes, probably there should be papers.

"You understand that this would make you less, well, desirable as a bride when you return? You would no longer be a virgin."

The girl smiles and her dimples show. "That has been true for two years," she says. "You would be taking nothing from me. And when I need to find a husband, upon my return, there are ways to remanufacture the appearances of virginity."

"There are?" says Ah Lee, not sure what she is talking about. He thinks that at some time later he might inquire about this matter.

"Would you like to start now?" she says. "I live less than a mile from this place. My landlady is blind and perhaps a bit deaf. She lives on my paltry rent and is glad for it. She does not ask questions."

"Would I like to start now?" Ah Lee echoes. He notes the shape of the young woman's dimple and the way that her dark hair persists in breaking free from the silver-colored ornaments at her temples. He notes the slight pulsing of blood in the girl's temples, pale against that sleek black hair.

He clears his throat. "I would like to start now," he says, and he rises and follows her out through the door of the tearoom.

11   Mindy Ji and Joe

TWO YEARS AGO, disgusted with the face he saw in the weird greenish light of his truck cab mirror one Tuesday morning outside Bentonville, Arkansas, Joe Cimmer had shaved off his beard. It was thick and black and, more than anything, a place to hide. You were always the same when you had a beard, and who cared anyway. Joe had decided to get out of what he called "rogue" trucking, the companies who bent the rules but maybe had more adventure going. He had had enough of adventure.

He had signed on with Wal-Mart, a "family-oriented" firm, two years before that, and he was driving their trucks, in their uniforms now, feeling a tad better about himself. He was heading to a conference for Wal-Mart in Bentonville, to receive an award for good service.

His paunch was pretty much gone. The year before that, he had met up with a guy in the world's biggest truck stop, in Walcott, Iowa, who drove for Transport America. The guy had a crinkly smile and pale blue eyes. He was wearing a block-M Michigan ball cap, and he came from the Upper Peninsula of Michigan too. Weirder things had happened, for sure.

The guy was a runner, he said, ever since high school. He'd make it the point of his day to find a good spot to stop and go for a run. Three miles, like clockwork. Summertime, winter, whenever there was hard ground, no ice. Either interesting terrain or just a clear straight shot. In an unaccustomed surge of friendliness, Joe paid for the guy's coffee. "But I'm not gay, okay?" Joe said. He laughed awkwardly because he rarely talked to anyone, thought that would make a joke, and listened to the almost audible *klunk* as it fell stupidly to the counter. "I just thought, hey, man, that's a great idea, running every day. I'll think about it. Thanks."

The pale-eyed guy smiled but seemed unsure what to make of Joe, this talky edginess, and Joe never saw him again. But Joe began running himself, a mile a day to start, huffing and puffing. It took more energy than he could have imagined, and his feet felt like lead. He thought: no more fries. He bought new sweats. He bought new running shoes. He started doing sit-ups in his bunk. He took in his belt, one notch, another.

This conference was a pretty good thing now. Every year they sent one driver from each distribution center and one so-called associate. Joe got picked. It made him nuts. For the past couple of years something in him was looking hard to catch up, to get out of the red with the universe. All his antennae were up. He'd see a woman stopped in her pickup truck with little kids crying, and he'd be the one to stop, even if cars whizzed by solidly. He'd put a star on the chart in his head. He thought: *Not all the stars in the sky would make up for what I've done. Dear Jesus.* But he would keep trying. Maybe he could fill the cup to the brim. How many stars.

In a snowstorm he saw through his windshield, as if on a big movie-theater screen, a car ahead of him go slithering off the road in thick twilight. He stopped and climbed down the embankment. He called the cops on his cell phone. He had caught his foot on a protruding rock, slipped in the slick snow himself on the way down, and cut his hand on a piece of scrap metal covered by the snow. He bandaged it badly with a sweat sock until the next day, when he got home and got himself stitches and a goddamn tetanus shot. He told himself this would make up for some of the bad stuff, a kind of truck driver's purgatory on earth. Then he called himself an asshole, in his rearview mirror, for thinking that.

This was an old lady, really old, in the car that had slid down the embankment. She was wearing a bonnet-type hat like a little girl's, with fake pink fur around it. Terrified, tears in her eyes. Joe got her to put down the window a couple of inches and just touch his hand. Her fingers were so bony. He stayed touching her hand till the cops came.

The old lady was taken to the hospital, and she was okay. Not even a broken bone. She got her son, who was an accountant, to write a letter to the company. Joe was commended. But this was uncomfortable. He wanted these stars to be only inside his skull. He tried to do his job, be invisible. Instead he had gotten himself noticed. Shit.

A couple of towns short of Bentonville now, Joe looked in the mirror at his bearded face and growled, "The hell with *this*." He pulled off the road, got out the utility scissors he kept for cutting rope or random articles out of *USA Today* or, he thought, an umbilical cord, yes! in case someone should be having a baby on the shoulder in an old car with a flat, in driving rain, in the middle of nowhere. He snorted contemptuously at this newest moronic superhero fantasy. He took the scissors and cut off the wiry beard close to the skin, then pulled out his electric shaver.

Underneath the beard, his face was greenish. There was something almost obscene about the nakedness of it. "God, why did I do that," he said out loud in the truck, looking at the mess he'd made, tiny loose whiskers all over the cab. No one answered. A voice in his head said: *Because you are sick of yourself, Joe Cimmer. But shaving won't fix that.*

When he got to the conference, the associate from his center was already there. She shrieked in hilarity when she saw him in the lobby of the hotel. "You *didn't!*" she said.

He groaned. "I look like a horse's ass, right?" he said.

The woman made a half-smile, a sister-in-law kind of smile was the best way he could put it to himself, and said, "No, not exactly. I wouldn't put it that way." But she didn't put it any other way.

Joe went through the conference self-conscious as hell. But he began to think of himself in a slightly different way. He got asked if he might think about moving into management. He thought about that. No, thanks, not me for a desk, nope. They asked him again the next year. He said he would think about it. But the antsiness in him was past handling. He had to be on the road until . . . until what? So now the Joe who had grown first a paunch and then a beard has lost them, in reverse order. He feels almost balloon light and something like new.

. . .

THE EVENING OF June 9, 2003, Joe is heading to a Super Wal-Mart
in Green Bay, Wisconsin. Last time he has come this way, he remembers as
he heads toward town, it was late October. The day was windy and dreary,
and rain had taken down most of the dried brown leaves clinging to roadside trees. Joe was carrying a load of Halloween costumes that trip. He was
also carrying many small boxes of all the replenishment stuff the scanner
had called up online, in this whiz of a system that all the other companies
envied: half a dozen tubes of Aquafresh toothpaste, half a dozen bottles of
Aussie hair gel, several Oral-B toothbrushes, this sort of mélange multiplied
dozens of times. There were a couple of dorm-room refrigerators. There
was White Stag stuff for ladies—skirts, sweaters. There were boxes of am-
munition for hunters, and camouflage gear, and three different sizes of
binoculars. There were boxes of candles that smelled like blackberries, and
a box of Johnson's Baby Soap. There were boxes of fill-in-the-blank party
invitations with pictures of happy mailboxes, and boxes of thank-you notes
with pictures of autumnal forests in which stood, serenely, high-steepled
white churches. There were pressed-sawdust fire logs and forty- and sixty-
watt lightbulbs; there were two lamps shaped like lighthouses, three with
dangling Victorian crystals, and one with pulsing neon fiber-optics. There
were a couple of dozen clock radios, and a little plug-in ceramic waterfall to
put on your dresser at night, to light up and soothe you with its sounds, like
the world's tiniest harp or piano.

But the Halloween costumes were what had occupied Joe's mind that day,
driving. He had walked through a store the week before while his truck was
being unloaded, and the costumes there were already out, hanging and
folded into boxes. A ballerina costume for a little girl, pink tarlatan tutu
with sparkles. Fairy wings and a wand. Spider-Man. A pumpkin with lights.
Frankenstein's monster. Something that looked like a space alien. He wasn't
sure. Maybe from a movie he hadn't seen.

But then that would be almost any movie, the last few years, except for
movies with Russell Crowe in them. Maybe it was the build of the guy that
Joe identified with. He had seen *Gladiator* at least a dozen times, and when
A Beautiful Mind came out he went to see it in the theater and cried right
there in his seat. He had no idea why. This had nothing to do with him and

probably nothing to do with the guy who it was supposedly about either, considering Hollywood. He rented *Mystery, Alaska* and watched it alone in his little apartment, his brown Naugahyde recliner pushed back into launch mode, a brew at his right hand.

Russell Crowe skated like a maniac in the movie and Joe remembered how well he skated in high school, when he was on the ice hockey team; Russell Crowe made crinkly smiles and charmed everyone, and Joe all of a sudden started crying, right there in his recliner.

A different voice entered then, through some labyrinthine passage. It sounded like Marlon Brando, and it said, *I coulda been a contender.* Joe sobbed, and a line of snot drooled down onto his shirt. "*Fuck* Marlon Brando," Joe said out loud, there in his little gray room. He was remembering Mindy and the baby again. He was trying to do the math but he was on his third beer and the math seemed to wobble in front of him like a mirage on the Silk Road. How old was Justin again? He decided what he needed was a good roast beef sandwich, with horseradish, and with more lettuce than anyone else would use, and hot pepper, and pickles. *Twenty-two? Jesus Christ,* he thought. *Not twenty-two?* No one answered. The answer at that point had been twenty-five, and that was four years ago.

Joe is heading hard for Green Bay again now, and last fall's load of Halloween costumes are dancing in his mind's eye as he drives. *Where the hell is this coming from?* he thinks. Then he realizes: he is remembering a dream he had that morning, after a couple of hours' sleep, a dream that began as a memory. Maybe it came because he was heading for Green Bay, and last time he had a run to Green Bay it was Halloween. Stupid.

In the dream Justin, age two, is running out in front of him in his Halloween costume. Justin is a pumpkin, in a homemade, puffy orange suit Mindy has stuffed with crumples of paper. Joe is trailing a few feet behind him, carrying the big trick-or-treat bag, as he shuffles along in the brilliant, soft leaves on the sidewalk. The weatherman has cooperated, and this Halloween is neither frigid nor rainy, but a clear, bright fall day turning twilight now. Around the corner comes a kid on a bike, not looking, just as Justin starts to step off the curb. Joe lunges, and Justin is caught.

The kid on the bicycle calls out a swear word and Joe thinks, What kind of parents has that kid got? He wants to give the kid a piece of his mind: *You could have hit this little guy*. He holds Justin close to him and feels his little heart pumping like a bird's. By the next Halloween, when Justin is three, Joe is already gone.

At this point in Joe's dream, everything shifts. All the Halloween costumes lying inert in their boxes in the back of the truck take on life and struggle out of their wrappings. In his dream he can see himself asleep and the costumes escaping. He can hear their noise: crunch, crinkle, *schiff.*

A ghost shapes itself liquidly in midair, a Frankenstein's monster grows to ridiculous proportions and stalks off down the highway. Rubbernecking drivers run amok; there is the squealing of rubber and brakes, and the terrible meeting of metal with metal, the shatter of glass. But no one is hurt. The drivers climb out of their cars and start dancing, a kind of fifties jitterbug, silly, incongruous. There is no music. A rabbit costume takes on life and starts leaping zigzag among the dancers, several of whom try to catch it. The space alien costume multiplies itself and scatters out into a cornfield, between the rows.

When Joe wakes up he is sweating peculiarly. He thinks: *What did I eat?* That dream is a fish-enchilada dream, and there has been no fish enchilada. Moreover, he insists to himself, *I'm not worried about anything, so it can't be anxiety. I have nothing in my life to worry about.* Then he hears himself and corrects himself, truncating, *I have nothing in my life.*

At Green Bay now it is ten at night when Joe backs his truck up to the loading dock, and the unloaders go right to work. He has a two-hour wait for the next trailer, so he hikes up the road a bit to McDonald's for a fish fillet sandwich. He has been thinking about that sandwich all day, ever since that stupid dream. Maybe he will have a dream sequel that will explain the first one. He would like someone to come in and explain everything.

Joe walks back to the Wal-Mart and roams in silence around the quiet, near-empty store. He likes it at night in a Wal-Mart. Very contemplative mood in the place, he thinks. The fluorescent lights and the high ceilings seem somehow to press down on him heavily, a kind of fluorescent-light pressure. He groans aloud with it and then wonders why he groaned. In the vacuum-cleaner aisle he stops to compare two handhelds. He has gotten persnickety about keeping his truck cab pristine these days. There is nothing so obnoxious as a slob reformed. He sighs and moves on.

At the jewelry counter he twirls a Plexiglas kiosk of earrings, sees a pair of earrings that are the most expensive Wal-Mart carries, silver danglers with pale blue stones. The clerk watches him inspect the display. "Can I show you something?" she says. So Joe points to the earrings. "They're simulated blue topaz," says the clerk. She turns the card over to show Joe the sticker that assures him they're not real.

"Simulated," Joe echoes.

"Yeah," says the clerk. "I don't know how much they'd cost if they were *real*. Probably a lot."

"What do you think of these?" he says to the clerk. "You like them?" He holds them out toward her.

"Oh, yeah," says the girl, who has no name tag. "They're nice. I like blue." The clerk is little more than a teenager. Her eyes are blue. She takes them from Joe, removes them from their card, and holds one up against each earlobe. She peers at herself in the mirror. "They're good," she says. "Look." She turns to Joe smiling, and the blue earrings make her eyes even more blue. She looks at his ring finger to decide whether to say girlfriend or wife. "Does your, um, girlfriend have blue eyes?" she says.

"Naw," Joe says. "She's Chinese. She's my wife." He is amazed hearing himself. "But she likes blue."

"Chinese is cool," says the girl. She pauses a moment and then adds, "I like egg rolls."

"Yeah," Joe says. "Chicken or shrimp, either one." He holds the earrings out in front of him. "I'll take these, then," he says.

He has a shiny black jewelry box lined in blue velvet back in his apartment bedroom, bought a couple of years ago at a Wal-Mart in Iron Mountain, Michigan. It holds several pairs of earrings he has bought over the years, most of them at Wal-Mart, all with Mindy in mind, as if he thought stupidly she might just stop in to watch a Russell Crowe movie with him. He didn't fucking know what.

He has never actually considered the internal contradiction in his scenarios: Mindy in that SUV, with the fat husband—Joe no longer has the paunch so is self-righteous as hell about other guys' potbellies—and the little twin daughters, damn it; and then again there is the Mindy who would welcome these earrings from Wal-Mart and hold him close in rushes of delayed grief and astonished joy.

He takes his little blue translucent plastic bag and moves on. He tries on a pair of shades he thinks Russell Crowe might approve and leans back to peer at himself in the down-slanted mirror on the tall kiosk. He wonders if Justin looks anything like him. He puts a new pair of sunglasses into a hand-basket. He wonders if Justin remembers him at all.

It does not occur to him to go further than that, to try to imagine Justin's life now. It is all too surreal. Now that the fat white businessman stepfather he invented has provided so well, Justin has gone off to college in . . . He couldn't go further than that. Gone off to college somewhere, yeah, he'd be about to graduate now, right? No, he would have already graduated, God, a long time ago. He picks up a package of Little Debbie brownies to eat in the truck. He picks up a three-pack of Fruit of the Loom briefs, size medium. Used to be large.

Joe wanders idly into the electronics department and inspects a CD player in a bright blue-and-purple case. *Ick,* he thinks. He turns to face the row of televisions and all the screens carry the same channel: a rescue attempt, apparently. He has been tuned out today. What is going on? He moves closer to the bank of TVs and stands in front of one with stereo speakers.

Brandi Chandler-Greene is off somewhere napping, and a red-haired guy with a great voice and an unfortunate look, as if his eyes are permanently crossed, has taken her place. His name is spelled out beneath him: STANIS-LAUS KECK. For real? Maybe so. We have gotten past the days of Hollywood names, right? Stanislaus Keck is reading from a prompter.

"The Meridel-Pflaum Corporation," says Stanislaus Keck, "was once the premier producer of taconite ore in the Great Lakes area, operating mines at Rovaniemi, Ishpeming, and Republic Mine, Michigan. The area is no longer an iron-mining center, having peaked in the first half of the last century." He knows this is a copper mine here, not iron. He knows the difference, for godsake. He hopes the next thing that comes onto the prompter explains to him what he means, so that he can adjust his inflection. No explanation is forthcoming, so he continues. "The area is populated by the descendants of immigrant miners, many of them Finnish, others Cornish or Greek or Italian." Someone off-camera holds up a hand-lettered sign for him. He tries not to squint as he reads it. "The great-great-grandfather of this little girl was a miner who died in the Meridel-Pflaum collapse at Rovaniemi in 1926." The sign actually says mining supervisor, but this is hard to do on the fly. "Little Ursula and her parents were up here in the Keweenaw looking for the mining camp, Camp Grit, where Jake Maki spent part of his childhood, and in the process of seeking out their family history—" He pauses and clears his throat. He continues lamely, "In the process of seeking out family history, new history was made." He sighs, sick at his inability to ad lib. Perhaps he should have gone into teaching voice. He almost laughs aloud. No one on the team thinks anything he has said is less than perfect.

JOE SPEAKS ALOUD to no one in particular. He has just heard a shuffle and thump and assumed a clerk was around the end cap from him. "Say, you know what's going on here?" he says. Here is this Keck guy out there in the dark in the middle of the night talking about iron-mining history. He looks around the corner and an already emptied box has just slipped from a stack, all by itself, and lies across the aisle. There is no one there. "I guess you don't," he says, to the air.

On the television, Stanislaus Keck, standing inside some sort of log-walled building of strange proportions, is interviewing an elderly woman who squints at the camera. "I'm talking here today with Mrs. Maidie Vennema, the daughter of Paavo Wisti, a foreman who died in the collapse of the Meridel-Pflaum mine at Rovaniemi in 1926." Mrs. Vennema nods and makes a sad face. "Mrs. Vennema simply happens to live in the vicinity, in Eagle Harbor, and met the Wong child's father this afternoon. This is not a Meridel-Pflaum mine. They were an iron-mining company."

At home in their living rooms, several viewers think, *Then why don't you shut up about it*, but of course he has to fill empty air space. "It is unknown to whom this shaft belongs," says Stanislaus Keck, "because it does not appear on the survey maps."

He hands the mike to Mrs. Vennema. "Yah," she says. "I was watching Judge Jayber on TV and that young man come banging on my door asking to use the phone. He called 911, and then he come back here to be with his wife, and I got my son to drive me down in his wife's Geo. It feels like a tunafish can when you ride in it," she says. "Oh, this is awful."

"Does this bring that terrible day in 1926 to mind, Mrs. Vennema? You must have been a very small girl."

"No, it *doesn't* remind me of that day at all," Mrs. Vennema says curtly. Stanislaus Keck seems taken aback. She looks at him as if to say, are you thick? "That was a whole different thing," she says.

"Well, yes," says Stanislaus Keck. "Yes, indeed. But a mine is a mine, and a rescue attempt is a rescue attempt, and given that there is nothing we can report at the moment about this, I wonder if you could tell our viewing audience about your memories of the collapse of the Meridel-Pflaum."

"Are you serious?" says Mrs. Vennema. Stanislaus Keck's eyes dart about as if asking for help. "Good Lord, I can see that you are. You just want me to keep talking because the camera won't go away, right?"

Stanislaus Keck is local, not network, only on the job for a matter of months now. He clears his throat in discomfiture. "Can you tell us about your father then?" he says.

Mrs. Vennema surrenders. Her father came over from Finland, she says, and he was a hardworking man. Didn't drink, she says, belonged to the Finnish Temperance Society. There were six children and a grandfather, and it was difficult after he died. "Stark," she says, rolling the word around on her tongue. Her mother, she said, remarried to a German who owned a grocery in town. "He was coarse," she says oddly, and Stanislaus Keck has no idea where to go with that.

"Can you tell us about the day of the disaster itself?" he says.

"Oh, sure, sure," she says. She has never been on television before and she hopes someone is taping this so she can show her grandkids in Grand Rapids. "We had oatmeal for breakfast."

Joe wanders off to the next department, where there is a clerk in a blue vest. "Hey," he says, "Do you know what this is on the TV?"

"Some little girl fell down a mine shaft out in the woods today. Over in Michigan." He looks past Joe's shoulder. "Terrible."

"How old?" says Joe. "Can they get her out? Is she alive?"

"Three, or maybe two and something," says the clerk. "They don't know anything else yet. The emergency crews are just barely getting their equipment to the site, I think. My God, can you imagine if that was your kid! Look!" he says, pointing to the screen. "That's the kid," he says.

It is a close-up snapshot of Ursula, just last week, Memorial Day, at the edge of Lake Superior, running across the sand. Justin took the shot, standing on a dune at the edge of the shore road at Munising, just as the sun was starting to go down. Ursula's dark half-Asian eyes twinkle, and her white blond hair, unbraided, blows in the breeze.

"Cute kid," Joe says. He remembers Justin running on that same beach, a place Mindy liked to go for the view, even if it was two hours' drive. The way the shore swooped in and out, the incurve of the sand up to the road, the green tufts of dune grass, the amazing expanse of blue dazzling lake. He's not thinking about the mine shaft, only about that little girl running on the same beach where Justin ran. Same big-ass lake, Gitche Gumee. His mind echoes back: Hiawatha. Old Nokomis. He thinks about filling his truck at a diesel pump, and he wonders how many gallons that lake holds.

Joe wanders off to the toiletries, picks up a tube of shampoo and sniffs it. Fruit. Some kind of fruit. He can't put his finger on it. The little girl's face imprints itself on his consciousness and will not go away. Those dark eyes, that Finn white hair. He picks up a new toothbrush. He has a half hour left before the truck is ready. He takes out the toothbrush and inspects it closely again. *Why do they put different-colored bristles in the middle?* he thinks. He is eking out second by second a semblance of something to fill a huge hole. He considers a purple handle rather than the emerald green. He puts both of them back and decides he does not need a toothbrush tonight.

Melon! he thinks. *That was* melon *shampoo. Good grief.* He wanders back to the row of televisions. Stanislaus Keck is outdoors in the dark now, with portable lighting. Trees in full leaf and bare trees and evergreens bunched in the background ground are lit eerily by the cameramen's lights. The branches dance, the wind whips the lights around.

Stanislaus Keck is interviewing the child's father, a young man with dark hair pulled back into a ponytail. The young man's coat is bright yellow, his face is clean-lined, good-humored, sober. Next to him, leaning up against the sleeve of his coat, is a short Asian woman. Joe cannot hear anything. Someone has turned down the volume on all of the TVs. As he comes closer the name flashes on the screen: JUSTIN WONG. Joe blinks. Did he see this? Then he looks at the woman beside the young man. Yes! It's Mindy Ji. Joe feels his legs ready to crumple out from beneath him. Some kind of liquid slosh back of his eyes—a brain?—swirls in response to all this. If that's Mindy Ji . . . and if that's Justin . . . then that child is . . .

He turns his back to the televisions, as if in some way that will make it all vanish. He walks away a few feet. He stands staring at a bank of country-western CDs across the aisle, a blur. A bunch of pale fake multimillionaire cowboys in cowboy hats, fake nonchalance on their fucking fake faces.

He turns back to the bank of televisions, two rows of them, upper and lower, two dozen in all. On the screen is the little girl's face again, two dozen times, bright on the summer beach, and now Joe recognizes that sweet almond look to her eyes, Mindy Ji's, Justin's.

It is also uncannily like the look of the eyes of Ming Tao, the daughter of Wong Shao-Long, the seventeenth-century minister of maps, with his estate bordering the Lake of the Fragrant Pomegranate, because the very specific combination of genes that shapes the cheekbones and forehead are a gift down the sluice of lineage, but of course Joe does not know that. Below the pale almond-eyed face, letters spell out her name, URSULA WONG.

"Oh, my God," says Joe. "Oh no, oh Christ." He does not realize that he is speaking this aloud, that he is in fact *very* loud.

"Yes, sir," says the earring clerk, who happens to be passing in the aisle en route to somewhere else. "Sir, is there something I can do for you, sir?"

Joe says, "Oh shit, oh Jesus, do you believe." Mindy Ji is on the screen again. He turns to the earring clerk. He points to the row of TV screens. He says, *"That"*—and then he points to each individual screen, one by one, down the line—"is my wife." He pauses to comprehend this, and in saying it makes it real.

"That boy is my . . . *son,* that's my Justin, goddamn, and that little girl is my . . . granddaughter." The word is too strange on his tongue, and he has an impulse to cough, as if he has inhaled a crumb down the wrong pipe. "My grandchild," he says. "That gorgeous little girl."

He looks around him confused, as if a bird had flown through and he were a searcher determined to find it. "Down that hole. My grandchild."

"Oh, mister," says the blue-eyed jewelry clerk.

"I didn't know I *had* a grandchild," says Joe.

"Omigod," says the clerk, clapping her hands to her face. She has no idea on earth what he means. She wonders how old you need to be to have a stroke. She wonders what having a stroke looks like. She peers at the dark hair poking out from beneath his cap. No gray she can see. *Older than my mom?* she thinks. Her mom uses Herbal Essences blond hair color, a shade called Crushed Pearl. She jokes about not knowing what color is underneath. The girl has no idea how old you get gray anyway. Past thirty is all the same to her: just old, omigod.

"I gotta call my dispatcher," says Joe. The jewelry clerk stands perplexed, squinting at him. "I gotta get there," he says. He is slapping himself loudly, clap, clap, pockets everywhere, looking for he doesn't know what. A number, a wallet, a phone?

"Oh!" says the girl. "Sure you do! Oh, mister!"

She runs to the closest blue-vested employee, a skinny guy with a tanning-booth tan who is mopping the aisle between hardware and lighting. "Hey, Wade!" she yells. "This guy didn't know he had a grandchild!"

And so, in domino effect, the bewilderment passes right down the line. Wade and the earring girl stand in tableau, looking stupefied at each other. Wade leans on his mop, and the girl stands with her hands stretched out as if checking to see whether it's raining.

Joe pulls himself together, out of necessity. After all, this is *his* deal. Not Wade's, not the jewelry girl's. He finds his cell, right there in its belt holster. He punches in a number. He talks. And he's off. The plan is to leave the tractor in the lot, at the back, and to get a rental car. Yeah, that should do it.

He's on the loading dock in a flash. The unloaders are done. The picnic baskets and rattan paper-plate holders are already on their way to the aisles. A tall bundle of patio-table umbrellas makes its way along the conveyor belt, and several boxes of Deep Woods OFF and Hawaiian Tropic tanning lotion. Here come some more of those dorm little refrigerators, maybe for some-body's boat or cabin, looking as if they are going to dwarves in a forest.

Joe stands in the half-light of the loading dock holding his little hand-basket with the brownies and the sunglasses and the Fruit of the Loom. He looks at it, thinking, *What do I do with* this? The jewelry clerk comes run-ning out.

"Hey!" she calls out ahead of herself. "What are you going to do *now?*"

Joe is trying to think. He is looking at his tractor. He is realizing car rentals don't open till morning, hours away. He says, "Jesus Christ, what *am* I going to do?"

The girl is one step ahead of him. She says, "Okay, so look, my mom's boyfriend, Josh, is the manager at the airport car rental deal. They don't open till morning." She pauses a minute. "I've got the number to his cell. He won't mind. He'll go in. Yeah. Josh is cool." She grabs Joe's slightly grimy phone. She punches in a number.

"Hey, Josh. You still up? Yeah, okay, but what are you doing watching *that?*" She rolls her eyes at Joe as if asking agreement. "That's a chick flick!" she says incredulously. She pauses. "Okay," she says, "I *told* you you were *whipped.*" She turns aside to Joe, covering the phone. "My mom is there. She's making him watch *My Best Friend's Wedding.* Omigod."

"Okay, so Josh," she says. "I'm going to need for you to do me a favor. Yeah, *now.* A customer here, at the store, well, his granddaughter is on the news. Over in the Keweenaw. She fell down a mine shaft. It's on the TV. Check it out if you want. But get your ass to the airport, quick. *Stop* the movie, Josh. This guy needs a car. Now. And give him your best." She smiles over to Joe, big re-assuring grin showing a little-girl gap between her front teeth. "Yeah, I'll drive him there. *Now,*" she says to Josh on the cell phone. She clicks off.

"Okay then, dude. Park your tractor—is that what you call it?—and let's haul," she says. Joe is astonished at all this. "I'll just check with the store manager, and I'll bring my car around back. Barf-green Cutlass, a million years old, from the eighties, okay?"

Joe hasn't had anyone do any favors for him in a long time. But it all goes so easily. Josh is a cheery guy, the jewelry girl's mom looks just like her but twenty years older, and the car Josh gets him is a red Ford Explorer. "It's all we had ready," Josh says. "I can give it to you for the price of a compact." He smiles a big manager smile. The jewelry girl tells Joe just to keep the briefs and the shades and the brownies, and she'll tell the store manager. "No, *really*," she says, insisting.

Joe blinks in surprise at the red Ford Explorer and remembers the old lady in the car with the pink fur like a flower around her pale, teary face as they waited in the snow for the ambulance. He remembers her telling him that her son had a red Ford Explorer. He thinks how wonderful it is that the human mind in moments of direst urgency runs around touching on factoids this way, like a child touching base in a game of tag.

Suddenly he thinks of Sacagawea, on Lewis and Clark's expedition. He thinks, where did *that* come from? From the word *explorer?* He realizes he is suddenly very exhausted. He climbs into the rental car, waves to Josh and the jewelry girl and her older-twin mother and pulls out into West Mason Street, empty of traffic, lit with lonely pink mercury-vapor lights.

Bleak middle of the night in Green Bay, Wisconsin, thinks Joe, *and I have a granddaughter, or I* did. He heads for the highway, which scrolls out ahead into open country unlit, black as a mine shaft. Six hours to Eagle River now, north through the forest, tiny towns, darkness, a million trees.

The Explorer feels light, like a toy, under his hands, after driving the semi. He drives through the same McDonald's where he had his fish sandwich and orders a giant-sized coffee. No, he says, not decaf, I've got to drive all night. When the girl goes back into the interior to get a stirrer, he says to himself, as if talking to her, "Yeah, my granddaughter fell down a mine shaft."

The girl inside the window is simultaneously wondering why her boyfriend gave her that look, whether she should quit school at the semester, and what time she should eat that great orange she brought in her lunch, pulling the sections apart with delight in her head. Joe imagines her smiling mindlessly in response to the news about Ursula by saying, "Thank you, drive through." It makes him furious, even if he hasn't told her, even if she hasn't ignored him. He hands her a five-dollar bill and says, "Keep the change," taking off before she can tell him she doesn't take tips.

His eyes are bleary. The coffee is perfect. He loves it when they put the sugar in for him, as if he were king. He turns up the radio, loud. Stupid hiphop noise to drown his thoughts. But he can't stand it longer than a few seconds. He finds a station with something that sounds like Brazilian violins and keeps it low. His mind races. He puts the Explorer on cruise control. He will spend the six hours beating himself up for leaving his family, trying not to think about this little grandchild he never knew he had, and then every once in a while reminding himself that he *has* lost one whole pants size, shaved off that damn beard and made sure his face was real, helped several people in trouble, and gotten a company commendation.

He tries not to consider what Mindy Ji will think of him. She looked the same on the TV, except older, not bad, just worried, did not look as if she had married some fat cat. Pooh! he says. What would that *look* like! He tries not to think about Ursula. He thinks: *Justin's wife—Wife? Did I say wife?— must be blond, eh, to judge from the little one.*

The trees whiz by. The stars overhead are bright. Deer dart occasionally through the trees or stand next to the road seeming to threaten to leap. Joe keeps driving. It is in fact a good deal less than the six hours Joe had calculated as driving time when he arrives. It is still dark. A one-room portable building the size of a playhouse sits brightly lit at the roadside. Joe parks the Explorer and walks toward it.

In the middle of the room, his arms crossed over his yellow jacket, Justin sits on a folding chair, blurry and ashen. Mindy Ji has asked him to go for a walk to clear his tension, and he has done that, but when he got this far, he had to sit down, and here was this damn building and nobody in it. Joe does not register on Justin's radar; to Joe, Justin is a fine, handsome boy, but certainly not one who could have come out of him. Joe does not know what to say.

Justin says, as if he were the host at a glum party, "What can I do you for?"

Joe has nothing to say. He sits down on another chair. "You're the little girl's father," says Joe.

"Yeah," says Justin. The corners of his mouth twitch slightly.

"I saw you on TV in Green Bay," says Joe.

"Green Bay," echoes Justin oddly.

"On twenty-four TVs in Wal-Mart. All at the same time."

Justin narrows his eyes and puts Joe in his crosshairs as if he will very soon figure this out.

"I was dropping a load of merchandise." Joe pauses and catches his breath. "I bought your mother some earrings too. Blue topaz. Just simulated."

"Hey," Justin says, half rising. "Who *are* you?"

"Look at me, Justin," says Joe. "I'm a crummy dad. But I never forgot about you. I just didn't know the way back."

Justin just stares.

"I'm sorry," Joe says.

Justin glares at him with a look between incredulity and pain unto death. He stands up. He pulls a dark wool toque over his head and walks heavily out the door into the chilly morning. His work boots are loud on the hollow floor, then thudding on the dirt. He starts running toward the RV, which is sixty or seventy feet from the hole, around which the rescue crew work in silence, in the surreal bright light from the road-crew setups.

A car with a pizza-place logo on the side pulls up. *How did the cops let them through,* Joe thinks, even though he himself has driven up and parked with an even easier sense of entitlement. It is two reporters from Sault Sainte Marie, operating on a shoestring and in a borrowed delivery car. The reporters hop out and head into Joe's silly building.

"You got the time?" says one. "We just switched from Eastern to Central, at Ishpeming, right?"

"Almost five," says Joe.

"Pretty light for five," says one.

"Yep," says the other.

"It must be some dark down that hole," says the first.

"God, you think that kid is still alive? Any chance?" says the second.

Joe stands and looks at the reporter with fury, as if the man had caused this. He thinks at that moment, *Who* did *cause this? Did I? If I'd stuck around, what would have happened?*

"She's my grandchild," he says, and he heads out into the morning, which is pale lavender and pierced with scattered birdcalls. He heads for the Explorer and sits in the front seat with the motor running and the heater and the radio on, thinking he is wide awake. He dozes just momentarily, the white noise of new age harp music on the radio, and he looks up.

Mindy Ji is standing outside in the morning staring into the car window at him as if he were a Madame Tussaud's display, crafted of wax, his head tipped toward the driver's side window, his mouth slightly open, wet at the left corner with drool.

It is perhaps the sense of being watched that awakens him. He clears his throat and leans forward to turn off the music, which seems false and horrid, something that might be piped into a coffin. *Coffin!* he thinks. *Ursula! What is happening?* He turns and is stunned to see Mindy Ji standing there expressionless, her eyes fixed on his face through the window. For a minute he wants to keep that wall of glass between them. He cannot think of what to say. Mindy Ji smiles, the smile he remembers—delight, wonder—and motions him to roll down the window. He does. Still he cannot think of what to say. Both of them breathe shallowly, as if afraid they will use up the atmosphere. Mindy Ji says, "I cannot believe—" and she knows at that second that she will believe anything, this is all so surreal.

Joe says, "I'm sorry." It sounds so stupid.

"You're here," Mindy Ji says. "That's good." She says it solidly.

"It is?" Joe says. He cannot imagine how anything can be good. He feels a cosmic nausea deep in his skull. He slides his fingers beside him on the seat, searching for the little blue plastic Wal-Mart bag. He rummages through it for the earrings on their card. Mindy watches him mystified. He pulls them out, peels off the price tag, and hands them to her through the window. "I was in Green Bay, at Wal-Mart," he says. "I drive for Wal-Mart. Five years now. I was making a drop. I bought these for you. I had no idea I'd see you tonight. Or ever again, really."

Mindy Ji takes the earrings and looks at them in amazement. "Well," she says again, "you're here. That's good."

Behind her, twenty feet off, Justin stands scowling. "Come inside, Ma," he calls, angrily, too loud.

She turns to him defiant. "This is your father," she says. "Justin, come meet your father." He turns and stalks away seething.

"He's mad," says Mindy Ji, as if Joe required subtitles.

"He has reason," Joe says mildly.

"No, no, this will be all right," she says. "He's a father now, and he needs to forgive. That's what fathers are for."

Joe doesn't understand this but it sounds wonderful. He changes the subject. "What, is his wife a Finn? Blond? I saw the little girl on the news. Beautiful."

Justin calls again to Mindy Ji from a distance, "Get over here, Ma." His voice almost sounds as if it will break.

She waves him off. She is telling Joe about how Justin met Annie, and Annie's legs, and the fact that she suspects Annie's mom died at Garrett's hand, though she cannot prove that, and how no one thought Annie could have a child, but then there was this C-section . . .

Justin calls out to Mindy Ji again. "Ma, I said *get in here.*"

She calls back to him, "I'm not taking orders today, Justin." She is surprised at herself. "He thinks I should—" She pauses. "What would he say? I should kick your Polish ass all the way to Manitoba? Maybe."

"You should," Joe says.

"I won't," she says. "Oh, Joe," she says, suddenly considering the possibilities here. "Do you have a new . . . family?"

Joe's eyes fill. "No, no, not anybody," he says.

"Good," she says, matter-of-fact.

12   The Woman Who Married the Baker's Friend

N O ONE BUT God is watching the girl sitting on the hill sloping down to the oat fields, so there is no photograph like this. No camera in use at the turn of the twentieth century could have used color film subtle enough to catch the breathtaking sudden shifts in the light as the breeze whips the leaves overhead, making brilliance, then shadow, and millions of quicksilver gradations of each. Nor could it have caught the flickering smile at the corners of this girl's mouth, in all its mobility. The light is the same light that surrounds Annie Wong on the morning of Ursula's fall into nothingness: clear and pure, jewel-like.

This girl's back is to us. Her hair is long, like Annie's, and equally bright, undimmed Finn blond. If we did not know better, we might mistake this girl, Marjatta Palomaki, for her great-great-grandchild, Annie, not born till almost a century later, across the wide ocean—even though, if we looked closely, we could see that there is a slight curl to this girl's hair that is not in Annie's, and a consequent wisping off into the sunlight like minuscule threads of curved lightning.

Marjatta's feet are bare, her brown clogs set aside neatly next to each other against the trunk of the nearest pine tree. She is the kind of Finn whose sensitivities to the nature all around her lead her to wake up each day in summer and set her feet on the morning-damp cool earth, treasuring the feeling of its warming toward midday and chilling toward evening. She counts the days of summer still left to her, loving the feel underfoot of the pine needles, caressing the warmth of the rounded extrusions of eons-old granite that punctuate the soil here. She loves winter equally: but it is summer now, and we will look at *this* snapshot only, which is regardless only in our imaginations, the only cameras anyone had before our own era.

The caption of this picture would likely be "Innocence." It would be a romantic oversimplification—hence falsification—like most of the tales in our own family histories.

It is late summer, the hot brightness of July waning to shadowy pink gold, preparing for autumn, and the slanting light surrounds and halos the girl. There is a slight arching up toward the light in the shape of her back: she is not relaxed into herself but stretching toward the sun, which will soon slip into its autumnal scarcity and winter vanishing. The babe in the sling of her apron skirt sleeps happily, baking in the sunlight.

The upcresting of earth where Marjatta sits is land that has never been cultivated, virgin land. Its soil, uphill from the oat fields, is decent but rocky. The shape of the land is a painter's delight. Were we to frame this scene photographically without including the brown-red windmill on the oat farmer's land down below, or the centuries-old church with its yard dense with gravestones, we might have a hard time distinguishing it from a snapshot of Annie a hundred years later, sitting on a hill outside Sault Sainte Marie, say the drop-off just past the edge of the trailer park.

A traveler might today drive the roads of Michigan—or Illinois or Wisconsin or Minnesota or beyond—and see again and again shapes of land that called up palpitations in the hearts of Scandinavian immigrants of Marjatta's day: *There! That incurve of the field there, where the land moves like hair in the wind, that is just like my grandfather's land! And there! I can imagine the church of my childhood nestling into that grassy gold slope! And there! That hill crests in precisely the way that the eskers line up outside of my home village! Oh, be still, my heart!*

Marjatta wears a white shift elaborately smocked at the neck. From behind her we cannot see the smocking, veiled by her pale silky hair. Typically she wears her hair in three thick coiled braids, one on each side and one low at the back. She has just washed it and is drying it in the sun. She has sat, late evenings, at the age of seventeen, by oil light in the dark log-walled room and done the smocking herself, as she has smocked other garments before. This one is different: this one is her wedding garment, meant to be worn with a bright flower crown and elaborate red-and-black apron shot through with bright green stitching. There are also touches of gold from the thread brought from Vaasa.

As she rode home from the Lutheran church in the open horse carriage with its top down, she looked like any other Finnish girl making the passage to what she assumed to be sober adulthood, a long pilgrimage toward death punctuated by the birth of several children, with that life's projected, imagined highlights being perhaps the construction of a new house not far from her family's, painted dark iron-oxide red, and her ultimate dream the purchase, in the city of Vaasa, of a new loom.

At the back of every dream of hers, there was the thwack and the clack of that new loom: it was the one possession that she desired in the world. She was at heart an artist in textiles. But in the meanwhile, she was very much in love with her new husband, Emil, solid in the carriage beside her, his thin ash blond mustache catching the sun in a way that tugged at her heart.

The wedding dress Marjatta is wearing is five years old now, presently only a Sunday dress. She has embroidered small indigo flowers at points in the smocking to make the dress somehow different. In front of her, cupped away from the wind in the bowl of her skirt, is her third child, a girl, only seven weeks old, wearing a dark wool cap tied tightly by ribbons under the chin. The baby girl's name is Emilia Kristiina.

The baby girl's father, Emil, has died of a fever before her birth. Only half-consciously, Marjatta has since his funeral ceased calling the baby by her first name, taken from Emil's, and now already calls her Stiina. The two older children, Jaako and Susu, had sweated and shaken briefly beneath their heavy quilts with the same germ but recovered. Marjatta nursed everyone but did not fall sick. This is her way now: as a little girl she had been sickly, but now she is called to nurse everyone and never takes ill.

As she sits silent on the hill and we watch from our own silence—whose shape locks into hers, puzzlelike—Marjatta recalls in unbearably painful vividness her failed trip to America. Time shuts down: she is not aware of the sun moving away behind the trees and the air turning chill.

She had gone with her father and brothers at the age of fourteen, the year after her mother died, and boarded a ship at Liverpool which also brought to America, among others, several Russian Jews, a Norwegian, three families from Italy near the Yugoslavian border, and one young woman from Liverpool itself, who lived not a mile from the point of embarkation and had walked to the docks. One Italian grandmother and a two-year-old boy from Greece died en route, but the rest survived the journey in various states of hardihood and debility.

At Ellis Island, Marjatta had been separated from the rest in a medical quarantine section. Her father and brothers had been passed on while she was held in the wire-caged area. Marjatta remembers the huge rooms, whose vastness—she thought at the time, upon entering them, sniffing the smells of the wood of the walls and the damp, somehow still clayey smell of the vast tiled floors—must be a faint echo of heaven. She remembers having said that to her father in the midst of their being herded about, before they were separated.

Her father, listening to a man with a megaphone shouting instructions, had not heard her. "What?" he had said, distracted. Marjatta repeated herself. Next to her in the formless crush, a short woman in a dark scarf doubled over with a stomach pain, as if to vomit, and a man next to the woman whispered warning and encouragement: "Don't look sick, or they'll send you back, Mama."

"Trachoma," said the doctor who came to examine Marjatta after hours and hours had passed. Marjatta felt sure her father and brothers had been forced to leave on the train for somewhere else they had never meant to go. This was not working out as planned. The doctor said this word soberly—"trachoma"—after probing Marjatta's eyes and, irrelevantly, listening to her heart with a stethoscope, which required not only that she sit cold in her chemise but that she let him see her that way.

In Finnish, she protested, "There is nothing wrong with my eyes!" She wanted a mirror to see: there was no crusting, no redness, no symptoms whatever. What *was* the doctor saying! She had been screened by the steamship company before they set sail. She had seen a girl once who had been afflicted by the ailment: it was clearly visible. The doctor turned to look at her as she expostulated in her strange, beautiful language. He stared into her eyes. She could see that *he saw* that her eyes were clear.

He smiled a strange smile, then laughed hugely. His mustache was dark, fat, obscene. Marjatta, whose spirit was generous and free and nearly devoid of normal human meanness, wanted nevertheless to spit at him. What was she, part of a quota of immigrants he had to send back every day? Had he not met his tally? He was likely an immigrant himself: had he no heart?

He looked into her eyes again, then turned to an assistant and said, almost without inflection, "Good Lord, her eyes are like blue water. Like a lake I saw once up in Minnesota."

The assistant said back, uneasy, unclenching his shoulders' tension, "She has no symptoms, Doctor." Marjatta saw the defiance, though she could not understand the words. The doctor smirked and moved on. Marjatta reminded him of a girl in St. Paul, where he'd grown up, who'd snubbed him and married a grain merchant from Red Wing. This ought just to pay her back, the wench.

Marjatta was far out to sea, on her way back to Liverpool, before her astonished and bereft father was told that she had been rejected and sent back. Her fare was, of course, forfeited, and she fell into servitude on her return. There was no family to take her in, so the pastor's wife claimed her and gave her a room in the attic.

From America, her bereft father wrote letters that praised the white-gold sweep of grain he could see from the window of the boardinghouse where he and the older boys lived now. "I am saving so carefully," he said, "I soon will have the fare for you, my beautiful daughter. Your mother watches from heaven and she will protect you as well."

Her brother Carl raged aloud about Marjatta's having been sent back. He raged and swore in English: he was determined to become an American quickly. He threatened to take the train back to New York and pull the mustachioed doctor's balls out through his throat. Carl could do that. He was strong and tall and had not yet developed the restraints that adulthood should have brought. But Marjatta's father insisted that Carl turn over his pay, so that Carl would not even be tempted.

Back in Kuortane, in the province of Vaasa, Marjatta Haapalehto did beautiful needlework and became known in the parish for it. White-on-white embroidery of the church linens, fine work for trousseaus, baptismal gowns. Her father kept sending letters that said soon there would be enough money.

Marjatta recalled, now and then during that time between, the black glitter of the water off Ellis Island. She was let out onto the roof garden for fresh air and walked and walked, peering out over the water at this new land, the door to which, the next day, slammed heavily as a bank vault's. That very night, not an hour before, a ten-year-old boy born in Romania, named Emanuel Goldenberg, had walked in wonder on the same roof garden, transfixed by the same stars on the water. He laid his hands flat on the wall that fenced the roof in the precise place Marjatta would stand, just moments later. Emanuel Goldenberg was not sent back to Romania. He reminded the doctor who checked him of no one against whom he carried a grudge. He went on to change his name to Edward G. Robinson, and to become a Hollywood hero, typecast as a gangster in a time when any financial success was applauded and lionized, even violent crime.

As Marjatta waited for her father to send for her, fares rose. Carl got into a fight in a bar and required a lawyer. The money came out of the passage fund. Marjatta's father was injured and could not work.

The second brother, Jonas, took off on a train westward. On his journey, he sat on a railway-station bench in Kansas where, not so many years before, Ah Lee Wong waited for a train, coming east. At the window, he talked to the same clerk to whom Ah Lee had spoken. The clerk had gone bald in the meanwhile and lost his right index finger in a station-platform accident.

No one would ever see Jonas again. He would be lost to the family, changing his name to John Martin Grove, not looking back. He would enter a California banking concern named Crocker and rise high in its ranks. When he thought of his father, brother, sister, all that mess, he would give thanks to a Lutheran god—in whom he no longer believed—that he had cut himself off from those ill-fated people. He would have become an American.

. . .

WHEN MARJATTA WAS seventeen, Emil Palomaki, the village teacher of Latin and Greek, came to call at the pastor's. He asked to court Marjatta, did so efficiently, quickly proposed to her. She accepted. Her father's letters had ceased sounding real to her, and she had given up hope of going to America. Emil took on more pupils, and he tutored privately also. They thrived, and then Emil so quickly died.

Marjatta remembers more than anything Emil's voice, reciting passages from Virgil and Julius Caesar and—of all things!—the Roman Catholic hymnal. She has only their wedding portrait and a studio portrait of Emil from two years before she met him. In her memory, while the voice stays alive, all the times she has seen Emil's face—mornings on the pillow next to hers, evenings frowning over student papers, in the broad light of day bargaining for white cheese with the farmer a half mile away who charges too much—distill down to these two faces in the portraits, both formal, and gentle, and much alike.

She can see Emil's quickness with language in Jaako and Susu. She can see the shape of his shoulders in the shoulders of the little one, Stiina. As she sits on the hill outside the village of Kuortane, she reframes her life once more: she determines that she will indeed now take the children to America.

There are no reserves of money, no inheritance, no insurance for Emil's death. So Marjatta sells her dead mother's silver-and-amethyst necklace to pay for the passage to America, but still there is not quite enough. Then Jaako takes ill: there are doctors to pay. Marjatta feels her breath, her hope, being sucked from her.

A wealthy woman from Turku who cannot have children visits, at the suggestion of someone in the parish who knows of the little family's plight. The woman offers to adopt Susu in exchange for a goodly sum of money. Marjatta's heart wrenches at the very idea. She cannot conceive of this! But then, in desperation, and against her own will, she travels with Susu to Turku at the woman's request to see her home and the life that the woman could give Susu.

The woman's husband is an industrialist whose factory makes wooden spools for thread and exports boatloads of them to America. Their home has every convenience and luxury: a huge bathroom with claw-footed porcelain tub and full plumbing, electric lights, built-in cabinets everywhere of an exotic wood that seems African or Polynesian in origin.

The woman explains: Susu will have a small Viennese violin of her own, and a violin teacher, from the age of four. She has just had her fourth birthday, and Marjatta's homemade birthday card sits propped on the sideboard back in Kuortane. Susu will have a four-poster bed here in Turku, made of black walnut. There will be pineapples carved everywhere on it. Susu will have a Saint Bernard dog who can pull her in a cart. The cart, sitting in a small barn on the property, has hearts and flowers on it, painted bright blue and fuchsia and stippled with gilt. When Susu sees the cart, she claps her hands in glee and climbs into the driver's seat. Marjatta's heart breaks like an egg as she watches her small daughter drive off with the blue-ribbon reins of the dog in her hands.

"I will send you photographs," says the woman. "Every birthday. Every Christmas." The woman is tall and has prominent cheekbones and dark eyes. The pale little blue-eyed girl does not look one iota like her, yet the woman will tell everyone that the child is her own enough times that people forget that Susu did not appear in Turku until she was four years old.

"May I stay? May I stay?" Susu begs. The woman has told her that this is a visit and that her mama will be coming back.

Marjatta's heart lies in ruins. "Of course, sweet girl," she says. She imagines at that moment that the lumbering little wooden carriage has run over her body and severed a limb: Susu has always, for her whole little life, been so much a part of her! And yet what can Marjatta do, any more than if that carriage had in fact severed a limb? She imagines herself staring dissociatively at a lost hand or foot of her own, lying there on the ground severed.

Susu is gone. And yet Marjatta can see her, here, right in front of her. The feeling of incredulity—she *must* do this thing, and not one cell in her wants to do it—makes her want to breathe out and not breathe in again. She is not the first woman, or the last, to have had to do such a thing or to feel this way. She wants to renegotiate. She cannot: the deal is done. Already Susu is reacclimating. Susu will never be told that she has been adopted. The industrialist's wife reconsiders her promise to write to Marjatta with news of the little girl. She will write not a single word.

When Susu remembers her mother, it is as a blurry image of a blond woman who once waved with great feeling when she rode by in her dog cart. This image recurs in her dreams until she is a teenager. "Who was that woman?" she asks her adoptive mother. "I keep dreaming this scene."

The woman shrugs and looks away. "Who can know?" she says. Her husband is so preoccupied with his factory that Susu has become the whole focus of her life. She is fiercely possessive of her.

When Susu is sixteen, she is sent to Paris to study. She is inexplicably drawn to the study of classical languages. She meets in a class in elementary Greek a young man who is the spit and image of her dead father, Emil. She falls desperately in love with him, her heart leaping out of her chest as if drawn by a massive suction. His name—is this coincidence?—is Emile de Villiers, and he has grown up in the suburbs of Paris. He has a delicate-boned face and a pale ash brown mustache. Had Susu laid a photograph of Emile de Villiers next to the photo of Emil Palomaki, which Marjatta kept in her palm-sized locket, she would have been astounded at the resemblance.

At eighteen, she marries this young man in Turku in a grand garden ceremony. Her "mother" is pleased at the match but distraught at losing the girl; her "father" is thinking about spool production and whether a more profitable deal can be made with the textile mill eight miles outside the city as well as whether the war in Europe, just getting under way, will interfere much with the spool trade. Susu thus becomes a Frenchwoman, Suzanne de Villiers. She will never know of her adoption.

When her parents die in a ferry accident and she inherits the factory, she entrusts the business to others, to manage at a distance. She throws herself for a period into the care of orphans at an orphanage run by Sisters of Charity. She cannot have children for several years—is told she never will have them—but she finds herself at a loss to ascribe the compassion she feels for these children to that fact alone. She does not know how very much an orphan she is herself or that she has a living family vanished into the polyglot chaos of the raw new American nation: she does not know that she has an uncle named John Grove who will make a fortune in banking, in California, an uncle named Carl who will die in a knife fight in a bar in Detroit, a mother named Marjatta who will be Annie Maki's great-great-grandmother.

When Susu/Suzanne has a child, a boy, when she is thirty-six and has given up, she will never mention to her son, who will die fighting for France in the Second World War, that she has half an inkling that something is lost in the family history.

MARJATTA TAKES THE money from the industrialist's wife and books passage for herself and Jaako and Stiina. While they wait for the ship, she secures Jaako to her own waist by a leather strap so that he cannot get lost in the crowd. On the ship, she finds the strap invaluable: the boy will not stay near her otherwise and wants to wander off to explore everywhere. She keeps thinking of Susu and begins to cry.

A Romanian woman, a gypsy, tells her through a go-between who somehow miraculously knows both Finn and Romany that Susu's life will go well. The gypsy says it melodramatically. Marjatta asks through the go-between whether she is saying this just to please her, to silence her.

Silence would be very nice, says the gypsy half-sourly. I would like to go to sleep. But no, I do not tell the future to silence anyone. It is a terrible burden, this knowing the future. The gypsy pauses, closes her eyes, seems almost to be asleep. She continues. So that you will know that I tell you the truth, I tell you also that your grandson, who will be your daughter's son, whom you will never know, this boy will die in a terrible explosion, on a beach, with fire falling out of the sky and men dying all around him. There, she says, looking at the blanched horror on Marjatta's face, did I say that to please you? Believe me, then.

They board at Göteborg, in the province of Bohuslän in southwestern Sweden. The ship sails for several days and then they disembark, at the very same wharf they had left, in the Göteborg harbor. The shipping company has gone bankrupt. There will be no refunds. Marjatta sits on a bench in a public park with Jaako beside her and Stiina in her lap and cries into her shawl. She is not good at crying, and so she cries only a moment, a matter of seconds.

She stands up resolutely, with Stiina on her hip and Jaako on his little strap, and she marches from door to door looking to hire into domestic service. She says that she is good at making pastries, that she can mend stockings without a visible thread, that she loves to wax wood. There is a large hole in the sole of her right shoe, and she has put a piece of cardboard there to buffer the skin of the ball of her foot from the rub of the pavement. No one wants a servant with two little ones to look after.

She sleeps in a hostel for poor unwed mothers, in a bunk with the two children under her coat, in the spoon curve of her sleeping body. She gets up—her limbs heavy with despair and fatigue—and goes out again to seek work. She feels exhausted and used up, so tired in her bones that she might be seventy-four rather than twenty-four now.

She takes in handwork in Göteborg and pays for a two-room flat this way. She drinks cup after cup of green tea and feeds the children bread and buns that the baker's assistant gets her at half price. He is a Finn too, from Pori, to the south of Vaasa. She works late by candlelight every night, embroidering, after the children are finally sleeping. She listens to their breathing in their shared bed. She gives thanks for them. Whenever she thinks of Susu, she cries.

The third month that she is in Göteborg, the baker's helper says he has a friend visiting from Finland and would she like to meet a nice young man? Marjatta stares at him wide-eyed with astonishment. This would be the last thing that she needs: romance. She shakes her head, no thank you. She tries not to laugh. The baker's assistant insists. This young man has seen you, one day, in the store, he says, and he believes you are very beautiful.

"Very beautiful!" scoffs Marjatta, to herself. She turns to look in the mirror that hangs on the wall of the bakery's back room, where she is talking with the baker's assistant from Pori. The mirror is curdled blue black with age, and Marjatta sees in it a curdled blue-black woman. She laughs out loud. Even without the mirror, she feels discolored, the blood sucked from her.

She remembers herself on the hill outside Kuortane, a year before, as if it were geological epochs ago. Yes, she has aged: the chubby, sweet cheek fat of youth has been siphoned down into her bones, or her children's, and around her eyes, blue shadows bloom like pansies. Her yellow hair seems to have been leached of some of its light. She wears it bound up to her head, in a single braid-crown that is less daily trouble than the triple braid she had worn in the vanity of her long-ago youth, the summer before.

My friend, he has money, the baker's assistant says. He is testing her for her response.

She tries not to sound interested. Very much? she says, tossing her head in a way that tries to seem insouciant and gay, as if she does not really care. It is hard to seem carefree when your cheeks and your eyes are so sunken.

Enough money to go to America, and this is where he is going, says the baker's assistant.

He must be very wealthy, I suppose, says Marjatta detachedly. Do you have some of that white cardamom bread you made last week? The baby liked it in soup.

Not wealthy, but frugal, says the baker's helper. He is wrapping a loaf of dark bread in white paper. He hands it to her. This is my gift, he says. No charge.

And why would you want so greatly for me to meet your friend that you give me free bread? asks Marjatta, testily. She thinks as well: *You are only the helper, and the bread is not yours to give away.*

Because he has no wife, says the baker's assistant. I do have a wife, but when you come into this store I don't remember that. You are too beautiful.

The baker's assistant is mixing a glaze for buns that sit in a row on a baking sheet, warm. Marjatta watches their steam rise in the chilly room. The man rotates his wooden spoon in the big metal bowl, *thurk thurk*, round and round. He does not take his eyes off Marjatta.

I should like to get rid of you, says the man. As a matter of caution, and as a favor to my friend, and perhaps I pretend that I am this man, and have a sweet dream for a moment but not for too long. Please do not make me forget that I have a wife. Marjatta stares at him fixedly, in disbelief. Please go with my friend to America, he says. The confectioners' sugar and butter and milk are all blended now, with his muscular whipping, and he sets down his bowl.

Out the window Marjatta can see the canal that runs along the street. The sunlight is the same sunlight that fell through the leaves outside the window of Kyllikki, daughter of Rauno, more than a millennium earlier, not far away. A small boat passes and she watches its wake in the green water. She can smell the green smell of the water lift onto the evening breeze.

"And is your friend elderly?" Marjatta says. "How has he managed to save so much money? Does he own factories? Is he a king or a duke?"

"He is a supervisor at the copper mine at Orijaarvi," the man says. "He is thirty-seven. He has never married."

Marjatta's hopes fall: A laborer? Crude, blackened hands and coarse features? A man who can doubtless not read. A man who at thirty-seven has not found a woman who will marry him. But a man with the money to go to America. He is not in danger of being drafted by the Russians. That is a real danger and motivator to many younger men who are leaving to go to America.

"Will you meet him, beautiful lady? He wishes to meet you." The baker's helper begins ladling the white glaze over the buns. Marjatta watches mesmerized as the frosting drools over their golden crust.

Then she is surprised to hear her own voice, for she has not realized she has made a decision. "I will meet him," she says. She sees herself again in the dark oily distortion of the baker's mirror and decides that she has no looks left anyway and cannot be picky.

The evening the baker's friend from Orijaarvi is due to come to call, Marjatta fusses with the yellow tablecloth in the front room, which will not stay straight. She fusses with the curtains, which hang badly and look threadbare. Then she closes the curtains a bit when she sees that on the yellow tablecloth there is a slight butter stain and that the drip from the beet juice a month ago really did not get bleached out. She fusses with the rugs, which ravel at the edges. She sighs a huge sigh and looks at herself in a hand mirror and cannot understand why this man wishes to see her.

Then the baby starts crying again, loud wretched goatlike bleats, and will not stop no matter how insistently her mother presses her into the comfort of her breast, no matter how many words of reassurance she whispers. Marjatta herself begins crying and cannot stop.

There is a knock at the door. Marjatta considers a leap out the window. Jaako has blessedly fallen asleep on the floor where he has been playing with a wooden elephant on wheels, and she has slid a small cushion beneath his head. Stiina continues to cry, and the knock comes again. Marjatta wipes her eyes.

Well. There is nothing to be done for this. She goes to the door. She opens it. There she stands, red-faced from crying and still slightly damp-cheeked as well, her feet set apart to balance the baby's weight, for as Marjatta has grown thinner the little girl has gotten plumper and as active as a furry little animal. The baby hangs there: she tugs at Marjatta's collar, she grabs at her hair, which has come loose from its pins. She drools slobber and baby slime everywhere, bleating and whining.

There the baker's friend Isak stands, with a handful of wildflowers, white and green and one bright coral red in the heart of the bunch. The baby stops crying suddenly, and her hand in midair clenches and unclenches like a small sea anemone. "I found these beside the street," says Isak. "In the grass by the canal." He clears his throat. Marjatta has not yet looked at him, only at the flowers. He's holding them away from himself as if they're dangerous.

"Good," she says. She is not sure what she means: that's a good place to find flowers? Stiina makes a terrible burbling sound in her diaper and a brown green stench rises. "Oh, my," Marjatta says. She is mortified, sure this is the wrongest choice she has ever made, to meet this man. It seems so ill-fated, in the details: the rug ravel, the slobber, the stench.

She has not yet even looked at him. She pulls her eyes up to meet his. She is taken aback. His eyes are deep-set and small. They seem kind. His brows are bushy blond white; his cheeks are creased with weathering wrinkles. He is not much taller than she is. She stands staring into his eyes and then she bursts out crying again.

"Perhaps this can be simple," Isak says. "I am not a romantic young boy. Let me just say, If you will marry me, I will take you to America."

Stiina makes another loud burble deep in her pants and belches a smell that is almost as bad as the diaper's. Marjatta giggles in mortification. "When will you do this?" she says.

"On the very next boat, if you like," says Isak. "The next boat on which we can book passage."

"My children as well," says Marjatta. It is a question. Isak's eyes shift to little Jaako lying peacefully on the floor with his arm draped across the wheeled elephant.

"We four," says Isak.

"Come in then," says Marjatta. "I have made some soup, and we can discuss this." She catches a glint in the eyes of this mining supervisor that says she is not the bluish old mess that she imagines herself. His brow is prominent and looks intelligent. His earlobes are perhaps too long. His hands are, yes, a laborer's—big knuckles, serrated nails that seem never to have been without grime—but also interesting, strong. His feet appear smaller than they ought to be, but perhaps they are pinched in these shoes, which he may have borrowed from his friend at the bakery.

"You know that I am a widow then?"

"Yes," he says.

"And this is all right with you?" she says. "That I have been someone else's before you?"

"If it is all right that I have *not* been anyone else's before. That I am an old bachelor who has nothing to recommend him but enough money to take you and your children to America."

Marjatta cannot stand the matter-of-factness of this. "Well, the flowers are lovely," she says. "And you seem kind. And your eyes are the palest blue that I have ever seen."

"I bleached them for this evening," he says, straight-faced, "along with this, my white shirt, and these, my white pants."

Marjatta hesitates a moment, then breaks into laughter so raucous that Jaako wakes up and Stiina begins again, crying and crying.

"How long do you think it will be before we can go?" Marjatta says. She lays down the baby on a pad on the floor, opens her diaper, and begins wiping the claylike stuff off Stiina's bottom with the dry end of the diaper.

Marjatta has at this moment a vivid image of herself in old age—she has, after all, only to exacerbate the blueing and loss of flesh—a vision of herself wiping the incontinent bottom of this man before her. After all, this is what wives do, and then they always survive their men.

In her peculiar reverie, wiping the mess from the baby girl, Marjatta wonders suddenly what this man's privates are like: whiter or browner or redder than the rest of him? Small tight balls to match his small pale eyes or big sacks of squashy stuff to match the peasantlike look of his knuckles? She blushes at her forwardness. Then she excuses herself to herself, as she has been with only one man, Emil. He is her only standard. She knows she will have to adapt. It is all just so horrible.

She recalls Emil in the dark, sliding over onto her like a sweet eel, and the things he would say, Latin epigrams, lines from Catullus, nonsense verses he had made up himself. In five years she had learned to distinguish the last, and she often giggled in bed at his silliness. This man in front of her: Would he make her laugh? Did he have more sly dry jokes like that one about bleaching his eyes with his laundry? Would he be silent in the act, as Emil had been, only his smooth rhythmic breathing discernible in the dark, or would he—as she had heard from other women of their husbands—be a grunter or a moaner?

"So that is how that is done," says Isak, watching the completion of Stiina's diapering in rapt fascination. "Tomorrow I will go to the steamship broker's office. Is that soon enough?"

Marjatta tries to remember what he is talking about: after all, she is thinking about the prospect of having sex with this man she does not even know, in order to keep her children fed. She pulls her attention back quickly to diapering, hoping he had not been reading her mind, then nods, then gags slightly at the smell.

"I thought mothers liked the smell of their own babies' shit," says Isak.

Again, Marjatta laughs uncontrollably, and she is not sure why. She wipes at her eyes with her sleeve. Tears of some kind of overflow—relief, terror, appreciation of the absurdity of it all—have spilled onto her cheeks. She wipes again, clearing her throat as a cover. She puts Stiina into her crib. The baby picks up a stuffed toy and throws it at Jaako, who starts crying and needs to be picked up.

"You must understand that I have money to go to America, but not much more," says Isak. "I know that I can get work there, in a copper mine in northern Michigan. My cousin has gone ahead of me. He says that it feels much like Finland. The climate, the land. Many Finns are there, as well. We can rent a house owned by the company."

"An entire house?" Marjatta says. She had not even had a whole house with her professor-husband, Emil. They had lived in half a house, the upstairs, and had to go up and down icy, wobbly outdoor steps, all winter. When the babies came, she seldom ventured out during the winter.

Isak has a piece of paper folded into his coat pocket. It is a piece of publicity for the mine, seeking workers in Finland. It pictures, in a fine line drawing, a lovely white house with a gable. There is a paved walkway to the small front porch. A willow branch drapes down to soften the lines of the house, and a flowering bush stands beside the door. Marjatta can almost smell the blooms. There are sketchy diagonal lines on the window of what must be the living room, and the shape of someone inside. Marjatta can almost hear a woman in there playing "Midsummer's Eve in Vaasa" on a dark piano with ribbons and flower crowns carved in the wood of the cabinet. The familiar chords are as sweet as the smell of the blossoms and make her want to cry.

"So," Marjatta says, her mind's eye aglitter with the light reflecting off the window of that little white house the copper mine owns, in the United States of America. "So. Tell me about where you are from."

"Rantsila," says Isak.

"Talk about Rantsila then!" she says cheerily.

"Houses, people," says Isak. "Horses, snow."

Marjatta sighs. "Then talk to me about mining. I know nothing about mining. It must be interesting to pull copper up out of the earth."

Isak shrugs his shoulders. "It is a job," he says. That seems sufficient.

It is three weeks before a ship can take them, and while Marjatta has agreed within minutes to the marriage, she insists on what she terms a proper courting in the interim. The more she knows of Isak the first week, the more she is appalled at herself for agreeing. There is nothing she can share with this man. His world seems to be a world of rock: hard, unyielding, absolutes everywhere. For any question that arises, Isak has an opinion, curt and binary and without a shadow of subtlety, so there is no discussion to be had.

Marjatta recalls long talks with Emil about whether Finland ought to appreciate Russia more, even in some sense to assimilate, about whether the Apostolic Lutheran Church, in its emotionalism, could be counterfeiting the true experience of communion with the Creator. Isak, if asked, would have two quick answers: no and no, and he would not be interested in elaborating. Emil's humming of sweet little songs and his poems in Latin and Greek: there is none of this, certainly, but there also seems nothing else that will compensate, no intrusion of his own culture. The man is quite silent but lets her talk on about anything, listening raptly. Thus, in some way his posture allows her to shape the relationship without his help.

Marjatta imagines a marriage in which the husband and wife do not meet in a clear intellectual space—she unconsciously pictures a green-lit poplar grove, or *haapalehto,* her maiden name—and feels a heaviness descend on her, but then she thinks of all the marriages she knows and considers that none of them, no, not a single one, has that clearing in the forest that she and Emil had. That fact does not comfort her one whit. She considers withdrawing her agreement: Could he then sell the tickets? Would she be morally obliged to provide a substitute in her place? Could she, should she, go out into the streets of Göteborg looking for a woman who would more willingly go off to America with this big-knuckled, small-footed, long-lobed strange man?

That night when he comes to call, she says, "I have something that I must say to you." She looks at him intensely. They are sitting in straight chairs, their hands in their laps.

"I am listening," he says somberly. Are his eyes twinkling? She thinks so. Is he teasing her? Does he know what she wishes to say, and is his very niceness a form of intimidation?

She cannot say anything. A boat passes in the canal and toots its horn, and she takes the occasion to break away. "Oh! It will wake Stiina." She goes to the window to close it. Isak does not point out that Stiina is fully awake, lying quiet and still in her crib. He knows full well what Marjatta wishes to say, and he will not help her say it. His heart is near asphyxiation with terror.

Marjatta shuts the window, and sits back down, and says, "Well, what were we talking about? Oh. I think you had asked me about my brothers. Well." She does not say: *While I was at the window, I looked out and thought, Dear Lord, I cannot stay here and I cannot go home. Must I then go to America at any cost?* They move on, having avoided the hole in the road for the time being, but with that question hanging like a spiderweb in the way of real progress.

The second week she goes to the baker's on Wednesday morning for her usual order, with Jaako pulling at her skirt and then letting go, tugging, then running away. She chides him in Finnish, and Swedes on the street look at her strangely: While she looks as if she might be one of them, her language is so different. It is not often, even in this port city, that they hear Finnish.

She warns Jaako shrilly, her voice rising in fear at the very real prospect: A carriage will come down the street and the horse's hooves will fly like devils and kill you. Stay back. Stiina is perched on her hip like a monkey, beneath a shawl. She sleeps through all the chiding. Jaako cries and babbles on about devils but holds fast to the skirt of her dress. Marjatta knows that her anxiety is about more than horses and carriages.

She tells the baker's helper: I fear I have made a mistake. I do not want to marry this man.

The baker's helper says back: Do you not want to go to America then?

She is taken aback by the simplicity of this. She cannot answer.

Please go to America, says the baker's helper. Do this for my wife.

Could you not find another woman who would go with him? Perhaps a Swedish serving girl? Göteborg is full of them, wanting to go to America. Is that not a fine idea? she says.

But my friend does not want a Swedish serving girl. He wants you. And you already said that you would. Would you break this man's heart? Are you that cruel? the baker's helper says.

In the bakery, standing next to the glass pastry case with her two children and her empty cloth shopping satchel, Marjatta bawls. The baker's helper whisks her off to the back room. He grabs her sleeve in a way that seems just too familiar, as if he were a chiding brother. She knows him only a little.

I said, Are you that cruel? he says, and his eyes are as cold blue as his friend's. And I said, Do you not wish to go to America? Unless you can place my wife's feelings before your own, and Isak's wishes before your own, and my own needs before your own, yes, indeed, you are a cruel girl, Marjatta. I would like to know that my passion for your beauty has not been misplaced, that your virtue is what it seems to be, says the baker's helper.

Marjatta feels a dark silence rise up in her, a response to inevitability. She nods, and she never tells Isak of this moment. Still, just after their quick wedding and before they embark, the baker's helper takes Isak aside and tells him a doctored version of this story, an impersonal version involving cold feet and then presenting the friendly assurance that once Isak has her in his bed, she will forget all that. The baker's assistant is telling him: Give this more than you thought you could, astonish her, secure quickly what you have won.

Isak nods soberly to the baker's helper, as is his way, but then there is that twinkle again. Then he makes a small lewd pantomime with the fingers of both of his hands, in the shadow between them, and both men laugh heartily. "That's the spirit!" says the baker's helper. "Name your first son after me!"

The wedding is the morning of the embarkation, at the registry office. Marjatta wears a dark blue-green dress printed with wheat sheaves; Isak wears a slightly ill-fitting and shiny secondhand suit he has bought for the occasion. No photographs are taken. Isak has suggested that this might be nice, but Marjatta is, at some place in herself, horrified at the idea of documenting this. Without putting it into words, she thinks of this as infidelity, even if a practical necessity, and so she is sad and embarrassed. Isak does not notice her dimmed countenance. He is proprietarily happy.

Marjatta is glad there is no time or place for the honeymoon. On the ship, there is no privacy. So they will wait till they get to America. There is all the time in the world, they tell each other. Marjatta harbors a small fear that she will arrive at immigration and be turned away again by the mustachioed doctor who turned her back ten years before. Marjatta fears that she will not find her father or brothers, but if she does not go, then she *surely* will not.

No one dies on the voyage, not even the elderly woman Marjatta has marked out from the first day. She is passed at immigration, and when she arrives in New York, she stops at the first patch of grassy earth she sees in the city—a wide space between the sidewalk and the brick front of a house —and she takes off her shoes and stands feeling the earth.

Jaako asks in English, "What doing?" Marjatta has been teaching him.

Marjatta replies in English, "This is America." She wiggles her toes in the warm, dry pale soil between the blades of grass.

"Your mother has wanted to come here a very long time," says Isak in Finnish. He seems filled with enormous pride that he has finally brought her here, that he is the one to fulfill her wish. He looks at the skin of her cheeks reflecting the American sun and he thinks: *I am a lucky man, and she does not know her own beauty, not even half.*

Jaako nods solemnly, as if he understands. "Long time," he echoes in Finnish.

While Isak and Marjatta and Jaako and Stiina have huddled in the cramped quarters of the ship, with the odd smells of spices and the pickled, dark music of the Romany Gypsies who are their neighbors, and the unbearable longing of all of them, in unison, like one huge oar, reaching out into the cold heavy green water and pulling them toward the far shore, Matti Haapalehto, Marjatta's father, has fallen into a dark funk out of which he will never quite rise. He has tried and tried and now he has given up trying and moved into a living death. He will not die for years, but there will not be a reunion. He will board with an Italian family and work as a laborer for the city of Baltimore. Marjatta will never see him again.

The train ride to the Midwest is difficult for Marjatta and Isak and the children. Interminable, tedious, exhausting to the children; exhausting, tedious, endless to the adults. Stiina seems to have caught a flu bug on the boat, and she starts coughing and wheezing and throwing up not a full day into the train journey.

In Detroit, they will have to spend two full days in a hotel because of the railroad's schedules. Isak asks tentatively, on the train an hour before the train pulls into the station there, "Would this be a proper time for a honeymoon?"

"I do not think so," Marjatta says. "Here are these children."

"Who will not be going away," Isak says. Marjatta angles a glance at him out of the corner of her eye: is there a note of annoyance in this? He answers her unspoken concern, but his answer does not have the calming effect he would like. There is no right thing to say here. "They will be with us always. While I have never been married, it is obvious to me that you were able to sleep with your dead husband while you had two other children, or you would not have conceived little Stiina."

He does not seem to intend to be mean, but simple envy and fear that he will not measure up to Emil in Marjatta's heart push him to push her. There is something in his economy as well that says, "I have paid for this," and Marjatta can hear that. It makes her afraid.

"I never slept with a dead husband," says Marjatta. "He was alive when I slept with him. Always." She does not look at Isak when she says this. She feels her teeth clenching. She wishes that he were more patient or she more clairvoyant. She remembers her moment of panic in Göteborg and her talk with the baker's helper.

She wishes she had met the gypsy that day in the park when she sat with the two little ones and the baker's helper had instead come along and suggested she come to the bakery to get warm and to have cardamom bread, and that the gypsy had warned her off. She recalls that he gave her dark bread, anyway.

She thinks: *I probably would not have listened. I am very stupid.* She wonders about her unborn grandson who will die on D day, all those years off, on the beaches of Normandy. She feels something like gratitude that little Susu is out of this wretchedness. She feels something like despair.

That night in the dark of the hotel room, when the children's breathing becomes a counterpoint—Jaako's slow puffing, then the intermittent wheeze of Stiina's waning flu—Isak lifts first Stiina and then Jaako to a pair of quilt nests he has made in two drawers of the dresser.

He covers them gently. Then he returns to the bedside. He relights the candle beside the bed. He takes off his nightshirt and stands naked there before Marjatta. She looks away. He commands her: "Look."

She is terrified at the raw, jagged edge in his voice.

Again he says, "Look. This is your husband now, woman."

She looks at his body. His shoulders are broad, his arms sinewy and thick, his chest as hairless and smooth as a boy's, but as muscular as any statue Marjatta has seen in museums. The candle flame moves in the draft and makes flickers of strange light and dark.

"Come here," he says. His voice is harsh. Marjatta wants to believe it is only the urgency of what must be his need. After all, thirty-seven years without a woman? She moves closer to the edge of the bed. "Out," he orders. She cannot quite comprehend what he means. "On your knees here," he says. The linoleum floor is bare. Marjatta remembers, irrelevantly, that in daylight its color is greenish. She needs to think about something else. Anything.

She is terrified. "I have already prayed, before I got in bed," she protests, feigning innocence, stalling.

He laughs, and his laugh is only half harsh. Or is it harsh at all? "You are no ignorant virgin," he says. "Take this into your mouth." He is holding his penis in his hand, and Marjatta can see it is fatter and longer than she might have thought. She thinks she might faint. She is wishing for Emil to come back, right now, from the dead, and break through the door and stop this.

Marjatta, obedient, kneels on the floor, her mind and her body at odds. Her knees are cold on the hard floor. She has never done this, not this way, not to order, like a whore, or like what she imagines a whore must do. She leans toward Isak, and, feeling weak, lifts her hands to steady herself.

Then she collapses forward, against him, bracing her hands against his hip bones. She nuzzles her mouth and nose into his groin like a little animal, avoiding his organ, touching anything else she can find. Hip bones: there! So she spends long minutes touching her tongue to his hip bones. He smells clean. She gives thanks for that. She is hearing a groaning. It must be that he is enjoying this then, these things she is doing to keep from doing what he wishes her to do. His hands clutch her braids, curled atop her head, his fingers digging into her hair and disheveling it. His penis brushes the side of her face. As she registers that, its insistence, its thickness, Marjatta lifts out of herself and pretends this is not going on. She watches the candle flame as she works. She bites softly into the fronts of his legs. Anything to avoid the thing she hopes she will not have to do.

He makes a moaning sound. He comes out of his trance just enough to unbraid her hair roughly as she kneels there. His fingers are not gentle, and they pull the long hairs at the scalp, although they do not mean to. Marjatta winces, and at one instant, against her will, a sound—*aii!*— escapes her lips. Her hair falls like a cape around her, kinked from the braids, and a mess.

She wonders, attempting to float outside herself, to float in air, what this must look like from an observer's standpoint, and then thinks, in her simplicity, *But nobody ever sees this anyway.*

Stiina turns in her drawer bed and coughs slightly. Isak notices nothing. He is lost in his own pleasure. Marjatta thinks: *I must hurry.*

She grimaces in the dark, lets out a slight groan of discomfort—the floor is so cold, so unyielding, so hard!—and she whispers to Isak, "My knees hurt." Matter-of-factly she instructs him, "Get up here." She climbs up onto the high mattress and lies back. He climbs up over her, and she takes the full length of him into her mouth, and she gags, and he notices nothing. Jaako moans, "Mama," and then turns back into his sleep. Marjatta prays silently, *Please. Let him hurry.*

She moves her lips over him to help him hurry. She reaches up to grab the pendulous sacks that flap against her cheeks—trying not to remember Emil, configured so differently, small, neat, and tight—and she squeezes, as if she were making a cooked-vegetable puree, and there he is, there it is, oh, dear Jesus, she splutters the bitter thick stuff in the dark. She can feel it all over her hair and her forehead. She is halfway down the bed and cannot move; he is collapsed on her; she cries silently and fights for breath.

It is a half hour later when he wakes momentarily and she can pull herself out from under him. Her neck hurts, and her left arm is asleep from being pinned down. She wipes her hair and her face and steps out of the bed. She picks up his nightshirt. She hands it to him without a word or demonstration of feeling. "Put this on," she says matter-of-factly. "The children will wake in the morning." She lies down beside him, perhaps more awake than she ever has been. He does not reach over to her or hold her. She watches the patterns the candle flame makes on the ceiling, and then she blows out the candle, remembering how Emil would talk to her in the dark. She wants just a few words now, something.

"Rrrr," Isak says into his pillow, at the bed's edge. It is almost a growl. "You would fetch a high price as a harlot." His tone of voice says he thinks this the highest compliment he can bestow.

Marjatta thinks: *Oh, I am more stupid than I knew. He said he had be-*

longed to nobody, and that is all. He did not say he was without experience. I am so stupid. She remembers the saying "You have made your bed, now you must lie in it."

She lies awake until dawn, and the minute she drifts off to sleep Stiina wakes howling. The day has begun. She looks at her new husband beside her. He sleeps with his mouth open, looking almost as a corpse might look, drained of life. She tries hard not to wish him dead. She chides herself. "He has brought you to America," she says under her breath. She adds, "I am losing my mind, I am, speaking aloud to myself this way."

She watches Isak sleep open-mouthed, drooling onto the sheet where his head has slipped from the pillow. She watches him detachedly, over the curly bright head of her little Stiina, hooked fast to her right nipple. She looks out the window at the Detroit morning, where the clattering of peddlers is just beginning. The sky is trying to turn from pink to blue, making it only as far as gray. She thinks: *Nevertheless, now my Stiina will have a home, my Jaako will have a home. And we are in America!*

The stopover in Detroit is extended to three days, then four, and Isak finds reasons to take a nap every day, when the little ones do, and insists that Marjatta lie down as well. He does not mean to sleep and she knows it.

Marjatta is shocked—in the same room with the children, in daylight?

Isak says, "Then let us simply be quieter."

"I have no problem being quiet," Marjatta says, with a hint, just a glimmer, of sullenness. Isak does nothing to cause her to be anything but entirely silent. She remembers wistfully all the sweet pleasurings Emil knew how to administer.

Isak is somewhat gentler than he was that first night and does not demand that she get on her knees again. But he seems insatiable: three times every afternoon and twice at night. Marjatta thinks she will wear out, like a pocket that carries too much, like a purse full of heavy and terrible things whose seams split and give way.

As she walks about Detroit keeping Jaako's curiosity occupied while Isak shops for new boots, she imagines herself breaking open, a split-seam purse, a pomegranate, her innards falling onto the sidewalk as she trots after Jaako, passersby clicking their tongues in American English: *Messy woman! Intestines all over the pavement!* She is chafed and she aches. When she walks she feels like flayed meat.

She is glad for their departure north. Dear God, thank you, she says, that there will be no privacy now for a while again. She remembers the brochure that Isak had shown her, the lovely little white house with roses clambering happy and helter-skelter up the porch trellis. She sees the roses in her mind's eye as a rich carmine red, then realizes that the picture was black and white. *In a week we will be there! All I have ever wanted is a home!* She remembers the music that wafted out the living-room window from the piano in the living room, and she sighs. Then she remembers that she invented both the piano and the music herself, and she laughs aloud at herself. *Truly, I have lost my mind. But in one week . . .*

In a week they arrive. The company agent meets them with instructions. They are to stay here at the station for seven or eight hours and then three more families will arrive and they will all take a train in the morning out to the camp. *Camp?* thinks Marjatta. She looks her question at Isak. There is nothing here but a makeshift village. No clapboard houses with rambling roses. Isak holds out his hands in a gesture that she knows is genuine. His gesture says, I am as confused as you.

He follows the company agent into a tiny ramshackle building. The door remains open. Marjatta can see Isak gesticulating broadly with his hands. The clerk is making the gesture that Isak had made: I don't know. Isak reaches into the pocket of his coat and withdraws a soft, folded page, dog-eared from being opened and closed many times, in anticipation. It is the recruitment poster for the mine. Isak is demanding clarification.

As she watches this, Marjatta is rocking Stiina to keep her awake, and shooing Jaako away from the tracks, though no train will be coming for hours. The child needs to learn.

Isak explodes in a torrent of swear words in Finnish. He throws the paper into the air and it drifts on the breeze and then falls to earth on the train tracks. He storms over to Marjatta. "The agent says this paper is from another mining company," he blusters. "We have been tricked."

Marjatta is silent, awaiting more explanation.

"My cousin who sent me this paper," he says, "he was always a bit of a weasel. I believed he had changed his ways."

"So this paper is for another mine?" Marjatta says. Her voice rises in hope. "In another place? Then we will go there."

Isak shakes his head no. "The mine on this paper, it is not a copper mine. It is an iron mine. I am a copper miner."

"You are a mining *supervisor*," says Marjatta.

It happens that indeed no longer is Isak a supervisor: in this place, the Cornishmen take precedence, and Finns' skills brought from the Old Country are not credited until proven. In any event, there is no supervisory position open, the company agent tells Isak, and that is that.

"I know nothing of iron," says Isak to Marjatta. "What I know is hardrock." His voice suggests there is no meeting ground on this matter.

A young woman is sitting on a bench outside the station nursing her baby and singing to it in Finnish. Her voice carries to Marjatta. She is singing the hymn "How Great Thou Art," its melody a Swedish folk tune seemingly from time immemorial.

Marjatta makes a small prayer inside herself: *Lord, if you are Lord, if you are great—Lord, I have sung this hymn to you so many times in my life—if you are who you tell us you are, clear up this business right now. You have said, 'Ask, and you shall receive,' so I am asking. Whatever it is that is your will right now, Lord, please—*Marjatta does not know the words to say—*show me, in Jesus' name.*

Marjatta assumes that the single desirable option is this: We will go to the other mine, where they have roses and trellises. Isak will decide that switching to iron mining is really no problem. We will go to the other mine. She thinks if she repeats it to herself again and again, it will happen. She cannot, she will not, stay *here*. She has picked up the flyer that Isak flung onto the tracks and folded it aside as a talisman, as a promise to which she will hold her Lutheran God.

She can imagine that that woman over there, that lovely young woman nursing her baby, can stay and be happy. She must have a husband she loves and a willingness to follow him to the ends of the earth. Marjatta has no idea why she thinks this, except that she knows she could have followed Emil anywhere and been happy.

But this is not acceptable: to be tricked into marrying this man, to come to a place it seems God himself has not even visited—a concept far past

godforsakenness!—and then to be denied even the pleasure of being furious with Isak for the trickery, for clearly he himself was tricked too! Marjatta wonders whether there is a way to undo this marriage, annul it. But
then it has been consummated. Still . . . perhaps she can keep Isak at a distance until she finds a way to get out of this.

She looks up at Isak. He has tears in his eyes, this strong, sinewy man.
"Oh, Marjatta," he says. "I am so very sorry."

She hates this. He is so sincere, she cannot keep her composure. "It is not
your fault, Isak." She doesn't want to be comforting him: she wants comfort
herself. She shouts to little Jaako, who is poking at birds with a stick, "Leave
those birds alone, Jaako! They are not hurting you! Let them eat in peace!"

"My cousin," says Isak. "I loaned him a good bit of money in gratitude
for his connecting me with this mine. All the rest of the money I had set
aside. He pled terrible hardship: his wife had a terrible illness, his house had
burned. I signed a contract. And where is my cousin? He has moved away,
the moment the money arrived, and no one knows where he has gone. He
had no wife, no house. He was still single, he lived at a boardinghouse, and
they say he had a reputation for drinking and getting loud and making no
sense at all when he drank." Isak sighs.

Marjatta asks herself: *Is this perhaps God's will? Has he indeed answered
my prayer, that he make his will known in the circumstances? Can he mean
this?* She remembers a passage from Proverbs she learned in her Sunday
school back in Kuortane. She remembers the pursed lips of the young in-
structress, a woman with striking brown eyes who could not—she had
thought at the time—be a Finn. There were no brown-eyed Finns except
up north in Lapland. Yet this woman had been born in the village.

She recalls focusing on the young woman's eyes as she intoned the verse:
"Trust in the Lord and lean not on your own understanding . . . ," and the
children repeated the verse, singsong, most of them parroting, few of them
thinking about what they said.

"In all your ways acknowledge him, and he shall make straight your
paths," intoned the young teacher. Marjatta remembers having in her young
mind that day an image of smoothed dirt, a path mildly curving through
beds of wildflowers that looked cultivated, all colors of flowers, a gentle rise,

and past the crest of the hill a green valley that she knew was Paradise. That image has stayed with her.

That day in Sunday school she had raised her hand. "Teacher, what does that mean, 'in all your ways acknowledge him'? What are 'ways'?"

"This means, everything you do, your actions, the thoughts you allow to possess you." The young woman had a slight otherworldly air about her.

Marjatta thought: *If I do not understand this now, I can take her words away and examine them later.* Marjatta said then, "And, teacher, what does this mean, 'He will make straight your paths'?"

The young teacher cleared her throat. Then she cleared her throat again. "It means just what it says," she said solemnly. "It is the Word of God." Her air of assurance seemed somehow less solid.

"Does it mean that we will not have trouble?" Marjatta asked.

"It means 'He shall make straight your paths,'" said the teacher, with an insistent edge to her voice.

"Does it mean that if we live well, live by the Word—"

"It is time to go back to the choir," the young teacher said. "Please mark hymns number 42, 61, and 107. I do not want to hear flipping of pages and whisperings, asking your neighbor the numbers. Now. Go."

Marjatta calls up the image of that beautiful wildflower valley where she had believed God would lead her, if she were a good girl. She is not sure now whether that valley lies just ahead, or whether she has invented it and God's will is something else altogether. She hopes the vision was correct. She wants her paths made straight, and she wants that now.

The "camp" is on land owned by the mining company. The company agent tells Isak that there are ten camps, widely spread to allow people room to farm to supplement their income from the mine. They are named Camp Jubilee, Camp Ambivalence, Camp Toivo Rooney, Camp Sweat, Camp Raspberry Briar, Camp Grit, Camp Pirkis, and Camp Principle. Then there is Camp Number Nine. No one knows what has become of the tenth planned camp, but people still talk of the "ten camps."

"Who is Toivo Rooney?" asks Marjatta. "Toivo is Finnish, of course, but isn't Rooney an Irish name?"

"For that matter, where is Principle?" says Isak.

Marjatta thinks at this moment, even though she still plans to keep a distance, now, from her new husband, that he seems somewhat worthier than she had thought in Detroit at the moment she was swiping his gluey white semen out of her hair. She is willing to think he is just a bit insensitive, but then, after all, he is a man, and a miner. Perhaps his remark about prostitutes, well intentioned as he had thought it, should not have been a surprise to her, and were all men this way? She hangs the question in midair a moment and answers it: *Emil was not this way.*

The other families arrive, though it is fourteen hours rather than six, and Isak and Marjatta and the children are hard asleep on their luggage in the station when the group comes in, none of them even waking at the ruckus.

They are going to Camp Grit. The name of the camp does not mean *sisu,* the determination, grit, perseverance that the Finns prize so highly and see as their national characteristic. Camp Grit is named after the literal grit from the millstone that finds its way into the porridge, the grit that the mine families sift out carefully with their tongues before they swallow.

At Camp Grit the families sleep on the floor and in bunks without mattresses for a week, until mattresses come on the logging train. They arrive in the same boxcar with the Kalliokoskis' cow, the Makelas' dog, several dozen brown and white chickens, a farm wagon, a sleigh, a plow, pots and pans, dishes and lamps, and a number of pieces of basic furniture for the three families.

The boxcar is shunted over onto a siding, and the logging train moves on to Camp Toivo Rooney, the next camp down the line, then to Camp Jubilee. There are no roads yet, and Marjatta understands why this is called a camp. She wonders momentarily who has named these camps: A fanatical Apostolic Lutheran awaiting the Second Coming? An embittered sardonic fellow employed by the company whose own life and dreams have come to naught out in these weeds?

Marjatta rejoices that there is no privacy, so she can protest to Isak that intimacy has to wait. Until when? Isak asks. Until fall, she begs, until they are in the cabins that the men are building all day every day, out of wood they are clearing from the land. But, says Isak, the Makelas and the Hiltunens and the Kalliokoskis seem to do all right. Can't you hear them going at it after we are in bed? Oh, Isak, says Marjatta. She tries not to look at him; then he catches her eye and she laughs.

Her project—to find her way out of this marriage somehow, to obtain an annulment and find a way to get back—where, to Finland? —seems ill-fated now. She has not had a menstrual period since the marriage, and summer's end is nearing. Isak knows nothing of this because they have not been intimate since their arrival. Soon she will have to tell him. She considers whether to take herbs that might make this go away, and then she thinks, *I have become a monster. I sell one child, and now . . .* She will wait to tell Isak until it is utterly unavoidable.

The children in the Makela and Hiltunen families are older, ranging from four years to sixteen, and they help the men clear the land. Even the little ones pick up dead twigs and bring them to the brush piles, carry rocks to the rock cart. Marjatta watches with amazement as the four-year-old Makela boy, little Arvi, carries to the cart a stone that must weigh as much as he does. Marjatta will not interfere, but she wishes his mother would. The child will break his foot!

"Put that down twice before you get to the cart!" shouts the mother. "Don't try to go all the way in one trip! That's the way!" And little Arvi does it.

Marjatta becomes friends with Sophie Hiltunen, and at a moment when the men are away putting the roof on the Hiltunens' cabin, the first to be finished, she tells her the situation: that she was tricked, though the trickery was Isak's cousin's, that she does not love Isak, and that she is pregnant.

Sophie laughs uproariously. "You do not *love* Isak?" She slaps her knees and chortles till she chokes. When the men are around she is far more demure. "Everyone can see that you love Isak! Everyone talks about you two, that this is so lovely, the new-married couple." There is something about the slant of Sophie's glance that says she is testing something here.

"I hear you and your husband at night," Marjatta says, looking away.

"And I do not hear you and Isak," says Sophie. "And I understand from my husband that Isak is vexed about this." Sophie *tsk-tsks*. "This is a . . . contradiction," she says. "But then life is complicated."

"Isak is vexed about this?" says Marjatta, attempting to feign surprise. "He talks to your husband? He has not said this to me."

Sophie looks darkly from under her eyebrows at Marjatta. "Indeed?"

"Well," says Marjatta, "perhaps he has stopped saying this for the past two months. He said it twice. He is not a talker."

Sophie laughs again and slaps her knees. Her husband is a silent man also. "The Stone," she calls him, to the other women, when she is irritated. She says to Marjatta, soberly, "You will not forget about your Emil, I know this. But that was another life, Marjatta. This is your new life."

"Well," says Marjatta. And that is all she can say. "I suppose I will tell Isak soon that there will be a child."

"Yes, I am certain you will," Sophie says evenly, firmly. "Stop thinking about whether you love Isak. Just decide that you do."

IT IS JULY, the peak of the wild-raspberry crop, and the children have been out picking berries, in enormous quantities. The Makelas' great-uncle Paavo, a barrel-chested older man with a milky white look to his eyes, a bent man who limps and uses a cane, supervises them on these hunts. He sits under a tree whittling and smoking his pipe while they gather. Each child has a tin cup, and when he has filled his tin cup he dumps it into a five-pound lard can the "captain" of his team—the oldest child—monitors. The lard tins in turn are dumped into a galvanized watering can whose top has been sawed off, its edges soldered smooth.

Uncle Paavo keeps up great enthusiasm among the children—who would after a few minutes rather play pitch-and-catch or jacks, or go stilt walking—by keeping score. After they have filled enough buckets, Paavo escorts them the quarter mile through the high grass, through the whirring green insect-filled air, to the river. In an intricate division of labor, the bigger girls and boys take turns watching the littler children in the shallows. Three of the children, who are better swimmers, are allowed to go around the bend together into the deeper water, where they can actually swim. Paavo can see them all from his post. After they swim, they eat dark bread sandwiches of canned meat and egg.

Uncle Paavo's cane has a head carved in the shape of the head of a bear. He bobs the cane up and down before himself as he pretends that the bear is talking to the children. They love it. Oh, my, Uncle Paavo's bear says if we eat more than five berries out of each bucket we pick, he will eat *us!* Paavo makes the bear's voice in his throat again—as a young man, he had shown a gift for ventriloquism but spent his life until his injury down the mine shaft. Gracious, oh, goodness, Uncle Paavo's bear says he will come in the window at midnight if I do not stop pestering little Manu!

The women and children have scoured the camp for any bottles discarded by previous inhabitants. They were evidently a less than savory lot, clearly not members of the Finnish Temperance Society, for a huge number of liquor bottles lie in the high grass around the camp. The women have saved and sterilized these long-necked whiskey bottles to hold the berry preserves. They discuss this. This is unusual, yes, but under the circumstances, if we cook the preserves down until there are no large pieces, this will be fine. For what is the alternative? Only three actual widemouthed canning jars—one quart each—have been found in the weeds. We cannot waste raspberries. The women joke about possible inebriatory effects of the raspberry preserves they will make in these liquor bottles, whether all of the Finns at the camp will be tootling and lurching around—husbands, wives, children—like common drunks, bumping into trees, after a breakfast of toast and jam, but no one considers the actual practical problem.

One night at the end of August, while everyone is asleep, and the raspberries have silently been fermenting for three weeks, one of the bottles pops its cork out of the paraffin that surrounds it. The bottles' shape means that it takes so long for the viscous preserves to make their way down through the funnel that bacteria can get in. So when this occurs, no one is alert to this or even aware it has happened.

The next night two more bottles pop their corks, and the next day, unheard, several more bottle corks pop, in near-unison. Everyone is out at work. The men are off at the homesteads, hammering and sawing to get everyone's home finished before the fall chill. The women are doing the eternal mending out under the trees in the shade. The bottles sit on their shelves at the far end of the large, shedlike cabin, slowly and silently drooling dark, thick, viscous stickiness.

That night the rats come. The rats have been thriving in one of the abandoned small sheds, locked up tight and thus unnoticed by the new families, where there are old stores of dried corn and flour. The new residents are careful with their food scraps, so the rats have stayed where they were. The rats have just now licked the last bit from the molasses vat in the storage shed and are hungry. These preserves, now: these are irresistible.

Marjatta is the first to waken. She rises on her elbow and listens. A thump and a rolling sound—one of the bottles has overturned. Several rats fight in the dark for the sweet preserves. There are squeaks and scratching sounds. Another thump. A heavy roll. A thud.

"Isak!" Marjatta whispers. "Wake up!" He lifts his head from his pillow, groggy. He is a heavy sleeper. Marjatta is irritated at this—or is she irritated at something else, at all of this? But then, she reminds herself, if he were not such a leaden sleeper, he would likely be crawling all over her in her sleep. Oh, my. And this would be worse. "Rats!" she hisses.

"Acch!" says Isak, and drops his head. "The cat will chase them!"

"We have no cat," she reminds him.

He waits a moment and lifts his head again. "Oh," he says flatly, seemingly trying to remember what "we" do have, in fact, who "we" are.

"They will bite the children!" she says. "They will ravage them! I have heard stories of children killed by rats, ripped into pieces!"

Isak points dopily in the direction of the sound, to the far end of the building. "The sound comes from *there*. We are *here*, between the rats and the children. They will have to run over us to get to them. The children are safe."

Marjatta is beside herself with frustration and fear. "*Hundreds* of fifteen-pound rats could run right over you as you sleep and you would not know! As for myself, I do not care to serve as a footbridge for rats, nor do I care to find Stiina and Jaako in the morning with their eyes eaten out of their heads, and their fingers gnawed off!"

"Oh, Marjatta!" scolds Isak. He gets up from the bed and he pitches a heavy boot in the direction of the noise. There is a great scurrying and then silence. Marjatta lies wide awake for an hour after Isak is back asleep and then is overcome by her weariness.

In the morning Isak tiptoes to the children's bed and beckons Marjatta. "You see? Four eyes. Twenty fingers."

Marjatta says disgustedly, "Go build a house, Isak. I will tend to the rats myself."

Marjatta does not consult with the other women, Sophie Hiltunen, Kaisa Kalliokoski, and Una Makela. She does as she has told Isak she will do: she deals with the rats herself.

She gathers up the several bottles the rats have knocked over and those on the shelves that have popped their corks but remained standing. She empties them of their preserves, being careful to make sure no dirt or leaves get into the jam. Then she begins emptying the other bottles of their rich sweet contents, one by one, into the same huge bowl. The other women are already gone, so there is no one to question her about this strange thing she is doing. The preserves that have not popped their corks may be fermented as well, but they are still useful, for pies or fruit soup to be poured in a bowl over custard or farmer's cheese.

Over the fire outside she hangs a huge kettle. She hauls water from the river, two trips, breaking a substantial sweat on her brow, and then she boils the water and lets the bottles swim around in it. She stirs them with a spoon. The sun is getting high now. She wipes her forehead with her apron.

She leaves the water to cool and goes and looks for Isak's small toolbox, the one he has not brought with him to the Kalliokoskis' homestead this morning, the one he uses for minor repairs.

Stiina is with one of the older girls, who has taken a liking to her, and Marjatta is feeling her breasts begin to tighten and grow hot with milk as the morning goes on. Stiina is a frequent nurser, but this morning Marjatta has given the bigger girl sweet dry toast for the baby to chew on so that she can get this thing done.

Marjatta goes back to the kettle of bottles. The water is cool enough now. She uses a wooden spoon to jostle the bottles and tries to withdraw them with a hook. She cannot, and she winds up rolling her sleeves to the elbow and pulling the bottles out individually. Some of them try to elude her. They bob and shift in the kettle. The raspberry residue is everywhere in the cloudy, warm water. She is determined to catch all the bottles, and she winds up with her sleeves wet and sticky all the way to her armpits. She lays the bottles on an outdoor table in the sun to dry while she looks again for

Isak's toolbox. She comes back with the toolbox. In the shed she has found an old horse blanket ruined by tar and ripped on a nail where it snagged. She drags this behind her. She tucks up her skirt and sits cross-legged on the brick floor, and she starts her strange project.

One by one, she inserts the bottles tidily into the folds of the blanket and begins pounding with Isak's hammer. She pulverizes the old whiskey bottles, one by one. As she begins the third bottle, she feels her eyes tearing up. *Blam!* She shatters the bottle inside its dark blanket wrap. This, she says inside herself, is for the doctor at Ellis Island, the one with the terrible mustache. She suggests to God that he might wish to give this man some dreadful disease, or reduce him to poverty, or send him to work in a sewer. And then she confesses her sin—this ill wishing—and repents of it, but hopes that God has meanwhile indeed answered her prayer. She pounds and she pounds, and the bottle is powdered glass. She takes out any larger pieces that refuse to be pulverized and puts them into a separate pile. She takes out another bottle. *Blam!* This bottle is for my father and all of his losses. He was a good man. He deserved to be cared for and not to die all alone. She does not know her father is alive. He feels dead to her. She feels more tears rise in her eyes. One more bottle. *Blam! Blam!* This one is for Emil's death, and the mystery of it, why the illness should seek him out. He was a strong man. Why could not the fever have taken some terrible person instead? One more bottle. *Blam!* This is for Susu. Marjatta, the woman who has seldom cried, bawls aloud. She reduces the bottle to finest powder. Another. For Isak's cousin, the liar. *Blam! Blam!* Yet one more bottle. For Isak, that night in Detroit. *Blam!*

The other women walk in, as one. "Marjatta!" they say in unison.

"Have you lost your mind?" says Una Makela.

Marjatta wipes at her eyes. "No," she says, firm, certain, sounding as sane as a Lutheran deacon. "Only my life and my hope and a number of other small items." Then she explains her plan. They stand staring wide-eyed and listening. Indeed, they are thinking: *She has lost her mind.* But they do not stop her.

She is making a cake for the rats. She measures out the glass "flour" and sets it aside. She takes sugar and eggs and wheat flour and yesterday's left-over soured milk from the Kalliokoskis' brown cow, and she mixes them in a huge bowl. Then she pours in the pulverized glass.

Kaisa is giggling in horror. "You cannot mean to do this!" she says.

"Indeed?" says Marjatta. "I do mean to do this, and do this I will."

It is not the plan itself so much as the look on Marjatta's face that is so frightening to the other women.

Marjatta pours her batter into two pans and she bakes it. The bodice of her blouse is drenched with her own breast milk now, and its fabric is stiff where the milk has dried. Her breasts have been leaking for two hours. The skin at the open neck of her bodice feels fevered.

"I'll go get your Stiina for you," says Kaisa Kalliokoski, skewing her thin yellow eyebrows above her pale eyes at Marjatta. "Please sit down. You will take a fever."

So while the cake bakes in the oven just outside the door, and its sweet, eggy smell fills the air of the yard, Marjatta sits with her little girl, now toddling and talking, and nurses her, smiling, as if all were very well, humming an old Finnish folk tune whose name she has never known. The melody reminds her of the oat fields and of Emil and of the candles on the graves in the Lutheran churchyard on Christmas Eve.

When the cake is baked, Marjatta puts the layers together carefully, flipping the second layer gingerly over on top of the first. Then she frosts it with a thick coating of the raspberry preserves and covers it with a pan. She puts it on a high shelf.

"We would not want any of the children to get into this," she says. To the other women, Marjatta's eyes look glazed. They are wondering, individually, whether this is a look of exhaustion or a look of insanity.

"Or the husbands," says Sophie. "My husband, he would get into it. Any good-looking food, he gets into. A roast, a custard, a cake. He is worse than a child." She says this with a glow of undisguised pride in her husband's appetites.

My husband, thinks Marjatta, *he* should *get into it.* And then she begins crying again. Isak is not to blame retroactively for all the terrible things in her life. He is a decent man. He is only a man, after all. And she bawls.

Sophie takes Stiina, who has fallen asleep at Marjatta's breast. "You must go to bed. Rest," she insists.

"I must finish my task," says Marjatta. "And then I will rest."

That night, Marjatta lies down with Isak as usual. She tries to make conversation. Her tone is that of a silly drawing-room play. Isak does not notice. "You never tell me about your work, Isak," she says. "I know nothing about copper mining. Tell me what you do every day. Is copper mining different here from in Finland?" This is guaranteed to put him to sleep.

"Copper mining is copper mining," he says laconically. He seems to get progressively sleepier in the space of those few words. He is snoring within half a minute.

When Isak is asleep, she rises and goes to the shelf where she has put the cake made of flour of glass. She takes down the cake and she removes the pan that has covered it. She places the cake in the center of the table. She wants to see this event in all its glory. Though rats normally hate the light, she has full confidence that her cake is so rat delectable that they will come right out into the spotlight, as if this were a stage in a fine theater in Helsinki or Turku, so that she can see them. She wants to watch them die, but she has not admitted this to herself fully. It is the same impulse that came alive in the head of her hammer that afternoon.

Then she feels eyes on her. Kaisa and Una have tiptoed up and are standing behind a clothes tree where the husbands have hung their big jackets. Marjatta throws a strange glaring look at them but says nothing. They look like silly children to her. The three hear a shuffling sound. It is Sophie, coming up out of the dark corner where she has been lying next to her husband, not sleeping.

"All right then," Marjatta says. She places a lit oil lamp next to the cake. "If we watch, so the lamp cannot be knocked over and start a fire, I think there is really no danger."

The table is right at the center of the room, near none of the children's beds. The women step back into the shadows. They stand waiting. The night is rapidly cooling. Kaisa goes for a blanket and then for a rocking chair. Marjatta brings two straight chairs. All of the women but Sophie sit down in a row in the shadows, as if this were indeed theater.

"Sit down," says Marjatta. "You'll frighten the little beasts. We must be very still." So Sophie brings a stool and crouches on it with her quilt wrapped about her, and the four women wait for the show.

A scuffling sound. A squeak. Then another. A thump, and a pan falls from somewhere. One of the husbands turns in his bed, mumbling a demand for quiet. A rat brushes past the skirt of Una's nightdress and she catches her breath in astonishment and terror. She looks over at Marjatta, who winks and flares her nostrils in an odd relish, showing no fear at all. Another rat rushes past, several, scampering up the legs of the table or jumping from the ground and the rafters, and all of them are on the cake, now a dozen, two dozen. The women sit frozen in terror. The rats lick up every crumb. When the plate is licked clean, every crumb swallowed, suddenly, silently, all of the rats are gone. The women gape at one another in amazement at this thing that they have witnessed. Marjatta says, "Well. I do not believe we will see those creatures ever again."

And they do not. At Kaisa's insistence, the Kalliokoskis get a cat from a family in Calumet, but it stays unemployed, lazing about in the sun, testing the patience of the Makelas' dog, annoying the cow, getting fat, making several of the inhabitants sneeze. One day the cat disappears and no one notices for a number of days, it is such a superfluous animal.

MARJATTA'S TIME TO deliver has not yet come when one day she goes into labor. The men are at work and Sophie and Kaisa have gone on the rails, in a boxcar with most of the children, to Camp Sweat to visit a friend who has just come from Finland. Una goes on the horse for the doctor, following the flattened grass that lines the railroad tracks. There is of course still no road. And as it turns out there is also no doctor: the doctor has gone somewhere else.

When she returns, three hours later, Marjatta has given birth to the child, there in the bed, only minutes before. The child is born blue, with its cord around its neck. Marjatta has, with the speed of light, risen from the bed, gotten scissors and cut the cord, which she has flung out the door as if it were dangerous, muttering spells in Finnish. She cannot imagine how she knows these spells: she cannot remember anyone teaching them to her.

"Breathe," she has said calmly to the infant, who lies limp and blue and motionless.

She has washed the boy and dressed him in a little white batiste dress she had used for the other three. She has laid him on the table, the same place she had put the cake.

When Una returns, Marjatta, her bulbous abdomen deflated to a flat slackness, with her nightgown knotted up around her hips, is going about her business, only slightly weak, holding a baby blanket she has drenched with blood between her legs with her left hand and with her right attempting to fold up the blood-sodden sheets that she has taken up from the bed. The child lies still and blue on the table, looking light as an eggshell and ready to levitate.

Una cries, "Marjatta! Lie down!"

"I think that the pastor had better come soon to bless the child," Marjatta says. "He is not looking well. Perhaps prayer will revive him." She turns to the child and again she says, "Breathe." Her voice is only an imperceptible bit more urgent, as if she had all the time in the world and did not want to rush the baby.

Then Marjatta stops as if she has remembered something. "*Is* there a pastor, Una? Do we have a pastor now or am I thinking of Finland?"

"Marjatta, the baby is dead. Don't you see?" Una stands staring in horror.

"Oh, no," says Marjatta. "He just has not quite come alive. Does he look like his father, do you think? What shall we call him?" Marjatta sets down the blanket pad that she has held between her legs and picks up a fresh blanket. "My, we will surely have laundry!"

"Marjatta!" Una thinks to shock her into attention.

Marjatta lifts the baby from the table and holds the limp thing tightly under its arms. She is displaying the baby to Una. She shakes it slightly, as if to make it dance. Una stares, and suddenly the baby moves, and sucks air, and coughs, and wails, and flails its small arms and legs.

"Do you see? The boy lives," says Marjatta.

Una is certain the child is bewitched or will be an idiot all its life, but in fact the boy thrives.

Isak is delighted with the child, whom he names Juhani.

"Is that the name of the baker's assistant?" says Marjatta. She never did learn the man's name.

"No," says Isak. He does not say what the baker's helper is named or where he is taking the name Juhani from: An ancestor? Thin air? She is too tired to ask, because when he finds her questions tiresome and gives her that look she feels as though she has been punched in the breastbone.

After the others are in bed, and the children have remarked on the new baby, and the men have congratulated Isak, Marjatta and Isak retire to their bed. They are sitting on their respective sides, she braiding her hair, he putting out his pipe. The child sleeps peacefully.

Marjatta says, "The men congratulated *you*."

"Yes?" Isak says.

Marjatta decides there is nothing to say. So she says, "Oh, nothing."

"Do you remember the first night we slept as man and wife?" Isak says. Marjatta does, yes, she nods. She does not meet Isak's eyes. She would rather not remember. "I said to you that you would bring a high price as a whore."

Marjatta holds her breath. He is about to apologize! Her heart is almost audible in her chest, fluttering like a small fat bird trying to break through the cage of bones. She turns her whole body to look at him now.

"Well, I say to you now you would bring just as high a price as a breeder. Perhaps higher."

Marjatta slaps his face harder than she would have imagined she could have. She walks out the door into the night in her nightgown. The door stands open, framing the moonlit clearing and dark trees in the distance.

Isak sits on the edge of the bed with his fingertips pressed to the sting on his cheek. He cannot imagine what he has said. He has just praised her to the skies! He goes after her, puzzled, but she has vanished into the forest. She is gone all night. The child sleeps through.

Just before dawn, Marjatta reappears. Isak stares at her silhouette in the doorway as she enters, a flat slate blue sky framing her, and a number of brilliant stars spilled loose there. Her nightgown is damp with the dew, and her hair is soaking wet. She has caught a cold in the night air. She sneezes. She sneezes again.

She picks up the sleeping child, who wakes amiably and goes for her nipple. Marjatta looks at the child. Yes, he does look like Isak, but there is some of her own look as well: perhaps the boy will resemble his brother Jaako. Marjatta decides that she will forget that the boys are just half brothers. They both are her sons, and she loves them both fiercely.

Then she looks up at Isak with a look that is cold and unclear.

"You will need to be going to work soon," she says. "We will need a house. Put the coffeepot on the stove. You are the first one up." He starts to say something and she says, sharp as a knife, "No words. No words. Please no words."

"I worried all night," says Isak.

"The child was fine," says Marjatta.

"But you are not fine," says Isak.

"I? I?" says Marjatta. She lifts her arm, she inspects her hand, holds it up before her face, stares at it as if it were transparent. She pulls her right braid up and holds it before her. Then her left braid. She is squinting at them as if she cannot see them at all. "I do not exist, Isak," she says. "I am a ghost. Build the house nonetheless. Even the dead need a place to live."

Marjatta hears the strange inturning of her language and frowns. Isak takes no notice of it. He goes off to his day's work. As he is hammering on the roof in bright midday, with the hot sun beating down on the top of his pale, thinning hair, briefly Marjatta's words come back to him, their weight almost imperceptible, like a dragonfly resting on the seam of his shirtsleeve: *Even the dead need a place to live.* But Isak is not a man of words, and the dragonfly lifts off and flies away.

With the coming of fall, all the families are in their houses and the men are off to the copper mine, coming home every two weeks or so. The women keep things going at home, and the men live in dormitories run by the mine. This is fine with Marjatta.

Occasionally she feels a twinge of guilt for her hardness toward Isak, but then she excuses herself. After all, she is not alone: Sophie calls her husband "the Stone," and Una bakes a celebratory plum-jam pudding, as if it were a wonderful holiday, each alternate Sunday night when the men go back to the mine. Kaisa complains that her husband will not wear a sheath and she is not yet ready for one more child—she now has six under the age of ten—and that this is all just too much difficulty.

Everyone heaves a sigh of relief to be settled finally in separate cabins. It is only a ten-minute walk between cabins, and after the women each day gather eggs and set up the day's work—baking one day, laundry another, mending another—they meet at one of the houses for a second cup of coffee, to share the previous day's tribulations and to laugh and to talk about dreams. They still do have dreams. Marjatta talks once or twice about the roses that climb the porch trellis and several times about the loom that she wanted in Finland and still may be longing for.

IN SEPTEMBER, WHEN the leaves are at their most beautiful, copper colored, pear yellow, unearthly luminous green and bright, unalloyed red, two new families come to Camp Grit. Their names are Rapajarvi and Kangas. The three women welcome them, but there is a collective sigh: now they will have to share cabins again, the whole winter, until in late spring the men can build two more homes.

Because the Kalliokoskis have six children—and now, in the last few weeks, Kaisa has discovered that there is one more on the way—they are excused by common agreement from hosting new people. The Makelas are contributing all the milk to the little settlement, so they too are excused.

Sophie and Marjatta find themselves hosting the two new families. Sophie is genial enough about this, and the Kangas woman is in fact a pleasant companion, but Marjatta has drawn the short straw, figuratively speaking: Mrs. Rapajarvi is unbearable, a whiner, a giver of orders, a patent malingerer full of good reasons why she cannot help with the work.

"I was not brought up to this!" she says, fanning her fingers out across her chest with a self-pitying thump.

"*None* of us was brought up to this!" Marjatta says. "I was second in line to become queen of Finland! Be quiet and do your share!"

"Paugh," says Mrs. Rapajarvi. "There is no queen of Finland."

"That is because I was shipped to this dreadful place," Marjatta says, wryly. "Had I not been, there would have been a queen of Finland. And I would have been wonderful at it." She does not crack a smile, though she thinks this is the funniest thing she has said in years.

Mrs. Rapajarvi does not think that this is funny at all. In fact, Mrs. Rapajarvi does not think anything is funny.

The second time Isak comes home from the mines, Marjatta takes him aside and says, "Tell Rapajarvi to take this witch back where she came from. I will not put up with this. She expects me to wait on her. She will not help cut wood. And—this I will never forgive!—she complains that my coffee is too bitter and my *nisua* too sweet! I will go live with the Indians first, before I will stay here with this horrible woman." She sits with her arms crossed in fury.

Isak tells Rapajarvi sanguinely that the women seem not to be getting along. Rapajarvi says, "Ohh! Women! It is their nature not to get along! Have a drink with me, Isak! They soon will adapt."

The third time Isak comes home from the mines, Marjatta whispers in bed, "Isak, I am not fooling. Get rid of this woman or I will go offer myself to the chief of the Chippewas. Nothing could be worse than this."

Isak laughs wholeheartedly. "Just turn over here," he says. "Hold this." He takes her hand and places it on his ready organ. "Do you think that the chief of the Chippewas could please you as your husband does?"

Marjatta complies in mute fury. But she thinks: *So you think that you please me, you fool?*

The second night Isak is home on this visit, he sits with Rapajarvi by the fireplace having a vodka. Mrs. Rapajarvi—she seems to have no first name, and the women would frankly just as soon not know—is mending her husband's socks by oil light at the other end of the room. Isak tells Rapajarvi, "Marjatta is not adapting well to your wife! She has threatened to give herself to the old Chippewa chief if this arrangement goes on!" And the men both laugh.

There is some lewd talk about Indian wife swapping. Isak hopes that Rapajarvi will not make a joke that involves their wives, because, damn it to hell, he will tell him that he has no idea how he can sleep with that harpy, and does she have teeth sharpened to a point in the place where women ought to be softest? And no thank, you, he will just keep Marjatta.

When it is bedtime, Isak looks for Marjatta. She has gone out with the children at sunset, leaving venison stew for the men, saying that she has something to bring over to Kalliokoskis. She has not returned.

In fact, with Juhani in a wool sling, Stiina on her back, and Jaako trailing along in his boots, coat, and muffler, Marjatta has stood in the trackside snow, in the glare of the headlight of the slow-moving engine of the logging train and flagged down the engineer with a bandanna. By bedtime she is at

Camp Jubilee, trudging through the snow to her friend the widow Vainionpaa, whose husband has died in a mine accident the year before, his
chest crushed by an ore car.

As she stomps off the snow in the cabin of the astonished woman, Marjatta says, "He will have to get down on his knees this time. Mrs. Rapajarvi
can go live with the Chippewas. I have reached my limit."

The matter is cleared up within the week. Isak guesses her whereabouts on
the third try, and he shows up at the widow Vainionpaa's door at midnight.

"Do you have my wife here?" he says.

"By her own will," says the woman. "She is not held hostage. And will not
be held hostage by you either."

Isak is taken aback. Is this what America does to these women? "Well,
then," he says, trying to sound firm. He is not sure what he means.

The men stay in camp an extra day before going back to the mine, to
hammer out an agreement. Mrs. Rapajarvi decides on her own that she is
going back to Finland. She tells her husband she plans to leave after the
snow melts.

"Oh, feel free to go sooner!" says her husband.

And so Mrs. Rapajarvi leaves, and Rapajarvi himself sheds no tears anyone can see, and Marjatta has her cabin back.

She remembers the eleventh chapter of Paul's Epistle to the Hebrews. It
is a chapter about faith. It catalogs all of the wonderful heroes of the Old
Testament, how great was their faith and their long perseverance. She grumbles inside herself. She cannot recall a single woman in that catalog. She
goes to the bedside table and picks up her Bible. She thumbs through it to
the passage in Hebrews. Ah, well, there is Sarah, but only peripherally. A
mention, as it were, out of the side of Paul's mouth.

In the last paragraph of the chapter she comes to the passage she has half
remembered. It disconcerts her. It answers the question the brown-eyed girl
teacher in Finland would not answer. It talks about all sorts of nameless folk
who, despite their great faith, never receive their reward on earth, who wander about in sheepskins and goatskins and live in caves and in holes in the
ground, who are beaten with chains, and yet are all commended for their
great faith.

Marjatta sighs and slams the book. This is not what she wanted to hear. She wanted to open her Bible and have it tell her that the little white house with the roses would come in the next post. There is a verse in the passage that says, "Women received back their dead, raised to life again." Prior to Juhani's birth she thought that this was just a thing that happened in what people call the old days, and she does not remember a thing of the first day of Juhani's life, despite Una's recountings of it, but she does believe that the infant boy was indeed raised from the dead. *Then,* she thinks, *why not Emil?*

She remembers the sister of Lazarus, Lazarus who has been dead for four days when Jesus comes. "Lord, he stinketh!" protests the woman. Emil has been dead now for three years. He is rotted away to white bone. "Shall these bones live?" asks the prophet Ezekiel in the Valley of Dry Bones. God's answer is yes. *So then,* she thinks, *why not Emil?* She begins to believe that there may be a miracle coming.

Isak picks up a hint of this and teases her one day. "My goodness, Marjatta, what would I do if that Emil fellow came back?"

She answers him reasonably, she thinks. "You would find someone else, Isak. All that you want is a sack of flesh, something to sleep with." She is not being ugly, she thinks, just matter-of-fact. Her very matter-of-factness disconcerts Isak. "Take the widow Vainionpaa. She makes very fine pasties as well, especially pork—do you remember that wild hog Makela shot and we shared the meat? she made the tastiest pasties of that—and moreover she tells me that she used to suck on her husband's . . . thing . . . whenever he wanted. Marry *her.*"

"Marjatta, do you really mean that?" Isak stares at her.

She turns away and busies herself with the baby. She speaks in a perfectly reasonable tone of voice, as if they were discussing a real possibility. "The settlement could use a teacher," she says. "Emil is a very fine teacher."

"Marjatta, my wife, Emil Palomaki is *dead.*"

"And so was your son, little Juhani," she says. "And here he is, alive." She pauses, then adds, light and clear and as if this were nothing but reasonable, "But if Emil returns, I will take little Juhani with me. You can start over with Mrs. Vainionpaa."

Isak stares at her in disbelief. It is clear she is serious. Wearied by all of this, he begins coming home no more than once a month, sending Marjatta home most of his miner's pay with Kalliokoski. By midwinter there is talk that Isak is drinking too much.

"Talk is talk," says Marjatta. "Isak is a decent man." She seems to mean it.

The following winter the widow Vainionpaa takes the train south. It is said that she has gone to Grand Rapids to work in a hospital. Then it is said that she has had a child. People say that the child is Isak's.

"Oh, well, talk is talk," says Marjatta. She thinks of the little white house that she thought she was coming to. She remembers the voice of Emil Palomaki, reading aloud in the evenings. She cannot think how it has all come to this.

Soon Isak is home again, talking as little as ever, impassive when Marjatta mentions the gossip. He raises an eyebrow at her. "Do you really think I would do that? With that woman?" He flares his nostrils as if there is a smell.

"How do I know what you would do, Isak Karajamaki?" says Marjatta. Her implication is that she does not know him, really, at all.

"You know you are the only woman who has ever interested me," Isak says.

"Except whores?" says Marjatta.

He spits. "Whores have never interested me."

"And still, what was this past you have?" says Marjatta.

"Stop talking about this," he says. "I am home. Past is past."

THERE HAS BEEN a good deal of talk about fairness of wages and frequency of accidents. Vainionpaa is not the only man to have died in this mine. In 1913 union organizers from the IWW come to town to rally the miners, and in August there is a strike.

The union assures everyone they will be taken care of. Strikers' families will receive clothing and food. At the end of this period of tightened belts there will be paradise.

"The green valley of Psalm 23," Marjatta says drily to Isak. He is coming home every two weeks again, for years now, and there is an arid and fragile peace in place.

Jaako is fifteen and has been sent to high school in Rovaniemi, boarding with relatives of the Makelas. He is after all Emil's son, a boy who will go far with his mind. Marjatta's fondest hope is that he will not ever go down the shaft of a copper mine.

"Finish high school," she exhorts him. "Get a good job."

Stiina is twelve, starting to sprout breasts. Her hair curls delicately. She seems to resemble her father Emil's sister who died as a child. She is fond of reciting Longfellow before the fire, and Marjatta encourages her. Her favorite poem is "The Skeleton in Armor." The ghost of a Viking warrior rises before the poet and tells of his amazing past. Stiina loves to mimic the booming voice rising from the empty rib cage of the skeleton.

"Then, from those cavernous eyes / Pale flashes seemed to rise / As when the Northern skies / Gleam in December," she intones.

When she speaks as the warrior, Juhani always breaks up in laughter. He thinks his sister so clever. Juhani is ten, bright and active, the pride of his father, the joy of his mother.

There is not a day when Marjatta does not think of Susu, in Turku. At the time of the copper miners' strike in Calumet County, Susu is packing her trunks for Paris, to go there to study. Marjatta wonders what she looks like now, what she does, what she thinks about. Every year she has written to the woman in Turku asking for news. The letters do not come back, but neither are they answered. Once Susu sees an envelope from her mother. She does not know the name on the return address: *Marjatta Karajamaki.*

"Who is this?" she says to her adoptive mother.

"A cousin of your father's," says her adoptive mother. "Twice removed."

"Pretty handwriting," Susu says. "Lovely, the way she makes curls on the *m* and the *k*. It looks as if they grew there, like a bud on a branch."

"She is an annoying woman," says the adoptive mother. There is something about the way she says it that piques Susu's curiosity for the moment. The woman's response—Susu thinks, her mother's response—seems out of proportion. But then there is all of this packing to do, and the subject does not come up again.

The strike goes on for months. By Christmas there is strain—the union has not been able to keep its promises, people are hungry, the children's clothes threadbare. There is an enormous amount of tension in the community between the families of the men walking the picket lines and the families of the men who cannot in conscience side with the union, or who do not trust it, and so go to work in the mine as "scabs."

Isak has stood with the union, as have Rapajarvi and Kangas and Hiltunen. Makela and Kalliokoski have kept working. Each has his logic and reasons. The women stay out of it and try to help one another, though often the men are underfoot now.

ON CHRISTMAS EVE the union is sponsoring a party at the Italian Hall in Calumet. There will be presents for all of the children. Marjatta begins, the week before the party, to try to find something for the children to wear. There are no older girls in the settlement of the right age to pass on hand-me-downs, and Marjatta has no old dresses that would remake easily into a dress for a twelve-year-old. There is no money for new cloth. So Stiina wears an old dress ornamented with a new collar borrowed for the occasion from Una Makela.

The Italian Hall is gaily lit and filled to capacity: ribbons, wreaths, lights, every child of a striker not bed-bound with illness. Marjatta delivers Juhani and Stiina early to the party so that they will be sure to be near the front of the line when the gifts are distributed. Even though they are ten and twelve now, she treats them as if they were still small: they are all she has.

Then she goes down the street to the Polish scissor sharpener and to the dry goods store, which is still open, because business has not been good and the owners are trying to make up for lost business by staying open late. She looks at everything in the store—as if she had money to spare!—and she decides there is nothing that means anything here. Her heart is overwhelmed with gratitude for the children she has, and she includes Susu in this. She resolves to be kinder to Isak this year.

She is coming back toward the hall when she hears the screams.

Afterward witnesses say they have seen a small, slight man on the stairs just before everyone hears the shout: "Fire!" The double doors of the hall open inward. The crowd pushes to get out, and no one can open the doors. People panic. Children and parents push and shove. Some trip and stumble. Many fall and are trampled. Some jump from windows. In all of this no one smells or sees smoke or fire.

Marjatta, coming back toward the hall, stands transfixed. *Fire?* Her mind is not putting the scene together. Then where is the smoke. No, where are Stiina and Juhani? *Inside there.*

She runs toward the building. She hears herself screaming. An ax! Get an ax! Break the door! She assumes that there is indeed fire. Then she realizes that, even if there is no fire, the children are just inside the door. An ax is not the answer.

They are trapped. Someone must know what to do. She sees children jumping from windows. She runs around the side of the building. A small girl, half Stiina's age, screams: "Mama!"

Marjatta says: "Jump to me, little one!" The girl jumps directly into Marjatta's arms and is safe, but Marjatta falls backward and hits her head. She is knocked unconscious. When she wakes, hours later, Isak is sitting next to her in an emergency shelter, his face blanched, his jaw set harder than she has ever seen.

"The children are dead," he says. "Stiina. Juhani." He sits in silence for what seems an eternity. Marjatta weaves in and out of consciousness, with the disconnectedness of the head-injured which feels like simple, dozy, sweet sleep to her. She is out awhile and then she tries to sit up. "No, be still," says Isak.

"What did you say? Before? I dreamed you said the children were dead."

"You were not dreaming," Isak says.

"Our children?" Marjatta says. "The children cannot be dead," she says. "This is not a joking matter, Isak. What are you talking about?"

"Juhani?" he says. "That baby that you raised from the dead, you recall? Well, he has gone back to the dead. And your beautiful Stiina? *Our* beautiful Stiina? As dead as her brother." Isak breaks down crying. Marjatta has never heard him put so many words together at one time.

"No," says Marjatta firmly. "You are mistaken. I'll get up and find out." She tries to get up and cannot.

"Trampled and smothered," says Isak. "Both of them."

Marjatta begins keening, rocking and keening.

"I should not have let them come to this party," says Marjatta. "For two little presents! My God!"

"God damn the union," says Isak. "God fucking shit damn the union."

The children and adults who perish in the panic are laid out like sardines on the floor of the Calumet Theater. Photographers take pictures of the dead, arrayed neatly, and make them into postcards. Today locals gather in that hall in the evening to watch films like *Eat Drink Man Woman*. Few visitors to the theater today even know about that grisly spectacle. People whose children have *not* died in the disaster send the postcards to their relatives elsewhere, as if these were photographs of a row of dolls: *Dear Aunt Hannah, There but for the grace of God go we all. Had good game of cribbage last night. Do you have word from Cousin Lou? Write soon and tell me. Best wishes, Ondine.*

The following year, the war in Europe begins. The union's power dwindles in response to people's fears of . . . *what?* Some sinister political thing. Marjatta does not understand, nor does Isak.

Isak reads Finnish newspapers that are passed around from hand to hand.

He shakes his head. "Confused," he says. "Finns don't know if they are Russians or who."

Marjatta thinks she is making a joke, parodying Isak's usual straightforward logic and syntax. "Finns are Finns," she says, mimicking Isak's voice. She expects him to laugh. He does not. He does not think one thing about this war is funny.

Since Juhani and Stiina's death, Marjatta can do nothing. She sits in her rocking chair like an old woman, though she is only thirty-four, knitting endless columns of chain stitches that go nowhere. Her long hair begins to go gray and turn wiry.

This goes on for several months and then Isak says, bluff and hearty, "Perhaps we should go for a holiday!"

She looks up at him as if she does not know him. A Finnish copper miner, a holiday? Surely he has lost his mind. She looks out the window. The sky is incredible, dazzling blue—it is autumn—and the cloud configuration above the trees might seem to resemble a coach-and-four, backlit in glory, to the Marjatta who sat on the hill outside Kuortane as a teenaged girl and then a young mother, only a few years before. Marjatta goes back to her knitting.

WHEN JAAKO FINISHES high school, he stays in Rovaniemi and gets a job. The First World War is over. He sends money. He does not say what the job is, and Marjatta does not ask.

Jaako has a job that has dignity. Marjatta tells this to Isak again and again. They sleep in the same bed, but they hardly speak. Marjatta has never recovered from the deaths of the children, and Isak lives in a somber space that is somehow cushioned by Marjatta's silence. The war in Europe may be over now, but Isak and Marjatta's truce does not seem totally solid.

Jaako's letters could hardly be called chatty, but it is clear they are meant to reassure his mother, and to some extent Isak, that his life is good. He writes little bits of information about people in Rovaniemi. He talks about functions at the Finnish Lutheran Church. Isak wonders about him nonetheless. Marjatta does not wonder. She is certain that he is fine.

When Jaako is twenty, he marries a girl named Katey O'Doul, and he sends an announcement. *What is this,* Marjatta thinks. This is not the way it is done, she says to Isak.

Isak says, Mother, perhaps this is how this is done now.

You may stop calling me Mother, Marjatta says. I am not your mother.

They are both straw people, leaning together in high wind, though to outsiders Isak looks solid.

Jaako writes and says, *Mama, I have changed my name to Jacob, and most people call me Jake now. This sounds much more American, and Katey likes it too.*

Marjatta does not write back. She is waiting for the world to cave in. What next? And was she not the one who so badly wanted to be an American?

Her son writes again. *I have changed my last name as well. I went to court to do this. It cost five dollars to do this. Palomaki I was born, Karajamaki I became when Papa Isak came into our lives, and now I will be simply Maki. This honors both of my fathers.*

Marjatta puts down the letter. "Jake Maki," Marjatta says. She walks to the mirror on the bathroom wall. "Jake Maki," she says. "So this is what it has come to. Jake Maki of Michigan. Well."

Later that year news arrives that Katey is going to have a child. "Isak, you don't need me here. I am going to Rovaniemi," she says, "to help Jaako's Katey."

"His name is Jake now," Isak says.

Something in Marjatta wishes that Isak would protest that, yes, he needs her. And yet if he did she would fight with him about that. She packs her bags, and as it happens, she will never come back to the copper mine.

Jake's Katey is an independent girl with, at the moment, an enormous pregnant belly. She has springy red hair that she inherited from her Irish father. She is astonished at Marjatta's appearing, one Sunday afternoon, on their doorstep, the porch of a small white house in a row of identical houses that curve along a neighborhood street without trees.

Katey has seen Marjatta only in Jake's wallet-sized copy of the studio portrait made at the time of her wedding to Emil. In that photograph Marjatta is a radiant young girl with rich, full lips and a smile that glows. The Marjatta who appears before Katey now is, in her midforties, an old woman: pucker-lipped, her face drained of all of its juice, her blond hair gone to white down half its length. Katey does not for a second connect this old woman with that picture.

"Who are you looking for?" Katey asks, sprightly and helpful and thinking this woman a stranger who is perhaps lost.

"My Jaako," Marjatta says, in English. Her Finn accent has never abated: she has never had to use English to any degree.

This does not register with Katey, who has known her husband as Jake since the moment she met him. Jake's accent is noticeable but not strong. Marjatta's words sound like a single strange word—myako—to Katey. She cannot think how this woman would be speaking Japanese.

The two women stand looking at each other, at an impasse. Then, from behind Katey, Jake comes to the door.

"Mama!" he exclaims in astonishment. It has taken him a moment to consolidate the passage of time, to refocus. Katey wheels, looking first at him, then at Marjatta. "What are you doing here?"

"I come to help," says Marjatta in English. It sounds like a plea: Let me feel useful, let me stay, please.

Katey looks first to Jake, and there is a plea in her eyes as well: she's not coming to stay, is she? She looks down at the two fat satchels Marjatta carries. She stands straight and tall and does not put her bags down.

Jake is flustered. "Oh! Mama! Come in then!"

Katey's eyes fill with consternation. Marjatta does not see this, though she senses it. She thinks she may talk her way through this. "I think Katey can use some help. So she can rest."

Marjatta is thinking that these young girls today are not like we were, strong. She decides this is okay, this is just the way time changes things. She thinks, at some deeper level, catastrophizing as is her sometime habit, *The end of the world must be near. All these hundreds of generations we were strong, and we come to America, then in just one generation . . .*

She says, "Laundry and anything else. I can help you with these, and with the baby when he comes, or she. And you, Jaako, you probably have not had cardamom cake in a very long time."

Jake settles Marjatta on a hard little sofa in the living room.

"This is a nice room," says Marjatta. Her eyes rove the walls and she thinks, *This Irish girl does not know how to make a real home for my son.*

Jake seems ready to jump out of his skin with discomfort, and Katey's mouth hangs slightly open in consternation. Marjatta will not look at her. No one says anything. Suddenly Marjatta begins crying silently. "I cannot live the life of the miner's wife anymore, Jaako. I hate the mine."

"But, Mama," says Jaako. "This is a mine as well."

Marjatta stares at him as if she has heard him wrong.

"Mama, these houses are owned by the mine. I work for the Meridel-Pflaum Mining Company, Mama. I'm a miner too," Jake says.

"No!" says Marjatta in disbelief. She looks to Katey as if to confirm this. Katey shakes her head yes, of course, fully confused as to what is distressing Marjatta.

"Yes, Mama," Jake says. "Look at my fingernails." Yes, the telltale black, though he is clean-scrubbed.

"Oh, Jaako!" she says, and as is usual with Marjatta, her accent grows stronger as her distress heightens. "I thought you had gotten your high-school degree!"

"A diploma, yes, Mama."

"Diploma, okay, okay. I thought you had gotten a good job, Jaako. Your father was a teacher. I thought you would be something lovely like that. Not a miner," Marjatta says.

Now Jake is taken aback for a moment: the only father he has ever known is Isak Karajamaki, and Marjatta's dismissal of Isak always takes Jake by surprise. "Papa Isak is a miner," he says.

"Exactly," says Marjatta, as if to say, Case closed.

"Mama, I will become a supervisor, as Papa Isak was in Orijaarvi. Though this is an iron mine. Meridel-Pflaum is a steel manufacturer," Jake says.

Marjatta sits silent, speechless.

Jake seems to be searching for something to reassure her. "Would you like it if I became a supervisor?" Jake asks hopefully. "I work very hard. I think I will do very well."

"I am sure you will do very well," says Marjatta. She wants to say, *You are my only surviving child. Everything rests on you.* "I want you to do one thing for me," she says to her son. "Find a job where you get yourself out of the ground. I do not like my son down a hole all the time."

Jake sighs. "Oh, Mama."

"Tell me you will think about this," says Marjatta.

"I will think about this," says Jake.

Katey seems to be ready to cry, and she leaves the room. Jake says, "Mama, do you remember that paper you had, folded up, that you kept in the Bible, with something from a mining company, that thing Papa Isak's friend in Göteborg had given to him?"

Marjatta nods yes, slowly, truculently.

"You said that was what made you marry Papa Isak. Am I correct?" Jake asks.

"I thought I was coming to that place," says Marjatta. "I felt very tricked when I got here. Oh, did I feel tricked." She pauses a moment and then says the word again, "Tricked!"

"But you know Papa Isak thought that too," says Jake.

"I know that," she says reluctantly.

"Do you still have that paper?" says Jake.

"I do. In my Bible. Right here," she says.

"These are the houses, Ma. This is the iron mine. You are right where you thought you were going. So . . . now are you happy?" says Jake. He peers deeply into her eyes, hoping the answer is yes.

Marjatta frowns. She rummages in her satchel and pulls out her Bible. She takes the folded paper from between the pages. It is placed right in the third chapter of Proverbs. The paper has been unfolded so often that it is deeply perforated along the creases and threatens to fall apart utterly. Marjatta stares at the picture.

Jake goes on. "We have an opera house here, Mama! Over a thousand seats! We have a Carnegie library! With twenty thousand books!"

"But there are no roses here, Jaako!" Marjatta protests, staring at the unfolded paper, though it is beginning to register that he is speaking the truth.

"Actually, there are roses," he says, "but seldom in January. In fact, I cannot remember a single rose blooming in January." He laughs. "The people who lived here before us, the wife did grow roses." He does not tell Marjatta that the husband died in a mine accident and the wife and the children went back to her parents.

Marjatta rises from her seat, and, coatless, walks out the front door to the end of the walk. She holds the paper up and compares the drawing to the house. She shakes her head in disbelief. "This is the house!" she says. "On the paper, it looks bigger, Jaako."

"Advertising, Ma," Jake says.

"So I can stay?" Marjatta says. The request is plaintive. Jake looks into his mother's eyes and says, Yes, of course, Mama. Katey will not be thrilled, he knows this, but he is Marjatta's only surviving child. What can he say?

"Look behind you, Ma," he says. Marjatta turns. The curve of the street is created by a broad circular park that the houses surround. There are shoot-the-chutes for the miners' children and two swing sets. There is a small fountain, now covered with ice. This is paradise. "Yes, Ma, of course you can stay," Jake says.

And so Marjatta comes to live in Rovaniemi, Michigan, where just over half the population is Finnish, and everyone works for the Meridel-Pflaum mine in one capacity or another. Jake and Katey's baby is born, a girl named

Helen, and she is a fussy child. Marjatta is tireless in helping and bakes for the family three times a week. Katey's resistance erodes to ambivalence, and then the roses come out on the porch. Those roses—Katey tells Marjatta that they are called Rose of Finland—are a more brilliant red than they ever were in Marjatta's mind's eye.

Isak comes to visit once a month. Katey cannot understand this peculiar arrangement, but Jake says, "It's not ours to understand, honey. We just need to do what we can. Maybe it will be okay with Isak and Mama again."

When Isak comes, he talks more than he has ever talked. Marjatta listens. She thinks she may be falling in love with this man whom she married seventeen years ago. He continues to visit. He sleeps overnight on the foldout bed when he comes, as if he were someone's cousin.

Katey is pregnant again, and the baby this time is a boy. They name him Willis. The following year, a girl, Emmeline. Two years later, another girl, Martha. And then, five years later, the last child, August, who will grow up to be called Gus and who will father Garrett. Each month, Isak visits and sleeps on the foldout bed kept in the front bedroom closet. Marjatta is happier than she has been since she came to America.

Jake has indeed risen to be a supervisor, but Marjatta, with Katey's full backing, says, "No, you are not finished. We want you *out of the mine* every day."

Jake runs for county mining inspector, and at the age of twenty-nine he wins, over the middle-aged Cornishman who had held the position before him. To the Finns in the mine, it is a national triumph. To Marjatta, it is a triumph of a different sort: it is not a degree from a fine university, but it will get her son out of the mine all the time. He will be in an office and out of the dark tunnels. He will be doing a valuable job, making sure on his periodic brief trips underground that conditions are safe for the miners, inspecting equipment, the hoists, cages, skips, ladderways, making sure ventilation is adequate and fire hazards are absent. He is well loved by the men because he has been one of them now for more than ten years. The Finns in the mine, especially, are proud: he is one of theirs.

Isak says, the week after the election, not as if it had never occurred to him, but in a tone that seeks some resolution, "Marjatta, all these years has it been that you do not respect me because I work with my hands?"

She looks at him guiltily, stonily. Without realizing why, she remembers that silly camp, Camp Ambivalence, which had never had more than one house and where nobody wanted to live. She almost laughs, thinking she lives there now, in some sense. She says, "We are not talking about you, Isak. We are talking about Jaako."

"Good," he says. "But the boy's name is Jake."

"And the boy is a man," she corrects him.

It is a Wednesday in August. The roses are past their peak, and the ladies in the neighborhood who do canning—Katey is not one of them, but a "modern girl" who despite her five children still looks young—have put up their raspberry preserves as well as their peach and their strawberry jam. They have canned tomatoes and corn for the winter. In the Maki household, Marjatta does this. She hums while she works. She sends some of her canning home to the copper mine with Isak when he visits.

Katey dresses in "flapper"-length skirts and has worn her bright red hair bobbed since her third baby. Campaigning for Jake's election, handing out little cards that carry Jake's picture, she has been an asset. Everyone thinks of the beautiful red-haired wife of Jacob Maki as part of the package: she seems to embody resilience and possibility.

Jake has been county mining inspector now since last November. He knows his job. Everyone is pleased: the company, the county, the miners, the family. There have been no fatalities in this mine since the freak accident that took the life of George Comely, the previous inhabitant of the house on Ore Circle where Jake and Kathryn O'Doul Maki now live with their little ones.

The house is owned by the mining company, and as an elected official Jake is no longer an employee of Meridel-Pflaum, but the company makes an exception to allow the family to live here: they are so solidly established, and they have improved the house, and Jake just might be back working for the steel company, come next election.

The morning is all blue and gold. Jake has left for his office at the usual civilized hour. This is so different from the days he worked the mine. A neighbor, Mrs. Seabloom, from the far side of the circle, has brought the family several jars of watermelon pickle she has canned the previous week. Marjatta and Katey remark on the jewel-like look of the fruit in the jars. Marjatta holds one jar up to the light in the living-room window. "Ooh, it is like that stone in your ring, Katey, that ring Jaako gave you when you got engaged. What do you call that stone?"

"Hmm?" Katey says. She is distracted. She is pinning up a hem on a school dress she is making for Helen. The dress is an odd red plaid, printed with apples. Katey is proud of her skill at keeping the children well dressed on Jake's salary. She takes a half-dozen straight pins from between her lips and says, "What stone? What?"

"Your engagement ring, Katey," Marjatta says.

"Oh, that's a peridot. It's my birthstone."

"A beautiful green," says Marjatta.

Willis and Emmeline and Martha have made a train out of cardboard boxes from the grocery store and are playing railroad on the rag rug in the living room. Willis is wearing an old hat of Jake's, a hat that got a burn hole in it from someone's cigar during the campaign. He is tootling very loudly.

"My goodness, Willis!" says Marjatta, laughing. "You are a noisy little boy!"

"I'm not a little boy," Willis says. "I am a enginer."

"Engineer, Willis," Katey says.

"That's what I said," Willis insists.

"Thass not an enginer hat," protests Emmeline.

"Yeah, thass not a engine hat," parrots Martha, in the caboose.

"Yesterday you sayed it was a king hat," says Emmeline.

"It's every kind of hat I want, whatever," says Willis, his voice rising. "If I say it's a enginer hat it's a enginer hat."

"Could you please not quarrel?" says Katey cheerily. "Or save it for something more substantive?"

Outside in the street there is a bit of commotion. The windows are open, and everyone inside can hear a car door slamming, hard-soled shoes slapping the sidewalk, hurried voices. No one inside is paying much attention.

"Could we play the Vitola?" says Martha.

Katey corrects her. "Victrola," she says.

"Yep," says Martha. "Thass what."

Emmeline says, "Play the 'Ma' song, Mommy."

Mrs. Seabloom says, delighted, "That girl is so precious! Those curls! That little pout!"

Katey says, "You mean the making-eyes song?"

From down the street there is a strange sound, a wail, a keening. It sounds only half human. Katey stops a moment and registers it. It must be the new family's four-year-old boy, brain-damaged at birth and susceptible to strange fits of terror. The mother has told Katey, "We never know what will set him off, oh, my. Last week the lettuce on his plate. One time, a picture in a book, of a moose. We could not get him to stop." The keening continues.

The three children shout, in small voices, in unison. "Yep! Do it, Mommy!"

Katey sighs and rolls her eyes and puts on the record. She winds the machine. She steps into the dining room so they can see her. She does a vaudeville-style routine they love. She says to the neighbor. "They've seen this a million times. This is such an old song. But they love it." She thanks God for her blessings, that none of the children is like that poor little brain-damaged boy. The keening continues.

Marjatta says to the neighbor, "This is the song that made my Jaako go heels over head at Katey. She was singing this song at a Finnish Lutheran dinner the night that he met her."

"Well, hardly, Mama. This is not the kind of song you hear at the Finnish Lutheran Church. And I'm not Finnish Lutheran anyway."

Marjatta says, "Oh. Well. I guess not."

Nearby—is it the house next door?—a girl's voice yells urgently, "Mother! Mother! Come down here! Oh, hurry!" and then the front door slams heavily.

Katey begins to think something is wrong in the neighborhood. What could it be? She will go see when she finishes this.

"It was some kind of picnic," says Katey. The song starts up, and Katey sings and mugs along with it.

Ma, he's making eyes at me!
Ma, he's awful nice to me!
Ma, he's almost breaking my heart . . .

There is a knock at the door. Katey stops singing. The record on the Victrola keeps playing. Marjatta is clapping along, slightly behind the beat. The three in the cardboard-box train clap their hands in insistent protest. "Sing, Mommy! Sing!"

Katey goes to the door. It is a man from the mine office. He speaks in a low, urgent tone, and Katey looks over her shoulder at Marjatta, a look that says, clearly, something is terribly wrong. She wobbles her head strangely, as she continues to talk to the man, as if pointing, for Marjatta's benefit, first to the children, then everywhere else, outdoors, upstairs, anywhere. The message is clear: send the children away.

There is silence for a split second, and then on the Victrola a new song begins,

Toot, toot, Tootsie, good-bye,
Toot, toot, Tootsie, don't cry . . .

Martha and Emmeline, in unison, applaud and cheer, and Willis, the engineer, pantomimes pulling his train engine's whistle. They love this song. They're not sure what this means, about sadness and jail, but they sing it with gusto.

The choo-choo train that takes me
away from you, no words can tell how sad it makes me,
Kiss me, Tootsie, and then
Do it over again . . .

Katey says to Marjatta, her voice level but striving to beat out the Victrola, "Upstairs, Mama. Get them into their rooms." Marjatta's eyes are wide in response, her brow lifted in terror.

Willis says, "Wait till the train comes!"

The man on the Victrola sings,

> Watch for the mail, I'll never fail,
> If you don't get a letter, then you'll know I'm in jail . . .

Katey starts keening, doubling over as she stands, and the children freeze, still as statues. What could be wrong?

> Toot, toot, Tootsie, don't cry,
> Toot, toot, Tootsie, good-bye!

Willis shouts at his mother, his voice breaking into a squeak, "Don't *cry,* Mommy! The song says don't *cry!*"

In fact, Jake Maki, father of five, first-term mining inspector, has been dead for over an hour now, trapped with his assistant, a union rep, a foreman, a motor brakeman, and two apprentice mechanics, in a horizontal passage—a "rise"—off the main shaft, fifteen hundred feet down, the very bottom of the mine. Jake has been knocked mercifully unconscious by a falling beam, and then—how can death be so matter-of-fact?—suffocated and drowned in an avalanche of water and rock and mud that fills the passageways.

The men had been standing together at the foot of the main shaft conferring about the noise like an explosion that they just heard up above. Someone was blasting, and this was normal, but something sounded very wrong. Then there was silence. Suddenly all the lifts and carts and pneumatic drills were swept, bundled together like asparagus, as a reporter would note later, by a violent and irresistible wave of sand, water, rock, mud, and debris two hundred feet down the slight incline of the deepest raise.

Relatives wait around the shaft all night, huddled in their jackets against the cool night, even though it has been announced midway into the afternoon that there are no survivors. Everyone hopes that his or her husband or father is not really down there, that he has been taken ill somewhere else, like the district inspector whom Jake was replacing today, and they will show up after a good long nap. That will happen any time now. Any time.

Jake Maki's funeral, at the Finnish Lutheran Church in the heart of Rovaniemi, is attended by three hundred people. The dirt that the shovelers lift out of his waiting grave sits looking dark, damp, and rich, heaped around the rectangular hole. He has been well loved in the community.

There is a newspaper photograph in the August 15, 1926, Finnish-language gazette's report of the disaster that shows Katey, in an ill-fitting borrowed black dress in the hot August day, holding baby Gus up against her shoulder as she leaves the church, trailing Jake's casket. Her face is washed clean of her pain and her loss. Several people in the crowd who have just come for the show, from another town, gawking, rejoicing that this funeral is not their father's, their husband's, their own, remark that this red-haired young widow doesn't seem properly grief-stricken. There is a slight clucking of tongues.

Marjatta is not visible in that picture. She is behind Katey, holding Willis's right hand. Isak holds Willis's left hand. Tears stream down the faces of all three.

That night, at Katey's, when Katey is hard asleep, thrown down by the sleeping tablets that the doctor has given her, Isak sits up in the living room with the light on, reading a magazine. The light in Marjatta's room soon will be switched off, and he will retire. But Marjatta's light does not go off.

Isak rises and goes to her door and knocks. "Yes?" she says. "Isak?"

He enters and sits on the side of her bed. "Yes?" she says again.

"Nothing," he says.

"Correct. What can one say?" says Marjatta. "Death is death?"

And they both laugh until tears form up in their eyes and spill over. "May I sleep here tonight?" Isak says.

"What will the children say?" Marjatta says. The corners of her mouth turn down in an attempt not to start laughing again.

"Likely, they will say 'Good morning,'" Isak says.

And that is indeed what the children say, and Isak visits regularly for five more years, until he is injured in the mine and put on a pension. He comes to stay with Katey and Marjatta and the children, and he lives with Marjatta as her husband once again. There is no discussion about this long, strange time apart.

Twenty years after Jake Maki's death, Finland is released finally from the terrible territorial tug-of-war between the Axis and Allies, in which there is no position that can make the American Finn happy. The mother country, with a total population of four million, has lost eighty-two thousand soldiers in the war. Half a million in Finland have been made homeless, refugees, by the Second World War. Isak says over his coffee and newspaper, "Maybe now." Marjatta does not ask now what.

Contrary to what everyone expects—Isak has seemed so frail since his injury—Marjatta dies first, at sixty-nine. She has had several small strokes and has been confined to her bed for seven weeks. As the end nears, Isak holds her against him as if thinking to cheat death.

Marjatta whispers something into the shoulder seam of his shirt.

"What?" he says. "I can't hear you."

"Kiss," she says. Her eyes closed, she lifts her soft, puckered mouth up to his. He looks at the flesh of her neck as she strains: soft, like old velvet.

He is astonished. He kisses her. Her eyes are still closed.

"Oh, Emil," she says, each word filled with a breathy, deep longing, and then she lies back on her pillow and dies.

13   Ursula Again

O N THE ROAD suddenly there are cars and cars, and nowhere to park them. On the shoulder of the road, one after the next, is vehicle after vehicle. It is still light, and the line of cars and pickups and SUVs stretches back to the curve in the road. Who knows how much longer it goes on.

The county sheriff is here now, and he radios to the state police for backup. There are so few people living up here now—in contrast to the days of the copper boom, when Calumet had mansions and millionaires, and was under consideration for the site of the state capitol. Then, it had over a hundred bars; now, it has not much more than that number of houses. So the sheriff and the state police work together well, no competition or territorial issues. The sheriff and the deputy are working the road, but more cars keep coming.

The deputy grumbles, "Kibitzers and gawkers and news vultures." He ambles down the road suggesting nicely, sanguinely, to people that they all just go home. Mostly, they thank him and say they'll just stay a short time. He grumbles again. "There is going to be some real action here coming up soon and you don't want to get in the way," he says.

A woman who has driven up from Phoenix, a few miles inland, with a hot pan of corn bread—she thought it just might come in handy—says to the deputy, "Now *that* was dumb." He looks a question at her: Huh? She says, like the mother she is, "If you want to get rid of folks who came to gawk, don't go telling them action is coming up soon."

"Oh," says the deputy, who is a sweet, well-intentioned big-muscled young man with a broad freckled face and little time on the job. "I'm sure you're right, ma'am."

When there is an opening, the deputy sidles over to the sheriff and says, "In the manual it says . . ."

The sheriff gives the deputy a penetrating look and says patiently, "Cody, it's all nice and wonderful to have that handbook, guy, but things just don't develop the way the book wants you to think." Cody wrinkles his nose in dismay, like a kid. The sheriff says, "You remember in training I said that at least sixteen times?" Cody just stares at him.

"But aren't we supposed to put up the yellow tape first?" he asks.

The sheriff says, "We're keeping these folks off the site for now, and someone will bring the tape later." They have put up a traffic barrier and parked two cars across the entrance. The look of perplexity on the young deputy's face makes the sheriff smile, but he tries to repress it. "I got to say one thing," says the sheriff. "These people are going to start to be a hazard to their own selves in no time at all, and I'm not in the mood to be baby-sitting this kind of stuff." There is a festive look on the faces of some of them. *Ghouls,* the sheriff thinks to himself.

He is remembering a call the week before, in which a man who had been drinking fell down somewhere near the railroad tracks, in an area where there had been mining years before, and there were rubble piles. The wife, who was almost as drunk, had called the sheriff from a nearby house well off the road—amazing, he thought at the time, that she could find the house, the state she was in—and when the sheriff got there, the man had disappeared from where he was. The couple from the house came down with flickering, dim two-cell flashlights and wandered around, and the sheriff started thinking, *Oh, Lord, oh, Lord.* The fire department in the next town—volunteer—had just come back from a call, a small fire easily put out—and fifteen guys there all full of energy came out to search the area, but these two-cell flashlight folk didn't want to go home. So the fifteen got added to the two, plus the sheriff, all clunking around in the dark, and the wife of the man who was lost sat on a stump crying drunk. And then the guy turned up asleep in a friend's house a mile away, and the sheriff got to thinking about all his youthful heroic dreams, him with a dazzling star on his chest like in some old Western. Aw, foo, he says, almost out loud.

The sheriff remembers the slag piles, the crying wife smelling like beer, and the flashlight beams slithering wormlike in the dark. He sees the lights of more cars moving toward the site of the accident shining on the road around the bend, then the lights go off as they park. *Damn,* he thinks, and that's all he can think. He can't think about that little girl down the hole.

He remembers the time thirty years ago—he had his own kids still little then—when that Lorelei Wolf kid fell down an abandoned mine shaft, south in Houghton County. It was in the sixties, before the regulatory push to get all of those shafts capped. *Lord,* he thinks, *terrible.* All of it comes back. And then he remembers a thing that makes him shudder inside. He thinks, *She was a half-breed too.* He makes himself urp sometimes when he catches himself. He had thought he'd grown out of that stuff.

Lorelei Wolf was the seven-year-old daughter of a Chippewa gal who worked as a janitor at the college, and who *knew* who the dad was? The talk was that whoever had gotten her pregnant was the son of somebody important—whatever important meant in a place like this, off the beaten track of the world—maybe somebody in town whose folks owned a business, maybe some professor at the college.

The talk was that the Indian gal, Lilah Wolf, had been paid off to keep her mouth shut. That didn't make a whole lot of sense, really, because she had to keep working pushing a mop on the night shift, the whole pregnancy, and then the whole time that the girl was little. Paid off indeed. The talk among regular white folks was that the mom had neglected her—must have, because how else could the child have fallen down a shaft? People wanted to think what they wanted to think, and the truth didn't matter much.

The truth, as the sheriff had been able to see for himself later, was that the mom was a fierce little gal, determined to hold up her head even though the guy—somebody pale and maybe redheaded, if you looked at the kid—had abandoned her. She had been really protective, and the day that the little girl fell down the shaft the mom was right there, just as Justin and Annie had been. LilahWolf had been baby-sitting somebody else's kid too, a boy, and the three of them were just out on a picnic. Same as the Wongs. Just too much the same for the sheriff's comfort. The sheriff thought: *I don't want to follow this thing through to its conclusion.* Lorelei Wolf had not been recovered, and Lilah Wolf had grieved her whole life and then died young. The shaft down which Lorelei Wolf had fallen had been capped, and Lilah Wolf's ashes were interred there too, with a bronze marker. The boy who was with Lilah and Lorelei Wolf that day is here tonight among the crowd, scared shitless for little Ursula down that hole. He works at the gas station the sheriff uses, but the subject of Lorelei Wolf has never come up between them. Just "Fill 'er up?" and a nod and a random remark, back and forth, about weather or sports.

Near that shaft—not a hundred yards away as the crow flies—through the trees was another shaft, same size. Say fourteen feet across, typical of the bigger ones: they had two, three chambers, one for the man cars, one for the ore, and he couldn't remember what the other compartment was for. But then they all weren't the same anyway.

That other shaft, the one they called Briar Rose, that was the one gave him the *real* heebie-jeebies. You wondered who was running things. The mining company had thrown ten or twelve cars—right, just regular old junk heaps of *automobiles*—down that one years ago, and a lot of mine tailings and who knew what else. One of the cars—an Oldsmobile—was poking up out of the mouth of the shaft, like a dead whale, just the grille and front wheels.

The sheriff had moved here from downstate no more than a dozen years ago, and this was a mystery to him. First time he saw this one, he thought it was the Lorelei Wolf shaft: he thought, *Oh God, no, the kid's down at the bottom of that hole and they're throwing the garbage in on her?* But this was the wrong shaft. At the real shaft was a bronze plaque her mother had put there, with a verse on it about her being an angel who flew into her life and then flew out. There were plastic flowers poked through the holes in the chain-link fence. Overbright pink and blue roses and a Barbie doll wired by its waist to the chain-link, wearing a wilted bride's dress. He wondered who'd put them there.

The sheriff thinks: *I've got to stop thinking about that Wolf kid.* But then he cannot think about Ursula either.

The sheriff says to his deputy, "Look, you go stand over there and look firm, kid. Feet apart, eyes like a soldier." Cody just stares at him. "Yeah, like that," says the sheriff, joking and then again not. "Zone out. Just stand like a zombie."

So Cody says, "Right, I can do this." He stands like a soldier, like a zombie.

On the road, the lights keep coming, and here comes a family of five, with their tent, setting it up in the woods across the road, and there come a couple of reporters from Minneapolis in a van, and now, in a white Navigator, the news crew from Fox, and the sheriff is swearing under his breath. There are more lights on the road, and then a helicopter, with its blades—*thuck-a thuck-a thuck-a*—reminding the sheriff of his time in Vietnam, and his throat closes up and for a split second as he walks away to the row of blue Porta Potti stalls that have been set up, and no one can see him, he starts bawling—silently, but a flood—for no reason that he can discern.

THE CREW FROM Fox is on Swede Maguire now, like blackflies. What does he think this shaft was, what was it connected to, or from, or what. "I will talk when you turn that equipment off," he says. Swede is tempted to swear every time he opens his mouth. He draws them a diagram on the back of an envelope. "Here, to the right, we've got the Keweenaw Fault, inland. Here at a thirty-two-degree angle, you see the lava flows, heading downward toward the lake. The earth shifted," he said.

He is thinking in millions and billions of years, and these people are thinking in sound bites. One of the Fox crew is remembering Gary Cooper and Ingrid Bergman in *For Whom the Bell Tolls,* in the moonlight, and he can't figure out why. The moon is beginning to rise now.

The state roads contractor has got the huge lights, which crews are unfolding like giant toy Transformers, to illuminate the area. The grass of the clearing is low, kept short by the cinders left there when the boiler house of the mine was taken down. The trees around have grown tall and thick, but the lights will make the area bright as day.

Someone from one of the networks is nattering at Swede Maguire again, and he is willing enough to talk, when their pesky equipment is off. They have him repeat what he says for the camera afterward, but Swede wants *no more surprises* here and tells them so firmly. Suffering fools gladly is not his strong suit. He is talking now about a man named George Trevelyan.

Trevelyan, he says, came here in the 1850s after inheriting his father's fortune, made from mining, and bought up the land on which this shaft has suddenly shown itself. Trevelyan, he says, was a quick one, not only born to money but ruthless in getting more, with an iron fist of control over his employees. Trevelyan's actress-wife, Corisande, who was not pleased with this venture, would have preferred to stay in Cornwall.

In the sixties, right after the Civil War, says Swede, at which time the mine had had an incredible boom in production—the Union forces needed copper for everything—Corisande apparently became involved with a foreman, a "swarthy Eye-talian," says Swede Maguire, burlesqueing the pronunciation of the day.

"That's the way they wrote about it," he says. "Swarthy. He's always called swarthy. Somebody has got to be low man on the totem pole and, you know, a lot of the time it's about color. So this 'swarthy Eye-talian' determined to do in Trevelyan, apparently . . . but soon enough the Italian was found murdered down near the harbor, clubbed to death, and Trevelyan boasted that no one dared try to best him again.

"But he was wrong. On a trip back east, New York State, Trevelyan was on a passenger train in the 1870s. Someone pulled the emergency chain, and the brakeman hit the brakes. Trevelyan was shaving, the story went, and his throat was slit, one side to the other. Except that no one believed for a minute that it was an accident, and a man was seen jumping from Trevelyan's car and running off into the forest. No one followed up." Swede clears his throat. He feels as if he wants to spit and swear and say things about the laziness and shifty motives of people with dollar signs in their eyes, but he says nothing, just blinks and goes on.

"After which the mine fell into other hands. Very shifty transaction it seemed, lawyers being lawyers. So what's new. In the fashion of the day it was renamed after an Indian tribe, the Sac Indians, way south and west into Iowa and Illinois. Lots of mines in those days took on Indian names, kind of 'romantic,' you know, the way a gal will name a panty boutique something French. We thought Indians were pretty romantic, while we were taking their lands and giving them smallpox and all that. So this mine became the Sac-Trevelyan. There are a dozen shafts we already knew about, and this system extends"—he sweeps his arm in the direction of the depths of the forest—"maybe a mile in that direction, a half mile that way." He points to the left. "You people can take a little ride afterward if you like, through some of these old mining roads in the forest—they just look like hiking paths now, snowmobile paths, and nobody ever asks, 'How did this get here?' This shaft would have had to be an early aborted attempt—or maybe an air shaft—we'll see about details later. After we get *this* done." And there is Swede Maguire again, spraying up dry conversational snow, at the end of one of his wild slaloms of exposition.

The reporter is stunned, standing holding his mike in the geologist's face. He blinks his eyes and repeats the name, as if simply having a label and a possible history for this hole in the ground has given the matter a new and more sober reality. "Sac-Trevelyan, you say?"

AND SUDDENLY THE crew from Traverse City arrives, two huge bright red vehicles, one pulling a trailer. It is technically sunset, eight forty-five, but it will stay light, a luminous purple sky, for two more hours. Traverse City is the closest team for Michigan Urban Search and Rescue. It has taken them six hours on the road, after an hour and a half getting the team and equipment together.

Justin's call has come in to 911 at noon; the dispatcher calls MUSAR and MUSAR calls back to confirm. She is ready to scream, but she knows the drill: if they don't call back, they don't know if the call is for real. The advantage in this team, as far away as they are, is that these people have trained for hundreds and thousands of hours for this and are a real model of teamwork. Moreover, they have *jurisdiction*.

Downstate, the teams from Ann Arbor and Pontiac are coming ahead as backup, planning a rendezvous at I-75, and then a caravan north. It will take them a few hours longer to get here. It all seems absurd, but they have skills that nobody else has. In both the lead team and the backup there is a sober concentration along with the usual pumping adrenaline: ask any one of them and they will tell you, no, they aren't daredevils, but they're adrenaline junkies, no question. In the minds of each of them is a photo of Ursula that someone scanned into the computer and e-mailed to their stations. In the picture she is mugging, on her second birthday, in her purple coat out in the snow in the yard behind Mindy Ji's little shingled house.

Yolanda Torres, the team doctor from Traverse, is knitting in the dark as they drive, "in Braille," she says, when the guys razz her. It's her way of handling the edginess. She is knitting an afghan for her grandmother, who speaks very little English, though she knows enough to get by at the grocery. Yolanda's father came to Traverse City as a migrant worker in the sixties for the cherry harvest and just stayed.

Yolanda is not too much older than Justin and Annie; she is engaged to a teacher of junior-high science who knows he is sterile because of mumps, and she is sad thinking she may never have a child. The face of that little girl out in the snow—such dark eyes, such a bright smile—hover before her in the dark of the red Suburban speeding through the night.

THE 911 DISPATCHER from the afternoon is off-duty now, but she has come back with her two oldest teenaged kids, wearing a sweatshirt and daisy-printed capris. She has her hands wrapped around a huge plastic mug of coffee, warming them. "The official incident commander got here maybe two hours ago," she tells the driver of the first vehicle, a career firefighter. "He flew in from Grand Blanc, way downstate. He's set up a command post in the lounge and they're putting the media in the tabernacle."

"Say what?" says the driver. *The media in the tabernacle?*

"That's a big meeting hall down at the camp."

"At the camp?"

"Gitche Gumee Bible Camp, about half a mile down M-26."

"Oh, jeez," says the firefighter. "I think I might ralph." He has a deep aversion to anything church connected, going back to childhood and a pastor with clammy hands and denture breath. No more, just that.

"Set up your stuff here and then go confab with the Grand Blanc guy." The dispatcher indicates the site with a grand sweep of her hand.

"I don't know about this guy," she says. "I hear they call him Lightning. This is the *slowest* thing I ever saw in my life, like being trapped in amber. Dear God, that poor little baby girl." She cannot imagine any realistic possibility that the child is still alive, and yet she keeps hoping. She is as invested as if this were her own kid.

THREE CREW MEMBERS start unloading equipment, and three head toward the shaft to take bearings. They are wearing getups that look like kids' action figures, thinks the dispatcher-mom. On their backs big square letters say TECHNICAL RESCUE TEAM. She thinks, *This makes the toy-ish effect* way *worse.* They are carrying all sorts of bulky equipment. The lighting towers are up now all the way. Someone flips a switch and the whole area dazzles bright as day. Out at the road, the spectators roar their approval, as if this were a soccer match ready to start.

The sheriff and his deputy have been reinforced by officers from the state police and from inland. Still, there is a feel of dangerous disorder here, not least in the coffee-buzzing head of Cody the deputy, who stands at the road, still on duty and wired, as if he fears the crowd might charge the site en masse.

He doesn't know any of these guys who've just gotten here from Traverse, but last year his friend Brian there had been out to keep order during the cherry festival, and all kinds of drunk guys were grabbing their equipment. Brian had had to get up in some faces. Cody is hoping that won't happen tonight. He doesn't like to deal with that stuff. The sheriff calls Cody "Barney" when he gets too far off to the wimp end, and that would be Barney of Mayberry.

Two of the Traverse City crew stay at the top of the shaft and begin organizing help among the locals who have been champing at the bit. They drop a line to check the depth of the shaft again, and again the line drops only twenty feet, then hits solid ground. There is no way of knowing yet whether the shaft simply angles off, or drops off, or connects with a horizontal shaft and continues on.

If the shaft does not stop dead, the prospect of danger lies not only in the fall but in the fact that when a mine is closed down, pumping ceases, and the hole—the vertical shaft, the tunnels, all of it—fills up with water. Few up above know this, and like Annie they are picturing an Alice in Wonderland sort of fall, down, and down, and down, buoyed as if by wings. Most

mines will fill nearly to the top with water, maybe a hundred-foot fall to the
waterline, which alone could have killed Ursula.

Swede Maguire is asleep on the front seat of his Jeep. The guy from Traverse City goes to rouse him. "Look," the Traverse guy says, puzzled. "Why
do you figure the plumb line *stops* at twenty feet? Is there something special about twenty feet that a shaft would take a jag in another direction?"

"Yeah, well, if bedrock is special," says Maguire. "That's about where you
hit bedrock. Might be another shaft off at an angle, yes. Very likely."

The guy heads back to the rescue team's vehicles and says, "Look, we're
going to need plywood." The dispatcher—who is only an observer but is in
this as much as anyone, and somehow they have let her inside the "warm"
zone, the intermediate zone where outsiders can't be—stares at him in disbelief. Does he think he's in civilization?

"Where's the nearest construction site where we could get, say, fourteen
four-by-eight sheets of plywood?"

"Say what?"

"We can't do *anything* in that shaft—not even exploratory—until we
shore up the soil there, with plywood and struts, good and solid. We've got
exactly *six*, which is what we carry with us. My calculator says we need
twenty. So where's a construction site?"

She is stumped for a second. Then she says, "Not far from where I live,
about ten miles. They're building a restaurant. I know the guy who owns the
construction company. He's my brother Roy's wife's uncle. I could get my
brother to get him for you."

"Okay," he says. "Call him and get him to do that *now*. But I've got to
have firsthand confirmation—meaning *I* have to speak to this guy—and
I've got to get one of *my* men there to pick it up."

She can see this is a matter of procedure, and she is seeing how critical is
every step. An unknown brother—not Roy, though, because Roy is as de-
pendable as sunrise—could fall back asleep, and the whole team be waiting
for nothing, and Ursula trapped in the dark, forever. Okay, she says, and she
takes one of the team and drives down to the command center at the camp
to use the phone.

The incident commander, set up in a tin-roofed former director's cabin just inside the front gate of Camp Gitche Gumee, is Matt Leitinen. Of all the half-dozen possible commanders who could have been sent, he has been sent because this is his home territory. He is a UP-er, born and bred: a Finn, moreover. He has a different kind of commitment here, no more really than if the child were not a Finn, but then again it feels as if she's family. He is neither fast nor slow: the name "Lightnin'" that everyone seems to hear is only Leitinen. He is methodical, has all his nerve ends up, and besides being able to see through lead, he says, he can leap tall buildings at a single bound. Naw, he says then with a big grin, when he tells this to people, a standard riff. Just wanted to see if you were awake there.

Roy and the guy from Traverse make arrangements, and the dispatcher is thinking, with a sense that her throat will close up, that this is taking an eternity. *Be okay, little one,* she says, deep inside her. *Just please be okay.*

BACK AT THE camp chapel, a building of logs with a tiny rose window at one end—far less elaborate than the one in René Josserand's family chapel in France—set deep in tall pine trees—the crew of counselors is singing hymns along with a CD player, praying for Ursula. "Thrice praying!" enthuses the energetic team leader, a ruddy, cheerful man in a sweatshirt that says NEXT YEAR IN JERUSALEM. The counselors are training for next week's descent upon the camp of fifty-plus grade-school boys and girls in Gitche Gumee T-shirts and bearing fat duffel bags.

The sound of the counselors' singing is eerie and pure in the plum-colored twilight. The fragrance of the forest is nearly identical to the smell of the trees outside the village of the sled dogs, when Kyllikki stood in the moonlight so long ago, praying to her spirits: identical, that is, except for the smell of camp lasagna that wafts from the mess hall when the wind shifts.

The crew at the shaft have set up what they call a "mechanical advantage system." The high point for leverage is provided by the boom of an emergency vehicle from Traverse City. The power and sensitivity will be provided by humans, in a finely tuned choreography of pulleying and belaying. The incident commander is busy explaining this to a press liaison down at the command center. Machines can't respond to a tug or a slackness the way human beings can, so the ropes will be always in the hands of real people. *Amazing,* the liaison thinks: *you'd think machines could do* anything *better than people.*

WHEN THE SHERIFF gets back to the clearing he can hear harmonica music coming out of the RV, whose door stands ajar for fresh air. Mindy Ji has brought Justin a couple of his harmonicas, ones he doesn't use for gigs. The song Justin is playing jerks at the sheriff's heart. He has no idea what it is. It is the theme from the French film that Annie likes. In the movie, the little blonde shepherdess's mom is an opera singer, and that's how this happens to be from Verdi, "La Forza del Destino."

It's *so* very sad that the sheriff is wondering how he can do that, how he can play that. But then, he thinks, what is he going to play, "Bluetailed Fly," "Riders on the Storm?" There is no right program music for a mine shaft rescue. At the rescue attempt at the Meridel-Pflaum mine in 1926, he had heard some Greek guy played a violin while they were waiting. Now he understood. You have to *do* something.

MINDY JI IS kneeling in the sleeping compartment of the RV. Kneeling is something she rarely does when she prays. She is reading the Letter to the Hebrews, on her knees. It is the mystery of it all. She is hovering like a hummingbird, trying not to land on the branch of fear that keeps beckoning. She reads about people who "went about in goatskins and sheepskins, destitute and persecuted and mistreated . . . the world was not worthy of them."

She whispers there at the edge of the sheriff's musty-blanketed camp bed, "Dear God, Jus and Annie have only this *one* little one. Don't take her away." That is all she can think to say.

She moves on to the next chapter. It begins, "Therefore, since we are surrounded by such a cloud of witnesses . . . ," and her mind leaps to that. She imagines a great "cloud of witnesses" like the crowd at an athletic event, a gigantic bleachers full of —who are these?—ancestors? She really cannot see clearly, but they feel like ancestors, and the Chinese blood in her rises up and petitions the ancestors too, "Dear ancestors, preserve this child. She is all you have to carry on your line. Do what you need to."

She breathes in, and the nasty-wool smell of the sheriff's bed, and the old melted-cheese smell of his microwave, and even the smell of some guy who keeps coming in and out of the next room smoking a cigarette, and nobody wants to chide, as if everything here were incredibly fragile—all these meld together in a tissue of hope, suddenly. Life is persistent. *Ursula will live.*

Mindy Ji blinks at the clarity of that. Her grandchild has been down the hole now for many hours: she could be dead that long. A voice says in her head: *She lives.* Mindy Ji argues, "Dear God, don't be yanking my chain like that, if it's not true." The silent voice says it again: *Ursula is alive.* Mindy Ji says out loud then to herself, "Okay, excellent." Her inflection sounds a lot like Justin's. This is the way Justin talks. In the next room, Justin is playing some old hymn he learned to please Mindy Ji, quietly, and Annie is crying into a wad of paper towels.

"She's alive," Mindy Ji announces.

"What did they tell you, Ma?" Justin says, leaping to his feet.

"They?" Mindy Ji echoes. "They, nothing. I just know it."

"Oh, *crap*," Justin roars, "that's just crazy. That's *cruel*, Ma."

Annie says quietly, "Justin, if I recall, it was *you* who said to me, how many minutes after the event, 'Would God just let her go like this?'"

Justin says, "I said *that?*"

"You did," Annie says. Annie looks down at the cover of a *People* magazine on the prickly plaid sofa. There is a young woman, a starlet of sorts, with a look about her that is not unlike Ursula's look—Eurasian, exotic, but now, in this new world, becoming the look of the future. Annie does not want Ursula on the cover of *People* magazine, for sure—not a starlet, with all of that dazzle and trouble and confusion about who she is, and what the world is about—but it's interesting to see that face, so like hers, that when Annie was a child was so very unusual. This is the kind of face that is all over the fashion pages of the *New York Times,* the sloe eyes, the almond complexion, the hair of every hue of the rainbow, the meeting of East and West.

• • •

PEOPLE HAVE BEEN sneaking from the road through the trees all evening to catch a glimpse, some taking snapshots of the site with their instant cameras in the dark. The snapshots of course will not come out: the dark is pretty dark, and the little flash pops are good only for eight or ten feet. What are they taking pictures of? Cody, the deputy standing guard, a clear space of thin grass shot with gravel. A couple of cars parked "all cattywampus," as the sheriff says. Nothing to see at all. Another instant-camera flash pops from somewhere in the trees and Cody calls out, almost petulant, "Aw, jeez. Give us a break here, folks."

Down on the road, a very elderly woman who was friends with Toby Root's grandmother when she was alive has come with her children and grandchildren to sit vigil. She was born in Austria, a gypsy, and escaped before Hitler took over. She learned to play accordion in childhood, and she has brought her accordion with her tonight. Her grandson's RV is parked just off the road, and he has hung up loopy jewel-colored Japanese lanterns, the ones they use when they go camping on vacation. Her great-grandchildren are asleep in the camper, but her children and grandchildren are sitting vigil with her, in the dark by the roadside. Rumors pass along through the crowd every now and again, but no news has come for a long while. The old gypsy woman is playing a dark, pained, but somehow oddly festive song there beneath a pine tree next to the road, sitting in a folding chair. Its key is minor, its cadence adagio, its melody repetitive but also wandering.

All who are listening find themselves seeing visions in their minds' eyes: sad things, dark things, ancient dances, and festivals. Is this rescue attempt a festival? Somehow the old lady thinks if she plays she will turn it into one. She is remembering her oldest son who died in Vietnam, whose son then lost an eye and a hand in Bosnia; she is remembering herself standing in the doorway when her middle son's youngest boy wanted to enlist to go to the Persian Gulf; she remembers herself crying with her head in her apron when her neighbor's grandson died two months ago in Iraq.

"Shock and awe," she said aloud at the time to the TV news. "Shock and awe. I give you shock and awe." So she plays her accordion, thinking it will —like a Hindu fakir's flute raising a cobra—raise Ursula from that grave.

Her mind shuts down when she tries to will the whole Middle East to peace and to healing, but she can at ninety-six play her accordion, even if stumblingly, to bring this little girl out of the ground.

It is almost midnight before all of the panels have arrived and the struts and the pumps to inflate the struts—they are pumping petroleum into them, grief—are prepared. Suddenly, as if in a dance, a half-dozen emergency workers wearing blue suits and complex harness systems form up around the hole.

They begin carefully lowering a hundred-pound sheet of double-thick plywood, with struts nailed across it. The panel hits the bottom of the hole and they let down one of their own number, reeling out purple-and-blue argyle rope that looks for all the world, in this fierce artificial light, like a silly toy snake. The man does not touch the sides of the shaft: there is no reason to trust them. He reaches the floor of the shaft and calls up for silence.

This is the first moment anyone has seen clearly what is down there: a shaft, eight feet high, eight feet wide, angling down into the earth at the slope of the copper ore body, about thirty degrees, angling off into the dark.

The noise continues: blower engine, truck engines, radio equipment. Roar, rattle, static, not to mention the noise of the road out there, and the kibitzers lining the shoulder. He calls up again: "Total silence, I need total silence." The engines cut out. The truck engine is turned off. The radio static ceases. The man at the bottom of the hole powers up the small three-pound black electronic box that he carries, a "life detector," seismic, acoustic, equipped to detect any slightest movement or sound.

This is the very same type of detector that was used at the collapse of the World Trade Center, to search for survivors in the rubble: Brandi Chandler-Greene would love it, but she is dead asleep now in the curve of a bunk in a campers' cabin down at Gitche Gumee, wearing camp logo sweats and covered by a prickly wool blanket. Her chic on-screen suit hangs across a folding chair, forlorn.

The detector hears nothing. The man with the machine sighs. He knows that does not mean nothing's there. If the little girl is at too great a distance, there will be nothing to hear. If she is unconscious, there may be no movement to hear, though breathing should be detectable if they are close enough. But he hears nothing.

He calls up to the crew on the ground, and he tells them to start up the engines again. The edge man relays the news and the order, and the noise starts up again. A second man is lowered, with six men up top fanned out into position: ropes, carabiners, elaborate pulleys, and all of the forces of muscle and gravity. The news that the life detector hears no noise is passed to no one but Matt Leitinen, down at the camp command post. They are not telling this to the parents, and certainly not to the public.

It is almost two before the panels are all in place. It all seems so ridiculous. The two-member rescue team has been champing at the bit, doing breathing exercises, meditating—Jack Bostian is Buddhist, Edie Faber does yoga—all this time. Finally the shaft is prepared and they are ready to descend.

Jack is an engineer with amateur weight-lifting credentials, Edie was a gymnast in high school and college and has yet to hit 110 soaking wet.

The team on the ground has to set up their mechanical advantage system, stabilization and leverage: they have decided on a tripod, balanced on timbers. This takes another half hour. Justin walks off into the forest as far as he can go in the dark and still find his way back, pisses wildly into the dark, roaring incoherent curses into the night just as loud as he can, zips his pants, wipes his eyes with his sleeve—there are tears—and saunters back out into the light.

At 2:37 the team begins their descent. It has been fourteen and a half hours now since Ursula disappeared down the hole. The deer after which she ran wanders nearby in the forest, wondering what all the noise is about, and all this odor of humans.

As Edie and Jack are descending, the team from Ann Arbor and Pontiac are finally pulling their vehicles in from the road, which has quieted down in the dark. These additional search-and-rescue people are superfluous at present but there is no guessing what might come next: the sloping shaft may very well lead to an internal vertical shaft down which Ursula may have fallen, and that is the worst-case scenario anyone can conceive.

The iron mine shaft down which Ursula's great-great-grandfather Jake

Maki descended was fifteen hundred feet deep, but many copper mine shafts out here in the Keweenaw plunge far deeper. At one point in this, Justin in all of his swearing at everything has cursed gravity itself: he wants Ursula to be able to float up to them, as if they were on the moon.

It takes a quarter hour to get the pair down the shaft. Matt Leitinen is in constant voice contact now, but all of the media people are on virtual news blackout except for brief blips.

The decision as to who will rappel down the second shaft has been easy: Edie, the lightest and most agile, will go. She has done urban search and rescue—collapsed buildings and construction-site trenches—and knows her stuff. She is also certified as a paramedic.

She gets only a few feet into the second shaft—hooked to Jack on the flat of the floor of the first shaft by a carabiner at her waist harness—before her flashlight shows her the next obstacle: blocking the passageway is all the rotted-out cribbing that has tumbled down from the vertical shaft and gotten stuck. It has to be secured before any progress can be made: any movement might dislodge the heavy timbers and send them rolling downhill to kill the little girl, if she is still alive. The pile of punky wood hangs to the right of the shaft; there certainly is more than enough space for Ursula to have fallen or rolled past on the left.

Edie calls up for the roll of chocolate brown Tensor fabric they have in the truck: a geo-textile, as they put it, incredibly strong and flexible. She will, as if she were not this tiny woman but rather a giant, tie off this huge pile of punky wood, that could fall apart if she breathes too hard. She will bundle it up as if it were a Christmas present. Insane, if anyone were to consider it; still, she will do it. She focuses on the wood to be tied back, but all she can see in her mind's eye is that little girl. *Please let her be just past this junk, and all right.*

Back at the command post at Camp Gitche Gumee, the director's wife is bringing cocoa to Matt Leitinen, and Matt Leitinen starts communication on what Edie and Jack are doing—the part about the Tensor fabric anyway—to the press, who want news news news any news, something to glom onto for a while.

Not all of the media people are still awake. The networks are playing old footage from yesterday, Brandi and Stanislaus, Swede Maguire, the elderly Eagle Harbor woman from whose living room Justin phoned 911.

Matt Leitinen is directing the moves of the various teams from the cabin where he has been set up. No one can do a thing without his instruction or permission. He has procured and had dropped to Edie the miraculously strong fabric, a huge bolt of it, and then a cordless drill and rock anchors.

Patiently, lightly as a small spider spinning her web, she crawls—trying to be weightless, holding her anal sphincter up high, breathing shallowly—up around the back of the woodpile. She drills half a dozen holes into the rock above the blockage and another half dozen into the floor of the passageway. The floor is wet from the earth's natural moisture, but in the darkness no moss grows to cause her to slip. She works at the bundle for a full half hour. "How you doing there, Edie?" says Matt Leitinen every few minutes. She's doing fine, thanks. She drills, she ties off. She drills, she ties off. "Doing good, Edie," Jack says. "You bet," she says. She is trying not to think what time it is.

The vibration of the drill is so minor—it is not after all a jackhammer—but Edie holds her breath as she drills, *willing* the rubble to stay in place. It is recalcitrant, and the pile seems to sigh every now and again, threatening to let loose. It is 3:40 A.M. by the time she has every rock anchor in place and the debris wrapped like a package. It will not come loose now.

She signals Jack Bostian and Matt Leitinen, and she moves carefully down the slope, setting each foot on the slippery rock with great care. She is anchored from above, but she cannot lose even a second on clumsiness. She shines her flashlight in front of her. The beam slithers around the walls and ceiling and suddenly down low there is a fluorescent red flash in her eye.

It is the safety chevrons on Ursula's purple coat, like geese flying in formation to safety, the little glued-on flashes to keep her safe in the dark . . . *What dark*, Justin had never been sure when Annie insisted on attaching them—Ursula has had someone with her every second, always, her whole life.

Edie calls out, "Ursula?" and Ursula's voice comes back, weak as a kitten's mew, "Mommy!" Edie's voice does not resemble Annie's. Ursula says firmly now, "I want Mommy."

Her voice starts to break. She has been mercifully unconscious until a few minutes before, when the sound of the drill brought her into consciousness. This is a concussion that doctors, despite all these hours of unconsciousness, the equivalent of a long night's sleep, term "minor."

Edie can see the child now. She is caught like a little bug in a webwork of debris just a few feet short of the point to which the water has risen. Edie can see the gleam of the water, not six feet down the shaft behind Ursula. Ursula is held firmly in place, in fact trapped, caught firmly, imprisoned, by the clanking decorative silver D-rings that Annie had said were so silly when Ursula saw the coat in the store and began clapping her hands in delight.

A hundred feet below her in the downsloping passageway there is indeed the vertical tunnel that was Swede Maguire's imagined worst-case scenario, an internal shaft that did not reach the surface and that surely would have been the immediate end of Ursula.

But before this diagonal downward shaft intersects with that one, just fifty feet beyond this blockage, water has risen to fill the mine, and it is impossible to imagine a good end if Ursula had fallen even a few feet farther. Drowning, surely, likely with no recovery of her body even possible.

But they will get her now. Surely they will.

Edie calls up to Jack Bostian to send down the mike so that she can feed it out on its cord to where Ursula is trapped. "Get the mom," she says. "I can see the little girl. She's alive and she's calling for the mom."

Matt Leitinen calculates whether to tell the press yet and if so, what to say. Judgement call, that's his business, eh, he will tell someone afterward. He purses his lips and peers into his half empty cup with the brown cocoa residue on its sides. He tells the press, "Edie Faber has made visual contact with the little girl and she's alive. Hold onto that for a sec, and I'll give you some more pretty quick here."

Talking to the mom will keep Ursula calm, Edie thinks, while these last stages are gotten through. Edie feels her own throat and chest tight with the tension. She does conscious relaxation yoga breathing. She listens to her own breath to quell her excitement and fear: her own little-girl trick.

It is five minutes before the mike comes down, and Edie stays very still, talking to Ursula in low tones about comforting things: her room at home, the fact that her mom and dad are up there waiting, that there are a lot of people working to get her out, and they will.

"Just stay still," Edie says. "Can you do that? Don't wiggle?"

"I want Mommy," says Ursula.

"She'll be here in a minute," says Edie. "Do you have a doggie at home?"

Ursula makes a small shriek. No, she does not have a dog, she is down this dark hole and she wants out.

"Get my daddy," says Ursula.

"Your mommy and daddy are coming," says Edie. "And your grandma too, I think."

"Grandma Mindy?" says Ursula.

"I guess," says Edie. "If that's her name." *Get me that mike,* she thinks.

"My head has a owie," says Ursula.

Edie says, "You just had a bump. It will be okay." She has no idea how serious this is. She's speaking this rescue into being, second by second.

"My arm hurts," says Ursula. It will turn out to be broken, and she will wear a cast for the rest of the summer. She will lose LEGOs down the cast, and a plastic picnic fork, trying to scratch herself. When the pediatrician removes the cast, they will all laugh so hard in the examining room that they feel near hysteria. It is simply relief, which will never end, Ursula's whole life.

The mike is dropped to Jack Bostian, who feeds it down to Edie. Edie tests it. Who's there? Nobody, yet. It's 4 A.M.

Edie will wait till the mother is there and then keep the little girl talking to her while Edie ties off the second pile, which should be simpler. This pile comprises a couple of huge timbers, which seem to be wedged firmly into the crevice where the wall of the shaft meets its floor, and splintered pieces several feet long braced by those huge timbers.

Edie calls up to Jack: "I can do this one with the rope I've already got. Piece of cake."

Up on the surface, Matt Leitinen at the command center is monitoring the conversation between Edie and the surface crew in the hot zone. A car passing on the road slows to a crawl to let a deer cross from one piece of forest to another. The deer seems terrified. The driver, who has had a good night's sleep and is just driving to work in Eagle Harbor, is paying no attention to the rescue attempt except to think it curious: his restedness, however, makes him pay attention to the look in the eyes of the deer. He thinks, *I've felt that way too.*

The deer that lured Ursula into the woods is a couple of miles away now, eating green leaves and blossoms, oblivious. It will live out its life and die of a hunter's bullet in maturity.

Edie speaks into the other mike. "Is this the mom yet? Are you there?"

Annie is there now. She says, "Ursula?" She has been told the number of feet the rescuers have traversed—not even fifty. Ursula has been so close all this time—not the hundreds or thousands of feet Annie had imagined— but the shaft had to be secured open or she would be buried forever, a mere fifty feet under the earth, like the men at the Meridel-Pflaum mine, who of course were entombed far deeper. *Six feet under is deep enough,* Annie has thought at one point, and then erased the thought.

Edie says, "Edie Faber here. I am going to feed the mike down to your lit- tle girl. I want you to keep her calm while I tie off this last rubble. Can you do that?" Edie Faber has no idea who these people are, the parents, what they are like. It is 4:11 A.M.

"Go ahead," says Annie.

Mindy Ji is marching up and down like—Justin observes—the mourn- ing doves who patrol her little front porch in the morning expecting the raggedy crusts of bread Mindy brings home from the restaurant for them. The family is in what the rescuers call the warm zone a few dozen feet from the shaft.

Annie and Justin are stationed inside Joe's rented Explorer now, with the mike. Joe stands, arms folded, leaning against the rear door, trying to as- similate at least *some* of this.

Edie feeds the line down toward Ursula, who is perhaps twenty feet be- yond the pile of debris in front of her. When the mike is near enough to Ur- sula, sliding along the wet floor and then coming to a stop, Edie calls out to her. "Talk to your Mommy now." Edie does not know how to do this, ex- actly. She has never been good with small kids. They're almost her size.

"Mommy?" says Ursula.

"Ursula," Annie says.

"Ursula," Justin says, "how about a nice song? Would you like a nice song? I've got my harmonicas."

"Okay," says Ursula, as if humoring him. "Play . . ." She fades, turning her head away from the mike to peer into the dark overhead, wondering what made a whirring sound she just heard. *It might be a bat,* she thinks excitedly.

"Echo?" Ursula says to the air, turning away from the mike. Only the week before Annie has read her a picture book about a bat pup named Echo. Ursula loved the picture of the mother bat hanging placidly upside down, wrapped—like a taco, Annie says, joking—around her pup, Echo.

The whirring sound is in fact a bat. Hundreds of them sluice in and out of the tiny hole Ursula fell through, each day: out at night to seek insects, back in with the coming of day, seeking darkness. They cling to the walls and the timbers downhill between Ursula and the black water, into which she could so easily have rolled, and drowned.

The split-second passes, and the whir is forgotten. Had the moment been mentioned to Mindy Ji afterward (it will not be), she would have said, "An angel! I'll bet that was an angel, and it saw that you were safe now and its job was done!"

Ursula says to Justin through the mike, her eyes still searching the dark for the source of the whir, "Play the whispering song."

Edie sighs and turns to her work, tying off the largest timber, drilling a hole into the wall of the chamber, and anchoring the timber to the rock. Justin plays "Whispering Hope" on the harmonica. Joe hears it and is astonished, riveted. He stands like a statue.

Edie Faber is drilling, and every time the drill stops she tries to think, *What is that song?* She can hear only snippets. It is all going beautifully, and suddenly a drill bit breaks. Edie makes a sound she cannot even interpret herself: disbelief, frustration.

"Don't say bad words," says Ursula, twenty feet away down the hole, loud enough for Edie to hear and firm as a teacher. Edie breaks into laughter. Tears of relief well up in her eyes.

"Send me down a replacement drill bit," she says. "I broke this fucker."

Ursula says, "Be nice, police lady."

Edie says, "You just hold on there, little one. Be really still."

"Okay," Ursula says. She has started to tug at the coat where it snags on the rubble and to twist her torso. She stops.

"Go on, talk to your mommy some more," Edie says. She moves back up the corridor on her rope to the crook of the shaft, where Jack Bostian stands guard. Edie looks downhill to Ursula and uphill to Jack. The drill bit is lowered to Jack. He passes it to Edie, along with an extra length of rope, in case.

She inches back down toward the pile. It is 4:32 A.M. now and growing light up on the surface.

In the camp chapel down the hill the counselors-in-training are gathered in their pajamas, sweatshirts, flannels, having been roused by the news that the rescuers have made contact. The trainer in the NEXT YEAR IN JERUSALEM shirt puts on a CD with wild guitars, tambourines, and African drums. The counselors dance in the early light, a modernized version of some black spiritual. They are claiming victory already.

On the road, people are moving from one RV to the next, waking one another up. They've found her, they say. She's alive. They're ready to bring her up.

Annie is talking to Ursula about books they have read together. Does Ursula remember *Alice in Wonderland,* in the pictures, drifting down the hole just as she did? Annie knows Ursula well enough to know this will not frighten her. Someone else wouldn't have tried this.

"I fell," Ursula says. Matter-of-fact. "I did sleep."

Annie thinks: *Good, she has not been awake all this time and lying there in terror.* Do you remember Peter Rabbit's house under the ground, Ursula?

Of course she does. "Flopsy and Mopsy and Cottontail and Peter," Ursula says, singsong.

Edie has drilled the first hole and secured the rope with the rock anchor.

And do you remember what happened when Winnie-the-Pooh went to see his friend Rabbit, who lived in a hole in the ground?

"He got stuck!" Ursula says, and she giggles.

But why did he get stuck? asks Annie.

"He did eat too much condensed milk," says Ursula.

And what else? Annie says.

"Condensed milk and honey and bread," chortles Ursula. "But he did tell Rabbit *forget about* bread." She giggles. She understands the joke.

Edie is nonplussed by this. Underground humor, har har. The child cannot move, and indeed if she did she'd go tumbling down the shaft into hundreds of feet of water. "You be still there, little miss," she says, feeling as if Ursula has taken over. Here she is, relaxed as can be, remembering stories, understanding the jokes, repeating them back to her mother.

Edie cannot pay attention to what is going on between the mother and child. She concentrates on drilling the second hole. She secures the rock anchor and calls up to Jack. "The bottom of this thing is secure as it is," she says. "I'm done drilling. I'm going down after the little girl." It is 4:57 A.M.

On the surface, Mindy Ji has stopped pacing like a mourning dove. Justin is out of the Explorer now and is glaring at Joe, who has put his hand on Mindy's back, comforting, tentative. Mindy squirms slightly at his touch, not rejecting, just astonished. Justin has never seen anyone touch his mother as if she were a woman, and he wants to deck Joe.

Edie inches down the slick rock until she can kneel next to Ursula. The webwork in which the child is caught seems solid, but her coat is pinning her there. "Hold still," Edie says.

On the mike, Annie is reciting Robert Louis Stevenson, a poem Ursula knows. Ursula will fill in the blanks.

"The friendly cow all red and white," Annie says.

"I love with all my heart," says Ursula.

Edie is amazed to see that Ursula is wearing mittens: a fine providence in the subterranean chill. She doesn't know children will wear what they want, when they want, and Ursula wanted this coat and these mittens and hadn't yet gotten hot enough to take them off. Edie removes the mittens, first one then the other. They hang free now from the ends of the sleeves on toothed silver cliplets. She takes out shears from her belt holster and holds the child's sleeve away from her tiny arm. She snips upward, snip, snip, whispering, "Be still, be still now."

"She gives me cream with all her might," says Annie.

"To eat with apple-tart," Ursula finishes.

The sleeve comes free. Edie leans over and speaks to Annie. "Ma'am?" she says. "I'm cutting her coat off to free her. We're almost there." It is 5:17.

"Good," Annie says, as if this is routine, and no problem.

Mindy Ji is pacing again like a soldier bird, and Joe is watching her with a frown of delight and awe that he has been carrying with him for twenty-plus years, to use this morning, a face he has not worn in all this time.

Edie snips up the other sleeve, all the way to the hood. "I'm afraid I've ruined your coat," she says to Ursula, as if this were all quite routine. "We'll have to leave it here in the hole."

"It's okay," Ursula says. "I am bigger now anyway. *Way* bigger."

Edie speaks into the mike again. "Ma'am," she says, "I am going to put her into a cervical collar for safety. Procedures. She seems to be able to move her head fine. Just keep talking, please, while I do this."

"That is my last year's coat anyway," Ursula says, discounting, "even if it is purple."

Annie intones another poem from *A Child's Garden of Verses,* the first thing that comes to her mind. "How do you like to go up in a swing / Up in the sky so blue?"

Ursula answers, antiphonal, singsong, articulate, "Oh, I do think it the pleasantest thing / Ever a child can do!"

"Lift up your head there, just a tad," says Edie. She secures the cervical collar on Ursula. She lifts her. Ursula grabs the mike on the way up and speaks into it like a performer.

"Up in the air and over the wall, / Till I can see so wide," Annie says.

Ursula finishes: "Rivers and trees and cattle and all / over the countryside."

Edie attaches a harness to Ursula, securing her to her own torso as they rise.

"Jack, we're coming up," Edie says. It is 5:23. She gives the rope a slight tug. Ursula is clinging to her like a monkey and holding the mike too. Edie takes it. "We're on our way," she says to Annie. "I'm going to let the mike go now."

She puts it down onto the damp floor and gives its cord a tug. The mike withdraws as if with a life of its own, up the slick slope ahead of them, pulled by Jack Bostian, who is standing, beaming, at the crook of the tunnel. Ursula squeals in delight, as if the mike were alive.

At the top of the hole, the edge man is lowering a Stokes basket, an adult-sized stretcher, to the bottom of the shaft. Edie and Jack are not aware of the clamor above them, the bustling: they are concentrated on getting this little girl into the Stokes basket, their last task. She is cool now, without her coat, and she sneezes once. It is 5:34.

Edie and Jack pack the stretcher with padding. Ursula lies still, under complicated weaves of webbing intended to immobilize her, gazing all around, staring up the shaft to the light. *She is so tiny,* Edie thinks. *She felt like a bird on my hip.*

It seems to take forever, the stretcher rising with excruciating slowness. The plywood that frames the shaft looks so superfluous and silly. Such care it took, while Ursula lay there unconscious, but if they had *not* taken all that time the shaft could have fallen in on itself. Ursula lies immobilized by all the webbing, gazing up at the sky, eyes wide, mouth pursed in silence.

Jack calls up to the edge man, and—despite Ursula's bird lightness—six men spread out in a formation like a web, like a star, winching her up, ever so slowly, inch by inch.

When she is lifted out of the hole and the stretcher is set on the ground, someone shouts, "Five forty-seven A.M." The crew yells to everyone to stay back, stay back.

Annie hovers, leaning on Justin. Mindy Ji jumps up and down in glee. Joe stands at a slight remove, shy and strange.

At the road, a roar rises from the crowd, and the sheriff is using a bullhorn to tell them they *still* need to stay back, please, *still.*

Swede Maguire, wild-haired with sleep, puts his arm around Joe. "So," he says, "you're the grandfather." Swede had heard earlier that the grandfather was gone, had not been seen in twenty years. He says nothing about this.

"I guess so," says Joe, blinking. He doesn't flinch away from Swede's hold on him.

He says to Mindy Ji, "I don't deserve this."

Mindy Ji says, "It's just grace, that's all," and she hooks her arm into his.

Yolanda Torres is checking Ursula's vital signs. Ursula has a black eye, her left. It is swollen nearly shut, like a bee sting, but she keeps forcing it open because she wants to see *everything.* The next day her face will be mottled purple, and then green and yellow, with bruises. Justin and Annie and Mindy Ji and Joe will hardly be able to take their eyes off her or stop touching her, lightly, featherily, with their fingertips, as if to make sure she is real and not an apparition.

She has several knots on her head, hematomas that swell but will subside by the next morning. Her lip is split, though not terribly. A scab has already formed. Her top front teeth have been knocked loose. The dentist says not to worry, that likely they'll settle themselves back in solidly, and they do. He adds, however, that trauma can make the roots resorb—dissolve—and they do that too. The teeth eventually work themselves loose at age four, and Ursula will be proud then to be a *big girl*, entering kindergarten with no front teeth, slick as a second-grader. The quilted coat has cushioned her fall somewhat: her trunk and limbs are only bruised, though her right arm is broken. The newspeople are growling back behind the barriers, chomping at the bit to get to all of this.

Edie frowns at Jack Bostian, as if asking why he is looking at her so strangely, with a kind of fierce pride. He will propose marriage three weeks later. They have mostly been friends until now, coffee dates. His argument will be, "We went through that little girl's rescue together," and that will seem a good enough reason.

JINX MUEHLENBERG WILL never know that "that half-breed trailer-trash kid" was the child of the little girl on the bike she hit at Greve Street and Easterday Avenue so many years ago, as well as the daughter of the young laborer on her porch and the granddaughter of Joe Cimmer, that guy she met the hell over in Big Bay, one summer in high school.

Jinx is drinking more now: one night next winter, after a good deal of wine, slumped in her chair before the TV, she will become confused and take her evening medications twice. She will already have taken her dose at dinner and a sleeping pill afterward. The pills interact badly with her migraine medicine and her allergy tablets, and the wine shuts her down. No one finds her until the next Monday.

None of the medications or their interactions is enough to account for cardiac arrest. The coroner rules that the death is from natural causes. He does not say that she has gotten her due, because autopsies do not discern this, and really, she hasn't. The lawyers will wrangle about the will's provisions, look for loopholes to their advantage, and find a few excellent ones. They will cobble up bills for a lot of hours. There is no one to whom Jinx has wanted to leave all her stocks and her properties, and she was sure she would live longer than her parents did anyway and thus hadn't locked things up tightly the way she might have, had she not forgotten she wasn't immortal. A good deal of the ready money, as much as they can cadge, will go to the lawyers, whom she chose for just this talent. The rest of her money will disappear into the state, in the same quick fashion that Ursula fell through her slot, chasing that deer.

Because Jinx's parents' estate is still in the fifteen-year transitional period, a minuscule provision transfers the house to the Sisters of the Virgin of Kraków, who taught Jinx in high school. The house will become a retreat center for a few elderly teaching nuns still alive and for their lay colleagues at the high school, who will find the treed acreage soothing and peaceful and the toile de Nantes wallpaper lovely. A gardener will landscape the grounds with winding walking paths for prayer and will place a scallop-shell grotto in front of the house, with a pale marble statue of the mother and child. Jinx would beat on the underside of her coffin lid in rage if she knew, even though the Virgin of Kraków is the one after whom she was named Virginia.

MINDY JI STOPS and suddenly remembers a dream she had had when she slept, briefly: over the forest, in the purple of evening, perhaps of the evening before, there is a vision of ancestors, that cloud of witnesses, cheering.

She does not know particulars. She cannot make out the myopic Sichuan alchemist in his green gown or his son, the imperial foot soldier; she has no way of identifying Kyllikki in her wedding dress or her dark-eyed, square-headed, speaking and hearing son, Aamos, in his prime as well. A dark-bearded Jesuit in his long black cassock is there, and a highborn Chinese woman in an odd cart because of her birth-injured legs. Violeta is there, her leprosy gone and her beauty restored, and Oscar Lucassen standing beside her because he belongs. Chen Bing is there, still a bit fey-looking; his grand-son Alabaster Wong, in his professorial tweed and the pince-nez that were just for effect, stands near him. Marjatta is there, again in her prime, and Emil, before he took fever. All of them, standing in mist thick as sun-rippled wheat to their waists, jostle for a glimpse of Ursula as she comes up out of the earth, bruised and beaming.

Many-colored robes, a murmur, a crowd of all of the people whose blood and lives went into this little girl. Behind them there seems to be music, perhaps an accordion, maybe a harp, and back of that, flashing, the north-ern lights.

ABERDEEN
CITY
LIBRARIES

Acknowledgments

DEEP APPRECIATION GOES to the National Endowment for the Arts for substantial support during the completion of this novel.

The nature and scope of this story required that I fling myself summarily down its shaft into an amazing darkness and then trust that help would come. Among those who helped in so many ways, supporting me with their faith in my work, or providing me facts or connectives of so many kinds, were: Shauna Ayres, Beth Belding, Melissa Belevender, Lyn Bromiley, Joseph Buckwalter, MD, Dave Carlson, Jane Carlson, Jason Chen, Dave Couillard, Lori Dahlen, Cathy Esser, John Feith, Jim Firkus, Mindy Fitch, Jude Grant, Greg Heffron, Emil Hill, Zachary Tobias Hill, Sulo Hiltunen, Mel Jones, Pasi Karppanen, Theresa Klingenberg, Brooks Landon, Reverend Lauri Maki, Elizabeth Mancke, Mary McInroy, Luke Nathaniel, Bode Okalanmi, Angie Phillips, David Ploof, Aaryn Richard, Detective Sergeant Stan Rogers, Peter "Madcat" Ruth, Eden Shambrook, Todd Shields, Ron Taylor, Dave Vahama, Dave Whiteman, and Marly Youmans. Many thanks are due Barry James and Thomas G. Friggens of the Michigan Iron Industry Museum. Invaluable technical advice came from Tom Ferguson, Jim Humston, and Brian Snyder. To Allan Johnson I owe enormous gratitude for research, ideas, referral to further resources, and tireless, intuitive help as a tour guide in the old copper-mining country of the Keweenaw Peninsula.

Thanks are also due to Lake Superior Writers for their awarding "Marjatta" a prize and to my audience at the awards reading at The Depot in Duluth, Minnesota, who laughed in local recognition at my rendition of Marjatta and Isak's Finn immigrant accents.

Any inadvertent omissions here, I regret. Any errors are my own.